Dorothy Simpson worked ~~~~ ~~ teacher and then for many years as a marriage guidance counsellor, before turning to writing full time. She is married with three children and lives near Maidstone in Kent, the setting for the Thanet novels. In 1985 she was awarded the Crime Writers' Association's Silver Dagger Award.

'Simpson can disinter the past with the best of them, and her portrait of a small community is matchless' *The Times*

'All the traditional home comforts of English village murder, with a final twist' *Observer*

'Dorothy Simpson is a contemporary Agatha Christie, renowned for weaving murder mysteries round credible characters in very English settings' *Annabel*

'Dorothy Simpson writes very good detective stories – tantalising . . . exasperating' *She*

'Thrillers that are both well written and crisply plotted do not come along every day, so a Dorothy Simpson novel is a welcome and engrossing treat' *The Lady*

'The creation of that most likeable policeman, Detective Inspector Luke Thanet, and his sidekick, Mike Lineham, was a stroke of genius' *Yorkshire Post*

The Third Inspector Thanet Omnibus

ELEMENT OF DOUBT
SUSPICIOUS DEATH
DEAD BY MORNING

DOROTHY SIMPSON

WARNER BOOKS

A *Warner* Book

This edition first published in Great Britain by Warner Books in 1998

Third Inspector Thanet Omnibus Copyright © Dorothy Simpson 1998

Previously published separately:
Element of Doubt first published in Great Britain in 1987 by Michael Joseph Ltd
Published in 1988 by Sphere Books Ltd
Reprinted 1988, 1989, 1991 (twice)
Published in 1993 by Warner Books
Reprinted 1996
Copyright © Dorothy Simpson 1987
Suspicious Death first published in Great Britain in 1988 by Michael Joseph Ltd
Published in 1989 by Sphere Books
Reprinted 1989, 1990, 1991
Published in 1992 by Warner Books
Reprinted 1994, 1995, 1996
Copyright © Dorothy Simpson 1988
Dead by Morning first published in Great Britain in 1989 by Michael Joseph Ltd
Published in 1990 by Sphere Books
Reprinted 1990
Published in 1992 by Warner Books
Reprinted 1994, 1996
Copyright © Dorothy Simpson 1989

The moral right of the author has been asserted.

A CIP catalogue record for this book
is available from the British Library.

ISBN 0 7515 1715 1

Printed and bound in Great Britain by Clays Ltd, St Ives plc

Warner Books
A Division of
Little, Brown and Company (UK)
Brettenham House
Lancaster Place
London WC2E 7EN

ELEMENT OF DOUBT

To Keith, again

ONE

As he swung into the drive Thanet felt distinctly smug. Joan had asked him to try to be home by six and it was one minute to. He was still smiling to himself at the thought of her surprise at his almost unprecedented punctuality when the front door was flung open and Ben came racing down the path.

'Dad! You just had a phone call. There's been a murder out at Ribbleden!' At twelve Ben was still young enough to relish the more sensational aspects of his father's police work and to enjoy parading his imaginary inside knowledge before his friends.

Thanet groaned. The fantasy of the long, lazy, thoroughly self-indulgent evening he had planned lingered tantalisingly in his imagination for a moment or two longer before fading reluctantly away. He gave Ben an accusing look. 'And you shouldn't have been listening, anyway.'

'Oh come on, Dad! I can't just go deaf every time the phone rings.'

'You know perfectly well what I mean. But as you did listen, not a single word about it at Scouts tonight, do you hear?'

'Oh, *Dad!*'

'I mean it, Ben. I don't want rumours flying around. If that's all it turned out to be, a rumour, there could be all sorts of complications.'

'Oh all right. If I must . . . On one condition . . .'

'Condition, my foot! If you think I'm going to submit to blackmail . . .'

1

'Blackmail?' said Joan, as they reached the front door. She looked harassed.

Thanet shook his head. 'A joke.' He kissed her. 'We've got a problem, I gather.'

Joan, a probation officer, was due at a meeting at six thirty and it had been arranged that Thanet should do the Scout run and, later, pick Bridget up from Doc Mallard's, where she and Mrs Mallard were having one of what they called their 'creative' evenings. Helen Mallard was a well-established writer of popular cookery books and Bridget's love of cooking had forged a strong bond between them.

'Not any more. It's all organised.' Joan was fishing in her handbag for her car keys. 'If you could manage to take Ben and the others to Scouts, as arranged, Jane Orton will fetch them home. And Helen will bring Bridget back when they've finished their session.'

'Fine. Thanks. Ben, disappear for a few minutes, will you? Go *on*. Your mother's in a hurry.' Thanet waited until Ben had gone into the living room and shut the door, then turned to Joan. 'So, what's it all about? Ben said something about a murder out at Ribbleden.'

'That's right – well, a suspicious death, anyway. I don't know the details, but here's the address. I hope I didn't jump the gun, but as I had to ring Helen Mallard anyway, I arranged for you to pick up Doc Mallard on the way, as she'll be needing his car to bring Bridget home. Hers is in for servicing.'

'Thanks, that's fine. Off you go then, love.' Thanet paused. 'What's the matter?'

Joan was hesitating.

'That address. High Gables, Ribbleden ... Damon Tarrant lives there.'

'Damon ... ? Ah ... Possession of drugs, right?'

Joan nodded.

'The poor little rich boy.'

'I wish you wouldn't call him that!'

2

Thanet held up his hands in apology. 'All right, I'm sorry. But why so uptight?'

Joan hesitated. 'He didn't turn up for his appointment this afternoon,' she said reluctantly.

'I see . . . And now you're worried in case he had something to do with this . . . suspicious death.'

'Well, not worried, exactly, not in that sense. Concerned would be a better word. He is only eighteen, after all.'

'Were you told who the victim is?'

Joan's mouth turned down at the corners. 'His mother . . . Of course, his not turning up for an appointment could be purely coincidental.'

'True. But in any case, there's absolutely nothing you can do about it at the moment, so you'd better get off. You're going to be late as it is. I'll let you know what the situation is when I get home. OK?'

Joan nodded. 'I suppose you're right. But . . . Oh goodness, it's twenty past already. I must fly.'

Thanet gave her a quick kiss and a gentle push towards the front door.

'Ben?' he called. 'Ready?'

Doctor Mallard, the police surgeon, was ready and waiting when Thanet's car pulled up outside the bungalow transformed since Mallard's recent remarriage by fresh paint, new curtains and a garden full of flowers instead of weeds. Every time he passed it Thanet would marvel at the difference this marriage had made to his old friend after the years of sadness and depression which had followed the death of the little doctor's first wife. The man himself had also taken on a new lease of life. Gone was the irritability which had made him so uncomfortable to work with, the scruffy, down-at-heel clothes and unpolished shoes. Watching him now as he walked briskly down the path to the car Thanet offered up a brief prayer of gratitude on his friend's behalf.

Helen Mallard and Bridget appeared at the front door,

waving. Thanet got out of the car. 'Thanks for helping out, Helen,' he called.

She smiled and made a dismissive gesture. 'Any time.'

'It's very kind of Helen to take so much trouble over Bridget,' said Thanet as they moved off. 'Joan and I really appreciate it, and I know Bridget does.'

'Nonsense. She really enjoys having someone to share her ideas with. It's a relief for me to get out tonight. I'm definitely persona non grata on Thursday evenings.' But Mallard's indulgent smile belied his words. 'She says Bridget is very talented.'

'The admiration is mutual, I assure you.'

'Anyway, tell me a bit more about this case. Joan didn't say much on the phone.'

'I don't suppose I know much more than you. A suspicious death at Ribbleden. A Mrs Tarrant.'

'Of High Gables? Good grief!'

'You know her, then?'

'I have met her a few times. Know of her, would be more accurate.'

'Well?'

'Well what?'

'Don't be tantalising. What do you know of her?'

'Far be it from me to pass on gossip,' said Mallard, primly.

Glancing at his companion Thanet caught the mischievous glint above the lenses of the half-moon spectacles. 'Don't be infuriating, Doc. If this turns out to be a murder case . . .'

'It's just that she has something of a reputation, that's all.'

'For what?'

'Promiscuity.' Mallard was no longer smiling. 'And as a matter of fact, it's not just gossip. I know of at least one marriage she destroyed. It's a number of years ago now, but the husband was a friend of mine. What I found so hard to swallow was the fact that she'd just been playing around with him. He thought it was the great love of his life, but when it came to the crunch and his wife left him, taking the children with her, and he suggested to Nerine Tarrant that

4

she get a divorce and marry him, she just laughed at him. He was left with nothing.'

'His wife didn't come back?'

Mallard shook his head. 'Said the whole experience had been so humiliating and so disillusioning that she could never trust him again.'

'So what happened to him?'

'He left the area, soon afterwards. Last I heard, he was thinking of emigrating.'

'Nerine . . . It's an unusual name.'

'Just what I said, when I first heard it. Apparently Mrs Tarrant's father was very fond of flowers and named his daughters after two of his favourites, Nerine and Daphne. He owned a nursery, but he died some years ago and Daphne now runs it – very efficiently, I believe.'

'A real mine of information, aren't you, Doc?'

'I get about . . . And don't forget, Luke, I've been living in the area since before you drew your first breath. Turn left here.'

Ribbleden lay at the heart of an unspoiled area of country-side south of Sturrenden, the country town in Kent where Thanet lived and worked. Protected from coachloads of tour-ists by the maze of narrow twisting country lanes which surrounded it, the village was a sight to gladden the heart of any photographer in search of calendar material. Village green, pond with ducks, picturesque pubs and period houses, they were all there. At this hour of a fine June evening the place was deserted. Presumably the entire population was either eating its evening meal or glued to its television sets.

A moment or two later Thanet was kicking himself for being so naive. As they rounded a bend he saw that the entire population of Ribbleden seemed to be clustered around some tall iron entrance gates.

Mallard frowned. 'The ghouls are out in force I see.'

'As usual,' said Thanet grimly.

The crowd parted reluctantly to allow the car through, closing behind it like the Red Sea behind the Israelites.

Ahead, a curving drive led to a substantial Victorian red-brick house ornamented with the gables, pinnacles and turrets so beloved of that era. A number of police and private cars were parked on the gravel near the front door.

'Lineham's here, I see,' said Mallard, nodding in the direction of a red Ford Escort. 'How is he these days? He seems a lot more cheerful, I must say.'

'Yes, he's pretty buoyant at the moment.'

'Recovered from not getting his promotion last year, has he?'

'I think so, yes.'

'Is he going to try again?'

'No, he seems pretty determined not to.' Privately, Thanet thought this a wise decision. Mike Lineham was a first-rate sergeant, but he lacked the extra flair essential for the higher rank. In Thanet's opinion Lineham would never have made the application in the first place if it hadn't been for his wife. Louise was both determined and ambitious.

'That'll suit you, I should think.'

'True. There's no one I prefer to work with.'

Thanet got out and stood for a moment taking in his surroundings. The drive continued around the left side of the house and disappeared, presumably in the direction of the garages. The whole place had an air of complacent prosperity. The gravel was weed-free, the lawns and flower-borders well maintained, the house itself, despite its size, in excellent order.

'What does Mr Tarrant do?'

'He's a surgeon at Sturrenden General, with a prosperous private practice.'

Thanet grinned. 'You're in the wrong branch of your profession, Doc.'

Mallard smiled back. 'Bit late to do anything about it now.'

'Ah, there's Lineham.'

The detective sergeant had appeared round the right-hand

6

corner of the house. He raised a hand in greeting, then beckoned. The two men began to walk towards him.

'Evening Mike. Not inside?'

'Evening, sir, Doc. No. This way. She fell,' the sergeant explained, 'from a first-floor balcony onto a stone terrace. Broke her neck, by the look of it.'

'And you don't think it was an accident, presumably?'

Lineham shrugged. 'Difficult to see how. The balcony rail is just that little bit too high for her simply to have overbalanced.'

'I see.' Thanet's tone was abstracted and unconsciously his pace had quickened. They were approaching the corner of the house and he was steeling himself for the moment he dreaded, that first sight of the corpse. He wanted to get it over with as quickly as possible.

'Here we are, sir.'

It was the familiar scene of disciplined activity. Sketches were being made, measurements and photographs taken. Trace, the Scenes-of-Crime Officer, was waiting for the police surgeon officially to pronounce death before launching on the painstaking task of taking his samples. And at the heart of it all lay the inanimate object that had once been the miracle that is a live human being. Thanet took a deep breath and moved forward to look as Mallard dropped to his knees beside the body.

Nerine Tarrant lay sprawled on her back on the wide stone terrace, limbs splayed, neck at an unnatural angle, feet pointing away from the house. She must have been in her early thirties, Thanet thought, and even now, in death, was one of the most beautiful women he had ever seen: classic oval face, high cheekbones, and a Dallas-style tumble of long dark expensive curls. Already, in mid-June, her skin was tanned to a rich honey (sunbed? he wondered), and her simple linen dress the colour of an unripe lemon enhanced the slim youthful body, the long shapely legs. A second, closer look told him that he had underestimated her age. The faintest lines at the corners of eyes and mouth reminded him

7

that Damon Tarrant, aged eighteen, was her son. Late thirties, then, he decided. But exceedingly well preserved. He would guess that a great deal of money had been spent on maintaining that youthful façade. And to what end? To die only half-way through her allotted span in the garden of her own home on this tranquil June evening. No one deserved an end such as this.

Thanet's gaze swung upwards. A white-painted wooden balustrade edged the covered balcony which ran right along this side of the house at first-floor level. An unusual feature for a Victorian house, surely? Perhaps this section had been added on later. On the ground floor two sets of french windows led out onto the terrace and stepping back he could see that there were two matching sets on the balcony above, one open, one closed.

'Her bedroom and sitting room,' said Lineham's voice in his ear. The two men had been working together for so long that the sergeant could gauge to a second the right moment to break into Thanet's thoughts. 'The open windows lead into the sitting room. The bedroom windows are locked.'

'And there's no other access to the balcony?'

Lineham shook his head.

'Have you looked at the sitting room yet?'

'Only a quick glance. There's no sign of a struggle, if that's what you're thinking. And the balcony rail is about three foot six high. At a guess, Mrs Tarrant was around five seven, so the rail would have come roughly to the top of her thighs.'

Thanet glanced from balcony to body and back again. 'From the way she's lying it looks as though she came over head first, wouldn't you agree?'

'Yes. Did a somersault, I'd say.'

'Did you bring up the question of suicide, with her husband?'

'Touched on it, that's all. He's pretty shocked, of course, I thought it could wait. But he dismissed the idea out of hand.'

'They always do,' said Thanet. 'All the same, in this case

8

I'd think it a pretty remote possibility. If you really want to kill yourself there are far more certain ways of doing it. That balcony can't be much more than — what? — fifteen feet from the ground?'

'Something like that, yes.'

'If you threw yourself from that height you'd quite likely end up in a wheelchair for the rest of your life . . . No, I think we can safely rule out suicide.'

'Or accident, sir, surely. I mean, if she'd been leaning on the rail and just fallen, either because she was dizzy, or drunk, or even drugged . . .'

'Are there any indications, up there, that she had either been drinking or taking drugs?'

'No, sir, not that I could see. But as I said, I only took a quick look . . . I was just speculating.'

'Right, sorry, go on.'

'Well, if she just toppled over, for whatever reason, surely she would be lying closer in to the house.'

'I would have thought so, yes. She could have been sitting on the rail, I suppose.'

'Most unlikely,' said Lineham promptly. 'It's too narrow, only about three inches wide.'

'Hmm. Well, it looks as though you're right, and she was helped on her way. If she was leaning on that rail, all anyone would have to do would be to bend down, lift her legs off the ground, give one hard shove, and that would be it.'

Mallard closed his bag with a snap and stood up.

'Well, Doc?' said Thanet.

'I'd be very surprised if the PM shows she died of anything but a broken neck. One never knows, of course, the unexpected is always a possibility . . . But there seems to be no sign of a struggle. Difficult to see how she could have fallen over of her own accord, though.'

'That's what we thought . . . If she'd taken any drugs, would you be able to tell?'

'Here and now, you mean?'

'Yes.'

'Unlikely – though it would depend on what they were and how and when they were taken. Most tablets dissolve pretty quickly and are absorbed into the bloodstream, so it's impossible to tell until the analyst has had a go at some samples.'

'What about constriction of the pupils?' said Lineham.

'Unreliable. It's quite normal for pupils to be either dilated or constricted after death, and you sometimes even get irregular dilation, with one pupil much larger than the other. Anyway, this woman's look all right to me.'

'And injection marks?' persisted Lineham.

'There are certainly no obvious punctures, but as you know, they're not always visible. Is there any suspicion that she was involved with drugs?'

'No, none, at the moment,' said Thanet. 'It's just that her son was up on a drugs charge recently.'

'Hard drugs?'

'No. Cannabis.'

'In that case, in the present economic climate, I think you'll find it difficult to make a case for drug tests to be done.'

'I doubt that we'd even suggest it, at the moment. We're just looking at possibilities. We might ask for an alcohol test, though.'

'Fair enough. Right, well if that's all ... Any chance of getting someone to run me home, Luke?'

'Yes, of course. Er, just one more question, Doc ...'

'I thought you wouldn't let me get away without asking. Time of death, of course ... When was the body discovered?'

'Five forty-five,' said Lineham.

'Yes, well I'd put it at any time within the last four or five hours.'

'From two o'clock onwards, then,' said Thanet.

'Something like that.'

The two men escorted Mallard to a car and then turned back to look up at the house.

'Have you had a chance to find out anything about the household yet, Mike?'

'Mr Tarrant, Mrs Tarrant, their son, Mr Tarrant's mother and her companion.' Lineham was ticking off his fingers. 'And Mrs Tarrant's sister lives in the coach house at the back of the premises with another woman. I'm not sure of her connection with the family, but the local bobby is here, PC Driver. He'll be able to fill us in, I'm sure.'

'I'll have a word with him later. You've been busy, Mike. Well done. Who discovered the body?'

'The husband.'

'Ah.'

The two men exchanged glances. There was no need to say what they were both thinking. In a domestic murder, the police always look first at the husband, then at the person who discovered the body. When the two were one and the same . . .

'And he's very cut up, you say.'

'Certainly seems it, yes.'

'Where is he?'

'In his study.'

'Right, we'll go and have a word with him. But we'll take a quick look at Mrs Tarrant's sitting room first. I just want to get the geography clear in my mind.'

As they set off briskly for the front door Lineham said, 'Surprising how often the old chestnut, comes up, isn't it, sir? You know, "Did she fall, or was she pushed?" '

'Yes. Though in this case there doesn't seem to be much doubt about the answer. The point is, why?'

TWO

The massive front door of High Gables was surrounded by panels of stained glass depicting the four seasons. The house faced west and as Thanet and Lineham entered the sun streamed in, creating a brilliant multicoloured archway on the white-tiled floor of the hall. Had this been the magical effect the architect intended? wondered Thanet as he and the sergeant paused for a moment to exclaim. Then Lineham led the way past tall green plants in huge white ceramic pots, up the green-carpeted stairs and along a corridor to Nerine Tarrant's sitting room.

Here, the predominant colour was blue: powder-blue carpet, pale blue curtains with deep blue patterned borders, and an entire wall covered with a collection of blue-and-white plates. The room was saved from coldness by touches of a deep vibrant pink in upholstery and cushions, and by the lavish arrangement of summer flowers in a glossy pink bowl on a table near the open french windows.

Thanet crossed to the balcony, which was about five feet wide and furnished with white cane chairs and table. Lineham was right. The rail was around three foot six high and it was difficult to see how Nerine could possibly have fallen over without being pushed, even if she had had a sudden attack of vertigo.

Thanet turned back into the sitting room and wandered around, hands clasped behind his back to remind himself to resist the urge to touch. It was an attractive room, yet now that he looked at it more closely there was something subtly wrong with it. What was it? Pondering the question, he

12

stooped to examine a photograph: Nerine Tarrant and her husband on their wedding day, posed against a background of silver birches and daffodils naturalised in grass. Tarrant was gazing adoringly down at his bride, while she ... She was directing a brilliant, seductive smile at the photographer. Was he being unfair? Thanet wondered. Was this impression of her unjustifiably coloured by what Doc Mallard had told him? He looked again, noting the determined tilt of the chin, the proprietorial hand laid casually on her new husband's arm. There was no doubt, looking at the photograph, who was going to be the giver and who the taker in this marriage.

Greedy whispered a little voice in his brain, and he thought, that's it, that's what's wrong with this room. It was too crowded, too cluttered with objects, as though Nerine hadn't known when to stop, how to say no to herself. Had this attitude carried over into her relationships?

'A real looker, wasn't she?' Lineham was peering over his shoulder.

'What's her husband like?' said Thanet. According to the photograph, tall and slim, as fair as Nerine was dark. How had the years dealt with this young man so patently in love with his fairytale bride? 'No,' he went on as Lineham opened his mouth to speak, 'don't tell me. I'd rather judge for myself.'

Down the stairs again, across the hall and around a corner. As they entered a corridor a young woman with long brown hair caught up in a ponytail closed a door half-way along, glanced at them, then hurried away in the opposite direction.

'Who was that?' said Thanet.

Lineham shook his head. 'No idea. Old Mrs Tarrant's companion, perhaps? In any case, she was coming out of Tarrant's study.'

It was a square, masculine room furnished with club-style leather chairs, tall bookshelves filled with leather-backed volumes and an impressive antique kneehole desk in glowing mahogany. There were two people in the room, a man and

13

an older woman. Tarrant was sitting at his desk, head in hands, in an attitude of despair, the woman standing beside him, hand on his shoulder. He glanced up as the door opened. He looked dazed.

Thanet immediately experienced a painful wave of empathy. How would he feel, in Tarrant's position? And how could he possibly question a man in this state, and at such a time? It was the part of his job that he hated most, tormenting people when they were at their most vulnerable. Many of his colleagues, he knew, disagreed. They took the view that now would be the time to press home the advantage. The end, they argued, justified the means, and in pursuit of the truth all other considerations should be put aside. Thanet was equally determined to get at the truth – but not in such a way that he wouldn't be able to live with himself afterwards. *What is a man profited, if he shall gain the whole world, and lose his own soul?*

'This is Detective-Inspector Thanet, Mr Tarrant,' said Lineham.

The man nodded. 'Do sit down,' he said, waving his hand at some chairs.

Thanet and Lineham complied, Thanet pulling a chair up to the other side of the desk, Lineham retreating to one against the wall.

'I'd better be going, then, Roland,' said the woman.

'Oh, Beatrix, forgive me . . .' Tarrant rubbed a hand wearily across his eyes and forehead. 'Inspector, this is Mrs Haywood, who has been kind enough to keep me company. She lives in the coach house, with my wife's sister. She . . .' He shook his head as if to clear it, preparatory to giving some apparently complicated explanation.

'I don't suppose the Inspector wants to hear about me,' said Mrs Haywood. Tall and angular, with untidy greying hair escaping from a bun, she was wearing what Thanet privately labelled 'arty' clothes: long flower-sprigged skirt with a wide flounce at the hem, shapeless white blouse, a felt waistcoat with flowers appliquéd down the front and

14

several indian cotton scarves, loosely tied and floating around her as she moved. She was, understandably, looking pale and shaken. 'I'll be back later, Roland.'

'Perhaps we could have a word with you afterwards, Mrs Haywood?' said Thanet.

'Oh . . . Yes, of course.'

Thanet waited until she had gone, then turned back to Tarrant. 'I'm sorry to trouble you at a time like this, Mr Tarrant, but I'm afraid that I really shall have to ask you a few questions.'

Tarrant waved a hand, wearily.

'I quite understand. Yes, of course I do.' It sounded as though he was trying to convince himself. 'You'll want to know when I found her . . .' His voice thickened and he swallowed, hard.

'That's right. And one or two other details . . .'

'Of course, of course.' Tarrant made a visible effort to pull himself together, sitting up straighter and squaring his shoulders.

The surgeon had not worn as well as his wife, Thanet thought. Although well groomed, there was a visible paunch beneath the expensive dark suit, and the abundant fair hair had receded and thinned to little more than a token covering of the scalp. The dryness which is so often the bane of the fair-skinned had created a network of fine lines on his forehead and around the pale blue eyes. He looked a good ten years older than her.

Thanet sat down again.

'Perhaps we could begin by asking you to tell us exactly what happened when you got home this afternoon, sir?'

'Yes . . .' Tarrant frowned and massaged the side of his forehead for a moment or two with tiny circular movements, as though trying to erase a pain – or perhaps reactivate a memory he had tried to blot out?

Behind him, through the open window, the garden stretched serene, the trees at the far end washed with an almost eerie crimson glow from the setting sun.

15

'I got home at about, oh, twenty to six, I suppose. I went straight upstairs. Nerine – that's my wife – was usually in her sitting room at that time of day. But she wasn't there, so I knocked at her bedroom door. It was locked, so I knew she couldn't be in there, either . . .'

'I'm sorry to interrupt,' said Thanet. 'But perhaps you could just clarify that statement?'

'Clarify . . . ?' Tarrant looked puzzled, then his brow cleared. 'Oh, I see what you mean. Well, my mother lives with us, and she has a passion for clothes, jewellery and make-up – especially my wife's clothes, jewellery and make-up, I'm afraid. She is suffering from Alzheimer's disease – senile dementia – so she's rather confused and finds it difficult, after living here all her life, to understand that some parts of the house are out of bounds, so to speak, and that everything in the house is not hers to do what she likes with. Once or twice she's made rather a mess of my wife's bedroom and eventually my wife got into the habit of locking the door whenever she left the room. So this afternoon, when I found the bedroom door locked, I knew she wouldn't be in there.'

'I see. Thank you.'

'So I went downstairs, looked in the drawing room and the kitchen, but I couldn't find her anywhere . . . Then I thought, it's a lovely afternoon, perhaps she's still sunbathing in the garden. So I went out onto the terrace and . . . and found her.'

Abruptly, Tarrant swivelled around in his chair to gaze out of the window.

Thanet guessed that he was fighting for control. 'I'm sorry, I don't suppose I can even begin to imagine how painful this must be for you.'

Tarrant swung back. 'At least you didn't say "I *know* how painful this must be for you." God, when I think of how often I've said those very words myself, to people whose relations had died . . . You just have no idea, no conception of what it's really like, until it happens to you – and of course, you never really expect it to. Tragedies are things that happen to other people.' He shook his head despairingly. 'I'm sorry. You don't want to hear all this. Please, go on. Ask me all the questions you want.' *Then go, go and leave me alone, for God's sake.* The man's unspoken cry was almost audible.

'Look, I'm not sure that you're really in a fit state to be questioned at the moment. Perhaps we could go away for a while, come back later, when you've had a little more time to recover from the shock...'

'Recover!' Tarrant gave a harsh, bitter, laugh. 'Oh, make no mistake about that. I'm never going to recover from this, Inspector. Never. I can't even begin to imagine life without her... So you might as well ask your questions. Now is as good a time as any.'

The outburst seemed to have helped. Tarrant was looking much more in command of himself.

'Very well... When you went into your wife's sitting room, did you go out onto the balcony?'

'Not actually out onto it, no. I did walk across as far as the french windows, just to see if she was out there.'

'So how long, in all, would you say this process of looking for your wife took?'

'Five minutes?'

Lineham made a note. Thanet could visualise it. *Body found 5.45p.m.*

'Did you see anyone during this time?'

Tarrant shook his head. 'No.'

'I understand that your mother has a companion?'

'Marilyn Barnes, yes. Perhaps I should explain that, contrary to the impression I may have given just now, we lead separate lives, Inspector. Fortunately this house is constructed in such a way as to make that possible. It is, broadly speaking, shaped like an H. The hall and staircase form the central section; my wife, my son and I live in one of the long, vertical arms, my mother, Miss Barnes and her small son in the other. My mother, as I said, does tend to wander, rather, but part of Miss Barnes's job is to try to prevent that happening.'

'What about your son? Was he home at the time?'

'No. I noticed his car was missing, when I parked mine.'

Thanet did not betray his quickened interest. For the first time there was something not quite straightforward in Tarrant's tone . . . Nothing as definite as a lie, but a reservation of some kind . . .

'Has he come home, since?'

'No.'

'So he doesn't even know about his mother's death yet?'

Tarrant shook his head.

'Do you know where he is?'

An uneasy laugh. 'You can't have any teenagers or you wouldn't be asking that question, Inspector. When he goes out, I never know where he is, how long he's going to be or who he's with.'

Then you have been far too lax with him. Battles or no battles, Thanet was determined that his children's adolescence was going to have some kind of positive framework, however long they had to spend hammering out the rules together. Freedom should be a common goal, independence something to be worked for by parents and children alike, not a dangerous weapon carelessly bestowed upon those too immature to know how to handle it.

'How old is he?'

'Damon? Eighteen.'

'He's still at school?'

'No. He's very bright, and took his A levels early, last year. He's having a year out while he tries to decide what to do.'

'He has a job?'

Tarrant shook his head, regretfully. 'Not at the moment.'

Thanet was thinking of that missed appointment with Joan. 'So you have no idea whether he was at home, earlier in the afternoon?'

'None, I'm afraid. Look here, Inspector, why all this

18

interest in Damon? If he'd been here earlier, and seen his mother fall, do you seriously think he wouldn't have reported it, or rung me, immediately?'

'I'm just trying to get a clear picture of the situation in the house, this afternoon,' said Thanet evasively.

'But why?' Tarrant's suspicions were aroused now and he was staring at Thanet as if trying to read his mind.

'In the case of a sudden death we have to investigate the circumstances as thoroughly as possible.'

'Now wait a minute. You're not suggesting – you *can't* be suggesting that my wife's death was anything but a simple accident? My God! That *is* what you're suggesting, isn't it?'

'I'm not suggesting anything at the moment, Mr Tarrant. I'm merely trying to find out what happened. But I think it only fair to tell you – and I'm sorry, because I know that this will cause you additional distress – that we have to take the possibility into consideration.'

Tarrant jumped up out of his chair and stood glaring down at Thanet, running a hand over his head. 'I don't believe I'm hearing this! You surely don't think she was . . .' But he couldn't bring himself to say the word and for a moment there was total silence in the room.

'Mr Tarrant, please, do sit down again. I assure you that at the moment I have a completely open mind. Nevertheless, you must see that I have to consider the possibility.'

'But why? Who could possibly want to . . . ?'

'That is one of the questions I have to ask you.'

Tarrant shook his head in bewilderment and subsided into his chair. 'The idea is preposterous. There's no one, no one . . .'

'Well, perhaps you could help us by giving us some idea of what your wife was going to do today.'

But Tarrant was still staring at Thanet, trying to adjust himself to this new and appalling idea.

'Mr Tarrant?' said Thanet, gently.

'Sorry . . . I . . . What did you say?'

Thanet repeated his question.

Tarrant made an effort to concentrate, blinking and again pressing his fingers into his temples.

'Nothing special, so far as I know. She always has . . . had her hair done, on Thursday afternoons.'

'Where?'

Tarrant told him, and Lineham made a note.

'But apart from that, you had no idea of how she was going to spend her day?'

'Sorry, no.'

'When did you last see her?'

'After breakfast. I went up to say goodbye to her. She always has a tray in her room.'

'And she seemed perfectly normal?'

'Yes.' Tarrant shook his head. 'If I'd only known that was the last time I'd see her alive . . .'

How often, Thanet wondered, had he heard these words from shocked and grieving relatives, anxious to have bestowed upon that final encounter some special significance. But he knew that this is possible only if one always treats one's loved ones as if seeing them for the last time, an impossible counsel of perfection.

'And she was well? No complaints about dizziness, for example?'

Tarrant hesitated and Thanet could almost hear him thinking. *If I say yes it would be such an easy way out . . .*

'No.' The regret in his voice was evident.

'She wasn't taking any medication?'

Tarrant shook his head.

'Or drugs of any kind, in fact?'

Thanet hoped he had slipped that particular question tactfully in, but Tarrant reacted strongly.

'Drugs? What do you mean? What are you implying?' But he didn't wait for a reply. 'Oh, I see . . . Now look here, Inspector, just because Damon had a spot of trouble over cannabis, it doesn't mean that this is a household of junkies. My God, you never miss a trick, do you?'

'I only meant . . .'

20

'I know damn well what you meant, and you're wrong. If Damon had been dabbling in the hard stuff, believe me, I'd know. I've been keeping a pretty close eye on him for any symptoms, I assure you, and as for Nerine . . . The idea is ludicrous . . .'

'Very well. I'm sorry. But I had to ask, you must see that.'

Tarrant glared at him for a moment or two longer, then sank back into his chair, his expression softening. 'Oh, I suppose so. But you must see . . .'

'Believe me, I do. And I don't like asking these questions any more than you like answering them.'

Tarrant gave him an assessing look. 'Then perhaps it's my turn to apologise . . .' He rubbed the back of his hand over his forehead. 'I don't usually lose my temper like that.'

'These are not usual circumstances.'

'No, thank God. Anyway, carry on, will you? I'd like to get this over with.'

'Right. Well, if we could go back a little . . . You spent the day at the hospital?'

'Sturrenden General, yes.'

'And you left at what time?'

'At around 5.15.'

'And you got home at about 5.40, you say?'

'That's right.'

'Did anyone see you arrive?'

'Not to my knowledge.'

Was there a hint of reservation there?

'You're sure?'

'Well I didn't see anyone myself. But with several other people living here I can't speak for them, naturally.'

'Apart from your mother, Miss Barnes and her son, does anyone else live in the house?' A reasonable question, in the circumstances. Nerine Tarrant could scarcely have run an establishment of this size without help.

'We have a housekeeper who comes in from eight in the morning until four in the afternoon. And a woman who comes in to clean three mornings a week.'

21

Their names were duly noted by Lineham.

'And your wife's sister lives, I gather, in the coach house. Where is that? I'm afraid I haven't had time to look around yet.'

'At the back of the house, near the garages. Yes, she bought it some years ago, when their father died. Daphne had lived with him until then, but it was a large house, much too big for one, and the coach house was empty . . . We offered it to her rent free, but she preferred to buy.'

'And Mrs Haywood . . . ?'

'Ah, yes. Well, Daphne is unmarried, but she was engaged, once. Her fiancé was killed in a car crash and she kept in touch with his mother, Mrs Haywood, who was at the time living in a rented house. When that was pulled down for a motorway project she had nowhere to go and Daphne suggested she come and live with her.' Tarrant shrugged. 'I must admit I wasn't too keen on the idea. I could see Daphne being saddled with an ageing woman who was strictly speaking no relation of hers, but she was very set on it and Mrs Haywood moved in. They've lived together — quite harmoniously, I might add — for some years now. Mrs Haywood runs the house, and with Daphne working full-time it seems to have worked out very well for both of them.'

'Fine. Well, I think that apart from one more question, that's about it for the moment, Mr Tarrant. Thank you for being so cooperative.'

'You're wrong, you know,' said Tarrant. 'Thinking that my wife might have been . . .' He steeled himself to say it. 'might have been . . . killed, deliberately.'

'I didn't say I thought that. I said, if you remember, that it is a possibility we have to take into account. But it does in a way lead on to my final question. And I apologise in advance for causing you pain by asking it.'

'What?' said Tarrant, warily.

'Your wife . . .' Hell, there was no way to cushion the impact. 'Did you have any reason to believe that she was not faithful to you?'

Tarrant stared at Thanet for a moment, his expression unreadable. Then he said quietly, 'I see that I was mistaken, Inspector. I thought that, contrary to my expectations, you were a reasonably civilised human being.' His voice rose. 'Get out, will you?' He made a violent, dismissive gesture. 'Just get out!'

Without another word, they left.

THREE

Outside the study door Thanet and Lineham grimaced at each other.

'You'd no option. You had to ask,' said Lineham.

'Yes, I know. Especially after what Doc Mallard told me about Mrs Tarrant.' Briefly, Thanet filled Lineham in.

'Ah, so you're saying that Dr Tarrant's reaction . . .'

'Mr.'

'But . . .'

'Up to consultant status, doctors are "Dr". After that, they're "Mr".'

'But why? They're still doctors, aren't they?'

Thanet shrugged. 'No idea. I've always assumed it's because when they become consultants they're so obviously important that they don't need a special form of address.'

'Stupid sort of system, if you ask me.'

'Anyway, what were you going to say, Mike?'

'I can't remember now.'

'Something about Mr Tarrant's reaction.'

'Ah, yes. Are you suggesting, then, that he reacted as strongly as he did not because he considered your question an insult to his wife but because you'd hit the nail on the head and he hated to admit it?'

'The thought had crossed my mind. Ah, here we are.'

They had arrived at a green baize door.

'I've only ever seen these in stately homes,' said Lineham. 'I didn't know they had them in houses like this.'

'Any house where there were lots of servants, I imagine.

To cut off noise and cooking smells . . . and I suppose also to draw a symbolic line between upstairs and downstairs.'

'Just as a matter of interest, where exactly are we going?'

'To see Mrs Haywood. And Mrs Tarrant's sister too, of course. I imagine she's home from work by now. Come to think of it, she should have been home from work some time ago . . .'

'That's a point. I wonder why she wasn't the one to rush over and give Mr Tarrant moral support.'

'Too upset, perhaps? Anyway, I just thought it would be interesting to go out the back way, see a bit more of the terrain.'

They were now in a short passage with doors along one side. Thanet glanced in: storeroom, flower room with sink and shelves of vases, and finally a large square kitchen. This was a sight to gladden any woman's heart, with custom-made pine units, acres of work surface and cupboard space and every imaginable gadget. It was immaculately tidy and spotlessly clean. On the pine table was a note, weighted down by a salt cellar. Lineham picked it up and they read it together. 'THURS: *chicken mayonnaise, potato salad, green salad, strawberries and cream, all in fridge*'.

'Note from the housekeeper?' said Lineham. 'Tonight's supper, I presume. Very nice, too. Just the job for a warm summer evening.'

'Mmm . . . Mike, I've just realised . . . When we get back from seeing Mrs Haywood I want to take a look at Mrs Tarrant's bedroom, but presumably it's still locked. Go and tell one of the men to get hold of a key in the next half an hour or so, will you? I'll wait for you outside.'

Thanet saw the coach house as soon as he stepped out of the back door, some fifty yards away on the far side of a gravelled yard. A sleek Porsche was parked in front. Daphne's, he presumed. He didn't know her surname, he realised. The nursery must be doing well.

He could understand her wanting to own this place rather than live in it by grace and favour. Solidly built of stone,

25

with a steeply pitched slate roof and dormer windows, it was an attractive little property by any standards. Ideally situated, too, away from the road and surrounded by the extensive gardens of High Gables. Over to the right were the garages for the main house, obviously converted from another outbuilding. Room for three cars, Thanet noted. One of the spaces was empty.

Lineham appeared around the corner of the house, predictably gazing in the direction of the garage. 'A Mercedes and a Jaguar XJS!' he said. 'And a Porsche 844! Not exactly short of a penny, are they?'

'I don't suppose that's much consolation to Mr Tarrant now.'

Lineham pulled a face. 'True. Bentley's going to track down the key, sir. Oh, and one interesting thing I noticed. There's a path which goes in the direction of the garden boundary, leading off the terrace where the body was found.'

'And there are french windows downstairs . . . So anyone wanting to get in unobserved . . .'

'Exactly, sir.'

Beatrix Haywood must have been watching for them; as they approached the front door, it opened.

She put a finger across her lips, adjuring silence. 'Come in,' she whispered. 'This way.'

She led them through a narrow hall into a large square sitting room and closed the door behind them. 'That's better,' she said, in a normal voice. 'I didn't want to disturb Daphne – Miss Linacre. She has a migraine . . . Sit down, won't you?'

She perched on the edge of a hard-backed chair.

She was getting on for seventy, Thanet estimated, and it was scarcely surprising that she was still looking upset. A sudden brush with violent death is liable to shake the hardiest of constitutions.

'Thank you. I'm sorry to hear that. Miserable things, migraines, aren't they? She suffers them regularly?'

'Oh yes, as far back as I can remember.'

'Brought on in this instance, I suppose, by the shock of her sister's death?'

'Oh no. That's just made it ten times worse. She came home from work early with it this afternoon, and went straight to bed.'

'What time would that have been?'

'Around twenty to five, I suppose.'

During this brief conversation he had been glancing around the room. It was comfortably and conventionally furnished with fitted carpet, chintz curtains and chair covers. On a small table near the fireplace pride of place was given to the photograph of a young man with a weak, rather effeminate mouth and a quantity of untidy brown shoulder-length hair. Mrs Haywood's dead son? he wondered. But the most striking feature of the room was the number of pictures, which covered every available inch of wall space.

'Yours?' he said.

'No, my son's.'

He had been looking for a way to put her more at ease and the pride in her voice told him he might have found it.

'He was an artist?' A somewhat fatuous question, in the circumstances, but it would serve. The tense he had used, however, made her frown.

'How did you know he was dead?'

'Mr Tarrant told me of his accident. I'm sorry.'

'Yes.' Mrs Haywood shook her head and sighed. 'It was a tragedy, as you can see.' And she waved her hand at the paintings, which she evidently considered a mute testimony to her son's talent. 'Such a *waste*. It was said, you know, that if only he'd had the opportunity to fulfil his potential, he could have been one of the world's great artists.'

That, Thanet thought, was a matter of opinion. Personally, he couldn't see that Haywood's work had an ounce of originality in it, in terms of composition, execution, or use of colour. Not that he was an expert, of course, but still . . .

'He was very prolific.'

'Jocelyn was devoted to his work.' She was warming to

her subject. 'Absolutely devoted to it. How different things would have been, if he had lived to marry Daphne ... She understood him, you see, recognised his genius. She would have allowed him to dedicate himself entirely to his work, instead of being forced to prostitute his talents ...'

Thanet's look of mild enquiry was enough to encourage her to continue. This was clearly her favourite theme, the subject nearest her heart, and her natural diffidence and hesitant manner fell away as she became engrossed in talking about her son. Listening to the enthusiasm in her voice and noting the sparkle in her eyes, the mounting flush on those pale cheeks, Thanet reflected that it must be rare for her to have so rapt an audience. Most of the people she knew must long ago have grown tired of listening to these exaggerated claims of his genius. His attention sharpened as she began to talk about his romance with Daphne.

He had met her, it seemed, when he had been commissioned to design a cover for the 1969 catalogue for Linacre Nurseries. Daphne was then nineteen. After leaving school she had done a business studies course and had gone straight into the office at the nurseries. Listening carefully to what was not said, Thanet deduced that by the time she met Jocelyn it was already obvious that one day she would be taking over the business.

'It was love at first sight,' sighed Mrs Haywood. 'Daphne has never even looked at another man. Not like ...' The flow of information broke off abruptly and she looked embarrassed, the temporary spell broken.

'What were you going to say, Mrs Haywood?' said Thanet gently.

Pause.

'Mrs Haywood?'

Again he waited for a reply, but she merely shook her head.

'Not like her sister, perhaps?' said Thanet, softly.

Another shake of the head, lips compressed.

Thanet rose, began to wander around, studying the paintings. A closer view did nothing to alter his opinion of them. 'Perhaps I should tell you, Mrs Haywood, that there does seem to be some question as to whether or not Mrs Tarrant's death was an accident.'

Her head snapped around, eyes stretched wide. 'Not . . . not an accident? What . . . what do you mean?'

Thanet did not reply and she was forced to break the silence.

'You don't . . . You can't . . . You're surely not implying that . . . someone killed her, deliberately?'

'It's a possibility we have to take into consideration.'

'But why? She fell . . . From the balcony . . . I always did say that rail was dangerously low . . .'

'But perhaps not low enough for an accidental fall . . .' Thanet returned to his chair and sat down. 'I'm sorry, this has obviously been a shock to you. And I must stress that we haven't made up our minds, yet. But you must see that if there is even the remotest possibility that Mrs Tarrant was murdered, we can't waste time by assuming that her death was an accident. If, later on, it is proved to be otherwise, well and good, but at the moment we have no choice but to proceed as if this were a murder investigation.'

Silence. Mrs Haywood's hands were clasped tightly together in her lap as she considered what had just been said.

'Yes,' she said at last, hesitantly. 'Yes, I see that . . . But why are you saying all this to me?'

'Because we need your help. Unlike Mr Tarrant and Miss Linacre, you are here all day. Even though you don't live in the house, you overlook the garages. You must know a lot more about Mrs Tarrant's movements than they do.'

Mrs Haywood chewed at her lower lip. Clearly, she was trying to reach some decision.

'We really would be grateful for any information you could give us.'

She sighed and shook her head. 'There's no point in pretending I had much time for Nerine . . . But it seems so wrong, to gossip about the dead.'

'We are not gossiping, Mrs Haywood. Far from it. We are merely seeking the truth, trying to find out who killed her – if indeed she was killed. I can understand your not wanting to discuss her when she can no longer defend herself, but try to look at it this way. Could you come to terms with your conscience if you refused to help bring a murderer to justice?'

He was laying it on a bit thick, Thanet knew, but you had to adapt your approach to the personality of the witness concerned.

And he had struck just the right note. He could see the lines of indecision in her face already beginning to harden into conviction.

'I suppose you're right,' she said at last. 'Of course you are . . . What is it you want to know?'

But there was still a reservation in her voice.

'Perhaps we could begin by going back to the point at which you broke off. You *were* going to say, "Not like her sister", weren't you?'

A reluctant nod.

'Perhaps you could explain what you meant?'

Mrs Haywood pulled one of the floating scarves from her neck into her lap and began to tug it, twist it around one hand.

Did she know, Thanet wondered, how revealing these movements were? She could not have mirrored the conflict in her mind more clearly if she had tried.

As if she had read his thoughts she laid the scarf down, smoothing it out across her knees, and raised her head to look Thanet straight in the eye. 'She was not a good woman. She . . . It was upsetting, the way she carried on.'

'Carried on?' echoed Thanet.

She lowered her eyes and murmured, almost inaudibly, 'With men.'

'You're saying that she was often unfaithful to her husband?'

She nodded, lips compressed.

'And at present?'

She glanced up at him quickly from beneath lowered eyelids, and shook her head.

'Mrs Haywood, please . . . This could be very important, you must realise that.'

She hesitated a moment longer and then mumbled something.

'I'm sorry, I didn't quite catch that.'

She sighed again, and raised her head, capitulating. 'Speed,' she said. 'Lance Speed.'

'He's local?'

She nodded. 'He runs the garage – in the village.'

'And this has been going on for . . . how long?'

'A few months.' And then, in an uncharacteristic outburst, added bitterly, 'Judging by her past record, I should say that any minute now Mr Speed would have found himself supplanted.'

'Was this affair general knowledge?'

'Oh yes.' She gave him a shamefaced look and said, 'I'm afraid Nerine's affairs always were. She never took the slightest trouble to hide them from anybody.'

Which, Thanet thought, was no doubt why Mrs Haywood had finally decided to be so frank now. If Nerine Tarrant's promiscuity was common knowledge, it wouldn't have been long before he had heard about it from other sources.

'From anybody, Mrs Haywood? What about her husband?'

Mrs Haywood shook her head so vigorously that a few more wisps escaped from her bun. 'Not even from him. I don't know how he stood it. In fact, I used to think, sometimes . . .'

She hesitated, then stopped.

'You were saying?'

'Nothing.'

'You were going to say, perhaps, that you sometimes wondered if Mrs Tarrant used deliberately to flaunt her lovers in front of her husband?'

'I didn't say that!'

But he had been right, he could tell.

'But in any case, you are saying that her husband had full knowledge of her behaviour?'

She inclined her head.

'And what was his reaction?'

She hesitated for a moment, then said earnestly, 'I can tell you this, Inspector. Mr Tarrant would never have hurt a single hair on his wife's head. He adored that woman, and didn't care what she did as long as she stayed with him.'

So that spurt of anger just now had been on Tarrant's behalf. She was obviously fond of him, thought highly of him.

'How did Mrs Tarrant get on with the rest of the household?'

'Well . . .' She hesitated. Discussing Nerine, whom she had disliked, and who was dead, was obviously one thing; talking about the other people with whom she lived at close quarters was another.

'I understand, for example, that there were . . . certain difficulties with Mr Tarrant's mother.'

'That's true, yes . . .' she said reluctantly. Then she added defensively, 'There are always problems, having parents living in the same house. And Lavinia – Mrs Tarrant senior – well, it's not her fault. It's her illness, you see. She can't help it if she's become a little, well, eccentric, as the disease progresses.'

'She is suffering from senile dementia, I understand?'

'That's right.' A sigh. 'Such a shame. When I think how lively and active she was only a few years ago . . .'

'But I understand that she and Miss Barnes, her companion, have what is virtually a separate establishment.'

'I know. But Marilyn, Miss Barnes, can't keep an eye on Lavinia twenty-four hours of the day. Lavinia has lived in that house for over forty years and genuinely forgets that she is not still mistress of it. It used to drive Nerine mad, especially when Lavinia used to get into her – Nerine's –

bedroom and try her clothes on as if they were her own. Like . . .' She stopped, abruptly.

It was obvious that she wished that last word had not slipped out. No doubt she didn't want to get the old lady into trouble.

'Like when?'

'I . . .' She shook her head. 'Nothing.'

'Like this afternoon, perhaps?'

She was still hesitating, but now she gave a little shrug. 'I suppose if I don't tell you, someone else will . . . Yes, there was a row this afternoon.'

If so, how had she come to overhear it? Thanet's puzzlement must have shown in his face and she forestalled his next question by adding, 'I only know because I went over to the house to look through the attic for some stuff for a jumble sale in the village on Saturday. With permission, of course.'

'I'm sure . . . What time was this?'

'Let me see. I went over just before two. I waited until I saw Nerine leave for the hairdresser's. That must have been about ten to two. She always has – had a two o'clock hair appointment on Thursdays. I intended finishing before she got back – she was usually gone about an hour – but there's so much stuff up there . . .'

'Mrs Tarrant was a compulsive hoarder?' Yes, thought Thanet. That would fit with the impression he had got from her sitting room.

Mrs Haywood grimaced. 'Yes.'

Thanet grinned. 'In that case I'm surprised she agreed to let anything go at all. People like that can't usually bear to part with a thing.'

She responded with a hesitant smile, her first. 'I know. She only agreed this time because the attic was getting so crammed with stuff that Roland absolutely insisted she part with some of it.'

'But a house of that size must have an attic as big as a warehouse!'

'Ah, but most of it has been converted into a flat for Damon – Mr Tarrant's son. So there's only a small space left for storage, about the size of an average room, I suppose.'

'I see.'

Mrs Haywood passed her hand across her forehead and rubbed her eyes. 'I'm not sure how we got onto this, surely it isn't relevant . . .'

'You were explaining how it was that you came to over-hear the row between Mrs Tarrant and her mother-in-law.'

'Ah, yes . . . Well, the point was, I became so engrossed up there I didn't notice the time. Not until I heard Nerine shouting at Lavinia.'

'And that was at what time?'

'Just after half past three. I looked at my watch. I didn't want to get caught up in the argument, so I waited until things had quietened down and then crept out, as quietly as I could.'

'I understand from Mr Tarrant that Mrs Tarrant usually kept her bedroom door locked, to prevent that particular problem occurring.'

Mrs Haywood shrugged. 'She must have forgotten, this afternoon. She would, occasionally. And Lavinia always seemed to know, when she did. She seemed to have a sixth sense about it. Extraordinary, really. The ideal solution would have been for Lavinia and Marilyn to have a separate establishment. I suppose, if this house had been free, they could have come here, but of course, at the time when Daphne bought it, there was no hint of the way Lavinia's mind was going to deteriorate. It's so sad . . . As it stands, well, High Gables belongs to Lavinia and she steadfastly refuses to leave. Why should she, after all? It's her home. She was there for many years before Nerine came on the scene.'

'But if she is becoming senile?'

'You cannot make people do things against their will, Inspector.' Mrs Haywood was reproachful. 'Lavinia's illness is erratic. She still has long lucid periods when, although she

34

is forgetful, she can converse quite rationally. And Mr Tarrant is far too fine a person to trick his mother into signing away her home . . .'

'And Mrs Tarrant?'

Mrs Haywood sighed. 'Would have been delighted to see her go. She made no bones about it. I think it's the only issue over which I have ever known Roland refuse to give her what she wanted.'

'So, did you by any chance see young Mrs Tarrant after the argument with her mother-in-law?' Thanet had spotted a photograph which interested him, over by the door. A woman, holding hands with two little girls, one on either side. Daphne and Nerine, as children?

'No. I came straight back here and started preparing supper. I usually try and do that in the afternoon, so that I'm free when Daphne gets back.'

'Which is usually at . . . ?'

'About twenty to six. But today, as I say, she was an hour or so early, because of the migraine.'

'Did you happen to see Mr Tarrant arrive home?'

'No. After Daphne got here, I'm afraid I was pretty occupied with looking after her. Until, of course, Mr Tarrant came across to tell me about the . . . about Nerine.'

'I understand that the Tarrants' son, Damon, whom you mentioned just now, has no job at present. Was he about at all during the day, do you know?'

'Oh, yes. He was working on that old car of his this morning, in the end garage.'

'And then he went back over to the house?'

'I don't know. I assume so.'

'Did you notice if his car was in the garage during the afternoon – when you went over to the house, for example?'

'No, I didn't, I'm afraid.'

'Or when you came back?'

She shook her head. 'Sorry . . . Oh, wait a minute. I do vaguely remember hearing him drive out . . . There's something wrong with the exhaust of his car. It makes a terrible din, we all complain about it. I think he likes the noise and keeps "forgetting" to get it attended to.'

'What time was this?'

She frowned, thinking. 'I'm not sure. Where was I, at the time? I think I was . . . yes, that's right. I was crossing the hall. I'd just come downstairs to fetch some ice for Daphne. She finds a really cold compress helps. And that was . . . yes, that was only five or ten minutes before Roland came across with the news.'

The memory clearly distressed her. Her lips began to tremble and she pressed the back of her hand against her mouth as if to hold in the potentially embarrassing sounds that might escape. Thanet judged that she had had just about as much as she could take, and that it would be best to bring the interview to a swift conclusion. But she was speaking again.

'He . . . he didn't know what he was doing,' she whispered. 'Like . . . I saw someone once, who'd been in a car accident . . . He looked just like that. In a complete daze.'

'What did you do?'

'When I realised what he was saying, I went to look at . . . at Nerine. Then I rang the police. By then I was beginning to feel a bit dizzy myself, what with the shock, and Daphne being ill and Roland in that state . . .'

'I suppose Miss Linacre still isn't well enough to be interviewed?' As soon as the words were out, Thanet could have kicked himself. Lesson number one in how not to phrase a question, he thought.

'No,' said Mrs Haywood, predictably.

Should he insist? What if Daphne Linacre didn't have a migraine? What if she had killed her sister then rushed across to her loyal friend and begged her to keep the police away until she'd had time to pull herself together? He ought at least to have some independent corroboration of her illness. 'You've called her doctor?'

'There's no point. We know exactly what to do when she has one of these attacks, by now.'

She was being unexpectedly firm. All her considerable maternal instincts were evidently now directed at Daphne.

'All the same... With the additional shock over her sister's death... Don't you think it advisable?'

'Possibly... We'll see.'

Thanet hesitated. But Mrs Haywood looked exhausted and he didn't want to put further, unnecessary strain upon her. No, he'd leave it for the moment. He could always come over later, if it became essential to talk to Daphne tonight.

'In that case, I'll see her in the morning.'

'Well... She usually has to have twenty-four hours in bed before the worst of the attack passes.'

Best not to press the point at present. Tomorrow would be a different matter. 'Well, thank you very much, Mrs Haywood. You've been most helpful.' Thanet stood up and Lineham closed his notebook and followed suit. On the way to the door Thanet paused, nodded at the photograph. 'Mrs Tarrant and Miss Linacre, as children?' he asked.

'Yes.'

The woman was middle-aged, smiling, good-natured, the girls aged perhaps six and nine. But surely she was too old to... 'Their mother?' said Thanet.

'Oh no. That's Mrs Glass, their housekeeper. Mrs Linacre died when Daphne was born. Poor little thing, she never knew her mother.'

Poor Nerine too, thought Thanet. It can't be much fun having your mother snatched away and a squalling new infant thrust at you, all on the same day. He studied the solemn faces of the two girls, Nerine beautiful even then, slim as a willow wand, and as graceful. And Daphne... Oh, dear. It couldn't have been easy for plain, lumpy Daphne, with a sister who looked like that.

'Mrs Glass is in a home now, in Sturrenden. Well, not a home, exactly. Sheltered accommodation. She's absolutely amazing for her age. She's well into her eighties by now.'

Thanet recognised in Mrs Haywood's tone the need to reassure herself so often displayed by elderly people seeking

37

to allay the spectres of old age. Look, they seem to say: so-and-so has managed to avoid dependence, sickness, and its attendant indignities, so surely so shall I?

He opened the door and was at once aware of sounds of retching from upstairs.

Mrs Haywood pushed past him. 'Oh, dear,' she said. 'Daphne. I must go . . .'

'I should give her doctor a ring . . . Don't worry about us, we'll let ourselves out.'

Thanet waited until they were a few paces away from the front door, then turned to Lineham. 'Well, what did you make of all that, Mike? You were very quiet in there.'

Lineham grinned. 'Too busy listening, watching and scribbling.' He tapped his notebook. 'You always say . . .'

'Yes, yes. I know what I always say . . . So tell me, what do you *think*?'

'Several interesting things, sir.'

Lineham's face was eager, bright with interest, and Thanet experienced the familiar sense of warmth and satisfaction which these discussions with the sergeant invariably gave him. He'd never found anyone else to work with whose mind was so in tune with his own.

'Such as?'

'Well, first of all, we guessed right about Mr Tarrant. He obviously knew about this affair his wife was having. So he was lying, back there.'

'Not exactly, Mike. He didn't actually say he knew nothing about it. He just refused to discuss it.'

'Well, it's the same thing, isn't it?'

'Not quite. After all, put yourself in his situation. Would you want to discuss your wife's infidelities if you loved her and had just found her dead, perhaps murdered?'

'Well, if I suspected her lover might have done it . . .'

'I don't think he'd got as far as that, Mike. In fact, I doubt if he was thinking rationally at all. No, I suspect that when we do tackle him about it, he'll suggest precisely that.'

'Mrs Haywood certainly seems to think a lot of him,'

conceded Lineham, grudgingly, abandoning that line of argument for the moment. 'And then there was what she said about the son, Damon.'

'Yes, the timing there was quite interesting, wasn't it? It sounds as though Damon left just a few minutes before his father got home.'

'Did you notice,' said Lineham eagerly, 'that when we were talking to Mr Tarrant, he was a bit, well, off, when we mentioned his son?'

'Yes, I must say I had the impression he wasn't being quite frank with us.'

'Say the son did it,' said Lineham. 'Say he has a row with his mother, shoves her over the balcony and then panics, decides to run for it . . .'

'Let's not get carried away, Mike. We'll probably find that he turns up as innocent as a lamb, later on this evening.'

'And if he doesn't?'

'Then we shall have to reconsider. But I think it's too early to jump to conclusions yet.'

'What about Miss Linacre, sir? D'you think that migraine's genuine?'

'She was certainly being sick, up in the bathroom.'

'Could have been guilt. Or remorse?'

'Slow down, Mike. We'll soon find out, when we do a bit of checking. I could hardly force myself into the sickroom, could I? We'll have a word with her doctor, if he comes, and first thing tomorrow you can send someone over to Linacre Nurseries, to ask a few questions.'

'Right, sir.'

Bentley appeared around the corner of the house.

'Ah, Bentley's found the key,' said Lineham.

'It was in her handbag, sir,' said Bentley, handing it over. 'In the sitting room.'

'Good.'

The key was smooth and hard in Thanet's hand, a symbol of secrets withheld, of revelations to come. Over the years, if his investigations into domestic murder had taught him anything, they had taught him that it is in the character of the victim that the seeds of his own destruction lie. A woman's bedroom can reveal much of her personality. Anticipation began to fizz through his veins.

'Let's go and take a look, then, shall we?'

FOUR

As the door of Nerine Tarrant's bedroom swung open two impressions were paramount: opulence and chaos.

Lineham gave a low whistle of astonishment and admiration as they stepped inside. 'Louise would love to see this. But what a mess!'

The bed dominated the room. An elaborate canopy was suspended from the ceiling, swathes of material cascading down to the four corners, creating a four-poster effect. In this room, too, the theme was blue and white. The flowered chintz of the bedhangings had also been used in the quilted bedhead and bedspread, and the two tones of blue in the floral design exactly matched the pale blue carpet and the deep blue range of fitted cupboards which stretched the length of an entire wall. Filmy white curtains hung at the tall french windows. The effect was both dramatic and romantic – clues to Nerine's character?

Clearly, much thought had gone into the designing of this room and no one could blame Nerine for being angry with her mother-in-law for making such a mess of it. Clothes were strewn everywhere – tossed on the bed, draped over the elegant blue velvet chaise longue, lying about in careless disorder all over the floor. And what clothes! Thanet didn't know much about fashion, but he could recognise quality when he saw it: silk, satin, velvet, lawn, wool, suede, leather, fur . . .

Also . . . 'Can you smell something, Mike?'

'Like what?'

'I'm not sure. Something . . .' Thanet shook his head. It

had been a whiff, no more, of something familiar, yet alien to this room.

Both men stood still, sniffing.

'No, it's gone . . .' Thanet shrugged, moved on. He and Lineham were being very careful not to touch or move anything.

'I bet she spent more on clothes in a year than I earn,' said Lineham, stepping gingerly over what looked like a mink coat. 'You think Mrs Tarrant senior really did this?'

'Sounds as if it was a regular occurrence. Anyway, it doesn't look to me as though it's the result of a struggle, wouldn't you agree?'

The clutter of open jars and bottles, some overturned, on the dressing table, the gaping wardrobe doors and half-open drawers, told their own story. They had been rifled by an eager, impatient hand, searching — for what? For some exquisite garment that would transform the ravages of age into an illusion of youth and beauty? Or, more sinister thought, for revenge? Had the old woman been seeking to strike where it would hurt most at the daughter-in-law who regarded her as nothing more than a nuisance?

Lineham was obviously thinking along similar lines. 'D'you think this really was just an old lady having fun, or d'you think she might have done it on purpose?'

'Just what I was wondering myself.'

'It doesn't sound as though they were exactly on the best of terms, does it? Sir, you don't think . . .'

'I sincerely hope not!' To have to arrest a senile old lady was the last thing Thanet wanted.

'Old people can be very difficult, when they're suffering from dementia,' Lineham persisted. 'I know a chap whose mother went like that and he said that if she was crossed, she used to go quite beserk. She'd be beyond reason, he said, and she was amazingly strong. It took two of them to hold her back, once, when she wanted to go shopping in the middle of the night, in January, in her nightdress!'

'Hmm . . . It was around half past three, wasn't it, when

Mrs Haywood said she heard Nerine Tarrant start shouting at her mother-in-law?'

'Yes. I imagine the companion, Miss Barnes, will be able to verify that. Doc Mallard put the earliest time of death at two o'clock, but it looks as though we can push that back at least an hour and a half . . . And another thing . . . Surely Mrs Tarrant must have been killed either during or soon after that row, or she would have tidied up in here?'

'Not necessarily. She might well have blamed Miss Barnes for allowing the old lady to give her the slip, and told her she expected her to do the clearing up. But I suppose you could be right . . . We'd better go and have a word with them.'

They relocked the door, gave the key to Trace, the SOCO, who would need it when he had finished working on the sitting room next door, and set off in search of old Mrs Tarrant's quarters. They were crossing the landing when Thanet put out a restraining hand.

'Wait,' he murmured.

He had glimpsed a flicker of movement ahead of them and now a figure appeared at the far end of the landing. The two men exchanged glances of astonishment. Nothing they had heard about old Mrs Tarrant had prepared them for this. The slack, puckered flesh of arms and neck, the knotted veins on the hand that now went up to her throat in a dramatic gesture of surprise, betrayed her age. But she was dressed like a young girl, in flowing white muslin skirt, very high heels, an off-the-shoulder blouse and, the final grotesque touch, a white velvet ribbon tied in a large bow on the top of her scanty curls. She had attempted, and failed, to conceal the deeply scored wrinkles of her face with heavy, garish make-up: thick, deep blue eyeshadow, symmetrical circles of rouge on either cheek and a scarlet cupid's bow of a mouth. Thanet experienced a powerful shaft of compassion as she gave them a brilliant, coquettish smile. Mrs Tarrant might appear to them to be a bizarre, almost clownish figure, but in her own eyes she was clearly beautiful. He and Lineham watched in painful silence as she dipped to gather up the hem of her skirt in her right hand and, wafting it backwards and forwards in rhythm with her steps, began to descend the stairs with an exaggerated, swaying walk. Half-way down she paused to cast the same smile back at them, over one shoulder.

'Now what?' said Lineham, in a low voice.

Thanet shrugged. 'We can but try. Mrs Tarrant?' he called, as they began to descend the stairs behind her.

She had reached the bottom now and she paused, putting one hand on the newel post to steady herself. When she looked back at them this time that terrifyingly flirtatious rictus had been replaced by a look of terror.

'Mrs Tarrant?'

She made a little choking sound in her throat and in a swirl of movement, a diminishing clatter of high heels along the passageway beside the stairs, was gone.

'This isn't going to be easy,' said Thanet grimly. 'Come on. With any luck, she's run to Miss Barnes.'

He was right. The sound of voices – or rather, of a voice – led them to a half-open door, and they paused outside.

'Come on, Lavinia, you tell Marilyn.' A coaxing tone. 'How can Marilyn help you, if you won't tell her what's the matter?'

Thanet knocked and pushed the door further open. 'Miss Barnes?'

It was a kitchen which had obviously been converted from a former sitting room; a heavy marble fireplace still dominated one end of the room. Seated in a rocking chair beside it crouched Mrs Tarrant, moaning, face in lap, hands clasped at the back of her neck, as if defying anyone to make her raise her head. The woman they had glimpsed earlier, coming out of Tarrant's study, was kneeling on the floor beside her, stroking her hair. It was, Thanet thought, a remarkably touching picture. He suspected that not many paid companions would in privacy treat their charges with such compassion.

The young woman scrambled to her feet, pushing long lanky brown hair back off her face.

'Who . . . ? Oh, you must be the policemen.'

'That's right.' Thanet made the introductions. No one would give Marilyn Barnes a second glance, he thought (and yet, someone had — the child existed, to prove it). She was neither pretty nor ugly, dark or fair, fat or thin, tall or short, but always somewhere in between. Even her eyes were an indeterminate bluish-greyish-greenish brown. 'I'm afraid we gave Mrs Tarrant a fright just now, appearing upstairs like that.'

Cautiously, the old woman raised her head, revealing eyes still drowning in tears, cheeks streaked with mascara.

'That's better!' said Miss Barnes with genuine pleasure in her voice, unconsciously displaying her best feature, a wide generous smile which illuminated her face and briefly gave an illusion of attractiveness. And to Thanet and Lineham, 'Perhaps you'd like to sit down? I won't be a minute.' Snatching up a box of tissues she tenderly wiped the old lady's eyes. 'There, that *is* better, isn't it?'

Mrs Tarrant's eyes, fixed until now on her companion's face, flickered briefly in the direction of the two policemen. She beckoned her companion to come closer. Her whisper was quite audible.

'Have they come to take me away?'

Miss Barnes laughed and patted her employer's hand. 'No, of course not. They just want to talk to us about Nerine, I expect. You remember, I told you, she's had an accident.'

The old lady's eyes clouded with incomprehension. 'An accident?'

'Yes,' said Miss Barnes patiently. 'She fell, from her balcony. I told you.'

Mrs Tarrant shook her head. 'I don't remember.' She clutched suddenly at Miss Barnes's arm. 'You won't let her send me away, will you?'

A firm shake of the head. 'No. No, of course not. No one

45

is going to send you away. You're going to stay here with me.'

Mrs Tarrant gazed doubtfully at her companion. 'She said she was going to.' Her face puckered. 'She shouted at me.' It was the whining, petulant tone of a child.

'I know. But it's all right now. I promise.' Taking up a shawl which hung over the back of a nearby chair, Miss Barnes draped it around the old lady's shoulders, covering up the unsuitable blouse, the scrawny, knobbly shoulders. 'There, that's better isn't it?' Then she sank down into a chair at the table, facing Thanet. 'I'm sorry, I'm afraid she's rather upset.'

'Because of the row with young Mrs Tarrant, this afternoon?'

Miss Barnes sighed. 'You heard about that, then. Yes. She's been very unsettled ever since.'

The old lady seemed to have withdrawn into herself. Rocking gently to and fro, she was stroking the soft, fine muslin of her skirt.

Thanet glanced at Lineham. *Your turn.*

'What time was this, Miss Barnes?' said Lineham. 'The row?'

'About half past three. Lavinia – I hope you don't mind if I call her that, but it's so confusing, with two Mrs Tarrants in the house, that we decided it was the sensible thing to do – Lavinia usually has a rest in the afternoon, from two until three thirty, then I get her up so that by the time Nicky – my son – gets home from school at a quarter to four, I'm free to attend to him.'

'So what went wrong, this afternoon?'

'How did Lavinia get into young Mrs Tarrant's bedroom, you mean?' Miss Barnes shrugged. 'Just an unfortunate combination of circumstances. I did look in on her at a quarter past two, to make sure she'd dozed off, but she must have been faking.' Miss Barnes shook her head and sighed. 'The trouble is, she absolutely adores dressing up – well, you can see that for yourselves – and Mrs Tarrant has such

46

beautiful clothes . . . That room is like a magnet to Lavinia. I don't know how she does it, but it's uncanny, she always seems to know, every time Mrs Tarrant leaves the door unlocked – which is rarely, I can tell you. Anyway, that hour and a half is the only time of the day that I get to myself, so once I'd satisfied myself she was settled I came back down here, made myself a cup of tea and read a magazine. Just before half past three I made a cup for Lavinia, and I was on my way upstairs when I heard Mrs Tarrant shouting.'

Marilyn Barnes broke off and glanced anxiously at the old lady, who was still rocking gently, stroking her muslin skirt and gazing blankly into space. She lowered her voice. 'I don't want to upset her again, now she's settled down.'

Thanet and Lineham leaned closer.

'Mrs Tarrant was dragging Lavinia along the corridor towards the stairs. She was really livid.

"*You bloody woman. You ought to be put away, you know that? Locked up, where you can't be a nuisance to anyone. And where the hell d'you think you've been, Marilyn? Lazing the afternoon away in the kitchen, I suppose, while this wretched old woman has been busy turning my bedroom upside down again. What d'you think we pay you for, that's what I'd like to know?"*

"*Don't cry, Lavinia. I'm sorry, Mrs Tarrant, I thought she was asleep.*"

"*You thought. You thought. Well, it's not good enough. I've had enough, I really have. I've told you, over and over again, you ought to lock her in, in the afternoons . . .*"

"*But I can't do that. I have no right . . .*"

"*You have every right. We have every right. We employ you and I'm telling you, you lock that bloody door or I'm warning you, for the last time, you'll be finding yourself out of a job and my dear mother-in-law can take herself off to a nursing home. Or the loony-bin, which is where she really belongs.*"

"*She can't help it, Mrs Tarrant. It's her illness.*"

"*Don't make excuses to me! Ill or not, no one in their*"

right mind would put up with this sort of performance for a moment longer than they had to . . . Oh, do stop snivelling, Lavinia. Here, take her away, for God's sake. But you needn't think you've heard the last of this. I shall speak to my husband tonight." '

They all glanced at the old lady as Marilyn reached the end of her story, but there was still no change. Old Mrs Tarrant had, consciously or unconsciously, decided that it was more comfortable to blank out reality for the moment.

'Do you think she meant it?' said Thanet 'About the nursing home?'

Marilyn shrugged. 'Oh, she meant it, all right. Whether Mr Tarrant would have agreed is another matter. The house belongs to his mother, you see. She wants to stay here and so far he has always refused to try to get her committed. You may not think it, looking at her now, but sometimes you can have a perfectly rational conversation with her. And she's really a very sweet person. So appreciative. And the rest of the time . . . Well, I just tell myself to treat her as if she was a child, and it usually works.'

'You don't find it very frustrating, at times?'

'Well of course. But what job isn't? And I can't be too fussy.' She glanced down at her left hand. 'I'm not married, as you'll have gathered, and jobs aren't exactly thick on the ground. Especially ones that keep school hours and allow you to be at home during the holidays. And this one pays bed and board for Nicky and me, too, so . . .' Again she shrugged. 'I've always thought, well, he's only got one parent, so I must try and be available when he needs me, to make it up to him . . . This suits me very well, until he's a bit older.'

'How old is he?'

'Ten.'

'Where is he now?'

'I've arranged for him to spend the night with some friends in the village.'

'Good idea.' Though if Nicky were anything like Ben, he'd

48

be furious at being summarily removed from the scene of the action, thought Thanet.

'Of course,' said Marilyn, 'the trouble is that every time this sort of thing happens, Lavinia lives in fear and trembling for ages afterwards.'

'In case she's sent away, you mean?'

'Yes. That's why she was so frightened when she saw you. She thought you'd come for her.'

Quite possible, thought Thanet. Though there could be another, more sinister explanation... He glanced at Lineham. *Take over again.*

'So what happened after all the fuss had died down?' said Lineham.

Marilyn grimaced. 'It was all a bit hectic. Lavinia was in a state and Nicky was due home, so I brought her down here and gave her a cup of tea, tried to calm her down, while Nicky had a glass of squash and an apple. Then he went out to play and I put Lavinia to bed for an hour – she hadn't had a sleep this afternoon, and the fuss had worn her out. She went up quite happily, and I sat with her until she dozed off. Before I came downstairs I knocked at the door of Mrs Tarrant's bedroom and when she didn't answer I checked that it was locked. I didn't want the same thing happening again.'

'And was it? Locked?'

'Yes.'

'What time was this?'

'About four thirty, I should think.'

'Did you see anyone about?'

Marilyn shook her head. 'Not a soul.'

'So what did you do then?'

For the first time she hesitated.

'What's the matter?' said Lineham.

'It's just that... Well, I suppose I'm wondering why you want to know all these details.'

Lineham glanced at Thanet, who gave an almost imperceptible shake of the head. 'It's simply that whenever there's an accidental death, we have to try to build up a complete picture of the movements of all the people in the household . . . In case one of them might have seen or heard something significant, you understand.'

'But I haven't. I didn't.'

'The point is, you can never tell. It may not seem significant or important to you, but it can be very helpful to us.'

Thanet was watching Marilyn closely. She seemed to be taking Lineham's explanation at its face value. It was, after all, true.

She shrugged. 'Fair enough. What was it you wanted to know?'

'What you did after putting old Mrs Tarrant to bed, and checking that her daughter-in-law's bedroom door was locked.'

'I came down and got Nicky's tea ready. I usually cook him something simple and he has it about a quarter to five. I did pop upstairs to check on Lavinia before I called him in, but she was still fast asleep. I sat with him while he ate it, then I washed up, cleared away, and went back upstairs, to get Lavinia up.'

'What time was it then?'

'About half past five.'

'And did you see anyone about, either then or on the earlier occasion?'

'No.'

'What about earlier in the afternoon?'

'I saw Mrs Haywood, going upstairs, soon after lunch. She was going to look out some jumble in the attic, I believe.'

'Ah, yes, she told us . . . Did you see her leave, later on?'

Marilyn shook her head.

'Anyone else?'

'I don't think so . . . Not in the house, anyway.'

Thanet saw Lineham restrain himself from pouncing too eagerly. The sergeant was doing very well.

'And outside?'

'Well, I did see Miss Linacre come home, not long before I called Nicky in for his tea.'

'Around twenty to five, then?'

'Yes. I noticed especially because I was surprised to see her home so early. She doesn't usually come until an hour or so later.'

'She has a migraine.'

'I thought that might be it. She goes down with them every few months or so ... Miserable things ... She looks like death warmed up for days afterwards.'

'Anyone else, outside?'

'Only Damon. At least, I assume it was Damon. I glanced out of the landing window when I was coming downstairs with Lavinia, the second time, and I saw his car backing out of the garage.'

'This was at half past five?'

'Well, five or ten minutes later, I should say. Because although I didn't have to dress Lavinia after her rest – I'd only slipped her shoes off, earlier – it took me five or ten minutes to coax her out of her room.' She glanced at her charge, leaned forward and lowered her voice again. 'She was very upset again. When I went into the bedroom I couldn't see her anywhere, and I almost panicked. I thought, Oh God, if she's somehow managed to get at Mrs Tarrant's things again ... But she made a little sound, and I found her. She was sitting on the floor in a corner, on the far side of the bed. She was all ready to come back downstairs – she'd put her shoes and cardigan on ... but I think she'd been afraid that if she went out onto the landing, she might meet Mrs Tarrant, and there'd be another scene.'

Lineham glanced at Thanet. *I think you'd better take over now, sir.*

'She was frightened,' said Thanet.

'In case there was another row, yes.'

'Or,' said Thanet delicately, 'possibly because she had already been out of her room, before you came up to fetch her, and had seen something to upset her ... ?' Or done

51

something to upset her, he silently added, mentally shuddering away from the picture of the old lady, with a strength born of desperation and dementia, grabbing the shapely legs of the woman who was threatening to lock her away for ever and heaving, tilting, shoving and finally watching, as Nerine's body smashed down on the paving stones and lay still, still . . . A moment of appalled clarity, as she realises what she has done, then flight, back to her room and into a corner to hide . . .

Marilyn was looking horrified. 'You're not suggesting she might actually have seen . . .' Her eyes swivelled to her employer, who was now frowning down at her lap. The blunt, varnished nails had scrabbled a hole in the gauzy material, Thanet noticed, and even as he watched, the old lady seized the torn edges on either side and with a twisting, rending movement ripped the skirt apart from waist to hem.

'Lavinia!' exclaimed Marilyn, springing up and imprisoning her employer's hands in her own. 'Why did you do that? Look what a mess you've made of your pretty skirt . . .'

'I'm thirsty,' said the old lady querulously. 'I haven't had my Horlicks. Where's my Horlicks . . . ?'

Marilyn stood up. 'Well, there's no need to show off like that, to get my attention,' she said, with understandable irritation. 'All you had to do was ask, and I would have got it for you.' Already she was pouring milk into a saucepan, spooning Horlicks from a jar.

But the old lady wasn't listening. Watching her, Thanet could see the beginnings of a tremor in her body, scarcely perceptible to begin with, like the first breath of wind stirring the topmost leaves of the trees in a forest, then gradually becoming more and more apparent. Marilyn, busy with the hot drink, had not yet noticed.

'Miss Barnes,' said Thanet softly, calling her attention to her charge.

Shoving the saucepan hastily aside, off the heat, Marilyn swooped forward and seized the old lady's hands, in a very

52

different manner from a few minutes previously. 'Lavinia!' she cried. 'What is it? What's the matter?' And leaning forward she gathered the frail, shaking body into her arms. 'Don't worry,' she murmured. 'Marilyn isn't cross with you. Really. Hush, now. Marilyn's got you . . .'

Thanet was more certain than ever that the old lady had seen something, heard something, done something that had terrified her. Which? he wondered. And what?

Her next words confirmed this.

'I'm frightened,' she quavered. 'Death . . .'

Marilyn looked helplessly up at Thanet, then turned back to her employer and began to murmur soothingly again, rocking her gently and patting her back.

Thanet stood up. 'She's obviously not up to being questioned now. Tomorrow, perhaps?'

Marilyn nodded. 'She might be calmer then, after a good night's sleep. Though there's no guarantee she'll remember anything, of course.'

'Just one more question . . . We noticed that no attempt had been made to tidy Mrs Tarrant's bedroom . . .'

Marilyn's eyes were hard as she looked up again. 'That was because she wanted her husband to see the grounds for her complaint. She told me she wasn't going to clear away a thing until he'd seen exactly what his mother had been up to.'

'I see. Thank you.'

They left.

FIVE

'Nice woman,' said Lineham, when they were out of earshot.

'Very.'

'I don't suppose there are many in her position who'd take so much trouble over a batty old lady like that. And she wasn't just putting it on for our benefit, was she?'

'I don't think so, no.'

'What's the matter, sir?'

'I'm just hoping you're wrong, in your suggestion that old Mrs Tarrant may have pushed her daughter-in-law off that balcony. Frankly, the idea appals me.'

'She'd get off,' said Lineham cheerfully.

'That's not the point.'

'What is, then, sir?'

Thanet shook his head. 'Never mind.' If Lineham couldn't see it for himself, there was no point in explaining it to him. The sergeant's occasional lack of sensitivity was something Thanet had had to learn to live with.

'Anyway, even if she did do it, sir, there's no guarantee we'd be able to prove it, unless forensic come up with something useful.'

'Well, it's early days yet,' said Thanet vaguely. 'Let's go and have a word with PC Driver, shall we? Where is he?'

'Down by the gate, holding back the ghouls.'

'Right. Of course,' Thanet added, as they headed for the front door, 'there's always the possibility that Miss Barnes did it.'

Lineham stride faltered. 'Why?' Clearly, the suggestion didn't appeal to him.

'Well, she'd just been threatened with being thrown out on her ear, hadn't she? And for a woman in her position that's a pretty alarming prospect.'

'I imagine she's very capable,' said Lineham. 'And people are supposed to be crying out for good domestic staff, house-keepers and such-like, these days. I shouldn't have thought she'd have too many problems in finding another job.'

'With a ten-year-old boy in tow? Not as easy as you're making out, I suspect, Mike. Let's face it, like old Mrs Tarrant, she had both motive and opportunity.'

'For all we know, they could have been in it together,' said Lineham sarcastically.

'Who knows? They say truth is often stranger than fiction.' But Thanet didn't mean it. He could accept that both women had a powerful reason to be afraid of Nerine Tarrant – who sounded more and more unpleasant the more he learnt about her – and that either of them could, in the last resort, have lost her temper and given Nerine that fatal shove, but he simply could not see them sitting down and carefully plan-ning the murder as conspirators.

Lineham gave a derisive snort. 'There are limits.'

Thanet enjoyed teasing his sergeant occasionally. 'To what, Mike? Our credulity? Their decency? Our gullibility? Their potential evil? I doubt it. On the contrary, I think that such limits are capable of infinite expansion and contraction. That's what makes people so fascinating. You never know where they're going to draw their particular line. I suppose,' said Thanet, becoming interested in pursuing the idea, 'it's what life is all about. Learning where to draw the lines.'

Lineham was not interested in philosophising. He made a polite sound of assent but mentally he had switched off, Thanet could tell.

'Then, there's the son, sir. Damon.' Lineham injected the name with the scorn of the conventional for the off-beat. 'Didn't someone say he's on probation?'

'That's right. As a matter of fact, he's one of Joan's clients.'

'Really? That could be useful.'

Thanet wasn't so sure. He could foresee difficulties ahead. He had always dreaded finding himself in the situation where a suspect in one of his cases was also Joan's client. Thinking about it now he experienced a premonitory tremor of unease. Already he was in a slight dilemma: should he tell the sergeant about that missed appointment this afternoon?

There was no reason why not, so far as he could tell. Joan could hardly regard it as a confidence broken. In the circumstances it would be routine to interview Damon's probation officer and this information would have come out as a matter of course.

'As a matter of fact, she's already told me something interesting. Damon had an appointment with her this afternoon, and he didn't turn up.'

'Really? What time was he supposed to have seen her?'

'I don't know the details. She was rushing off to a meeting, there was no time to talk.'

'Was he in the habit of breaking appointments?'

'No idea. But I imagine not, or she wouldn't have been so concerned. In any case, the timing of his departure was interesting, didn't you think?'

'You mean, that was what his father was hiding? The fact that he met Damon driving out as he was driving in? So as to avoid implicating him?'

'It's quite likely, don't you think?'

'Possible, certainly. But I wonder why. So far there hasn't been any suggestion that Damon and his mother didn't get on, let alone that he hated her enough to kill her . . .'

'Perhaps it's just a natural paternal reaction – try to keep your offspring out of trouble if you can – and especially if they've already had a brush with the law. Anyway, it sounds as though Damon might well have been here over the crucial period.'

'Yes. It'll be interesting to hear what he has to say . . . Ah, there's Driver, sir.'

It was now just after nine thirty and the light was seeping out of the sky. Sharp-edged silhouettes of trees were etched against the pearly brightness which still lingered above the western horizon, and the crunch of their footsteps on the gravel sounded unnaturally loud in that strangely cathedral hush which falls over the land as day fades into night.

Most of the crowd had dispersed by now, resigned to the fact that there was to be no more drama tonight, and only five or six die-hards were still lingering on the far side of the tall gates. PC Driver was chatting to them through the wrought-iron scrolls and curlicues, his stance relaxed, a man at ease among old acquaintants. He was in his mid-twenties, tall and thin, with a hooked nose and a frizz of tight, fair curls. As Thanet and Lineham approached he turned, unconsciously stiffening to attention. Lineham made the introductions and the three men strolled a little way up the drive, out of range of all the eager ears flapping on the other side of the gates.

'We're hoping your local knowledge is going to be of some use to us,' said Thanet. 'How long have you been living in Ribbleden.'

Driver pulled a face. 'A couple of years, sir. That's only five minutes – less – by rural standards.'

'But you've got a good idea of what goes on here, by now.'

'I make it my business to keep my ear to the ground, sir. And my mouth shut.'

'Good. So tell us what you know about the people who live in High Gables. And especially about young Mrs Tarrant.'

Driver shuffled his feet. 'She had a bit of a reputation, I'm afraid, sir.' He looked uncomfortable, as if he felt it slightly improper to gossip about his social superiors. Thanet knew that in the country such distinctions were still more clearly delineated than in the town.

'She played around, you mean.'

'She certainly did.' Driver rolled his eyes, warming to his subject. 'It's common knowledge that she'd have a new man every few months or so. You'd have thought she'd have run out by now, in a place this size.'

'And the current candidate?'

'Lance Speed, sir. Owner of the local garage.'

'What can you tell us about him?'

'He's married, with one son, Tim, aged eighteen, who's a friend of Damon Tarrant. Mrs Speed is very popular, does a lot in the village organisations.'

'She's aware of this liaison?'

'Opinion is divided, sir. But the majority view is that no, she doesn't know about it. Sometimes the wife is the last person to know, especially if she's well liked, and I'd guess that in this case there was a sort of conspiracy of silence, to prevent her getting hurt. Mr Speed has a reputation as a bit of a lad with the ladies, but to my knowledge until now it hasn't gone beyond a bit of harmless flirtation at the petrol pumps.'

'Where do they live?'

'In a bungalow at the entrance to the village. I expect you passed it on your way in. Shangri-la.'

'What about the rest of the people in High Gables?'

'The son's a bit wild, Damon. Got put on probation a couple of months ago, possession of drugs. Mr Tarrant is pretty well liked, I've never heard anything against him — except that most people think he's a bit of a fool to put up with his wife's behaviour.'

'There was no talk that they were on bad terms?'

'Not to my knowledge, sir. Beats me how he stood it. She never made any attempt to be discreet.' Driver shrugged. 'He was potty about her, if you ask me.'

'What about the old lady?'

'Eccentric but harmless. She did a lot for the village, in her time — ran the Darby and Joan club, chairman of the WI, that sort of thing, and there's a lot of goodwill towards her. The general feeling is that it's sad, the way she's gone downhill.'

'And her companion? How long has she been looking after her?'

'Since just after I came. There was a drawing aside of skirts to begin with, on account of her being an unmarried mum, but she keeps herself to herself and people have accepted her by now. Seems a nice enough woman.'

'What about Miss Linacre and Mrs Haywood?'

'Miss Linacre is out at work all day, so we don't see much of her, but Mrs Haywood helps out at church events — jumble sales, cake stalls, that sort of thing. She's regarded as harmless but a bit odd, partly because of the way she dresses and partly because of the way she goes on and on about that son of hers, the one who died, years ago. I don't think she has any close personal friends in the village.'

'Right, well what I'd like you to do is see if you can find out anything more about the Speeds. DS Lineham and I are going to go along and have a word with them now, and I'd be interested to know what you can pick up. People in the village know you, they're more likely to talk freely. Also, I'd like you to compile a list of Mrs Tarrant's previous boyfriends, with addresses if possible. Mark those with whom she is thought to have parted on bad terms, and those who were said to be jealous. Let me have a report, tomorrow morning.'

'Right, sir.'

'The pub'll be the best place for you, tonight. Mike, nip up to the house and arrange for someone to relieve PC Driver at the gate in, say, half an hour.'

Lineham was back in a few minutes. 'I assume you didn't want me to bring the car, sir?'

'No, we'll walk. Take a look around. Perhaps drop in at the pub ourselves, on the way. I don't know about you, but I'm starving.'

'I could do with a bite. Haven't had anything since a sandwich, at lunchtime.'

The hangers-on at the gate fell silent as the three policemen approached. Driver opened the gates, slipped through with Thanet and Lineham, then resumed his I'm-your-approachable-local-bobby attitude, leaning back against the gates with his arms folded. The people held back until Thanet and

Lineham had gone a little way down the road, then turned back to cluster around Driver, eager for titbits.

'*What did they say?*'

'*What's the news?*'

'*What's the latest?*'

'*Come on, Billy-boy, give!*'

Thanet and Lineham exchanged grins.

'He's got his head screwed on the right way,' said Lineham.

'Yes. Though in fact he didn't tell us much we hadn't learned already.'

'No. But it was interesting to have it confirmed by an outsider.'

'True.' Thanet's tone was abstracted. He had come to a halt and was looking around, trying to absorb his surroundings. High Gables was on the edge of the village in what Thanet now realised was an interesting and unusual position: private yet not isolated, and not directly overlooked by any other house, it stood on what could be described as a peninsula of garden, between two sharp bends in the road. If this had been a main road no doubt it would long ago have been re-routed to cut across behind the house, but such alterations to minor roads in the country are always being shelved in favour of other, more urgent repairs or innovations.

Glancing back, by craning his neck Thanet could just see another chimneystack, poking up above and beyond the trees in Tarrant's front garden. And on this side, once he and Lineham had carefully negotiated the bend (there were no pavements), the narrow country lane widened out and the village began. The domestic architecture was typical of villages all over Kent, a picturesque juxaposition of Tudor black and white, mellow brick and tile, crisp white-painted weatherboard. Thanet studied the houses with an appreciative eye as he walked by. He himself would have loved to live in one, with its crooked walls, uneven floors and, above all, individuality. Alas, such aspirations were not matched by a policeman's pay. The price of houses like these had rocketed over the last twenty years and the dwindling supply ensured that such properties were certain to climb even higher in value, as time went on.

'Pretty little place,' said Lineham.

'Mmm.'

Here, the road divided, the right fork going straight on, the left sweeping round in front of the church to encircle the village green. Thanet's men were hard at work on their house-to-house enquiries.

'That looks promising,' said the sergeant, nodding at a colourful inn sign depicting a labrador with a somewhat garish cock pheasant in its mouth. Inside the pub the excited roar of conversation stopped abruptly as the two men entered, only gradually resuming and at a much lower, more subdued level.

'Oh, to be a fly on the wall,' murmured Lineham in Thanet's ear as they carried their sandwiches and beer across to a small corner table which had miraculously become vacant.

It was obvious that they weren't going to learn anything useful by attempting to eavesdrop and it was impossible to discuss the case; they ate their sandwiches, drained their glasses and departed. By the time the door swung to behind them, the noise level had already increased perceptibly.

'Let's hope Driver does better than us,' said Lineham.

They walked on, passing in turn the post-office-cum-shop, the village school (still functioning, Thanet noticed; the tide of closures had been stemmed in recent years, owing to the soaring cost of transport), the village hall and a seedy-looking garage, somewhat pretentiously called Ribbleden Motors. Three second-hand cars, none of them less than three years old, were drawn up on the forecourt, price stickers on windscreens. There was a solitary petrol pump.

'I thought they went out with the Ark,' said Lineham, nodding at the overhead swing bar and trailing rubber hose. 'If this is Speed's place, it doesn't exactly seem to be thriving.'

'Not enough custom, out here. Too far off the beaten track.'

Another few minutes brought them to the far end of the village and Shangri-la, which had been squeezed into a narrow slot between the last of the older houses and the inevitable council estate. Thanet noted that this was undergoing the by now familiar transformation process. The original Airey houses, ugly dwellings hastily erected after the war and apparently constructed of horizontal pre-cast concrete strips, had recently been discovered to have some design fault which rendered them unsafe, and all over the country were in the process of being pulled down and replaced. The new houses, he noted with approval, were much more attractive and in keeping with their setting.

Unlike his business premises, Speed's home looked spruce enough. Paint gleamed, windows shone and well-tended flowerbeds full of newly planted summer bedding surrounded the close-cropped lawn. Mrs Speed's handiwork, Thanet guessed.

'If she really doesn't know what's been going on between her husband and Nerine Tarrant,' he said, 'then this is going to be a bit tricky.'

This was the part of his job that he hated, the damage done to innocent people peripherally involved in his cases. Mrs Speed, by all accounts, was a nice woman protected until now by a consensus of goodwill from knowledge which would cause her considerable distress, and he, Thanet, was going to be the one to have to disillusion her.

'She's bound to wonder, if we ask to talk to him privately,' agreed Lineham. 'But what else can we do?'

Musical chimes sounded as he pressed the bell and a moment later a light went on in the hall. The man who opened the door stood back resignedly when Thanet introduced himself.

'Come in.'

Geometric was the word which blinked on like a neon sign in Thanet's brain. Speed had a square head, and a square body, with oblongs for trousers and arms. The head was adorned with thinning hair and a curly moustache which drooped a little on one side, spoiling the symmetrical effect. He was in his mid-forties, and was wearing designer jeans and a shirt unbuttoned half-way to the waist. A gold medallion winked coyly in the sparse hair of his chest. Thanet spared a moment to marvel at the attractions between men and women. What could Nerine Tarrant have seen in this ageing Lothario?

The room into which he had led them was hazy with cigarette smoke and rather too gaudy for Thanet's taste: brown-and-white striped Dralon suite, multi coloured floral carpet and fluorescent orange velvet curtains, which a woman was drawing across the large picture window. She turned as they entered.

'My wife.'

If Speed was all straight lines, his wife was all curves. Short and plump, with billowing breasts overflowing the tight brassiere clearly visible beneath the thin material of her dress, she looked a prime candidate for Weight Watchers. Noting the double – no doubt soon to be triple – chin, the sausage-like arms and legs, Thanet wondered if PC Driver had been wrong, if Mrs Speed had known of her husband's affair (affairs?) all along and had been stuffing herself with food to compensate. But he had been right about the good nature. Despite the anxiety in her face the lines were benign, the mouth generous.

She watched the two policemen warily as they all sat down, the Speeds side by side on the settee, Thanet and Lineham in easy chairs facing them. Speed stubbed out his cigarette in an overflowing ashtray and lit another.

'Actually, I was wondering if I might have a word with you in private, Mr Speed,' said Thanet.

It was their very lack of reaction, their careful, frozen stillness, which betrayed the unspoken message which passed between them.

So Mrs Speed had known of the affair, thought Thanet with relief. The question now was, how long had she known? For some time? Or just since this afternoon, when having

63

killed his mistress her husband had anticipated the possibility of a murder investigation, and had decided to throw himself on his wife's mercy?

'There's no need for my wife to leave,' said Speed. 'We haven't got any secrets from each other.'

Mrs Speed's hand sought her husband's, squeezed it.

Thanet noted the stubborn line of her mouth, the defiant angle of her head. Good. Whatever happened, she was not going to faint or have hysterics. She was preparing for battle and he didn't mind that – welcomed it, in fact. He enjoyed a good fight. Better get on with it, then.

'As I expect you've guessed, we're looking into the death of Mrs Nerine Tarrant. We . . .'

'Just a minute.' The colour came up in Mrs Speed's face and she shifted uncomfortably on her seat. 'I'm sorry, but can I ask you something?'

She was not, Thanet guessed, a woman who was used to asserting herself in the presence of men. Her husband was watching her with surprise.

'By all means.'

'How . . . How did she die? I mean, there's all sorts of rumours flying around the village but nobody really knows . . .'

No reason why the information should be withheld. 'She fell from her balcony.'

'Oh.' A wave of colour again, stronger this time. She glanced at her husband, for the first time. 'Then . . . Are you saying it was an accident, after all? We'd heard . . . We thought . . .'

'I'm afraid we don't know yet. And won't know for sure, until various tests have been done and we have the post mortem results. But as there is an element of doubt . . .'

'There is, then?' she pressed. 'An element of doubt?'

'At this stage, in this particular case, yes, there must be. But,' he went on, as Mrs Speed squeezed her husband's hand and shot him a reassuring glance, 'as there is a *strong* element of doubt, we can't afford to waste time doing nothing, we have to proceed as if the death were murder.'

The word dropped into the conversation like a stone, and there was a brief, appalled silence on their part. Then they both spoke together.

'But . . .'

'So . . . ?'

Thanet waited. Let them sort it out. It would be interesting to see who deferred. It was Mrs Speed. From habit? he wondered.

'So what did you want to say to me, Inspector?'

'Can't you guess, Mr Speed?'

Speed glanced nervously at his wife and Thanet could guess what he was thinking. *There's a chance they don't know. If I assume they do, I could drop myself right in it for no good reason.* He cleared his throat. 'I'm sorry, no, I can't.'

'Oh, come on, Mr Speed. Let's not play games.' Thanet glanced at Mrs Speed, who bowed her head as if to shield herself from the blow which she knew was coming. 'Well, if you insist on making this painful for your wife . . . It is common knowledge that you have been having an affair with Mrs Tarrant. Naturally, in the circumstances, there are some questions we would like to ask you . . .'

Speed shrugged and tried to look confident. 'Like what, for instance?' He was beginning to sweat, Thanet noticed.

'Well, let's begin with an account of your movements today. From, say, lunchtime.'

'Since lunchtime?'

Had there been a hint of relief in Speed's tone? If so, why? The testimony of both Mrs Haywood and Marilyn Barnes confirmed that Nerine Tarrant had still been alive at half past three. But Speed ran a garage. Perhaps he had been up to something shady with second-hand cars this morning. Thanet knew that in the course of a murder investigation people often acted in a guilty manner for reasons which had nothing to do with the case, simply because they had some other secret to hide.

'That's easy,' Speed was saying. 'I was at the garage all afternoon – and all morning too, for that matter.'

'You're sure?'

'Oh, yes. Absolutely.' A thought struck him. 'Oh, except for a test drive, late this afternoon. We'd changed a gear-box.'

'What time was this?'

'Let me see . . .' Speed stubbed out his cigarette, leaned sideways and, with difficulty, extracted a handkerchief from the pocket of his tight jeans. He mopped his forehead. 'It must have been about a quarter or twenty past five when I drove off. So it would have been around twenty to six when I got back. I usually take the same route for test drives, and the circuit takes about twenty minutes.'

And Nerine's body had been found at a quarter to six. The garage was only minutes away from the Tarrants' house. Speed could well be in the running, then. 'Which route do you take?'

Lineham took down the details. And yes, Speed's route had indeed taken him past High Gables.

'Did you see anyone at the house, as you passed?'

'I was doing a test drive, Inspector. I was concentrating on the car.'

True, perhaps. But wouldn't it be natural for a man to glance at his mistress's house, however briefly, as he went by?

'There are two very nasty bends, near High Gables,' said Speed, as if Thanet had spoken his thoughts aloud. 'You can't afford to let your concentration slip. There've been a number of accidents there, in the past.'

'Can anyone corroborate these times?'

This provoked a definite though almost undetectable reaction from both of them. A sideways flick of the eyes from Speed, a determinedly wooden look from his wife. What now? wondered Thanet.

'My son will bear me out. He's helping at the garage at the moment. He's just finished his A levels,' Speed went on, forced to continue by Thanet's silence, 'and they're allowed to stay at home if they want to. He'll tell you I was at the garage all day.'

'And at lunchtime?' said Thanet, softly.

Again he picked up a tremor of reaction.

'My husband was at home for lunch,' said Mrs Speed firmly. 'And a neighbour of ours can verify that. Mrs Shrimpton. She called in to pick up some stuff for the jumble sale on Saturday.'

Lineham noted Mrs Shrimpton's address.

'And what did you do after lunch, Mrs Speed?'

'Me?' She was taken aback.

'Just for the record,' said Thanet, smiling.

'Well,' she said, a little flustered, 'let me see. From half past two till four I was at a meeting in the village hall. Afterwards I went to visit someone who is sick. I left there about five.'

But she was holding something back. Thanet was intrigued; but he wouldn't probe any further at the moment, he decided. Better do a little digging and acquire some ammunition, first, in case he was met by blank stares and flat denials.

'Is your son at home? What's his name?'

And yet again he had touched a nerve, hard though they tried to conceal it. What on earth was going on here?

Speed cleared his throat. 'Tim? Er . . . No, he's out, I'm afraid.' He gave an apologetic smile. 'You know these young people. The minute they've got some cash in their pockets, they're out spending it.'

'You know where he is?'

They shook their heads in unison, two clockwork figures. 'With friends,' said Mrs Speed. 'That's all we know.'

'Not to worry,' said Thanet, rising. 'I'll have a word with him tomorrow.'

This time they were even less successful in hiding their consternation.

Lineham waited until he had closed the front gate behind him before bursting out, 'What on earth did she see in that slimy little creep!'

'You're talking about Nerine Tarrant, I presume?'

'I mean, she was gorgeous, wasn't she? Really beautiful. Surely she could have done better for herself than that.'

Thanet forbore to point out that she had in fact done better for herself than that; she had married Roland Tarrant, who was handsome and successful and by all accounts as devoted a husband as she could wish for. 'Nothing better around?' he suggested.

'All the same . . .'

'Interesting interview, though, Mike, didn't you think?'

'I bet he's our man,' said Lineham enthusiastically. 'It was obvious that he was covering up, and I can just imagine him creeping up behind her and shoving her off a balcony.'

'Why?'

'Why what? Why should he shove her off?' Lineham shrugged. 'He was tired of her? Or, much more likely, she was tired of him? That's probably it, sir. Mrs Haywood and PC Driver both said her affairs never lasted more than a few months. Perhaps he nipped in to see her on the way back from that test drive of his. She tells him to get lost, she never wants to see him again. She stalks off onto the balcony and leans against the rail, turning her back on him. He's in a blind rage, determined that if he can't have her, nobody will. He goes after her, bends down, lifts her by the legs like you said, and gives a good shove. Then, naturally, he scarpers . . .'

'Maybe,' said Thanet thoughtfully. 'But I think there was a lot more going on back there than just covering up a murder.'

'Just!' said Lineham. 'Just! Now if I made a remark like that you'd be having my guts for garters! *Sir*.'

Thanet laughed. 'I stand rebuked, Mike. But you know what I mean.'

'The way they nearly had heart attacks every time their son was mentioned, you mean? Yes, I noticed that, all right. I wonder what he's been up to.'

'Something to do with Damon Tarrant, you think?'

'Could be. We'll have to find out, obviously.'

'Along with a million other things,' said Thanet.

Unconsciously, both men speeded up. There was indeed a great deal to do.

SIX

It was one o'clock in the morning before Thanet got home and he was surprised to see a light still burning in their bedroom. Joan was coming downstairs in her dressing gown as he entered the house.

'What on earth are you doing, still up at this hour?'

'I couldn't sleep.'

'Worrying about your protégé, I suppose.'

As soon as the words were out Thanet realised that he had been tactless; impartiality was the probation officer's golden rule.

'Don't call him that!' And then, more gently, 'I left your supper in a low oven, if you feel like eating it.' She went ahead of him into the kitchen and stooped to open the oven door. 'Really, Luke, he's a client, nothing more, nothing less. But I was worried about him, yes. I was just about managing to get him onto an even keel, and now this happens . . . How is he?'

Thanet shook his head. 'No idea. He hasn't turned up yet.'

'Not turned up yet?' she echoed, turning plate in hand. 'Do you want this?'

'Sorry, love, no. I'm past being hungry. I picked up a sandwich, earlier, so I won't starve.' He sat down heavily at the kitchen table. 'I'd like a cup of tea, though. No, Damon apparently left home in his car at about twenty to six, and hasn't been seen since.'

'So does he know about his mother's death?'

'That's what we would like to know,' said Thanet grimly. 'Amongst other things.'

70

'You're not suggesting he had anything to do with the murder, are you? It was murder, I gather, or you wouldn't be so late.'

'We think it was, yes.' Thanet explained about the balcony, the height. 'But as far as Damon is concerned . . .' He shrugged. 'Who knows?'

'But that's preposterous! You're not seriously suggesting he *killed* her?'

'Darling, you ought to know by now that at this stage I'm unlikely to be suggesting anything so specific. I'm just saying we don't know. How can we, if the boy isn't even available for questioning?'

'But . . .' Joan broke off to make the tea, maintained a thoughtful silence until she poured it. Then she sat down opposite him. 'Look, Luke, I don't want to seem over-biased, but I really can't believe Damon would have had anything to do with it. He's just not the violent type.'

'What is the violent type? You know as well as I do that everyone has potential violence in them, if they are pushed hard enough. Then there's the question of drugs . . .'

'But he's off drugs! That is, he was never really on them. It was only cannabis.'

'Only cannabis! My God, I never thought I'd live to see the day when you said, "only cannabis"! What would you say if we caught Ben smoking it? Is that what you'd say? "Only cannabis"?'

'All right, darling, calm down. You know what I mean, I simply meant, it wasn't an hallucinatory drug. Those are the ones that are dangerous in the kind of situation we're talking about.'

'We both know that once people get into drugs there's no telling where it'll end. Let's face it, he's just the type, isn't he? Rich parents, more money than love . . .'

'You're over-simplifying and you know it.'

'No, I don't know it. I know very little about him. Why don't you tell me, then I can make up my own mind.'

Silence.

71

With a shock, Thanet realised that Joan had no intention of doing so.

He had been right, then, to feel apprehensive. It had indeed come upon them, the moment he had been dreading for years, when their respective jobs would erect a barrier between them. He was appalled at how suddenly and stealthily it had arrived, catching them unawares, vulnerable, complacent, even. He and Joan had never held anything back from each other before; there had never even been any need to discuss the matter, it was implicit in all they said or did. Thanet had seen too many of his colleagues' marriages eroded by resentment and mistrust to allow even a hint of such destructive emotions to creep into his own, if he could help it. Now, it seemed, he had no choice in the matter.

Joan looked up at him and their eyes met. She was thinking the same thing, he could tell.

He put out his hand to cover hers. 'No,' he said. 'We mustn't let this happen. I know you can't talk about clients, especially in circumstances like this. I shouldn't have asked. And I'm sorry I snapped at you. I'm a bit tired, I suppose. Forgive me?'

She smiled, squeezed his hand. 'Of course. Anyway, there's no need to apologise. I shouldn't have overreacted.'

'And we're not going to allow it to come between us?' *But it had. It already had.*

She shook her head, smiled again. 'No.'

He only hoped their good resolutions would hold, if things became sticky. 'I wasn't really saying we suspect him, you know. It's just that there is this unexplained absence . . .'

'I appreciate that. But there could be a dozen reasons for it. The most likely one is that he's gone to a party, some distance away, and he's simply late getting home.'

'Quite.' Or he could have had a row with his mother, and killed her.

They decided to call it a day. But in bed, Thanet couldn't sleep. He and Joan might have managed to build a temporary bridge over the chasm which had suddenly opened up beneath their feet, but he could foresee all sorts of problems ahead. And his mind was crammed to bursting point with all the information he had accumulated that day, with all the new people he had met and with endless speculation about the relationships between them. And at the heart of it all, an enigma yet, was Nerine, possessing everything a woman could want – health, beauty, a handsome successful husband who adored her, a son, a beautiful home, a life of ease, of luxury, even . . . yet restless, dissatisfied, apparently heartless and egocentric . . .

At least, this was the façade which she presented to the world.

What had she really been like?

Thoughts of death and murder seemed singularly inappropriate when Thanet set off for work next day. It was a golden morning, with clear blue skies and brilliant sunshine gilding the feathery new foliage of the Gleditchia tree in the front garden. It was Thanet's turn to take the children to school and all along the suburban streets there was evidence that high summer had arrived at last: climbing roses in full bloom, early Dutch honeysuckle rioting over fence and porch, stately blue spires of delphinium towering over campanula and phlox, catmint and valerian.

Ben was in the back of the car, engrossed in last-minute revision for a History test that morning. Thanet glanced at Bridget.

'How did you and Mrs Mallard get on last night?'

'Oh, it was great! We dreamed up this new chicken dish – chicken breast cooked in cider with onions, herbs and tomato puree. We're going to have it for lunch on Sunday.'

'Sounds terrific.' Thanet hoped he would be at home to enjoy it.

'And guess what, Dad! Mrs Mallard said that the *Kent Messenger* had rung up the other day. They wanted to know if she would do a cookery corner for children – you know, something simple the kids could make for themselves. She said she didn't really have the time, as she's trying to finish her new book, but she could recommend someone . . .'

'You?' said Thanet.

Bridget nodded, face glowing. 'They were a bit dubious at first, when they heard I'm only fourteen, but she reminded them about my winning the Young Chef of the Year competition last year, and told them about the column I'd been writing for the school news-sheet and they said if I sent some back copies they'd take a look at my stuff and let me know.'

'Delia Smith, beware!' said Thanet. 'That really is good news.' And just the sort of thing to look good on her c.v. later on, when Bridget was job-hunting.

For several years now Bridget's interest in cookery had grown and flourished and she was determined to pursue a career in it. Though reasonably bright, Bridget, unlike Ben, was not academically minded, and like all parents in the current unemployment situation Thanet and Joan were worried about their children's future prospects. Anything which helped was to be wholeheartedly encouraged.

'I'm going to go through the news-sheets tonight, look out the best recipes, then I'll get them off tomorrow.'

'How long will it be before you hear? Did they say?'

'Within the next week or two. They want to get this column started quite soon, apparently.'

'We'll keep our fingers crossed,' said Thanet. 'Come on Ben, take your nose out of that book, we're here. I hope that wasn't the only revision you've done for this test.'

'Cool it, Dad,' said Ben. 'I'll do OK.'

Thanet shook his head and sighed as he watched them go. If only Ben would realise that it was not enough to be bright, you had to work hard too. And this academic year was crucial for him. Next spring he would learn whether or not he had been selected for the upper schools – the modern-day equivalent of the old grammar and technical schools. If not, his chances of going on to university would be sadly reduced. Whatever the claims for comprehensive schools, the fact was that the standards they achieved frequently fell far short of those required for university entrance. Somehow he and Joan had to get the message across to Ben.

Joan . . . This morning they had been carefully polite and pleasant to each other, but Thanet's apprehension had not diminished. He hated the idea of any note of falsity in a relationship which had always been open and honest on both sides. What could he do about it? Nothing, so far as he could see, but remain aware of what was happening and deal with the situation as best he could, as it unfolded.

On the way up to his office he ran into Detective-Sergeant Bristow. 'Heard about the robbery out at Nettleton Grange yesterday afternoon, sir?'

'No. Much taken?'

'A few thousand quid's worth of jewellery, apparently.'

'Any leads, yet?'

'Not so far. What about your case?'

'It's early days yet.'

They chatted for a few minutes longer before going their separate ways.

In Thanet's office Lineham was already hard at work, sifting through the reports which had come in since yesterday. He gave Thanet a beaming smile.

'Morning, sir.'

'Morning. Won the pools?'

Lineham grinned and laid down the folder he was holding. 'Heard some good news this morning. My mother rang up, before breakfast.'

'Oh?' said Thanet. Lineham's reaction to his mother's early-morning telephone calls was not usually so enthusiastic. Mrs Lineham senior had never reconciled herself to the fact that her son was a married man with a wife and two children and she could no longer take first place in his life.

'She's getting married again!'

'Mike! That's terrific! Good for her!' Good for Lineham, too. With another focus in her life, the sergeant would at last be free of her undivided attention and the running battle between wife and mother.

75

They talked for a moment or two about Mrs Lineham's plans, then turned their attention to work.

'Has Damon Tarrant turned up yet? said Thanet.

'No. There was one report which mentioned him, though. Someone saw him driving away from Ribbleden at about 5.45 last night. Apparently he was in a tearing hurry and going along those winding lanes much too fast.'

'And there's no word from him since?'

'Not so far. Do you think we ought to put out a call for him, sir?'

Thanet strolled across to the window and stood gazing out, absentmindedly admiring the mist of fresh green which now enveloped the silver birches at the far side of the car park. Obviously, if there had been any evidence that Damon had killed his mother, it would have been necessary to track him down without delay, but so far there was nothing to implicate him but the fact that he had been around at the time of the murder and had made a hasty departure just before the body was discovered. Thanet had to allow for the possibility that Damon had been unaware of his mother's death – might still be unaware of it, for that matter. But if so, at some point during the day he should surely hear about it, and if he were innocent he would presumably get in touch. If he didn't, well, that would put a different complexion on matters. Meanwhile, Thanet felt he had to give him that chance.

Suppressing the suspicion that he might also be influenced by Joan's reaction if he didn't, Thanet said, 'Not at the moment. We'll give him till this evening, I think.'

Lineham shrugged acquiescence.

'All the same, I think his room should be searched for drugs. We'll arrange for that to be done later on today.' Thanet nodded at the reports. 'Anything else of interest?' He sat down at his desk and began to fill his pipe. He was almost out of tobacco, he noticed. He must remember to get some more.

'They haven't finished the house to house yet, of course,

but there are one or two interesting bits and pieces, yes. For one thing, a witness has reported seeing Mr Speed's car parked in the entrance to a field just around the bend from High Gables at lunchtime yesterday.'

'Empty?'

'I assume so, sir. The report doesn't actually say.' Lineham was shuffling through the pile. He found and scanned it. 'No, it doesn't.' He handed it to Thanet.

Thanet skimmed through it. 'Benson, I see. Of course, he wasn't to know the significance of this particular car, at that point . . . Get on to him. Tell him to interview the witness again and get a really detailed report. I want to know if Speed was actually seen, where he was going, what he was doing, what time it was, whether the witness saw the car arrive and leave, how far away the witness was, the lot . . .'

Lineham made a note. 'You think it's that important, sir? We know she was still alive a couple of hours later.'

'I just can't really understand why Speed didn't come clean about this. I noticed we got a reaction, when lunchtime was mentioned . . . But why not own up, if he saw her then? It isn't as if he was denying the affair with her.'

'Mrs Speed claimed he had lunch at home, sir. And she mentioned a neighbour . . .'

'Make sure the neighbour is interviewed this morning.'

'Right, sir. I assumed that reaction you mentioned was to do with his son — that there'd been a family row he didn't want aired in public, or something.' Lineham shuffled through the pile of papers again. 'PC Driver's report seemed to suggest something of the sort. He remembered after talking to us last night. Yes, here we are. Apparently he called in at the garage for some petrol yesterday afternoon, sensed a bit of an atmosphere between Speed and his son.'

'What else does he say?'

'Not a lot. He went to the pub last night, as you suggested, but most of what he heard just confirmed what he already knew. Speed's affair with Mrs Tarrant was common knowledge but opinion was divided as to whether Mrs Speed knew about it or not. The consensus of opinion was that she didn't. People agreed that although Speed had always enjoyed the odd harmless flirtation, he'd never strayed to this degree before, and there was a general feeling that it was Mrs Tarrant who was really to blame for initiating the affair and that she had probably now got what she deserved.'

'Any suggestion as to who might have done it?'

'I don't suppose they'd have named names with Driver there, even though they do know him. But nods and winks hinted at Tarrant or Speed being strong favourites, apparently.'

'Surprise, surprise. No talk of any previous lovers muscling in on the act?'

Lineham shook his head. 'No. According to Driver, it was well known that her affairs usually only lasted a few months and the men he knew of who'd been involved with her seemed to take the attitude that they'd take what was on offer, enjoy it while they could and shrug their shoulders when it was over. The last one, a chap called Browning, moved out of the area a couple of months ago.'

There was a knock and Doc Mallard put his head around the door. 'May I come in?' But he hadn't waited for an invitation, he was in already. 'Just to let you know the PM is scheduled for this afternoon. Not that I'm expecting any surprises, but you never know, do you?'

Smiling benignly at them over his gold-rimmed half-moon spectacles, he clasped his hands behind his back then turned to gaze out of the window. He gave a little bounce on the balls of his feet. 'Beautiful morning, isn't it?'

Thanet and Lineham still hadn't got used to this benevolent version of the tetchy, irritable little man they had worked with for so many years, and they exchanged indulgent smiles behind his back.

The phone rang and Lineham answered it. 'Ah, good morning, Mr Tarrant . . . You have?'

Lineham's glance and the upward inflexion of his voice alerted Thanet and Mallard to the fact that some interesting

78

information was coming in. Mallard raised his hand in a gesture of farewell and left.

Lineham was listening intently. 'Yes . . . Yes . . . I see . . . Hold on a moment, please.' He covered the receiver and said to Thanet, 'Mr Tarrant says he's thought of someone with a grudge against his wife. He wants to know if we're coming out to the house this morning.'

Thanet nodded.

Lineham brought the conversation to a close and had just replaced the receiver when it rang again.

'DS Lineham . . . Hullo, Mick. Oh? What's that? Really? What time was that? Yes, thanks, that's very interesting. Cheers.' He put the phone down again and said, 'Well, well!'

'Mike, stop being infuriating. Well what?'

'Mr Tarrant's car was seen parked in his drive yesterday, at lunchtime. Around twelve thirty.'

'Lunchtime, again. Why didn't he tell us, either? What the hell was going on?'

'Perhaps,' said Lineham, his eyes beginning to sparkle with the familiar enthusiasm, 'Speed had arranged a lunchtime tryst with Mrs Tarrant, at her house. Then Mr Tarrant returns home unexpectedly, catches them at it . . .'

'Then what? Goes away and thinks about it for four hours, then comes home and pushes her off her balcony?'

'Something like that. Why not?' Lineham was warming to his theme. 'He comes home at lunchtime. Speed is already there. Mr Tarrant hears them together, but doesn't actually show himself. It's not as though it's a complete shock, he's known about the affair all along, his wife had made no attempt to hide it. So he says nothing, does nothing, just goes away, back to the hospital. But during the afternoon he finds he's getting more and more angry. Somehow, hearing them at it had really brought it home to him and he feels he can't put up with it any longer, he must have it out with her. When he gets home he goes straight upstairs to his wife's sitting room. She is out on the balcony. They quarrel, and . . .' Lineham shrugged. 'The scenario as before.'

Thanet remembered the crushed, defeated man he had interviewed the previous day. Could Tarrant be guilty? It was quite feasible, he supposed. A moment's anger can bring a lifetime of remorse. And the surgeon had lied to them – or at least, deliberately given the impression that he hadn't been home all day. 'I suppose it could have happened like that. And if it did . . .'

If it had, one way or another he and Lineham would get at the truth.

He began to shuffle the papers on his desk together. 'We'll just tidy up a few loose ends here, then we'll be on our way.'

SEVEN

'No! I didn't see her yesterday, I swear it!'

They were all crammed into Speed's tiny office at the garage. There was a pungent reek of oil and grease, and a whiff of the expensive hair-oil which Speed used to glue those carefully separated thinning strands of hair to his scalp. There was, too, another smell that Thanet recognised: the smell of fear.

'We have a witness.' Thanet, seated on the edge of the littered desk, was implacable. In between questions he had taken in the small, cluttered room: girlie calendar on wall, mess of papers on desk, dirt on floor, grime on windows. If a man's environment said anything about his personality, then Speed was both lazy and disorganised. Was he also, perhaps, a dreamer, oblivious of his surroundings because his mind was busy elsewhere? Was that what Nerine had been to him? Thanet wondered: fantasy made flesh and blood, a taste of the glamour for which his soul had hungered?

In any case, it wasn't surprising that the man's business was foundering. An office like this was scarcely designed to inspire confidence in prospective customers.

Speed was staring at him, eyes bulging slightly as if he were straining to see into Thanet's mind and find out how much the inspector knew. 'But that's impossible! I didn't see her yesterday din – lunchtime, I tell you. No one could have seen me because I wasn't there.'

'Weren't you?'

'No! I . . .' Speed broke off abruptly, and the lines of his face began to reassemble themselves into a new expression: dismay.

'Yes?' said Thanet, politely.

Lineham, squeezed into a corner behind Speed, shifted slightly and Thanet sensed that the sergeant was hoping to catch his eye, exchange a triumphant glance. But Thanet knew that it was essential to keep his attention focused on Speed. Minute beads of perspiration were beginning to break out on the man's forehead and nose.

'I . . .' The sound was strangled, as if Speed's windpipe had closed up.

Thanet waited.

'I'd forgotten,' Speed brought out at last.

'That you'd been to visit her at lunchtime yesterday?'

'No! That I'd stopped . . .' Suddenly the words began to tumble out. 'That's why I was so sure I hadn't seen her . . . I mean, because I'd intended seeing her, and then . . . then I couldn't, because her husband was there.'

So further corroboration that Tarrant had lied, that he had indeed been home during the day, yesterday. Of course, it was still possible that he hadn't lied about seeing his wife; she might have been out . . .

'You had arranged to see her at lunchtime, then?'

'Oh, no. No.' Speed put up a hand and wiped his forehead, leaving a long black horizontal smear. He had been working on a car when they arrived, and had given his hands no more than a token wipe on a rag. 'I just happened to have a few minutes to spare din – lunchtime and thought I'd drop in, give her a surprise . . .'

Some surprise, thought Thanet, if Speed had looked as scruffy as this. He thought of Nerine's cool well-groomed beauty, tried – and failed – to visualise Speed in the silken elegance of her bedroom.

Speed glanced at a grubby door in the corner of the room. 'I gotta shower here,' he said, as if he had read Thanet's thoughts. 'I couldn't've gone to see her like this, of course.

Anyway, I needn't've bothered. Like I said, I didn't go in because her husband was there.'

'How did you know?'

'His car turned into the drive ahead of me.'

'So what did you do?'

'Drove on past, of course.'

'And then?'

Speed swallowed, his prominent Adam's apple bobbing nervously. 'That's what had slipped my mind. I parked for a short while in the usual place, a farm gateway just around the bend from the Tarrants' house. I thought Mr Tarrant might not be staying long, that he'd just called back at the house to pick up some papers or something. It was most unusual for him to come home dinnertime . . .' He clicked his tongue in exasperation and shook his head. 'I suppose that's when someone saw me. You can't blow your nose in this bloody place without someone knowing it.'

He seemed much calmer now. He had stopped sweating and had relaxed a little, sitting back in his chair and folding his arms. 'Sorry, Inspector. Looks as though I misled you without intending to. It had just slipped my mind . . .'

'You told us you spent lunchtime at home.'

'But I did. After going to try to see Ner . . . Mrs Tarrant.'

'How did your wife react?'

'To what?' Unaccountably, Speed was looking nervous again.

'To your appearing at home unexpectedly.'

'Oh, yes, well . . .' Speed shrugged, composure recovered. 'I'd told her I might be home dinnertime, so she wasn't too surprised.'

What other, more alarming area had he brushed against unawares? Thanet wondered. What was the question he should have asked, just then? He had no idea. 'Was she surprised that you had showered and changed?'

Speed gave a complacent shrug. 'Told her I'd had to see an important customer.'

And without more details from the witness who had seen

Speed's car, that was about as far as they could go, thought Thanet.

The boy who had been helping Speed when they arrived had now gone out onto the forecourt – too grand a name, really, for the small apron of oil-stained concrete which separated the workshop and office building from the road – and was serving a customer with petrol.

'Is that your son?'

Speed's slightly smug expression was instantly erased. He glanced uneasily out of the window. 'Yes.'

'I'd like a few words with him. May we have the use of your office?'

Speed rose clumsily to his feet. 'Yes, of course.'

'What did you say his name was?' said Thanet pleasantly. 'Tim?'

Speed cleared his throat. 'That's right.' At the door he paused. 'Er . . . Will you be wanting me?'

Thanet shook his head. 'No, that's all, thank you, Mr Speed. For the moment.'

He watched through the window as Speed approached the boy and spoke to him. Tim glanced over his shoulder at the office and said something. Speed shook his head vigorously.

'What d'you think is going on out there, Mike?'

Lineham shook his head. 'I'd give a lot to know.'

Despite their attempts to conceal the fact, it was obvious that they were arguing now, the boy with his head down, glowering up at his father from beneath lowered eyelids, Speed with chin thrust forward, hands gesticulating. Both of them kept shooting nervous little glances in the direction of the office. Eventually Tim nodded and, head drooping, began to walk towards the office, reluctance in the sag of his shoulders and dragging feet.

He pushed it open. 'Dad says you wanted to see me.'

He was a good-looking boy, handsome even, with regular features, firm chin and a tumble of curly brown hair. Well built for his eighteen years, too. A rugger player, perhaps?

He looked tired, though, as if he hadn't had much sleep last night.

Thanet gave a reassuring smile. 'Just one or two things we thought you might be able to help us out with. May I call you Tim?'

The boy nodded.

'Sit down.' Thanet waved a hand at the desk and Tim perched stiffly on one corner. He reminded Thanet of a bird poised for flight as danger approaches.

But Tim was no bird and there was nowhere to fly to. What was he afraid of? In the course of his work Thanet had met countless boys – young men, really – of Tim's age. They came in all shapes and sizes and ranged from the innocent to the depraved. Thanet would have guessed that Tim tipped the scales well down on the innocent side, but his behaviour indicated otherwise. What on earth could he be hiding? The fact that his father was lying? Tim was supposed to verify Speed's alibi. What if he didn't want to, felt it would be better to tell the truth? Was that what the argument had been about, just now?

Thanet introduced himself and Lineham. 'Actually, it's the sergeant who wants to have a word with you.' Then he turned, folded his arms and leaned casually on the window ledge, apparently dissociating himself from the proceedings. At this stage he wanted the atmosphere to be as unthreatening as possible. As Lineham and the boy started to talk he edged himself imperceptibly around so that he could see the boy's face.

'We understand you're a friend of Damon Tarrant.'

Lineham had selected the right opening. Tim relaxed slightly.

'That's right.'

'A close friend?'

Tim shrugged. 'We know each other quite well, yes.'

'Did you know that he had disappeared?'

'What do you mean, "disappeared"?'

Lineham lifted his shoulders. 'Perhaps that's too ...

dramatic a term. Let's say that he left his house yesterday afternoon at about twenty to six, and he hasn't been seen since. Did you know that?'

'I had heard something of the sort, yes.'

Naturally, thought Thanet. Every last detail would have been around the village before the last police car had left last night. He was well aware of that strange osmosis whereby news in a village is transmitted without apparent means of communication.

'You didn't see him yourself, last night, then?'

'No. I haven't seen him since Wednesday.' Tim gave a sheepish grin. 'Several of us finished our A levels that day, and we had a bit of a celebration in the evening. I asked Damon along.'

'Do you have any idea where he might have gone?'

Tim shook his head. 'Haven't a clue.'

'Could you make some suggestions?'

'Not really. He could be anywhere.'

'Where, for example?'

But Tim merely shook his head.

'Look,' said Lineham, 'it really would be to Damon's advantage, if he could be found quickly.'

'Why?'

'Has it occurred to you that he might not even know his mother is dead? How would you like to learn that your mother had been murdered by reading about it in a newspaper, or hearing it on the radio?'

Thanet mentally applauded. That shot had really gone home. Tim's face had darkened and he was gazing down, all his concentration apparently bent upon picking at a piece of loose skin beside his thumbnail.

'Well,' demanded Lineham. 'Would you?'

Tim sighed and glanced up at the sergeant, eyes narrowing. 'You don't suspect him of being . . . involved, then?'

Lineham shot a little sideways glance at Thanet as if seeking guidance, but Thanet avoided his gaze. Mike was doing very well without any help from him.

86

'I'll be honest with you,' said Lineham 'We just don't know. There's no point in my swearing that we've discounted him as a possible suspect because at the moment we just don't know how things will turn out. But . . . Look, can I trust you not to let this go any further?'

Tim nodded. Lineham really had his attention, now.

'Well,' said the sergeant, leaning closer to the boy and lowering his voice in conspiratorial fashion, 'it's obvious that there are three possible alternatives. One: when Tim left, his mother was still alive; two: when he left she was dead and he didn't know it; three: when he left she was dead and he did know it. In the first two, he's innocent. It's only in the last that there's any question of his being involved, and I can truthfully say that at the moment we have heard nothing whatsoever to suggest that he might be. Quite apart from the fact that we'd like to find him and break the news gently before he hears it some other way — contrary to popular opinion, we are human, you know — you must see that whichever of these possibilities applies, he just might know something that could be very helpful to us.'

There was a pause while Tim considered what Lineham had said.

'Well?' said the sergeant.

A further hesitation, then Tim said, 'You really mean that? You honestly have no reason to suspect him?'

'Cross my heart,' said Lineham, smiling. 'That's right, isn't it, sir?'

Thanet nodded. 'It's true, Tim.'

'OK. Not that I can help you, really . . .'

'If you could just make some suggestions,' said Lineham, 'we would at least have some idea where to begin . . .'

'There are one or two friends he might have gone to,' said Tim doubtfully.

'Good. Let's start with them.'

Tim managed to come up with four names and, after some thought, two of the four addresses.

87

'Thanks. Now, if he isn't with any of them, have you any other ideas where he might be?'

'A party?'

'Where?'

Tim lifted his hands in a helpless gesture. 'Anywhere. A friend. A friend of a friend. Who knows?'

'OK. Well, if you come up with any other ideas, could you let us know?'

'Right.' Obviously under the impression that the interview was over, Tim slid off the desk and stood up.

'Just one other point . . .'

At once the wariness mingled with apprehension was back. 'What's that?'

'We understand from your father that you're helping out here at the moment.'

'Yes . . .' Tim was obviously on the defensive. 'I've finished my A levels, as I said, and we're allowed not to go in if we don't want to, so Dad asked if I'd give him a hand. He's a bit pushed at the moment. It's a waste of time going to school after exams are over, so I agreed. It's all above board.'

'I wasn't suggesting otherwise,' said Lineham. 'It's just that this garage is in a pretty central position in the village and you are very well placed to see all the comings and goings . . . We were wondering if you noticed anything unusual, yesterday, while you were here?'

'Not really, I'm afraid. I have thought about it.'

'You were both here all day, you and your father?'

'Most of the time, yes. Dad had a big job on for Mr Horton. A new gearbox for his Escort. The housing was all cracked, too.'

'Ah yes, he told us about that. I understand he took the car for a test drive, at around ten past five.'

'Somewhere around then, yes.'

'And he was away about twenty minutes.'

'Approximately, I suppose.'

'What happens at lunchtimes?'

'We stagger it. We both have an hour. I go first, at twelve, then Dad goes at twelve thirty, so the garage is only shut for half an hour or so.'

'I see. And this was what you did yesterday?'

'Yes.' But Tim was looking uncomfortable.

'I suppose, as you're so close to home, you go there for lunch?'

'Usually.'

'And yesterday?'

'We both went home.'

Thanet could have sworn the boy was telling the truth, and yet . . .

'I see. Well, I think that's about all I wanted to ask you. Unless the Inspector . . . ?'

Thanet shook his head. 'I don't think so, no.'

'Right.' Lineham smiled. 'Thank you, Tim, you've been very helpful.'

When they were in the car Lineham said, 'I really would like to know why they're so on edge about yesterday lunchtime.'

'So would I. The trouble is, it might be completely irrelevant, as far as we're concerned.'

'Or it might not.'

'Quite.' Thanet sighed. 'Well, I suppose we'll find out, eventually.' Or it might always remain a mystery, he thought, one of those intriguing little puzzles thrown up by an investigation. Most people have secrets which they would prefer other people not to know about. If only they wouldn't get in the way like this . . .

'You did very well with young Tim in there, by the way, Mike.'

'Thank you sir.'

'Couldn't have handled it better myself.'

'Where now, sir? High Gables?'

'Yes.'

'I wonder what Mr Tarrant'll have to say about this

character who's supposed to have had a grudge against Mrs Tarrant.'

'Mmm. But apart from that, I think he has some explaining to do, don't you?'

EIGHT

Bridget was longing for a pair of Benetton jeans. Life, Thanet had been assured, was not worth living without them. *Everyone* was wearing them, and after several excursions in which Bridget relentlessly drew his attention to everyone who was wearing them, he was beginning to believe her. All the same, he was surprised to be confronted by them here, worn by the girl who answered their knock at the front door of High Gables. They were topped by a shocking-pink teeshirt, a round cheerful face liberally spattered with freckles, and a mop of unruly brown curls anchored by a shocking-pink bandeau and an assortment of pink hair slides in the shapes of – Thanet peered while trying not to look as though he was peering – yes, animals. She was in her late teens or early twenties.

'Morning. Inspector Thanet?' A wide, uninhibited grin.

Housekeepers these days came in unexpected shapes and sizes, it seemed. Victoria Cunningham ('Call me Vicky') was nineteen, had spent a year at the highly respected, long-established (and expensive) Eastbourne College of Domestic Economy (Cordon Bleu Diploma in the third term) and had at once landed this very well-paid job at High Gables. She had worked here for six months, lived in a neighbouring village, drove to work in a Ford Fiesta Daddy had given her for an eighteenth birthday present, and was altogether very pleased with life. All this Thanet learned within a few minutes of being invited into the kitchen (Mr Tarrant being in the middle of a lengthy telephone call), where delicious smells filled the air and Vicky tied a white nylon triangle over her hair before resuming her culinary activities.

'You don't mind if I go on with this pud? Oh, sorry, I expect you'd like some coffee. I took some to Roland half an hour ago.' The Christian name was another surprise, but Thanet accepted it along with the excellent ground coffee bubbling away in a coffee machine as part of the ambiance of expansive middle-class living which Vicky exuded.

'Thank you. Were you on duty yesterday afternoon?'

Vicky's face grew sombre. 'Yes and no. I was on duty, but on Thursday afternoons I go into Sturrenden to do the week's food shopping.'

'When did you leave?'

'About twelve. I usually meet a friend who's doing the same sort of job for a quick snack, and we go around Sainsbury's together afterwards. Then I do any other errands they want me to do in the town before coming home – going to the dry cleaners, that sort of thing. I usually get back about three, as I did yesterday.'

'Just before Mrs Tarrant got back from the hairdresser's.'

'That's right.'

'You heard the ensuing row with old Mrs Tarrant?'

Vicky grimaced. 'Couldn't have missed it. When I'd finished putting the shopping away I went out into the hall. I was going to go up to Mrs Tarrant's sitting room to ask her something. But I kept well out of it, I assure you, turned around and went straight back to the kitchen.'

'Did you go up to see Mrs Tarrant later?'

'No. It hadn't been anything very important and I decided it could wait until the next day.'

'Would Mrs Tarrant have blamed you at all, for not keeping an eye on the old lady?'

'How could she? She knows I'm always out on Thursdays while she's at the hairdresser's, and anyway that's Marilyn's job.'

Vicky finished piping an elaborate pattern of minute cream whorls on what looked like a strawberry mousse, added a few fresh strawberries as a final decoration and put the dish into the refrigerator. Then she sat down at the table, pulled the white triangle off her hair and gave her head a little shake, as if relieved to be free of the restriction.

'And you finish work at four, I understand.'

'That's right.'

So Vicky had not only been away over the lunch hour yesterday, but had probably left before the murder.

'Look, Vicky, I know it's normally not on, to talk about your employers, but in the circumstances I'd be grateful if you could answer a few questions.'

She frowned. 'Depends what they are.'

She had been willing enough to talk about herself, but now the flow of information became a grudging trickle. She was prepared to supply facts about household routine, but not to discuss the relationships within her employer's family. Reluctantly, Thanet gave up.

'Could you find out if Mr Tarrant is free, now?'

He was.

'Don't bother to come with us, we know the way.' On the way out Thanet paused. 'That was a delicious smell, when we came in. What had you been cooking?'

Vicky reverted to her former expansiveness. 'Chicken breast with paprika and onions. I don't suppose Roland'll have much appetite, poor man, he didn't touch his breakfast, but I thought I'd make an effort, just in case.'

Thanet mentally filed away the ingredients of the dish for Bridget's benefit as he and Lineham pushed through the baize door and walked along the corridor to Tarrant's study.

'Come in.'

Tarrant was standing at the window with his back to the room, and swung around as they came in.

'Ah, good morning, Inspector, Sergeant. Sit down, won't you?'

Thanet had expected to find Tarrant crushed, bowed down beneath the burden of sorrow and pain, but here was a man simmering with a barely suppressed excitement. In complete contrast to yesterday's formal attire, he was wearing crumpled cotton trousers and a navy sweatshirt. He had cut himself shaving, Thanet noticed. It was just as well he hadn't gone into work today.

Tarrant plunged straight in. 'Sergeant Lineham will have told you why I rang. It came to me while I was shaving.' With a rueful grin he pointed to the small red mark on his neck. 'I didn't get much sleep last night, as you can imagine. I kept on thinking and thinking about what you'd said . . .'

He began to pace restlessly to and fro in the space between his desk and the window, pausing occasionally to look directly into Thanet's face while making a telling point.

'At first, of course, I'd assumed it was an accident. Then, when I came to think about it . . . I know that rail isn't very high, and my wife was tall, but even so . . . I just couldn't see how she could have fallen just by overbalancing . . .

'Then, I knew she would never have thrown herself off that balcony deliberately. For one thing, she wasn't the type to commit suicide. She loved life too much. She was . . . greedy for it. Oh yes, Inspector, I was under no illusions about my wife. I loved her for what she was . . . Anyway, if she had wanted to kill herself, she would have had enough common sense to choose another method. After all, how high is that balcony? Fifteen, twenty feet? She would have run the risk of injuring or even paralysing herself, and life in a wheelchair would have been unthinkable to her . . . No, I felt I could rule suicide out, straight away.'

Thanet nodded. 'I came to much the same conclusions myself.'

'So that was when I began to take your suggestion seriously . . . That she might have been . . . murdered.'

Tarrant turned his back on them and stood facing the window, though Thanet doubted if the man was seeing anything. Although he was trying hard to conceal it, he was fighting for control of himself. Those deliberately deep, even breaths, and clenched, white-knuckled fists told their own story.

When he continued his throat was hoarse, his voice ragged. 'I didn't want to believe it, of course. In fact, even now, I . . . It scarcely bears thinking about. But if it did happen, then the first question to ask is the one I did ask, yesterday.'

His voice was gaining in strength and momentum and now he swung around to face them again, his eyes glittering. 'Who? Who could possibly want to do such a thing? Nothing had been taken, so far as we could tell, it couldn't have been a burglar. So it must have been someone she knew, or who knew her, someone with a grudge against her. I thought and thought of all the people she knew, and all the possible reasons they could have for wanting to do such a thing . . . And I just couldn't believe it, of any one of them. And then as I said, when I was shaving, it suddenly came to me!'

He sat down abruptly and leaned forward across the desk, lowering his voice. His quiet, even tone and lack of histrionics gave his words credibility and impact. 'I thought of someone who wouldn't have hesitated to kill her, if it suited him. Someone, moreover, who had actually sworn to kill her – well, "get" her was the actual word he used . . . Have you by any chance ever come across a man called Buzzard, Inspector?'

The unusual name immediately rang a bell with the two policemen and they glanced at each other.

'Halo Buzzard?' said Lineham. 'Armed robbery.'

'Post office raids,' said Thanet. 'A spate of them, about ten years ago.'

'Right!' said Tarrant, triumphantly. 'And I'll bet you anything you like that with the crazy parole system they have nowadays he'll be out by now, for being a good little boy.'

'Quite possible,' said Thanet.

'Well,' said Tarrant, obviously nearing the climax of his revelation, 'you may or may not be aware, Inspector, that it was my wife's evidence that put him away.'

'Really?' Now that *was* interesting.

'Yes. What happened was this. Buzzard used to wait until the coast was clear and the post office deserted, then he'd pull on one of those stocking masks and go in, armed with a sawn-off shotgun, to carry out the raid. He was a one-man band, if you remember, so he'd leave his engine running and when he came out he'd pull off the mask before driving away.

'In the raid on Nettleton post office, my wife had just pulled up across the road when he emerged. Luckily for her, she dropped her handbag as she was getting out of the car, and she was bending down to pick it up. Buzzard glanced across at her car, couldn't see anyone in it, and assumed the driver was gone. He got into his own car, pulled off the mask, and drove off. But she had seen him quite clearly, wearing the mask, through the windows of her car as she was straightening up. Realising what was happening she sensibly crouched down again, out of sight. Buzzard was naturally in a hurry and having satisfied himself that her car was empty, didn't even glance in her direction again. But she got a clear view of his face when he pulled off the mask, took the number of his car and went straight into the post office and rang the police. Of course, Buzzard claimed he had an alibi, and paraded several of his unsavoury friends to back him up, but my wife's evidence got him convicted. And when he was sentenced, he shouted out, in court, that he'd get her for this, one day. Now . . .' Suddenly the excitement in Tarrant's eyes faded and his voice trailed away. He shook his head despairingly. 'Now it looks as though he has, doesn't it?'

'We'll get onto it right away,' said Thanet. 'We'll soon be able to find out if he's still inside. And it shouldn't be too difficult to pick him up if he's not.'

'I blame myself,' said Tarrant. 'There were all sorts of things I could have done. I could have made it my business to find out where he was, exactly when he was coming out . . . I could have made sure she had more protection, more security measures in the house . . . We could have moved, so that he wouldn't have been able to find us . . . And above all, I shouldn't have just forgotten about it, let it fade away in my mind so that it wasn't a threat any longer . . . I should have known, people like that don't forget, and they don't forgive, and they don't care about human life, it has no value for them.' He looked pleadingly at Thanet. 'But it was so long ago . . . Ten years . . .'

'These things are bound to fade, in time. You mustn't blame yourself. Criminals often make threats, in circumstances like that, but very few of them actually carry them out, so many years later. If that is what happened . . .'

'But if it wasn't him,' said Tarrant, 'who was it?'

'I'm glad you recognise that we have to look at all the other possibilities, sir.'

'Other possibilities?' The dazed look was back in Tarrant's eyes, as if the sustained effort of telling his story had used up his meagre reserves of concentration.

'I'm afraid so. As I said, we will most certainly follow up your theory. But meanwhile, we have to take a closer look at the movements yesterday of all the people connected with your wife.'

Unexpectedly, Tarrant gave a harsh bark of laughter. 'Beginning, I suppose, with me?'

Thanet's silence gave him his answer.

He shook his head in disbelief. 'I don't believe I'm hearing this. I don't believe any of it.' His voice rose. 'My God, I don't really believe she's dead, even, although I saw her lying there, with my own eyes . . . And now you're suggesting . . .'

'No,' said Thanet, cutting in. 'We are not suggesting anything, sir. Merely asking. As we must, however unpleasant the task may be.'

'Unpleasant!'

'Yes,' said Thanet, more quietly. 'Unpleasant, Mr Tarrant. There is no pleasure, believe me, in appearing to harass people who are already suffering, as you are . . . But it has to be done, whether we like it or not. Your wife is dead, and if she was killed we have to try to find out who did it, you must see that.'

'What's the point? It won't bring her back.'

'Mr Tarrant. You are a surgeon. Your whole working life is dedicated to saving life, isn't it? You must therefore believe, as I do, that it is of paramount importance. The difference is that whereas your work ends with a patient's death, that's when mine begins. If people were allowed to kill whoever they liked without any attempt being made to bring them to justice, the whole fabric of society would disintegrate.'

Tarrant waved a weary hand. 'All right, Inspector. Spare me the sermon. I'm well aware of all that. And I also know that in the case of domestic murder it is the husband who is most likely to have committed the crime. It just seems so . . .' He shook his head again. 'Ah well . . . Go ahead. Let's get it over with, shall we?'

It was Tarrant's very capitulation that made Thanet hesitate. It was true that in the majority of such cases it proved to be the husband who had committed the crime. It was therefore essential to question Tarrant, to treat him not merely as a suspect but as the chief suspect. Thanet knew that he would have to do it, knew that he *would* do it, but part of him hated himself for knowing this, fleetingly despised the man who voluntarily undertook such work. He was convinced that whether or not Tarrant had killed his wife, perhaps in a fit of anger which he now bitterly regretted, he had loved her, was genuinely grieving for her, and it was inhumane to consider treating him like a common criminal.

Thanet could feel the comforting knob which was the bowl of his pipe in his pocket and he longed to take it out and smoke it. Tarrant, however, would no doubt disapprove; there wasn't an ashtray in sight.

No, there was only one possible outcome to his dilemma: he must get on with the job, whether he liked it or not. He became aware that the silence in the room had taken on a puzzled quality. Lineham and Tarrant were both staring at him, waiting for him to speak. Thanet was tempted to signal to Lineham to take over, but the knowledge that it would be a coward's way out prevented him from following what would normally be accepted procedure.

He cleared his throat.

'You may remember, Mr Tarrant, that just before we left you, yesterday afternoon, I asked you a question to which you took exception, to the degree that you asked us to leave, at once.'

Tarrant was nodding his head, wearily. 'Stupid of me. I should have known you'd find out about Speed from the first person you asked.' He gave a resigned shrug. 'My wife never bothered to conceal her little . . . amusements.'

'Is that how you saw them? As amusements?'

'I've just said so, haven't I?' There was an edge in Tarrant's voice now.

'Many men would find it difficult to be so tolerant.'

'I am not many men.' Tarrant made a *moue* of distaste. 'I'm sorry, that sounds very arrogant, and I didn't mean it to be so. I simply meant that it is impossible to generalise in that way. I am myself, my wife was herself, together we were a unique combination, as every couple is a unique combination. And as far as I was concerned, yes, that was precisely how I did see my wife's lovers – and you will notice the plural, Inspector. I have lived with this sort of situation for many years, practically since we were first married, as a matter of fact.'

'And it didn't worry you?'

'Of course it worried me! I'm only human, and I loved my wife – hell, I still love her, you don't stop loving a person just because you'll never see them again . . . But if you mean, did it make me so mad with jealousy that I killed her, then no, it didn't. I've always thought such jealous rage self-defeating. After all, by giving in to it you simply succeed in losing the very person you are trying to keep.'

It was all very well to sit there being coolly analytical, thought Thanet, but had Tarrant actually been able to put his theories into practice, maintain an iron self-control in the face of what at times must have been extreme provocation? What if, as Lineham had suggested, the surgeon had come home at lunchtime yesterday and found his wife in bed with the garage owner? Perhaps the long habit of years would have sent him away again, but was it not possible that he had had to endure this particular humiliation once too often? During the afternoon, could he not have stewed and sweated over what he had seen or heard until at last, driven by an impulse which was beyond reasoning away, he had gone home, had one final row with his wife, and pushed her off that balcony at a time when he was simply not in control of his behaviour? It was all too uncomfortably credible. It was and always had been human nature, to make good resolutions dictated by common sense which prove impossible to keep when confronted by the situation which prompted them.

It was time to put this theory to the test.

'Why didn't you tell us you came home at lunchtime yesterday, sir?'

Tarrant stared at Thanet for a moment. What was he thinking? Was he going to deny it?

Then he shrugged. 'For one thing, you didn't ask me. And for another, I didn't think it relevant.'

'You certainly gave us the impression you had been away from the house all day.'

'I'm sorry if you were misled. But if you remember, you asked me when I had last seen my wife and I told you: at breakfast. That is the truth.'

'You didn't see her at lunchtime?'

'No! I told you . . .'

'Strange,' said Thanet. 'She was here, wasn't she?'

No reply.

'Wasn't she?' Thanet insisted.

Still no reply.

'And if she was, are you really asking us to believe that you didn't look for her and find her? That you simply came home and left without seeing her?'

Again that long, considering stare. Then, once more, the resigned shrug. 'All right, Inspector. I can see you're not going to leave me in peace until you're satisfied. I'll tell you what did happen, at lunchtime.'

NINE

Tarrant paused for a moment, as if marshalling his thoughts. Then he sat back in his chair, folding his arms.

'When I left home yesterday morning I forgot to take with me some papers I needed for a meeting in the afternoon, so I decided to pop back at lunchtime to fetch them. I got here just after half past twelve. I thought my wife would probably be in, so I naturally went upstairs to her sitting room to look for her. She usually had lunch about that time and she liked to eat it on the balcony, it was her favourite place.'

For a moment it looked as though his composure would slip, but he recovered. 'She wasn't in the sitting room and I could see through the open french windows that she wasn't out on the balcony, but all the same I went across and put my head out, to check. It was empty. I wondered where she was. Although it was a bit early – I knew that her hair-dressing appointment wasn't until two – I thought she might be changing, so I went out into the corridor and along to her bedroom. I put my hand on the doorknob and was about to turn it when ... when I heard a voice, from inside. A man's voice. Speed's.'

Tarrant gave Thanet an assessing glance and said drily, 'Naturally, I decided not to go in. I simply turned away, went downstairs, collected the papers from my study, and left.' He lifted his hands. 'End of story.'

And not surprising, thought Thanet, that Tarrant had been reluctant to tell it. Most men would listen to such a tale with amazement tinged with disbelief, and he himself found it very difficult to swallow.

How would he, Thanet, have reacted in a situation like that? An unwise question, he realised. Slamming a mental door upon the turmoil of violent images which immediately sprang into his mind, he forced himself to concentrate.

Cuckold.

The old term, with all its derogatory overtones, floated into his mind and was hastily suppressed. He wasn't here to make moral judgements, indeed had no right to make them, except insofar as they affected his work. And he did feel genuine sympathy for Tarrant. It must be hell to be forced to admit to a complete stranger that you had found your wife in bed with another man and had done nothing about it.

If that really was what had happened.

Perhaps Tarrant had picked up the overtones of incredulity in Thanet's silence. He said with wry amusement, 'I see you find it difficult to believe that I just turned and walked away, Inspector, but I do assure you that that is precisely what I did. For a very good reason.'

Tarrant's tone changed, became earnest. 'You see, I loved my wife, Inspector. Really loved her. Which means that I knew all her faults and weaknesses and loved her not in spite of them but *because* of them. She couldn't help herself, you see.' He leaned forward, as if anxious to convince Thanet of the truth of what he was saying. 'That was what nobody else could ever understand, not even Daphne, her own sister. They haven't seen her in tears, as I have, over her infidelities. After every affair she'd say how sorry she was, swear it would never happen again. Of course, we both knew she'd never be able to keep that promise.' He shook his head. 'She really couldn't help herself,' he repeated.

'I know you may find it difficult to understand my attitude, but I always felt that if she had been less insecure, hadn't been – how shall I put it? – so hungry for love, she would never have married me. She would have been . . . unattainable to me. So you see, I could hardly have rejected her for the very weakness which brought her to me in the first place.

103

In some strange way it forged a bond between us which kept us together all these years where many more apparently stable marriages have long since broken up. She knew, you see, that no one else could have accepted her as I did, that whatever she did, I would never leave her. And I knew that always, every time, she would come back to me. I was prepared to accept her upon any terms, rather than not have her at all.'

It was a cry from the heart.

Taken aback at first by Tarrant's unexpected frankness, Thanet had by now realised that the surgeon was seizing what was perhaps the first opportunity he had ever had to attempt to vindicate his wife. Death had released him from the bonds of loyalty and propriety which would have prevented him from openly defending her while she was still alive.

Nevertheless, thinking of the endless humiliations which Tarrant must have had to endure over the years, Thanet wondered if it was possible that the surgeon had truly never felt the need to punish her for all the suffering she must have caused him. Tarrant's sincerity was obvious, but his determined tolerance would have had to falter for only a few moments yesterday afternoon for the damage to be done.

'Have you any idea what gave her this . . . need for love?'

For the last few minutes Tarrant had been gazing down at his clasped hands as he spoke, absentmindedly revolving his thumbs. Now he raised his eyes and gave Thanet a look of gratitude, aware that the Inspector was making a genuine effort to understand. 'I've always assumed it was because her mother died when Daphne was born, when Nerine was only three. Her father, of course, was very busy and presumably didn't have much time to spare for the children.' He shrugged. 'I did try, but I never managed to get her to talk about it, and I honestly don't think she had any idea why she was the way she was. But I always felt that if her mother hadn't died when she did, my wife would have been a very different person. I know she never wanted for anything material, but nothing can compensate for emotional deprivation. I always hoped that one day she would come to realise that she had found what she was looking for in me.'

Now, that day will never come.

Thanet responded to the unspoken words. 'I'm sorry.'

Tarrant stared at him, nodding slowly, as if having come to a decision. 'Yes, I believe you really mean that.'

'I do.' Something now needed to be done to lighten the atmosphere. Thanet thumped his chest and grinned. 'Beneath this grey flannel suit beats a heart of gold.'

It had been the right response. Tarrant smiled with relief and leaned back in his chair, more relaxed than at any time so far. He steepled his fingers and said, 'Was there anything else you wanted to ask me, Inspector?'

'Just one or two small points to clear up . . . To get back to yesterday lunchtime . . .'

'Yes?'

'You're sure that it was Mr Speed, with your wife?'

Tarrant looked surprised. 'Yes, of course. Why?'

Thanet shook his head. 'No reason.' *Except that the gentleman in question swears he never came near the house.*

'How long were you in the house, would you say?'

'Ten minutes, perhaps. Certainly no longer than a quarter of an hour.'

'I see . . . Have you by any chance heard from your son yet?'

Tarrant shook his head.

'You're not worried about him?'

'I told you yesterday, Inspector. Damon is something of a law unto himself. All the same, I am very worried that he doesn't yet know about his mother, and I must admit he isn't usually away as long as this, without contacting us.'

'I was going to ask you . . . I'm sorry, but I'm afraid we shall have to search his room.'

Tarrant suddenly woke up. 'What for? He'd absolutely loathe the idea of anyone poking about in his things . . . Ah, I see. Drugs, I suppose . . . My God, one mistake and you have the police on your back for the rest of your life, don't you?'

'Not in normal circumstances. But you don't need me to remind you that these circumstances are not normal. You must see that this is a routine precaution we must take.'

Tarrant's brief flare of anger died away and he slumped back in his chair and waved his hand. 'Oh, very well. Just get on with it.'

'Thank you. But before his room is properly searched, I'd like to take a look at it myself.'

'Why?'

'I just want to reassure myself that there are no signs of anything other than a normal departure.'

'What do you mean?' Tarrant was alert again. 'What are you suggesting?'

'I'm not suggesting anything.'

'Oh, but you are, aren't you? You're suggesting he might have something to do with . . .' He broke off, clutched his head as if to control thoughts spinning out of control.

'Mr Tarrant. I'm not suggesting anything of the sort. I am just being careful, that's all. There could be a very simple, innocent reason for Damon's departure. On the other hand, not knowing as yet the exact circumstances under which your wife met her death, we have to consider the fact that Damon could, quite innocently, have got caught up in it.'

'Witnessed it, you mean?' Tarrant was appalled. 'My God, you could be right . . . What if this . . . this criminal, Buzzard, was here, and Damon saw something which aroused his suspicions, went after him . . .'

It was a possibility which had not occurred to Thanet, having heard of Buzzard's possible involvement only a short while ago, but he had to admit that it was as likely an explanation as any other.

Tarrant was staring at Thanet, obviously thinking furiously. 'That could explain . . .'

'What?'

Tarrant looked a little shamefaced. 'I forgot to mention it

106

before, but I saw Damon leave myself. He drove out of the gates just as I drove in. And I must admit he did seem to be in a tearing hurry.' He stood up, suddenly infused with energy. 'Come on, let's go and take a look.'

Thanet despatched Lineham to arrange for the drugs search and to radio in for enquiries to be made in regard to Halo Buzzard, and followed Tarrant to the servants' stairs at the back of the house.

'We converted the attic into what is virtually a self-contained flat for Damon's sixteenth birthday present,' said the surgeon as they climbed. 'Young people value their independence, don't they? I know I did.'

Thanet murmured assent. He certainly agreed that independence was the aim of parents and children alike, but he thought that, special cases apart, sixteen was much too young for such a degree of autonomy. He was beginning to wonder if this family had ever lived together, in the accepted sense of the word. They seemed so . . . fragmented. Nerine Tarrant had her own sitting room, bedroom and bathroom and so, apparently, had her son. What about Tarrant? Had he, too, had his own quarters? Then there was old Mrs Tarrant and her companion, again in a separate wing. Had they ever congregated, as families do (or should, in Thanet's opinion), in the kitchen, dining room or sitting room? Or had they all pursued their own separate existences, divided from each other by physical as well as emotional barriers? It wasn't surprising, he thought, that Damon had problems.

'How did he get on with his mother?' he asked.

Tarrant shrugged. 'You know what adolescents are.'

'There were arguments?'

'My wife wasn't a very maternal person.'

No, thought Thanet, if all Tarrant had told him were true, Nerine had been too engrossed in her own search for love to have any to spare for anyone else.

Perhaps he was being unfair, and Nerine had been more to be pitied than condemned, but he couldn't help feeling anger on behalf of this boy he had never seen. What was it that Tarrant had said, just now, about his wife? 'She never wanted for anything material, but nothing can compensate for emotional deprivation.' Couldn't the man see that the very same pattern was being repeated in the life of his son? Perhaps he could, but had felt helpless to do anything about it, at least as far as his wife was concerned.

'Here we are.'

They were at the foot of a white-painted wrought-iron spiral staircase, its intricate design stark against the slate-blue walls of the landing.

'More interesting than simply putting in another flight of stairs, we thought,' said Tarrant proudly.

'It's beautiful.' Thanet paused on the way up to admire the clusters of iron grapes, the delicate entwined tracery of vine leaves and tendrils. Nerine Tarrant might have been unable to give or receive human love, but she had obviously had a love of beauty for its own sake, and an unerring eye for visual effect.

A moment later this impression was heavily reinforced.

They stepped from the circular opening at the top of the staircase into a dazzle of light and space. Thanet drew in his breath sharply and stood quite still, taking it all in. It was one vast room, perhaps sixty feet by forty, taking up perhaps two thirds of the entire attic space of the house and visually divided by the timbers which supported the roof. Sunshine was pouring in through some of the huge skylights, spilling over the grass-green of the fitted carpet which covered the entire room and creating the illusion that the profusion of tall plants was actually growing outside in some enchanted garden, where the geometric shapes of the furniture were really futuristic sculptures, carefully sited for maximum impact.

'Everything looks pretty normal to me,' said Tarrant. He glanced at Thanet, saw his expression. 'My wife designed it,' he said sadly. 'She had an eye for that sort of thing.'

'It's amazing,' said Thanet. 'I've never seen anything quite

108

like it, outside magazines. She should have taken it up as a career.'

Tarrant looked at him, startled. 'You think so?'

'She must have considered it, surely?'

The surgeon didn't answer, just shook his head and then stood gazing around as if, for the first time, he were seeing the place as revealing a dimension of his wife's character.

Thanet began to wander about, careful not to touch or to disarrange anything. A closer look told him that although Damon may have valued (or hated) the privacy (or isolation) that this flat gave him, he certainly hadn't appreciated it in any other way. The grease-stained cooker, the scarred wooden work surfaces in the tiny kitchen area, the numerous stains on the carpet where liquid of one kind or another had been spilt, the drooping leaves of some of the taller shrubs and plants, the scatter of dirty clothes in the sleeping area, the general litter of books, records, unwashed mugs and plates and overflowing ashtrays all told their own story of indifference and neglect.

Tarrant was now keeping pace with Thanet.

'It's only cleaned once a month,' he murmured apologetically. 'Damon hates anyone else coming up here. But as I say, it all looks pretty normal to me ... Have you seen all you wanted to see, Inspector?'

Thanet took the hint. He turned back towards the spiral staircase. 'Yes, thank you.'

'And you're satisfied?'

Thanet nodded. Though after such a cursory examination it was impossible, given the general untidiness, to detect signs of a hasty departure.

'We'll just have to hope he turns up soon, sir. If he's not back by this evening we may have to put out an appeal.'

'Oh. Oh, dear. But if he hasn't heard about his mother's death ...'

'That's what's worrying us. But against that, you have to consider his safety. It would be good to know that he's all

109

right. Also, of course, we're very anxious to hear what he can tell us.'

Lineham was waiting for them at the foot of the spiral and Tarrant excused himself, disappearing down the next flight of stairs. Thanet and Lineham followed slowly, talking as they went.

'The dog handler will be out later on this morning, to search for drugs,' said Lineham. 'And I've put them on to Buzzard. They'll get back to us as soon as they have anything. Oh, and you remember that neighbour the Speeds mentioned?'

Thanet nodded.

'She confirms that she saw all three of them at lunchtime yesterday, at around 1.15.'

Thanet frowned. 'I thought Tim said that his lunch hour was from 12 to 1.'

'He did. But the interesting thing is this. You remember what PC Driver said, about noticing an atmosphere between Tim and his father yesterday afternoon? Well, this neighbour says that when she went into the house she had the impression she was interrupting a full-scale family row. She felt so uncomfortable she only stayed a few minutes.'

'Hmm. Yes, that is interesting. She had no idea what it was about?'

'No, unfortunately. Anyway, she saw Tim leave about ten minutes later, but his father stayed on for another hour or so.'

'Until after a quarter past two, then. And he distinctly gave us the impression that he'd taken only his normal lunch break, from 12.30 to 1.30!'

'Quite. What d'you think was going on, sir? I mean, what possible reason could he have for lying about the length of time he spent with his wife?'

'Search me. And I still don't understand why he lied about seeing Mrs Tarrant earlier on in the lunch hour, either. And why tell us Tarrant's car turned into the drive ahead of him,

when he must already have been in bed with Mrs Tarrant
by then?'

'Perhaps it's Mr Tarrant who's lying.'

'Why should he? Surely no man would lie about something
like that. No, I think Tarrant was telling the truth. But in
any case, the problem is that there's no way of knowing, at
the moment, whether or not any of this is relevant to our
investigation.'

'I know. To be honest, sir, I can't really see why we're so
bothered about what happened at lunchtime. After all, we
know she was still alive at half past three.'

Thanet paused, turned to face the sergeant. 'Oh, come on,
Mike, you can't be serious. You know perfectly well that
murder is always the end of a process, sometimes brief,
sometimes lengthy. You've only got to think back over some
of the cases we've been involved in to see just how lengthy
that process can be. Speed was deeply involved with Nerine
Tarrant. You must see that anything out of the ordinary in
his behaviour only a few hours before the murder could well
be highly relevant.'

Lineham was looking sheepish. He mumbled an apology
and they continued on down the stairs. At the bottom the
sergeant came to an abrupt halt and gave Thanet a warning
nudge.

Ahead of them, silhouetted in the light spilling out through
the open study door, were Tarrant and Marilyn Barnes, deep
in conversation. Tarrant was leaning against the doorpost
and Marilyn was talking, looking up at him. Then they both
turned, their startled faces quickly assuming expressions of
polite enquiry.

'Ah, there you are, Miss Barnes,' said Thanet. 'How is old
Mrs Tarrant today?' And then, to Tarrant, 'We've arranged
to have a chat with your mother this morning, if she's up to
it.'

'As I was just saying to Mr Tarrant, much better, thank
you,' said Marilyn with a little smile. 'Much calmer and
more rational.'

111

Was that really what they had been talking about? Thanet wondered. 'Good. If you'll excuse us, then, sir?'

Tarrant waved a hand. 'By all means.'

A startling idea had come into Thanet's mind at his first glimpse of those two figures and he studied the girl leading them up the stairs with new eyes. She certainly couldn't compete with her former employer in looks, but in terms of warmth and kindness she was, by all accounts, streets ahead of her. What if Tarrant had become tired of endlessly struggling to create something positive out of the sterile relationship with his wife and had turned to a more sympathetic ear? It would be easy to imagine the nondescript Marilyn being bowled over by the attentions of an attractive, successful and wealthy man like Tarrant. And even if Tarrant had remained completely faithful to his wife and had never even glanced in Marilyn's direction, there was nothing to stop Marilyn falling hopelessly in love with him. And if she had . . . How would she have felt about Nerine, in view of the constant humiliations inflicted upon Tarrant by his wife?

Thanet put out his hand and touched her gently on the arm. 'I wonder if we could have a brief word together first, before I see Mrs Tarrant senior?'

She hesitated. 'All right. But I don't like to leave her alone for too long . . .'

'Just a few minutes,' said Thanet.

She pushed open a door. 'In here, then,' she said.

TEN

The bare dressing table and general air of emptiness indicated that this was an unused guest room. Nerine Tarrant's flair for interior decoration was evident in the combination of ivory carpet, jade-green silk curtains and ivory-and-green wallpaper with a delicate, almost Oriental design of herons.

Marilyn closed the door and stood awaiting Thanet's questions with an air of slightly impatient resignation. Her eyelids drooped, and the flesh beneath her eyes looked slack and bruised, as if she had slept badly. The strain of yesterday was clearly taking its toll.

'Before I speak to old Mrs Tarrant,' said Thanet, 'I just wanted to ask you . . . You remember you told us that when you went back upstairs at half past five yesterday afternoon, to get her up after her delayed rest, she seemed frightened. It took you five or ten minutes to coax her out of her room, you said . . .'

Marilyn nodded. 'That's right.'

'Have you by any chance talked to her about this, asked her just what she was afraid of?'

'No. I told you, at the time I simply assumed she was frightened of another scene with Mrs Tarrant. And it's usually pretty pointless to try to discuss any recent event with Lavinia. She often can't remember things from one moment to the next.'

Not very promising, thought Thanet, though scarcely unexpected.

'You said, "often". Sometimes she does remember?'

'Sometimes, yes.'

113

'So it might be worth a try?'

Marilyn gave a little shrug. 'Try, by all means. Her memory is so unpredictable that you can never tell . . . Her long-term memory is quite good, of course. But her short-term memory is hopeless. You can have virtually the same conversation with her over and over again within the space of minutes. And then sometimes you think to yourself, "She'll never remember that", and she astonishes you by having total recall. You'll see what I mean, when you talk to her.'

'How do you think she would react, if I tried to discuss it with her?'

'It really is impossible to tell, in advance.'

'I was wondering . . . Would it be kinder, d'you think, if you were to question her about it?'

'Perhaps. I could try, if you like.'

'Thank you. It might not be necessary, of course. Perhaps I'll be able to do it. I'll have to play it by ear. In any case, I'd like to have a general chat with her first, and I'd like you to be present.'

'Of course.' She turned away, evidently under the impression that the interview was over.

'Er . . . There are just one or two other small points, Miss Barnes . . .'

She turned back with a little sigh. 'Yes?'

'I wanted to ask you . . . You were here at lunchtime, yesterday?'

'Yes, I was.'

Had he imagined the wariness in her tone? 'Did you happen to see Mr Tarrant? He tells us he came home briefly at lunchtime, to fetch some papers he'd forgotten . . .'

This time there was a definite hesitation. 'Yes . . . Yes, I did see him. I didn't speak to him, though.'

'This was at what time?'

'Soon after half past twelve, I think. Yes, it must have been.'

'And where was this?'

114

'Where . . . ?'

Was she prevaricating in order to give herself time to think? Thanet wondered.

'Where was he, when you saw him?'

'In . . . In the corridor, outside Mrs Tarrant's bedroom.' A faint flush was creeping up her neck and into her cheeks.

Could her reluctance be simply due to embarrassment, that she had caught Tarrant listening outside his wife's door when she, Marilyn, knew that Nerine had been entertaining her lover?

'Did he go in?'

She shook her head. 'I saw him try the door handle, then he hurried away downstairs.' She avoided Thanet's eye. 'I assumed the door was locked and he decided she wasn't in there,' she murmured.

Marilyn Barnes was a very poor liar, thought Thanet.

'Miss Barnes, I do understand your commendable sense of loyalty to your employer, but I assure you that there's no point in trying to cover up Mrs Tarrant's . . . unfortunate behaviour. We know that Mr Speed was her lover, Mr Tarrant himself told us so, and he also told us that he didn't enter his wife's room at that point because he realised that Mr Speed was in there with her.'

She was nodding slowly, as if relieved that the burden of decision had been taken from her.

'So I wanted to ask you. Did you, yourself, see Mr Speed in the house at lunchtime yesterday?'

'No.'

In that case, why the hesitation, earlier? And had he imagined the gleam of relief in her eyes, just then? Yet the monosyllable had been unequivocal and to Thanet's ear had the ring of truth about it. He decided to leave it, for the moment.

'I also wanted to ask you . . . Having thought over the events of yesterday, as I'm sure you have, can you recall anything else that you think might be of the slightest interest to us?'

She gave a quick, tight shake of the head and avoided his eyes again.

Yes, there definitely was something . . . Something to do with Roland Tarrant?

But the stubborn set of her lips told him that, whatever it was, she wasn't going to tell, at the moment anyway.

It was time to move on to old Mrs Tarrant.

Marilyn led them along the corridor to the next room and entered without knocking.

'I've brought you some visitors, Lavinia. Some gentlemen. You met them yesterday, remember?'

The room was cluttered with furniture, pictures and ornaments and there were photographs scattered about on every available surface. Thanet guessed that when Nerine moved in as mistress of the house and began to redecorate to her own taste, old Mrs Tarrant had gradually accumulated in her own quarters those things which were of special sentimental value to her. She was sitting in a wing chair in the sunshine, gazing out of the window.

'Hullo, dear. Visitors, how nice.' She smiled without recognition at Thanet and Lineham, put her hands on the arms of the chair and began to lever herself up.

Thanet smiled back. 'Please, don't get up.'

He would scarcely have recognised her as the extraordinary vision he and Lineham had seen on the stairs yesterday. She was still wearing make-up but it was discreet and carefully applied, probably by Marilyn, Thanet thought. Her clothes were sober, a navy linen dress and thick white cardigan, sensible flat-heeled navy sandals. Her faded blue eyes betrayed uncertainty. 'I'm sorry, I don't remember . . .'

Thanet shook his head. 'It doesn't matter.'

She waved a gracious hand. 'Do sit down.'

They complied, Marilyn perching on a low stool beside her employer, Thanet choosing an armchair and Lineham a more upright one a little further away.

Marilyn put an affectionate hand on Mrs Tarrant's arm.

116

'Inspector Thanet is a policeman, Lavinia. He is trying to find out about the . . . accident.'

'Accident?'

'To Nerine.'

'Has Nerine had an accident?'

Marilyn glanced at Thanet. *You see what I mean?*

'Lavinia,' said Marilyn patiently. 'I told you. Yesterday. She fell from her balcony and . . . and died.'

'Died?' The old lady stared at Marilyn. 'Nerine is dead?'

Marilyn nodded.

How many more times, Thanet wondered, would she have to break the news to the old lady? Senility was a terrible disease. In this particular case it didn't matter so much. By all accounts there had been no love lost between old Mrs Tarrant and her daughter-in-law. But what must it be like when it is the news of the death of a much-loved husband, wife, son or daughter that has to be broken over and over again, when the shock of hearing it must be suffered not once but many times by someone already enfeebled by age and illness?

'I did tell you,' said Marilyn.

Mrs Tarrant shook her head. 'I don't remember.' She sighed, and glanced at Thanet. 'My memory isn't very good these days, I'm afraid . . .'

She was silent for a few moments and then she said, 'But I can't pretend I'm sorry — that she's dead, I mean.' She leaned forward and said conspiratorially, 'She was trying to get rid of me, you know.' She glanced at Marilyn for confirmation. 'Wasn't she, dear?' One claw-like hand clutched at Marilyn's for reassurance. 'She wanted me to sign some papers, so she could put me in a home. But Roland wouldn't let her. My son.'

Automatically she reached for a photograph which stood to hand on a small table beside her chair. She glanced at it before handing it to Thanet. 'That's him,' she said proudly, 'with Damon, my grandson, on his first birthday.'

The snapshot had been taken in the garden. Tarrant was

117

squatting in a patch of sunshine under the trees on a carpet of autumn leaves, both hands supporting the baby standing with splayed legs in front of him.

'Damon took his first step that day,' said the old lady reminiscently. Roland was so proud.' Her face darkened. 'He's a good boy and deserves better than that wife of his.' She glanced at Marilyn, a curiously arch, knowing smile. 'Doesn't he, dear?'

So the old lady either knew of Marilyn's feelings for Tarrant or at least suspected them, thought Thanet.

Marilyn was attempting to cover up. She patted the old lady's hand and said quickly, 'The Inspector is trying to find out how the accident happened, Lavinia.'

'Accident?'

'To Nerine.' Marilyn glanced at Thanet again. *Now you really must see what I mean*. With commendable patience she explained it all again. Mrs Tarrant listened with an almost child-like air of trust, then sighed. 'It's so frustrating, when you can't remember things . . . So Nerine is dead . . .'

Again she was silent for a few moments and Thanet was waiting for the conversation to follow the same track as before when she nonplussed him by impaling him with a sharp, knowing look and saying, 'Are you sure it was an accident, Inspector? Knowing Nerine, it wouldn't surprise me in the least if someone helped her on her way.'

Marilyn was looking amused and rather proud, like a parent whose offspring unexpectedly walks off with a prize at speechday.

'That's what we're trying to find out,' said Thanet. 'And we wanted to ask you. Did you by any chance see anyone in the house, yesterday afternoon?'

Mrs Tarrant stared at him, her eyes opaque with – what? Thanet wondered. Concentration? Indecision? Briefly, so briefly that Thanet wondered if he had imagined it, they darkened as if a shadow had passed across them. She shook her head. 'I'm sorry, I can't recall . . .'

'What about your daughter-in-law? Did you see her at all, yesterday afternoon?'

The old lady shook her head. 'No, I don't think so.' She turned to Marilyn. 'Did I, dear?'

Thanet and Lineham exchanged glances. *She doesn't even remember the row in the bedroom.*

Marilyn gave Thanet a questioning look.

He nodded. *Go ahead.*

'You don't remember the . . . argument with Nerine, early in the afternoon, Lavinia?'

'No. No, I don't.' Mrs Tarrant cast at Thanet a look composed of a curious mixture of guilt, embarrassment and glee. Then she leaned towards Marilyn and said in a near-whisper, 'Was it because . . . ?'

Marilyn nodded. 'I'm afraid so.'

Mrs Tarrant's hand went to her mouth, the gesture of a naughty child caught in some trivial misdemeanour. 'Oh dear. Was she cross?' It was obvious that she was hoping the answer would be 'Yes'.

Marilyn's nod was emphatic, her tone full of reproof. 'Very cross, Lavinia.' She hesitated, then said, 'That's why I wondered if you'd seen her again, later. When I went to get you up after your rest you seemed rather . . . upset.'

'Did I?' Mrs Tarrant stared at Marilyn as if she held the key to her locked-up memories. She shook her head helplessly. 'I don't remember.'

This was pointless, Thanet decided, a waste of time.

'Never mind,' he said gently. 'It really doesn't matter.' Not true, but still . . . 'Perhaps, if you do remember something, Miss Barnes would be kind enough to let me know?'

Marilyn nodded. 'Of course.'

Mrs Tarrant seemed to have lost interest in the conversation. She was leaning forward, gazing down out of the window. Something had obviously attracted her attention.

Curiosity brought Thanet to his feet. This room must be at the back of the house. It overlooked the converted coach house and the garages. A woman wearing a blue skirt and white sweater was walking aimlessly away across the drive towards the left-hand corner of the house, head down, hands clasped behind her back.

'Is that Miss Linacre?' he said to Marilyn.

'Yes. It looks as though she's feeling a bit better today.'

Well enough to be interviewed, Thanet hoped.

He turned back to the old lady. 'Well, thank you, Mrs Tarrant. You've been very helpful.'

She gave a gratified smile. 'Have I? Good. Do call again, won't you? It's lovely to have visitors. Oh . . .' She glanced at Marilyn. 'What am I thinking of? We haven't offered our guests any refreshment, dear. Could you arrange some coffee for us?'

'I'm afraid we have to go now, Mrs Tarrant,' said Thanet. 'Next time, perhaps?'

She beamed. 'Next time, yes. I shall look forward to that. Marilyn, see the gentlemen out, would you?'

'No, it's all right, thank you, we know the way.'

Outside Lineham said, 'Whew, stuffy in there, wasn't it!'

Thanet agreed. 'Let's go and get a breath of fresh air.'

At the front door he paused to light his pipe and exchange a few words with the constable on duty before making for the terrace where Nerine's body had been found.

'Is that the path you were talking about yesterday?'

Beyond the terrace was a rectangular lawn, enclosed on three sides by tall, well-clipped yew hedges. The path, which was of crazy paving, ran along the base of the left-hand hedge and disappeared through a gap at the corner.

'Yes. That report said that Speed's car was parked at the entrance to a field just around the bend from High Gables, didn't it? He could easily have got into the house through the garden and no one would have been any the wiser.'

'Is there a gardener?'

Lineham grimaced. 'Yes, but unfortunately he wasn't here yesterday. He doesn't come in on Thursdays.'

'Pity. Let's take a look, shall we?'

120

They set off along the path. After a few paces Lineham said, 'I think I'd rather be dead than senile.'

'Wouldn't we all.'

'I still think it's possible that the old lady might have shoved her daughter-in-law off that balcony, even if she has forgotten all about it. You must admit it's obvious there was no love lost between them. I got the impression she enjoyed messing up Mrs Tarrant's bedroom, just to spite her. If so, Mrs Tarrant could have sensed that it was deliberate, and that would have made her even more mad. Though the old lady certainly hasn't lost all her marbles, has she, sir? Once or twice she seemed pretty sharp. I was wondering . . . Did you notice that look she gave Miss Barnes, when she was talking about Mrs Tarrant being an unsuitable wife for her son?'

'Ah, you spotted that too. Yes, I did.'

'Well, it's obvious that she's fond of Marilyn Barnes. Apart from being afraid that her daughter-in-law might persuade Mr Tarrant to get rid of Marilyn, don't you think it's possible she might also have thought that with Mrs Tarrant out of the way Mr Tarrant might marry Marilyn? I should think she'd be delighted at the prospect. And if so, it would certainly strengthen her motive for getting rid of Mrs Tarrant, wouldn't it?'

'True.' Much as he disliked the idea, Thanet was forced to acknowledge its plausibility.

'D'you think there might be something going on between Mr Tarrant and Miss Barnes, sir?'

Thanet shrugged. 'Who knows?'

'If he is in love with her, it would give him an even stronger motive, wouldn't it? Because he can swear black and blue that he didn't care about his wife's lovers, but I find it impossible to believe he could go on year after year and never want to do anything about it.'

'I'm not sure I agree with you there, Mike. I think I'm prepared to give him the benefit of the doubt, for the moment, anyway.'

Lineham looked sceptical, but didn't argue. 'But as far as Miss Barnes is concerned ... If she is in love with him, it gives her an additional motive too, doesn't it? If she was in danger of losing her job, I mean ...' Lineham caught Thanet's eye and, obviously recalling his own attitude the last time they had discussed this particular possibility, gave a slightly embarrassed grin. 'I still don't like the idea that she could have done it, I must admit. I'm just trying to keep the open mind you're always on about.'

'Just as well at this stage. There's certainly no shortage of suspects.'

Thanet stopped walking. They had reached the corner of the yew hedge and he stood gazing about. Here the crazy paving gave way to gravel and the path divided. To the left it started to curve away between densely packed beds of tall shrubs towards the edge of the garden; to the right it ran along the back of the hedge and disappeared in the direction of the front gate. Thanet supposed that in a garden of this size it was necessary to have a whole network of paths; there would be a great deal of wheeling about of rubbish, tools, fertilisers and so on.

They took the left fork, ducking and side-stepping occasionally to avoid stray branches of philadelphus and shrub rose, viburnum and holly. Fifty yards or so further ·
the gravel became beaten earth, the shrub borders ended and a narrow belt of silver birch and Scots Pine began, stretching away to right and left and creating, Thanet imagined, a windbreak around the entire garden. Beyond the trees was a tall, close-boarded boundary fence and here again the path divided, running along the base of the fence in both directions and presumably providing, at intervals, access to different areas of the garden.

They paused.

'I imagine that the field where Speed parked his car is on the other side of this fence,' said Lineham. 'There must be a gate somewhere.'

They followed the path to the right first, but the fence

122

continued in an unbroken line as far as the hedge which bordered the road. Retracing their steps to the point at which they had emerged they walked on in the opposite direction.

'There it is!' said Lineham triumphantly.

The gate was almost invisible until they were upon it, being constructed of the same close-boarding as the fence. There was no lock, only a latch.

'You'd think they'd take a bit more care over security,' grumbled Lineham as he opened it.

Thanet was not surprised to find a footpath on the other side. It was obvious that long before High Gables had been built on its little projecting spit of land, people from the village would have established a right-of-way across this short cut behind it. A couple of minutes' walk confirmed that after leaving the boundary fence the footpath cut across a field to the gateway in which Speed must have parked his car. Over to the right a country hedge of hawthorn, dogwood, field maple and wild rose delineated the sharp bend in the road.

'No problem, then,' said Lineham. 'He had a nice little private route to the house, whenever he wanted to visit her. When are we going to talk to him again?'

'All in good time,' said Thanet. 'I want to read a full report from the witness who saw him park, first.' He turned and began to walk back in the direction of the gate, hands in pockets, head down, shoulders hunched. Lineham, recognising the signs, followed in silence.

Just before they reached the gate Lineham hesitated, then reached out to pluck at Thanet's sleeve.

'Sir,' he whispered.

Thanet turned, still abstracted. 'What?'

Lineham nodded in the direction of the village.

Approaching them along the footpath was the woman they had seen earlier from old Mrs Tarrant's window.

They were at last about to meet the elusive Daphne.

ELEVEN

At the sight of the two men Daphne Linacre's step had faltered.

Scarcely surprising, thought Thanet. The soaring statistics of rape, muggings and crime in general had resulted in fifty per cent of the female population being afraid to go out alone at night. And here, on a deserted country footpath . . .

He stepped forward boldly and raised a hand in greeting.

'Good morning, Miss Linacre,' he called. 'Detective-Inspector Thanet, Sturrenden CID. I hope we didn't startle you.'

She had stopped when he first spoke. Now she started walking again. Thanet had already noticed that despite the dense shade along the footpath she was wearing sunglasses, and he cursed the migraine which had presumably made them necessary. He hated talking to people without being able to see their eyes. More than any other feature, eyes reveal what their owner is feeling.

Close to, he could see that Daphne Linacre's clothes were expensive, the blue linen skirt elegantly cut, the white cotton sweater handknitted in an intricate design. Unfortunately their owner's body did not match up to them. It was as if nature had used up all her skill, all her art, in creating the physical perfection that had been Nerine. Daphne was too stocky, her waist too thick, her breasts too flat, her hips too lumpy. But there was plenty of character in her face: determined jaw, firm mouth, and a resolute tilt to the head which went some way towards explaining why she had become such a successful businesswoman.

'Not at all.' She patted a bulge in her skirt pocket. 'I was out of cigarettes. And, to be honest, I wanted an excuse to get out of the house for a while. I loathe being cooped up with nothing to do.'

Thanet admired her honesty. He knew that death imposes a strait-jacket of conventions and inactivity on those who are left behind. An unspoken conspiracy, born of love and desire to alleviate the burden of grief, frequently exists to prevent the bereaved from performing even the simplest task, like making a cup of tea. Many people, of course, both enjoy and appreciate such attention, but some find the strain well-nigh intolerable. Few, however, can bring themselves openly to admit it.

'I'm glad to see that you're feeling better today. Mrs Haywood told us about your migraine attack. Oh, sorry. This is Detective-Sergeant Lineham.'

She nodded a greeting at Lineham and said, 'Much better, thank God. Sometimes I'm laid up for days.'

'We were on our way back to the house . . . Do you feel up to answering a few questions?'

'Yes, of course.'

Thanet opened the gate and stood back for her to precede him. She turned right, followed the path along the fence for a short distance and then cut off to the left. Thanet and Lineham walked behind her in single file and they all emerged eventually onto the drive, opposite the north side of the main house and about seventy-five yards from the coach house.

Beatrix Haywood was crossing the open space between the two houses, carrying a large cardboard box overflowing with clothes. They all converged at the coach-house door.

Lineham took the box from her.

'Thanks,' she said, puffing slightly. Her cheeks were pink and there was a sheen of perspiration on her forehead. Today she was wearing a shapeless dress made out of what looked like sacking, several strings of multicoloured beads and long, dangling earrings. 'It's surprisingly heavy. More jumble,' she added as she let them in. 'Just put it with the rest of the

125

stuff, will you? The vicar's supposed to be picking it up before lunch.'

There were three more boxes lined up in the hallway.

'You'll take some coffee, Inspector?' said Daphne. 'I could do with a cup myself.'

'That would be very welcome, thank you.'

Without a word Mrs Haywood disappeared into the kitchen. Mr Tarrant may have thought that it was rash of Daphne to offer a home to her dead fiancé's mother, thought Thanet, but he suspected that Daphne had known what she was doing. Good domestic help is like gold dust these days: expensive and difficult to find. A devoted, unpaid housekeeper is a prize indeed.

Daphne led the two men into the sitting room and they all sat down. The paintings on the walls appealed to Thanet even less this morning, their only distinction being that so many of them hung in one room. He wondered how Jocelyn Haywood had managed to secure the commission for the Linacre Nursery catalogue in the first place.

'Now, how can I help you?' she said.

'It's fairly simple, really,' said Thanet. 'We're trying to build up a picture of everyone's movements yesterday afternoon. There are just a few routine questions we'd like to put to you.' He glanced at Lineham. *Take over.*

It didn't take long for Daphne to confirm what Mrs Haywood had told them. She had gone to work in the morning as usual and during the afternoon had begun to feel unwell. By four o'clock she knew she was starting a migraine attack and had decided to go home. She had finished up one or two urgent tasks before leaving the nursery at around twenty past four, and had arrived home at about twenty to five.

'When I got here I went straight to bed.'

Mrs Haywood came in with a tray. Only three cups, Thanet noticed.

Daphne smiled up at her as Mrs Haywood handed her the coffee. 'Thank you, Beatrix.' She patted Mrs Haywood's hand and said, 'Of course, Beatrix is wonderful when I have one of my attacks. I don't know what I'd do without her.'

Mrs Haywood gave a gratified smile.

'Beatrix, you've only brought three cups,' said Daphne. 'Aren't you having any?'

'I . . .'

'I know, you've already had one,' said Daphne with a little smile. 'But I'm sure you could do with another.'

'I won't be long,' said Beatrix in a stifled voice. She hurried out.

Thanet had watched this little exchange with interest. What, exactly, did it signify? Was Daphne perhaps ashamed to see Mrs Haywood behaving like a servant and apparently expecting to be treated as one, in front of outsiders? Or was this self-confident, capable woman more vulnerable than she looked, and in need of moral support?

'Did you see anyone about, when you arrived home?' asked Lineham.

Daphne frowned, then shook her head. 'No. And even if I had, I don't suppose it would have registered. At that stage all I could think of was lying down in a cool, dark room.'

'What about later on?'

She shook her head. 'Sorry, no. I can see you're not a migraine sufferer, Sergeant. If you were you'd know that during an attack you're pretty well deaf and blind to anything else.'

'So when did you hear of your sister's death?' said Thanet.

Mrs Haywood came back into the room with a cup of coffee and sat down on an upright chair near Lineham, glancing apprehensively at his notebook.

Daphne grimaced. 'Some time during the evening. I've no idea when, exactly. I think Beatrix would have preferred to wait to tell me until the worst of the attack was over, wouldn't you, Bea? But during one of my sorties to the bathroom I happened to glance out of the window and see that the place was crawling with police, so . . .'

127

'Sorry to interrupt,' said Lineham. 'but I thought you said that at that stage you were virtually deaf and blind . . .'

'Aha,' said Daphne theatrically. 'Ze vitness contradicts herself.' Then, in her normal voice, 'Sorry to disappoint you, Sergeant, but I think you will have to agree that it's one thing to register that your garden is overrun with police, another to notice a given individual at a given time . . .' She waited for Lineham's nod before saying, 'Anyway, at that point I naturally asked her what was going on. So . . . so she told me.'

Suddenly there was a tremor in her voice, a huskiness in her throat. It was the first hint of grief she had displayed.

If only he could see her eyes, thought Thanet.

'You were fond of your sister, Miss Linacre?' he said. He could see himself reflected in her dark glasses, a distorted little mannikin with bulging eyes in an elongated pale oval of a face.

Daphne shrugged. 'She was my sister, the only blood relation I had left.' The moment of weakness had passed and she was in control of herself again. She glanced at Mrs Haywood. 'Beatrix told me of your suspicion that Nerine's death was no accident, and frankly, the idea wasn't too much of a shock. To put it bluntly, the way she carried on, she was asking for it.'

'You think one of her lovers, past or present, was responsible?'

Daphne shrugged. 'It would seem to be the obvious answer, wouldn't you agree? *Crime passionnel* and all that.'

'Did you have anyone special in mind?'

'Not really, no. But I'm sure you won't have to look far.'

Perhaps you could help us out with some names?'

'Sorry, no. I'm afraid my sister's grubby little affairs had no interest for me.' She brushed an imaginary piece of fluff off her skirt, as if trying to erase the memory of Nerine's never-ending string of lovers.

'You do realise, Miss Linacre, that most crimes of this nature are carried out by a member of the family?'

128

'I have a great respect for statistics, Inspector, but they can be misleading. If that is an indirect way of asking if I suspect Roland of having done it, or Damon, even, then you're barking up the wrong tree. And as for myself...' Daphne shrugged. 'Well, I can't pretend Nerine and I were bosom pals, because we weren't, but all I can say is, I really cannot see why I should suddenly decide to shove her off her balcony for no apparent reason. After all, if there had been bad blood between us I'd never have come to live here in the first place. It wasn't as though I was hard up, I could have bought a house anywhere I liked.'

This was unanswerable.

'You'll make up your own minds, of course, but let me tell you this...' Daphne leaned forward, the huskiness back in her voice. 'My mother died when I was born. Nerine was only three, but I can still remember... She was mother and sister to me, all through my childhood. She looked after me, watched over me, and I adored her. I'd have done anything for her. Anything.' She glanced away, out of the window, as if looking into the past and seeking to recapture the intensity of that passionate childhood devotion. Then she sighed, shrugged. 'Things changed, of course, as we grew up. Our interests, our tastes were so different... And I can't pretend to have approved of the way she played around with men...'

Briefly, there was an ugly, bitter twist to Daphne's mouth. Inspired, perhaps, by jealousy, thought Thanet, the jealousy of a plain spinster unfortunate enough to have lost her one and only suitor by a cruel twist of fate, for a beautiful older sister who all her life had had only to crook her little finger for men to come running after her?

Daphne shrugged again. 'But there we are. That was her affair and didn't affect me in the slightest. I had my own life to live. I enjoy my work, get a lot of satisfaction out of it, and Bea and I get along like a house on fire, don't we, Bea?'

Mrs Haywood gave a quick, nervous smile and cleared her throat. 'Oh, yes, we *do*,' she said.

129

'So I'm sorry, Inspector,' said Daphne. 'I'm afraid you'll have to look elsewhere for your murderer – if there is one.'

'You have no further suggestions to make?'

'Only the advice I gave you earlier. *Cherchez l'homme.*'

At the door Thanet hesitated. 'You mentioned Damon just now . . . He hasn't turned up yet and I was wondering . . . Have you any idea where he's gone?'

Daphne shook her head. 'Sorry, no . . . You mean, he hasn't even rung Roland, to say when he'll be back?'

'Not so far.'

'Oh. Oh, dear.' For the first time her composure was shaken, and she glanced at Beatrix Haywood, who had moved up to stand close behind her. 'That's not like him. I hope he's all right . . . My God, it's only just occurred to me . . . You mean, he doesn't even know his mother's dead yet?'

'It looks that way,' said Thanet.

'Poor boy,' said Beatrix. Her lips were trembling and she put her hand up to her mouth.

'With any luck he'll turn up soon,' said Thanet, hating the note of false reassurance in his voice. 'But I thought I ought to warn you – if he's not back by late afternoon, we might have to put out an appeal, on TVS. Anyway, if either of you comes up with an idea as to where he might be, let me know, will you?'

'Of course.'

Outside, Lineham said, 'Not much sisterly devotion there now, is there, whatever she says about the past.'

'True. But lack of love is different from positive hatred. She made a good point, I thought, when she said she wouldn't have come to live in the coach house if there'd been ill feeling between them. And it's difficult to see why, after all these years, she should suddenly decide to come home from work in the middle of the afternoon and shove her sister off a balcony.'

'She'd be capable of it, though, don't you think?'

'If she had a strong enough motive, yes. But there's been

130

no hint of any quarrels between them. They seemed to lead such separate lives, I can't really see what could have been such a burning issue between them.'

'What now, sir?'

'Mmm?' Thanet was abstracted. He had just thought of someone else he would like to interview, but he wasn't going to mention it to Lineham yet, not until he'd mulled the idea over for a little while longer. But it could prove very interesting.

He smiled with satisfaction. Yes, very interesting indeed.

TWELVE

Thanet felt like a schoolboy playing truant, an especially delicious sensation after the long and tedious afternoon.

Conscientiously, he and Lineham had spent hours catching up on the reports which had come in, checking and cross-checking all details which could conceivably have any significance.

The most promising item of information was that 'Halo' Buzzard had been released from prison the previous week. Was it possible that the solution to the case was going to fall into Thanet's lap? Stranger things had happened. Thanet had at once set in train extensive enquiries to trace Buzzard's movements and especially to find out if he had been seen in the area.

Daphne Linacre's story seemed to check out. Her secretary said that although Miss Linacre had been in good spirits most of the previous day, around ten past four she had called the girl into her office to say that she had begun to feel ill and had decided to go home. This was not unusual. Miss Linacre would have a migraine attack once every three or four months, and they usually seemed to descend with very little warning. No, nothing had happened to upset Miss Linacre, so far as she knew. No unusual letters, or phone calls . . . Phone calls? Miss Linacre had had several in the preceding half an hour, three business calls and one from Mrs Haywood, to be precise.

Thanet rang Beatrix Haywood. Yes, she had rung Daphne at around four o'clock, but she hadn't mentioned it because she hadn't thought it important. She'd made up some pretext to ring – some trivial shopping request – because, knowing Daphne very well, she had suspected the imminence of a migraine. There were certain signs, if you only knew how to recognise them – a tightness around the eyes, a particular facial expression – and she had wanted to know how Daphne was. And she'd been right, of course. By that time Daphne was feeling distinctly unwell and she, Beatrix, had done her best to persuade her that it would be sensible to come home immediately, while it was still safe to drive. Daphne had agreed.

The next loose end to be tied up was that there were now two witnesses to confirm that Tarrant had indeed arrived home at around twenty to six the previous afternoon, as he claimed. The same two witnesses had seen Damon leave ('like a bat out of hell', as one of them graphically put it) a minute or two earlier.

Which reminded him . . . Thanet glanced at the dashboard clock. One minute to six. He switched on Radio Kent.

All day, whenever Damon's name had come up, Thanet's thoughts had fleetingly returned to the uneasy conversation with Joan last night and the invisible barrier that had suddenly sprung up between them. No trace of drugs had been found in Damon's room, but late this afternoon, in view of Damon's continued absence and silence, Thanet had reluctantly been driven to take the step he had been hoping to avoid, and had authorised an appeal on both TVS and Radio Kent this evening. Here it came.

'Police investigating the death of Mrs Nerine Tarrant, found dead in the garden of her home at Ribbleden yesterday afternoon, are anxious to trace her son, Damon Tarrant, aged eighteen. It is thought that Damon may have gone to spend the night with friends and may as yet be unaware of his mother's death. He is driving a red Vauxhall saloon, registration number BJZ 189J, and anyone with information as to his whereabouts is asked to contact Sturrenden Police on Sturrenden 265. I repeat, Sturrenden . . .'

Thanet switched the radio off. It had come over very well,

he thought. There was a clear implication that Damon was not a suspect. Surely Joan couldn't raise any objections?

Anyway, he refused to worry about her reaction at the moment. Instead, he savoured the thought of the interview ahead, just as a woman, tired after an exhausting day, savours the prospect of a leisurely hot bath. It was, quite simply, his reward for duty done, a self-indulgence justified only by the merest thread of necessity.

Lineham had thought it a waste of time.

'What's the point of going to see her? It's years since she set eyes on any of them.'

But Thanet couldn't resist the idea. Who could give him a better insight into the dead woman than the housekeeper who had virtually brought her up?

And here he was. He pulled into the parking area and switched off the engine.

Thanet was aware that sheltered housing for the elderly, both private and council-funded, is the biggest 'growth area' in new building these days. By the end of the century the population of Great Britain will be heavily weighted in favour of the over-sixties, and Thanet sometimes wondered if the younger generation would be able to carry the crippling burden ahead. The Government was doing its best. Traditional nursing homes were out, community care and other schemes which enable pensioners to maintain their independence to the last were in.

Rainbow Court was typical of the latter.

Only a few minutes' walk from the centre of Sturrenden with all its amenities, old people could continue to shop, enjoy their chosen entertainment and generally live a full and independent life (health allowing) long after they could no longer afford expensive public transport or bear the expense of running a car. Four blocks of clearly numbered low-rise flats, one no doubt occupied by a warden, were grouped around a paved courtyard attractively furnished with wooden benches, tubs of bedding plants and a central, raised rose-bed full of pink floribundas in bloom.

Ignoring the lift, Thanet climbed the stairs to Flat 15 on the third floor.

The door was wide open.

'Is that you, Ellie?' called a cheerful voice as he approached. 'I've just finished it. Come and see. Oh,' a different inflection as the woman realised her mistake. 'Sorry, I was expecting someone else.'

Thanet had recognised her at once. The transition from middle-age to old-age does not bring about nearly such a radical transformation as youth to middle-age. She must, Thanet had worked out, be in her eighties by now but the years had treated her well. She was neither shrunken nor obese, and although the wrinkles on her face had multiplied and the brown hair gone grey, her carriage was still upright, her eyes alert and intelligent. She was wearing a long-sleeved floral cotton shirt-dress and a white apron. A vivid memory of the pathetic, confused figure of Lavinia Tarrant flashed through Thanet's mind and he understood why Beatrix Haywood found the thought of this woman so reassuring.

'Mrs Glass?' He paused on the threshold, took out his ID card and introduced himself.

Her welcoming smile faded. 'Oh.'

She took the card and compared the photograph with the reality before taking off her apron and saying, 'You'd better come in. It's about Nerine, I suppose.'

'I'm afraid so.'

'I heard about it on the wireless.'

She moved aside and he stepped into the small, comfortably furnished room, his attention at once drawn to a round table near the window. On it were displayed all three tiers of a beautifully decorated wedding cake, the smallest tier still on a revolving icing stand, familiar to Thanet from Bridget's attempt at decorative icing. The sheet carefully spread beneath the table to protect the carpet, the bowls with their tell-tale traces of icing, the clutter of icing nozzles and piping bags all told the same story.

Thanet pursed his lips in admiration and moved to take a

closer look. The top tier was edged with alternating minia-
ture footballs and bunches of flowers.

'You did this?'

Mrs Glass nodded, with justifiable pride. 'I like to keep
my hand in.'

'It's magnificent! A work of art.'

'It's for the granddaughter of a friend of mine. She's getting
married on Saturday.' She grinned. 'As you may have gathered, she's a florist and he's a footballer. I work in here
because I like to have a bit of elbow room when I'm icing,
and my kitchen's so tiny I fall over my own feet if I'm
not careful. Though I mustn't grumble. This place suits me
perfectly.'

'I've never been in one of these sheltered housing flats
before.'

Clearly anxious to delay discussion of Nerine's death, Mrs
Glass seized on this as an excuse to show him around, and
Thanet was given a guided tour of the only bedroom, the
minute kitchen and even smaller bathroom. Every room had
an alarm cord which would summon help in case of emergency, and the warden apparently did a quick round of her
protégés night and morning to check that they were all right.

'At my age, you can't imagine the sense of security that
gives you.'

By now they were sitting down, the atmosphere was
relaxed and Mrs Glass was chatting freely.

'Have you always lived in this area?'

Gently, Thanet led the old lady through the years, from
her impoverished childhood ('I always longed to be educated,
these days I'd have gone to university') and her entry into
domestic service at the age of fourteen, past early marriage
and widowhood in the 1914–18 war to her eventual appointment in 1944 as housekeeper to the Linacres.

At this point her eyes grew troubled, her manner hesitant.
If only he could help her to keep up the flow of reminiscence,
thought Thanet . . .

'You never remarried?' he asked, striking off obliquely.

'No. I got used to being independent . . . Look, Inspector, I've enjoyed our chat and it's helped me to relax. I appreciate your taking the trouble, a lot of men wouldn't have bothered, I'm sure, they'd just have barged in, asked their questions and been off . . . I'm just trying to say that if you want me to talk about Nerine, I'm ready now.' And she gave an apprehensive smile.

Thanet was touched. It was a declaration of faith, after all. *I trust you not to upset me too much.*

'Thank you,' he said gently. 'I appreciate your frankness.'

Her smile was a little bolder now. 'To be honest, I can't really see why you want to talk to me at all. It's so many years since I saw Nerine. Daphne visits me once a month, though, regular as clockwork.'

'Does she?' Thanet was surprised, he wasn't sure why. Mrs Glass, after all, would have been Daphne's mother-substitute.

'I understand they were very close, as children.'

Mrs Glass's eyes glazed reminiscently. 'They certainly were. Inseparable. Nerine had adored her mother, you see, and Mrs Linacre used to make such a fuss of her . . . So did her father, for that matter, but then he would have done anything to please Mrs Linacre and later on, after Mrs Linacre died, I did wonder whether he'd only been pretending affection for Nerine to please his wife.'

'You mean, after his wife's death he took no interest in Nerine?'

'That's right. No interest in either of them, for that matter. In fact, he couldn't bear the sight of Daphne, blamed her for her mother's death, I think. He'd worshipped Mrs Linacre and it hit him hard.'

'How did Nerine react?'

Mrs Glass grimaced. 'It was pathetic, really. To begin with, she used to follow him around like a little dog, but he just couldn't be bothered with her and eventually she got the message. She went through a very bad time – well, you can imagine how she must have felt, losing her mother and, to all intents and purposes, her father, both at once. Poor little scrap, I was really worried about her for some time. I could scarcely get her to eat anything, or take any interest in anything — she just used to lie around on the floor, sucking her thumb and gazing into space . . .'

'She was lucky to have you. At least there was some continuity in her life.'

'I suppose so. The trouble was, I had that big house to run and I couldn't really give her the time and attention she needed . . . Mr Linacre got a nanny for the baby, of course, but babies need a lot of care and Nerine tended to miss out there, too. And I don't think the girl really understood what the child was going through. She was good-hearted but not very bright . . . Anyway, after a while Nerine turned her attention to Daphne, and soon you couldn't have prised them apart with a shoe-horn. Nerine used to spend all her time with her, played with her, pushed her about in her pram, created a terrible fuss if ever they were separated . . .

'I remember when she started school. When the day came, she couldn't believe that Daphne wasn't to be allowed to go with her. The scene she created! I honestly thought she was going to scream herself into some kind of fit! We had to call the doctor, to give her a sedative. And every morning it was the same, until in the end her father got really fed up and said it was nothing short of emotional blackmail and if she carried on like this he'd jolly well send her away to boarding school and she wouldn't see Daphne at all . . . Well, that did the trick and she gave in. But I'll never forget her little face looking back over her shoulder at Daphne as she left for school each morning. She looked so lost and bewildered, as if she simply couldn't understand why she had to be sent away. I honestly think she thought she was being punished for something, and couldn't understand what.'

'Didn't the situation improve when Daphne started school?'

'Well, to some extent, of course. But Nerine always hated school, never did a stroke of work. Daphne was a very different matter. She absolutely loved it, took to it like a duck to water – well, I think she was bored and lonely after Nerine started, and couldn't wait to get there.'

'So how do you think this experience affected Nerine, in the long term?'

Mrs Glass paused, eyes narrowed, thinking. Then she sighed. 'I think it made her very self-centred. As if the only thing that mattered was to look after number one. And yet, it wasn't her fault, you see. She didn't start out like that. Before Daphne was born she was the sweetest, sunniest little girl you could imagine. It was such a shame. Oh dear. I hate talking about her like this, when . . . I mean, she's not here to defend herself any more, is she?'

'I know. Will it make you feel any better if I say that all this is invaluable to me? In order to find out why she died I really need to understand her, as a person . . .'

'Is it true, what they're saying? That she might have . . . That it was . . .'

'That someone might have killed her, you mean? I'm afraid it's all too likely. Everyone seems to agree that she was the last person to commit suicide, and from what you've just been saying . . .'

'Oh, I agree,' Mrs Glass broke in vehemently. 'Nerine would never have killed herself. Never.'

'And it's very difficult to see how it could have been an accident. She fell from a balcony, you see, and the rail was too high . . . We haven't entirely ruled out the possibility, but . . .'

Mrs Glass was nodding. 'I see. Oh dear. But I suppose . . .'

'What?'

'Well . . .' She was speaking slowly, working it out. 'I was just thinking that Nerine's problem was that she was so . . . engrossed with herself that she was incapable of taking thought for anyone else's feelings, or even beginning to understand them. She didn't want to understand them. She was so . . . insensitive, that way. I remember when she and Daphne were in their teens . . . Nerine was a beautiful girl, quite exceptionally so, whereas Daphne . . . Well, I suppose you've seen her, haven't you? I'm fond of Daphne, but she's no oil painting, is she? Nerine used to have hordes of boy-friends, they used to fall over each other trying to get her to go out with them, whereas Daphne was always ignored, passed over, as if she was invisible or something. And Nerine never seemed to realise how Daphne must have felt about it. I honestly don't think it ever entered her head to wonder.'

'How did Daphne react?'

Mrs Glass shrugged. 'She just seemed to accept it. But I couldn't help feeling sorry for her, especially when her fiancé was killed in that car crash. A real tragedy that was. He was the first man ever to take an interest in her, and she was on cloud nine from the day they started going out together.'

'What happened?'

'Oh, it was awful. Terrible. Even now, after all these years, it upsets me to think about it.'

She wasn't exaggerating. The memory had clouded her eyes, sharpened the lines in her face. Absentmindedly, she took a handkerchief from the pocket of her dress and began to pick at one corner, tiny, suppressed, agitated movements which mirrored only too clearly both her distress and the struggle to control it.

Thanet said nothing, waited.

'Daphne met him at work. He'd been commissioned to do a cover for the Spring Catalogue. He was an artist . . . She kept very quiet about him, but I knew something was up. She was . . . transformed. Radiant.' Her eyes flickered towards the wedding cake. 'Like a bride.' She pulled a face. 'I don't think either Nerine or her father ever even noticed. Anyway, a couple of months later they got engaged. There was a terrible row, when she told her father. I was there. She guessed there'd be trouble and she asked me to be with her, for moral support. I'd been with them twenty-five years by then, and I suppose she thought of me as family. He was furious. Called Jocelyn a jumped-up little fortune hunter. Daphne was so angry . . . I'd never seen her really stand up to her father before, but she certainly did then. I think, by that stage, they'd both forgotten I was there.

"*To be honest with you, Father, I don't care what you think. You've never taken the slightest interest in my welfare, and I have no intention of allowing you to influence such an important decision.*"

' "*Never taken the slightest interest in your welfare! I've fed you, haven't I? Clothed you, educated you . . .*"

"*Loved me? Ah, I see you can't answer that one. Oh, I grant that you have maintained me, materially speaking, because it was the done thing to do. But Jocelyn is the first person in my life ever to love me for myself, and nothing, I repeat nothing, will make me give him up.*"

"*Love you for yourself? Daphne, I don't want to be unkind, but didn't you say he was an artist? And therefore a lover of beauty? I hate to say this, but I think you only have to look in the mirror to see that you must be deluding yourself.*"

"*I won't listen to this! I told you, Father, I don't care what you think and I don't care what you say. I'm going to marry him and that's that.*"

"*He can smell money, that's the trouble. Perhaps he wouldn't be so interested if he didn't think you'd get the business when I'm gone.*"

"*Father, you are fifty-two years old and in perfect health . . .*"

"*Now, maybe. But looking to the future . . .*"

"*Who's interested in the future, at our age?*"

"*I'll tell you who. Artists. Artists are interested in only one thing, the freedom to paint. And if the future can be manipulated to provide that freedom then believe me, they are very interested indeed.*"

"*The trouble with you, Father, is that the nursery has been your life for so long you've forgotten what it's like to love someone.*"

"*Oh, no, Daphne. You're the one who's forgotten. I lost the person I loved and got you, instead.*" '

Mrs Glass shook her head. 'As soon as the words were out, he knew he'd gone too far. I'll never forget her face, when he said that. She just stared at him for what seemed like ages. Then she said, "I rather think you've just proved my point, Father, don't you?" And she turned and walked out.'

'But if they didn't get on, why did she go to work for him in the first place? She's obviously a very capable woman, she could easily have found a job elsewhere.'

'Oh, don't misunderstand me. Until this row blew up they'd got on well enough. They lived together in the same house, worked in the same place, and they were always perfectly polite to each other. Unnaturally so, I always thought. The thing is, the nursery was Mr Linacre's life. After his wife died he spent all his time there, and he built it up into a really successful business. They've got an international reputation, you know . . . And I'm sure the reason why he encouraged Daphne to take that Business Studies course and then to work for him was because he wanted her to take over the nursery after he died. There was no one else, you see. It was obvious that Nerine wouldn't make a businesswoman in a million years. I suppose he'd always hoped Daphne would marry someone who'd be able to help her run the place.'

'How did Nerine react to the news of Daphne's engagement?'

'She just grinned and said, "Well done, little sister. Looks as though you'll beat me to the altar after all." She'd been going out with Mr Roland for several months, by then, and I know he was keen to get her to agree to marry him. But at that point there'd been no news of an engagement. I think she was just enjoying having a good time.'

'So what happened, after the row when she told her father she was going to get married?' Thanet found himself as eager to hear the next instalment as a soap-opera fan waiting for his daily fix. Except that this, he reminded himself, was real life, these the people with whom Nerine had spent her days.

Mrs Glass shrugged. 'Things seemed to settle down, after a while. Mr Linacre raised no more objections, to my knowledge — I suppose he could see it was pointless. A couple of months later, Daphne had a perforated appendix. She was desperately ill — nearly died, as a matter of fact — and she was away in hospital for six weeks. Then, the night before she was due to come home . . .'

She hesitated, fingers once more picking away at the corner of the handkerchief. It was starting to fray, Thanet noticed.

'Yes?'

'It was March, I remember, and a wild night, with a strong wind blowing and gusty rain. The coroner thought the weather conditions may have contributed to the accident . . . Mr Roland was at the house. He'd only come back from Australia a few days before, he'd been out there since just after Christmas. An aunt had died and left him all her money, and he'd had to go out to sort out the estate with her lawyers. When he arrived I let him in and half an hour later Nerine brought him into the kitchen, where I was preparing dinner. There was a . . . glitter about her that I'd never seen before. "Ah, there you are, Mrs G," she said. "We've got some news for you." And she held out her left hand. "How d'you like my ring?" she said. It was the biggest diamond I'd ever seen in my life. Mr Roland was smiling all over his face and looking so happy. "It was my grandmother's," he said. I couldn't help feeling glad for him, though I must admit I thought he'd have a difficult time of it, with Nerine for a wife. "So come on, Mrs G," says Nerine. "Dig a bottle of champagne out of the cellar, and bring it into the drawing room. This is a celebration. Daddy's like a dog with two tails."

'Well, I couldn't help remembering how poor Daphne's news had been received, and feeling glad she wasn't there to see the contrast, but I did as she said and we were all drinking a toast when there was a knock at the door. It was Jocelyn, carrying a huge bunch of red roses for Daphne's homecoming. My first thought was, oh dear, how awkward, but

143

I couldn't shut the door in his face and it was far too windy to leave it open, so I invited him in and was just about to ask if he'd like me to put the flowers in water when Nerine came into the hall. "Who is it, Mrs G?" she says. "Oh, Jocelyn. Come along in and have a glass of champagne. Roland and I are celebrating our engagement." And she held out her hand, to show the ring.

'Just then Mr Linacre and Mr Roland burst out laughing, in the drawing room, and Jocelyn . . . Well, I suppose he couldn't help remembering how Daphne and he had been treated when they got engaged . . . He went white, and said, "No thanks. I wouldn't want to intrude." And he pushed the flowers into my hands and was gone. Nerine just raised her eyebrows at me, shrugged, and went back into the drawing room. A couple of hundred yards down the road Jocelyn's car skidded, went out of control and hit a tree. He was killed instantly.'

'And Daphne?'

Mrs Glass shook her head. 'She never got over it. Oh, she pulled herself together after a while, but it was a bad time for her. She was only just getting over her illness, and then, on top of Jocelyn's death, to have to put up not only with the news of Nerine's engagement and their father's obvious pleasure at the prospect of having Roland as a son-in-law, but all the preparations for the wedding . . . It was just too much.'

'Nerine didn't think of postponing the wedding?'

'I don't think the idea would have entered her head. I told you, she was completely insensitive to other people's feelings.'

'When you said that before . . . Were you trying to say that you think this insensitivity might have caused her death — that she had hurt someone so badly that he — or she — was driven to kill her?'

Mrs Glass shrugged. 'How can I tell? As I said, I haven't seen Nerine for years. But I shouldn't think she's changed much.'

'D'you think Daphne ever forgave her sister, for going ahead with the wedding so soon after Jocelyn's death?'

Mrs Glass sighed. 'Oh yes. You see, I don't think Daphne ever forgot those early years, when Nerine made so much of her. I suppose you'd find that difficult to understand, but to have Nerine's exclusive attention was like . . . like . . . well, it was as if the sun was shining especially for you. It's a feeling that's difficult to describe, and I've never experienced it with anyone else. She could make you feel you were the most important person in the world, at that particular moment, and even though you were aware of all her faults, that feeling would keep you . . . bound, to her, somehow.' Mrs Glass shook her head. 'I'm not putting this very well, I'm afraid. But the point is, Daphne never forgot how much she'd meant to Nerine, when they were little. And after Mr Linacre died, of course, Nerine was the only family Daphne had. That was why, when the opportunity of living in the coach house came up, Daphne jumped at the chance to buy it.'

'She didn't give me the impression that she was deeply distressed over Nerine's death.'

'No, I don't suppose she would. She and Nerine haven't been particularly close for years now. But don't be misled. She'll be upset in her own way, it's just that she's always been good at hiding her feelings.'

There was a clatter of feet on the staircase, a knock at the door.

'Yoo-hoo, Barbara. It's me.'

Mrs Glass rose stiffly to her feet, betraying her age for the first time. 'That'll be the friend I was expecting. The one whose granddaughter is getting married.'

Ellie was a tiny, bird-like woman, with a restless, eager air. She came in with a rush, apologising for her lateness, widening her eyes at Thanet's presence and finally twittering over the cake, dragging him into further admiration of its beauties.

Eventually Thanet managed to make his excuses, thank

Mrs Glass and leave. He walked slowly down the stairs, thinking over all that she had told him. He was glad he had come. For the first time he was beginning to feel genuine sympathy for Nerine, the 'sweetest, sunniest little girl you could imagine', whose life had overnight become transformed from a joyous, secure existence to a wasteland devoid of warmth and love. Small wonder that she had spent the rest of her life searching for those dimly remembered joys, flitting from lover to lover, restless and dissatisfied. And too blind to see that they had been right there beside her, all the time.

THIRTEEN

As Thanet drove home that evening he couldn't help remembering how he had felt the night before: at peace with the world.

Tonight it was very different.

For one thing, he was tired. It had been a hectic day; stimulating of course, but requiring intense and unremitting concentration, crowded with new people, new impressions, and filled with that sense of urgency unique to the start of a murder case. True, things had gone reasonably well, but at the moment he had no inkling of who the murderer might be. As he'd said, there was certainly no shortage of suspects.

Secondly, his back was aching. In the privacy of his car he allowed himself the luxury of a little groan as he tried to ease himself into a more comfortable position. Twice in the past he had managed to injure his back. On the first occasion he had foolishly tried to heave a lawnmower into the boot of his car and on the second – well, he preferred not to think about the second, if he could help it. About to escort a newly arrested murder suspect back to the police station, he had stooped to open the car door and found he couldn't straighten up again. The suspect and Lineham had actually had to help him into the back seat. And as for his arrival back at the station ... It had been one of the most humiliating experiences of his life.

Thirdly ... well, of course, this was where the root of his depression lay. Thirdly, there was Joan, and this clash of interests and loyalties which was threatening to undermine his marriage. It was pointless to remember that he had never really wanted Joan to go back to work in the first place, or to remind himself that he had foreseen precisely this sort of difficulty from the moment when Joan had first told him she wanted to train as a probation officer. The fact remained that for one reason and another (primarily the fear of losing her if he continued to oppose her wishes) Thanet had given in and until last night, he had to admit it, things had gone reasonably smoothly. There had been difficulties, true, but sensible discussion and a determination to overcome them had always won the day. But now ...

He could see Joan's point of view, of course. Here she was, with a first offender whom she had every hope of putting permanently on the straight and narrow. Then along comes something like this, a disaster perhaps not of the client's making, and the whole fragile edifice comes tumbling down, negating months of careful, sustained effort.

She's bound to be angry over the television appeal, Thanet told himself, forgetting his earlier optimism. It's perfectly natural. I must just be prepared for it. It'll blow over, in time.

Anyway, what choice did I have? he asked himself.

You could have left it another twenty-four hours.

'No!' he said aloud, glad that there was no one in the car with him to look at him askance.

Look at the circumstances, he argued. A woman is dead. Her son is on probation. He is missing from the moment of the murder, and despite all attempts by the police to trace him, he still hasn't turned up a day later ...

No, he had had no choice.

Ben was mending a puncture, his bicycle upturned on the drive. Thanet edged the car carefully in alongside it and chatted with his son for a few minutes. Delaying tactics, he thought sadly as he let himself into the house. Who would ever have believed the day would come when he was reluctant to meet his wife?

The kitchen was empty and in the living room Bridget was

sitting on the floor, school magazines spread out all around her. She was snipping away at one, tongue between her teeth.

'Hi,' she said, greeting him with a smile. 'I'm cutting out some recipes for the *KM*. And I've written them a letter. D'you think you could have a look at it after supper, see if you think it's OK?'

'Yes, sure. Er . . . where's your mother?'

'Upstairs, in the study.'

This was the grandiose title given as a joke to the shoe-box of a fourth bedroom where both Thanet and Joan worked in the evenings, when necessary.

'She's finishing a report for tomorrow.' Bridget hesitated, scissors stilled. 'I don't know what's up, but she's in a pretty grim mood.'

Thanet pulled a face. 'I'd better go and see.'

'Your supper's in the oven,' Bridget called after him as he left the room.

'Thanks.'

But the thought of food made his stomach churn as he climbed the stairs, feet dragging. At the top he paused for a moment and then, without allowing himself to hesitate further, flung open the 'study' door, said 'Hullo, darling,' took the two necessary paces to arrive at the desk and stooped to kiss her.

Instead of turning her head to kiss him on the mouth as usual she remained quite still, staring at the papers spread out on the desk, and the kiss landed on her temple.

'What's the matter?' he said, and was immediately angry with himself. What was the point in pretending?

Slowly, now, she turned to look up at him. 'Need you ask?'

He perched on the edge of the desk. 'The television appeal, I suppose.'

She nodded. 'The television appeal. Oh, Luke, couldn't you have waited just another twenty-four hours?'

'No, I couldn't. I'm sorry.' Then, as she remained silent, he said with quiet intensity, 'Look, I did everything that

149

could be done. We've consulted you, as his probation officer, tracked down his friends, followed up every lead we've been given, and there's been nothing. Not a trace of him, anywhere. He's just disappeared off the face of the earth. And there's been plenty of publicity over the murder. I imagine he has a radio in his car, most young people seem to, these days ... So why hasn't he come forward? He really should have heard by now.'

'And if he hasn't? It'll be enough of a shock for him to find out his mother's dead, without hearing that he's wanted by the police.'

'He's not wanted by the police – not in the way you mean at least! Didn't you notice how carefully worded the appeal was, to avoid giving that impression? We just want to talk to him, that's all.' Thanet shook his head. 'Look, love, I can see your point of view. I was thinking about it on the way home in the car, and I can understand how concerned for him you must be, and how disappointed you must feel that all the work you've done with him might be wasted, if he reacts badly to all this. But you must try and look at it from my point of view, too. And the one thing I cannot allow myself to do is behave any differently towards him just because he happens to be your client. You must see that. So this afternoon, when I was debating whether or not to put out that appeal I had to ask myself why I was debating it at all. And I realised that if he hadn't been your client I wouldn't even have hesitated. The fact is that he disappeared around the time of the murder, and even if he is not implicated himself, he could have vital evidence ...'

'If he had, I'm sure he would have come forward with it.'

Thanet shrugged. 'Perhaps.'

Joan shook her head stubbornly. 'I still think you could have given him another twenty-four hours. I'm sorry, Luke, I'm afraid we have to accept that we just aren't going to agree over this, however much we talk about it.'

I knew it, Thanet wanted to say. *I knew this would happen*

150

one day, if you went into the probation service. Don't you remember my saying so, right at the start?

But nothing was to be gained by an I-told-you-so attitude and he left it at that. Over supper he brooded, his mind ranging to and fro between the various interviews he had conducted today, but always returning at intervals, obsessively, to Joan. At the moment he could see no way out of their predicament. He could recall that conversation seven years ago as though it were yesterday.

"It would be ideal, Luke, don't you see?"

"Ideal for whom?"

"Well for me, of course. What do you mean?"

"Have you thought how it could affect us?"

"Us? In what way?"

"You haven't thought that there could be a certain, well, clash of interests?"

"No. Why should there be?"

"Look, the probation service and the police, they're often poles apart in their attitudes to criminals."

"But they're both on the same side really, surely? They're both concerned to maintain peace and order in society?"

"Maybe. But that doesn't stop them frequently being in conflict. I don't suppose you've had much to do with probation officers, but I have. And I grant you they do very fine work, many of them. But that's not the point. The point is, as I say, that their attitudes to criminals are different. Don't you see that it's impossible to shed one's working attitudes in one's private life? They become an integral part of one, as basic as breathing. I can see all sorts of situations in which this thing could become a barrier between us."

"How, for example?"

"Well, for one thing, I've always shared my work with you, haven't I? Told you everything, without reserve, knowing that I could trust you not to talk about it."

"But I still wouldn't. You know that, surely?"

"Maybe you wouldn't talk about it, but your attitude to what I tell you would be bound to be different, don't you see?

151

It's inevitable that you'd be looking at the whole question of crime from a different point of view, from the side of the criminal, his guilt, his rehabiliation, whatever . . . Darling, don't you see that? You must, surely."

"Not necessarily. Probation officers have to be detached, they can't afford to identify with their clients or they couldn't work properly."

"And what if it turned out that we were both working on the same case . . . ?"

"I would think that the chances of that happening would be very slight. And if it did happen, couldn't one or the other of us request that we should be taken off the case?"

"And that would create a barrier between us, too. Joan, you must see that. It would limit us, put restrictions on our work. We'd be bound to resent it. And there would be other barriers — just in ordinary life, in casual conversation, we'd have to be guarding our tongues, watching what we say to each other . . ."

And now it's happening, thought Thanet. All my worst fears are being realised.

'Did you enjoy that?' Bridget had come in, gesturing at his plate and clutching a piece of paper.

The plate was empty, so presumably he had eaten his supper, though he had no memory of doing so.

Bridget was laughing. 'Oh Dad, your face . . . Did you even notice what you were eating?'

'Well . . .'

'I knew it! I work my fingers to the bone and look what happens! I might just as well have made you a cardboard sandwich.'

'Ah, well, now that I might have noticed. By the way, I came across an interesting dish today — at least, it smelt delicious. Now let me see, what was it . . .'

They chatted for a while, and Thanet looked over the letter she had written to the *Kent Messenger*. He was impressed, and said so. 'If that doesn't make them take you on, I don't know what will.'

'D'you think so? Oh, Dad, I do hope so.'

'Well don't get too excited about it, just in case.'

Ben came in to wash his hands.

'Finished?' said Thanet.

Ben nodded. 'Took me ages.'

'How was the History test?'

Ben shrugged. 'OK. Seven out of ten.'

'Good.'

And so the evening passed. Joan did not come down to join him later on as she usually did. Instead she took a leisurely bath and went straight to bed. When he went upstairs she was either asleep or pretending to be so.

It took him a long time to get to sleep himself.

Next morning they again kept up a pretence of normality for the sake of the children, a simple matter in the fragmented bustle of bathroom, breakfast and departure. Joan kissed him goodbye as usual, but there was no warmth in it, merely a brief contact of flesh against flesh, as impersonal as a social kiss at a party.

It was another glorious summer morning, but today Thanet was not in the mood to appreciate the beauties of nature. He arrived at the office early, determined to drown his private sorrows in work. Lineham was late, and by the time he bounded into the room whistling the Wedding March Thanet had already skimmed through the reports which had come in overnight. His heart sank as he noted the sergeant's bright and smiling face. He hoped Lineham wasn't going to be overpoweringly cheerful this morning, he didn't think he could stand it.

'Any news of the boy, sir?'

'Quite a number of possible sightings, but none of them has come to anything, as yet.'

'But not a word from the lad himself?'

'Not so far.'

Thanet slapped the report he had been reading down on his desk. 'Why on earth can't people tell the truth?'

He knew the answer, of course: because they were afraid.

But it was a time-wasting business trying to get people to be frank. There was something about a murder investigation which made them clam up, innocent and guilty alike. The lengths to which people would go to conceal some very minor peccadillo never ceased to amaze Thanet. The problem for the police was trying to sift the wheat from the chaff.

'Why, who's been putting up smoke screens now?' Lineham perched on the edge of Thanet's desk, looking as keen and alert as a labrador awaiting the word of command.

Thanet flapped an irritated hand. 'Do go and sit down, Mike. I can't think with you looming over me like that.'

At once he was angry with himself, the look on Lineham's face a silent reproach as without a word the sergeant slid off the desk and retreated to his own.

The phone rang and Thanet answered it: Beatrix Haywood, enquiring after Damon. Thanet assured her that he'd let her and Miss Linacre know the moment there was anything definite, and rang off.

'Sorry, Mike, I didn't mean to snap at you. I seem to be in a bit of a mood this morning, I can't think why.' *Liar.* 'You'll just have to try and ignore it if I let fly from time to time.'

Lineham was looking mollified. 'Nothing wrong, sir, is there?'

The negative question provided Thanet with his escape route. 'Oh no . . .' He managed to grin. 'I expect I just got out of bed on the wrong side.' He glanced at the reports scattered on his desk. 'And now I find that not one but three of our main suspects have been either lying to us or misleading us.'

Lineham leaned forward, the eagerness back in his face. 'Which?'

'The oh-so-innocent, butter-wouldn't-melt-in-my-mouth Mrs Speed, for one. You remember she went sick-visiting after her meeting, in the afternoon? That's been confirmed. What she didn't tell us was that she also paid a call on Nerine Tarrant.'

'Really? At what time?'

'Well, that's the interesting thing. It sounds as though she was in two minds about it. First of all she was spotted just after four o'clock, when the meeting in the village hall ended, standing by the gates of High Gables, staring up the drive towards the house. Then later on, about ten past five, presumably after she'd finished her sick visit, she was seen actually walking up the drive.'

'Two different witnesses?'

'Yes.'

Lineham pursed his lips in a silent whistle. 'Interesting.'

'Also,' said Thanet, shuffling through the papers for the appropriate report, 'there's confirmation that Speed was lying about his movements at lunchtime on the day of the murder. Remember he gave us the impression he hadn't put a toe outside his car while he was parked in that field? Well we guessed that couldn't be right for a start. If he'd been watching for Mr Tarrant to leave he wouldn't have been able to see a thing from there. As you know, the witness who reported seeing the car lives in that little cottage further on around the bend from High Gables. She was away most of yesterday and couldn't be contacted until evening, but she says that the car was parked from about twenty-five to one to around ten to one that day. About a quarter of an hour, in fact. The reason why she's so sure is because Speed always parked in that farm gateway when he went to visit Nerine Tarrant, and he usually stayed much longer – forty to forty-five minutes, on average. And she swears that on Thursday he got out, locked the car and walked along the footpath towards High Gables as he always did.'

'A quarter of an hour,' said Lineham thoughtfully. 'Not long, even for a quickie.'

'Quite. And by then, Mr Tarrant was already in the house.'

'And if *he's* telling the truth, and went straight up to his wife's rooms . . .'

' . . . who was it he heard in the bedroom with his wife?'

'Exactly.'

155

The phone rang again: Tarrant, this time, also enquiring about Damon. After a brief conversation Thanet replaced the receiver and said, 'He's really getting worried about the boy now.'

The two men stared at each other in silence, thinking.

'If Mrs Tarrant had taken a new lover,' said Lineham at last, 'and Speed knew about it, it would certainly give him a motive, wouldn't it?'

'I would have thought so, yes. Though if you remember, according to PC Driver it was extraordinary what a knack she had for discarding her lovers without turning them against her.' Thanet remembered what old Mrs Glass had said. *To have Nerine's exclusive attention was as if the sun was shining especially for you.* 'Despite her reputation it was almost as though they regarded it as a privilege to have been admitted to her bed at all, and went into the affair accepting from the beginning that it was too good to last. Though, come to think of it, I know for a fact that that certainly didn't always apply.' And he told Lineham about Doc Mallard's friend.

'But it's surely unlikely that she should have been killed by a past lover. I mean, the time when that sort of violence erupts is when feelings of jealousy and rejection are still running high, not months afterwards. And Speed has been the current favourite for some time.'

'I remember Beatrix Haywood saying that a few months was par for the course and any minute now he would be finding himself supplanted. It looks as though it might already have happened.'

'And he suspected it!' said Lineham. 'He probably sensed she was going off him and got suspicious when she started trying to put him off. I expect he was desperate to find out who the new man was, and thought he'd do a bit of spying.'

'Maybe.'

'So then, later on in the afternoon, he goes back to have it out with her.'

'Could be . . . If we're right about all this, Mike, I wonder if Tarrant knew about this new lover.'

'I doubt it. If he realised the voice wasn't Speed's, why should he lie about it?'

'I'm not so sure. It can't be much fun admitting that your wife was having an affair and that you actually walked away from her bedroom door knowing she was with her lover. But to put her in an even worse light by informing us that, well, as a matter of fact it wasn't the lover we knew about but yet another one . . . It would have made her look a bit of a whore, wouldn't it?'

'Well, let's face it, sir, that's what she was, practically. High-class, perhaps, choosy – well, yes, to the extent that she only had one man at a time, but . . . '

'Perhaps. But it's one thing for her husband to have to admit that to himself, another to have to acknowledge it to the police.'

'Possibly . . . I suppose that if Mr Tarrant realised that the voice he heard wasn't Speed's that could have been the straw which finally broke the camel's back. He could have gone away, brooded over it all afternoon and finally decided he'd had enough.'

'On the other hand we have to accept that he might just have assumed the man with his wife was Speed, and still genuinely believe it. Well, there's not much point in wasting time speculating. We'll have to see them both again, obviously. Mrs Speed, too. What was she up to, I wonder?'

'Anything else of interest come in, sir?'

'Yes.' Thanet grinned. He had kept the most dramatic bit of news until last. 'There's a possibility that our outsider might be coming up fast on the rails.'

'Buzzard?'

'Yes. There's been a sighting in the area, on the afternoon of the murder. He was driving an old green van. An alert PC who happened to be involved in Buzzard's trial recognised him waiting at the traffic lights by those major road works on the Ashford Road just outside Sturrenden, at around five o'clock.'

'Really? But that's only a few miles away from Ribbleden!'

'Exactly. I want him picked up and brought in, Mike. Who knows? We might have to look no further, and we can leave all these people in peace.'

'I'll get on to it right away, sir.'

'But meanwhile we can't sit about twiddling our thumbs. As soon as you're ready we'll go and see Mr Tarrant again.'

FOURTEEN

The lawns of High Gables had just been cut and the scent of new-mown grass hung on the air. Thanet inhaled appreciatively as he and Lineham crossed the gravel to the front door.

Vicky Cunningham answered their knock. Today she was wearing red-and-white striped trousers, a white teeshirt decorated with red hearts and red butterfly clips in her hair. The gravity of her expression belied the gaiety of her attire. 'He's in the garden. He's . . .'

'What?' prompted Thanet.

She pulled a face, shrugged. 'You'll see for yourself.'

'Where is he, exactly?'

'Around the back. He said he was going to have a bonfire.'

'Not exactly bonfire weather,' said Lineham as they walked along the front of the house and turned the corner onto the terrace where Nerine Tarrant's body had been found. 'It must be in the seventies by now.'

Thanet stopped. 'I wonder . . .'

'What's the matter?'

'I was just thinking . . . If we're right, and Speed came here on Thursday not to meet Nerine, but to spy on her, he must have found himself a vantage point . . .'

Thanet set off purposefully along the path they had followed the previous day. When he reached the gap in the yew hedge he turned right instead of left, walked as far as the corner, then paused. Here there was no gap; the hedge was a dense, impenetrable right-angle. Ahead, the path continued, curving past a border of tall shrubs which backed

159

onto the third side of the hedge, and skirting a huge clump of rhododendrons.

The rhododendrons were the answer, Thanet decided. He approached them, then turned to look back at the house. Yes, from here there was a clear view of both the front door and the gap in the yew hedge through which any clandestine visitor would have to emerge in order to get out of the garden via the gate in the back fence.

Thanet turned to study them. At their tallest they were perhaps fifteen feet high. Here and there late flowers still bloomed, the spectacular purity of their candy-floss pink enhanced by the glossy dark greens of the dense foliage and the withered bracts of dead blossoms. Stooping, Thanet thrust his way into the heart of the bushes. It was like stepping into a low cave. Green filtered light penetrated the canopy of leaves, imparting to the thick gnarled branches a mysterious, almost sinister air. Despite the oppressive warmth of the enclosed space, Thanet shivered.

'Find anything, sir?'

Lineham's face, suspended like that of the Cheshire Cat, appeared in a gap in the foliage.

'Just a minute. Ah . . .'

Thanet took some tweezers and a plastic bag from his pocket and bent to retrieve a small object from the ground. Then he thrust his way back through the embrace of the branches onto the path and handed the bag to Lineham.

The sergeant's nose wrinkled in distaste. 'Fag end. Pretty stupid if you ask me, smoking while he waited. I mean, anyone could have seen the smoke and come to investigate.'

'Still, potentially useful evidence. If it's his. It could have been thrown there by anyone. We'll get a saliva test done.'

'Talking of smoke, sir . . .' Lineham nodded in the direction of the back boundary, where a murky, dun-coloured cloud was swirling up between the tops of the trees. 'Mr Tarrant's bonfire, presumably.'

As they drew nearer the crackling of the fire grew louder, punctuated by the irregular thud of an axe and a sharp crack of snapped branches. At the edge of a small clearing they paused. Tarrant was burning up the remains of a dead tree, felled some time ago, judging by the weathered look of the exposed end of the trunk. Stripped to the waist, he was working like a man demented, and his body glistened with sweat. The frenetic energy with which he was attacking a recalcitrant branch, the leaping flames and billowing smoke all combined to impart to the scene a disturbing air of violence, of passion unleashed. A picture of Tarrant as he had first seen him, the suave, sophisticated man of the world, flashed across Thanet's mind. It was difficult to reconcile the two images.

Thanet stepped forward. 'Mr Tarrant?' he called.

Tarrant gave a final wrench at the branch before glancing over his shoulder, staggering a little as it finally parted company with the trunk. Then he laid it on the ground and wiped his forehead with the back of his arm before slowly straightening up. He was breathing heavily, his sparse fair hair dark with sweat.

Thanet advanced, holding up a hand to shield his face from the intense heat. He was conscious of sweat breaking out all over his body. 'Could we have a word?'

'Is it Damon?'

Thanet shook his head. 'No further news yet, I'm afraid.'

Now that Tarrant's impetus was broken, the energy seemed suddenly to drain out of him, and he put out a hand to steady himself against one of the few remaining branches of the dead tree. Then, body sagging with fatigue, he walked heavily to the edge of the clearing and picked up a checked shirt lying on the ground. He pulled it on.

'Perhaps we could find somewhere cooler?' suggested Thanet.

'We'll go indoors.'

Tarrant led the way to the back door of the house and then to the study, pausing in the kitchen to ask Vicky to bring a jug of iced lemonade. He slumped into his chair

161

behind the desk and indicated that Thanet and Lineham should sit down.

'What is it now?' he said wearily, taking a red spotted handkerchief from his pocket and mopping at his forehead again.

What had driven Tarrant to that bout of frenetic activity? Thanet wondered. Had he been trying to blot out misery, or guilt?

Thanet didn't want to believe that this man had killed his wife. Tarrant, he was convinced, had loved her deeply. But he had to acknowledge that the surgeon was one of the prime candidates. Over the years Thanet had seen many a reasonable man or woman ultimately driven to violence, the trigger factor sometimes so apparently trivial that others gaped in disbelief that so minor an offence should have such disastrous consequences. If Tarrant had realised that the man in his wife's room wasn't Speed . . . Well, Nerine might well have taken one lover too many. Thanet knew that if this man were innocent he should be allowed to mourn in peace, that it would be inhuman to cause him further, unnecessary pain. But he might be guilty and the professional in Thanet knew that he had no choice. Much as he hated the idea, it was his duty to get at the truth. And if Tarrant had lied . . .

'You remember, when we spoke to you last, you told us that when you came back to the house at lunchtime on the day your wife died, you heard a man's voice from her bedroom?'

Tarrant's lips tightened. 'Yes.'

'You told us that it was Mr Speed.'

'That's right.'

'You'll have had more time to think about it, by now. Would you care to amend that statement in any way?'

Thanet caught the flicker of a glance from Lineham. *You're being too soft with him. Sir.*

There was a knock at the door and Vicky entered with a tray, ice-cubes chinking. She set it down on a side table and poured three tall glasses and handed them around. Thanet

162

would have preferred not to accept the drink. In the circumstances he didn't feel comfortable about enjoying Tarrant's hospitality. But it would have been churlish to refuse and besides, it looked like fresh lemonade. Thanet could see the bits of lemon floating around in the cloudy liquid. His throat suddenly ached for the delicious coolness of it.

He smiled up at Vicky. 'Thank you.'

Tarrant had already drained his glass and was holding it out for more. 'God, I needed that. Delicious, Vicky.'

'Good.' Vicky refilled his glass then held up the jug, raising her eyebrows at Thanet and Lineham.

They shook their heads.

'I'll leave it here and you can help yourselves if you change your minds.'

Thanet waited until the door had closed behind her before saying, 'Well?'

'I'm sorry, I've forgotten what the question was.'

'I asked if you'd care to amend your statement in any way . . . That you'd heard Mr Speed's voice in your wife's room.'

'That's what I thought you said. I don't know what you mean. How could I "amend" it, as you put it?'

'You're sure, that it was Mr Speed's voice?'

'I told you, yes.' Tarrant was impatient now, and Thanet was pretty sure that he was sincere.

'What are you getting at, Inspector?'

Thanet sighed. There was no going back. 'I'm afraid it couldn't have been Speed.'

'But . . .'

'Mr Speed tells us that he did intend to visit your wife that lunchtime, but that he didn't do so because he saw your car turn into the drive ahead of him. That was at twelve thirty-five. You did say you got here just after half past twelve, didn't you?'

'Yes. But . . . Just a minute. Let me get this quite straight. You're saying that he arrived *after* me?' Tarrant paused, his

163

eyes going blank as he focused on the next, inevitable question. 'But in that case,' he said slowly, 'who . . . ?'

'Exactly, Mr Tarrant. In that case, who was with your wife?'

Tarrant gave an uncomprehending shake of the head, then rubbed his hands over his face as if to erase his confusion. 'I have no idea. None.'

'Any conjectures?'

'No!' It was almost a shout. 'Look here, Inspector, there must be some mistake. You must have got this wrong.'

'I'm afraid not, sir. We have an independent witness who confirms that Mr Speed was definitely not in this house at twelve thirty-five that day.'

Tarrant swivelled his chair to look out of the window, and Thanet wondered what he was thinking. If he was innocent, his thoughts must be bitter indeed. Even after her death, it seemed, Nerine's promiscuity had the power to reach out and turn the knife in the wound which had given him so much pain all his married life. And if he was guilty . . . Well, thought Thanet, if Tarrant was guilty he deserved an Oscar.

Tarrant shook his head and his voice was tight with suppressed emotion as he said, 'I'm afraid I can't help you, Inspector. So if you don't mind . . .'

Outside, Lineham said, 'What d'you think, sir?'

Thanet shrugged. 'For what it's worth, I'd say he was telling the truth. But I've been wrong before and no doubt I'll be wrong again. What did you think?'

'Same as you. What now?'

'Another word with Miss Barnes, I think. She saw Tarrant knock on his wife's door that lunchtime, remember. And I distinctly recall feeling that she was holding something back.'

'You mean, she might know who the new man was?'

'Well, she's around the house all day, isn't she? We don't know how long the new affair had been going on, and even if she didn't see him on that occasion, she might have seen him on another.'

'True. There is one odd thing, though . . .'

'What?'

'Well, everyone seems to agree that Mrs Tarrant never tried to hide her affairs, so why the secrecy surrounding this one?'

'Perhaps she wanted to be sure of the new lover before casting off the old? Or perhaps...' Thanet came to an abrupt halt. Suddenly, all was clear to him. And yes, it would explain so much...

'Perhaps what?' said Lineham.

'Come on. Let's go and see Miss Barnes.'

But finding her took a little time. Eventually a murmur of voices led them to the room next door to the sitting room in which they had interviewed old Mrs Tarrant that morning. The old lady's bedroom? wondered Thanet as he knocked.

'Just a minute.' Marilyn's voice. A moment or two later the door opened a few inches. 'Yes? Oh... Sorry, you can't come in. Lavinia's in one of her dressing-up moods and she's changing.'

'Could you spare us just a few moments?'

Marilyn glanced back over her shoulder. 'If you'd wait, I'll be as quick as I can.'

Thanet nodded. 'Fine.'

The door closed. Lineham leaned against the wall beside it, gazing into space and whistling tunelessly between his teeth. Thanet strolled along the corridor to a window at the far end. Daphne and Beatrix Haywood were standing at the door of the coach house, deep in conversation. Beatrix was carrying a wicker basket over one arm and as he watched she set off purposefully down the drive. Going to the village, presumably. Shopping, perhaps? Or possibly to help prepare for the jumble sale this afternoon. He and Lineham had seen the notice outside the church hall as they had driven past, earlier. Daphne stayed watching the older woman until she was out of sight, then turned back into the house, closing the door behind her. They certainly seemed to get on well, thought Thanet. But then, their needs dovetailed beautifully. Daphne needed someone to run her home and Beatrix needed a home to run. But in addition they were linked by a powerful emotional tie: Daphne's only lover had been Beatrix's only son.

'Sir,' called Lineham.

Marilyn Barnes came out into the corridor, closing the door behind her as Thanet hurried back.

'She'll be all right for a few minutes now,' she said. 'What did you want to ask me?'

No point in wasting time. 'It seems that Mrs Tarrant had taken a new lover,' said Thanet. 'Could you tell us who he is?'

Marilyn gave him a long, considering look. 'Who told you that?'

'Shall we just say that it has . . . emerged, during the course of our investigation.'

She sighed, shook her head, lips compressed. 'Have you talked to Mr Tarrant about this?'

'Yes.'

'And what did he say?'

'He denies all knowledge of it. He seemed distressed.'

'He didn't know. I was hoping he wouldn't find out.'

'You're sure he knew nothing about it?'

'Pretty sure, yes. Mr Tarrant rarely comes home in the middle of the day.'

'So who . . . ?'

The bedroom door opened and Lavinia Tarrant stood dramatically framed in the opening, posing with one foot forward, like a fashion model.

'Is that you, Jack?'

Thanet suppressed a gasp. Could this really be the sweet old lady they had talked to the previous day? She was heavily made-up and might have stepped straight from the fashion pages of the late nineteen twenties. Her dress was of pale orange crêpe, with a low, boat-shaped neckline, a very short, gathered, two-tier skirt and a low-waisted, tubular bodice decorated with a geometric design of brightly coloured sequins. Pointed shoes, dangling earrings, and a waist-long

166

string of pearls completed the flapper image. But once again the effect was merely grotesque, the contrast between the bright young clothes and the shrunken body within them a tragic reminder of mortality. Thanet remembered a conversation he'd had once with an old lady in her nineties. 'The sad thing is,' she'd said, 'I still feel sixteen inside.' Would Lavinia Tarrant say the same? he wondered.

'No, Lavinia,' said Marilyn. 'Jack's not here yet.' Then, in an undertone, to Thanet, 'Jack was her husband.' She turned back to the old lady. 'You said he wouldn't be here until this evening, remember?'

Lavinia frowned, eyes clouded with the effort to resurrect the memory. She shook her head. 'Did I? I don't remember.'

Marilyn took her arm. 'Why don't we go into the sitting room?' She began to steer her charge along the corridor.

'Miss Barnes,' said Thanet urgently. 'You still haven't told me who he is.'

She paused, glancing back at him, her expression wry.

'It was *Tim* Speed,' she said.

FIFTEEN

Thanet raised a hand in a gesture of acknowledgement, then hustled Lineham away. At times like this, even after all these years in the force, the sergeant's streak of puritanism tended to surface. Sure enough, as soon as the door had closed behind Marilyn Barnes and Lavinia, Lineham hissed, 'But she was old enough to be his *mother!*'

Thanet glanced around, then frowned at Lineham and shook his head. Lineham took the hint and remained silent as they went down the stairs, across the hall and through the front door into the sunshine.

They both blinked and screwed up their eyes against the sudden transition to brilliant light.

'What's the time, Mike?'

Lineham squinted at his watch. 'Quarter past twelve, sir.'

'Right. Speed starts his lunch hour at twelve thirty. There's time for a sandwich and a quick pint at the Dog and Pheasant before seeing what he has to say for himself.'

'OK, sir.' Lineham set off across the gravel.

'Where are you off to, Mike?'

'The car.'

'Mike, do you realise how far away the Dog and Pheasant is?'

Lineham shrugged. 'Four hundred yards, sir? But I thought we were going on to Mr Speed's house after that.'

'We are. And that's another four hundred yards or so. Half a mile in all. You'll lose the use of your legs one of these days.' And Thanet set off at a brisk pace for the gate.

'I just like driving, that's all,' Lineham protested, falling in beside him.

'There's more to life than a gleaming bonnet and a powerful engine, Mike. Anyway, we'll have time to talk.'

'He's only eighteen,' said Lineham, instantly slipping back into gear again. 'And her son's friend.'

'Not unheard of,' said Thanet. 'Come on, Mike, don't be naive. You've come across far worse than this. They're both consenting adults, after all. He's a good-looking young man and she was a very beautiful woman.'

'You don't seem too surprised, I must say. You'd already guessed, I suppose.'

'The possibility did cross my mind, I must admit, while we were talking after seeing Mr Tarrant just now. I could kick myself for not seeing it before. No, what I find much more interesting are the implications.'

'You mean, how the other people involved would have reacted if they knew.'

'Yes. I rather think that's the crux of the matter. Did they know?'

The two men walked in silence for a few moments, then Lineham said, 'I'm not sure about Mr Tarrant. I think I believed him, but . . . I suppose, if he did know, it would be understandable if he hoped it wouldn't get out. It would make his wife's reputation sink to an all-time low, if it was generally known she'd been cradle-snatching.'

'Quite. But as far as the Speeds are concerned, I'd guess they do know, wouldn't you agree? And I shouldn't think they'd want it to get out, either. It would certainly explain why they were so touchy every time Tim was mentioned.'

'I bet they only found out that lunchtime,' said Lineham. 'Yes,' he went on excitedly, 'if you think about it, it all fits. Remember the family row the neighbour overheard, and the atmosphere between Speed and Tim which PC Driver noticed, that afternoon? And if Speed had known before then, why would he have been lurking in those bushes? No, I'd guess he suspected she'd found someone else – perhaps because she'd put him off once or twice, whatever – and wanted to find out who it was. So he hung about until Tim came out and then . . .'

'What?'

Another silence, while they speculated.

'It must have been an awful shock for him,' said Lineham. 'It's one thing to suspect you're being given the push, another to know you've been supplanted by your own son. I should think he'd have gone after him there and then, caught him up in the garden.'

'That neighbour of the Speeds, Mrs Shrimpton . . . What time did she say she heard them having that row?'

'One fifteen I think, sir. And she saw Tim leave ten minutes later.'

'Yet his lunch hour is supposed to be from twelve to one. It looks as though they both went straight home from High Gables.'

'They didn't leave together in the car, though, sir. That witness who saw Speed park in the field would surely have mentioned it, if he had arrived alone and left with someone else.'

'But as we were saying a few minutes ago, it's only a short distance to the Speeds' bungalow. Perhaps Speed didn't want to get into the car with Tim after what he'd just learned, and told him to walk home.'

'And he did! Pretty obedient of him, don't you think?'

'Perhaps he thought he might as well face the music and get it over with. What are you drinking?'

On this lovely summer Saturday the Dog and Pheasant was crowded with weekend drinkers. Lineham spotted a sign to a rear garden and they carried their beer and sandwiches outside. The tables under their striped umbrellas were well spaced out, affording more privacy.

All the same, they automatically lowered their voices, leaned together like conspirators.

'Well,' said Thanet, 'It would certainly strengthen Speed's

170

motive, that's for sure. He must have been in a real turmoil, that afternoon.'

'I bet he was mad with Mrs Tarrant, for choosing Tim of all people ... It wouldn't be in the least surprising if he grabbed the first chance he had and slipped back to the house during that test drive, to give her a piece of his mind.'

'And what about Mrs Speed, Mike? This would give her a much stronger motive too.'

'Yes. But wait a minute. That's a thought. Don't you think it's a bit odd, that Mr Speed would have chosen to have it out with Tim at home, when he knew his wife would be there?'

'He probably wasn't thinking straight. As you say, he'd just had a pretty nasty shock. The garage would have been a bit public, too, for the sort of conversation he would have had in mind. Customers could have kept walking in and interrupting them.'

'True. I suppose, in the heat of the moment, he could even have forgotten his wife would be there. Or maybe he did remember, and deliberately chose to have it out with Tim at home, knowing that she'd be as outraged as he was, if for a different reason, and would back him up.'

'She would certainly have been furiously angry with Nerine. First of all stealing her husband and then seducing her son ... During the afternoon she must have been plucking up the courage to go and tell her what she thought of her. If you remember, she was first seen hesitating outside the gates of High Gables just after four. Obviously her nerve failed, on that occasion. But later, at about ten past five, she was actually seen going up the drive ...' Thanet drained his glass. He was eager to hear what the Speeds had to say about all this. 'Ready, Mike?'

The hall of Shangri-La smelled of boiled cauliflower. Mrs Speed reluctantly invited them in. She was wearing a pink nylon overall and looked hot, her plump cheeks mottled an unhealthy shade of red. She showed them into the living room and left to fetch her husband. By daylight the garish

171

colours of the carpet, upholstery and curtains could not conceal the fact that the room was shabby and much in need of refurbishment. When she returned with Speed she had shed her overall. They were both looking apprehensive.

As they sat down Speed pointedly consulted his watch. 'I've got to be back at work in half an hour.'

'We'll try not to keep you too long.'

Thanet had been trying to make up his mind over which tactics to employ: the shock approach or the more subtle one? Which would be most effective with these people? On the surface they appeared ordinary, inoffensive types, but Thanet had long ago discovered just how deceptive appearances can be. It is always difficult to tell how people will react in a crisis, and the situation in this house both now and last Thursday could certainly be described as that. If they were both innocent what they now needed was a period of calm in which to regain their equilibrium. Unfortunately this was just what he could not allow them. If one of them were guilty . . . It was the same old dilemma and he knew that once again he had no choice in the matter. He had to find out the truth, and to do so he would have to press as hard as was necessary. But, how best to do it?

He looked at them sitting side by side on the settee staring at him, Mrs Speed perched uncomfortably on the edge, Speed even now a prey to vanity, running a hand over his balding head to check that the thinning strands were evenly spread out. It was difficult to visualise either of them pushing Nerine off that balcony, and even if one of them had, Thanet was prepared to believe that it was in the heat of the moment rather than in cold blood. But the fact remained that each of them had a classic motive for murder. Revenge and jealousy are emotions which only too easily get out of hand.

Unfortunately, if one of them were his quarry, there was so far not a single scrap of evidence to prove it. He had to hope for a confession. If he tried the shock approach and failed, there would be nothing left to fall back on. But if he

172

proceeded cautiously, eroding their defences bit by bit, he might in the end succeed in winkling the truth out of them.

Thanet was not perturbed that the silence had become uncomfortably protracted. The Speeds were obviously finding it difficult to cope with and were showing signs of tension. Speed was smoking a cigarette with quick, nervous puffs, and now he stubbed it out, cleared his throat and opened his mouth to speak. Mrs Speed shot him a quick glance and caught his eye. The message that passed between them was clear: *wait*.

But after only another minute or two Speed couldn't stand it. With a defiant look at his wife he burst out, 'Well? How much longer're we going to have to sit here like a couple of lemons?'

'We were just waiting for you to begin, Mr Speed.' Thanet's tone was conversational, courteous.

'Me, begin? Why should I begin? This is your idea, not mine.' Speed lit another cigarette and sucked the smoke in greedily.

'We thought you might have something to tell us,' said Lineham.

The belligerence drained out of Speed's face and although he and his wife did not so much as glance at each other Thanet picked up their unspoken thought. *Oh God, how much do they know?* He had noticed it many times before, this telepathy between married couples in times of stress.

'We've told you all we know,' said Mrs Speed. But her attempt at firmness was a dismal failure and the statement almost became a question.

'Really?' Thanet sat back, folding his arms and looking from one to the other and back again, as if searching for something he failed to find. 'I really don't understand it, Sergeant, do you?'

'Understand what?' Speed was sweating now and the reek of motor oil was growing stronger as his body temperature rose, an emanation as distinctive as a fingerprint.

Suddenly Thanet remembered: the first time he had entered

173

Nerine Tarrant's bedroom he had caught an elusive whiff of something incongruous. Now he realised what it was. It is notoriously difficult to recognise smells out of context and he supposed that he might be excused for not having been able to identify motor oil in all that silken, feminine elegance. Although Tim had only been working at the pump and in the office garage his clothes must have picked up the smell and left that almost undetectable imprint upon the air.

'Why is it, do you think, Sergeant, that when people wish they hadn't been in a certain place at a certain time, they seem to manage to convince themselves that they were invisible?'

'Beats me, sir.'

'Invisible? What do you mean? What are you talking about?'

But they had both understood him. Thanet could read it in the flare of a nostril, an averted eye, a whitening of the knuckles.

'Oh, I think you know what I mean, Mr Speed.' Abruptly Thanet abandoned his jocular, almost benign tone and leaning forward said accusingly, 'Don't you?'

'No!' Speed glanced at his wife for support. 'No, we don't, do we, Ceel?'

Celia Speed did not reply for a moment. She gave Thanet a level, assessing look, then said, 'I think we'd better hear what the Inspector has to say, don't you? I think he's rather angry with us.'

'Yes,' said Thanet. 'You could say that. I'm angry because this is a murder investigation and I don't like people wasting my time. Both of you, I find, have lied to us. No,' and he raised a hand as they both made to speak, 'don't say anything at the moment. Just hear me out. Now it's always very difficult, when people do lie to us, to work out their motives in doing so. They might be innocent of the crime we are investigating and merely trying to conceal some little family secret they don't want broadcast – no, I'm sorry, you really will have to wait until I've finished, you had your opportunity to speak and you didn't take it – or, *or* they might be lying because they are up to their necks in the crime in question and are trying to wriggle out of being suspected. I'm not sure which it is, in your case.'

'The first,' they said together, and stopped.

'But naturally, you would say that, wouldn't you?' said Thanet. 'Being the lesser of two evils.'

'But it's true!' said Speed. 'I did explain to you, at the garage . . .'

'Oh no, Mr Speed,' said Lineham. 'We're not talking about that. This is something else.'

'Something else . . . ?'

'Suppose you come right out and tell us what we are supposed to have done, Inspector,' said Celia Speed.

'No. Suppose you try to set the record straight. Suppose *you* tell *us* anything you "forgot" to tell us the first – or in the case of Mr Speed, the second – time around.'

Mrs Speed made as if to rise. 'Do you mind if I get a glass of water?'

'Sergeant Lineham will get you one.'

While they waited for Lineham to return Thanet said, 'Let me just say this. If you are innocent of this crime, you have nothing to fear. Unless what you tell me is relevant to the investigation and eventually has to be used in court, I assure you that it is not going to become a matter of gossip amongst your neighbours through any indiscretion on our part. I think you understand me.'

They exchanged glances. *They do know about Tim.*

'But,' Thanet went on, 'this time I really want the whole truth and nothing but. Otherwise . . .'

There was no need to spell it out. *Otherwise you'll find yourselves in deep water indeed.*

Lineham returned with a cup of water. 'Sorry, I couldn't find the glasses.'

Mrs Speed took the cup with a murmur of thanks and drained it at a draught.

'So who's going to begin? Mr Speed, perhaps?'

SIXTEEN

'Let's start from the moment you parked your car in that field, shall we, Mr Speed? And remember, we're not just guessing at all this. We do have witnesses.'

Mrs Speed closed her eyes tightly, as if to shut out the view of a too harsh reality, and swallowed hard. But this did not succeed in stopping the tears which now began to force themselves between her closed eyelids. With an exclamation of impatience she flicked them away with the back of her forefinger, groped in her pocket for a handkerchief and failed to find one. 'Sorry,' she said. 'There are some tissues in the kitchen . . .' And again she dashed away the tears with her finger.

Thanet waited until Lineham had fetched the tissues and she was rather more composed, then said, 'Look, Mrs Speed, I can guess how painful all this is for you. There's absolutely no need for you to be here while we're talking to Mr Speed. Why don't you go and lie down for a little while? Your husband will call you for us, when we need to see you . . . And if you're not feeling well enough, then we'll leave it until another day.'

Long before he had finished his little speech she was shaking her head.

'No, I'd rather stay, thank you. Really.'

Thanet guessed that she would prefer to know exactly what was going on in here than lie on her bed in a torment of uncertainty and speculation. He gave a slight shrug. 'As you wish.' He glanced from wife to husband and then said, 'Perhaps it might help and perhaps hurry things along a little if I openly state what I hinted at just now. We do know about Mrs Tarrant and your son.'

He had guessed that this would produce more tears, and he was right. Mrs Tarrant briefly turned her face into her husband's shoulder and he put his arm around her. After a moment she sat up again, blew her nose and whispered, 'I'm sorry. It's just that . . . I can't . . .' And she shook her head, at a loss for words. Finally she raised her head and looked directly at Thanet. 'I still find it difficult to believe.'

'I can imagine. I'm sorry.'

She studied his face, and after a moment said with a note of surprise, 'Yes, I believe you are.'

'It must have been a tremendous shock to you.'

'Yes.' She glanced at her husband and added bitterly, 'To both of us, in different ways.'

'There was a row, I believe,' said Thanet.

'Yes.' She frowned at the memory, and blew her nose again. 'Tim . . .'

Thanet said nothing, waited.

She gave a little shrug. 'Tim says it was *her* doing. That the idea would never have entered his head, if she hadn't made the first move. To him she was just Damon's mother, that's all. And then . . . But I don't want to go into all that. It happened, that's all, and somehow I'm going to have to learn to accept it.'

'How long had it been going on?'

She was studiously avoiding looking at her husband now. 'A couple of weeks, so far as I can gather.'

'And you suspected something of the sort, Mr Speed?'

'Yes. But . . .' His voice was hoarse and he paused to clear his throat. 'But not that it was . . . him, of course.' He obviously couldn't bring himself to say his son's name in this context.

'So you decided to try to find out who had supplanted you.'

Speed nodded.

It had been exactly as they thought. Speed became

177

suspicious when Nerine started putting him off. He knew her routine for entertaining her lovers over the lunch hour and on the day of the murder he decided to spy on her, to try to find out who his rival was. In the normal way of things Tarrant never returned home during the day and Speed had been disconcerted to see his Mercedes turn into the drive. But it had occurred to him that Tarrant's return home might have been unexpected. If Nerine were entertaining a lover it would be interesting to see what transpired. And he might yet learn who his rival was.

So he had carried out his plan, parking in the field and entering the garden via the back gate as usual, then hiding in the rhododendron bushes, a vantage point which gave him a good view of both front and side entrances.

He had been there only a minute or so when Tarrant came out in a hurry, jumped into his car and drove off. He had looked upset and Speed wondered what had happened in the house. He knew that Nerine always locked her bedroom door when entertaining, and thought that Tarrant had perhaps heard voices inside and jumped to the obvious conclusion.

'You didn't think that in that case he might have forced some sort of confrontation? Hammered on the door? Gone around onto the balcony and tried to get in through the french windows?'

Speed shook his head. 'No.' He shifted uncomfortably. 'He . . . His attitude to Nerine's boyfriends was very peculiar. I mean, he used to behave as though it wasn't happening, even when it obviously was, right under his nose! I could never understand it.'

Mrs Speed was sitting tight-lipped, nostrils pinched as though there were a bad smell in the room.

Speed cast her an apologetic glance, then said, 'Anyway, I thought it was worth hanging on a bit longer, just in case there was someone with her. And then, about ten minutes later . . .'

'All right,' said Thanet. There was no point in rubbing salt into the wound. 'We can guess what happened next. You saw Tim come out, realised you couldn't have a shouting match there and then in Mrs Tarrant's garden, and ordered him home. Why? You knew your wife would be here. I should have thought she'd be the last person you'd want around, in the circumstances.'

'She wasn't supposed to be here,' said Speed sullenly. 'I'd told her I wouldn't be back, dinnertime, and she said in that case she'd ring up a friend of hers, go shopping with her in Sturrenden and have a bite to eat in the town.'

'But Betty had already made other arrangements,' put in Mrs Speed, 'so I didn't go.'

'I see.' *More lies*, said his tone. He distinctly remembered both of them giving the impression that Speed had all along intended going home for lunch that day.

'So what happened?'

Speed was studiously avoiding looking at his wife. 'She could see something was wrong, straight away.

"*Lance! I thought you said you weren't coming home? I haven't got anything ready for . . . What's the matter? What is it?*"

"*I . . . Oh God.*"

"*Lance. Tell me.*"

"*It's Tim.*"

"*Tim? What's happened to him? Has there been an accident? He's not . . . He's not . . . dead?*"

"*No, nothing like that. He's all right. But . . .*"

"*But what? Lance, just tell me, will you?*"

"*I don't know how to. I've just found out . . .*"

"*WHAT?*"

"*That he's been . . . having it off, with Mrs Tarrant. Oh God, Ceel, I'm sorry. Don't look at me like that. He'll be here any minute. I sent him home. I thought you'd be out.*"

'And then Tim came home,' said Speed, 'and there was the most almighty row. He didn't stay long, walked out in the middle of it.'

179

'I'm surprised he went back to work in the garage that afternoon, after all that.'

'I said he'd bloody better, or he could say goodbye to his nice little holiday job, and they don't grow on trees these days, you know. I stayed behind with Ceel for a while. She was in a bit of a state.'

Scarcely surprising, thought Thanet, after that little bombshell had landed in her lap. 'And then what?'

The staccato question made them exchange a look of surprised alarm.

'What do you mean?' said Speed. 'You know what happened then. We told you, last time you was here.'

'You mean, you went back to the garage as if nothing had happened, worked there all afternoon, took a car out for a test drive for twenty minutes at around a quarter past five, then shut up shop and came home as usual.'

'Yes. Yes!'

'No little detours to High Gables, to see Mrs Tarrant?'

'No! Look, Inspector, you wanted the whole truth and now you've got it.'

'Have I? How do I know you're not lying, Mr Speed?'

'Because I'm not! I swear it.'

'That's what you said last time. And the time before. That's the trouble with telling lies, you see, Mr Speed. You destroy your own credibility.'

This was unanswerable. Speed's lips tightened, but he said nothing.

Thanet turned to Speed's wife. 'And you, Mrs Speed?'

Without looking at her husband, Celia Speed said calmly, 'After the row with Tim I was furious with Mrs Tarrant.' Her chin lifted a little 'I had every reason to be, I think you'll agree. First my husband, then my son . . . I decided I'd go and tell her exactly what I thought of her.'

Speed obviously knew all this. He shook his head in resigned exasperation. His wife ignored him but there was a note of defiance as she continued.

'I couldn't go straight away because of the meeting in the

180

village hall. I'd been asked to give the vote of thanks, to the speaker. Afterwards, well, I wanted to get it over with and in fact I walked as far as the gates of High Gables . . . But old Mr Parkin was expecting me. He's got arthritis and we all take it in turns to give him a hand. I always go on Thursday afternoons, and I was already late because of the meeting. So I visited him first, then went back to High Gables again. This time I actually got as far as walking up the drive.'

'And then?'

Mrs Speed's plump cheeks quivered as she shook her head. 'I couldn't do it. I . . . I'm not the sort of person who goes in for rows, and I was still feeling all churned up after the one at dinnertime. And, well . . .'

She gave her husband an uncertain, embarrassed glance, and Thanet wondered what was coming. 'You may think me stupid, Inspector, but people like Mrs Tarrant always make me feel nervous. Well, inferior, I suppose. I mean, she was so beautiful, always so elegant, so confident . . . I just lost my nerve. I told myself I hadn't given up the idea, but I'd do it another day, when I was feeling better, and, you know, had got myself ready.'

Had had her hair done, armoured herself in her smartest clothes, and was feeling her unconfident best, Thanet supposed. He winced at the thought of such a confrontation and was glad that Celia Speed had at least been spared that. There was no doubt in his mind as to who would have come off best.

'And then . . .' She shrugged. 'I just came home.'

And nothing could shake either of them. These were their stories and they were sticking to them. After a while Thanet decided that it was pointless to continue.

He and Lineham walked back to High Gables to pick up the car. It was very hot, the sun high in a sky of the purest cerulean blue. The cottage gardens were a brilliant kaleido-scope of colour, canvases crowded with the strawberry pink of foxgloves creamy-white at the throat, the frothy gold of alchemilla, the sprawling mauve of catmint and everywhere

181

the pinks and reds, yellows and apricots of roses in full bloom.

'Well, if either of the Speeds did it, it looks as though we're going to have to produce some pretty cast-iron evidence before they'll admit it,' said Lineham.

'Mmm.' Thanet paused to inhale the fragrance of a clump of sweet rocket growing through a white picket fence. 'Let's hope forensic come up with something useful. Let's see, it's Saturday. With any luck we might have something through from fingerprints on Monday. And the PM should be finished by now, so I expect Doc Mallard will give us a verbal report this afternoon. Not that I'm expecting too much from that.'

It was just before two o'clock and outside the village hall a little queue had formed.

'Didn't know jumble sales were so popular,' said Lineham.

Thanet grinned. 'Quite a lot of people become addicted, I believe. Joan tells me that lots of dealers comb the local paper for jumble sale ads and get in there fast, in the hope of bargains. She usually runs the white elephant stall at our church bazaar and the second the doors open people come streaming in as if it were the first day of Harrods' sale. They know exactly what they want. There's one chap who always hunts for brass, makes for her stall like a homing pigeon, turns everything over, grabs what he wants and is off, presumably to his next target, within a matter of minutes.'

'Scavengers.'

'Quite.'

'Look, I bet that's one, sir.'

Among the straggle of determined women with carrier bags was a seedy-looking character in stained corduroys, a grubby checked shirt and greasy anorak.

'No prize for that observation, Mike.'

'There's Mrs Haywood.'

Beatrix Haywood was approaching from the other direction, scarves a-flutter. She spotted them, raised a hand in greeting and came to ask if there were any news of Damon before pushing past the queue. She knocked on the door and was admitted.

'Helping on one of the stalls, I expect,' said Lineham.

'Mmm.' Thanet was trying to decide what to do next, but he needn't have bothered; over the car radio they learned that Halo Buzzard had been picked up and brought in for questioning.

'Who knows?' said Thanet as they sped back to Sturrenden. 'We could have been running around in circles for nothing. Buzzard is, after all, the only person known to have uttered threats against her.'

In most murder cases, as Thanet knew well, the most obvious suspect usually turns out to be the murderer. He had had just such a case himself, only last year. This might well turn out to be another.

'Yes, ten years ago! That's why I doubt if it'll come to anything. For one thing, ten years is a long time to cool off. For another, no one who has spent ten years inside is going to risk spending another ten unless there's a pretty hefty profit in it.'

'It's also a long time to brood over a grievance.'

'I know. But still . . .'

Buzzard was in a belligerent mood. As soon as Thanet entered the room he jumped to his feet.

''Ere, what the 'ell's going on? There was I, behaving meself, 'aving a nice quiet drink with me mates and in come you lot and before I know where I am I'm stuck in 'ere and left to cool me 'eels for an hour. I got better things to do with me time, you know.'

'And so have I. So let's get on with it, shall we, Buzzard?'

The reason for the man's nickname was immediately obvious. Thanet knew that 'Halo' was thirty-two, but his face had the unmarked smoothness and texture of youth, and his blue eyes and fair curls gave him a deceptive air of innocence. It was all wrong, Thanet thought, that a man who had been convicted of armed robbery and grievous bodily harm should look so angelic.

183

'Get on with what? I'm not getting on with nothing. I know my rights and I demand my phone call and my solicitor.'

'Don't worry, you'll get your rights. All in good time. If that's what you want. But don't you think you might be overreacting a bit? I merely wanted to have a little chat with you. Afterwards, if you're in the clear, you can go.'

'A little chat!' Buzzard almost spat the words. 'Very cosy, I'm sure. Oh, no, you ain't catching me out like that. I ain't saying a word until my brief is here.'

'Pity. You could have been away in a matter of minutes. Still, it's up to you. As it is, I'm afraid you'll just have to accept our hospitality for a bit longer.'

'Why? I told you, I ain't done nothing.'

'I seem to have heard that song before,' said Thanet. 'And you ought to know by now that we don't pick people up without good reason.'

'Pull the other one. Once you've been inside you can't even crap without the rozzers breathing down your neck . . . Anyway, what good reason? Go on, you tell me that. What good reason?'

'You were seen in the area where a crime was committed, on Thursday afternoon.'

'So what? What crime? Where?'

Had there been an overtone of unease, there? Of fear, even?

'On the outskirts of Sturrenden.'

'Mistaken identity.'

'No mistake. The witness is reliable.'

'I don't care if the Pope hisself swears he saw me. He's lying.'

'You were somewhere else, of course.'

'Of course. Playing poker with some mates.'

'Time, place, names, addresses?' said Thanet wearily.

Lineham took them down.

Thanet stood up. 'We'll have to check these out of course.' He turned to go.

''Ere! You're not going to leave me twiddling me thumbs while you check all that lot? It's Saturday. They could be anywhere ... football match, taking the kids to the seaside ... They could even be away for the weekend!'

'That's just too bad, I'm afraid. Come on, Buzzard. You're not seriously suggesting we let you go so that you can rush off and contact these mates of yours, make sure they back up your story? You must be joking.'

'It's harassment, that's what it is. Harassment. Dragging me in off the street and interrogating me ...'

'You weren't dragged, and a five-minute conversation can scarcely be called interrogation.'

'You haven't even told me what I'm supposed to have done!'

Thanet had reached the door, and he turned to face Buzzard.

'Murder,' he said quietly. 'That's what.'

Buzzard's expression changed. His eyes narrowed and his mouth pinched up in apparent disbelief. 'Murder? What the 'ell you on about? Whose murder? When? Where?'

'If you're telling the truth,' said Thanet, 'you don't need to know, do you? You've got an alibi, remember?' And he turned and walked out. As Lineham closed the door behind them he heard Buzzard say, ''Ere, 'ang on a minute ... !'

'We'll leave him to stew for a while,' said Thanet. 'You'd better get a team onto checking up on these "mates" of his. I've no doubt they'll back him up, but we'd better go through the motions.'

'What d'you think, sir? D'you think he's our man?'

Thanet sighed. 'I doubt it, worse luck. But there was something ... Underneath all the bluster I thought I detected a distinct note of nervousness.'

'I agree. I was wondering ... Even if he's not involved in our case, it's possible he was up to something else that afternoon.'

'Let me see ... Thursday ... Thursday ... Of course! The burglary out at Nettleton Grange! Mike, I bet that's it. And

185

if so . . . Look, go and have a word with Bristow, he's in charge, tell him what we think and suggest it might be worth getting a search warrant sworn out, while we've got Buzzard safely tucked up here. It's a long shot, but we might just be lucky.'

Thanet knew from past experience that a criminal pulled in on suspicion of one crime might well prove guilty of another.

'Surely he wouldn't have stashed any stuff in his room? He's too old a hand for that.'

'You never know. He hasn't been out of prison that long, he might not have built up enough contacts yet to have been able to dispose of everything. It's a long shot, of course, but worth a try.'

'I'll get on to it right away.'

On the way up to his office Thanet ran into Doc Mallard, coming down.

'Ah, Luke. I heard you were back. I've just been looking for you.'

'The PM results?'

'Verbal report, yes.'

'Come along to my office.'

Someone had come in and shut the window while Thanet and Lineham were out, and the room was stifling, airless. With an exclamation of annoyance Thanet went to open it. 'Place is like an oven.' He took off his jacket and slung it on the back of his chair. 'Well Doc, what's the news?'

SEVENTEEN

Mallard perched on the corner of Thanet's desk, picked up a report and began to fan himself with it. 'If you're hoping for a sensation you're going to be disappointed. We didn't learn anything we hadn't already guessed. She was in very good shape, vital organs all healthy. Cause of death, as we thought, fracture-dislocation of the cervical spine – or, to put it in layman's terms, a broken neck.'

'No signs of a previous struggle?'

''Fraid not. Sorry to be so unhelpful.'

Thanet sighed. He was longing to flex his back, which was beginning to ache again, but he tried never to draw attention to his weakness in front of other people. 'Not your fault. Ah, well . . . Not that I really expected anything, but still . . .'

'How's the case going?'

'So-so. It's early days yet, of course.'

'Has the boy turned up yet? What's his name? Damon? Damon! What an outlandish name. Fancy saddling any child with a handle like that.'

'No, I'm afraid not. There's been not a sight nor sound of him.'

'But you're not worried about him, are you? In the sense that he could be in danger? I understood he was seen leaving of his own accord.'

'That's right, yes, he was. But I'd give a lot to know *why* he went. He's not in any of his usual haunts.'

'Didn't you say he was up on a drugs charge, recently? You've talked to his probation officer, of course.'

'Yes, we have.'

Mallard frowned at Thanet's tone. 'Sorry, I didn't mean to tell you how to do your job.'

'Oh no, Doc, please don't misunderstand me. It's just that . . . well, his probation officer is Joan.'

There was a brief silence while Mallard took in the implications. 'Ah,' he said at last, heavily. 'I can see that that might cause . . . complications.'

So there it was, the opportunity Thanet needed, to unburden himself. Should he take it?

Thanet himself had often been the recipient of confidences. He liked people and it showed. He was approachable, sympathetic and percipient and inevitably he had found himself in the position of having to try to sort out the all-too-frequent marital difficulties of his men. Despite his apparent openness, however, he was really a very private person and the prospect of discussing his relationship with Joan with an outsider, however trustworthy, appalled him. Over and over again, presented with an apparently insoluble marriage problem, he had given the same advice: talk about it with her (or him), as honestly as you can. Sooner or later, he realised, he and Joan were going to have to do just that.

'It is a bit tricky, yes. We've never encountered this particular problem before. In the circumstances, I suppose we're lucky to have escaped up to now. Still, we'll cope, no doubt.'

Mallard took the hint. 'Yes.' He put down the report with which he had been fanning himself and slid off the edge of the desk. 'Well, I'm sorry I couldn't have been more help. Let me know, if there's anything I can do.'

Left alone, Thanet stood up, crossed to a filing cabinet and grasped it firmly with both hands, at shoulder level. Then, feet apart, he raised himself on his toes and slowly, carefully, arched his back, clenching his teeth as the dull ache sharpened into an edge of pain. Then he straightened up, relaxed. He repeated the exercise five times and returned to his chair, careful to sit upright, with the base of his spine hard against the back of the seat. Then he lit his pipe, closed his eyes and began to think.

He was convinced that Damon was somehow at the root of the problem. What had caused him to shoot off like that, 'like a bat out of hell', as one witness had put it? It was possible, of course, that there was some perfectly innocent explanation, that he had gone away by previous arrangement and had left in haste because he was late. But with every day that passed this possibility seemed less and less likely and in any case smacked too much of coincidence for Thanet's liking. There was that missed appointment, too.

The other explanation was that something had happened to make him run away.

But what?

Thanet ran over the alternatives. One (the most obvious): Damon had killed his mother and was in hiding from the police. But if so, what could have driven him to it? There must have been a quarrel, obviously, but what about? Any of the usual things, Thanet supposed: late nights, loud music, girls, rudeness, inconsideration . . . But a row over any of these would escalate into violence only if there had been a long, accelerating history of clashes, and surely somebody, at some point, would have let slip a hint if Damon's relationship with his mother had been as stormy as that. No, if there had been a quarrel, it must have been about one specific issue.

What?

Of course! Thanet's eyes snapped open as a possible explanation occurred to him. Damon had been in the house all day. Which presumably meant over the lunch hour. What if, by chance, he had happened to come downstairs at the wrong moment and had seen Tim, his friend, emerging from his mother's bedroom?

Thanet considered the idea. How would Damon have felt? Knowing so little about him, it was difficult to tell. Would he have been shocked, censorious, disgusted, or amused, resigned, even titillated?

189

In any case, Thanet simply couldn't believe that the shock would have been enough to cause an eighteen-year-old to leave home and to stay away despite the considerable publicity surrounding the murder. Nor would he have hung around for hours before departing in a hurry.

So what would Damon have done? Thanet felt that his most likely reaction would have been to say nothing. Or, if he decided he must speak, to have blurted it out immediately.

But just say, for the sake of argument, that Damon decided to tell his mother what he thought of her behaviour but found he needed time in which to pluck up his courage to do so. Why take so long about it?

Tim had left High Gables at around ten to one. Nerine had been in the house for another hour before leaving for the hairdresser's, had returned at half past three and had been around for another couple of hours (dead or alive) before Damon's departure. Surely the most likely time for Damon to have tackled Nerine would be as soon as she got back from the hairdresser's. Why wait a further two hours? And if Damon had in fact killed his mother soon after her return at half past three, surely he wouldn't have hung about so long before departing in such a hurry?

No, Thanet decided. It hadn't been such a brilliant idea after all. The timings were all wrong. If Damon had had a quarrel with Nerine, it must have been about something else.

But what?

There was no way of telling.

Thanet abandoned this line of thought and moved on.

Why else might the boy have run away? Thanet couldn't imagine that it was simply because he had found his mother's body. In that case he would have been shocked, yes, but surely his natural reaction would have been to assume an accident and call for help? No, if Damon had not committed the murder himself, and if he yet knew that a murder had been committed, the only possible reason why he could have disappeared was because he knew who had killed his mother *and wanted to protect that person.*

190

So, who would Damon wish to protect?

His father?

If Roland Tarrant had committed the murder, it must have been later on in the afternoon. Nerine had certainly been alive and well until half past three and there were witnesses enough to confirm that Tarrant had been fully occupied at the hospital until he left at a quarter past five. No, if Tarrant had done it, it must have been after his return home at twenty to six, and Damon couldn't have known; he had left the house just before his father arrived. Did this mean that Tarrant was in the clear? Not necessarily. Thanet still had to allow for the fact that Damon's departure might have nothing to do with the murder.

So who else might the lad have been trying to protect? Certainly there was one obvious person, much as Thanet disliked the idea: Damon's grandmother. She had had both motive and opportunity. And it sounded as though during that second rest period from four thirty to five thirty the old lady had seen something, heard something, done something that had frightened her badly. Why else, when Marilyn went to get her up from her rest, should she have been crouching in the corner of her bedroom, like a terrified child? Had she just returned from her daughter-in-law's room after a quarrel which had got out of hand and resulted in an outburst of senile frenzy?

Thanet's neck prickled as he remembered Lavinia's face when she had whispered, '*Death*'.

Thanet shook his head. So much speculation, so much frustration, in not being able to follow up essential lines of enquiry. If only Damon were available, if only Lavinia were rational, her memory undimmed by the disease gnawing away at her brain . . . But if it was a sense of loyalty which had driven Damon away, there was no doubt about it, Lavinia was the most likely candidate to have inspired it.

Who else had been on the premises during the afternoon? Thanet mentally checked them off.

Beatrix Haywood had been in the attic sorting out things

for the jumble sale, until just after the quarrel between Nerine and Lavinia over the mess in Nerine's bedroom, at half past three.

Vicky Cunningham had returned from her shopping trip at three and had been working in the kitchen until four.

Daphne Linacre had arrived back at the coach house at twenty to five and claimed to have gone straight to bed, with a migraine.

Then there was Marilyn Barnes, who had been in the house all afternoon. There was, too, Thanet reminded himself, one other person: Nicky, Marilyn's ten-year-old son. Perhaps he should be questioned again. Children were astonishingly observant and Nicky had been in the house or out in the garden from a quarter to four right up until the time the murder was discovered.

Thanet considered the list. Of all these, the only other person he thought Damon might have been tempted to protect was his aunt, Daphne Linacre. She seemed to be fond of the boy . . .

The door opened and Lineham came in, glowing with satisfaction.

'All fixed, sir. DS Bristow was very keen to cooperate. As he said, we've nothing to lose by taking a look and maybe a lot to gain. We managed to contact a JP and she's satisfied that there are sufficient grounds for a search warrant.' He plumped down at his desk, and looked eagerly at Thanet. 'Anything new? Have we heard about the PM yet?'

'Yes, but there's nothing of any use to us. Cause of death a broken neck.'

Lineham pulled a face. 'Pity. So where do we go from here?'

'I think it's time we put our heads together, tried to thrash things out.'

'OK. Where do we start?'

'Well, I've been thinking about Damon.' Briefly, Thanet summarised his conclusions.

Lineham said slowly, 'You could well be right, about him

192

disappearing so that he couldn't be questioned. But it's a pretty short-sighted thing to do, surely? I mean, he couldn't hope to vanish permanently.'

'Maybe not. But that hasty departure smacks of impulse, of panic, even. And if he had in fact seen his mother murdered by someone he knew and loved, his grandmother for instance, he would have been in a state of shock. But he'd know that if he stayed he'd be questioned and might well have felt that he wouldn't be able to lie convincingly. Perhaps he hoped we'd simply accept that it was an accidental fall. In any case he'd have hoped that if he kept out of the way long enough the thing would be resolved without his evidence being instrumental in bringing about the arrest of someone close to him. In which case he's lying low until it's all over.'

'If that's what happened we ought to be concentrating on the latter part of the afternoon. I can't see him hanging about for hours after witnessing a murder, before taking off in that kind of a hurry.'

'If.' Thanet sighed. 'The trouble is, it's all speculation and doesn't get us any further.'

'And there's still a possibility that he took off for some reason unconnected with the murder.'

'Quite.'

'Well, the one thing that seems pretty certain, unless Buzzard did it, and I think we both tend to agree that that's unlikely, is that it was an unplanned murder. Someone with a grievance against Mrs Tarrant had a quarrel with her and it got out of hand.'

'That seems the most likely explanation, Mike, I agree.'

'The trouble is, there are so many candidates. If it was old Mrs Tarrant, it must have been because of the threat either to put her in a nursing home or to get rid of Miss Barnes.

'If it was Marilyn Barnes, it was either because she wanted Roland Tarrant for herself or because she was afraid of losing her job – which in her case means losing her home, too. And she has her son to think of.

193

'If it was Mr Tarrant, it was because he'd finally snapped, after overhearing his wife entertaining her lover – especially if he realised it was Tim Speed in there. Tim is Damon's friend. Mr Tarrant might well have recognised his voice.'

'I don't know, Mike. I'm inclined to believe him, when he says he thought it was Tim's father. Their voices are very alike, you know.'

'True. All the same, I'm still not convinced about all this turning-a-blind-eye stuff. And it's one thing to know it's going on, another to have your nose rubbed in it.

'Then there are the Speeds. Now there are two juicy motives, if you like. It can't be easy for an ageing Romeo like Speed to realise he's been chucked out of his mistress's bed by his own son. And as for Mrs Speed . . . Well, I know she seems inoffensive enough, and she's generally well liked and all that, but even if she managed to come to terms with the fact that her husband was having it off with Mrs Tarrant, when it came to finding out that the woman had now got her claws into young Tim . . . Mrs Speed's only got the one chick, sir, and it's generally accepted that even the mildest of mothers can turn into a tigress when defending her young. We only have her word that she didn't actually go into the house and see Mrs Tarrant, that second time. I'm not saying she necessarily went there intending to kill her, but I can just imagine the sort of a scene there might have been between them, can't you?'

'Yes.' Thanet could imagine it, quite clearly: Nerine, cool, elegant, amused, scornful, and Celia Speed, dowdy, hot with anger, frustration, humiliation . . . 'There's Nerine's sister Daphne, too, don't forget, Mike. We might yet turn up some reason why she could have done it.'

Lineham frowned. 'It's difficult to see what could have triggered it off in her case. She wasn't even there until late afternoon. And she and Mrs Tarrant did seem to live pretty separate lives. Unless we're wrong about thinking it was an unplanned murder, and Daphne Linacre had just been waiting for the right opportunity to come along. Bit of a coincidence though, in that case, that she just happened to hit upon the very afternoon when her sister had seriously upset a whole lot of other people, don't you think?'

'I suppose so.' Thanet felt dispirited. All that seemed to be happening at the moment was that the list of suspects was growing longer and the chances of nailing any one of them seemed to be becoming more remote. 'What we really need is just one little bit of hard evidence, Mike.'

'Well, we'll just have to keep hoping forensic come up with something.'

'Yes. Meanwhile, I think we ought to have a word with Nicky Barnes. It occurs to me that he was around in either the house or the garden from a quarter to four right up to when the body was discovered.'

'Carson seemed satisfied that the boy hadn't seen anything suspicious.'

'I'm aware of that. All the same, you never know. It might not have seemed suspicious to Nicky, but with what we now know about the comings and goings in the house that afternoon . . .'

'You think we ought to try and talk to him today, sir?'

'Might as well. Come to think of it, it's odd that we didn't see him around earlier on, when we were out at the house. It's Saturday, he wouldn't be at school.'

'Perhaps Miss Barnes is still keeping him out of the way, sir.'

Thanet grinned. 'If so, I can't imagine he'll be very pleased about it. If he's anything like Ben he'd want to be where the action is.'

But apparently Nicky had gone on a school trip to Windsor Safari Park and wouldn't be back until late. Marilyn Barnes was not keen on the idea of the boy being interviewed at the end of such a long day.

Lineham arranged to see him at ten next morning.

EIGHTEEN

Talk it over with her.

All the way home snatches of Thanet's own advice to those with marital problems kept coming back to him. He'd always known, of course, that it is far easier to give counsel than to follow it. Now, for the first time, he was on the receiving end and a very uncomfortable sensation it was.

It was a quarter to midnight and in the centre of town there were still people about. It was, after all, Saturday night. But the suburban streets through which Thanet was now driving were virtually deserted, most of their windows in darkness. He turned left, catching up with an old Vauxhall which was limping along at twenty-five miles an hour. Thanet was about to overtake when without warning it swung out in a curve before turning into a narrow driveway. He considered stopping, to remonstrate, but couldn't be bothered. He was too tired, too preoccupied, too engrossed in his private dilemma to have any energy to spare for minor misdemeanours. He drove on.

Pick your moment. Don't, above all, choose a time when you're both upset, in the middle of an argument. Easier said than done. If you were working long hours, as he was, time with your wife was at a premium, especially time alone with her. If you were tired after a heavy day, and she was already in bed and asleep when you got home, she was scarcely going to appreciate being woken up and asked to have a serious discussion, in the middle of the night. And mornings were always such a rush, with both of them getting ready to go

196

to work, and the children around . . . But I must *make* time, he told himself fiercely. We can't go on like this.

All day, whenever he had allowed his concentration to slip, a wave of misery had washed over him at the memory of the rift between them. There had been arguments before, of course, times when one or the other of them – sometimes both – had been tired, contentious or on edge. But except for those distant, premonitory rumblings seven years ago, when Joan had chosen probation as her career, there had never been anything as serious as this. He could certainly never remember a time when she had gone off to bed without even saying good night to him – it had always been a matter of principle with them to follow the advice from Ephesians 4:26 drummed into them by both sets of parents: *Let not the sun go down upon your wrath*. It had, they found, never failed to work.

I can't let this happen, he thought. There must be some way around it.

But if there was, he couldn't see it. Perhaps he should simply climb down, make an abject apology and leave it at that?

But why should he?

If a man close to the victim disappears virtually at the same time as a murder is committed, the inference is obvious: there is a strong possibility that in some way he is involved. Surely Joan ought to be able to see that, after giving Damon twenty-four hours' grace, Thanet had had no option but to publicise the boy's disappearance?

He had arrived home. Joan usually liked to be in bed by half past eleven, but the muted glow behind the curtained window of the living room told him that she was still up. Thanet got out of the car, locked it, then stood for a moment, hesitating. Despite his eagerness for a reconciliation he found that he was reluctant to go in and face her.

It was very quiet; only the occasional roar of a distant car and the orange globes of the street lamps punctuated the wan midsummer darkness. The full moon was encircled by a band of milky, opalescent cloud and even as he watched a few high, ragged wisps drifted across it. Rain tomorrow?

Light suddenly spilled across the front lawn as a curtain in the living room was pulled back, and Joan peered out. She must have heard the car and was checking that it was indeed her husband out there, not thieves on the prowl. She drew the curtain again and a few moments later the front door opened.

'Luke?'

'Coming.'

She was wearing the blue silk kimono he had given her for her last birthday. As he came up to her she said, 'I wondered who it was, lurking about out there.'

Good resolutions were at once swamped by an irrational uprush of indignation. 'I was not "lurking"!' He brushed past her.

'Sorry! Lingering, then.' She followed him into the kitchen. 'D'you want anything to eat?'

'No, thanks. I picked something up in the canteen.' He took a can of lager out of the fridge, held it up. 'D'you want one?' The note of forced politeness in his voice gave him a jolt. What was he doing? Here he was, presented with the very opportunity for which he had been hoping. The fact that Joan had waited up for him showed that she must be in a conciliatory mood.

She was shaking her head. 'I had a cup of tea, half an hour ago.'

He put the can down on the table and reached for her hands. 'Joan?'

She returned his gaze steadily, defiantly, almost. 'Yes?'

'We've got to talk.'

'I know.'

'Sorry I was so bad-tempered just now.'

A little shrug, a barely perceptible movement of her shoulders. 'That's OK.' She attempted a smile. 'You've had a long day.'

'No reason why I should take it out on you . . . Truce?'

198

The smile was warmer now. 'Truce.'

He tugged her towards him and gave her a brief hug. 'Let's go into the other room, shall we?'

He kept his arm around her as they crossed the hall. Surely, with goodwill on both sides they ought to be able to sort this out? Suddenly he felt more optimistic than he had all day. They sat down side by side, his arm falling from her shoulders as she curled away from him into her favourite position in the corner of the settee, legs tucked beneath her. The coffee table nearby was littered with photographs.

She gestured towards them. 'I really must get around to sticking them into an album.'

'Mmm.' He took a long, grateful drink of lager and leaned forward to set the can down on the table. There it was, spread out before him, a pictorial record of their married life together: their summer wedding, honeymoon in the Dordogne, Bridget's christening, Ben's, holiday photographs, children's parties, family gatherings at Christmas . . . He picked a photograph out at random: Ben and himself, in the garden. He was squatting beside his son, who was holding a bright red balloon on the end of a string. It had been taken on Ben's second birthday, he remembered. What had made Joan indulge in this orgy of nostalgia? he wondered. Regret for happier days gone by, fear of the future, or a need to reassure herself that with so much shared happiness they had a solid foundation on which to build a bridge over the chasm that now yawned between them?

He risked a glance at her. She was watching him solemnly. What was she thinking? She was as apprehensive as he, he realised. How best to begin?

'I don't know where to start,' he said helplessly.

She shrugged. 'There's no point in beating about the bush. Let's start with the TVS appeal, shall we?'

'Why not. All right. Let's. You first.'

'I just don't know why you acted so . . . precipitately.' Her tone was reasonable, unaccusatory. 'I should have thought it could easily have waited another twenty-four hours, if not longer.'

She was, he could see, trying very hard to follow all the precepts he had been laying down for himself. His own voice echoed in his head. *Try to see her point of view.* 'I don't see that I had any choice. I couldn't – I still can't – believe that it was sheer coincidence that Damon disappeared on the very afternoon his mother was murdered. I'm convinced there must be some connection.'

'But as it turned out, the appeal had no effect. He still hasn't turned up.'

'That's beside the point. We couldn't know that. The point is, we had to try.'

'I'm not saying you didn't have to try, but why then, at that particular moment? Why not give him a little more time?'

'But why should I have?' In spite of himself a note of indignation, of belligerence, almost, was creeping back into his voice. 'Look, Joan, I think what you're really saying is that I should have treated him differently simply because he was – is – your client.'

Her frown deepened. 'That's not true.'

'Isn't it?'

She hesitated. She was, he could see, making a real effort to be honest with herself. 'I'm not sure,' she admitted at last.

'You see, what I had to ask myself was, if Damon was not your client, would I have put out that appeal when I did? And the answer was yes, I would.'

'Are you sure, Luke?'

'Yes. Yes! Of course I am.' But, was he? He glanced at Joan. She was frowning down at her lap, rolling the sash of her kimono round and round her forefinger. 'You don't believe me.'

A tight little shake of the head. 'It's just that . . .'

'What?'

She looked up, met his accusatory gaze. 'Oh never mind. Forget it.'

'No!'

There was a brief silence. Thanet told himself that nothing would be achieved and everything might be lost if he couldn't control his irritation, and he took a deep calming breath before saying, 'Look, I'm sorry, love. We'll get nowhere if we just stop talking every time things are getting sticky. Maybe you're right and I just can't see it yet. So tell me what you think, and we'll take it from there.'

She looked at him doubtfully, then said, 'Well, there wasn't any reason to believe that he might have committed the crime, was there?'

'No.' He tried hard to be fair. 'There still isn't, for that matter.'

'So . . . Did you feel that you were stuck without his evidence?'

'No, not exactly.'

'That you couldn't progress any further without talking to him?'

'No, but . . .'

Joan shook her head. 'Then I'm sorry, I still can't see why you couldn't have waited a little longer. It's not like you, Luke. You knew the boy might not know his mother had been killed . . . What a way to hear news like that! With the implication that he might somehow be involved.'

'There was no such implication!'

'Oh, come on, darling. What do you think people think, when that sort of appeal goes out? "The police are anxious to talk to . . ." It's the first thing they think of, that that person is under suspicion.'

'I can't help it, if people misinterpret.'

'Luke,' said Joan softly. 'A minute ago you asked me if what I was saying was that I thought you should have treated him differently because he was my client. I'm still not sure of the answer to that. Now I would like to ask you . . . Do you think you *did* treat him differently because he was my client?'

Thanet recognised the prickle of shock which ran through

him in reaction to her question; he had experienced it before, in facing an unpalatable truth. He suppressed the instinctive 'No!' which sprang to his lips. He owed it to Joan, to himself, to both of them, to try to match his honesty with hers.

'Perhaps,' he said at last. 'But if so, I certainly wasn't aware of it, at the time.'

'I didn't suppose for a moment that you were. But,' and her tone was gentle, 'that isn't quite the point, is it, darling?'

'What is, then?'

'The point is, that — assuming that he did in fact hear of the appeal — it's Damon who's been the loser, as a result of our private . . . war, conflict, disagreement . . . whatever you like to call it.'

That was true. The thought pained him. He had acted unprofessionally and an innocent boy might have suffered. But why had he really gone ahead when he did? It wasn't enough, simply to say that he had overreacted. If Joan had been a little more forthcoming, in the first place, it might never have happened, he thought defensively. He said so.

'You mean on Thursday night, when you wanted me to talk to you about Damon?'

'Well I did feel you could have been a little more helpful.' Thanet's sense of grievance had returned in full force. 'After all, I've always talked freely about my cases to you, knowing that I could trust you implicitly never to talk about them. Surely you could have done the same?'

'But it wasn't the same, was it?'

'Why not?'

'Our cases have never overlapped before. I've never needed to use any of the things you've told me, in my work.'

'But this was a murder case. A woman had been *killed* . . .'

'I know. D'you think it was easy for me, to withhold information which could have been useful to you? But I had to, don't you see? I couldn't betray my client. It's a question of . . . well, of loyalty, I suppose.'

'And what about your loyalty to me?' The words were out before Thanet could stop them.

'But that's different, isn't it?'

'Is it?'

'Of course it is!' Joan was beginning to get angry too, now. 'Have you ever had any reason to doubt my loyalty to you, in our private life?'

'No, of course not.'

'Then just tell me this. I said a minute ago that I've never needed to use any of the things you've told me, in my work. If I had, if a client of mine had been involved in one of your cases as a prime suspect, would you then have been prepared to talk to me so freely? Have you in fact talked to me as freely, in this case, even though Damon is not seriously under suspicion?'

'I've scarcely seen you.'

'Maybe not. But even if you had, I bet you would have edited what you'd told me.'

Thanet didn't answer. She was right and they both knew it.

'And tell me this too. If, on Thursday, I had in fact given you any information about Damon upon which you could act, would you have acted upon it?'

He had to admit that he would. And Joan would have known that he had betrayed her confidence. There seemed to be no end to the complications and ramifications of this issue. Perhaps, after all, hers was the wisest course.

'I suppose I would.' He wasn't proud of the grudging reluctance in his tone, but at least he had managed to admit that he was wrong. He forced himself to say it. 'You're right, it could have caused all sorts of difficulties.'

She sank back against the settee, as if the argument had sapped her energy. 'I've always dreaded this happening, you know.'

'What, in particular?'

'Clashing, over our work. You warned me, didn't you, right at the beginning. And I was so confident we could handle it, so . . .' She shrugged. 'So naive, I suppose. The truth was, I wanted so much to go into probation that I just didn't want to listen to anything that might put me off.'

'And have you ever regretted it?' But he knew the answer.

'No, never. I really enjoy it – though "enjoy" isn't perhaps the right word. I find it satisfying, fulfilling.'

And that, thought Thanet, with a sudden spurt of insight, was what he had never really been able to accept: that his wife should need anything beside himself, their children and their home, to feel fulfilled. Was he really so egocentric? He professed to love Joan, but if he truly loved her he would want above all to enable her to develop every aspect of her potential. True, he had paid lip-service to the idea, but even his capitulation had been brought about by selfish motives: he had known that, if he didn't give in, he would bring about a breach between them that would never be healed.

Was this, then, the root cause of their difficulty? Not that she was wilful, lacking in loyalty or understanding, but that he was childishly self-centred, jealous and spiteful. He saw now that it was he, not she, who had erected that barrier between them. From the moment he realised, on Thursday, that one of Joan's clients was a possible suspect in this case, he had anticipated trouble. Worse, it was almost as though, deep down inside, he had welcomed it.

Had he needed so much to be proved right in warning Joan against her choice of profession that after all these years he had seized the first opportunity of trying to force her to admit that it had been a mistake?

The thought made him squirm.

She was watching him apprehensively, as if she were aware of the private struggle going on inside him and were nervous of the outcome. He felt deeply ashamed that he, who had always prided himself on his tolerance, his compassion, his understanding of others, could have been so prejudiced, so punitive, so blinkered in this, the most important area of his life. Humble, too, that Joan, who was so wise, had continued to love him despite it all.

It wasn't enough, he realised, to attempt to come to terms

with this unwelcome insight himself. He owed it to her to bring it out into the open. Perhaps, then, they might at last attain the peace which had always eluded them over this issue before. He turned to her, took her hand.

'I know you do. Find your work fulfilling, I mean. And I suppose . . .' Oh, God, it was hard, very hard, to expose one's weaknesses to anyone, especially hard when all along he had felt that he was the one with the grievance. He tried again. 'I suppose that's what I've found so hard to accept. That I – we – weren't enough for you.'

He could tell that she knew how much the admission had cost him.

'Yes. Men do find that difficult, I think. Women have always accepted the importance of a man's work, made allowances for it.'

As she had, he thought – all those late nights, broken promises, last-minute phone calls, cancelled excursions . . . A policeman's wife was called upon to make more sacrifices than most. To think that he had always prided himself on overcoming this problem by talking about his work to her, thinking that this would compensate for the demands it made upon her. How condescending could you get! Why should she, an intelligent woman with so much to offer, have been expected to be satisfied with the crumbs that fell from his table?

'I think,' Joan was saying, 'that the next generation will find it easier. Ours was brought up in the transition period, and there have been a lot of casualties along the way.'

And we could well have been one of them. It was a chilling thought.

'I'm sorry. Can you forgive me?'

She opened her arms to him. 'Need you ask?'

NINETEEN

Thanet set the tray down on the dressing table and drew back the curtains, frowning at the dismal scene outside. The ring around the moon had fulfilled its promise and it was raining heavily, a continuous drenching downpour discharged by an unbroken ceiling of leaden cloud. But this morning not even this dreary prospect could lower his spirits for long. Their reconciliation last night had been sweet indeed, and today he was glowing with the well-being of a man restored to full health after a long and serious illness.

Joan stirred and opened one eye. Quickly, Thanet picked up the tray and crossed to stand at attention beside the bed.

'Room service, madam.'

She blinked and looked up at him, taking in his pose, the tray. She shot up in bed. 'Darling!' And as he lowered it onto her lap, 'Breakfast in bed! What a luxury! Thank you.' She raised her face for a kiss and Thanet obliged with alacrity, breathing in the warm, sleepy smell of her skin and regretting the impulse that had driven him early out of bed to prepare her breakfast before leaving for work. But the appreciation on Joan's face as she surveyed the carefully laid tray reassured him that it had been the right thing to do, and he surveyed his handiwork with satisfaction: flowered traycloth, best bone china, chilled orange juice, a pot of freshly ground coffee (decaffeinated, Joan's latest fad) and a hot croissant.

'No red rose in single holder, I'm afraid,' he said in mock apology. 'It would have dripped all over the place.'

She glanced at the rain streaming down the window-panes.

'A wet Sunday. Horrid. Still, at least it makes it not quite so bad that you've got to go to work.'

'True.'

'Are the children up?'

'Still asleep, I think.'

'They can have a lie-in. As long as they're up in time for church . . .'

Thanet kissed her goodbye and peeped into the children's rooms. Humped shapes slumbered on. He smiled indulgently, closing the doors softly behind him. It would do them good to sleep late for once.

As he drove through the deserted streets he remembered what it was that had woken him up so early: the knowledge that in his sleep he had been dreaming, and that the dream had been trying to tell him something important, something to do with the Tarrant case. He had struggled to reach back into it, to fix it in his memory before it faded, but he was already too late, it had gone. What had it been about? He frowned, trying to remember. Briefly, a green image flickered across his mind, and was gone. What had it been? Garden, field, wood, park, landscape? Mentally, he shrugged. Perhaps it would come back later, when he wasn't thinking about it.

On the way up to his office he ran into DS Bristow.

'Thanks for the tip, sir. We nailed him!'

'Buzzard?'

'Yes. Would you believe it, one or two juicy little items from Thursday's robbery tucked away under a loose floorboard! They never learn.'

'Good. That's excellent. Make sure some credit goes to the PC from traffic, who spotted him in the first place.'

'Of course, sir.'

'What time was the robbery committed?'

'Between four and half past, on Thursday afternoon. Does that clear him, as far as your case is concerned?'

'I doubt it. The trouble is, we still haven't been able to pinpoint the exact time of the murder.'

The phone was ringing as Thanet entered his office:

Tarrant, again enquiring for news of Damon. It was obvious that by now the surgeon was really worried about his son.

'Isn't there anything else you can do?'

'I assure you, sir, that everything that can be done is being done. And I promise that the moment we have any news of him, we'll let you know.'

By now Thanet was himself becoming concerned about the boy. Considering the amount of publicity it really was becoming very difficult to believe that Damon hadn't heard of his mother's death. And if so, why hadn't he been in touch?

Thanet was still studying a large-scale map of the area when Lineham arrived.

'Morning, Mike.'

'Morning, sir. You're looking very cheerful today. Don't tell me you've had one of your bright ideas overnight.'

'No such luck, I'm afraid.'

The phone again. Daphne Linacre, this time, also enquiring about Damon.

'Still no news of him, then?' said Lineham, when Thanet had crashed the receiver down in a thoroughly disgruntled mood at having had to communicate the same bad news twice in ten minutes to anxious relatives.

Thanet shook his head.

Lineham evidently considered it politic to change the subject. 'What are you doing with that?' He nodded at the map.

Thanet told him, and for a while they discussed whether or not it might have been possible for Buzzard to have committed the murder either before or after his foray to Nettleton. On balance, Thanet was inclined to dismiss him as a suspect.

'I can't really see him committing a murder, then calmly going on to do a robbery ten miles away. Or vice versa. I should have thought his main aim would have been to put as much distance as possible as quickly as possible, between himself and the scene of either crime.'

208

'I agree.'

'Anyway, it's time we were leaving for Ribbleden, to see Nicky Barnes. I've arranged for WPC Fernley to come with us.'

A woman police officer has to be present when a child is interviewed.

'Right, sir.'

Even on the main road there was very little traffic about and after turning off into the country lanes they had the drowned countryside to themselves. Ribbleden looked as though it had decided to turn its back on the weather; doors and windows were firmly shut and apart from a bedraggled paper boy there was not a soul about. Not everyone was lying in bed late, though; a number of cars lined the road outside the church.

'Must have an early service,' said Lineham.

'They have to stagger them. The vicar has four parishes to look after, I believe.'

'How on earth does he manage at festivals?'

'With difficulty, I imagine. I was talking to one country parson last year and he told me he'd conducted ten harvest festivals at different churches, schools and organisations.'

'I should think he was ploughing the fields and scattering in his sleep,' said Lineham with a grin.

They drew up at the gates of High Gables but before Lineham could get out to open them a small wet figure emerged from the shelter of a tall shrub and performed the task for him.

'Nicky, I presume,' said Thanet. 'Waiting for us, obviously. Stop when we're inside.'

The car drove in and Thanet wound down his window, waited for the boy to approach. 'You must be Nicky. I'm Inspector Thanet, and this is Woman Police-Constable Fernley and Detective-Sergeant Lineham. Want a ride?'

Nicky nodded eagerly. He was well equipped for the weather in hooded anorak and wellington boots. He clambered into the back and leaned into the gap between the front seats, dripping water everywhere.

'Ever been in a police car before?'

'No.'

Thanet explained how the radio worked. 'There are two frequencies, one for transmitting, the other for reception. Those pips you hear mean that someone in another patrol car is talking to the control room . . .'

After they drew up outside the back door Thanet spent several more minutes chatting to the boy. If the ice was broken it would be far easier to get Nicky to open up to him, if there was anything to tell. Besides, he liked boys, was used to having them around. Ben's friends were always in and out of each other's houses. Not, he thought, that there were any signs of this one being difficult to handle. His expression was open, alert, and he was clearly storing up every word in order to impress his friends.

'We'd better go in, I suppose,' Thanet said at last. 'I expect your mum will have seen us arrive and she'll be wondering where we've got to.'

'OK.' Nicky scrambled out, reluctantly.

They had arranged that Lineham would wait in the car; three police officers, they agreed, might be a little overwhelming for the boy. Nicky led them into the kitchen where Thanet had first met the old lady and her companion.

Marilyn Barnes was alone. 'I've arranged for Lavinia to have coffee with Mr Tarrant,' she said, noticing Thanet's enquiring glance around the room. 'I thought it would be easier.'

'Good idea.'

'I made some for us. You'd like a cup, I expect.'

'Thank you.' Thanet introduced Jessica Fernley and they all sat down. He waited until the coffee had been poured and then turned to Nicky, who was watching him expectantly.

'Now then, Nicky, I expect your mum's told you what we want to talk about.'

'Thursday afternoon,' said the boy promptly.

He was of average height for his age, and rather thin, with bony elbows and narrow wrists, his very short hair emphasising the shape of skull and jawline. The brown eyes so like his mother's were eager and intelligent.

'That's right. Now I know one of my men has interviewed you already, so I'll just explain why it is I need to talk to you again. As I'm sure you know, after a major crime like this, we have to spend a lot of time building up a picture of exactly what happened in the period leading up to it. It's very painstaking work, rather like putting together a huge jigsaw puzzle, and the pieces are supplied by all the people we talk to. The trouble is, some of them can be pretty vague, but in the end, by checking one person's version with another's we usually manage to fit it all together. But it is often necessary to see people more than once – take your mother, for instance.' He glanced at Marilyn. 'I've talked to you several times, haven't I?'

She nodded. 'To most of us, I should think.'

'The other thing, of course, is we often find that after people have had time to think they remember things they didn't the first time around.'

Nicky was nodding sagely.

'But I must emphasise that I want you to try to remember everything, every single thing, that you saw and did on Thursday afternoon after you got home from school, from the moment you walked through the gate – I assume you came in the back way, along the footpath? – right up to the time you left to stay with your friends.'

'Everything?'

'Everything. Step by step. I'll try not to interrupt too much. Close your eyes, if you like, if it would make it easier.'

But that wouldn't be necessary, Thanet could tell. Already Nicky's eyes were glazing in recollection.

'Now, you got home at about a quarter to four, I believe?' He waited for the boy's nod. 'And it was very hot. Was there anyone about, in the garden?'

'No. I came along the footpath and in through the gate in

211

the back fence, like you said, then through the garden and across the drive to the back door. I was thirsty . . . Is this the sort of thing you mean?'

'Yes, exactly. Go on.'

'There was no one in here, so I made myself a drink of squash. Then Mum came in, with Mrs Tarrant – old Mrs Tarrant, that is. She, Mrs Tarrant, was in a state and Mum was trying to calm her down, so I grabbed an apple and went out to play.'

'Did you go to a friend's house, or stay in the garden?'

'I stayed in the garden.'

The flow of information seemed to have come to an abrupt halt. Why?

'So what did you do, in the garden?'

Nicky glanced at his mother. 'I . . . er . . .'

'Well?' said Marilyn, breaking in impatiently. 'You what?'

'I went to my den,' he mumbled.

At once Thanet understood. This was the boy's secret place and he didn't want his mother to know about it. A glance at Marilyn Barnes told him that she had also cottoned on.

She rose. 'I think I'd better just pop along to see Lavinia for a moment, Nicky. You'll be all right?'

He couldn't hide his relief. 'Yeah, sure.'

As soon as the door had closed behind her Thanet said, 'I had a den, too, when I was a boy. It was crammed in between the back of the garden shed and the hedge – our garden wasn't anything like as big as yours. I got hold of some old planks, and a bit of corrugated iron for the roof . . . No one was allowed in there unless they were invited. It was my own special, private place . . . I expect yours is the same.'

'Yes.' Nicky lowered his voice, glanced at the door. 'Mum doesn't even know where it is.'

I shouldn't be too sure of that, thought Thanet. 'Look, Nicky, I don't want to pry into your secrets, I really don't. And I promise that if you tell me roughly where it is, I won't tell a soul, neither of us will, not without your permission, anyway.'

He glanced at WPC Fernley, who shook her head vigorously. 'Of course not.'

Nicky shrugged. 'OK. It's over behind the coach house, in some big bushes.'

'Far behind?'

'A fair way. A hundred yards or so, I suppose.'

Thanet wasn't sure if this estimate could be trusted. Distances are difficult to estimate, especially where there are trees and shrubs about.

'Can you hear any sounds from the coach house?'

'Not really, no. Unless there are people talking in the garden at the back.'

'And were there?'

'No. Miss Linacre was at work, anyway, till later.'

'We're getting a bit ahead of ourselves. Can we go back to when you first went out, just before four o'clock. You went straight across to your den?'

'Yes.'

'Did you see anyone on the way?'

'Only Mrs Haywood. She was just going into the coach house as I came out of our back door.'

That fitted, Thanet thought. Beatrix Haywood had told them that after overhearing the row between Nerine and her mother-in-law she had hung about in the attic for a further ten minutes or so before returning to the coach house, for fear of meeting either of the protagonists.

'Did she see you?'

'No. She had her back to me.'

'Then what? Go on. You're doing very well.'

Nicky looked pleased. 'The next thing was that just as I got to my den I heard Vicky drive away.'

Vicky of the Benetton jeans. 'How did you know it was Vicky if you were that far away?' Thanet could guess the answer, but it was best to take nothing for granted.

'I know the sound of her Fiesta.'

'Right. So then what did you do?'

'I've been trying to construct the walls – you know,

weaving branches in and out.' He pulled a face. 'It's not as easy as it sounds.'

Thanet grinned. 'I know, I've tried it myself ... So you were moving about, I expect, fetching branches ... Or did you have a pile already gathered?'

'No, I was moving about, like you said.'

'So, and I want you to think very carefully, did you see anyone about, at any point, while you were working?'

Nicky shook his head regretfully. 'No, sorry.'

'Never mind. What happened next?'

'I heard the bell, for tea ... The garden's so big I often didn't hear Mum when she used to call me, so now she comes to the back door and rings that.' Nicky nodded at an old-fashioned hand-bell which stood on the windowsill by the sink. 'No, hang on ... Was it before, or after ... ?' His forehead creased as he tried to remember. 'No, it was before, I remember now ... A few minutes before the bell rang I heard Miss Linacre arrive home – I know the sound of all the cars.'

'That would have been at about twenty to five?'

'Yes.'

Again, it fitted.

'And a few minutes afterwards, you heard your mother ring the bell. Did you go in straight away?'

'No. I was in the middle of a tricky bit, and I wanted to get it finished.'

'And that would have taken how long?'

'Another five minutes or so. Then I came back to the house. I saw Miss Linacre going into the coach house as I came out onto the drive.'

Suppressing the sudden flare of excitement Thanet kept his tone carefully casual as he said, 'Going in, you say?'

Nicky nodded. 'I thought she must have gone out to fetch something she'd left in the car.'

'You saw her come away from the car?'

'Oh, no, just go into the house. Anyway, then I came back here and had my tea.' He grinned. 'It was hamburgers.'

214

'Your favourite, by the sound of it . . . Then what?'

'Mum went to get Mrs Tarrant up from her rest, and,' he grimaced, 'I washed up the tea things. While I was at the sink I saw Damon go across to the coach house.'

Again, this was news but once more Thanet betrayed no special interest. 'That would have been at what time?'

Nicky frowned. 'Twenty, twenty-five past five, I suppose.'

'Did he go in?'

'Yes. The front door was open. They often leave it open in the hot weather.'

'Did he seem in a hurry? I'm only asking, because as you know, Damon's disappearance is a bit of a mystery, and very few people seem to have seen him that afternoon.'

'You don't think . . . ?'

'That he had anything to do with his mother's death? No, not for a moment. But we are afraid that he might be rather upset, and we're anxious to find him.'

'No, he didn't seem to be in a hurry. He didn't stay, though. He was only in there a minute or two and he came out again, back to the house.'

'How did he seem?'

Nicky shrugged. 'On the way back he was walking slowly, with his hands in his pockets, looking at the ground. Then, as he got nearer the house, he suddenly speeded up. Mum and Mrs Tarrant came in then and I'd finished my washing up, so I went back out to the den. Not long afterwards I heard Damon drive off – his car makes a terrific din – and then, only a minute or two later, Mr Tarrant came home. Soon after that all the fuss began, and Mum rang Mrs Rice and she came to fetch me.'

Thanet nodded with satisfaction. 'Well Nicky, all I can say is that I wish all witnesses were as concise and as helpful as you.'

On cue the door opened and Marilyn came in. Perhaps she had been waiting tactfully outside? Thanet turned to her. 'I was just saying how helpful Nicky had been, Miss Barnes. Thank you for letting me talk to him.'

'Oh, good.' But she didn't sound too sure. 'You've finished, now?'

'Yes, we have.' Thanet rose and WPC Fernley closed her notebook and followed suit.

'Oh, just one small point, Miss Barnes. Could we confirm the time at which you called Nicky in for tea?'

'A quarter to five,' she said promptly. 'I always call him at a quarter to five.'

'Thank you.'

Outside, it was still raining hard and they made a dash for the car, flung themselves in. All the windows were steamed up, giving the illusion of total privacy and isolation.

'Well?' said Lineham. 'Any luck?'

'Some.' Thanet glanced at Lineham's impatient face and grinned. He knew the sergeant hated being kept in the dark.

'There were two interesting points. One: Nicky heard Daphne Linacre's car arrive at twenty to five. He was playing in his den, in the garden, and didn't actually see her at that point. Five minutes later, at a quarter to five, his mother called him in for tea, but he was busy doing something and didn't actually go in for another five minutes or so. But when he did, he saw Daphne Linacre going into the coach house. He assumed she'd left something in her car, and had gone out to fetch it, and of course, there might be some perfectly innocent explanation, but . . .'

'She gave us the impression she was so prostrated by migraine that she could scarcely totter up the stairs to bed!'

'Precisely. And if she did have a migraine I can't see her running any trivial errands herself. It seemed to me that Miss Haywood was only too willing to be at her beck and call.'

'I agree . . . Yes, that is interesting. What was the other thing?'

Thanet related what Nicky had told him about Damon.

'I wonder why he went across to the coach house? Sir, you don't think . . .'

Thanet recognised the dawning sparkle in Lineham's eyes. A theory was being born. 'What?'

'Well, you know what you were saying about Damon disappearing because he wanted to protect someone? And one of the people you thought he might have wanted to protect was his aunt? Just suppose that earlier, soon after Daphne Linacre got home, he overheard a quarrel between her and his mother? And that for whatever reason he decided to go and see his mother half an hour later? He goes into her room, finds it empty, and walks out onto the balcony, calling her. She's not there, but he crosses to the rail to see if she's in the garden and sees her lying on the terrace. He rushes down, finds that she's stone dead and comes to the conclusion his aunt must have shoved her over during the quarrel. He's very shocked, naturally, and he goes straight across to the coach house, to tackle her. But Miss Haywood says his aunt is ill, she's got a severe migraine, and can't be disturbed. He doesn't know what to do, so when he comes out he's in a bit of a daze, walking slowly, as Nicky said. Then, on the way back to the house, he makes up his mind. If his aunt has killed his mother he doesn't want to be any part of the uproar that's bound to follow. He'll keep well out of the way for a few days until the fuss has died down. He rushes up to his flat, throws a few things in a bag and takes off.'

Lineham folded his arms and sat back with an air of satisfaction. 'What d'you think, sir?'

'Could be. Of course, he could have gone across to the coach house for a dozen different reasons, none of them anything to do with the murder: he could have wanted to confirm an arrangement, borrow some money, return a book, ask a favour ... He might simply have wondered why his aunt was home from work so early, gone across out of curiosity.'

'You'll be suggesting he went across to take afternoon tea with them, next. Sir.'

'No need to be sarcastic, Mike. It could well have been as innocent as that. They were on pretty good terms. Look at

217

the way she and Mrs Haywood keep ringing up to enquire about him.'

'And I suppose he only stayed a minute or two because Miss Haywood was busy looking after Miss Linacre and wouldn't have had time to talk to him.'

'Quite.' Thanet enjoyed baiting Lineham occasionally. 'Actually . . .'

'What?'

'Well, let's say, for the sake of argument, that it did happen as you suggest, that the two sisters had a quarrel which got out of hand . . . I suppose that the strain and the shock might well have brought on a genuine migraine – or the beginnings of one, anyway, by the time Damon went across, half an hour later.'

'If you ask me, she never had one at all.'

'And the vomiting we heard from upstairs, when we went across that first evening?'

'Emotional reaction,' said Lineham triumphantly. 'From having committed a murder.'

'There's still something you haven't explained, in this neat little theory of yours, Mike.'

'What's that?'

'Motive, Mike, motive. Why, in the middle of a sunny June afternoon, should Daphne Linacre suddenly rush home from work and kill her sister? Any suggestions?'

'I'm sure I can come up with something, given time.'

'I've got a better idea than that.'

'What?'

'We'll go across to the coach house and ask her.'

TWENTY

Daphne Linacre answered the door herself.

'You've got news of Damon?' she said, apprehensively.

Without her sunglasses she looked older, perhaps more vulnerable, Thanet thought. Her eyes were a bleak pebble-grey, flecked with brown. Once again she was smartly dressed in crisp cream linen skirt and matching blouse, with a soft, caramel-coloured cardigan slung loosely around her shoulders.

Thanet shook his head. 'Sorry, no. We'd like another word with you, if we may.'

She stood back without a word, silently waiting while they removed their dripping raincoats.

'You can hang them there.' She nodded at a row of hooks behind the front door. Then she led them into the sitting room.

Sunday newspapers were scattered around the armchair in which she had sat last time they were here, and a half-empty cup of coffee stood on a small table nearby.

'I've been having a lazy time, as you can see. Nothing much else to do on a morning like this. Do sit down. Would you like some coffee?'

'We've just had some, thanks.'

Where was Beatrix Haywood? Thanet wondered.

As if she had picked up his unspoken thought Daphne Linacre said, 'Bea's at church. I told her she was crazy to go out in this weather if she didn't have to, but she insisted.'

Her concern evidently hadn't extended to offering Mrs Haywood a lift, Thanet thought.

'Well, how can I help you?'

'A minor point,' said Thanet. 'A small discrepancy. We thought you could clear it up.'

Despite his dramatic announcement to Lineham that they would go and ask Daphne Linacre why she might have killed her sister, Thanet was well aware that it would be pointless to do so. She would simply deny it, or laugh it off, as she had last time. And they would have revealed more than they wished of their suspicions.

She smiled. 'Oh dear, the third degree. What have I done, I ask myself? Do go on.'

'Perhaps you could bear with us and tell us once more exactly what you did when you got home on Thursday afternoon.'

She gave him an assessing look. 'Why should I? I've been through it once, that should be enough, surely.'

Thanet sighed. 'Often, when people have had time to think, they remember details they forgot the first time around. It's understandable. Nobody thinks very clearly, in a state of shock.'

There, he had given her a way out, if she needed one. Would she take it?

Apparently not.

'I'm afraid I have nothing to add.' Then, noting his waiting silence she said irritably, 'Oh, very well, then, if I must. I came home from work with a migraine. When I got here all I wanted to do was go upstairs, undress and lie down in a darkened room. Which was precisely what I did.'

'You came through the door and went straight up the stairs?'

'Got it in one, Inspector.'

'You're sure you didn't, for instance, talk to Mrs Haywood for a minute or two?' Thanet persisted.

'No.'

'Or go into the kitchen, for a drink of water, perhaps?'

'No, I did not! Look, when I drove up Bea was waiting at the door. She knew I was feeling ill, we'd spoken on the telephone earlier. She helped me up the stairs. I went to the bathroom to pee – if we must have the sordid details – then into my bedroom, where I undressed, got into bed and closed my eyes with a huge sigh of relief. Does that satisfy you?'

'According to a witness you were seen entering this house some ten minutes after you got home.'

She raised one eyebrow and said with amusement, 'Really? Well, all I can say is, he's either mistaken – to put the charitable interpretation on it – or he's lying in his teeth. And if it's the latter, I should say his motives require investigation, Inspector.'

'You deny it, then.'

'I certainly do! Surely I can't spell it out any more clearly than I already have!' She folded her hands and cracked her knuckles, a habit which Thanet had always abhorred. But he refused to allow himself to be distracted. He was trying to make up his mind if she was lying. Sometimes it was easy to tell – a facial expression, a false note in the voice, certain gestures such as rubbing the side of the nose, but at others it is well-nigh impossible and this, he decided reluctantly, was one of those occasions. Daphne Linacre met his gaze stare for stare and it was obvious that nothing was going to make her change her story in even the slightest detail.

He was certain that Nicky hadn't been lying, but was it possible that the boy had been mistaken? Thanet didn't think so. But there was no way at present to prove or disprove his story.

They would have to leave it there.

'Very well.' He stood up. 'But if you should suddenly recall . . .'

'I shan't.' The extent of her resentment showed in the sudden surge of energy with which she swung herself up out of her chair. 'Who is this . . . informant, anyway? I have a right to know, don't you agree?'

Thanet shook his head. 'I'm sorry, I can't tell you that.' The last thing Thanet wanted was to expose Nicky to ill will.

'Then there's nothing more to be said.'

Back in the car Thanet looked at Lineham and grinned. 'Well? Still as keen on your latest theory?'

The sergeant grimaced. 'I still think it could have happened like that.'

'That's the trouble with this case, Mike, there are too many credible possibilities, too many suspects with means, motive, opportunity, and no way at present of proving anything against any of them.'

'Miss Linacre doesn't seem to have a motive, as you so rightly pointed out. And as far as she's concerned we keep coming up against the same old question: why on earth should she suddenly decide to come home from work one afternoon and kill her sister?'

'If she did do it, something must have happened, to make her. But what?'

'And why? What possible reason could she have?'

What possible reason?

The windows had misted up again and Thanet stretched out a finger and absentmindedly cleared a small space on the glass. A small cameo appeared, of a young beech tree, its fresh green summer foliage drooping with the weight of unshed water. Something flickered at the back of Thanet's mind. What was it? He cleared a little more space on the glass, his finger switching from a circular movement to straight lines. The picture was larger now, revealing a rose-bed encircled by grass and a line of trees in the background, their tossing, heaving branches a mass of greens in every shade and tone.

Again there was that flicker at the back of his mind.

This time the sensation was unmistakable. Thanet had experienced it before, not frequently, but sufficiently often for him to recognise it when it happened. His unconscious mind had, quite independently, been sifting, weighing, sorting, assessing, and had come up with a conclusion of its own. It was now in the process of passing it on, up through the layers of his consciousness to the point where he was

222

able to acknowledge it. He closed his eyes and sat quite still, trying to blank out the sound of the rain drumming on the roof, the awareness of Lineham tactfully silent in the seat beside him . . . He had a brief, vivid image of the picture he had seen through the window just now, and then, without warning, he was seeing another picture, himself and Ben, in the photograph he had held last night – and then another, and another . . . Illumination came, bringing elation and a sense of triumph. Already, in his dream last night, he had made the connection . . . His eyes snapped open.

Lineham was watching him eagerly.

'Of course, Mike!'

'What?'

'Her motive. Daphne Linacre's motive. I think I've got it!'

'Well, are you going to tell me or not?'

'Naturally.'

Thanet explained, enjoying the dawning comprehension in Lineham's face. He had just finished when his bleeper went.

'There's a phone box near the village hall,' said Lineham.

It was a message from Joan. She'd had an idea where Damon might be and had decided to follow it up herself. She had taken the children to her mother's for the day.

'Did she say where she was going?'

'No, sir. It can't be too far away, though. She said that all being well she hoped to be back by mid-afternoon.'

All being well.

'She said it was a long shot, sir, but that if she found him and managed to persuade him to come back with her, they'd go straight to your office. She said not to raise your hopes too high, though.'

Thanet looked at his watch. Eleven o'clock.

At least four hours to go, then.

TWENTY-ONE

Thanet glanced at his watch. Twenty to four. Only three minutes had passed since the last time he looked. Time was crawling along so slowly it seemed virtually to have stopped.

Where was she?

His eagerness to talk to Damon was overshadowed by his anxiety about his wife. He knew that this was irrational, that Joan spent much of her working life dealing with criminals of every kind, but he didn't like not knowing where she had gone or what sort of a situation she might have walked into.

It was impossible to concentrate, and he tossed the papers he had been pretending to study onto his desk and got up, walked restlessly across to the window. The rain had stopped about an hour ago and the cloud ceiling was breaking up, the first patches of blue sky appearing.

'We should hear something soon, sir.'

Thanet gave a tight nod.

'In fact, I'd say it was looking quite hopeful. If she'd had a fruitless journey she'd have been back by now.'

'We can't say that if we don't know where she's gone.'

'No, but she did say mid-afternoon. She must have had some idea of how long it would take.'

'Mid-afternoon is so vague. It could mean anything, from two thirty to four thirty.'

'Even if it meant four thirty, at the outside, if she hasn't managed to find him we should hear from her before long. In that case she'd probably go straight back to your mother-in-law's and ring from there.'

'I imagine so. There'd be no point in coming here if she hadn't had any luck.'

'But if she did manage to find him, we might have to wait a good while longer. It could take some time to persuade him to come back with her.'

'Impossible to tell.' Thanet swung away from the window and returned to his desk. He picked up a report, riffled through it, put it down. His hand strayed to his pocket and came out holding his pipe. He didn't usually smoke in the middle of the afternoon but he felt that the occasion warranted a relaxation of the rules.

Lineham watched resignedly as Thanet filled his pipe and got it going.

'Anyway, she must have thought there was a good chance of finding him, sir, or she wouldn't have gone off like that.'

'True. Though she did say it was a long shot.'

They were going around in circles. Thanet stood up. 'Come on, Mike. There's no point in sitting around speculating like this. A change of scene will do us good. Let's go up to the canteen and have some tea. We can easily be contacted there.'

They were carrying the cups across to a table when the message came through.

'I've been told to tell you your wife has arrived, sir.'

Relief was sweet. 'Is she by herself?'

'I don't know, sir. I haven't actually seen her.'

'Where is she? Downstairs?'

'Yes, in the entrance hall. Shall I bring her up to your office?'

'No, I'll go down myself.'

Thanet sent Lineham back upstairs and went down alone. Outside the glass doors leading into the entrance hall he paused for a moment. Joan hadn't seen him yet. She looked tired. She was sitting with her eyes closed, leaning her head back against the wall. There was a young man beside her whom Thanet recognised immediately from the photographs released to the media. So she had brought it off. He experienced an uprush of pride and excitement. Damon, too,

225

looked tired. He was sitting forward, elbows on both knees, clasped hands dangling loosely between.

Thanet pushed open the door and entered the hall. Damon must have seen him heading towards them and stirred because Joan opened her eyes. She smiled up at him.

'Ah, there you are. This is Damon Tarrant. Damon, my husband, Detective-Inspector Thanet.'

Damon nodded but did not respond to Thanet's smile. His photograph hadn't done him justice. His resemblance to his mother was striking, her dark beauty translated here into masculine planes and angles. He looked strained, apprehensive and slightly dazed.

Thanet wondered if Damon had indeed learnt of his mother's death only a few hours ago. If so he must still be in a state of shock.

'Damon would like to make a statement,' said Joan.

'Good.' He looked at the boy. 'But are you sure you're up to it?'

Damon glanced at Joan, who said, 'You could leave it until tomorrow, you know.'

The boy shook his head. 'I'd only lie awake all night worrying about it. I'd rather get it over with.'

'All right. We'll go up to my office, then, shall we?' His office would be less impersonal than an interview room. 'This way.'

Joan rose too, but Damon said, 'There's no need for you to come, Mrs Thanet.'

'You're sure? I'm very happy to be present during the interview, if you'd like me to.'

'No. Really. I'll be fine.'

'I'll wait here, then, in case you want to see me afterwards.'

'That's not necessary, really.'

'If you're sure, Damon,' said Thanet. Secretly he was relieved. Questioning a witness with Joan present as the probation officer was not a prospect he relished. Then, to Joan, 'I think it would be a good idea if you went home. You're looking tired.'

226

'I am, a bit. All right, then, if you're sure, Damon.'

'I'll be fine,' Damon insisted.

Thanet and Damon set off towards the glass doors, then Thanet turned back with a murmured word of apology. He had to speak to Joan privately. Damon nodded and stood waiting, listlessly. Thanet cast a worried glance back over his shoulder as he said to Joan, 'Are you sure he's fit to be questioned?'

Joan shrugged. 'You saw for yourself. He's adamant that he wants to get it over with. I think he'll feel a lot better, if he does.'

'Did he know his mother was dead?'

'No. No radio, television or newspapers. He'll explain.'

'Did he tell you why he ran away?'

Joan pulled a face. 'Yes. He's going to tell you that himself.'

'Legitimate reason?'

She nodded sadly. 'Oh yes, only too legitimate.'

Thanet took her arm and gave it a quick squeeze. 'Don't worry, I'll be gentle with him.'

'I know.'

'Bye then, darling, and thanks.'

Thanet arranged for some tea to be brought up to his office. It arrived almost immediately and Damon cupped his hands around the mug as if to warm himself.

Where to begin?

'We've been very worried about you, you know.'

Damon attempted a cynical smile. 'Nice to know someone is.'

'Everyone is. You must know that, surely. Your father, your . . .'

'My father.' It was a sneer.

Thanet knew why the boy was taking this attitude, but he wasn't going to say so, at this point.

'Yes. He's very fond of you.'

Damon said nothing, merely jerked his head sideways in a gesture of repudiation.

227

It was time to tackle the first hurdle. 'My wife tells me you didn't know of your mother's death until this afternoon.'

'No.' For a moment Damon's self-control hovered in precarious balance, then he put the mug clumsily down on the edge of Thanet's desk and covered his face with his hands. 'Oh, God . . .'

Thanet and Lineham exchanged glances.

'Look, Damon – if I may call you that – I'm really not sure that this is the best time for us to talk to you. You've had a pretty severe shock. Are you sure you wouldn't prefer to wait until tomorrow?'

'No!' Damon rubbed his hands over his face, as if to clear his mind, pressing thumb and forefinger into his closed eyelids. Then he raised his head and met Thanet's eye. 'Sorry. I'm all right, really. Go ahead.'

Thanet waited a moment, then said, 'As you wish. Well, we couldn't understand, you see, how you could have avoided hearing the news. It's been in all the papers, on the radio and television . . .'

'We didn't have any of those, where I was.' Damon gave a reminiscent sigh and shook his head, as if in disbelief that such a place existed. 'It was great. So peaceful, so cut off from everything . . .'

'Where was this?'

'It's a commune, down on the Surrey/Hampshire border. One of my friends went off to live there, last year. They're into self-sufficiency, that sort of thing.'

'A religious community?'

'No. Unless you call believing in peace and sharing everything in common a religion . . . It was the only place I could think of, to run to, where no questions would be asked and I'd have time to . . .'

'To what?' said Thanet gently.

Damon shrugged. 'To sort myself out.'

Thanet waited, but the boy was silent.

'What was it that needed sorting out, Damon?'

No reply.

228

Thanet decided to try a different tack. 'From our point of view, the problem was that we couldn't think why you had taken off like that. We guessed you might not have known about your mother's death, of course. We assumed that if you had, you would have called for an ambulance. Unless . . .'

Damon glanced up sharply. 'Unless what?'

Thanet hesitated. 'Did Mrs Thanet tell you that it wasn't an accident?'

Damon swallowed, nodded.

'Then you must appreciate that we are trying to find out who was responsible.' Thanet was picking his words carefully, trying to avoid emotive words like 'murder' and 'killed'. 'So we did wonder if one possible reason why you disappeared was because you were trying to protect someone.'

Damon stared at him. 'Trying to . . . Are you saying that someone in the family might have done it?'

'We have to take that possibility into consideration.'

Damon was shaking his head slowly, in disbelief. 'That's impossible! I assumed it was an outsider. A burglar, a tramp . . .'

'I'm afraid it doesn't look that way, Damon. So you see, we thought that it was just possible you might have witnessed the crime and run away because you couldn't face being questioned about it. Especially if it had been committed by someone you were fond of.'

Damon was shaking his head again, vigorously this time. 'You're saying you really thought I might have seen my mother killed and done nothing about it?' He gave a disbelieving laugh. 'That's crazy. That really is absolutely crazy.'

'It may seem so now that we've met you. But you must remember we didn't know you, or anything about you . . .'

'Mrs Thanet did.'

'Mrs Thanet knows her job. Without your permission she wouldn't tell us anything about you which we couldn't easily learn from someone else.'

'Even when it's her husband in charge of the case!'

'Even then, Damon. I mean it.'

There was a brief silence while Thanet gave the boy time to digest this, then said, 'Anyway, to get back to the point I was making, it was very difficult at first for us to think of any other reason why you should suddenly just drop out of sight like that.'

Silence.

'So, why did you?'

'I don't have to tell you that.'

'No.'

Damon was gazing miserably into space.

Thanet waited a moment, then added gently, 'You don't have to tell me, Damon, because I already know.'

The boy's attention snapped back with an almost audible twang. 'That's not possible!'

'Yes, it is. All sorts of things come to light in the type of investigation we've been conducting.'

'In that case, there's no need to talk about it, is there?'

'But there is. I have no way of knowing for sure, of course, but I have a feeling that in some way your reason for leaving home on Thursday is very important to our understanding of this crime.'

'But how can it be? It concerns no one but myself.'

'Does it? Does it, really? If you think for a moment, I believe you'll see that that simply isn't true. There are other people who are bound to be affected by the fact that this information has come to light, several of them.'

Damon was silent for a while, gazing down at the floor. Finally, he shrugged. 'I suppose you're right.'

'In that case, would you tell me the whole story? It really would help. I gather you only found out about this on the afternoon of your mother's death?'

Damon nodded. 'Yes.' He hesitated, shrugged. 'OK. If you already know . . . Where d'you want me to begin?'

TWENTY-TWO

From the corner of his eye Thanet saw Lineham give an anticipatory stir. The sergeant was as eager to hear Damon's story as he was. Thanet knew the What but he very much wanted to know the Where, the When and the Who. He must be careful not to rush things, now that Damon had at last capitulated.

'You could start by telling me how you spent the day.'

'OK.' He paused, thinking back. 'I slept late. Some friends of mine had finished their A levels the day before and I went out with them in the evening, to celebrate. I didn't get up till around eleven, then I had some breakfast and went out to do some work on my car. I was out there for about an hour, then I went back up to my flat, had a beer, and crashed out on my bed. When I woke up it was well after three and I was hungry. I made myself some scrambled eggs, then I, well, just bummed around doing nothing much – played some tapes, looked at some motor magazines, that sort of thing . . .'

'Usually, when you were at home during the day, you didn't go down for lunch with your mother?'

'No. She doesn't eat lunch, just has a pot of yoghurt or something. Sometimes I go down to the kitchen and eat with Vicky, but on Thursdays she goes into Sturrenden for the weekly shop, and has lunch with a friend.'

'I see. Go on.' Thanet was filled with compassion for the strange, isolated life this boy had led, but he was careful not to show it. Damon might have had every material luxury

231

but he had been sadly lacking in the warmth and support that only a close family can give.

'By late afternoon I was getting a bit fed up with hanging around, so I thought I'd go along and see a friend of mine who lives in the village, get something fixed up for the evening.'

'That would be Tim Speed?'

'That's right, yes.'

'And this would have been at what time?'

'Around a quarter past five, I should think.'

'Right. Go on. No. Just a minute. Didn't you have an appointment with my wife, on Thursday afternoon?'

Damon looked sheepish. 'Yes, I did. I forgot it, I'm afraid. Normally, of course, I'd have rung her as soon as I realised, but in the circumstances it went clean out of my mind.'

So it was as simple as that. He had forgotten.

'Anyway, when I went out of the back door I saw my aunt's car outside the coach house. I was a bit surprised, because she doesn't usually get home until around a quarter to six. Anyway, I'd promised to fix a new aerial on for her – her old one was snapped off by vandals last week – so I thought I'd pop.in and arrange a time to do it. The front door was open, so I went in. The sitting room door was ajar and she and Mrs Haywood were talking. I was about to walk in when I heard my name.

"I still can't believe that Damon is my grandson."

"Even though you're holding the proof in your hand? I can. Oh yes, I can believe it all right. I ought to have known that, with me out of the way, my dear sister wouldn't have been able to resist the opportunity of seducing my fiancé."

"D'you think Roland knows, Daphne?"

"If anyone does, he should! I bet he was so besotted with her he just turned a blind eye to the fact that Damon arrived well ahead of schedule."

"But why didn't you guess? You knew Roland had been away in Australia for a couple of months before they got engaged. You could have worked it out for yourself."

232

"I agree, I could. I was a fool, that's why. At the time I couldn't think of anything but the fact that Jocelyn was dead. It never even entered my head to think that he might have been having it off with Nerine while I was safely tucked up in hospital. God, what an innocent I was."

"Do stop pacing about like that, Daphne. You're giving me a headache."

"Oh, shut up, Bea, for God's sake. I'm trying to think. I've got to work out what to do now."

'I didn't wait to hear any more,' Damon said, miserably. 'I just backed out, as quietly as I could, and went back up to my flat.'

A wounded animal seeking sanctuary, thought Thanet.

'But when I got there, I felt I was going to suffocate. It was as if the walls were . . . sort of closing in on me.' He looked at Thanet with mild surprise. 'Funny really. It's a big room with lots of light . . . I don't know what I did next. Paced about a bit, I think, trying to take it in . . . that I was a . . .' He shook his head, unable to say the word. 'I wasn't really thinking straight. I kept hearing their voices — my aunt's and Mrs Haywood's in my head. Suddenly I couldn't stand it any longer. I felt I had to get out, right away from there. But where could I go? I threw a few things in a bag, and all the time I was trying to think of somewhere. Then I remembered the commune. So I just . . . took off.'

'You didn't leave a note, or try to tell anyone where you were going?'

'Why should I? I didn't owe them anything, I reckoned, not after what they'd done to me.'

'What had they done to you, Damon?'

'Lied to me!' the boy shouted. He put his head in his hands. 'The lot of them,' he mumbled.

It was obvious that, much as Damon might have enjoyed his stay in Surrey, it had done nothing to restore his peace of mind. Thanet was now regretting having persuaded Joan to go home. She and Damon had driven back in separate cars, and she would have had no opportunity to talk to him

233

at length, try to enable him to come to terms with what had happened.

Perhaps I should ring her, Thanet thought, ask her to come back, so that she can spend some time with Damon after the interview is over. He had a vivid mental image of her in the waiting room, eyes closed, head leaning back against the wall. She had looked so tired . . . No, he really didn't want to bring her back if he could help it. On the other hand, he certainly couldn't allow the boy to leave in this state. Many of his colleagues, Thanet knew, would have had no qualms about doing so, but he knew, too, that he wouldn't be able to live with himself if he did.

Thanet glanced at Lineham and nodded towards the door. The sergeant got up and went out. The sound of the door closing softly behind him made Damon glance over his shoulder and, Thanet hoped, register that they were now alone.

Thanet abandoned his chair and went to perch on the edge of his desk.

'That isn't true, you know. Your aunt and Miss Haywood, for instance. They didn't lie to you. It's obvious that they'd only just heard the news themselves.'

But how? Thanet wondered. How, after all this time, had they stumbled upon this long-buried secret?

Damon shook his head dismissively. 'I wasn't thinking of them.'

'Your mother, you mean?'

'For one, yes.'

'Could you really have expected her to tell you the truth, in the circumstances?'

Damon was silent for a moment. Then he shrugged. 'Maybe not. Though it does explain one thing.'

'What?'

'Why she couldn't stand the sight of me.'

'I'm sure that's not true.'

'No? In that case, why did she avoid me? Why didn't she ever spend time with me? Or take me on outings, like other

mothers do? Or come to sports days and speechdays and . . .'
Damon shook his head, hard, as if to suppress the unruly
emotions which were threatening to swamp him. 'Oh, no,
don't try to make me believe she cared about me, because I
wouldn't believe you, not in a million years.'

'Damon,' said Thanet quietly.

His tone brought the boy's head up with a jerk.

'I'm going to tell you something about your mother, something that I think might help you to understand her better.
You see, in the course of an investigation such as this we
learn a great deal about the people involved, and especially
about the person at the heart of it, the victim. Now I'm not
going to try and pretend your mother cared about you,
because by all accounts she didn't. But,' he went on quickly
as the boy flinched, 'I do want you to understand this. *It
was nothing to do with you.*'

Damon frowned. 'What do you mean?'

'I mean that it wasn't that she found you unlikeable, or
unlovable or personally repulsive or anything like that, but
that she was incapable of caring, really caring for anyone.
Even for someone who loved her as deeply as your father.'

The boy was silent, trying to absorb this new and unfamiliar interpretation of a situation he had always understood
differently.

'I know that when people don't seem to like us much we
always take it for granted that it's because of something
we've said or done, or not said or not done, or just because
of the way we are, but the fact of the matter is that quite
often it's nothing to do with us at all, but with the person
himself – or, as in this case, herself. You see, your mother
was so badly hurt when she was a little child, that I think
she built a wall around herself so that she would never have
to suffer in the same way again. I'm not saying that she said
to herself consciously, I shall never allow myself to love
someone for fear that they will hurt me, because small children just don't think in those terms. But I'm convinced that,
deep down, unconsciously, she decided never to allow herself

235

to become vulnerable again – and that meant not allowing herself to care. The trouble is, of course, that people like that can do a great deal of harm to the people around them, especially to those who are dependent on them, like children . . . Like, in this case, you. May I make a suggestion?'

Damon nodded dumbly.

'Have you ever heard of Mrs Glass?'

'My aunt goes to see her sometimes. Wasn't she their housekeeper when they were children, she and my mother?'

'Yes. She knew them both well, virtually brought them up. I think if you heard the way she speaks of your mother, and the things she could tell you about her, you may come to feel very differently about the way she treated you. After all, you know yourself, from your experiences of the last few days, how shattering it can be when your world falls apart . . . Just think how much worse it is if you're little more than a toddler, and can't begin to understand what's going on . . . Go and talk to Mrs Glass, Damon. She'd be delighted to see you, I'm sure. She's a very interesting old lady and loves having visitors . . .'

Thanet paused for a moment and then said, 'But I have a feeling that the person you were really talking about, when you mentioned people lying to you, was your father, wasn't it?'

Damon's subdued mood was at once swept away by a gust of anger. 'Don't call him that! He's not my father! My father was someone I never knew, someone I'd scarcely heard of!'

'Jocelyn Haywood might have been your natural father, but Roland Tarrant was – is – your real father, and you know it.'

'Do I? Then why didn't he tell me the truth?'

'For two reasons, I think. First of all, he loves you, and he wouldn't have wanted to hurt you . . .'

'Loves me,' said Damon scornfully.

'Yes, loves you. He's been very worried indeed since it became evident that you hadn't just gone to spend the night with friends. He's rung up every day, twice or three times, to ask if there was any news of you . . .'

Damon was listening as if he would like to believe what Thanet was saying but found it impossible to do so. 'If he loves me why wasn't he honest with me from the beginning? Surely he must have known I'd find out some time. It's like when you're adopted. Everyone knows it's best to tell kids they're adopted right from the start.'

'Maybe. But you weren't adopted, were you? Your situation was a bit more . . . delicate than that. What would you have wanted him to tell you? That your mother became pregnant by another man but he married her just the same? Also, he had to consider the other people involved, people who might be deeply hurt by the knowledge, like your aunt. If he'd told you from the start, as you suggest, how could he be sure that you wouldn't have let slip the truth inadvertently? And you can hardly swear a small boy to eternal silence, can you?'

'It's all very well for you to say that! You can't know what it's like, to find out that no one is who you thought they were. Your father isn't your father, your grandmother isn't your grandmother . . . And, worst of all, you yourself are not the same person, but someone else . . .'

'That's not true, Damon. You are not someone else. You are yourself, you have the same genes, the same personality, the same appearance, the same mind, as you've always had. Oh look, I'm not saying this new knowledge doesn't change things, of course it does, but it need not change them for the worse if you don't let it. Your relationship with some of the other people around you will be different, yes, but maybe, and I'm thinking especially of your father, maybe things will be even better between you, now that this is out in the open. Just think how worried he must have been, that somehow you would find out, that it might drive you away from him.'

Had Roland Tarrant even suspected that this might have been what had happened on Thursday? Thanet wondered. Surely not. After eighteen years he must have thought the

237

secret was buried for ever. And yet . . . the clues had been there, scattered about, for anyone to read, as Thanet had read them . . .

'I think, you know, that the best thing you could do would be to talk to him about it, as honestly as you can.'

Damon was shaking his head. 'I can't do that.'

'Why not? Because it would be difficult, uncomfortable, embarrassing? Maybe it would be all those things, but one thing's certain, it wouldn't be nearly as difficult, uncomfortable or embarrassing as living the rest of your life saying nothing about it and trying to pretend none of this had ever happened. Because it has happened and nothing's going to change that. You can't wave a magic wand and make everything as it was before.'

Damon was silent.

'Won't you at least give it a try? After all, what have you got to lose? And just think what you have to gain! I haven't exaggerated his feelings for you, you know, as I think you'll see when you discover how relieved he is to see you back. What's more, with your mother gone, he'll need you more than ever.'

The boy glanced up, a gleam in his eye. 'That's true.' His eyes glazed and he looked away, over Thanet's shoulder, perhaps into a distant place where he and Tarrant encountered each other as equals for the first time. 'I suppose you're right,' he said slowly. 'What have I got to lose?'

The battle, it seemed, was won. Thanet breathed an inward sigh of relief and then said carefully, 'If you like, I could give you a lift. I have to go out to Ribbleden anyway . . . Ah, no, I suppose you have your car.'

'Yes . . . But I think, if you don't mind, I'd prefer to go with you.' Damon shook his head in disbelief. 'You're not like any other policeman I ever met.'

'Policemen are people, like everyone else.' Thanet slid off the desk, rubbing his buttocks, which had gone numb. 'We even get pins and needles,' he said with a grin.

Damon grinned back at him. The smile transformed him,

making him look much younger and, for the first time, carefree.

Thanet felt a warm glow of satisfaction. Social-worker Thanet, he told himself wryly. Perhaps I've missed my vocation.

TWENTY-THREE

Beatrix Haywood had come to the door. 'She's in the garden. If you go around the side of the house . . . '

It was six o'clock and a perfect June evening. The last of the clouds had rolled away and the sun had come out. Even though it was late in the day there had been enough heat to dry roads and pavements, roofs and driveways. Vegetation was another matter and gauzy veils of mist hung over the saturated landscape.

After delivering Damon to a delighted and relieved Tarrant, Thanet and Lineham had come direct to the coach house. Now they followed the narrow stone path which ran along the side of the house towards the back garden. Backed by tall shrubs, its edges were softened by an overhanging tapestry of foliage plants in gold and silver and many shades of green. Over the end of the path, at the back corner of the house, was a trellised archway spangled with the shimmering white stars of clematis.

At first the vista through the archway was blurred, indistinct, like the glimpse of a garden through a wrought-iron gate in an impressionist painting, but as they drew closer the view became more defined, blurs of colour resolving themselves into individual bushes or clumps of herbaceous plants. Even so, Thanet caught his breath as he stepped through the arch.

It was, quite simply, the most beautiful garden he had ever seen. It was deceptively small and Thanet could not have analysed its charm, but it was obvious that nothing short of genius and an instinctive love of plants and knowledge of how to use them had shaped the magical harmony of form and habit, foliage and flower which lay about them. He had taken it for granted that Daphne Linacre must be knowledgeable about plants; despite the fact that she had had no formal training, the nursery was, after all, her living. But there had been no hint of the creative talent beneath that brusque, business-like exterior.

She was bent double over a flower border, pulling out weeds. 'Oh, no, not again', she said as she became aware of the two policemen. She was wearing faded jeans and a cotton shirt, its sleeves rolled up above the elbows, and her face was flushed with exertion. She wiped her forehead with the back of her wrist and put her hands on her hips, squinting at their faces against the slanting sunlight. 'What is it this time?'

'We thought you'd like to know that Damon is safe and sound,' said Thanet.

'Really? Oh, that's wonderful! He really is all right?'

'Yes, he's fine.' Thanet gestured at a white-painted table and some chairs set out on a small paved patio near the back door. 'Shall we sit down?'

As he turned he caught a flicker of movement behind the open kitchen window. Beatrix Haywood was obviously anxious to know what was going on. He had every intention of ensuring that she did.

There was a tray on the table with two glasses and a half-empty jug of lemonade.

'Would either of you like a drink?' said Daphne, raising the jug, obviously wishing to make amends for their rather cool reception. 'I could easily get some more glasses. Or you could have something stronger, if you like.'

Both men shook their heads and she poured a glass for herself and drank it off in one draught.

'Phoo, that's better. Gardening's hot work in this weather.'

'It's beautiful,' said Thanet, gazing around. 'The most beautiful garden I have ever seen.'

She looked pleased. 'I'm glad. But I'm sure you didn't

come here just to discuss horticulture, Inspector, much as I should be delighted to do so. You were saying about Damon . . .'

'We've just brought him home. He's with his . . . father.'

If Daphne had been aware of that deliberate hesitation she didn't show it.

'Where's he been?'

'Staying on a commune, in Surrey, apparently.'

The heavy eyebrows went up. 'A *com*mune? How on earth . . . ?'

'He'd heard about it from a friend of his.'

'But why did he go off like that, without telling anyone?'

'Ah,' said Thanet. 'Now we come to it.' He paused, then said, slowly and deliberately, 'He went because of a conversation he overheard between you and Mrs Haywood.'

He was certain he hadn't imagined the alarm in her eyes as they flickered towards the open window behind them.

But she must have prepared herself for this moment and her expression was merely of amused disbelief as she said, 'Really, what an improbable story, Inspector! I'm afraid he's been having you on. He's rather good at that.'

'I believe not, Miss Linacre. He was most specific. And what he told me merely served to confirm what I had already worked out for myself.'

'I haven't the faintest idea what you're talking about.'

'Oh, I think you have, Miss Linacre. In fact, I'm certain of it. And I think it was as much of a shock to you as it was to him . . . to find out that his father was not Mr Tarrant, as he has naturally always assumed, but Jocelyn Haywood, your former fiancé.'

Despite her carefully maintained façade the bald statement affected her, as he had hoped it might; briefly, the lines of her face sharpened as her jaw clenched. Then she said, 'What a ridiculous idea! I don't know what fairy stories you've been listening to, Inspector, but I think it's thoroughly irresponsible of you to come here making wild accusations without an atom of proof.'

242

Unfortunately, she had hit the nail right on the head. He had no tangible evidence that Damon's story was true. He was certain that it existed, in some shape or another – unless, of course, it had already been destroyed – and by now he had a shrewd idea of how they had happened to stumble upon it, but the fact remained that his only real weapon against her was subtlety. Somehow he had to extract a confession, and it was obvious that this wasn't going to be easy. She had had several days now in which to plan her strategy and it was clear what it was going to be: denial and more denial. It was, after all, only Damon's word against hers and that, in the final account, would not be enough.

'Accusation, Miss Linacre?' He kept his tone, too, light and amused. Two could play at that game, he thought. 'What accusation?'

Briefly, she looked disconcerted. But she quickly recovered. 'That it was my fault that Damon went away like that, of course.'

'So you deny that any such conversation ever took place?'

'Categorically.'

'Strange.' Thanet seemed to muse. 'First we have one witness whose evidence suggests that you have been lying to us, now we have another ... How many more people are you going to claim are "mistaken" before you admit the truth?'

'Which is what?'

He had to admire her nerve. She was actually trying to force him to a premature accusation! He considered: should he allow her to appear to do so? He came to a decision and sat back in his chair with every appearance of relaxation, aware that Lineham was watching him. The sergeant knew from past experience that when Thanet looked at his most relaxed, he was at his most devious.

'Very well. I'll tell you the truth as I see it. Please feel free to interrupt, whenever you wish.'

'Last Thursday, the day your sister was killed, Mrs Haywood spent the afternoon up in the attic of the main house, sorting out stuff for the jumble sale yesterday. Now your sister, as we all know, was a compulsive hoarder, and my guess is that when she got married all her stuff from your former home came with her, and that much of it was never even unpacked but put, still in its boxes, up in the attic.'

Thanet paused, expecting a denial, but it didn't come. Daphne Linacre was listening with a tolerant, almost indulgent expression. He sent up a little prayer that his strategy was going to work and that he wasn't making a humiliating mistake.

'You've already told me that it was only after much persuasion and with considerable reluctance that your sister finally agreed to part with some of her discarded clothes, and that she stipulated which boxes Mrs Haywood was allowed to sort through.

'Now my guess is that those were the oldest boxes, and that at least one of them contained stuff which dated from before she was married. And that in that box was something, I don't know what – a letter, perhaps – which gave away the secret that Mrs Tarrant had carried for so long – the fact that her son Damon had been fathered not by her husband, but by another man, Jocelyn Haywood, her sister's fiancé. Not a very pleasant thing to have happened, especially as her sister – you – had been away in hospital at the time, recovering from a perforated appendix.

'And of course, the point is that Beatrix Haywood, who found this evidence, whatever it was, was the young man's mother. She's getting on a bit now, and this was all a tremendous shock to her. She'd had no idea that her son had had an affair with his fiancée's sister, and certainly no suspicion that all these years she'd had a grandchild of whose existence she had been unaware. Also, of course, she was very angry on your behalf – you've been extremely kind to her, taking her in when she was homeless and generally treating her as the mother-in-law she would have been if her son had not died long ago.'

Daphne was leaning back in her chair, apparently as

relaxed as he, her fingers steepled across her stomach. Now Thanet noticed that the tips had gone white and that her hands were trembling slightly with the pressure she was exerting. Encouraged, he continued.

'So, once Mrs Haywood had recovered from that initial shock her first instinct was to tell you what she had discovered. She came back here and rang you at work. I'm pretty certain she told you the news then and there, because you at once made an excuse for leaving work early and all the way home you brooded on what you'd learnt, working yourself up into a fury against your sister. Jocelyn Haywood had been the only man you ever loved, whereas Nerine had had countless admirers, serious or otherwise. For her to have stolen him from you, in your enforced absence, was betrayal of the worst kind. And for him to have given her the child that should have been yours by right . . . You simply couldn't bear the idea.

'You reached here at twenty to five, went indoors and demanded further details from Mrs Haywood, who showed you the evidence she had found in the attic. As soon as you had satisfied yourself that the story was true you stormed across to the main house, determined to have it out with your sister. You quarrelled, and during the course of that quarrel you lost control of yourself and threw her from the balcony.'

Thanet paused, breath held, alert for the slightest sound from behind him. Was it going to work, was his gamble going to pay off?

He prepared to play his last card. If this failed . . . He nodded at Lineham, who stood up.

'Daphne Linacre, you are not obliged to say anything unless you wish to do so but what you say may be put into writing and given in evidence.'

The kitchen door flew open with such force that it rebounded against the wall, and Beatrix Haywood came rushing out. 'No!' she cried. 'No! You've got it all wrong.'

Daphne was out of her chair in a flash. 'Bea, shut up!'

Mrs Haywood squirmed away from the arm which Daphne had flung around her shoulders. 'No, I won't. I can't let you . . .'

'Bea, stop. They've no proof, I tell you.'

'I don't care!' It was a cry of total despair. 'I can't go on like this, not for ever. It . . . I . . .' She took a long, ragged breath and once again freeing herself from Daphne's constraining arm turned to face Thanet. 'It was me,' she said. 'I did it.'

'What nonsense!' cried Daphne. 'She's overwrought, she doesn't know what she's saying. Bea, you must go and lie down.' Daphne took Mrs Haywood by the arm, presumably with the intention of propelling her towards the house, but yet again the older woman shrugged her off.

'Daphne, it's no good, can't you see? They'd be bound to find out sooner or later, and in any case I couldn't go on living like this for the rest of my life, I simply couldn't.'

Daphne shook her head in despair. 'She doesn't know what she's saying. It's all been too much for her.' But there was no conviction in her voice now.

There was a brief, exhausted silence.

Then Beatrix Haywood sank down on one of the chairs, limbs splayed like a rag doll. 'You have to believe me,' she said. 'Daphne had nothing to do with it.'

'Would you like to make a verbal statement now?'

She nodded, and once again Lineham delivered the caution. Then he sat down and opened his notebook.

Beatrix was looking down at her lap, fingers plucking nervously at a loose thread protruding from a seam of the same flounced, flowery skirt in which Thanet had first seen her, topped today by a heavily embroidered white peasant blouse with long sleeves and draw-string neck. Her hair, as usual, was escaping from its bun. Eventually she said, as if it were all the explanation necessary, 'She laughed at me, you see.'

'Nerine did? When you went to see her?'

A nod.

'When was that?'

'Just after she had that row with Lavinia. I'd found the letter not long before. It was in the pocket of a yellow dress, and the envelope was still stuck down, it hadn't even been opened. She hadn't even cared enough to open it . . .

'I recognised Jocelyn's handwriting and although I knew I shouldn't, I couldn't resist reading it . . .' She shook her head and rubbed her hand wearily across her forehead. 'I'd give anything to turn the clock back and leave that letter unread, so that we could go on the way we always were, not knowing.' She gave Thanet a despairing look. 'They say that knowledge is power, but power can be evil . . .'

'What did the letter say?'

'That she killed my son,' said Beatrix Haywood simply.

Thanet nodded.

'You guessed?' she said sharply.

'Shall we say I put two and two together? Though I confess I wouldn't have put it in quite those terms.'

'How else could you put it?' Little by little she was recovering. She was already looking more composed and now she sat up in her chair, straightening her shoulders, crossing her legs and folding her hands in her lap. 'She was a bad woman, an evil, wicked woman, and Jocelyn would be alive today if he hadn't got tangled up with her.'

'Could you tell me what the letter said, exactly?'

'You can have a look at it, if you like.'

Daphne sat up with a jerk. 'You told me you'd destroyed it!'

Beatrix shook her head sadly. 'I know. I'm sorry. I was going to, but . . . It's the only letter I've ever had from him.'

'But it wasn't even written to you, it was written to Nerine!'

'It's no good, Daphne, I just couldn't do it.' She reached into her pocket, took out an envelope and handed it, almost reverently, to Thanet.

It was addressed to Miss Nerine Linacre, and had an old fourpenny stamp on it. Thanet extracted the single, folded sheet of paper inside. It was covered with myriad creases as though someone — Beatrix? Daphne? — had savagely scrumpled it up and then smoothed it out again. The handwriting was sprawling, unformed, immature.

Wed. March 20th '69

My darling Nerine,

I've been so worried about you. Every time I've called or phoned for the last couple of days, you've been out, and you were so upset the last time I saw you ... Please, try not to be. I hope you're not still angry with me for suggesting an abortion, I was only thinking of you and honestly, truly, I'm glad you feel the way you do.

I'm writing because we really must talk before Daphne comes home on Friday. We have to decide what — and when — to tell her about us. Because we do have to tell her, don't we, now that we'll be getting married as soon as possible? I promise I shall try to be the best husband and father in the world.

Please, my darling, get in touch with me soon. A day when I don't hear your voice is a day wasted, and life without you would not be worth living. If I don't hear from you before then I'll call round at 7.30 tomorrow (Thursday) evening.

All my love, for ever and ever,
Jocelyn

Thanet handed the letter to Lineham, then asked the question which had been puzzling him ever since he first worked out what had happened.

'I wonder why she didn't have an abortion.' He couldn't see Nerine refusing the easy way out on moral grounds.

Daphne gave a cynical laugh. 'That's easy. She was scared stiff. One of her schoolfriends got pregnant when she was sixteen, had an abortion and died. She always swore she'd never take the same risk herself.'

'I see ...'

'But you can see now what happened, can't you?' Beatrix

Haywood leant forward in her chair in her eagerness to make sure he understood. 'Daphne and I have worked it all out. While Roland was away in Australia and Daphne was in hospital Nerine got bored and thought she'd amuse herself with Jocelyn. Then she discovered she was pregnant. She would have had no intention of tying herself for life to a struggling artist, so she took the obvious way out and when Roland got back and proposed to her again, she accepted. No doubt that's why Jocelyn couldn't get hold of her, she was out with Roland. And when Jocelyn's letter arrived she didn't even bother to open it, just shoved it in her pocket and forgot about it.

'So, when Jocelyn turned up to see her on the Thursday evening, the day before Daphne was due back from hospital, he was greeted by the news that she and Roland were engaged.'

Thanet remembered the scene as it had been so graphically described by Mrs Glass who, in her innocence, had misinterpreted the whole incident: Jocelyn's arrival with the red roses meant for Nerine, not Daphne; and Nerine's cruel welcome: 'Oh, Jocelyn. Come along in and have a glass of champagne. Roland and I are celebrating our engagement.' Then the hand held out to display the ring, and Jocelyn's reaction: a white face and 'No, thanks. I wouldn't want to intrude.'

'It was on the way home that he was killed.' Mrs Haywood's face was pinched. 'His car ran into a tree and exploded. He was burnt to death.' Her fists clenched in vicarious pain.

'You think he did it deliberately?'

She shook her head. 'Suicide, accident, it makes no difference. She was responsible, as surely as if she had been at the wheel herself. A pity she wasn't.'

Lineham handed the letter back to Thanet, who folded it carefully and put it back into the envelope.

'So after finding this and realising its significance, you went to see Nerine?'

'Not immediately. By that time she was in the middle of

the row with Lavinia. I obviously couldn't tackle her then and there, so I waited until everything had quieted down and Marilyn and Lavinia had gone downstairs. Then I went along to Nerine's sitting room.

"Oh, it's you, Beatrix. Have you finished upstairs yet . . . What's the matter? You look as though you've seen a ghost."

"I have."

"What is this, some kind of joke? Why are you looking at me like that?"

"If you read this, you'll find out. Even if it is eighteen years too late."

"What on earth are you talking about? What is it? It's addressed to me . . . It's from . . . from Jocelyn. Where did you get this? How dare you read my private correspondence!"

"Never mind where. You never even opened it, did you, at the time?"

"So what? Surely I have the right to open or not open letters that are addressed to me? Look, I've had enough of this. I see no reason why I should be interrogated in my own sitting room. I'd like you to leave, now, if you don't mind."

"Oh, but I do mind. I mind very much. I have no intention of leaving until this is sorted out."

"Until what's sorted out? I really don't know what you're going on about, Beatrix."

"Don't you? Don't you really? Look at the date on that letter."

"Oh, very well. Right, I've looked. So what?"

"So it was written the day before Jocelyn died. And the Thursday he was referring to was the day before Daphne was due home from hospital."

"So?"

"It was also the day you and Roland got engaged, I believe?"

"What about it?"

"And the day Jocelyn had his accident."

"I really don't . . ."

"The day my son was burnt to death."

"You're not suggesting ... Oh, now look, wait a minute. I think you're getting things a bit out of proportion here. I know Jocelyn and I had a bit of a fling ..."

"A bit of a fling? A bit of a fling? A fling that ended in one person's death and another person's birth. You call that a bit of a fling?"

"Well, what else was it? I certainly wasn't serious, Joss knew that ..."

"Don't call him Joss. His name was Jocelyn, and he was never called anything else."

"Well he was by me. I'll call him what I damn well like. For God's sake, Beatrix, he's been dead for eighteen years."

"Yes. And I've only just learned that, but for you, he'd be alive today."

"You can't be serious."

"Oh, but I am. Deadly serious. Jocelyn had a serious nature too, he took after me. And when he said life wouldn't be worth living without you, he meant it."

"So you're suggesting ... My God, you are, aren't you? You're suggesting that it wasn't an accident at all. That it was suicide. That Jocelyn killed himself because of me ... You're crazy, d'you know that? Crazy. Getting worked up like this over something that happened nearly twenty years ago. Just look at you! Honestly, Beatrix, if you could only see your face ..."

'Then she began to laugh,' said Mrs Haywood grimly. 'She just went on and on, louder and louder, till tears ran down her face, she couldn't stop. We were out on the balcony. She'd stalked out there earlier, when she asked me to leave, and I'd followed her. She was laughing so much she had to cling on to the rail for support, and she sort of doubled up over it, so that the upper part of her body was hanging over. She went on and on laughing until my head felt as though it was going to explode.' Beatrix put her hands over her ears as if to shut out the sound of it, echoing down the days. 'I can still hear it, now,' she whispered. 'I couldn't stand it. I took hold of her shoulders and shouted at her to stop, but she wouldn't. So I . . . I bent down, swung up her legs and . . . gave her a little push.'

She shook her head wonderingly. 'That's all it took, just one little push.'

TWENTY-FOUR

The village of Biddenden, with its broad cobbled pavements and black-and-white timbered weavers' cottages, is one of the most picturesque in Kent. The sign which hangs outside 'Ye Maydes', Thanet and Joan's favourite restaurant, perpetuates the memory of Eliza and Mary Chalkhurst, a celebrated pair of Siamese twins, unique in that they survived, joined at the hip, well into middle age – a notion over which Thanet's imagination always turned somersaults. How was it possible to live in such indissoluble intimacy with another person? he wondered. Never to be able to take even the smallest independent action without the full consent and cooperation of somebody else . . . ?

'Just one little push?' said Joan as they parked opposite 'Ye Maydes' and got out of the car. 'Mrs Haywood is deceiving herself, surely. It would take a lot more than that to tip a grown woman over a rail three foot six high.'

'Not necessarily. She says that Nerine was "doubled up over the rail" in a bout of hysterical laughter. The rail could therefore have acted as a fulcrum, and very little force indeed would have been necessary, to tip the balance one way or the other. Think of a see-saw.'

'Yes, I see.'

'Good evening Mr Thanet, Mrs Thanet.'

Mrs Daniels, the owner, came forward to greet them as they stepped into the heavily beamed exterior and turned left into the little bar, where in winter a log fire always burned in the huge inglenook fireplace.

Supplied with drinks they settled down to serious study of

the menu and, orders given, Joan sank back into her chair with a sigh of contentment. 'I love celebrations,' she said.

'Me too.' And on this occasion there was more than one reason to celebrate. It was an immense relief to have brought out into the open and satisfactorily resolved the issue which for years had been festering away beneath the surface of their marriage.

After they had chatted for a while Joan said, 'Anyway, there are a million things I want to ask you.'

This was their first opportunity to talk at length. Thanet had no desire to spend the evening discussing the Tarrant case, but he didn't want to disappoint Joan. He resigned himself to their usual 'post mortem'.

'Such as?'

'Well, before we get bogged down in complicated explanations, just tell me first what you think frightened old Mrs Tarrant so much?'

'Almost certainly she went along to Nerine's sitting room, wandered out onto the balcony and saw Nerine lying on the terrace below, very obviously dead.'

Joan grimaced. 'Poor old thing. I suppose it's one of the few occasions when she can be grateful for her erratic powers of recall.'

'True.'

Joan sipped at her drink and grinned. 'Now comes the tricky bit. I want you to explain how you managed to put two and two together and come up with four.'

'Tricky is the word. The answer is, I didn't, at first. In fact, to begin with, I began to wonder if I ever would. There seemed to be so many people with legitimate reasons for quarrelling with Nerine – her husband, both the Speeds, her mother-in-law, Marilyn Barnes . . .'

'You say, "quarrelling with", not "killing". You thought from the beginning, then, that it wasn't a premeditated murder.'

'Yes. It did look very much like an unplanned attack.

Anyway, it was you who eventually put me on the right track.'

Joan's eyebrows went up. 'Me?'

'Yes. And talking about you ... Did I tell you how beautiful you are looking this evening?'

Joan was wearing a dress in misty greens scattered with wild flowers – buttercups, ox-eyed daisies and cornflowers. It conjured up visions of long, lazy summer afternoons in the country. Thanet said so.

She smiled back at him and squeezed his hand. 'Romantic!'

'Have I ever denied it?'

Mrs Daniels approached. 'Your table is ready now, when you are.'

'Thank you.'

They were shown to a table for two near the window and Joan gazed about with satisfaction at the red-and-white colour scheme which contrasted so effectively with the abundance of dark beams. 'I love this place.'

'It's the nicest we've ever found, I agree.'

Their first course arrived: a fanned avocado topped with Atlantic prawns marinaded in a blue-cheese dressing, for Joan. And for Thanet, melt-in-the-mouth deep-fried breadcrumbed slivers of veal served with three different dips: horseradish, tomato and garlic, and chive. For a while there was complete silence punctuated only by murmurs of appreciation.

'Anyway,' said Joan eventually, 'what did you mean, when you said that it was me who put you on the right track?'

'Well, you remember when I got home on Saturday, you'd been looking at photographs? There was one that I picked up, of Ben and myself in the garden ... I didn't realise at the time, but it was that photograph that started to make things come together.'

'In what way?'

'Well, there were two particular photographs amongst those I'd seen at High Gables ... One of them, a wedding photograph of Nerine and Roland Tarrant, was in Nerine

255

Tarrant's sitting room. The second, which was really rather similar to the one of Ben and me, was in her mother-in-law's room, a photograph of Roland Tarrant and Damon in the garden, on Damon's first birthday.'

'So?'

'So, the first had been taken in the spring, because the daffodils were out, the second in the autumn. And when I got Lineham to check Damon's date of birth we learnt that he had been born only six months after his parents' marriage, and there'd been no whispers of his being a premature baby. I knew that Roland Tarrant had been away in Australia from soon after Christmas until the middle of March that year, so the conclusion was obvious: someone else was Damon's father.'

'Jocelyn Haywood, her sister's fiancé.'

'That's right. Daphne was in hospital, remember, and Nerine didn't seem to have had any other man in tow at the time. I checked with Mrs Glass — the woman who more or less brought Nerine and Daphne up. She's an amazing old dear. Still icing wedding cakes at the age of eighty-one!'

Joan laughed. 'Really?'

'She's a curious mixture of wisdom and naivety — she seemed to understand the girls very well indeed, but when it came to their relationships with men . . . She confirmed that Jocelyn had been around a lot while Daphne was in hospital, but put it down to the fact that he was lonely — that he had no family down here and with Daphne away naturally turned to Nerine for company.'

'I gather you think that Jocelyn meant no more to Nerine than someone to amuse herself with, at a time when she was at a loose end.'

'Yes, I do. Though that makes her sound very cold-blooded, and I don't think she was. I think that she just had a driving need to feel important to somebody — anybody, to reassure herself of her own worth.'

'You wouldn't say she was a nymphomaniac, then?'

'Oh, no, definitely not, though I daresay a lot of people

thought she was. No, I'm inclined to agree with her husband, who saw her as so damaged by the sudden and total withdrawal of love she suffered as a small child, that she spent the rest of her life looking for it, without being able to commit herself completely to any one person for fear of being hurt again. He told me he'd always hoped that one day she would wake up and see that she could find all she wanted or needed right there in her own home, in him. He really did love her, you know, darling. He was prepared to put up with anything as long as she stayed with him, convinced that in the end she'd come to her senses and find him waiting.'

'Poor man. He must be absolutely shattered by all this.'

Thanet had a brief, vivid image of Tarrant, sweat running down his body, attacking the dead tree with an axe in a vain attempt to exorcise the demons of pain and loss which were his constant companions. 'Yes, he is.'

'What I don't understand is why nobody else, at the time, seemed to have realised that he couldn't have been Damon's father.'

'Oh, I think they must have. But Nerine's father wouldn't have cared enough to make much of a fuss about it, as long as his daughter was respectably married, and Roland Tarrant certainly wouldn't have let the fact that Nerine was pregnant by another man deter him from marrying her. He would have taken Nerine on any terms. And his mother . . . Well, I think Lavinia Tarrant would have been glad to see Roland get the woman he wanted, but bitterly resentful of the fact that he had been cheated. Not that she seems to have held it against Damon, she seems very fond of him, but I suspect that she might well rather have enjoyed being a thorn in Nerine's flesh. Those little forays to create chaos in Nerine's private territory, for instance, I'm not sure they were as innocent as Marilyn chose to make out . . . No, the one person who would have been deeply hurt by the knowledge was Daphne, and I think she was too upset by Jocelyn's death to give any thought to the matter. I imagine she simply took it for granted that Roland was the father. I don't suppose she ever knew that Roland was away in Australia for quite so long. The latter part of his absence coincided with her stay in hospital and for much of that time she was very ill indeed, almost died from that perforated appendix, I gather . . . Anyway, to get back to what we were saying, I think looking at that photograph of Ben and me set me off. I remember waking up the next morning knowing that something had clicked, and not being able to put my finger on it. That came later on in the day.'

'Why? What happened then?'

'I talked to Nicky Barnes. I think I told you, he's the son of the woman who looks after old Mrs Tarrant. He's ten . . . Children are often remarkable witnesses. They seem to see things with an uncluttered vision most of us lose as experience piles on the preconceptions and prejudices . . . And it's usually easy to tell when they're lying.'

'And Nicky wasn't?'

'Oh, no. He's bright, and observant, too. Now Daphne Linacre had told us that the reason why she came home from work early that afternoon was because she had a migraine. She also said that when she got there she could think of nothing but lying down in a cool, dark room and had gone straight up to bed. But when I talked to Nicky he told me that he heard her car drive up and that ten minutes later, when he went across to the house for tea, he saw her going back into the coach house. When I challenged her about this, she flatly denied it, and I couldn't see why, unless she had something to hide.'

'You thought she might have been coming back from seeing Nerine – from killing her, in fact.'

'I certainly thought it possible, yes. But what I couldn't understand – which was why I hadn't seriously considered Daphne as a suspect up to that point – was why, after living next door to Nerine in reasonable harmony all those years, she should suddenly take it into her head to leave work early, come home and kill her. It seemed such a wildly improbable thing to do. Now I realised that there could be a proviso – *unless she had just learnt something - which completely changed her attitude towards Nerine.*

'That was when it clicked, about the photographs. If Nerine and Jocelyn had had an affair while Daphne was in hospital, if Damon was their son and Daphne had only just found out . . . At first I couldn't imagine how she could have found out, but then I remembered that it was after receiving a phone call from Beatrix Haywood that she suddenly decided to go home – and Beatrix had been up in the attic of High Gables that afternoon, sorting through boxes of Nerine's old belongings for stuff to send to a jumble sale . . .'

'So you suspected she might have come across something, a letter, some papers, that told her the truth . . . But wait a minute . . . Why wouldn't Mrs Haywood have guessed at the time, when Damon was born?'

'I checked on that. Apparently she was living up north then, so she wasn't involved with the Tarrant family – she didn't know anything about Roland being away while Daphne was in hospital, and so on. And in fact it wasn't until several years later that she moved down here. She'd kept in touch with Daphne and when the house she was renting was pulled down to make way for a motorway project Daphne offered her a home.'

'Kind of her.'

'Yes. Though I suspect her motives weren't entirely altruistic. Daphne doesn't exactly strike me as the domesticated type, and she gained a devoted, unpaid housekeeper for the duration.'

'Cynic!'

Thanet grinned. 'Realist, I'd say.' He smiled at the waitress who had come to clear away the first course. 'That was delicious.'

They waited until the girl had gone, then Joan said, 'So at that point you thought that it must have been Daphne who had killed Nerine?'

'To begin with, yes.'

'So what made you change your mind?'

'I didn't change my mind, exactly . . . It was just that, when I really started to think about it, work out what must have happened if Daphne were guilty, it didn't make sense.'

'Why not?'

'Daphne got home at twenty to five – several people have verified this. Allow five minutes for her to hear Beatrix's story, two minutes to get over to the house, another two to get back . . . Nicky saw her when he went in to tea at ten to five, and his mother confirms the time. So that would have given Daphne just one minute in which to quarrel with Nerine and push her over the balcony.'

'It only takes a second to push someone off a balcony . . .'

'Yes, I know, But I couldn't see Daphne rushing over to the main house having made up her mind in advance to kill her sister. I think she'd have gone because she wanted to verify the story, hear the truth of it from Nerine herself . . . She would have wanted to *know*, as much detail as possible. Wouldn't you agree?'

'Yes, I think that's true. Most women would.'

Thanet shrugged. 'So I began to have doubts whether she could have done it.'

'You didn't discount her entirely, then?'

'Oh no, I couldn't afford to do that. But I did think that it was much more likely to have happened as in fact it did happen.'

Their main course arrived. Joan had chosen sautéd pieces of beef fillet topped with caramelised Dijon mustard, and Thanet was having Paillard de Saumon a l'oseille – a flattened piece of Scotch salmon quickly pan fried and served with a wine and sorrel sauce. His mouth watered as the delectable aroma drifted up to his nostrils, and once again there was a reverent silence as they savoured the first mouthfuls of food.

'How was that?' said Joan eventually.

'Mmm?' They had been married long enough for Thanet to know at once that she was simply picking up the conversation again as if there had been no hiatus. 'Ah, yes, well it

260

was very simple, really.' He briefly narrated Beatrix Haywood's story. 'When she realised what she had done she went straight back to the coach house and rang Daphne. She can't remember a single word of the conversation, but according to Daphne she simply said, "Daphne, something really terrible has happened. Please come home at once," and put the phone down. Daphne knew that Beatrix would never make such an appeal unless there was something seriously wrong, so she left immediately. When she got home Beatrix poured out the whole story and Daphne hurried over to check for herself that Nerine really was dead – she didn't go into the main house at all, just around to the terrace. Then she went back to the coach house and spent some time planning what they should do and say when the inevitable investigation began, confident that any strangeness in Beatrix's behaviour would be put down to shock over the murder – as, indeed, it was. On the face of it, you see, there was nothing to connect Nerine and Beatrix other than that they were next-door neighbours. Later on, of course, Daphne had a delayed reaction. Mike and I heard her being sick upstairs when we were there talking to Beatrix Haywood – who, incidentally, after the initial panic, remained remarkably cool and level-headed for someone who usually gives the impression of being a bit scatterbrained. It had all been a terrible shock to Daphne, of course, learning of Jocelyn and Nerine's betrayal and the baby, then discovering that Beatrix had actually killed Nerine . . .'

'But why didn't she report the murder? After all, she'd had nothing to do with it, and now she's made herself into an accessory after the fact.'

'I know . . . I think it was partly because she's genuinely fond of Beatrix – they're both a bit odd, and they suit each other; partly because Beatrix is Jocelyn's mother, and over the years Daphne has come to think of her as family; and partly, I think, because Daphne felt no loyalty to Nerine after what she had just learned about her. Also, of course, I think she accepted that it was an accident, in the sense that

Beatrix hadn't gone to see Nerine with the intention of killing her, and that Beatrix therefore didn't deserve to go through all the pain and suffering that an arrest for murder would entail.'

'It was very strange, don't you think, the way it happened?'

'You mean, why Nerine should have had that bout of hysterical laughter? Yes, it was. Disastrous, too, of course, in that Beatrix just couldn't take the idea that Nerine should think any of this funny. In fact, I don't think she did. I think she was still in a state of considerable tension after the row with Lavinia, which had taken place immediately before. Then Beatrix stalked in like an avenging angel and, well, as I said, Beatrix is a bit odd – hair always escaping from a bun and arty, peasant-style clothes most inappropriate to a woman of nearly seventy . . . I can quite see she might have looked a bit comic, and I suspect that what was initially no more than a mildly amused reaction turned into one of those bouts of uncontrollable laughter we all experience from time to time – you know, the more inappropriate it seems, the harder it is to stop.'

'Like getting the giggles in church, you mean.'

'That sort of thing, yes.'

'So you're saying that when you finally went to see Daphne, you really weren't sure which of them had done it?'

'If either of them had! I tell you, Joan, I was taking a most almighty risk. Looking back, now, I go cold when I think about it. You see, as I said, there were a number of other people who had equally strong motives and opportunities, and there was no logical reason why one of them shouldn't have done it.'

'So why take that risk? Why not just wait, and see if anything more conclusive emerged?'

Thanet grinned. 'It's good to live dangerously, sometimes. And the longer I considered Beatrix as a suspect, the more likely it seemed that she was the culprit.'

'Why?'

'Well, she's pretty obsessive about Jocelyn, still, even after all these years – convinced that if he'd lived he would have been another Picasso. You should see their sitting room – it's like a third-rate art gallery.'

'You don't seem to have a very high opinion of his talent.'

'I don't know much about art, as you know, you're the expert there, but I must admit I wasn't impressed, no ... Anyway, as I say, Mrs Haywood didn't see it that way. And of course, he was her only son. The point is that people with obsessions can be dangerous – it often doesn't take much to tip them over the edge, if they're in a highly emotional state at the time.'

'As she was, because she was convinced that it was Nerine's fault that Jocelyn died.'

'That's right, yes.'

Their plates were cleared away and the pudding trolley appeared, loaded with tempting dishes.

'I honestly don't think I can manage anything else,' said Joan.

'What about a sorbet? You could make space for that, surely,' said Thanet.

'Well ... possibly, yes. Orange, perhaps?'

Thanet chose trifle, always his favourite, and Joan's sorbet arrived in the hollowed-out shell of an orange, with a little lid of orange peel on top.

'And was it?' said Joan. 'Nerine's fault, that Jocelyn died?'

'Perhaps not in the sense that Mrs Haywood meant. She was convinced – still is, for that matter – that he killed himself because of the shock of learning of Nerine's engagement.'

'You don't agree, though?'

'I just don't know. It could well have been an accident. The weather was bad that night – heavy rain, and a strong, gusting wind ... But in the sense that after such a shock he might have been driving carelessly then, yes, perhaps Nerine was at least partly responsible.'

'What will happen to his mother, now that she's confessed?'

'Well, she's been charged with murder, but my guess is that it will be reduced to manslaughter by reason of provocation and she'll probably get a two-year suspended sentence.'

'Let's hope so, anyway.'

'Yes. Certainly the jury will be able to see that she's appalled by what she did. The trial will be a pretty nasty experience for her, but I think she'll come through it all right. Then, all being well, she'll be able to sink gently back into obscurity as Daphne's housekeeper. Though I suppose they'll have to move. I can't really see them wanting to go on living in Roland Tarrant's back garden.'

'No. How's he reacted to all this?'

'Shocked – stunned, in fact. I don't think he's taken it in properly yet ...'

'I can imagine ... Mmm. This is really delicious,' said Joan. 'Would you like to try some?'

She held out a loaded spoon, and Thanet tasted.

'Yes, it is good. Cointreau in it, d'you think?'

Joan tasted again, considered. 'Yes, I think you're right.'

'I hope you're remembering all these culinary details for Bridget. She'll want chapter and verse tomorrow.'

'As usual.'

They grinned at each other, and for a few minutes discussed Bridget's prospects of getting a positive response from the *Kent Messenger*. Then Joan said, 'All right. So for one reason and another you became convinced that it was Beatrix who had killed Nerine. But why, in that case, did you choose to accuse Daphne?'

'As a matter of fact, I didn't actually accuse her. I admit I gave the impression of accusing her, but that's quite different. And I did it with the express intention of trying to manipulate Beatrix Haywood into a confession.'

'But why not tackle Beatrix? Daphne sounds much less likely to cave in.'

'Ah, it was all rather subtle, really. I thought that Beatrix would be much more likely to "cave in", as you put it, if she thought Daphne was going to be arrested for a crime she, Beatrix, had committed. I made sure she could hear the interview, and I knew how hard she would find it to stand by, saying absolutely nothing, while it seemed that Daphne was getting in deeper and deeper. Whereas if I'd accused her directly all she'd have had to do was keep on flatly denying it.'

'How devious can you get!'

Thanet grinned. 'But of course, it was you who really helped me to bring it off, by finding Damon like that.'

'Sounds to me as though you had it all worked out without him.'

'Maybe, but that isn't the same as *knowing*. I couldn't possibly have talked to Daphne as I did on the basis of mere speculation. Having Damon's confirmation made all the difference. I was convinced all along that his disappearance was somehow central to the case, and of course it was. And I was very grateful indeed to you, for producing him.'

'I wasn't at all sure it would come off.'

'But it did. And although, at the moment, he's naturally in a bit of a state, I have a feeling that he'll settle down, in time. Have you had a chance to talk to him yet?'

'Yes, I saw him today. He'd had quite a long talk with his father, I gather. And if we're handing out bouquets, I think you deserve one, for persuading him to do so.'

Thanet smiled. 'Social-worker Thanet in action. I thought at the time perhaps I'd missed my vocation. You would have been proud of me.'

'Oh, I am,' said Joan. 'Make no mistake about that, I am.'

Their eyes met in a lingering, loving look which saluted the value of each to the other.

'Mutual admiration society, then,' said Thanet.

They raised their glasses and drank the last of the wine in a silent toast.

SUSPICIOUS DEATH

To Mark and Janet

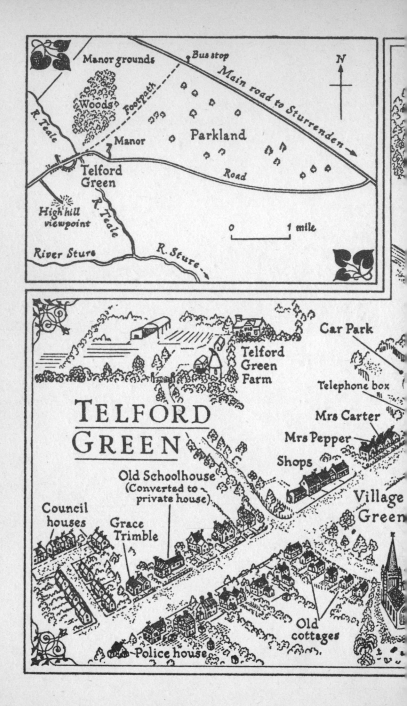

Telford Green map (upper panel)

Manor grounds · Bus stop · Main road to Sturrenden → · N

Woods · Footpath · Parkland · R. Teale · Manor · Telford Green · Road

High hill viewpoint · R. Teale · River Sture · R. Sture →

0   1 mile

Telford Green (lower panel)

Car Park

Telford Green Farm

Telephone box

TELFORD GREEN

Mrs Carter · Mrs Pepper · Shops · Village Green

Old Schoolhouse (Converted to private house)

Council houses · Grace Trimble

Old cottages

Police house

Woods

Coach house

Gardens

Gate

Manor

Parkland

rry's
ut

Footpath

Postbox

ardens

Steps

Bridge

High wall

Gatehouse
(Lodge)
[Edith Phipps]

Mrs Hammer's
cottage

Public
House
'The
Crooked
Door'

Bench

(Where Bernard sat)

Footpath

Bench

New Vicarage

River Teale

Old Vicarage

Bench

Churchyard

Peter McClure 1988

ONE

Thanet lay awake, staring into the darkness, ears tuned to catch the slightest sound from along the corridor. Beside him, Joan's deep, even breathing told him that she was sound asleep. He glanced at the luminous dial of the clock. Midnight.

This was ridiculous.

Moving stealthily, so as not to disturb her, he set aside the bedclothes and padded to the door, shivering slightly as the cold night air penetrated his pyjamas. No one would have believed it was April. Since the rain stopped at around six o'clock the temperature had rapidly plummeted to below freezing point and the house was cooling fast. All the more reason to take a firm stand now.

He eased the door open and glanced along the corridor to Bridget's room. Yes, as he thought, she was still up.

She was sitting at her desk, staring at the open book before her. Not by look, word or gesture did she acknowledge his presence as he came in.

'Sprig,' he said softly, the memory of past confrontations causing his resolution to crumble. 'Don't you think it's time you gave up for the night?'

She stirred, then, like someone awakening from a long sleep, and glanced up at him. 'I haven't finished yet.'

'But it's past midnight!'

Her mouth set stubbornly. 'I must finish this section.'

'What is it?'

'Biology. I told you. We've got this massive test tomorrow.'

'But . . .'

'Dad, leave it alone, will you? If it's got to be done, it's got

1

to be done. If I go to bed without finishing I'll never get to sleep.'

Her voice was rising, the familiar edge of near-hysteria, near-desperation creeping in, and once again, in the face of it, he was powerless.

'All right. But try not to be too long.' He bent to kiss the top of her head and switched on the electric fire before leaving.

What else could he have done? he asked himself as he returned to his own bed, snuggling up to Joan's comforting warmth. If he had persisted there would have been floods of tears and when Bridget did get to bed she would have been too upset to sleep. How many other parents all over the country, he wondered, were at this very moment faced by precisely the same dilemma? He had heard plenty of tales of pre-examination traumas, but who could have guessed that the imminence of GCSEs would turn his cheerful, extrovert Bridget into a wan, anxiety-ridden ghost of her former self? The situation had been deteriorating steadily since Christmas, when she had failed several of her 'mocks', and lately a combination of overwork, lack of sleep and general listlessness had been giving Thanet and Joan real cause for worry. Endless discussions had brought them no nearer a solution and time and again they had reached the unsatisfactory conclusion that there was nothing they could do other than offer her reassurance and moral support, grit their teeth and stick it out.

Another couple of months and it would all be over, Thanet told himself yet again as he tried to compose himself for sleep. Until it was Ben's turn . . .

Next morning Joan and Ben were brisk and energetic, Thanet and Bridget heavy-eyed and lethargic. It was Thanet's turn to do the school run and when he dropped the children off he again noted Bridget's dragging reluctance as she headed for the school gates. If only there were something he could do to help her. But you couldn't fight all your children's battles for them, he reminded himself as he drove off. Learning to cope alone was part of the painful process of growing up.

At this point, normally, his spirits would begin to rise. He loved his work, enjoyed the constant and varying challenge of it, the comforting familiarity of well-known faces, long-term relationships. But at the moment even this solace was denied him. After twenty years Superintendent Parker had retired, and the winds of change were sweeping through the sub-divisional police headquarters of Sturrenden, the small country town in Kent where Thanet lived and worked, in the shape of Superintendent Draco, a Welshman recently promoted from Cardiff.

Thanet glanced at his watch. He'd better get a move on, or he'd be late for the 8.45 morning meeting which Draco had instituted as part of the new regime.

Pater, the duty officer, greeted him with a grin. 'Morning, sir. You'll be pleased to hear they've decided to start on redecorating your office today.'

'Oh, no . . . I thought it wasn't going to be till next month.'

'Change of plan, sir. DS Lineham is directing operations.'

'What do you mean, "directing operations"?'

'They thought it would be quicker and easier if your desks were moved next door.'

'Oh, great.'

Upstairs the CID section was a hive of activity. In the main room a corner was being cleared to accommodate Thanet and Lineham and the corridor was crowded with desks, chairs, filing cabinets, noticeboards, stacks of files and decorators' equipment.

Detective Sergeant Lineham, carrying a chin-high stack of folders, grimaced as Thanet advanced, scowling.

'How are we supposed to get any work done, with all this going on?'

'It won't take long, sir. By the time you're back from the meeting, we'll be more or less straight.'

'There are times, Mike, when I find your optimism positively nauseating. How long will they take to do our office?'

'Two days, they say. Cheer up, sir, it's all part of our new image.' But all these upheavals were having an effect even upon the normally cheerful Lineham. His usual mischievous grin was conspicuous by its absence.

Thanet snorted in disgust. 'New image! Stop provoking me, Mike. I was perfectly happy with things as they were.'

'I must admit I'll miss the map of Australia on the ceiling myself.'

'Anything important come in since last night? I'm due at the meeting in five minutes.'

There was only routine stuff, however, and Thanet's report to Draco was brief. He had to admit that the new Superintendent was efficient, and seemed to know exactly what he was trying to achieve. If only he didn't have the unfortunate knack of putting people's backs up . . .

'One last point . . .' Draco's eyes, dark and diamond-bright as the anthracite in his native hills, glittered as he glanced from one man to the next, deliberately allowing his gaze to rest for a moment on each one. 'I've said it before and I'll say it again: I want to know everything that goes on in my patch. Everything. So if someone nicks an old lady's pension book or there's a fight in a school playground, I want to be told about it. Vigilance is the key word, vigilance and efficiency. And efficiency, as far as we are concerned, means reports. Detailed, literate and accurate reports, which we will all actually read. So just make sure that everyone gets the message. That's all for today. Thank you for your time.'

The phone rang as they began to file out and he snatched it up. 'Draco.' He listened for a moment then covered the receiver and called Thanet back, waving him into a chair.

Thanet studied him as he waited. Typically Celtish in appearance, Draco was short – barely regulation height, Thanet guessed – and thick-set, with close-cropped curly black hair and sallow skin. Even when, as now, he was in a passive role, he emanated controlled energy. It was in the tilt of his head, the intensity of his concentration, the rhythmic tapping of his forefinger on his desk.

'Yes. Yes, I see. When was this? Yes . . . Yes . . . Definitely. Inform the SOCO and the CCTV sergeant . . .'

Thanet's interest sharpened. If the Scenes-of-Crime Officer and Closed Circuit Television operative were being notified, it could only mean . . .

'Yes, of course, the police surgeon too. DI Thanet will be along shortly. Yes.'

The phone went down and Draco focussed his attention on

Thanet. 'As you'll have gathered, there's been a suspicious death. Woman pulled out of the river at Donnington Weir. Found by an old lady walking her dog. You'd better get over there.'

'Any sign of foul play, sir?'

'That,' said Draco, impaling Thanet with his glittering stare, 'is what you're going to find out.'

'Yes, sir.' Thanet turned to leave.

'Oh, and Thanet . . .'

'Yes, sir?'

'When you have found out, I want to know about it. The lot.'

'Right, sir.'

As he hurried upstairs, Thanet spared a moment to wonder if Draco was going to be able to content himself with being a mere administrator. This was what had always deterred Thanet from seeking promotion. He loved the investigative side of his work, the interviewing of witnesses and suspects, the intellectual challenge and supreme satisfaction of solving a difficult puzzle. To have found himself stuck behind a desk for most of his working life would be anathema to him. At this moment, he wouldn't have changed places with Draco for all the incentives in the world.

In the CID room Lineham had managed to establish some sort of order and was busy sorting through files on Thanet's desk. Thanet glanced around. All six Detective Constables were present, each conspicuously busy.

Thanet addressed the room at large. 'Well, it looks as though we're going to be stuck with each other for the next two days, and we'll just have to make the best of it. Anyway, with any luck you won't be seeing much of me. There's been a suspicious death. A woman's body, pulled out of the weir at Donnington.'

Heads turned and glances were exchanged as a ripple of excitement ran around the room. The unspoken word vibrated in the air. *Murder?*

'Of course,' Thanet went on, 'we have no idea yet whether it was accident, suicide or murder; so don't get too excited about it. Initially, Lineham and I will go and take a look, and

Bentley and Swift will come with us.' Swift was new to the section and his thin, dark face lit up with a look of ill-concealed satisfaction. Bentley, his usual phlegmatic self, merely nodded. Thanet tried to ignore the others' evident disappointment. It was understandable, of course. Sturrenden was a fairly law-abiding community and possible murder cases were few and far between. 'Naturally, if this turns out to be a potential murder investigation, you'll all be involved, one way or another. So get your heads down and clear off as much routine stuff as possible.' He turned to Lineham. 'Anything urgent we've got to deal with before we go?'

'Not really, sir, no.'

'Right. We'll be off, then.'

Thanet and Lineham took one car, Bentley and Swift another, in case they needed to divide forces later. It was market day in Sturrenden and the town was crowded with pedestrians thronging down the High Street to the large cobbled area of the Market Square, where traders who made their living moving from market to market would have been setting up their stalls since early morning. Donnington Weir was about two miles out of town but unfortunately was accessible by road only from the far side of the river. It was therefore necessary to cross the one and only river bridge, which as usual on market days was congested with traffic.

'About time they found a new site for the market, if you ask me,' grumbled Lineham as they queued to cross the river.

The policeman in Thanet agreed with Lineham, the private citizen thought that it would be a shame to sweep away a centuries-old tradition merely because of the inconvenience it caused. He contented himself with a non-committal grunt. In any case, there was no desperate rush. The SOCO and CCTV officer would have to get to Donnington and carry out their routine procedures before Thanet and his men could do very much. He gazed around at the colourful market scene. After yesterday's rain it was good to see blue skies and sunshine. Canvas awnings flapped, clothes on display swung to and fro on their hangars in the brisk wind which had sprung up overnight and puffy white clouds scudded gaily eastwards towards the coast and the sea. Thanet spotted Helen Mallard, the wife of the police surgeon, buying fruit from one of the stalls and according its selection her customary care. A professional writer of cookery books, she shared with Bridget, Thanet's daughter, a passionate interest in anything and everything to do with the preparation of food. She saw him and waved, came across.

He wound down the window.

'Hello, Luke, how are you all? I haven't seen Bridget for ages.'

Until Christmas she and Bridget used to get together once a week for what they called their 'creative evenings'. It was also through Helen Mallard that Bridget had managed to land a commission to write a children's cookery corner in the *Kent Messenger*. Lately, Thanet thought sadly, her interest even in that had waned.

He pulled a face. 'The prospect of GCSEs is really getting her down.'

'I gathered as much. Well, if she wants me, she knows where to find me. It might make a change, for her to come over one evening.'

'I'll mention it to her. Thanks, Helen.'

The car in front began to move.

'See you.'

''Bye, Luke. Love to Joan.'

Ten minutes later they turned off the main road and drove down the gentle incline into the large public car park at Donnington Weir, a well-known local beauty spot on the river Sture. A grassy meadow studded with mature oaks stretches between car park and river, and on the far side the land rises in a wide landscape of gently rolling pastureland scattered with farms, oast houses, barns and cottages. It is a favourite place, especially in summer, for family picnics and local artists. On this brisk April morning, however, the parking area was occupied only by a few police cars, an ambulance and the old Rover which Doctor Mallard, Helen's husband, stubbornly refused to part with.

Bentley and Swift pulled in alongside them and all four men put on wellington boots.

Thanet greeted the uniformed PC on duty beside the swing gate leading into the field. 'Morning, Weaver. Which way?' Thanet had been scanning the wide, grassy expanse, but could see no sign of activity. From here the river was invisible.

'Over there, sir.' Weaver pointed to a small stand of trees over to the left.

'Right.'

The heavy frost had thawed, but the wind had not yet dried out the residual moisture and their boots made a swishing, squelching sound as they moved through ankle-high grass across ground still sodden from the winter rains. Nearer the water the ground fell away, sloping down to the footpath along the river bank which in summer was rarely without its complement of dog-walkers and strolling couples. This morning it was deserted save for the flurry of activity near the trees. A small, nattily dressed figure was approaching, bald head gleaming and half-moons twinkling in the sunshine.

'Ah, reinforcements have arrived. Morning, everyone.'

'Morning, Doc,' they said, Thanet smiling with genuine pleasure. He was very fond of the little police surgeon, whom he had known since boyhood, and it always delighted him to see Mallard in the ebullient mood which had enveloped him since his second marriage. For many years before that Mallard had been a lonely embittered figure after the lingering death of his first wife.

'You beat us to it, I see,' said Thanet. 'What's the story?'

'Well, she's dead, all right.' Mallard peered mischievously at Thanet over his glasses. 'That what you wanted to know?'

Thanet tutted. 'Come on, Doc, stop playing games.'

'The young are always so impatient,' murmured Mallard, putting down his bag and pulling out a notebook. He flipped it open. 'Female, white, mid-forties, height 5′ 6″, weight about 9 stone, cause of death . . .' He paused.

'Well?' demanded Thanet.

Mallard shut his notebook with a snap. 'I'm not too sure I want to commit myself, as yet.'

'She didn't drown, then?'

'She might have. On the other hand, she . . .'

'. . . might not have!' finished Thanet.

'Precisely. Look, I'm sorry, but I can't pronounce yet on this one. You know how tricky drownings can be. She might have had a cardiac arrest or a laryngeal spasm as a result of the shock of falling into the water, or . . .'

'Or?'

Mallard shrugged. 'There's a nasty gash on the right temple. It's difficult to tell, at the moment, whether or not she got it before or after she went into the river.'

'You'll do a diatom test?'

'Definitely, yes.'

Thanet knew that this test would settle whether or not the woman had died before or after entering the water. Diatoms are microscopic algae, found in both sea and fresh water. Water is sucked into the lungs during drowning, and diatoms enter the bloodstream and are pumped to the heart, entering the body tissues. The presence of diatoms in these is therefore proof that the victim was alive on entering the water.

'How long had she been in the river?'

Mallard shrugged. 'Difficult to tell. But by the condition of her hands and feet . . . she went in some time last night, I'd guess.' The doctor picked up his bag. 'Well, must go now. See you later.'

As they made for the trees, Thanet was interested to note that he was feeling none of his usual qualms at viewing the body. The first sight of a corpse normally filled him with a complex and uncomfortable mixture of emotions, soon past but hard to endure while they lasted. This morning, however, his stomach was steady, his mind clear of the customary clogging apprehension. Why was that? he wondered. Because all signs of violence would have been washed away by long immersion? Or was it possible that at last he had outgrown his weakness?

Trace, the Scenes-of-Crime Officer, came to meet them. 'Morning, sir. It looks as though she went into the water somewhere further up river. The undergrowth along the bank just here is pretty dense and there's no way anyone could have dragged her through and dumped her without leaving traces of her passage. I understand they had problems enough getting her out . . .'

Thanet nodded a greeting at the two ambulancemen waiting near by before moving towards the body which was stretched out at the foot of a tree. Mallard's description had told him what to expect, but the bald facts had conveyed no image of the reality. The woman, even in death, had an interesting face: high cheek-boned, with jutting nose and powerful jaw. Deep vertical creases between her eyebrows hinted at bad temper, short sight or periods of intense concentration. A strong character, he guessed, and perhaps a difficult one. He noted the gash on the right temple, mentioned by Doc Mallard, and stooped to look more closely. Yes, it had been quite a nasty blow. Her long hair, he saw, had been dyed; it darkened perceptibly at the roots.

Closer proximity made him notice her jewellery too: large, tear-drop pearl earrings with gold mounts and a triple choker of pearls. If genuine, they would cost a packet. He glanced at her left hand. Yes, there was a wedding ring, plain gold, and a modest engagement ring with three small diamonds. On the same hand she wore two other rings, both apparently gold, one of a twisted rope design, the other elaborately chased. And on her right hand she wore a large diamond cluster which, again if genuine, would probably pay the deposit on a modest house.

Her shoes were missing but her clothes, too, were interesting: a quilted anorak over a peacock blue cocktail dress with a heavily beaded and sequinned top. A strange combination, surely? He pointed it out to Lineham.

'Hardly the sort of coat to wear over a dress like that.'

Lineham frowned. 'Perhaps she was entertaining at home and just slung the anorak on to go outside for some reason?'

'Possibly.' Thanet glanced up at Trace, who was watching him. 'Anything in the pockets?'

'Just a handkerchief and a set of car keys, sir.'

'Car keys ... Did you notice any cars belonging to members of the public back there, Mike?'

Lineham invariably noticed cars.

The sergeant shook his head. 'No, sir.'

'We'll check on the way back. So,' mused Thanet, 'no means of identification, so far.'

'Sir?' It was Swift, looking uncomfortable.

'Yes?'

'I don't know whether I ought to say anything, as it's so vague, but . . . I'm sure I've seen this woman before, somewhere.'

'But you can't remember where?'

'No sir. It's so frustrating. I've been racking my brains.' Swift stared down at the dead face, as if willing it to provide him with the information. He shook his head. 'It's no good.'

Thanet clapped him on the shoulder. 'Don't worry, it'll come. Just put it out of your mind, that's the best way.' He walked across to the river bank. To his right, a couple of hundred yards upstream, was the weir; eight or ten feet below him the swollen waters of the Sture, obscured by a dense tangle of undergrowth. Broken branches and trampled twigs confirmed Trace's words about the difficulties of retrieving the body. 'This where you got her out?'

'Yes, sir.' One of the uniformed PCs pointed. 'If it hadn't been for that tree, she'd be miles down river by now, we reckon. Her hair had caught on that tangle of branches. Apart from that she was floating free.'

The tree in question must have come down during the winter storms; it projected some fifteen feet into the river, its upper branches submerged and well out into the main current. Thanet could visualise the scene clearly, the body carried along by the swollen waters, accelerating as it approached the rush of water over the weir, the twisting tumble as it was carried over the lip into the churn of waters below, the sudden check as the woman's abundant hair caught in the web of branches lying in wait beneath the surface . . .

'Have you checked the bank upstream?'

'We had a quick look, sir, but there's no sign of a struggle, or of anything out of the ordinary.'

'Good.' But they would take another look all the same, thought Thanet. In any case, there was little point in cordoning off the area or setting up screens. He told the ambulance-men they could take the body away, then turned back to the uniformed men. 'Who was first on the scene?'

11

'We were, sir.'

Thanet addressed the older of the two patrolmen. 'I assume it was a member of the public who discovered the body?'

'Yes, a woman out walking her dog, sir. She lives in the cottage on the corner just up there, where you turn off the Sturrenden road to come down to the car park. We thought it would be OK for her to wait at home to give her statement. She was pretty shaken.'

'Fine. Right. So this is what we do.'

Thanet despatched young Swift to take a statement from the witness, then ordered a further search of the river bank upstream, both above and below the weir.

'Any news, report back to me. DS Lineham and I are going back to headquarters.'

Trudging back across the field Lineham said, 'Looks as though we might have a problem with identification, sir.'

'Mmm. I don't know. It wouldn't surprise me if it's not too long before someone reports her missing. She looks pretty well-heeled, don't you think? I should say she's come up in the world.'

'What makes you say that?'

'Those rings. Modest engagement ring, the rest of her jewellery — if it's genuine — pretty expensive. Either her husband has had a successful career, or she has.'

'She could have come downriver for miles,' said Lineham.

Something in the Sergeant's tone made Thanet glance at him sharply. Now that he came to think about it, Lineham had been unusually subdued all morning. Normally the prospect of a possible murder investigation aroused all the Sergeant's enthusiasm.

'Anything the matter, Mike?'

'No. Why?'

Now Thanet was certain. He knew Lineham too well. But if the Sergeant didn't want to talk about it . . . 'Just wondered . . . Anyway, I think we'd better take a good look at a map. Come on.'

Back in the CID room they were still studying a large-scale map of the area when Pater, the Station Officer, came on the line. 'I've got someone on the phone, sir, says his wife is missing. Sounds as though she could be the woman we pulled out of the river this morning.'

'What's his name?'

'Salden, sir. Lives at Telford Green.'

Which was in the right direction, upriver from Sturrenden on the river Teale, a main tributary of the Sture. 'Put him on.'

'Mr Salden? Detective Inspector Thanet here. I understand your wife is missing?'

'Yes. I didn't find out till this morning, but her bed hasn't been slept in.'

'I wonder, could you describe her for me?'

'She's five six, slim, long blonde hair, brown eyes . . .'

'How old is she?'

'Forty-five.'

'I see. And do you happen to know what she was wearing last night?'

There was a pause. Then, 'A deep blue cocktail dress, with those shiny things on the top . . . What d'you call them. . . ?'

'Sequins?'

'Yes, that's right, sequins.' The man's voice suddenly sharpened. 'Why?'

Thanet sighed. This was one of the worst parts of his job, and he especially hated having to communicate news like this over the telephone. But it would be unfair and rather pointless to keep Salden in suspense while they drove out to Telford Green.

'I'm sorry, Mr Salden, but I'm afraid I might have some bad news for you.'

TWO

'Here we are, sir.'

For the last few minutes the two police cars had been running alongside the tall red brick wall of Telford Green Manor, where Salden lived, and now the gates had come into view. Lineham turned in past the little octagonal gatehouse and as arranged the other car continued on into the village.

Salden was due back shortly from a visit to the mortuary where, Thanet knew, he had confirmed that the dead woman was his wife. Thanet wasn't looking forward to the interview. Above all things he hated questioning the newly bereaved, having to probe at a raw wound when the witness was least able to bear the pain. It had to be done, however, and if this turned out to be a murder case . . . well, Thanet was as aware as the next man that in cases of domestic murder it is the husband who is the most likely suspect.

Meanwhile, he and Lineham had been doing their home-work and studying a large-scale map of the Telford Green area. The main road to Sturrenden, which lay five miles to the east, ran at this point more or less parallel to the river Teale, which flowed into the Sture two miles downriver. The road to Telford Green, a small community with a population of around 500, cut away diagonally, crossing the Teale in the centre of the village. The Manor grounds were sandwiched between the two roads and ran right down to the Teale on the far side of the bridge in the village.

The rest of Thanet's team had been detailed to go into the centre of the village and work their way along the river bank, looking for signs of anything out of the ordinary.

The driveway to the Manor was about half a mile long, curving to the left between impressive mature oaks and copper

14

beeches before straightening out in an avenue which afforded a fine view of the house, which was black and white, long, low and timbered.

Lineham whistled as it came into sight.

'They can't be short of a penny.'

As this was the Sergeant's standard reaction to every dwelling bigger than a four-bedroomed detached, Thanet ignored it. What interested him much more was what was going on in front of it. A bulldozer was parked between a car and a police motorcycle, and a group consisting of a uniformed policeman, three men and two women seemed to be having a heated discussion. All six turned to look as Thanet's car approached.

'Wonder what's up?' said Lineham, parking neatly alongside the bulldozer.

They both got out.

'Detective Inspector Thanet, Sturrenden CID,' said Thanet, addressing the company at large. 'What's going on?'

They all started to speak at once, and Thanet raised a hand. 'One at a time, please.'

One of the women stepped forward. 'Is it true?' she said. 'About Mrs Salden?'

She was around fifty, short and dumpy, with untidy fluffy brown hair, a round ingenuous face and unfashionably uptilted spectacles. Her clothes were drab — brown tweed skirt, cream blouse with Peter Pan collar and a shapeless brown speckled cardigan.

'Sorry,' said Thanet, 'you're . . . ?'

The woman flushed, an ugly brick red. 'Edith Phipps,' she said. 'I'm Mrs Salden's secretary. And this is Mrs Pantry, the housekeeper. And will you please tell these men that in the circumstances nothing can be done, for the moment, now that . . . Is it true?' she repeated. 'Is Mrs Salden really. . . ?'

Thanet dragged his attention back from the fact that, without a single word being exchanged, he had taken an instinctive dislike to Mrs Pantry the housekeeper. 'Er . . . yes, Miss Phipps, I'm afraid it has been confirmed. Mrs Salden is dead.'

'Then I should think that settles it,' said the uniformed PC to the other three men. 'Sorry, sir, PC Kimberley. This is my patch, and Miss Phipps called me in to try and settle a dispute. These men are bailiffs. Mrs Salden has an order for possession against a chap called Greenleaf who's been living in her woods and they've come to enforce it, as he's been refusing to move after the notice expired.'

'And the bulldozer?' said Thanet.

'Greenleaf lives in a ramshackle sort of hut, sir, that he built himself. The bulldozer was to demolish it.'

'And I'm simply saying,' broke in Edith Phipps, 'that they can't go on with this, now that the circumstances have changed.' She was holding herself under a tight control, her hands, tightly clasped and white-knuckled, betrayed her agitation. 'We don't know if Mr Salden will still want to go ahead, and anyway he certainly won't feel like being bothered with all this, when he gets back, he'll be too upset. Please,' she said to Thanet, 'send them away. Otherwise there'll be so much trouble . . .'

'Trouble?' Thanet looked at PC Kimberley.

'The village people are opposed to the eviction, sir. A number of them are waiting down in the woods, near Harry's – Greenleaf's hut. I've sent to headquarters for reinforcements.'

'Then I agree,' said Thanet. 'The eviction should be postponed. Mr Salden will have too much on his mind to be bothered with this sort of problem.'

The taller of the two bailiffs shrugged. 'So long as you're willing to take the responsibility, Inspector.'

'I am.'

'OK.' He glanced around, as if reassuring himself that there were plenty of witnesses, then said, 'Come on then, Ted, we'll be off.' And to the bulldozer driver, who had been standing by smoking a cigarette and looking bored, 'You too, mate.'

The bailiffs got into their car and drove off. The other man shrugged, took his cigarette out of his mouth, spat, replaced the cigarette and then climbed into the seat of his cab.

'Right,' said Thanet. 'If you'd just wait here, Kimberley, I'd appreciate a word with you later.' He turned to the two women. 'Shall we go indoors?'

16

His words were drowned by the full-throated roar of the bulldozer starting up, and he had to repeat them. Mrs Pantry led the way through the heavy oak front door into a huge entrance hall open right up to the roof rafters. A wide, highly polished oak staircase led up to a galleried landing. The stone-flagged floor was incongruously adorned with a modern bordered carpet square in strident tones of orange and green.

'May I enquire which of you two ladies saw Mrs Salden last?'

The women looked at each other.

'I did,' said the housekeeper, reluctantly.

'What time would that have been?'

'About twenty to ten last night, when she left to visit her mother, in the village.'

'I haven't seen her since yesterday afternoon,' said the secretary.

'Right, well perhaps I could have a word with you later, Miss Phipps.' He looked at the housekeeper. 'Is there some-where private, where we could talk?'

'We could go into the kitchen.'

'Fine.'

Thanet's sitting-room and dining-room would both have fitted comfortably into the kitchen, which had evidently been built on to the house in the days when there was no servant problem and there would probably have been eight or ten people sitting down for meals at the long pine table. A row of bells, each labelled with the name of a room, hung near the door. Apart from its size it would be a pleasant room to work in, with a chestnut brown Aga exuding a comforting warmth, a more than adequate supply of oak-faced units, and yellow and white checked curtains at the windows, which looked out on to the back garden. A smell of baking hung in the air.

They all sat down at one end of the table.

'Now then,' said Thanet, 'perhaps you could tell us about last night?'

While she talked he studied the housekeeper, seeking a reason for that apparently irrational recoil he had experienced upon being introduced to her. She was a big, raw-boned woman in her sixties, heavily built and . . . no, not clumsy, exactly . . . He sought the word. Graceless, yes, that was it, graceless in all her movements. Although she was wearing a flowered dress beneath a blue nylon overall she looked as though she would have been much more at home in trousers, her feet planted firmly apart on the quarry-tiled floor. Her hair was cropped, the ends chunky and uneven as though she had cut it herself, standing in front of a mirror. It was an unbecoming style, emphasising the strong masculine planes of her face, the heavily unplucked brows and beginnings of a moustache. Thanet wondered about the circumstances that had brought her here. Was she a live-in housekeeper or a daily, imported from the village? He asked her.

'Oh, I'm full-time, live-in.'

'And how long have you been with the Saldens?'

'Eighteen months, now.'

Thanet was intrigued by the note of bitterness in her voice and he glanced at Lineham. *Take over*. He and Mike had worked together for so long they were like an old married couple, Thanet reflected as Lineham went smoothly into action. In this sort of situation there was rarely a need for them to communicate in words and Lineham was used to having to take over without warning. Thanet knew that one can often learn more about a witness by watching and listening than by conducting the interview oneself.

Mrs Salden's disappearance had apparently been discovered at 7.30 a.m. when Mrs Pantry took up a tray of early morning tea. Her bed had not been slept in and although the housekeeper was surprised she was not really alarmed. She simply thought that Mrs Salden must have spent the night at her mother's cottage in the village. It had happened before, from time to time.

'Where was Mr Salden?'

'They have separate rooms.' The housekeeper's mouth tightened in disapproval.

'So what did he say, when you told him that his wife's bed hadn't been slept in?'

'He seemed, well, confused, like. Put his hand to his forehead, as if he was trying to pull his thoughts together. He had just woken up, you know,' she added defensively.

18

So Mrs Pantry's loyalty lay with Salden rather than his wife, thought Thanet. Interesting, but scarcely surprising. Remembering the dead woman's strong, determined face, he couldn't really imagine her getting on well with this woman. What had soured the housekeeper so? he wondered. He tried to imagine her face transfigured by a smile or softened by tenderness, and failed. What a joyless life she must lead.

'In fact, he told me he hadn't got home till four this morning,' she added.

'Where had he been?'

'At his mother-in-law's place. She died about half-past three.'

'And his wife was there, too?'

'No. But I didn't know that then, did I?'

'Look,' said the sergeant, 'I'm getting a bit confused. Let's go back, start at the beginning. Were Mr and Mrs Salden both here last evening?'

'Early on, yes. They was having a dinner party, see.'

Hence the beaded dress, thought Thanet.

'Many guests?' said Lineham.

'No, only two. Mr Lomax and . . . *Miss* Trimble.'

An interestingly scornful inflection, there, Thanet thought.

Lineham frowned. 'Lomax . . . An unusual name . . . That wouldn't be Mr Douglas Lomax, the borough councillor, by any chance?'

'Yes, that's right.'

Well done, Mike.

'And Miss Trimble?'

'Lives in the village. She's always round here. Mrs Salden encouraged her.' Mrs Pantry gave a disapproving sniff and brushed an imaginary piece of fluff off her nylon overall as if dismissing the undesirable Miss Trimble as of no importance.

'She works here?'

A derisive snort. 'She's a hairdresser in Sturrenden. That unisex place at the bottom of the High Street.'

It certainly sounded an ill-assorted dinner party, thought Thanet. With an unusually small number of guests. A married couple might invite another couple for an informal supper,

19

but to give a dinner party for a borough councillor and a hairdresser . . . He scented intrigue. What had been going on?

'I see,' said Lineham. 'So what time did these guests arrive?'

'Josie — Miss Trimble — came first. Bang on 7.30.' *Unfashionably punctual*, her expression said. 'Mr Lomax got here about a quarter of an hour later.'

Mrs Salden, it seemed, had come downstairs shortly after Josie's arrival and had come into the kitchen to tell Mrs Pantry that dinner might have to be delayed, as the nurse had rung from old Mrs Carter's cottage to say that the old lady was asking for Mr Salden. He had left at once, having arranged to ring at about eight to tell his wife what time he was likely to be back.

'Odd, wasn't it?' said Lineham. 'Asking for him, rather than for her daughter?'

A reproving look. 'Mrs Carter was very fond of Mr Salden. Like a son he was, to her.'

'I see. So it wasn't unusual for the nurse to ring up and ask him to go and see the old lady?'

'Well . . .' For the first time, Mrs Pantry seemed unsure of her ground. 'I dunno. I can't say, I'm sure. I don't know what half their phone calls is about. It's just that last night I had to know, see, because of dinner getting spoiled.'

'Quite . . . So what happened then?'

At eight o'clock Mr Salden had rung to say that he would be staying on at the cottage for a while, and that dinner should proceed without him.

'Mrs Salden didn't think of cancelling the dinner party?' said Lineham.

'Oh no. Why should she? She wasn't to know it'd be any different this time. Mrs Carter has been ill for over a year, very ill . . . Cancer . . . There's been many, many times when they thought she wouldn't last the night, but she did. And when that keeps on happening, you get to expect just another false alarm, don't you?'

Lineham nodded. 'True.'

Mrs Pantry had then served dinner, and as soon as they had finished the last course, at about half-past nine, Mrs Salden had apparently rung the cottage, because a few minutes later she had come into the kitchen to say that she was just going to pop down to see her mother and to ask Mrs Pantry to serve coffee in the drawing-room. She didn't expect to be long.

'The guests didn't leave at that point?'

A disapproving sniff. 'Not they. Anyway,' she added grudgingly, 'as I was carrying the tray of coffee through I did hear Mrs Salden ask that Josie to wait till she got back, as she especially wanted to speak to her.'

'But she didn't come back?'

'Not to my knowledge. Mr Lomax left about a quarter or twenty past ten, and I went to bed soon after.'

'So you didn't hear either Mr or Mrs Salden come in, or Miss Trimble leave?'

'No. But she stayed till eleven, I believe.'

'What makes you say that?'

'There's a note for Mr Salden, on the table in the hall. I was dusting,' she added defensively, 'and couldn't help seeing it.'

Lineham was looking at Thanet. *Anything else you want to ask?*

Thanet gave an imperceptible shake of the head and stood up. 'This note, Mrs Pantry. Is it still on the table in the hall?'

'I think so, yes.'

'Let's go and see, shall we?'

He waited while she reluctantly dragged herself to her feet.

THREE

Mrs Pantry led them to a long oak table set against the wall at the far side of the hall and picked up a piece of paper. 'Here it is.' She handed it to Thanet.

10.35.   *Marcia*
Bernard rang. Is staying on at Holly Cottage. Don't wait up.

> Josie.

P.S.
Waited until 11 p.m. then gave up. See you tomorrow, after work. J.

Edith Phipps had been hovering near the stairs and now she approached them. 'Excuse me, Inspector. I thought you'd like to know. Mr Salden's home.'

Thanet turned. 'Oh, thank you. Where is he?'

'In the drawing-room. Through there.' She pointed.

A knock at the door, then a second, brought no response. Thanet waited a moment longer, then lifted the latch and went in.

The room was long and low, ceiling and walls striped with ancient, honey-coloured oak beams infilled with white-painted plaster. Thanet didn't think much of Marcia Salden's taste; instead of the old rugs, mellow colours and antique furniture which the room demanded, it was furnished with a heavily patterned fitted carpet, modern dralon three-piece suite and – most incongruous of all – in the far corner, a cocktail bar. Salden was slumped in an armchair beside the inglenook fireplace. As they came in he raised his head in a dazed fashion and then put his hands on the arms of the chair

22

preparatory to levering himself up, as if his legs alone were incapable of taking the strain.

'Please,' said Thanet, trying not to stare too obviously at an enlarged photograph hanging on the wall near by. Surely that was Princess Anne shaking hands with Salden? 'Don't get up.'

He introduced himself and he and Lineham sat down.

'I understand that you have identified your wife?'

Salden nodded.

'I'm sorry.'

Salden said nothing. He was considerably older than his wife, in his late fifties, Thanet guessed. Short and overweight, with round face, thinning hair and an aura of soft living, he would have passed unnoticed in any group of middle-aged businessmen, his conventional dark suit, sober tie and well-polished shoes almost the uniform of his class and status. Only the dazed look of someone in shock would have singled him out.

'I don't understand,' he said. For the first time his eyes focussed on Thanet's face. 'What happened?'

Thanet shook his head. 'That's what we're trying to find out. Do you feel you can answer a few questions?'

A nod.

'When did you last see your wife, Mr Salden?'

Salden's forehead wrinkled, as if this were an impossibly difficult question. 'I . . . Oh God, I can't seem to think straight. I'm sorry.' He rubbed his hand across his eyes. 'It must have been, oh, between a quarter and half-past seven last night.'

'When you left to go down to the village, to visit your mother-in-law?'

'Yes.'

'But you spoke to Mrs Salden after that, I understand.'

Salden stared at Thanet. 'Did I? Oh, yes, you're right, I did. On the phone. I rang to tell her not to hold dinner for me. We had guests, you see.'

'You were sufficiently worried about your mother-in-law not to want to leave her?'

'Well, it was partly that. But she'd been asking for me, and when I got to the cottage she was asleep. I thought I'd better

23

wait until she woke up. Over these last few months there's been little enough we could do for her except be there, when she wanted us.'

'Yes, I see. But you spoke to your wife again later, I believe?'

'Did I?' repeated Salden. He frowned, shook his head. 'No I didn't. I'm sure I didn't.'

'Didn't she ring the cottage herself, soon after half-past nine?'

'Ah, I see what you mean. Yes, Mrs Pantry told me . . . No, she must have spoken to Nurse Lint. I'd gone out, by then.'

'But I understood you stayed with your mother-in-law until she died, in the early hours of this morning.'

'Yes, I did. But I went out for a walk, earlier. Just for some fresh air . . .'

'So you didn't see your wife, when she went down to the cottage, after dinner?'

'No. Nurse Lint told me she'd left shortly before I got back.'

'And then you decided to stay on at the cottage.'

'That's right. It seemed to me that my mother-in-law had taken a turn for the worse, so I rang home to tell Marcia – my wife – not to wait up for me. But she hadn't arrived back, so I left a message with Josie – Josie Trimble, one of our guests.'

'You wouldn't have expected her to want to come back down to the cottage herself, to be with her mother?'

'No. It was my turn, you see. Win – my mother-in-law – had cancer, the lingering sort, and over the last few months we've both spent many nights at the cottage, thinking that she wouldn't last until morning. In the end we arranged that we'd take it in turns to sit with her. I assure you that my wife did everything possible to make her mother's life as comfortable as she could. She even got her a full-time nurse, to live in . . .'

'Please, Mr Salden . . . I wasn't criticising your wife, merely trying to understand what happened last night. So you're saying that she left your mother-in-law's house at – what time?'

'I'm not sure. Nurse Lint would be able to tell you, I expect. Before I got back from my walk at about half-past ten, anyway.'

'And how would she have got there?'

Salden frowned. 'Well, normally she would have gone by car. But there must be something wrong with it. It's still in the garage. It was the first thing I checked this morning, when we found she was missing, and I tried it. It wouldn't start.'

'These keys were in her pocket.'

Salden leaned forward to look at them. 'Yes, those are hers. So she must have decided to walk. It only takes a few minutes to get to the village, cutting across by the footpath. And I noticed the torch was missing from her car.'

A footpath . . . 'Does it run near the river, at any point?'

'Yes. It emerges into the village just beside the bridge.'

Salden's gaze suddenly became blank, fixed. His mouth quivered. Then slowly, almost imperceptibly at first, the contours of his face began to blur and slacken. His eyes glistened, then tears began to spill out and trickle down his cheeks.

'Mr Salden . . .'

Salden gave no sign of having heard. The silent tears continued to run unchecked down the plump, quivering cheeks and then, abruptly, his face contorting into a gargoyle mask of grief, he dropped his head into his hands and began to sob, a harsh, broken, ugly sound.

Any further questioning of Salden would have to wait for the moment. Thanet glanced at Lineham then rose and crossed to lay a consoling hand on the man's shoulder. After all these years in the force he still found the sight of naked grief hard to bear.

In the hall Mrs Pantry was just answering the front door. 'Oh, Mr Fothergill. Do come in.'

'Thank you.' The small, wiry figure of a man in his late twenties stepped briskly into the hall. He was wearing corduroys, a tweed sports jacket and a clerical collar. 'Is this true, what Jack Kimberley tells me? That Mrs Salden has been drowned?'

The vicar had presumably run into PC Kimberley outside. The housekeeper nodded.

Thanet came forward. 'I'm afraid so. I'm Detective Inspector Thanet of Sturrenden CID, and this is Sergeant Lineham.'

Mrs Pantry quietly withdrew.

'Richard Fothergill. Vicar of Telford Green.' He extended a hand and Thanet shook it.

'I'd just come to offer my condolences to Mrs Salden, on her mother's death. But this . . . This is terrible. Terrible.' The thin mobile face was clouded with genuine distress. 'First Mrs Hammer, then Mrs Carter, now Mrs Salden. Three deaths in one week . . .'

'Mrs Hammer?'

'An old lady who lived in the village. She'd been failing for some time, like Mrs Carter, Mrs Salden's mother. But Mrs Salden . . . This is terrible,' he repeated. 'What happened?'

'She was pulled out of the river at Donnington Weir this morning. The police surgeon thinks she must have gone in some time last night. More than that we don't know, as yet.'

'And Bernard . . . Mr Salden? How is he? How is he taking it?'

'Badly, by the look of it. He seems very distressed. I'm glad you've come, perhaps you'll be able to help him.'

'Of course. I'll call the doctor, if necessary. And between us Edith Phipps and I will be able to manage the administration to do with his mother-in-law's death, arrange for the undertakers to come and remove her body and so on. Where is he?'

'In the drawing-room . . .'

Thanet watched the vicar knock softly on the door and go in, then turned to Lineham. 'Did you notice where Miss Phipps disappeared to, Mike?'

'In there.' The Sergeant nodded at a door on the opposite side of the hall.

'Right. Look, give these keys to Kimberley and ask him to see if he can get Mrs Salden's car started. Tell him I want to talk to him after I've seen Miss Phipps. Then join me.'

'Right, sir.'

Thanet crossed the hall and knocked at the door Lineham had indicated.

'Come in.'

FOUR

It was another beautiful room, with leaded lights, huge fireplace and oak-panelled walls. Thanet guessed that it had once been a dining-room, or a library, perhaps. Now it had been downgraded to an office, and Edith Phipps, surrounded by all the paraphernalia of a thriving business, was seated at a modern desk using a computer.

The desk looked strangely askew, thought Thanet. Then he realised why: there was a second desk in the room, Marcia Salden's, presumably, and Miss Phipps had pushed hers into a position where she would no longer permanently have it in her field of vision.

She rose, looking apprehensive, as Thanet came in, and he waved her back to her seat. 'Please . . .'

He crossed to the window and stood with his back to the room gazing out. The avenue of tall trees was immediately ahead, and to the left there was a fine view across sweeping lawns flanked with shrub borders to parkland dotted with mature specimen trees. Over to the extreme right was a wood.

Thanet nodded towards it. 'That where Harry Greenleaf lives?'

Miss Phipps looked surprised at the unexpected question. 'Yes.'

'How long has he been there?'

'About ten years, I suppose. He just sort of, well, materialised. One day we just heard he was living there, and he's been there ever since. Mr Gentry — the former owner of the Manor — didn't mind.'

'There was no formal tenancy agreement?'

'Oh no, nothing like that.'

'I see. And the Saldens, I understand, have been here only eighteen months or so.'

'That's right.'

'Which is why local feeling is so strongly on his side? I suppose people feel he has a prior claim, so to speak.'

Miss Phipps hesitated. 'It's not that, exactly. It's difficult to explain, really. I suppose they feel that Harry isn't doing anyone any harm and there's no reason why he shouldn't be left in peace. He keeps himself to himself, seems quite content with his chickens and his goat . . . And I suppose people feel sorry for him, too.'

'Why?'

'He was in some sort of accident . . . A fire . . . Nobody knows the details. But it must have been a bad one. He had to have plastic surgery, and the result is . . . Well, I think he's probably pretty self-conscious about it. People can understand him wanting to live like a hermit . . .'

'So why was Mrs Salden so determined to evict him?'

Miss Phipps shook her head. 'I'm not sure.'

'You must have some idea, surely?' He glanced at the other desk. 'As her secretary you'll have spent a good deal of time together. She must have talked to you about it?'

There was a knock at the door. It was Lineham.

'Sit down, Sergeant. We were just talking about Harry Greenleaf.' Thanet sat down himself, in one of the chairs provided for visitors, swivelling it around so that he was facing her.

'Yes, she did, of course.' Miss Phipps was leafing through some papers. 'But she never actually told me why she was so keen to get rid of him. You might like to see this.' She held out a single sheet. 'I typed it yesterday afternoon.'

Thanet took the paper but did not look at it immediately. 'She may not have told you, but I suspect you had a pretty shrewd idea . . . ?'

Miss Phipps lowered her eyes, gave a self-deprecating little smile and began to fiddle with a loose thread on one of the buttons of her cardigan. 'Well . . .'

Thanet waited.

She darted a brief, assessing glance at him. 'It's only a guess, mind . . .'

Thanet gave an understanding nod.

'I think,' she said, abandoning the button and meeting Thanet's gaze squarely, 'I *think* it was because . . . Marcia liked to be in control, you see. She liked things to go her way . . . I think the fact that Harry was living on her land, cocking a snoot at her, so to speak, if you'll forgive the expression . . . She didn't like it. He was a, well, a thorn in her flesh.'

Thanet was nodding. 'Yes, I see . . . Thank you.' He glanced down at the paper in his hand. It was a carbon copy of a letter from Marcia Salden to Harry Greenleaf pointing out that it was now two weeks past the date when he should have left her land and informing him that she had taken steps to enforce the court order. Bailiffs would therefore arrive to evict him tomorrow morning and they would be accompanied by a bulldozer which would demolish the hut in which he lived.

'How would she have got this to him? Did the postman deliver?'

Miss Phipps looked amused, displaying an irregular and misshapen set of teeth. 'Oh no. I shouldn't think Harry ever has any letters. No, Marcia — Mrs Salden — was going to walk down and give him the news in person. I typed the letter so that, if he were out, she'd be able to leave it there for him to see. She wasn't taking any chances that he could claim he hadn't been informed.'

'Why do it herself? Why not send someone else?'

Miss Phipps shrugged. 'No idea. Except that getting rid of Harry had become something of an obsession with her.'

'So when did she intend going down?'

'After tea, yesterday afternoon.'

'Do you know if she did?'

'No. But I assume so. If Marcia said she was going to do something, she did it.'

Interesting overtones there, thought Thanet. A hint of — what? Suppressed emotion of some kind, certainly. 'Are you thinking of anything specific?'

'Oh no. No. But this business with Harry Greenleaf was

29

typical. If she set her mind on something, nothing would sway her.'

The denial had been too swift, too emphatic. There was more, Thanet could tell. He was about to pursue the matter when she distracted him by adding, 'She's always been the same.'

'What do you mean? Did you know her before she moved into the village?'

Edith Phipps gave a superior, knowing smile. 'I certainly did. I can see you don't know . . . What you said just now about the Saldens being relative newcomers wasn't strictly true. Not as far as Marcia was concerned, anyway. She was a local girl, born and bred in one of those little terraced cottages next to the pub in Telford Green. We went to school together. The village school . . .' She paused, watching him to gauge the effect of what she was telling him. 'Yes, Marcia certainly came up in the world, didn't she? But then, she always said she would. Take this house, for instance . . . She always loved it, admired it, from a distance. I think that's why she cultivated me, as a friend. I had access to the grounds, you see, because of my father . . . He was head gardener here, in the days when there were proper gardens, extensive glass houses and so on. We lived in the gatehouse – still do. Mr Gentry let us stay on, my mother and I, when Father died. Marcia never got tired of wandering around the gardens. She's lie for hours in the grass, just gazing at the house . . . Mrs Gentry complained about it once, to my father, and after that we were careful to keep out of sight. We weren't allowed indoors, of course, except for the kitchen . . . Marcia always said she'd live here one day, and I just used to laugh at her. But she did, didn't she? That's what I mean about determination.'

'So how did she bring about this dramatic change in her circumstances?' Thanet already had a good idea of what she would say. DC Swift had remembered where he had seen Marcia Salden before – in a TVS series on success stories of the South-east.

'She and Bernard own a chain of health food shops. They started with one, back in 1963, now they have a chain, all over

30

the South-east. Marcia foresaw the health food boom, she had an almost uncanny ability to see which way the wind would blow tomorrow, as far as business was concerned. Together with an eye for an opportunity, when it presented itself, and a tremendous capacity for hard work . . .' Edith shrugged. 'She was a very successful businesswoman, believe me.'

'Would you say she was ruthless?'

'Oh yes, undoubtedly.'

And there was no love lost between you, thought Thanet. He would be willing to bet that Edith Phipps had at some time been one of the victims of that ruthlessness.

'Ruthless people tend to make enemies,' he said. 'Did Mrs Salden?'

She hesitated, and a wary look crept into her eyes. 'Why do you ask?'

'We have to take into account the possibility that her death may not have been an accident.'

Thanet watched a slow tide of colour creep up Edith Phipps's neck and into her face. She took out a handkerchief and pressed it against her upper lip. Did that flush have any significance? Thanet wondered, or was she going through the menopause? She was the right age.

'You're not implying that . . . that it could have been murder?'

Thanet admired her for managing to bring the word out. Most people shied away from actually saying it.

There was a knock at the door. It was Mrs Pantry, with a tray.

'I thought you might like some coffee.'

'Very kind of you.'

The housekeeper poured in silence, handed the cups around and was about to leave when Thanet thought of a question he wanted to ask her.

She shook her head. No, Mrs Salden hadn't come back into the house last night to say the car wouldn't start. Mr Salden had tried it this morning, though, it was the first thing he thought of checking, and he'd said he couldn't get it to go.

'Thank you.'

As soon as she had gone Edith Phipps said, 'Inspector?'

'Officially,' said Thanet, 'this is a suspicious death, and we are treating it as such. It could be accident, it could be suicide, or it could be murder. We shan't know for sure until after the *post mortem*, and we can't afford to waste the interim period doing nothing.'

'But you must have some reason, for thinking it might have been . . .'

'I'm sorry, I can't tell you any more.'

'Marcia would never have committed suicide. Not in a thousand years.'

'That's what people usually say.'

'But it's true. If you'd ever met her you'd agree with me.'

'Perhaps. But if so, we're down to two alternatives, aren't we? Could Mrs Salden swim?'

She shook her head. 'No. She hated the water.'

She fell silent, staring at him, eyes blank. If only he could have known what she was thinking . . .

'So one of the things we have to do is try to build up some sort of picture of Mrs Salden's movements yesterday. Perhaps you could help us there?'

Edith gave her head a little shake, as if to tug her attention back to the present, and reached for a book at the edge of her desk. 'Yes, of course. This is Mrs Salden's appointment book.'

'May I see?'

She handed it to him. It was a conventional desk diary. Some of the entries were made in a neat, precise script, some in a bold scrawl. He glanced quickly through it. Marcia Salden seemed to have led a very busy life.

The previous day held several entries. In the morning there were three: Tunbridge Wells, Tonbridge and Sevenoaks, all bracketed together. At 12.30 she had met someone called J for lunch. The afternoon was blank except for the scrawl: Deliver letter Greenleaf.

Edith Phipps explained. Marcia made a point of visiting all her shops at least once a fortnight. It kept her managers on their toes, she said. Accordingly, every morning was spent in a different area of the South-east and yesterday had been the turn of Tunbridge Wells, Tonbridge and Sevenoaks. J was Janet, the manageress of the Sevenoaks shop. Marcia always called on the shops in a different order, and made a practice of taking the manager of the last shop visited in the morning out to lunch. If made for good public relations, she believed, as well as keeping her up to date with local problems. In the afternoons Marcia would work here, dealing with administration.

'And Mr Salden? You seemed to imply just now that they owned the businesses jointly. Does he take an active part, or is he a sleeping partner?'

'Oh active. He deals with the financial side – he's a chartered accountant. There's plenty for him to do, believe me.'

'I can imagine. We must be talking about substantial sums of money.'

'There's an annual turnover of just over £2.5 million.'

'I see.' He also saw that as sole owner Bernard Salden would now be a wealthy man.

'Husbands and wives don't always find it easy to work together,' he said cautiously.

'True. But Marcia and Bernard seemed to get along pretty well. I think because they had clear demarcation lines, and didn't actually spend much time together during the day. Bernard has a separate office.'

'Did they never disagree about policy?'

She hesitated. 'Not usually, no.'

'But sometimes?'

'Not as far as the business was concerned, no.'

'But in other ways?' he pressed.

Colour stained her neck and face yet again, and once more she dabbed a folded handkerchief at her upper lip and at the sides of her nose with quick, almost furtive movements.

'I'm sorry,' she said primly. 'I don't mind answering questions about the business, but I'm not prepared to talk about their private life.'

'Even if it does turn out to be murder?'

'If it does . . . then I'll have to reconsider, won't I?'

'Very well . . . Though there is one question about Mr Salden I shouldn't think you'd mind answering . . . Sheer curiosity on my part, really . . . There's a photograph in the drawing-room. Is that Princess Anne, shaking hands with him?'

She smiled and the atmosphere in the room lightened, as Thanet had hoped it would. 'Yes. Bernard is heavily involved in children's charities and as I'm sure you know the Princess Royal is chairman of the Save the Children Fund. The picture was taken at a fund-raising event last year.'

'I see. Thank you. Well, I think there's just one other matter, Miss Phipps . . . You yourself last saw Mrs Salden – when?'

'At half-past five yesterday afternoon, when I finished work.'

'How did she seem?'

'Fine. She said she was just going to have a cup of tea, then she was going to walk down and see Harry Greenleaf.'

'And you went home to the gatehouse.'

'That's right.'

'You live with your mother, you said?'

'Yes. She is elderly and unable to look after herself. It's very convenient, living so close, it means I can pop home in the lunch hour to see her. We were very lucky, being able to stay on when Mrs Gentry sold the house to Marcia, after Mr Gentry died. I used to do secretarial work for him and Marcia needed a secretary on the spot. There I was, so . . .' She shrugged. 'She sort of inherited me, so to speak.'

'Very convenient for both of you.'

'Quite.'

'Did you find it difficult, working for an old school friend?'

She looked surprised. 'No, not at all . . . I was only too thankful to be able to stay on.'

But there was a reservation in her voice. What was she holding back?

Thanet rose. 'Well, I think that really is all for the moment, Miss Phipps.' He and Lineham handed her their empty cups and she put them on the tray.

As they walked to the door Thanet said, 'Mrs Pantry tells me she has been with the Saldens for about eighteen months. I assume they engaged her when they moved in.'

'That's right, yes.'

'She seems . . . Well, I know we couldn't expect her to be

very cheerful this morning, in view of what's happened, but she does strike me as being a rather unhappy person.'

Miss Phipps grimaced. 'Yes, she is. She had rather a bad time of it before she came here.'

'Oh?'

'I believe her husband left her. It was a tied cottage and she found herself homeless. She went to live with an unmarried daughter, who then got married. The new son-in-law and Phyllis – Mrs Pantry – didn't get on, so she decided to find a live-in job as housekeeper – she'd trained as one when she was younger. I believe she had one or two jobs before coming here. She may seem a bit, well, dour, on first acquaintance, but she's all right when you get to know her.'

They had reached the door and Thanet turned. 'Oh, there was just one other point . . .'

'Yes?'

'As you live in the gatehouse . . . When you're at home, I suppose you must be aware of the comings and goings at the Manor?'

'To a certain extent, I suppose, if I happen to be in the kitchen, which looks out on to the drive. But there's quite a lot of traffic noise from the road to the village, you can't always distinguish.'

'I can imagine. But in the evening . . .'

'It's pretty quiet, yes.'

'And you were in, last night?'

'Oh yes.'

'All evening?'

She nodded.

Had there been the merest hesitation there?

'So, did you hear any vehicles at all entering or leaving the Manor drive last night?'

She considered, head on one side. 'I saw Bernard – Mr Salden – drive out just before half-past seven. I was in the kitchen, washing up after supper. And then I saw Mr Lomax's car drive in, about twenty minutes later. But that's all.'

Thanet was more convinced than ever that she was holding something back.

FIVE

In the hall Lineham said, 'What now, sir?'

What Thanet would really have liked was a good, long discussion with Lineham about his impressions so far, but that would have to wait. 'Down to the . . .'

'Oh, Inspector . . .' Edith Phipps had appeared at the door of the room they had just left. 'I forgot to tell you . . . I hope you don't mind, but I took it upon myself to telephone Nurse Lint and tell her about Mrs Salden. I thought she ought to know, because of Mrs Carter, and the arrangements that have to be made.'

'I believe the Vicar is going to have a word with you about that. What, exactly, did you tell Nurse Lint?'

'Only that Mrs Salden has been drowned. And I asked her to stay on at the cottage until the undertakers have been.'

Thanet smiled. 'Good. That's fine.'

Edith Phipps gave a satisfied little nod and retreated into her office.

'You were saying . . . ?' said Lineham.

'Mmm? Ah, yes. That I think we ought to take a stroll across to the wood.'

'Take a look at this chap Greenleaf?'

'Amongst other things, yes. And I'd like to see the lie of the land, especially around the river, and have a chat with Kimberley to get some local background . . .'

PC Kimberley was waiting patiently outside. He was in his early thirties, tall and well-built, with thick straight fair hair and broad flattened features. At first sight he could well have been taken for a lingering shade of the archetypal rural PC

36

Plod, but Thanet had already noted the alertness of those sharp blue eyes and guessed that there was more to Kimberley than first impressions conveyed.

'Been having some interesting thoughts, Kimberley?' said Thanet.

Kimberley grinned. 'Some, sir.'

'Then I'd like to hear them. Manage to get that car started?'

'No, I think the battery's flat.' He handed the keys back to Thanet.

'Hmm. Well, it seems that Mrs Salden was last seen alive just after half-past nine last night, when she left to go to the village to see her mother — who, incidentally, died in the early hours of this morning.'

'Yes, I'd heard, sir. She's been very ill for some time.'

'So I understand. Anyway, Mr Salden seems to think that if Mrs Salden couldn't start her car she'd have walked to the village via a footpath. A torch is missing from her car and of course she'd be familiar with the terrain.'

'Probably, sir. It wouldn't take much more than five minutes.'

'Does this footpath run anywhere near where Harry Greenleaf lives?'

'Depends what you mean by near. He lives in that wood over there. The footpath runs direct to the village. I suppose it passes within, oh, let me see, perhaps four hundred yards of Harry's hut, as the crow flies.'

'I see. Fine. So we'll be able to kill two birds with one stone. Come on.'

'You want me to come too, sir?'

'Of course. To show us the way . . . And give me a chance to pick your brains, as well.'

Kimberley fell in alongside them with alacrity.

'You lead the way, then.'

'Right.'

Kimberley set off at a brisk pace along the broad path in front of the house and across the lawn beyond. Thanet inhaled appreciatively. It was good to be out in the open air on such a fresh spring morning. Fallen blossom from a flowering cherry tree lay scattered like confetti on the grass, a few tenacious clusters of the delicate sugar-pink petals still clinging obstinately to the branches which here and there were breaking into leaf.

Beyond the lawn Kimberley cut around the end of a border of tall shrubs and they came to a high hawthorn hedge on which the buds were just bursting into tender green, the dense thicket of spiky branches broken by a small flimsy rustic gate made of split chestnut palings and secured only by a metal hook and eye. Kimberley unhooked the latter and pushed it open.

'This is the footpath, sir.'

'Don't think much of their security,' muttered Lineham as they stepped through. The path was of beaten earth and although muddy after yesterday's rain was well-maintained, clear of weeds and encroaching branches. On the other side of it a stretch of open grass sloped gently up to the edge of the wood.

Thanet glanced to the right. 'I presume the footpath goes across to the Sturrenden road?'

'That's right, sir.'

'Used a lot, is it?'

Kimberley grimaced. 'That's a bit of a sore point locally. Mrs Salden has just closed it to the public.'

'Can she do that? I thought it was virtually impossible to close a public right of way.'

'Well, it was all gone into, as you can imagine. Apparently, if a specific route has been in regular use for in excess of twenty years, then that's it, a public right of way is presumed, *unless* there is a notice on the path saying Private, or Permitted Path. In which case, permission can be withdrawn at the owner's discretion.'

Thanet turned left and the others fell in, one on each side. 'I gather there is such a notice?'

Kimberley sighed. 'Oh yes. There's a rotting signboard at each end. They must have been there since the year dot. I don't think anyone's really noticed them for years but of course, when this business came up, we couldn't deny that they were there, even if they were barely legible. There was quite an uproar about it in the village, they even had a public meeting. There's no bus service through Telford Green any more, so people without cars have to walk to the Sturrenden road to catch a bus into the town. This footpath saves a good mile or more.'

'And now you say they're up in arms over this Harry Greenleaf business?'

'They certainly are. They can't see any reason why Harry should be made to go. He's absolutely harmless, never bothers anybody, just seems perfectly content to keep himself to himself. You'd hardly know he was there, really . . . To be honest, sir, Mrs Salden seems to have managed to stir up an awful lot of bad feeling in the time she's been here.'

'You're not telling me there's more?'

'Where would you like me to start?' said Kimberley with a grin.

'Good grief.' Thanet waved a hand. 'Wherever you like.'

'Well, the latest thing is Telford Green Farm.'

'What about it? Where is it?'

'Ah, well, that's the point. It's where it is that's caused the trouble.' Kimberley came to a halt and pointed. 'You see those farm buildings, over the other side of the river?'

Thanet and Lineham looked. The hawthorn hedge on their left had ended abruptly, giving way to open parkland across which in the distance could be seen the avenue of trees leading up to the Manor. Half a mile ahead of them in the shallow valley of the Teale lay the village of Telford Green, its mellow roofs strung out on both sides of the old stone bridge for which the footpath was obviously heading. It was almost certainly somewhere along this stretch of water that Marcia Salden had gone in. To the right the wood which Thanet by now thought of as 'Harry's Wood' curved gently away, petering out a couple of hundred yards short of the river. From here this was glimpsed merely as a sparkle of fast-flowing water between the trees and shrubs which lined its banks. In the open space between woodland and river was a small group of perhaps ten to fifteen people, all staring up in Thanet's direction. This, he realised, must be the welcoming committee prepared for the bailiffs, on Harry Greenleaf's behalf. Kimberley's request for reinforcements had been met; two uniformed policemen were standing by.

Thanet followed the direction of Kimberley's pointing finger. On the far side of the river, opposite Harry's Wood and between the line of village houses and the water, was a cluster of farm buildings surrounded by neatly fenced fields — empty fields, Thanet realised. The place, in fact, looked deserted.

'Old Mr Tiller died about six months ago,' said Kimberley, 'and Mrs Tiller sold up. Went to live with her daughter the other side of Sturrenden . . . You couldn't blame her, of course, for taking what she could get.'

'What do you mean?' said Lineham.

'Well, the village has never had a hall and they've been fund-raising for years and years. Apparently, if a village has no hall the County Council will help out with grants and loans to build one, but you've got to have a certain amount of money in hand and of course you've also got to have the land on which to put it, first. So the Parish Council negotiated with Mr Tiller for a piece of land behind the pub — the Crooked Door, look, you can see it there, right next to the bridge. It would have been an ideal spot, right in the centre of the village. But before the negotiations were complete Mr Tiller died. Everyone naturally thought that the deal would still go ahead, but unfortunately that was where Mrs Salden stepped in. As soon as the farm was put up for sale she offered to buy it well above the asking price, on one condition — that Mrs Tiller also sell her the piece of land earmarked for the village hall.' Kimberley shrugged. 'I suppose, as I said, you couldn't blame the old lady for accepting. It wasn't as if she was going to go on living here any more — and, to tell you the truth, I think she was in such a daze she didn't really realise what she was doing, it all happened so fast. Anyway, you can imagine how people in the village felt, when they heard.'

Two people, a man and a woman, had detached themselves from the group by the river and started up the slope towards Thanet. The man was carrying something bulky.

'But why was Mrs Salden so determined to get that one little bit of land?' said Lineham.

'Ever heard of Naboth's vineyard, Mike?' said Thanet with a grin.

'She made it quite clear why she wanted it, sir. She hoped to get planning permission to build over the entire farm. The village hall, she said, would lower the value of the properties — there's always a certain amount of noise from discos, cars starting up late at night and so on . . . A delegation from the Parish Council went to see her, and she was quite blunt about it. Wouldn't budge an inch, apparently.'

'She certainly seemed to have the knack of making herself unpopular, didn't she?' Had this knack extended to her personal relationships? Thanet wondered. If Marcia Salden had trampled carelessly all over the feelings of those closest to her in the same way as she had totally disregarded the local climate of opinion, it wasn't perhaps surprising that she had ended up in the river.

'Went out of her way looking for it, if you ask me,' said Lineham.

The bulky object, Thanet now saw, was a hand-held television camera. No doubt TVS had been told of the eviction and had come along to film the fun. There was no way that the film unit van could have gained access to the site of Harry's hut, he realised, without entering the Manor gates and driving across the open parkland of the Manor grounds. No doubt these two had decided to proceed on foot via the footpath from the bridge. For the first time he wondered how, if the hut was deep in the woods, the bulldozer would have got to it.

'Anyway, she'd never have got planning permission to build there, surely,' Lineham went on. 'I mean, it's prime agricultural land and outside the village envelope . . .'

'Hmm. I don't know,' said Thanet. 'Controls are not quite as strict as they used to be. And I remember my mother-in-law telling me that someone she knew of had got a planning permission everyone had thought was out of the question because he had donated part of the land to the community for a village hall and children's playground.'

'You think that's what Mrs Salden might have had in mind?' said Kimberley.

'Could be why she was so insistent on wanting that bit of land too. If she could swing the larger issue by appearing to be a public benefactor . . .'

Lineham was looking puzzled. 'I don't get it.'

'Well,' said Thanet, 'as I understand it, in order to get planning permission you have to get first the approval of the Parish Council, then of the Borough Council. I'm just saying that maybe Mrs Salden was determined to have the village hall site included in her purchase of the farm because she wanted later to be able to offer it as a gift to the Parish Council as an inducement to them to approve her application for planning permission on the rest of the land.'

'I see what you mean,' said Lineham. 'It would certainly be worth her while financially. How big is the farm?'

'Three hundred acres,' said Kimberley.

Lineham whistled. 'If she paid two thousand an acre and got — what? — a hundred thousand an acre, with planning permission . . .'

'Big money,' said Thanet. It had just occurred to him. Wasn't Lomax chairman of the borough planning committee? Surely, if Marcia had been hoping to influence him, she would have been more discreet than to invite him openly to her house? Suddenly that odd dinner party began to make rather unpleasant sense.

The girl reporter, wearing what she no doubt considered to be appropriate country gear of green wellies, Burberry and a checked scarf which matched the lining of her raincoat, reached them first.

'Tessa Barclay, TVS. Can you tell us what's happening?' She had selected PC Kimberley as being in charge, no doubt because of his uniform.

Perhaps, thought Thanet with amusement, she thought that he and Lineham were bailiffs. She was a good candidate for the small screen, with excellent bone structure, winning smile and pleasant manner. She must be new. He knew most of the regular TVS *Coast to Coast* reporters.

The photographer came puffing up beside her. 'Cor,' he said, patting the flabby flesh which hung over the waistband of his trousers, 'it really is time I started to lose some weight.'

He was older than the girl, in his forties, perhaps, and beginning to lose his hair.

The girl flashed him an impatient smile and turned back to PC Kimberley. 'Can you?'

Kimberley glanced at Thanet, who hesitated. He didn't really want to find himself giving a television interview on the subject of Marcia's death just yet. On the other hand, the villagers down there were not going to disperse without being given a good reason why the eviction had, temporarily at least, been postponed. 'There'll be no eviction today.'

'Why is that — sorry, Mr. . . ?'

Thanet sighed. 'Detective Inspector Thanet, Sturrenden CID.' He saw the hungry look flare in the girl's eyes as she scented news. She glanced at the man beside her and the camera swung up.

'What are you doing here, Inspector?'

He could give some evasive answer, of course, but she would no doubt find out about Marcia Salden later today in any case. And it was never wise to antagonise the media, particularly TVS, who were always very helpful towards the police, both in putting out bulletins when necessary and in *Police 5*, a weekly programme dedicated to solving crime by the reconstruction of past cases. 'Mrs Salden was found drowned this morning.'

The girl glanced down the slope at the river. 'Down there?'

'No, at Donnington Weir.'

'It was Mrs Salden who was going to evict Harry Greenleaf and bulldoze the little hut he built, and in which he has been living for ten years?'

She was spelling it out for her potential viewers, Thanet realised.

'Yes.'

'And you suspect foul play?'

'We suspect nothing and no one at the moment. All cases of sudden death have to be investigated, as you know. We are merely trying to find out how it happened.'

'And Mr Salden has called off the eviction?'

'Mr Salden is in no state to make any kind of decision, as you can imagine, or to deal with the kind of problems that might have arisen if the eviction had gone ahead. I gave the authorisation for the eviction to be postponed.'

'Postponed . . . Then does that mean. . . ?'

'I'm sorry. I really can't say any more at the moment. Excuse me.'

Thanet set off down the slope at a brisk pace, Lineham and Kimberley following. The cameraman trotted alongside him on one side, the girl on the other, alternately speaking into the microphone and holding it out in front of his face.

'Who found the body, Inspector?'

'Where, exactly, was it found?'

'What time was it found?'

Thanet stopped, turned to face her. 'Look, Miss Barclay . . .'

'Tessa,' said the girl, showing very white teeth in a ravishing smile.

'. . . I really cannot release any more information at the moment. And I have a great deal to do, so . . .'

'OK.' She shrugged, turning up her hands in a gesture of surrender. 'I give in. If we could interview you later. . . ?'

'Ring my office, late this afternoon,' said Thanet, privately resolving not to go anywhere near Headquarters at that time.

'Right.' Another melting smile. 'Thanks.'

She fell back, allowing Lineham and Kimberley to flank him once more.

Kimberley at once left the footpath and cut off diagonally down the slope. The villagers, Thanet noted, had disappeared. A minute or two later, he saw why. As he rounded the edge of the trees near the river he saw that to his right a long tongue of grassy meadow protruded into the wood. At its tip, some two hundred yards away where the trees began again, was a ramshackle wooden hut of tarred boards, with a corrugated iron roof. Harry's, no doubt. And now he saw where the people had gone. They had obviously assumed that he and Lineham were bailiffs. Strung out across the width of the meadow, sitting cross-legged on the ground, hands linked, they were waiting in silent protest for the confrontation to begin. Here and there a hand-held notice sprouted: HANDS OFF HARRY; HAL'S OUR PAL; JUSTICE NOT LAW.

Fleetingly, Thanet wondered how they had heard about the eviction. From Edith Phipps? From Marcia herself? (Unlikely, surely.) From Harry? For the first time he began to wonder what sort of man this was, that he could arouse such strong feelings of loyalty. Or was it simply that he had, by virtue of his peculiarly unfortunate circumstances, unwittingly enlisted the crackpots, the sensation-seekers and the misguided?

Thanet stopped, raised a hand in greeting to the two uniformed men waiting nearby and, cupping his hands around his mouth, called, 'All right, you can go home now. The eviction's been postponed.'

A buzz of excitement ran along the line, like lightning conducted through their linked hands. But no one moved.

'It's true.' Thanet waved a hand. 'You all know PC Kimberley. Ask him.'

'Is it, Jack?' shouted one of the men in the middle of the line, a stringy man in his sixties, wearing (symbolically?) a combat jacket and ancient corduroys.

Kimberley nodded. 'True enough.'

Looks were exchanged, then the line broke up as people began to struggle to their feet.

Their self-appointed spokesman was the first to reach them.

'Why?' he demanded. 'What made 'er change 'er mind? Get cold feet, did she?'

'You'll wish you hadn't said that, Dan,' said Kimberley. He raised an eyebrow at Thanet, who nodded. 'This is Detective Inspector Thanet, Sturrenden CID. Mrs Salden is dead.'

The word caused a sudden hush, and an uneasy exchange of glances. Most of the villagers, Thanet noted, were either pensioners or middle-aged women, with a sprinkling of presumably unemployed youths.

The man's hairy eyebrows met in a fierce frown. 'Dead, you say?'

Kimberley nodded. 'She was pulled out of the river at Donnington Weir this morning.'

''Ow did it 'appen?'

'Your guess is as good as mine. But as Inspector Thanet says, there'll be no eviction today. You can all go home.'

However anti-Marcia they had been, the news had subdued

them and they began to drift off in twos and threes. The man called Dan, however, began to march purposefully off up the slope towards Greenleaf's hut.

'Just a moment,' Thanet said.

The man halted. 'I was only going to tell 'Arry. It does concern 'im, you know.'

Thanet ignored the sarcasm. 'I'll do it myself.'

The man's lips tightened but he said nothing, turning away and hurrying to catch up with some of the others.

'Right, the excitement's over,' said Thanet to the uniformed policemen. 'You can get off back to Headquarters. Have you seen any of my team?'

'Only in the distance, working along the river bank.'

'Where are they now, do you know?'

'They only came a short distance from the village, then turned back.'

It looked as though they might have found something. 'Tell them I'll be along shortly, will you? I just want a word with Greenleaf, first. Kimberley, I'd like you to stay with us for the time being.'

'Sir . . .' said Kimberley as they started up the grassy slope to Harry's hut.

'What?'

'I just thought you might like to know . . .'

'Well? Come on, spit it out, man.'

'I saw Mr Salden last night.'

Thanet stopped walking. 'Oh, where?'

'In the pub. Must have been somewhere between half-past eight and nine.'

'Was he alone?'

'Yes. Looked a bit down, I thought.'

'Does he often go to the pub?'

Kimberley shrugged. 'From time to time.'

'By himself?'

'Usually. But he'll have a pint and a chat. Last night he . . . Well, he gave out the impression that he didn't want to be sociable. Nothing was said, but it was interesting that apart from saying hello, people gave him a wide berth. And I noticed he was drinking whisky. Doubles.'

'Don't miss much, do you?'

Kimberley grinned. 'Try not to, sir.'

'He'd just have come from his mother-in-law's house,' said Lineham. 'Remember, he said he went out for a walk.'

'Yes . . . Did anyone in the pub comment, Kimberley?'

The policeman shrugged. 'I imagine they just assumed, as I did, that he was upset because of Mrs Carter. It was common knowledge that he was very fond of her — his own mother's long dead, I believe — and she thought the sun shone out of his eyes, by all accounts.'

'They wouldn't have thought he'd had a row with his wife?'

'No, I'm pretty sure not. I haven't heard any rumours in that direction.'

'How long did he stay in the pub?'

'Not much more than twenty minutes, I'd say.'

'And he had how many drinks?'

Kimberley thought. 'Three.'

Thanet turned and began walking up the slope again. 'What's he like?'

'I don't know him that well, but he's pretty well liked in the village.'

'Unlike his wife.'

'Yes. I don't know if you realised, sir, but Mrs Salden was a local girl.'

'Miss Phipps told me.'

'I think people found it difficult to accept her as lady of the manor, so to speak. And she made it worse by not making any attempt to enter village life. I mean, she didn't come to church or take part in any village events, or offer the Manor grounds for the village fête, or buy her groceries at the village shop . . . And of course, there's been all that trouble over the footpath and the village hall and now over Harry. Mr Salden is a different matter — he's on the PCC, gives a hand at village events . . .'

'And patronises the village pub,' Thanet said absent-mindedly. His attention was now focussed on the hut, about twenty yards away.

Throughout the brief conversation with Kimberley he had been keeping an eye on the primitive structure, but had so far

47

detected no sign of life. It was about fifteen feet long, the boarded wall punctuated only by a window festooned with what looked like an old army blanket. In front a neat little vegetable patch had been carved out of the meadow: weedless rows of spring cauliflowers and sprouting broccoli and a seedbed with a row of fluttering seed packets at one end stood as mute testimony to the care lavished upon it. Over to the left, tethered by a long rope to a stout post hammered into the ground, was a goat, and to the right of the hut was a wired-off enclosure where chickens scratched in the earth around a large chicken hut.

The door, which was on the right-hand side of the hut, facing the chickens, was shut and padlocked. They looked around, but there was no other entrance, the window was not made to open and any view of the interior was obscured by the blanket.

'He's gone, then,' said Lineham.

Their eyes met, each knowing what the other was thinking. Had Harry left because of the bailiffs, or because he was implicated in Marcia's death?

Beside the door was a worm-eaten Windsor armchair with broken slats, its surface bleached grey by exposure to wind and rain. Thanet could imagine the old man sitting in it, gazing contentedly down the slope to the river and across to the rising land on the other side. His seemed a harmless enough existence. Why had Marcia been so determined to get rid of him?

SIX

'We think we've found where she went in, sir.' Swift was looking very pleased with himself.

It was half an hour later. Thanet had decided that, in view of the fact that Harry no doubt knew the woods like the back of his hand, it would be a waste of time for just three of them to search for him, so they had retraced their steps to the footpath, then continued on to the village. Swift had come to meet them.

Ahead of them to the left of the bridge the high brick wall which edged the grounds of the Manor delineated the road to the village. At this end of the bridge, near an ominous gap in the parapet, the rest of Thanet's men were awaiting his arrival. A number of people, many of whom Thanet recognised as Harry Greenleaf's supporters, were lined up along the parapet at the far end, gaping at the policemen.

'I assume you're talking about the broken parapet.' Thanet glanced at Kimberley. He had been impressed by the local man and was surprised and slightly disappointed that such an obvious possibility had not been put forward. Kimberley flushed and opened his mouth to speak, but Swift forestalled him.

'Yes, sir. A heavy lorry skidded into the wall in all that rain yesterday, apparently.'

They had reached a short flight of stone steps leading up on to the road at the damaged end of the bridge, and Thanet stopped to take a good look. The parapet was of Kentish ragstone and a section about five feet long had been broken clean off, right down to road level. The chunk of masonry which had fallen out was visible in the river below.

'Hope it's not going to be another "Did she fall or was she pushed?" case,' muttered Lineham, gazing up at the gap.

He was referring, Thanet knew, to the Tarrant case, a murder they had solved the previous year in which the wife of an eminent local surgeon had fallen to her death from the balcony of her bedroom.

'Somewhat different circumstances, Mike.'

Kimberley was now very much on the defensive. 'Sir . . . I personally checked the safety precautions after the incident with the lorry yesterday. You can come and see for yourself. The Highways Authority put up a temporary barrier and promised to give priority to the repairs, to come back today if possible.'

They climbed up on to the road.

'Look, there's a POLICE ACCIDENT sign, and a big DANGER sign on the road at both approaches to the bridge, warning lamps around the gap and a temporary barrier — '

Kimberley broke off, and it was obvious why. Two metal rods had been driven into the road, one on either side of the gap, and ropes had been strung between them, one at the top, one halfway up. The latter must have been carelessly attached; one end was trailing loose, exposing a three-foot gap.

'Not your fault,' said Thanet, after a glance at Kimberley's appalled expression.

'I should have checked this morning.'

'You had your hands full, with Harry Greenleaf's eviction. And the erection of the barrier was not your responsibility.'

'All the same . . .'

Thanet squatted to examine the gap more closely. Halfway down the broken section of wall a solitary spike of rock stuck out, some five inches long. Caught in a split in it were some long blonde hairs and its tip was discoloured by a brownish stain. He peered down into the river below. At the edge of the water, at the bottom of the river bank, was a woman's brown walking shoe.

Marcia Salden's?

It certainly seemed likely that this was where she had met her death.

Thanet stood back and tried to visualise what had

happened. Was it possible that it had been a simple accident? Surely not. Anyone walking across the bridge from the village towards the entrance to the footpath in the dark would obviously have to be careful, yes, but Marcia would have known of the danger; she would have seen the damage and the warning lights on her way to her mother's cottage. Unless the accident had happened while she was there, of course. He turned to Kimberley and asked the obvious question.

'At 4 p.m. yesterday afternoon, sir.'

'And it took you how long to get it sorted out?'

'A couple of hours.'

So the temporary barriers would have been up by about six. Thanet glanced at Lineham. 'What do you think, Mike?'

'I really don't see how she could have fallen in by accident. Those red lights are a good three feet out into the road.'

'She could have stepped back to avoid a car?'

'Only a lunatic would drive fast over this bridge, especially at the moment, with all these warning signs.'

'Oh come on, Mike. There are plenty of lunatics about, as we know too well.'

'True. But surely anyone walking across this bridge and knowing about that gap in the parapet is going to be hyper-careful. He probably wouldn't even walk on that side of the road.'

'Unless he – or she, as we're talking about Mrs Salden – had to pass that gap, in order to get to the top of the steps leading down to the footpath.'

'Even so . . .'

'And the road might well have been icy, remember, Mike. The temperature dropped like a stone last night, and after all that rain . . .'

'Well, I suppose it's just possible she could have slipped,' said Lineham doubtfully. 'But one thing's certain. If anyone wanted to get rid of her, he would have had the perfect opportunity, with the parapet down and a slippery road surface. One little shove and she'd be gone.'

'Yes, well, obviously we'll have to go on considering the possibility, so we'd better go through the motions and get the rest of the team out. The CCTV team as well as the SOCOs.

They've been warned they might be needed.' His stomach gave a loud, protesting rumble and he glanced at his watch. A quarter to four. He'd had no idea it was so late.

'Have you all had something to eat?'

'We took it in turns to have sandwiches in the pub.'

'Sir . . .' It was Kimberley. 'If you and the Sergeant would like a bite . . . I'm sure my wife wouldn't mind rustling up a few sandwiches.'

'You're sure?' It was a tempting thought. Thanet suspected that they would be here for hours yet and the pub wouldn't be open again until six.

'Absolutely.'

Thanet issued his instructions: house to house enquiries were to begin, and the river bank was to be searched when the SOCOs and CCTV crew had finished. A couple of divers were to search the river bed and Mrs Pantry asked if she could identify the shoe. Also, someone must fetch his car and Kimberley's motorcycle from the Manor. 'We'll walk to your house. I want to take a closer look at the village.'

Most of Telford Green lay on the far side of the bridge. Only a few cottages straggled back along the road opposite the boundary wall of the Manor. Behind them lay open fields through which the Teale rushed eagerly towards its union with the Sture.

Once past the bridge, the road widened. On the right the pub, the Crooked Door, lived up to its name, the hinges on the front door sloping downwards in a way reminiscent of the famous door of the old King's School shop in Canterbury. The black and white building itself was equally eccentric, with every wall out of true and a roof which looked in imminent danger of collapse. Thanet suspected that this quaintness had been carefully nurtured as an attraction to customers, and Kimberley confirmed this. Behind it, well-tended lawns optimistically sprinkled with benches and parasolled tables led down to the river.

Facing the pub was the village green, the road dividing to sweep around it in a half-circle and join up again further on. On the far side of the expanse of rough grass was the church, flanked on one side by a couple of large detached houses, one of which was presumably the vicarage, and on the other by a row of pretty brick and tile-hung cottages with white picket fences and well-tended gardens.

On the right past the pub were two short rows of terraced cottages, with four houses in each. In the second cottage of the first terrace, Kimberley told them, had lived Mrs Carter, Marcia Salden's mother. It stood out by virtue of its well-groomed air – its crisp paintwork, newly pointed brickwork and neat front garden now a mass of many-coloured wall-flowers. Their sweet, musky scent, liberated by the sun, drifted out to greet the policemen as they passed. All eight cottages had once belonged to Telford Green Farm, having been built for the men who worked on it, but Marcia had bought her mother's cottage from Mr Tiller some years ago – at a grossly inflated price, rumour had it. The rest of the cottages were still tenanted and now presumably belonged to Bernard Salden. Just beyond them was a narrow metalled road leading to the farm – Thanet could just glimpse the conical roof of an oast house with its white-painted cowl sticking up beyond some trees. Beyond the green, on both sides of the road, were some rather larger houses, a mixture of old and new, the latter, Thanet guessed, having been built in the gardens of the former, this being the only possible way these days to acquire building plots in rural areas. The village ended with the usual cul-de-sac of council houses. Opposite them was the police house, a typically unimaginative square brick box, with a noticeboard outside.

Mrs Kimberley, a plump little woman with a frizz of black hair and bright dark eyes welcomed them warmly and half an hour later, fortified by roast beef and pickles with homemade bread, Thanet and Lineham set off with renewed enthusiasm to interview Nurse Lint.

From some distance away they could see that a hearse was parked in front of old Mrs Carter's cottage, and as they approached two men carried a canvas stretcher bag out of the front door, deposited their burden in the van and drove off.

'The undertakers,' said Lineham.

'Mmm. The doctor must already have been and signed the death certificate.'

53

A woman in nurse's uniform had been standing at the front gate gazing after the departing vehicle and now she went back into the cottage and shut the door. A minute or two later, when she answered Thanet's knock, he could see that she had been crying.

'Mrs Lint?'

'Miss.'

He introduced himself and Lineham and she stood back. 'Come in.'

The front door led directly into a small sitting-room with a brightly patterned brown, orange and yellow carpet, green curtains and a mustard-coloured settee and matching armchair. Thanet wondered how people could stand the effect of so much pattern and colour in so small a space. He found it overwhelming, claustrophobic, even.

She blew her nose and perched on the edge of the chair, gesturing at the settee. 'Do sit down.'

'Thank you.'

Thanet could see that she was making an effort to compose herself. She was much younger than he had expected. He had visualised a plump, matronly woman, a widow perhaps, whose children had grown up and moved away and was therefore free to devote all her time to a patient. Nursing someone terminally ill in a village miles from anywhere wouldn't have much appeal for most young people. Presumably this girl preferred to work in a one-to-one situation. She was in her late twenties and woefully plain, with lank brown hair caught back at the nape of her neck with an elastic band, and metal-rimmed glasses.

'It's about Mrs Salden's death, I suppose. Miss Phipps rang . . .'

'Yes. We're trying to find out what happened – ' He broke off. 'What's that?' There was a scratching sound at the door which presumably led to the kitchen.

'Oh, that's Spot. Mrs Carter's dog. He's upset, he knows something's wrong. I don't know what I'm going to do with him. D'you mind if I let him in?'

'Not at all. Perhaps,' Thanet added as she got up and opened the door, 'Mr Salden will take him.'

54

It was a mournful-looking spaniel, ears down and tail drooping. It followed Nurse Lint back to her chair and flopped down beside her, burying its nose in its paws.

'Possibly. But I don't feel I can bother him at a time like this; he'll have enough to worry about as it is.' She rubbed her eyes wearily before leaning over to stroke the dog's head. 'Perhaps Mrs Pepper will look after you for a few days, eh, boy? At least you're used to her.'

'Mrs Pepper?'

'Mrs Carter's friend. She lives next door. She used to take over, from time to time, so that I could get out. They're old friends, they've known each other for years.'

She stroked the dog for a moment or two longer, then looked up at Thanet. 'I'm sorry, what were you saying?'

'Only that we're trying to work out Mrs Salden's movements last night. She came here to visit her mother, I believe?'

'That's right.'

'What time did she arrive?'

The girl frowned. 'I'm not sure.' She rubbed her eyes again. 'Sorry, I didn't get much sleep last night.'

'So I gathered. Surely you're not on duty night and day?'

A shadow of a smile. 'More or less.'

'But that's ridiculous!'

'No, not really. It's not as bad as it sounds. In fact Mrs Carter didn't need a lot of attention during the night. And she was a very easy patient, a real sweetie, so looking after her wasn't the strain it sometimes is.'

'You were fond of her.'

'It's difficult to live with someone as nice as she is for nearly a year and not get fond of them. Oh, I know nurses aren't supposed to become emotionally involved with their patients, but when there's only one, and you spend all your time with her . . . It's easier said than done.'

'I can imagine . . . Look, it really is rather important that we work out the timings of Mrs Salden's movements last night. Perhaps it would help you to remember if you started earlier in the evening, and worked on from, say, when you rang Mr Salden, to tell him Mrs Carter wanted to see him. That wasn't unusual, I understand?'

'Oh, no. She was very fond of Mr Salden, he was more of a son . .. more like a son than a son-in-law.'

Had she been going to say 'more of a son than Mrs Salden was a daughter'? Thanet wondered.

'And he of her, I believe.'

'Yes. Mind, she didn't often actually ask him to come. He used to call in regularly anyway, so there was no need.'

'When did he last come, before yesterday?'

'The previous day. Yes, he was here at teatime.'

'Do you know what she wanted to see him about last night?'

'No.' She hesitated. 'She'd been restless all afternoon. I think she knew, really, that she was near the end.' She bit her lip. 'I think she just wanted to say goodbye.'

'To him and not to her daughter?'

She shook her head. 'She knew Mrs Salden had a dinner party, and she wouldn't have wanted to upset that. She was . . . proud, like that. Hated to ask.'

'She was prepared to ask Mr Salden.'

'Yes.' Miss Lint considered. 'I know it sounds odd if you didn't know her, but she was like that, where Mrs Salden was concerned. I imagine she probably thought that if Mr Salden saw how poorly she was he'd go back and tell Mrs Salden and she would come.'

'You're saying it was an indirect means of getting her daughter to come?'

'Yes. Don't misunderstand me, Mrs Salden was very good to her, bought her this house, I understand, and made sure she had everything she could possibly want . . . Including,' she finished, with an attempt at a smile, 'me.' She leant over to pat the dog again. 'Didn't she, Spot?'

Thanet returned the smile, glad to see that the girl was becoming a little less stiff. And now indeed she did relax, sitting back in the chair for the first time and leaning her head against the back. She looked very tired. The last twenty-four hours must have been a strain.

'And of course that is precisely what did happen, isn't it?'

She frowned. 'Well, not exactly. By the time Mr Salden got

here, Mrs Carter had drifted off to sleep, and he didn't want to wake her up. So he hung around until she did wake.'

'Perhaps we could just recap a little. What time did Mr Salden arrive?'

'I rang the Manor at twenty past seven. I remember that, because I looked at the clock. I was wondering if he'd have time to get down and back before the guests arrived. And he came straight away, so he must have got here about half-past. Unfortunately, as I said, Mrs Carter had dropped off to sleep by then. I told him I was sure she wouldn't mind if he woke her up – she had been asking for him, after all, but he said no, he'd wait. He'd promised to ring Mrs Salden at eight, so he did. I heard him say not to wait dinner.' She glanced at the telephone, which stood on a small table near the door to the kitchen. 'I couldn't help hearing. This is a very small house.'

Thanet nodded. 'So then what happened?'

'Mrs Carter went on sleeping for a little while longer, another twenty minutes, perhaps, and then she rang the bell. She has – had – an electric buzzer, Mrs Salden had it put in for her. Mr Salden had come downstairs and I'd made him a coffee, while he waited. I went upstairs, to make sure she was all right, and she asked if he'd come. I said yes, and she asked me to fetch him. So I did.'

'How long was he with her?'

'A quarter of an hour or so. When he came down he was upset, I could tell. He looked sort of . . . as if he was trying hard not to show what he was feeling, you know what I mean? He didn't say anything, just grabbed his coat and went out. To be honest, I thought he might be going to cry and wanted to get out of the house quickly, so I wouldn't see. Men don't like crying in front of women, do they? I know that, from other jobs I've done.'

Thanet remembered what Kimberley had told him. In fact, Salden must have gone straight to the pub.

'What did you do then?'

'I went up to make sure Mrs Carter was all right. She was sleeping again.'

'Did you expect Mr Salden to come back?'

She shrugged. 'I suppose I half thought he might. I

wondered if he might go and fetch Mrs Salden, but he didn't, apparently. When she rang at half nine she hadn't heard from him. He told me later he'd been walking. Said he wanted to come back later to see how Mrs Carter was, and couldn't face going home and being sociable in between.'

'What did Mrs Salden say, when she rang?'

'She asked to speak to her husband.'

'I'm afraid he's not here, Mrs Salden.'

'Not here? What time did he leave?'

'About three quarters of an hour ago.'

'Did he say where he was going?'

'No. I'm sorry. I assumed he was going home . . . He seemed rather upset.'

'About my mother?'

'Yes. She . . . I'm afraid she doesn't look too good.'

'Oh God. You think I ought to come down?'

'It's up to you, Mrs Salden.'

'Does she look any worse than she has before, when we've . . . When she's been OK, afterwards?'

'It's awfully difficult to judge. But I am quite worried about her.'

'I'd better pop down. Just for a few minutes, to see for myself. I'll be there in five minutes.'

'And was she?' said Thanet.

'No. Nearer ten or fifteen, I'd say. She had to walk. Her car wouldn't start, she said.'

'Did you tell Mr Salden that?'

'No. Should I have?'

'I just wondered . . . So she came via the footpath?'

'She didn't say. I assume so. It would have taken her much longer, if she'd walked all the way down the Manor drive and along the road.'

'So she must have arrived at what time? Around a quarter to ten?'

'I suppose so, yes.'

'How long did she stay?'

'Getting on for half an hour, I should think.'

'Until a quarter past ten, then?'

'Must have been. Perhaps Mrs Pepper can be more precise.'

'She was here?'

'She popped in five minutes or so before Mrs Salden left. She stayed about half an hour till around a quarter to eleven.'

'If Mrs Carter was as ill as that, why didn't Mrs Salden stay longer?'

'I think she thought it was another false alarm . . . We've had a number of them. And on the face of it there wasn't really much point in her staying. Her mother was asleep when she got here, and didn't wake up all the while she was here.'

'And then Mr Salden got back, I gather?'

'That's right. Not long after she left.'

'How long, do you think?'

Nurse Lint put up a hand and began to massage her right temple. 'Sorry, I've got a bit of a headache . . .' She frowned, her mouth turning down at the corners. 'Ten or fifteen minutes?'

Perhaps Mrs Pepper could confirm that. And if so . . . Sitting close to Lineham on the small settee, arms touching, Thanet was aware of the involuntary tremor of excitement which had passed through the Sergeant's body. He knew what Lineham was thinking. If Marcia Salden had left only ten or fifteen minutes before her husband arrived back, it was quite feasible that they could have passed each other on the bridge. Say that they quarrelled . . .

'Bernard! Where the hell have you been?'

'I went for a walk.'

'A walk?'

'I repeat, a walk. I was . . . upset.'

'Look, I didn't mind you deserting our guests to visit my mother . . .'

'I should hope not!'

'. . . but I think it's a bit much to spend the rest of the evening going for a walk!'

'Oh, you do, do you? May I ask where you're going now?'

'Home, of course.'

'I see. Home. We mustn't be rude to our guests, of course,

even if our mother is dying. My God, if they had any sensitivity they'd have taken themselves off hours ago.'

'As a matter of fact they offered to leave, but I asked them to stay on. And aren't you being a little melodramatic? If we dropped everything, cancelled everything, every time my mother rings up, we'd have given up living our own lives a year ago, and camped on her doorstep. Anyway, you know perfectly well that after all the false alarms we've had we agreed to take it in turns to sit up with her. And in case you've forgotten, it happens to be your turn.'

'No, I hadn't forgotten. But this isn't just another false alarm.'

'How can you be so sure?'

'It just isn't. I know it, she knows it, Nurse Lint knows it . . .'

'What nonsense! How can you possibly "know".'

'Please, Marcia, I'm serious. Let's sit up with her together tonight.'

'Look, I left her just a few moments ago, and she was sleeping peacefully . . . Let go of my arm, please.'

'Marcia, I am dead serious. I want you to come with me. Please?'

'No! I'm going home. I asked Josie to wait till I got back.'

'Never mind Josie. You can ring her from the cottage.'

'How many times have we been through this? It's pointless both of us staying . . .'

'Marcia . . .'

'Let go of my arm.'

'Please . . .'

'Let go, will you?'

'Marcia? Marcia? Oh, my God . . .'

Thanet blinked. The whole conversation had been so convincing that it was difficult to believe he had imagined it. Words hung in the air, and both Nurse Lint and Lineham were staring at him. 'Sorry?'

'I said, I told him he'd just missed his wife.'

'What did he say?'

'He asked me how long she'd stayed, and whether Mrs

60

Carter had woken up while Mrs Salden was here. I said no, she hadn't, which was why Mrs Salden only stayed half an hour or so, then decided to go home.'

'Did you tell him Mrs Salden's car wouldn't start, and she'd had to walk down?'

'No. He was already halfway up the stairs by then, and I went into the kitchen. Mrs Pepper was making a pot of tea. A minute later he came down again and made a phone call.'

'You heard what was said?'

'No. Mrs Pepper was clattering cups and saucers. But he came into the kitchen when he'd finished and said he'd rung home to say he was going to stay on here . . . He sat up with Mrs Carter until she died, you know.'

'What time was that?'

'Twenty-five to four. All those hours, he just sat there, holding her hand . . .'

'When he told you he'd rung home, did he say that he'd had to leave a message for Mrs Salden because she hadn't yet arrived back?'

'No.' *Why should he?* her expression said.

Why, indeed? Nurse Lint was his employee. He owed her no such explanations.

And of course he wouldn't have wanted to draw attention to Marcia's absence, if he'd known that she was already at the bottom of the river.

SEVEN

As they emerged from the front door of Mrs Carter's cottage a loud backfire from across the green, followed by a throaty roar and a cloud of exhaust smoke, caused Lineham to pause and click his tongue in disapproval. Putting his hand up to shade his eyes, he squinted in that direction.

Apart from that brief frisson of excitement a few minutes ago, when they had realised that Bernard Salden had been in the right place at the right time to have murdered his wife, this was the first spontaneous sign of animation that the Sergeant had shown all day. He had functioned efficiently, true, but his enthusiasm, one of his most endearing qualities, had been conspicuous by its absence and Thanet was beginning to find his unnatural silence unnerving. What on earth could be the matter?

For the second time today he decided to try to find out.

'Mike, are you sure you're all right?'

'Yes, fine, thanks.' A brief, flickering glance. *How much does he know?*

Come on, Luke, Thanet told himself. You're imagining things. What could Lineham possibly have to hide? The most obvious answer was marital problems. Louise, Lineham's wife, was anything but easy to live with. Bossy and demanding, when they married she had taken over where Lineham's domineering mother had left off. It was a mystery to Thanet why the Sergeant should have chosen a wife so similar in nature to the mother whose rule he had found so irksome. Presumably there was something in him that needed to be dominated — or at least needed to kick against being dominated. In any case, Thanet had no intention of prying. If

62

Lineham wanted to confide in him, well and good; if not, there was nothing he could do about it.

The offending car was heading in their direction and now screeched to a halt by Mrs Carter's gate, belching noxious fumes. It was, Thanet saw, an ancient Mini, painted what Ben would have called puke green, and it was driven by the Vicar.

'Afternoon, Inspector, Sergeant.' Fothergill glanced at their faces and clowned disappointment. 'Don't you like her?' He stuck his arm out of the car window and patted its flank. 'Don't be insulted, old girl, they're just jealous.' Then he put his hand up to his mouth and hissed. 'Don't want to upset her, just got her back from the garage.'

Thanet had been wondering how they could possibly have missed noticing this car up at the Manor this morning. All was now explained. Fothergill must have gone up on foot or by bicycle, the 'old girl' being out of action at the time.

'Got her *back*!' said Lineham.

'Certainly. Have to maintain an appropriately poverty-stricken image, you know, Sergeant. Doesn't do for the clergy to appear too affluent, people don't like it.'

'There must be a happy medium,' said Thanet, smiling.

'This is it.' Fothergill's expression changed. 'How's it going?'

'Slowly. Nothing definite yet. Except that we think we know where she went into the river.'

Fothergill nodded. 'The broken parapet. It did cross my mind, this morning. But the warnings and barriers were so obvious I didn't really consider it a serious possibility. Though the road was very icy last night . . . You're satisfied that it was an accident, then?'

'We still have to try and find out exactly what happened, if anyone saw her, and so on,' said Thanet, neatly side-stepping. The manoeuvre had not been missed by Fothergill, he noticed. The Vicar was no fool.

'Yes, well . . . I did what I could for Bernard Salden, by the way. He'd calmed down by the time I left. I got his doctor to come and take a look at him and he gave him a sedative. I gather the undertakers have been to collect Mrs Carter. We've postponed making the arrangements for her funeral until tomorrow or the next day.'

'Very sensible.'

'Well, better get on. Got a meeting in Maidstone.'

And with a smile and a wave he was off, leaving a trail of black smoke behind him.

Thanet and Lineham stepped back to avoid the fumes, waving their hands in front of their faces and coughing.

'Ought to be in the scrapyard, if you ask me,' said Lineham. 'I'm sure we could get him for public nuisance.'

'If we didn't have better things to do, Mike. Come on, I want a word with Mrs Pepper.' Thanet had high hopes of Mrs Pepper. If she and Mrs Carter had been friends for as long as Nurse Lint seemed to think, the old lady might be able to fill him in on Marcia's background.

This cottage, being tenanted, was not in such good structural repair as Mrs Carter's next door, but the little front garden was ablaze with the purple spires of honesty and regimented rows of pink and scarlet tulips. A straggling bush of *Kerria japonica*, most of its yellow globes now faded, was tied up against the wall between door and window. There was not a weed to be seen.

The woman who answered the door looked as though she would have no problem in buying her clothes from the children's sections of department stores. She was well under five feet tall and although she must have been in her late sixties was wearing what Bridget would call a jumpsuit, an all-in-one sort of tracksuit in vivid green with orange trimmings at shoulders and neck. Her hair was dyed orange. To match? Thanet was relieved to see that her eyes were bright, her manner alert. Excellent. She should make a good witness.

Formalities over, she led them into the sitting-room. It was immediately obvious that Mrs Pepper had two passions: indoor plants and crochet. The former all but obscured the light from the window, scrambled up the walls and trailed from the numerous containers suspended from the overhead beams, and the latter greeted the eye wherever it happened to fall, in gaily coloured circular woollen cushion covers crocheted in concentric rings, lacy white antimacassars on the backs of chairs and little round mats on every horizontal surface. Mrs Pepper had evidently found a solution to the problem which dogs every such hobby, that of what to do with the end product: on a table in the window were perhaps a dozen piles of crocheted squares in different colours.

'Blankets,' she said, following his gaze. 'For Age Concern. They're always desperate for them, come January.'

She insisted on providing them with a cup of tea. There was one in the pot, she assured them, she'd just made some for herself. A steaming cup on the arm of the chair beside the fireplace confirmed this. Finally they were all seated, sipping.

'Very welcome, Mrs Pepper,' said Lineham.

'Nothing like a nice cup of tea, I always say . . . I suppose you've come about Marcia – Mrs Salden. I've seen your men about all over the village.'

'That's right, yes. We understand you saw her briefly last night.'

'When I went next door to see Win – Mrs Carter, that is. Yes.' Mrs Pepper's mouth quivered and she set down her cup, picked up a large ball of green wool with a crochet hook stuck through it and began to work. 'You don't mind? It helps to keep my mind off . . .' She compressed her lips and shook her head fiercely as if to frighten grief away. 'Win – Mrs Carter – and me had been friends for getting on for fifty years.'

'That's a very long time,' said Thanet gently.

'It certainly is. I can hardly imagine life without her . . . Yes, I did see Marcia last night.'

'I don't suppose you realise this, but in fact you must have been one of the last people to see her alive.'

'Really?' The crochet needle was temporarily stilled as she took this in.

It didn't take long to check that the information Nurse Lint had given them was correct: Marcia had been at the cottage when Mrs Pepper arrived, and had left about five minutes later, at a quarter past ten. Mrs Pepper was fairly sure of the time because she had watched the headlines on *News at Ten* before going next door. Bernard Salden had arrived about ten or fifteen minutes after his wife left. His car had been parked outside all evening, since half-past seven or so, and had stayed there until a quarter to four in the morning. She had looked at her clock when she heard the engine start up – she hadn't been able to sleep because she had been worried about Win and feared that his departure in the early hours could mean that her friend had died. In the past, when Bernard had sat up with his mother-in-law, he had always stayed all night.

'Really loved her, he did. Like she was his own mum. He'll be ever so upset . . . And now this, with Marcia. Poor Bernard, I feel really sorry for him. He hasn't had much luck.'

'Oh, I don't know. He doesn't seem to have done too badly up to now,' put in Lineham.

She sniffed. 'Oh, him and Marcia have done very well in their business, I grant you that, but money isn't everything, it don't bring you happiness, do it?'

Knowing the value of silence, Thanet said nothing, praying that Lineham would also keep quiet. He was well aware that if he appeared too curious Mrs Pepper might well clam up, whereas nothing encourages confidences more than a sympathetic and attentive listener.

It worked.

'No,' she said, answering her own question. 'It don't. And Bernard's had a lot of bad luck. I mean, we all have to go through it, don't we, one way or the other, none of us can get away without losing someone we love, but Bernard . . . His parents were both killed when he was just a young lad, you know, and he didn't have no brothers or sisters, neither, so he was all alone, with no one to fall back on. But he stuck to his studies and got his accountant's exams, and got married – no, not to Marcia, he was married before, you know. But they'd only been married a couple of years and she died, having a baby. Hardly ever happens these days, of course, but this was over thirty years ago. The baby was still-born. Win told me all this later, when the other little girl died. I don't know why I'm telling you all this.'

Thanet ignored this last remark. Mrs Pepper, he knew, was now well launched, and needed only a guarantee of her audience's interest to continue. 'Other little girl?'

'Him and Marcia's. So you see what I mean, don't you? He seems to lose everyone he loves, his parents, his first wife, his first baby, his second baby, his mother-in-law what he loved like a son, his second wife . . .'

It was indeed an appalling catalogue of death.

She shook her head. 'I don't know how he survives, I'm sure.'

'I didn't know he and Mrs Salden had had a baby.'

'Oh yes, they did. Clare, she was called. Well, I don't suppose there's many around here would even know about her or care if they did, but I know because I went to the funeral.'

Their rapt attention encouraged her to elaborate and she stuck the needle back in the ball of green wool and laid down her work.

'You see, what happened was this. When Marcia and Bernard got married – she was only eighteen at the time, and pretty as a picture. A lovely bride she was, I went to the wedding. Got a picture somewhere . . .' She looked vaguely around as if it might materialise, but made no effort to get up and show it to them, she was too engrossed in her story.

Thanet would have liked to see it, to have looked upon that dead face when it was still young and vital with all life's promise still untapped, but he was afraid of disturbing the flow of reminiscence. It was clear that, like so many elderly people, Mrs Pepper rarely had such a receptive audience and that on this particular occasion she especially welcomed the opportunity to be distracted for a short while from her grief over her friend's death.

'Anyway, like I said, when they got married they moved up North. Bernard had been a lecturer, see, at the college where Marcia went to night school. He was one of her teachers, and of course it would have been a bit awkward for him to stay on there, marrying one of his students and all that. I don't suppose people'd pay all that much attention nowadays, but things was different then. So he got himself a job up North and it wasn't long before Marcia fell for the baby. I don't think she was too pleased at first, it being so quick and all, but of course she soon got used to the idea, like they all do, and the following year the little girl was born. Bernard was like a dog with two tails, Win said, absolutely over the moon. He's always loved kids and of course, with his first one being still-born . . . Well, you can imagine, can't you?

'Anyway, a couple of months later he was sent abroad by his firm, and while he was away, the baby died.'

Mrs Pepper paused for an appropriate reaction.

Thanet had no problem in showing his very real sympathy for the man. 'That's terrible. What happened?'

'She got pneumonia. But the worst of it was, Bernard couldn't come home for the funeral. He'd been in a car crash and fractured his pelvis and he was stuck in hospital abroad for months. And Win couldn't go, either, she was in bed with 'flu, it was a terrible winter, that one, people dying like flies . . . Poor Marcia had to cope all by herself, and she was in such a state, well, you can imagine, can't you? The next we knew, she was on Win's doorstep, ashes and all. Said she couldn't stand being all by herself up North a minute longer, she hated it, especially with no hope of Bernard being back for months and she'd decided the only thing to do was come home . . . It's the only time I've really felt sorry for Marcia. To tell you the truth, I've never had much time for her, hard as nails she was, but that time . . . I saw her, the day she got here. Thin as a rake and looking as though she hadn't slept for a month, and clutching that box with the baby's ashes in it. D'you know, she'd just walked out of her house, shut the front door behind her and left it all. Just like that. No arrangements made, nothing. And she never did go back. Said Bernard could see to it all when he came home but nothing would induce her to set foot over the threshold ever again. Nothing but bad luck it had brought her, she said, which was why she'd brought the baby's ashes home. She wanted them to be buried here, in Telford Green. Mr Greenhorn was vicar here at the time, I remember. Lovely service it was, too.'

'Why didn't you like her, Mrs Pepper?'

'Marcia?' She wrinkled her nose and turned up her upper lip, as if she'd just come across a bad smell. 'I told you, hard as nails, she was. Never did have much time for her mother – No, I tell a lie. She did care about her, must have, since she made a lot of money she's been very generous, bought Win everything she could possibly need. But the truth is – though it

68

took me a long time to work it out – Marcia never really forgave her mother for not standing up to her father.' She rolled her eyes. 'Now there was a right one, believe me.'

'In what way?'

'Drink, mostly. He didn't earn much – him and Bert, my husband God rest his soul, both worked on the farm, so they got the same wages and, believe me, the money didn't go far – and George, Win's husband, used to pour most of it into the pockets of the landlord of the Crooked Door on a Friday night. Then he'd come home and beat Win up. Our bedrooms was next to each other on either side of the party wall and many's the Friday I've lain with the bedclothes pulled up over me head to shut out the noise. Nowadays, of course, people call in the police over that sort of thing but forty or fifty years ago it'd never have entered your head to do that. You never heard about "battered wives" and such like in those days. Anyway, the point was, Marcia really' – she paused, seeking the right word – 'despised,' she brought out triumphantly, 'yes, despised her mother for putting up with it. I heard her going on at her about it more than once. "Why on earth don't you stand up to him?" she used to say. "He's only a bully, and bullies turn tail when you stand up to them." She proved it, too, as she got older. Many's the time I've seen her stick up for herself, and for her mother, too, and George'd shout and bluster, but she'd get away with it. But Win never could, she was too gentle. I always thought that was why Marcia got married so young.'

'To get away from home, you mean?'

Mrs Pepper nodded. 'Couldn't wait to be independent. And that was Bernard's attraction for her, I reckon. He was able to afford a wife. I mean, he was much older than her, he had a house, a car . . . It was just too good an opportunity to miss. And Marcia always was ambitious. Determined to make her way in the world.'

'And she certainly did,' said Lineham. 'How did she manage it?'

Something in the Sergeant's tone made Thanet glance at him sharply.

'Well,' said Mrs Pepper, picking up her ball of wool again,

'it was like this. After the baby died and Marcia came home, she didn't do nothing for a while. To give her credit, she'd always been a hard worker, went on working right up till six weeks before the baby was born . . .'

'What sort of work did she do?' asked Lineham.

'Secretarial. She always was bright, did well at school – wanted to stay on after her O levels, but her father wouldn't let her, said she was sixteen and it was time she got out in the world and started to earn a living. Terrible rows there was about it, but he wouldn't give in. So when she left school she got a job as a receptionist in some office, but she enrolled straight away at night school, like I told you, for a course in – what do they call it? – business studies. Yes. Like I said, that was where she met Bernard. Anyway, after they got married she found a good job as a secretary up North, but after the baby died and she come home, she just used to sit about all day doing nothing, staring into space. Often I'd go in there and she'd just be sitting there with the tears rolling down her cheeks, not making a sound. Win was that worried about her.'

It sounded like a bad case of post-natal depression, exacerbated by grief at losing the baby, thought Thanet.

'What did the doctor say?'

'Gave her tablets and that, but they didn't seem to do much good.'

'What about her father?'

'Oh, he was dead by then. Died not long after she got married, as a matter of fact, in an accident on the farm. His tractor overturned and of course in them days there was no safety cabs. He was crushed to death.'

'Nasty . . . Sorry, I didn't mean to interrupt. You were saying, about Marcia . . .'

'Well, she went on like that for months, we was beginning to wonder if she'd ever come out of it, and then at last she started to improve. Not long after, Bernard came home and took her off abroad for a holiday. He was still walking on sticks at the time, but he could get about all right and off they went. It worked wonders for her. By the time they came back she had it all worked out. They would sell their house up North and move back down here, because that's where the money was. They would buy the lease on a shop with a flat above, and open a health food shop. We thought she was mad at the time, but when Marcia set her mind on something nothing would budge her and of course she was right, wasn't she? Look at the business now!'

Marcia must really have got in on the ground floor, thought Thanet. The health food business had boomed in recent years, especially since the Government had started taking an interest in the nation's health and had launched the campaign for healthy eating. But in the late sixties it had been an unusual choice to make.

Lineham's thoughts had been running along similar lines. 'Whatever gave her the idea?' he said.

'No idea. But she was sharp, Marcia, very sharp. I remember she talked a lot about a gap in the market. And of course, once she was launched, nothing could stop her.'

'They didn't want any more children?' said Thanet.

'Oh yes, I think so. Bernard was very keen, I know. But they just never seemed to come along. After a while he even suggested adopting one, but Marcia didn't want to do that, said she'd never given up hope of having another of her own, but it wasn't to be.'

So Salden had turned to charity work with children as second best, thought Thanet. He'd certainly had more than his fair share of grief. He stood up, ducking to avoid a trailing spider plant. 'Well, Mrs Pepper, I really am very grateful to you for filling us in like this.'

She came to her feet slowly, one hand in the small of her back, betraying her age for the first time. 'I really have been rambling on, haven't I?'

'Not at all.'

'It's very kind of you to say so. But I can't see that it has anything to do with Marcia's accident.'

If it was an accident, thought Thanet.

The more he heard about Marcia Salden, the more likely a murder victim she seemed.

EIGHT

They paused outside Mrs Pepper's gate.

'What now?' said Lineham.

'I think it would be a good idea if we chewed things over a bit.' Thanet took out his pipe, inspected the bowl, scraped it out, inspected it again, blew through it a couple of times and started to fill it. Lineham watched him with resignation.

'Back to headquarters, then?' The Sergeant glanced at his watch. 'You realise it's nearly half-past five, sir? You did tell that TVS reporter to contact your office late in the afternoon.'

'Ah, but I didn't say I'd be there, did I? Anyway, we can't talk properly cramped up in the corner of the main CID room with phones ringing and people going in and out . . .' Thanet lit up. 'No, we need somewhere nice and quiet. The car's as good a place as any, I suppose.'

The car was in the pub car park, as arranged, with a piece of paper tucked under the windscreen wipers. *Keys in pub.*

Lineham fetched them. 'D'you want to stay here and talk?' he asked. With a glance at Thanet's pipe, he wound down the window. 'Or go somewhere else?'

'Somewhere else, I think. I never have found brick and tarmac very inspiring.'

'I know a place that'd do.'

Instead of turning left over the bridge towards the Sturrenden road, Lineham turned right. Shortly after leaving the village he swung left into a narrow rising lane, the branches of the trees on either side meeting overhead to form a tunnel. The sun was sinking but still bright and the road surface ahead was dappled with pools and patches of light laced with intricate patterns of shadow cast by still-bare twigs and branches. In summer it must be even more beautiful, thought Thanet, and promised himself that one sunny afternoon he'd bring Joan to see it.

'Where are we going, exactly?'

Lineham grinned. 'Nearly there.'

A few minutes later the trees gave way to hedges and they emerged into a wide expanse of open fields dotted with sheep and cattle. The lane bore around in a wide arc to the left and a few hundred yards further on Lineham pulled into the entrance to a tractor lane and switched off the engine.

'This do?'

Thanet said nothing, simply nodded then sat taking in the view, which was as fine as any he had seen in Kent. They were now looking at the valley of the Teale below them from the opposite direction, and from much higher up. To right and left the river wound lazily away into the distance, its surface mirror-bright and stained with the colours of the setting sun, the road through the village bisecting it at the bridge in a graceful curve. Immediately below them was the church, its spire casting a long shadow on the green beyond, the roofs of the cottages to either side russet red tinged here and there with purple, ochre and a rich, warm sepia. To the left, in the fields between village and river, lay Telford Green Farm, and beyond, on the far side of the Teale, the densely packed trees of Harry Greenleaf's wood. Thanet's gaze lingered here; a tiny figure was walking up the tongue of meadow which led up to the hut. Greenleaf, secure now in the knowledge that his sanctuary was safe for at least a little while longer? Thanet transferred his attention to the Manor, serene in its setting of gardens and parkland and wondered whether Salden had yet awoken from his drug-induced sleep and if he would proceed with the eviction now that Marcia was dead.

Here, spread out for his inspection, was Marcia Salden's world – or part of it, at least, the part in which she had functioned as a private individual. Was her murderer also a part of this tranquil scene, even now going about his daily tasks beneath one of those roofs down there and wondering if his crime would be detected?

Lineham's voice broke into his thoughts. 'Beautiful, isn't it?'

73

In deference to the Sergeant's aversion to pipe smoke Thanet wound down his window. The brisk wind of earlier in the day had abated and a light, cool breeze blew in, redolent of earth, trees, cattle and young green crops.

'How did you discover this place?'

'We were out looking for a picnic spot one day, years ago. I'd forgotten about it until we drove into the village this morning, I can't think why. It would be hard to find a better.'

'I agree . . .' Thanet wrenched his eyes away from the landscape below and looked at Lineham. 'Well, Mike, what do you think? Have we got a case, or haven't we?'

The Sergeant was gazing straight ahead out of the window. Free to study his profile at close quarters, Thanet took in Lineham's pallor, the fine lines of strain around eyes and mouth, the restless tapping of his fingers on the steering wheel. What *was* the matter with him? Normally, at this stage, the Sergeant would be bubbling over with ideas, suggestions.

'I'm not sure.' He turned to face Thanet, leaning back against the driving door. 'What do you think, sir?'

'Oh come on, Mike, don't throw it back at me like that. I'm asking for your opinion and I want to know what it is.'

'But that is it. I just can't make up my mind. Perhaps when we've got a bit more evidence . . .'

'Evidence, evidence . . . What's got into you, Mike? I'm usually the one falling over backwards saying take it easy, don't let's jump to conclusions . . . Of course we haven't got any evidence yet. If it's there to be found, we'll find it sooner or later. Meanwhile, you know perfectly well I'm not talking about evidence, I'm talking about impressions of people, about possible motives, opportunities.'

Lineham shifted uneasily in his seat and his eyes drifted away from Thanet's. 'Sorry.' He frowned, obviously making an effort to focus his mind.

Thanet opened the car door, put one foot out and emptied his pipe by tapping it against his heel. The familiar action soothed him a little, but he still couldn't entirely suppress the anger in his voice as he said, 'I don't know what sort of a fool you take me for, Mike, but it's as plain as a pikestaff that something's wrong and I'm fed up with asking what it is.

Now, your private life is your own affair and I have no wish to pry. If something's wrong between you and Louise, then it's up to you to take steps to sort it out. But your work's another matter. In this state you're as much use to me as a wet flannel and I feel I have every right to ask. So come on, tell me. What's the matter?'

While Thanet was speaking Lineham had been looking more and more uncomfortable. Now he glanced uneasily at Thanet, opened his mouth, shut it again.

'Mike . . . Come on, man. Spit it out.'

Thanet waited. He was sympathetic to the Sergeant's predicament, acutely conscious of the conflict raging in his mind, but he could say no more. The issue had been brought out into the open and if Lineham still chose not to confide in him there was nothing he could do about it.

Lineham was staring down at his hands, picking away at a piece of loose skin alongside the thumbnail of his right hand. The silence stretched out and Thanet was just beginning to think his appeal had failed when the Sergeant stirred.

'Louise wants me to leave the force,' he muttered. He glanced briefly at Thanet's blank face, then down at his hands again.

Thanet was first astounded and then, as the shock receded, furiously angry with Lineham's wife. His lips tightened as if to contain the spate of words which threatened to tumble out. Here was a minefield and he would have to tread carefully indeed.

'I see.'

Lineham glanced at him again, assessingly this time.

With an effort, Thanet kept his voice non-committal. 'May I ask why?'

Lineham shrugged, grimaced. 'The usual reasons, I imagine. Long, unpredictable, anti-social hours . . . But mainly, I think, the fact that the prospects are poor.'

I might have guessed, of course, thought Thanet. He had always suspected Louise of being ambitious. A couple of years back Lineham had sought promotion to Inspector. Thanet hadn't been surprised when he failed to get it. Lineham was an excellent second-in-command, but had always lacked that extra edge which would lift him above the rank of Sergeant. Thanet had thought at the time that it had been Louise who had pushed Lineham into applying, and he had sympathised with the demoralising effect the failure had had upon Lineham, privately approved the Sergeant's decision not to try again. It was obvious that Louise, balked at having one avenue closed, had determined upon another.

On impulse, Thanet swung open the car door and got out. 'Let's walk for a while, shall we? The car should be all right; I shouldn't think there'll be many tractors around at this time of night.'

Without speaking, Lineham followed suit, and they set off at a leisurely pace along the narrow lane between tall country hedges of hawthorn and blackthorn, field maple, dogwood and hazel, some distinguishable only by their bark, others just breaking into leaf.

'Does she have anything specific in mind?' Thanet asked, eventually.

Lineham shrugged again. 'She seems to think it would be a good idea to start our own business. Says that's where the money is these days and that the opportunities to do so have never been better, what with all the advice you can get free from the Government, and the ease with which you can get funding.'

'What sort of business?'

'She . . . We haven't made up our minds, yet.'

'But you, Mike?' said Thanet softly. 'Have you made up your mind?'

Lineham shook his head miserably.

'I can see what a dilemma you must be in . . . Worrying about what your mates'll say if you leave the Force, worrying about what Louise'll say if you don't, but Mike, listen' — Thanet stopped walking and turned to face Lineham, to emphasise the importance of what he was saying — 'you've got to ignore all that. There's only one question you have to ask yourself and that is, "What do *I* want to do?" '

Lineham gave a mirthless snort of laughter. 'You don't think that's a somewhat selfish attitude to take?'

'No I do not! Look, Mike, you're what? Thirty? All being well you've got another thirty-five years of working life ahead of you. Now I know, as well as you do, that you enjoy your work. Really enjoy it. Oh, I know it has disadvantages, all the things you mentioned plus an awful lot of frustration, hassle and danger at times, too, but all the same you do enjoy it. As much as I do. Don't you realise how privileged we are? To wake up in the morning and actually look forward to going to work instead of waking up and thinking, Oh God, another day, how can I face it, how can I get through it? You can't buy satisfaction like that, Mike, not if you're a millionaire. Now, if there were something else you wanted to do more than this, or as much as this, and you could earn more doing it and please Louise at the same time, I'd give you my blessing, say go ahead, you've everything to gain. But if you give up work you enjoy for something in which you haven't really the slightest interest, I'm afraid you'd end up in far worse straits than you are now – not financially, perhaps, but emotionally. Because for the rest of your life you'd resent being forced into a false position, and that resentment would gradually poison your relationship with Louise.'

Lineham had been listening intently, nodded now and then as Thanet made some particularly telling point. Now he said, 'I know that. I know all that. But I just can't seem to get Louise to see it.'

'You've actually put it to her, in those terms?'

'More or less.' Lineham shook his head despairingly. 'I just don't know what to do.'

They had come to a five-barred gate and in mute accord they turned to lean on it, gazing out over the serene landscape below. Colours were darkening and deepening in tone, edges becoming blurred and shadows lengthening fast as the sun sank towards the western horizon.

Thanet didn't know what to do either. It was obvious that this discussion could go no further without venturing into the very private territory of Lineham's marriage, and Thanet was unsure of the wisdom of taking this step. Marriage guidance, he felt, should be left to the experts. On the other hand, now that his initial reluctance to discuss the matter had been overcome, Lineham seemed anxious to pursue it further, was even now casting anxious glances at Thanet, awaiting his response. What to do? If only he could think of a way to give the Sergeant something positive to hang on to, some new and constructive way of looking at the situation . . . Suddenly he saw how it might be done.

'Mike,' he began cautiously.

'Yes, sir?'

The eager look in Lineham's eyes gave Thanet the courage to continue.

'Look, I don't want to pry, and I'll quite understand if you prefer not to answer, but I was wondering . . . Would you say that Louise is happy?'

Lineham compressed his lips, sighed and said bitterly, 'No, I don't mind you asking. And I don't suppose you'll be too surprised to hear that she hasn't been happy for a long time.'

'It's just that I was wondering . . . Do you think she misses her work?'

Before their marriage, Louise had been a nurse, working as a sister in Sturrenden General Hospital.

Lineham was nodding. 'Oh yes. Always has. I think you've hit the nail on the head, there. She's very fond of the children, mind, but she always has missed it. If I'd had a job with regular hours, of course, she'd have been able to go back before now, do a bit of night duty, to keep her hand in. But as it is it's just not possible.'

Thanet nodded, then shivered. As the light seeped out of the sky the breeze seemed to have freshened again. Perhaps there would be another touch of frost tonight. He dug his hands deep into his pockets and turned back towards the car, Lineham falling into step beside him. 'Has she ever considered finding someone to look after the children during the day?'

'Not seriously, no. For one thing, she thinks – we both think – that kids under the age of five really need their mothers and that you're asking for trouble later on if you duck out of your responsibilities by dumping them on someone else – at least until they're of school age. For another, from the purely economic point of view, she'd practically be working for nothing. Nurses are so badly paid she'd have to hand over most of it to the child-minder. Then there are the hours – they're impossible, as far as child-minding is concerned. You'd really think,' said Lineham bitterly, 'that if they're that desperate for nurses at Sturrenden General, they'd set up a crèche.'

'I agree . . . Louise has never considered doing anything other than nursing, something part-time, just until the children start school? How often does Richard go to playgroup?'

'Three mornings a week.'

'And Mandy will be starting in September, won't she?'

'Yes . . . I don't know whether it would have entered her head. Nursing's her first love, always has been . . .'

'I know. But it might just be worth discussing the possibility, stressing that it would only be a temporary measure. It must be very hard for a woman like Louise, who's had a successful career, to be stuck at home all day staring at four walls and looking after two young children.'

'You almost sound as if you've been through all this yourself.'

Lineham was looking much more relaxed, Thanet noticed. At this point he even managed an echo of his usual cheeky grin.

'Oh, I have. Not in quite the same way. But there was a point, when Ben finally started school and Joan was contemplating a career in the probation service, when I had to do some re-thinking. Up until then I'm afraid I'd just taken it for granted that she was one hundred per cent happy looking after the house, the children and me. A real MCP, in fact. And having my eyes opened was, as recall, distinctly painful.'

'Really?' Lineham was looking at Thanet as though the confession had enhanced rather than diminished him in the Sergeant's eyes.

Thanet grinned. 'Cross my heart. It took me years to adjust, really adjust, to having a wife whose career was as important to her as mine was to me. Until last year, as a matter of fact.'

'Last year? But Joan's been a probation officer for – how long? – six years now!'

'Marriage is a funny thing, Mike. People who are going through a bad patch seem to think things will never change, or

79

if they do they can only get worse. But the fact of the matter is, none of us is static, we're all changing all the time, and when two people are involved there is tremendous potential for change, given goodwill on both sides. You know, I've often thought that in marriage there seems to be a kind of natural ebb and flow, as feelings fluctuate, situations alter and attitudes change. So that sometimes things get better and sometimes things get worse, for no apparent reason but simply because of this fundamental – what shall I call it? – groundswell, going on underneath all the time. And this is perfectly normal, perfectly natural. The trouble nowadays is that people seem to take it for granted that if they're having a bad time it means their marriage has broken down for ever. And this simply need not be true. Take your situation, now. It might seem to you that there is no way – no acceptable way, that is – out of it. But it would need only one of you to change his attitude slightly and the other would begin to react to that change, and the possibility of breaking the apparent impasse would be there.'

They had reached the car now and Lineham automatically unlocked it, climbed in and reached across to release the catch on Thanet's door. Then he sat quite still for a minute or two, gazing sightlessly out of the windscreen. 'I don't think,' he said slowly at last, 'that I've ever really tried to look at the situation from Louise's point of view before. Oh, I know she's not happy stuck at home all the time, much as she loves the kids. But we've never really talked about it, it just comes out in other ways, as though she's trying to pin her dissatisfaction on something else . . .'

Like her husband's lack of ambition, thought Thanet.

Lineham was getting there himself. 'Perhaps she feels that the only way she can change things is through me.'

'Possibly. But if so, it's quite likely that it's unconscious, she doesn't realise she's doing it. In any case, it might help if you brought it out into the open, talked about it.'

Lineham turned to look Thanet full in the face and gave a resolute nod. 'I will. Yes.'

'In any case, I should stop worrying about having to make an immediate decision about leaving the force.'

'I don't want to leave. I really don't. As you say, I really enjoy my work, I've never wanted to do anything else.'

Thanet wondered if Lineham was remembering the battle he had fought with his mother over his entry to the police force. A widow who had brought up her only son single-handed, she had fought long and hard against his entering what she considered to be a dangerous profession. And if he did remember, would he now make the inevitable comparison with his current situation?

'But I was beginning to wonder if there was any other way out. Now . . . Well, I think I feel there may be a light at the end of the tunnel. Thank you, sir.'

Thanet recognised the note of finality in Lineham's voice. The Sergeant had had enough of discussing his private problems for the moment.

'All in a day's work,' said Thanet with a grin. 'And talking about work . . .'

'Ah, yes.' Lineham glanced down at Telford Green, where lights were coming on in the houses. Then he gave Thanet his usual mischievous grin and said, 'Well, one thing's certain, it seems to me. If Mrs Salden didn't manage to get herself murdered, it wasn't for want of trying.'

NINE

'So what did you mean, wasn't for want of trying?' said Thanet, settling back into his seat with a mental sigh of relief that their talk seemed to have been of some use and Lineham was showing every sign of reverting to normal.

They had decided that it was about time they returned to Headquarters and the car now plunged into the entrance to the tunnel of trees which was transformed by approaching darkness into a place of mystery; menace, even.

Lineham braked as a rabbit, momentarily transfixed by their headlights, squatted in their path before scuttling off into the undergrowth beside the road, white tail bobbing. 'Well, OK, we don't know yet if it was an accident or not. It could have been − though, as I said earlier, it's unlikely. I can't see how anyone could have been unaware of the lights and the barriers Kimberley set up on the bridge or how Mrs Salden could accidentally have fallen in without being pushed. But in view of the knack she seems to have had for stirring up trouble . . .'

'Trouble in general, or trouble with individuals?'

'Both, I should say. It's just the way she was. If she wanted something, she went for it, regardless of what anyone else felt. It wasn't surprising she was unpopular in the village. First she closes off a right of way . . .'

'Her right of way, remember, Mike.'

'Technically, maybe. But you can understand how the people in the village feel, with no bus and having to walk an extra mile or more. That's not much fun if you're an old age pensioner or a young mum. And they'd been using it for years. Why should she have been so determined to close it anyway? The footpath doesn't overlook the Manor gardens, the hedges are much too high and thick for that. It just seems mean and petty-minded. Then there's the business of the village hall and the planning permission. Imagine how they must have felt! They'd been slogging away raising money for years, they'd got the promise of a grant from the Borough Council, set up the purchase of the land with Mr — what was his name? — Tiller, and then, at the eleventh hour, Mrs Salden snatches the whole thing away from under their noses. Can you blame them for being mad at her? I bet that demonstration down there against Harry Greenleaf's eviction was as much an expression of their resentment against the way she's treated them as against the way she was treating him.'

'I thought the same thing myself. But I'm not so sure that she was just insensitive. I'm beginning to wonder if some of this provocation may have been deliberate.'

'Deliberate?' They had reached the bottom of the hill and Lineham paused to check that the road was clear before pulling out. 'Why?'

'Ah, that's the intriguing question, isn't it? And I think I'm only just starting to get the glimmer of an answer. But if you think about Marcia Salden's background, it does all begin to make sense.'

'Not to me it doesn't.'

'Just consider, Mike.' Thanet glanced out of the window as they entered Telford Green and then gestured at the row of cottages ahead, next to the Crooked Door. 'She was brought up there, in a farm worker's cottage. Her father was a drunk. That means that as far as this community was concerned she was the lowest of the low. Then, just as in all the best rags-to-riches stories, she finds fame and fortune — well, fortune, anyway. And what does she do? Does she go as far away as possible from the place where she suffered all the humiliations of the child of an alcoholic? No, she buys the house she fell in love with as a child, the house she swore she would one day own, and in fulfilment of all those childhood dreams comes back as Lady of the Manor. Quite a touching, romantic story, I think you'll agree. But unfortunately she didn't live happily ever after. The sequel wasn't at all what she had imagined. Country people are very conservative, Mike, and the older ones are still very conscious of hierarchy. I can't imagine that they were too pleased to see the daughter of a drunken cottager ensconced in the Manor.'

All the lights were on in the Crooked Door and the place looked warm and welcoming. As they passed, two men went in. Thanet thought he recognised them from this morning. He resisted the temptation to suggest stopping for a pint.

'Those warning lights are clearly visible from way back up the road,' said Lineham, slowing down as he drove over the bridge.

'Yes, I'd noticed.'

Lineham glanced at him. 'So you think they gave her the cold shoulder?'

'Let's be charitable and say that they would have been slow to accept her. Given time, they might well have done so. But I'd guess that she wouldn't have been prepared to wait. With her background she would have been hyper-sensitive to snubs, real or imagined, and when she found that they were not exactly going to welcome her with open arms she would have said, right, I'll show you, damned if I don't. And proceeded to do just that.'

The Manor gates flashed by on the left. The lights were on in the lodge but the main house was invisible from the road by virtue of the curve in the drive.

'So you're saying that closing the footpath and scuppering the plans for the village hall were a way of getting her own back on them?'

Thanet shrugged. 'It's possible, don't you think?'

'And evicting Harry Greenleaf?'

'Well, if what I've been saying is true, and I think it quite likely, it must have been galling for her to see Greenleaf accepted and tolerated – even liked – by the villagers, while she was shunned.'

'So out he had to go.'

'As good a suggestion as any, don't you think?'

'Unless she had some personal reason for wanting to get rid of him.'

'Such as?'

'No idea.'

84

'Anyway, to get back to what you were saying, Mike, about the general ill-feeling towards her, you're not by any chance suggesting that the people of the village collectively decided they'd had enough of her and grabbed the chance to shove her off the bridge?'

'No, of course not! I'm just talking about the way she steamrollered her way over people's feelings. And if she could do that on a big scale, why not on a small one?'

'Are you thinking of anyone in particular?'

'Not really. But surely you've noticed that no one we've yet met has shown any real grief over her death? They've been shocked, yes, but that's all. Mrs Pantry obviously didn't have much time for her, Edith Phipps wasn't exactly broken-hearted even though they went way back together, Nurse Lint wasn't too impressed by her even though she tried to hide it by talking about her generosity towards her mother, and Mrs Pepper — though she did sympathise with the rotten life Mrs Salden had had as a girl — didn't have much to say for her either.'

'Her husband seemed pretty upset.'

'Well, yes. But if she treated him the way she treated everyone else, he couldn't have had much of a life. Didn't you notice Mrs Pantry said they had separate bedrooms?'

'Lots of married couples have separate bedrooms for all sorts of reasons — he snores, she's an insomniac . . .'

Lineham's face showed that he couldn't accept this proposition. In his book, separate bedrooms meant only one thing: marital disharmony.

'So that show of grief . . . You think he was putting it on, then?'

'Not necessarily, sir. I don't know. I'm just saying he could have been.'

'True. But even if you're right, and they didn't get on too well, it doesn't necessarily mean he killed her. He could still genuinely have been in shock. After all, if you've lived with a woman for — what? — twenty years, you're bound to feel something when she dies suddenly, even if the first fine careless rapture has worn off. And there doesn't seem to have been any talk about trouble between them, in the village.'

'No, that's true. Miss Phipps wasn't too comfortable, though, when you asked her about them. In any case, you must admit he seems the most likely suspect so far, if only because he seems to have been in the right place at the right time.'

'True.'

'I mean, if he had a reason for wanting to get rid of her that nobody knows about and the opportunity to do so just shoved itself under his nose when they happened to pass each other on the bridge . . .'

'It's certainly possible, Mike, I grant you. Obviously we'll have to see him again tomorrow, when I hope he'll be in a fit state to talk . . .'

They had arrived back at Headquarters and Lineham parked the car and switched off the engine. Engrossed in their discussion, neither of them made any move to get out.

'The other likely suspect at the moment, of course, is Greenleaf,' said Thanet. 'You weren't there, were you, when Miss Phipps was telling me about him? Apparently he's badly disfigured after an accident, which I imagine is one of the reasons why he leads the life of a recluse.'

'No, I didn't know that. Poor chap. I wonder if Mr Salden will let him stay on, now.'

'Yes, it'll be interesting to find out. I imagine it wouldn't have been easy for him to find somewhere else to go, if the eviction had gone ahead. If the disfigurement is as bad as Miss Phipps says, it's understandable that he doesn't want too much contact with other people. He'd probably have been forced into a life on the road. All of which adds up to a powerful motive for wanting to get rid of Mrs Salden.'

'Honestly, sir, I know you were trying to excuse the way Mrs Salden behaved towards the people of the village, but with respect . . .'

'Not excuse, Mike. I was merely trying to understand her reasons. And every time you say, "With respect," I know you're about to disagree with me. So go on, disagree.'

'No, not disagree, exactly. I was only going to say that in my opinion she sounds a nasty bit of work. This Greenleaf business was typical. Why couldn't she have left the poor man alone? He wasn't doing anyone any harm, was he? And he wasn't exactly under her nose all the time, he was tucked well away out of sight. It just seems a bit of gratuitous unpleasantness to take him to court and threaten to tip him out like that.'

'Maybe. Nevertheless, Mike, if you can try to be a little more dispassionate about this, you'll concede that he has very good reason to be thankful that she is permanently out of the way.'

'That's not the same as saying he might have shoved her off the bridge.'

'Mike! I'm not suggesting it is, and you know it! Merely that the possibility exists.'

Lineham was silent for a moment or two, then said awkwardly, 'It does, of course. Sorry, sir, don't know what got into me.'

'Forget it. So we'll have to interview Greenleaf tomorrow, as well. Meanwhile, there were one or two other interesting points, I thought.'

'Such as?'

'That dinner party . . .'

'Yes. A bit of a mixed bag, wasn't it? A county councillor and a hairdresser?'

'Quite. It did just occur to me . . . Isn't Lomax chairman of the Planning Committee?'

'Yes, you're right, he is, I'd forgotten that . . .' Lineham's lips pursed in a silent whistle. 'You mean . . .'

'That Mrs Salden might have been using Josie Trimble as bait in order to swing that planning permission. Yes. What d'you think, Mike?'

'Sounds quite likely to me, after what we've heard about Mrs Salden. I wouldn't put anything past her, if she wanted something badly enough.'

'It would explain why she didn't want to cancel the dinner party, wouldn't it? A quarter of a million is a high stake.'

'And also why she didn't mind leaving them alone while she went down to the village to visit her mother. And,' said Lineham, warming to his theme, 'why the housekeeper was so sniffy when she was talking about the girl. I wondered what all that was about. I thought perhaps it was just because Mrs

Pantry was a bit of a snob, but if she was aware of what was going on . . .'

'I agree. Also, it surprised me a bit that Salden was so ready to disappear for the evening, that he didn't go back to the house to apologise to his guests and spend some time with them between his first and second visits to his mother-in-law. But if he knew what his wife was up to and disapproved of it he might have been only too glad of an excuse to keep out of the way. Anyway, if we're right, it does open up certain interesting possibilities, don't you agree?'

'I do. Blackmail, for instance. If Lomax had got himself entangled with Josie Trimble and Mrs Salden had started putting pressure on about the planning permission . . . Lomax could have found himself in a very nasty position.'

'If it had got out it wouldn't have done him much good, that's for sure.'

'It'd certainly have made the headlines in the local paper. It's got all the ingredients of a first-class scandal – sex, bribery, corruption in local government . . . I can just see the headlines. BOROUGH COUNCILLOR . . .'

'All right, Mike, no need to get carried away. The point is, we'll need to pay a little visit to those two tomorrow, too.'

'Don't you think we ought to see Miss Phipps again as well?'

'Ah, I wondered if you'd spotted that. Yes, she was holding something back, wasn't she, when I asked her about her movements that evening. I wonder what she'd been up to.'

No doubt they'd find out, sooner or later.

TEN

After spending several hours on the 'detailed, literate and accurate' reports Draco would expect next morning, all Thanet wanted to do when he got home was fall into bed and sink into oblivion. As he pulled into the drive he was surprised to see a light still on in the tiny shoebox of a bedroom which he and Joan used as a study. He went straight upstairs, pleased to note that tonight the light was off in Bridget's room.

Joan was sitting at the desk, which was strewn with papers. She turned as he came in and lifted her face for his kiss. 'How's the case going?'

He shrugged. 'So so. You're working late, love.'

'I know.' She laid down her pen, took off her recently acquired spectacles and rubbed her eyes. 'I've got to finish this report by tomorrow, and I didn't have a chance to tackle it earlier on.'

'Why was that?' Thanet perched on the edge of the desk. Joan, too, looked very tired. There were lines of strain around her eyes, her mouth drooped and her short fair curly hair was dishevelled, as though she had been running her hands through it. From where he sat looking down at her Thanet could see a glint of grey here and there. We're neither of us getting any younger, he thought.

She pulled a face. 'Vicky was here for a good couple of hours, in floods of tears most of the time.'

Vicky Younghusband lived next door. Her husband, Peter, was a travelling salesman and Vicky had given birth to their first child six weeks ago. She had worked in the offices of a local estate agent until a month before the baby was born, and had always been a cheerful, outgoing girl. She and Peter had been delighted when she found she was pregnant at last. They had been married for eight years and for the last five had been hoping that Vicky would conceive. On the day the pregnancy was confirmed they had brought round a bottle of champagne, and they had all drunk a toast to the next generation of Younghusbands.

'At least three of them!' Vicky had declared, radiant with happiness.

'Wait until you've had one,' Joan had teased. 'You might change your mind.'

Often, during the last few weeks, she had had reason to remember that light-hearted remark, for since the baby's arrival Vicky was a changed woman. Gone were the smiles, the cheerfulness, the unfailing optimism, replaced by endless tears and a dragging, debilitating depression. More than once Peter had come round to see the Thanets in despair.

'Post-natal depression, the doctor says. But how long is it going to last? I sometimes feel I can't take much more.'

Joan and Thanet had made consoling noises but had felt powerless to help. What could they do, except provide a sympathetic ear and a shoulder to cry on?

Instead of the fortnight he had arranged to take off to help Vicky after the baby was born, Peter had taken a month, using up all his annual leave in one fell swoop, but at the end of this time Vicky was no better. Worried though he was, Peter had had to go back to work, and although he had tried to arrange his schedule so that Vicky was not alone more than two nights in succession it wasn't always possible; his area was large and his employers understandably becoming a little tetchy. He could not afford to risk losing his job.

Thanet and Joan had promised to keep an eye on Vicky, but at the end of a working day it wasn't always easy to call up the reserves of emotional energy which she demanded.

Joan sighed. 'Honestly, Luke, I'm sure her doctor doesn't realise just how ill she is. From what she says he's one of the old school who tends to think women are a bit hysterical and everything would be all right if she'd just make an effort and pull herself together. I really am worried about her. I even wonder if . . .'

'What?'

Joan shook her head. 'Oh, nothing. I'm being silly, I suppose.'

'You're not suggesting she might try to commit suicide?'

'Well, it has crossed my mind, I must admit. And I feel so helpless, Luke. D'you know, I went in there the other day after I got home from work, about six o'clock it must have been, and there she was, sitting in front of the television set in a sort of trance, still in her dressing gown. No make-up, her hair uncombed . . . I had the impression she'd been there all day. The baby was screaming his head off, he was hungry, his nappy was soaking wet. She really is deeply and clinically depressed.'

'What about the health visitor? Surely she must be aware of the situation?'

'So far as I can gather, Peter has always made an enormous effort to get the house straight and make sure things look as normal as possible when she's coming. He hasn't actually said so, but I think he's afraid they might take the baby away if things look too bad. Which is understandable, but very misleading.'

'When's he due back?'

'The day after tomorrow.'

'I'll try and have a tactful word with him, point out that although it may have been done with the best of intentions, it's not really in Vicky's best interest to give a false impression of how she's coping. Meanwhile . . . Wait a minute, aren't they with the Thompson and Merridew practice?'

'Yes. Why?'

'I heard the other day that they'd just taken on a new partner. A woman in her thirties. One of the lads was complaining that he'd never get used to a woman doctor. Perhaps we could manoeuvre an appointment with her, for Vicky. She might be a lot more understanding and constructive. We'll suggest it to Peter, when he gets back. So cheer up, love. It's not all doom and despair.'

Joan grimaced. 'That's not the only thing that's worrying me, I'm afraid.' She laid a hand on his. 'Oh darling, I am sorry to throw all this at you the second you walk through the door.

You look so tired. And I suppose your back is playing up again?'

Thanet admitted that it was. It always did, when he was tired. An old injury had left him with a permanent weakness in the lumbar region. It was little consolation to know that there were 2.2 million other sufferers in the British Isles. 'But never mind that. What else is bothering you? You might as well tell me the worst.'

Joan glanced uneasily towards the door and lowered her voice. 'Did you notice if Bridget's light was off?'

Automatically Thanet leaned closer. We must look like a couple of conspirators, he thought. 'Yes, it was. Why?'

'Mr Foreman rang me at work this afternoon. He wants me to go and see him.'

Thanet frowned. Mr Foreman was Bridget and Ben's headmaster. 'Why?'

'He wouldn't say — except that it's about Bridget.'

'Perhaps he's as concerned as we are that she's pushing herself too hard.'

'Why wouldn't he discuss it over the phone, then?'

'No time?'

Joan shook her head. 'I felt it was more . . . how shall I put it? More as if he wanted to discuss some definite misdemeanour on her part.'

'What, for instance?'

'No idea.'

'There you are, then. You're imagining things. Bridget isn't the type to cause trouble, you know that. In fact, she's too conscientious by half. Did you ask her if she could guess why Mr Foreman wanted to see you?'

'Yes. She said she'd no idea. But . . .'

'What?'

'Well, I had the impression she wasn't being frank with me.'

This was bad news. Thanet had great faith in Joan's powers of intuition. 'Did you fix up an appointment?'

'Yes. Two thirty tomorrow afternoon.'

'I'll come with you.'

'No, there's no need. Really. It might look as though we're

taking the whole thing far too seriously if we both turn up. And it might be about something quite trivial.'

But the same thought was in both their minds: in that case, why hadn't Mr Foreman been prepared to discuss it over the phone?

Thanet stood up. 'Come on, time for bed. We're both tired.'

She shook her head, picked up her spectacles and put them on. 'I really have to finish this report tonight.'

'How much longer will you be?'

'Half an hour or so.'

For the second night running Thanet lay awake worrying about his daughter.

Next morning he set off for work early. He wanted to skim through as many as possible of the reports that would have come in on the Salden case before the morning meeting with Draco. He cast a wistful glance into his own office as he passed. Dust sheets covered the carpet and someone had been having fun spattering Polyfilla over the walls. The map of Australia on the ceiling had disappeared. Thanet found that like Lineham he mourned its passing.

It was difficult to concentrate in the main CID room, partly because the DCs were trying to be so considerate. They came and went as though walking on eggshells, held telephone conversations *sotto voce* and consulted each other in voices barely louder than whispers. It was all highly unnatural and therefore very distracting. All the reports were brief, however, and Thanet had just finished when Lineham arrived.

'Anything, sir?' said the Sergeant.

'Just a few odds and ends. There doesn't seem to be much doubt that Mrs Salden fell from the bridge, though of course we'll have to wait to hear from Forensic before we're absolutely certain. The divers found her torch in the river below the gap in the parapet, and Mrs Pantry identified the shoe. It was one of a pair kept for outdoor use in a small cloakroom near the back door. She also found Mrs Salden's evening shoes, which she'd obviously discarded when she discovered her car wouldn't start and she'd have to walk to the village.'

The telephone rang and Lineham answered it. He mouthed, 'Tessa Barclay, TVS' at Thanet, and proceeded to apologise for the fact that Thanet had been unavailable the previous afternoon and to promise regular daily bulletins.

'Got yourself a new job then, Mike,' said Thanet with a grin as the Sergeant put the phone down. 'Press correspondent.'

Lineham shrugged. He didn't always take kindly to being teased. 'Someone's got to do it,' he muttered.

'And who better?' Thanet glanced at his watch. 8.43. 'Look, get on the phone and check that Mr Salden will be at home around nine thirty, will you? As soon as the morning meeting's over we'll go out to the Manor again.'

But Draco had other ideas. At the end of the meeting he once again called Thanet back and waved him into a chair.

Thanet betrayed none of his sudden unease. He had an uncomfortable feeling that he knew what was coming.

Draco sat back in his chair, picked up an elastic band and started fiddling with it, winding it around his finger, rolling it on and off his wrist. He seemed incapable of sitting still and once again Thanet wondered how a desk job was going to accommodate all that nervous energy.

'Correct me if I'm wrong,' said the Superintendent in a casual manner which did not deceive Thanet for one moment, 'but am I right in thinking that at the moment you haven't got one single speck of evidence that Mrs Salden's death was anything but an accident?'

Thanet's guess had been correct. Draco wasn't the kind of man to back non-starters. He wanted Thanet to pull out. Thanet prepared to do battle, if necessary. But first he would have to cut Draco down to size in his own mind. He stared at the Superintendent. Draco's promotion was recent and his Welsh accent had been especially noticeable just now. This would be the first clash of wills with his Detective Inspector. Perhaps he, too, was a little nervous and wasn't such a formidable opponent after all.

'That's true, sir.'

'So would you mind explaining to me how I can justify using the entire resources of my CID department on an exercise that could turn out to be a complete waste of time?'

Thanet noticed an involuntary twinge of jealousy at the word *my*, and his determination to win his skirmish hardened. But what ammunition did he have? None. Except . . . 'Doesn't it rather turn on the word "could", sir?'

Draco's thick black eyebrows suddenly clamped together like two hairy caterpillars overcome by passion. 'What do you mean?'

'Well, sir, we have to acknowledge that, equally, it *could* turn out that she was murdered. In which case, if we had just let the matter drop after only twenty-four hours, when there were still obvious lines of enquiry to follow up . . . The Saldens were pretty big fish in the business world down here, and were getting bigger all the time, I gather. It seems to me that you could put that question another way: Can we afford *not* to pursue the matter, for at least a little while longer?'

Draco gave Thanet a penetrating stare, pinged the elastic band a couple of times, then tossed it on to the desk. He steepled his hands beneath his chin. 'Convince me,' he snapped.

Thanet recognised the first sign of capitulation and breathed an inward sigh of relief.

'Well, to begin with, it's difficult to see how she could have fallen through that gap in the parapet by accident . . .'

Thanet reiterated all the conclusions he and Lineham had reached and Draco listened intently, black eyes glittering. He then asked Thanet for details of the lines of enquiry he would follow up today if further investigations were made. Finally he said grudgingly, 'Well, I suppose it won't do any harm to carry on for a bit longer. When's the PM?'

'We're trying to fix it for this afternoon, sir.'

'Right. We'll review the situation again tomorrow morning.' He raised a hand as Thanet started to get up. 'There is just one other thing.'

'Yes, sir?'

'The media. Press, television and so on. We had TVS around yesterday afternoon, claiming an appointment with you. You weren't here.'

'It wasn't exactly an appointment, sir, I just said . . .'

'Never mind what you said. It's important to keep the press sweet, Thanet. It's good for our image.'

'Yes, I know, sir. And TVS is particularly helpful. But you know what's it's like on this sort of enquiry, it's very difficult to say you'll be in a given place at a given time . . .'

'I'm aware of that. That is why I have a suggestion to make.'

Thanet waited.

'On enquiries like these I suggest that you find time, each day, in the late afternoon, to report to me, either in person or by phone, and I can make the appropriate response to the media.'

So Draco was publicity hungry, too. That was fine by Thanet. 'Right, sir.'

Draco reached for a file and opened it.

Thanet took the hint. He was dismissed. He hurried back upstairs still seething with resentment. If he was going to have to face this kind of hassle every morning before he could get on with his work, he'd find himself applying for a transfer before long.

ELEVEN

Mrs Pantry showed them into the big sitting-room. 'I'll tell him you're here.'

While they waited Thanet wandered around, struck once again by the unsuitability of the furnishings. His work took him into many private houses and he firmly believed that a person's home said much about him. This room baffled him. Marcia Salden had obviously been hard-working and ambitious. She had made a resounding success of her business and had fulfilled her childhood dream of owning this house. Why, then, had she not made an effort to furnish it in an appropriate manner? He thought of the gracious room across the hall, downgraded to office. Surely, in a place this size, some other room could have been utilised for such a mundane purpose?

Was it insensitivity, he wondered, that had caused her to treat the house she had yearned for with so little respect? It could have been ignorance, of course, but then she would have been able to afford the best of advice, had she chosen to seek it. Perhaps she simply couldn't be bothered? But that didn't fit in with what he had learnt about her so far. She sounded a woman who paid meticulous attention to detail. Could it perhaps – unpleasant thought – have been a kind of contempt, exercised to demonstrate to the local community how little she valued what they prized so highly, the most beautiful and imposing house in the area? Or perhaps it was simply that it was her work alone that really mattered to her and it was computers and office equipment, rather than carpets and curtains, which monopolised her attention.

What had she and Salden *done* in here? Thanet wondered. There was a television set, true, and the hideous cocktail bar, but none of the clutter which gives a room a lived-in appearance – no books, magazines or newspapers, no photographs apart from the one of Salden shaking hands with Princess Anne, and virtually no ornaments either. What sort of life had she and Salden led together?

The door opened and Salden came in. Thanet guessed that he had put on the first clothes that had come to hand – formal grey worsted trousers that looked as though they belonged to a suit, green open-necked shirt and a navy sweater with a pattern of blue and white diamonds and a logo of crossed golf clubs. He seemed to have aged ten years overnight. If Thanet had met him for the first time today he would have put him in his late sixties. His plump cheeks sagged, his eyelids drooped and below his eyes the pouches of slack skin betrayed the fact that after the sedative wore off he must have spent a sleepless night. But it was his eyes that revealed most clearly his state of mind. They were dazed, veiled. Salden had understandably hidden himself behind the invisible barrier erected in self-protection by those who are trying to survive the aftermath of sudden death.

Thanet experienced a twinge of self-disgust. It was going to be his job to break that barrier down. This particular type of interview, with a bereaved husband or wife who was also a suspect, was the one he hated most of all. At times it had even made him consider changing his job. If Salden were innocent, he deserved the utmost sympathy; if not, sympathy could get badly in the way. Thanet had to walk the tightrope between compassion and inexorability, knowing that whatever the outcome a human being least able to cope with life was having his defences stripped away.

'Good morning, Inspector . . .' Salden shook his head. 'I'm sorry, I've forgotten your name.'

'Thanet. And this is Detective Sergeant Lineham.'

Salden walked slowly across to the wing chair – he was still wearing slippers, Thanet noticed – and lowered himself into it. He waved a hand at the settee opposite. 'Please . . .'

Thanet complied, but Lineham retreated to the matching armchair, moving it back a little and turning it slightly so that he was at right angles to the other two and out of Salden's direct line of vision.

'Have you found out what happened?' said Salden. The dazed look was still there, but behind it was a spark of animation. The process was beginning.

'We think so. We believe she fell through the gap in the parapet of the bridge in the village, where the lorry crashed into it.' Thanet was watching Salden's reaction closely. Was that alarm, or simply surprise?

'But that's not possible, surely? The gap was roped off, and there were warning lights . . .'

'You saw them when you went through the village that night.'

'Yes, of course.' Salden shook his head in apparent puzzlement. 'I don't understand.'

'I agree, it does seem odd. Obviously, we're trying to find out exactly what happened . . . You said you went for a walk that evening?'

'That's right, yes.'

'What time did you leave your mother-in-law's house?'

The brief flare of interest had burned itself out and there was a pause before each answer now as if remembering were a process only to be achieved by will-power.

'Let me see . . . Somewhere around half-past eight, I should think.'

'Which way did you go?'

'Through the village. I went for a drink at the pub first, then I carried on, over the bridge towards the Sturrenden road.'

'The warning lights and rope barriers . . . They were all in position then?'

A long pause, this time. 'So far as I can remember, yes. I think I would have noticed, if they hadn't been. But I was rather preoccupied. I was thinking about my mother-in-law. We . . .' He turned his head aside and took in a deep breath, held it. 'We were very fond of each other and it always upset me, to see her as she was that night.'

'Yes, I can imagine. I'm sorry, you've had a really bad time over the last few days.'

The words of sympathy penetrated Salden's fragile defences and his eyes filled with tears. He blinked several times in rapid succession and brushed a forefinger across each eye. 'Sorry.'

'Don't apologise, please.' *Remember, a man is innocent until he is proved guilty.* 'I'm sorry to have to ask you all these questions, but we've been trying to talk to everyone who was out and about in the village that night . . . We understand you didn't get back to your mother-in-law's house until about half-past ten. It must have been quite a long walk.'

'Well, I wasn't walking all the time. As I said, I went into the pub for a while, twenty minutes or half an hour, perhaps, then I strolled along as far as the junction with the Sturrenden road and back.'

'That would have taken how long?'

Salden shrugged. 'I wasn't walking very quickly. I wasn't looking for exercise, just fresh air and a chance to think.'

'About anything in particular?'

Salden frowned. 'Not really, no. Look, Inspector, I'm sorry, but I don't quite see where all this is leading.'

'I assure you that everyone in the village is being asked similar questions.'

'That may be so. But the point is, why are they necessary, if you already know how the accident happened?'

Thanet said nothing, just cast a deliberate glance at Lineham.

Salden's face changed, its slack lines firming up into much more positive contours. His eyes narrowed as the glazed look finally disappeared and he leaned forward.

Thanet could predict what was coming next. He had heard it so many times before.

'You're not suggesting. . . ? My God, you are, aren't you?'

'Suggesting what, Mr Salden?'

'That Marcia . . . That it wasn't an accident?'

'We're treating this as a suspicious death, Mr Salden, that's all. Before we can dismiss it as an accident we have to consider all the other possibilities. Suicide, for example.'

Salden was shaking his head vigorously. 'Marcia would never have committed suicide.'

'You'd be surprised how many of the relatives of suicides say just that.'

Salden waved a hand. 'Ask anyone you like . . . The housekeeper, Mrs Pantry . . . Edith Phipps . . . the Vicar . . .

Anyone who knew her. I don't think you'll find a single person who'd countenance the idea for one second. Marcia really just wasn't the type. She had too much to live for.'

'I must admit that that was the impression I had already gained from talking to people. So in that case, you see, we must at least consider the third possibility.'

Salden shook his head again. There was a beading of sweat on his upper lip and he was hugging himself as if to stop himself falling apart. 'I can't believe it. Who would want to do such a thing?'

'Have you any suggestions?'

Salden frowned, thinking.

There was a knock at the door. Salden appeared not to have heard. Thanet and Lineham exchanged irritated glances. Should they ignore it? But it could be important. 'Come in,' called Thanet as Salden, simultaneously, said, 'There's only – '

Edith Phipps put her head around the door. 'Sorry to interrupt, but I thought you'd want to know . . . The Vicar's on the phone, about the arrangements for Mrs Carter's funeral, and he's got to go out, you won't be able to ring him later.'

Salden glanced at Thanet. 'Sorry, Inspector . . . Would you excuse me for a moment?'

Thanet had no choice but to agree.

When Salden had left, Lineham burst out, 'He was just going to give us a name!'

Thanet nodded. 'Yes, but I bet you anything you like it was going to be Greenleaf's.'

Lineham pulled a face. 'Probably.'

Thanet got up and strolled across to the window. Earlier on the sky had been overcast but now the cloud cover was beginning to break up and patches of blue were appearing. Thanet leaned forward to look diagonally across to the right at the smudge of trees that was Harry's wood. It was foolish to ignore the obvious. Greenleaf had the only discernible motive so far for killing Marcia Salden. He would almost certainly have had opportunity, too. He was accountable to no one for his movements and could well have been in the right place at

101

the right time without anyone being the wiser. Yes, a visit to Harry was high on their list of priorities. Thanet half turned, propping one elbow on the window ledge, so that he could see Lineham's face. 'Well, what d'you think now you've had the chance of a second look at Salden? Still think he might have done it?'

'Might have. I don't think we're any further forward, to be honest.'

'I must admit he intrigues me, Mike.'

'Why? He seems a very ordinary sort of bloke to me.'

'But that's precisely it! What makes a man like that tick, Mike? He is ordinary. So ordinary that he practically disappears into the wallpaper.'

'The last person you'd suspect of murder, in fact.'

'Exactly.'

Lineham grinned. 'According to all the detective novels, then, he's bound to be our man.'

'Not such a joke in fact, Mike. Think of all the quiet little men who have upped and killed their spouses when they've had enough.'

'You think Salden had had enough?'

'Not necessarily, no.'

'If he did do it, it looks as though he killed the goose that laid the golden eggs, doesn't it? I'd guess she was the one who was the driving force behind the health food shops and all this.' Lineham waved a hand to encompass the Manor, the grounds outside. 'Not that it would matter too much, I suppose. There should be a tidy little sum to keep him in comfort in his old age.'

'Not necessarily, Mike. For all we know they could be mortgaged to the eyeballs. We'll have to look into it. But there's no doubt that at the moment Salden's a prime suspect. He's the only person we know of so far who was definitely in the right place at the right time.'

'So far.'

'True. But — and it's a big but — if his motive wasn't financial it's difficult to see what it could be.'

'Does he need one, sir? As the music-hall comedian would say, he was married to her, wasn't he?'

'Don't tell me you're becoming a cynic in your old age, Mike.'

'I was only kidding. No, the point I was trying to make is that, as you've said so often yourself, no one really knows what goes on between a married couple but the two people themselves. And in this case, well, they're an odd pair, you'll agree.'

'True. Though they must have got on reasonably well to have worked in the same business under the same roof for twenty years or so.'

'They weren't exactly under each other's feet, were they, in a place this size?'

'Maybe not, but they'd only been here eighteen months, remember. I bet that for years they were tripping over each other all day and every day in some poky little flat above the shop.'

Across the hall a door slammed. Thanet strolled back to his seat.

'Sorry I was so long. There was a lot to discuss.' Salden was moving more briskly, as if making decisions had nudged him one step further back towards normality. He sat down, frowning. 'What were we saying?'

'I'd just asked if you could think of anyone with a grudge against your wife,' said Thanet.

'Ah, yes . . . Well, as I was going to say, there's only Harry Greenleaf. I suppose you've heard about him?'

'We have, yes. In fact, we arrived yesterday just as the bailiffs were about to evict him. I hope you don't mind, but I took it upon myself to delay the eviction. I thought you wouldn't want all the fuss and commotion that would follow. A lot of the villagers turned up, you know, and formed a protest line. They'd have had to be removed bodily before the bulldozer could have got through to the hut.'

'Really? Good grief. I didn't know that. Edith – Miss Phipps – told me you'd sent the bailiffs away. Thank you. A minor riot was the last thing I'd have wanted on my hands yesterday.'

'What will you do now, about Greenleaf?'

Salden shrugged. 'Let him stay on, probably. If the local people feel as strongly as that . . .'

'It was your wife who was so keen to get rid of him?'

Salden looked embarrassed. 'Yes. I never did understand why. Still . . . although, as I say, he's the only person I can think of who could be said to have had a grudge against her, I really can't believe he would have gone to the sort of lengths you're suggesting. He's always struck me as being a quiet, gentle sort of chap, the kind who wouldn't squash a fly without having qualms about it. He's always taking wounded animals under his wing and patching them up before releasing them into the wild again, that sort of thing.'

Thanet decided to backtrack a little. 'To get back to your walk . . . Even allowing for your time in the pub, it wouldn't have taken you an hour and a half to stroll as far as the Sturrenden road and back.'

'There's a footpath running alongside the river, on the other side of the bridge, and a bench or two here and there. I went and sat on one for a while.'

'It was freezing, that night.'

'I was well wrapped up . . . Look, Inspector, all this interest in my movements . . . I'm not stupid, I can see where it's leading . . .'

Thanet said nothing. He was interested to see how Salden would deal with this.

Salden was watching him closely. 'I'm right, aren't I?' His voice rose. 'That is what you're getting at, isn't it?' A rush of indignation drove him to his feet and he stood confronting Thanet, feet planted firmly apart and hands shoved into his pockets. 'My God,' he said, glaring down at him, 'you really are the lowest of the low, aren't you?'

Inwardly, Thanet winced but, knowing that in circumstances like these silence is the most powerful weapon of all, he still did not respond.

'How can you do it?' said Salden, working himself up into a real fury. 'How would you feel if your wife had just been dragged out of the river and some grubby little policeman came along and said you'd shoved her in yourself, tell me that?'

This accorded so well with what Thanet himself felt that he was stung into speech. 'I said no such thing.'

Salden brushed the denial aside. 'Said, implied, what's the difference? It all comes down to the same thing, doesn't it? You think I might have killed her.' He shook his head in disgust and began to blunder blindly about the room, as if trying to find his way out of an impossible situation.

Lineham tensed, but Thanet shook his head. *Let him be.*

Salden clutched his head. 'I don't believe this. I just don't believe it.'

'Mr Salden.'

The note of command in Thanet's voice was so powerful that Salden was stopped in his tracks.

'Mr Salden,' Thanet repeated, more gently. 'Look, I know this is an unpleasant situation . . .'

Salden gave a great bark of mirthless laughter. 'Unpleasant, he says!'

'For both of us. And for you most of all. But . . .'

'Oh, I'm glad you recognise that! Very glad! You're right, it is *unpleasant* to be accused of murdering your wife when you're still trying to grasp the fact that she's gone for ever. Do you have even the first glimmering of what that can be like? Of course you haven't. No one can, if they haven't actually been through it themselves. There's this huge gap, this vast empty space, which has always been filled by one person . . . And you know that no one can fill it ever again, that you're going to have to live with that gap for the rest of your life. How can you even begin to understand? It's as if life itself has hit you with a sledgehammer and you know you're never going to get over it, never . . .'

Salden was fighting for control. Thanet and Lineham sat frozen into silence. What can you say in response to grief so raw and unconcealed?

'And then,' said Salden, his voice still shaking, 'you're expected to sit down meekly and face the allegation that you killed her yourself!'

'Mr Salden . . .'

'I don't want to hear any more! Get out, will you? Just get out!'

Thanet and Lineham consulted each other with a glance. They'd inflicted more than enough pain on the man for one day, Thanet thought. He nodded and they both rose, walked silently to the door. Thanet had his hand on the knob when Salden said, 'No!'

They turned.

Salden was chinking the change in his pockets, his restless fingers unconsciously betraying his jangled nerves. 'If I don't answer your bloody questions now you'll only come back another day. I've changed my mind. I want to get it over with.'

Thanet hesitated. He wasn't sure that there was any point in continuing, with Salden in this state.

Salden misread him. 'Oh, don't worry, I won't blow my top again. I can see that it's in my own interest to satisfy your curiosity' – he practically spat the word out – 'as soon as possible.' He sat down decisively in the wing chair and folded his hands in his lap. 'So I'm ready when you are.'

'If you're sure . . .'

'I've said so, haven't I?'

Thanet and Lineham returned to their seats.

'Right,' said Thanet briskly. 'We'll be as quick as possible. This walk . . .'

'We've been over all that once,' interrupted Salden impatiently.

'Please . . . bear with me for just a moment. This bench you were sitting on. How far away from the bridge was it?'

'Quite a long way. Three or four hundred yards, perhaps?'

'It was dark, of course. Would you be able to see anyone walking across the bridge, from that distance?'

'No. Not clearly, anyway, not to recognise anyone.'

'There's a lamp on the pub side of the bridge, isn't there? What about on the other side? I'm not too clear on that.'

'It's a sore point. We've been trying to get another one installed. The nearest one is a hundred yards away, where the houses start.'

'I see . . . Now I'd like you to think very carefully. While you were sitting on your bench, did you in fact see or hear any noise at all from the direction of the bridge? Voices, for example, or footsteps?' *Or sounds of a struggle, or a splash?* Thanet shuddered at the thought of Salden's wife fighting for her life with her husband sitting innocently on a bench only a quarter of a mile away. 'It was a clear, frosty night, so sound would have carried quite a long way, I imagine.'

The brief, factual questions were calming Salden down. He was frowning hard, trying to remember.

'I'm sorry,' he said at last. 'I just can't remember. I wasn't taking any notice, you see. I vaguely remember the odd car going by, but that's all.'

It was pointless to ask if, on his way back to Mrs Carter's cottage, Salden had seen his wife. He would obviously deny it. 'On your way back to your mother-in-law's house, did you see anyone?'

'Not a soul.'

'This walk you took . . . I must confess I'm a little puzzled.'

Salden raised his eyebrows.

'As to why you didn't go home instead? Especially as you had guests to dinner that evening.'

'I just wasn't feeling particularly sociable.'

'Even so . . .'

'To be blunt, Inspector, I just couldn't face the prospect of making polite conversation. My mother-in-law and I were very close, I told you . . . It really upset me to see her like that. At that particular moment I couldn't have cared less how discourteous it looked.'

'That dinner party . . .' Careful now, Thanet told himself. He didn't want to set Salden off again. On the other hand, he had to find out . . . 'I did have the impression it wasn't just a normal social occasion.'

'Oh?' Salden's eyes were wary.

'One of your guests was Councillor Lomax, I understand.'

'Yes he was.'

'I believe he is chairman of the Planning Committee. And your wife was hoping to get a rather tricky planning permission . . .' The implication was clear and Thanet awaited Salden's response with interest and some trepidation. Would he pretend not to understand, feign ignorance, become angry, bluster. . . ?

Salden sighed. 'Yes . . . Perhaps I should explain . . . My wife was an amazing woman. If you knew the kind of background she came from . . . Her father was an alcoholic, and they never had two pennies to rub together. I think that was why she had this tremendous drive to succeed. She was one of my students, you know, that was how we met. I was lecturing at the time on a Business Studies course, and this was what singled her out from all the rest. She was so determined . . . I couldn't help admiring her for that, it was what attracted me to her in the first place. I've always admired people who knew what they wanted and were prepared to work hard to get it. So I could hardly complain if, from time to time, she set out to do something I didn't really approve of. She never was the type to rest on her laurels, she was always looking for some bigger challenge to move on to and usually I just let her get on with it.'

'And this particular scheme?'

Salden shrugged. 'I told her I didn't like it. But if you think I shoved her off the bridge to stop her going on with it, I'm afraid you're way off the mark. There were other ways to show my disapproval.'

'Like ducking out of the dinner party, for example?'

For the first time there was a flicker of amusement in Salden's eyes. 'Exactly.'

'The other guest, Miss Trimble. . . ?'

'We all call her Josie. She spends quite a lot of time here. She's only eighteen and she comes from the village, her mother's a widow so they've had a bit of a struggle to manage. Josie was . . . well, I suppose you could call her a protégé of my wife's. We never actually discussed it, but I think Marcia saw herself in the girl, and was trying to help her to better herself – teaching her table manners and so on.'

'So she was often invited to dinner parties? To put into practice what she'd learned.'

'Yes. Well, not often, exactly. We don't – didn't – entertain much.'

'In that case, wasn't your wife annoyed, that you didn't go back to join them?'

Salden blinked. 'How should I know? I never saw her

again . . . Oh, you mean earlier, when we spoke on the phone? No, I don't think so. In fact I think at that point she was just relieved that she wouldn't have to go down to the village herself. It had been too late, earlier, to stop Lomax coming, Nurse Lint didn't ring until just before half-past seven.'

'Your wife went down to see her mother later though, leaving her guests entirely on their own.'

Another shrug. 'In the normal way of things she'd only have been away ten or fifteen minutes, if she'd gone by car.'

'But she still went, even though the car wouldn't start.'

'True. But she'd have expected to find me there, remember. No doubt she thought I'd be able to give her a lift back, or that she could borrow my keys and drive back in my car . . . Look, Inspector, I really can't see why we're dredging all this up. Yes, she did go, and yes, I agree it did look odd, leaving her guests by themselves like that, but it happened and I can't see any point in discussing it further.'

'Why did Mrs Carter want to see you?'

Salden lifted his shoulders. 'She was convinced she was dying. Wasn't that a good enough reason?'

'In that case, wasn't it strange that she didn't ask for your wife in the first place?'

'She knew I'd get Marcia to come when I felt the time was right. My mother-in-law was a very proud woman in some ways, especially where my wife was concerned. It was as if she didn't want it to look as though she was making any kind of claim on her. I could never understand it myself. She really hated asking Marcia for anything. Anyway, I decided to ring Marcia from the cottage when I got back from my walk and tell her I thought she ought to come down. I knew dinner would be over by then and she'd be able to get rid of Lomax and Josie without too much difficulty. But of course, when I got back to the cottage, she'd already been and gone.'

'I understand you missed her by just a few minutes.'

'Yes.' Salden shivered and wrapped his arms around his body. 'If only I'd started back a few minutes earlier she'd still be alive . . .'

'There's never any point in saying "If only", Mr Salden,' said Thanet gently.

'Maybe not. But how do you stop yourself, in circumstances like these?'

The pain in Salden's eyes was so intense that it was almost unbearable to meet them and there was no doubting his sincerity.

'Just one more question, and we'll leave you in peace. When you got home, why didn't you go into your wife's room and tell her that her mother had died?'

'It was four in the morning, Inspector. Her room was in darkness and I assumed she'd been asleep for hours. What was the point in waking her up? She couldn't have done anything.'

This was unanswerable.

They left.

TWELVE

'Well, that was no act, was it?' said Lineham. 'He really did care about her, didn't he?'

Thanet had decided that a visit to Greenleaf was definitely next on the agenda and they were crossing the lawn towards the entrance to the footpath. It was a relief to get out into the open air, away from the claustrophobic atmosphere of the house. He sniffed appreciatively and turned his face to the sun, which had just broken through. 'Mmm.' His feet scuffed through the lake of fallen petals beneath the cherry tree. 'Doesn't necessarily exonerate him, though.' Violent crime, he knew, stirred strong passions in those caught up in its aftermath – guilt, anger and frustration as well as sorrow and regret.

'He seemed pretty cut up, to me.'

'Oh yes, I agree, he is.'

'And not so ordinary after all.'

'True. Just shows it never pays to judge by outward appearances.'

They walked on in a companionable silence, Thanet wondering if the Sergeant had yet managed to have that talk with his wife. He certainly looked much more cheerful this morning.

Lineham unhooked the gate and held it open.

A young woman was coming up the footpath from the village, leaning forward with the effort of propelling a toddler in a pushchair up the hill. She checked for a moment when she saw the two men, then came on again more slowly. It looked as though Marcia's death had encouraged people to start using the short cut again. Perhaps this girl thought she was about to be accused of trespassing. Or perhaps, Thanet thought as they stepped aside on to the grass for her to pass, she was simply nervous of meeting two strange men out here where there was no one to come to her aid if she were attacked. She had scuttled past, barely returning their greeting, and he thought how sad it was that nowadays women felt so vulnerable that even an innocent chance encounter such as this became an occasion for fear.

As they rounded the trees near the river and glanced up the grassy slope towards Greenleaf's hut, Lineham gave Thanet an excited nudge.

'He's there, sir.'

It was logical to assume that the figure stooping over the vegetable patch was Greenleaf. A black and white mongrel which had been lying near him leaped up and started to bark the moment it spotted them and Greenleaf turned to look. He straightened up, shoving his fork into the ground, and, hands on hips, watched them approach. Thanet realised with surprise that the recluse was much younger than he had expected. For some reason he had visualised Greenleaf as an old man, in his sixties or seventies, but even from a distance it was obvious from the vigour of his movements that he was a good decade or two younger.

It was, of course, impossible to tell his age from his face.

Even though Thanet had been prepared for the man's disfigurement, he still experienced a shock of pity when they drew close enough to see him clearly. The fire in which he had received his injuries must have been horrendous. Despite the miracles which plastic surgery is now able to achieve, Greenleaf's face was barely human, its contours unnatural, the skin stretched and shiny, the nose virtually non-existent, the mouth lipless, the eyes mere slits. He was wearing worn but clean corduroy trousers and a collarless shirt rolled up above the elbows. His hands and arms had been badly burned too. Thanet could see why he lived in self-imposed isolation. It would be impossible for him ever to go out without attracting glances of fascinated horror, aversion or pity. Deliberately, Thanet kept his face impassive, and hoped that Lineham was managing to do the same.

The dog was still barking frantically. Greenleaf made no

move to quieten it until the two men were only a few yards away, then he extended the forefinger of his right hand and pointed briefly at the dog's muzzle. It fell silent at once, sitting down close beside him. His hand moved over its head in a brief gesture of praise before he said, 'Who are you?' He obviously didn't believe in wasting words. His voice was hoarse, rusty perhaps with disuse. He would have no one to talk to but the animals. He listened to Thanet's introductions, his eyes moving to Lineham and back again. It was impossible to tell what he was thinking.

'Thought you might be more of those danged reporters. Or the bailiffs, come to chuck me out.'

Thanet shook his head. 'We're looking into the death of Mrs Salden.'

'Ah . . . Yes, I heard about that . . . Falled in the river, didn't she?'

'Yes, she did. We wondered if you knew anything about it.'

'Knew anything?'

The dog growled low in its throat, a barometer perhaps of its master's emotions. Thanet could not remember ever having to interview a witness without being able to try to gauge his reaction from his face.

'She was drowned in the river down there.' Thanet gestured at the waters of the Teale in the valley below, sparkling innocently in the spring sunshine. 'We thought perhaps you might have seen or heard something.'

'I heard tell that there's a lot of questions being asked,' said Greenleaf. 'In the village and all.'

'A woman is dead,' said Thanet. 'Of course we're asking a lot of questions. And until we find out how and when she died, we'll be asking a lot more.'

'You're thinking, perhaps, that someone might have helped her on her way.'

'It is one possibility, yes.'

'And you asks yourself, "Now, who would be glad to see the back of Mrs Salden?" And back comes the answer, "Harry Greenleaf, that's who. Him what was about to be turned off her land and made to join the ranks of the homeless." Am I right?'

113

'Of course.'

'Just so long as we know where we are.'

'So . . .' Thanet was brisk. 'Now that we're quite clear about it . . . Perhaps you could tell us where you were, that night.'

'Well now, which night was that, can you tell me?' Disfigured hand came up and rubbed travesty of a chin in a gesture of mock puzzlement.

No point in allowing yourself to be riled, Thanet told himself. 'Oh, come, Mr Greenleaf,' he said lightly, 'your memory can't be that short, surely. It was only the night before last.'

'The night before last,' Greenleaf said thoughtfully. He looked down at the dog and stroked its head. 'Do you remember what we was doing the night before last, Jack?'

He and the dog gazed at each other in silence for a moment or two. 'Ah, yes, that's right. Thanks, Jack.' Greenleaf's slits of eyes turned in Thanet's direction again. 'I was busy packing up, of course. On account of expecting to be turfed out next morning.'

'It must have been a relief, to find that the proceedings had been called off.'

'Oh it was, wasn't it, Jack? That Mr Salden's all right.'

'It wasn't Mr Salden who called them off,' said Lineham, interrupting. 'It was Inspector Thanet here.'

Thanet shot Lineham a furious glance.

Greenleaf said with mock humility, 'Oh, it was, was it? Then we has every reason to be grateful to the kind Inspector, hasn't we, Jack?'

Thanet was amused to find that the last vestiges of pity for Greenleaf had vanished, to be replaced by reluctant admiration. The man was obviously more than capable of looking after himself. 'So you claim you were in your hut all evening?'

Greenleaf's eyes, glittering through the narrow openings in the puffy flesh, met Thanet's squarely. 'I was.' He looked down at the dog. 'As Jack is my witness.'

He was lying, Thanet was sure of it. But it was impossible to tell whether it was because he had indeed been responsible for pushing Marcia off the bridge or because he'd been up to something else he didn't want the police to know about. In any case, it was obvious that there was no point in pursuing that particular line of questioning.

'I believe Mrs Salden came down to see you in the afternoon.'

'In a manner of speaking.'

'What do you mean?'

'She did come, but she didn't see me.'

'Why not?'

Greenleaf addressed the dog again. 'Saw her coming, didn't we Jack.' He met Thanet's eye again. 'Guessed she meant trouble, so we slipped away, come back after she'd gone.'

That was Harry's story and clearly he was going to stick to it. They left.

Lineham waited until they were halfway down the slope before he spoke. 'Insolent so and so.'

'You shouldn't have interfered, Mike.'

'I know, sir. I'm sorry. But it just made me mad to see him taking the mickey out of you like that.'

'I'm quite capable of looking after myself, you know. I don't need protecting.'

'No, I know. But . . .'

'No "buts", Mike. Did it occur to you that it's probably his way of coping with his disfigurement in front of strangers? By all accounts he's popular enough with the locals.'

Lineham looked a little shamefaced. 'You think so?'

'Could be. If people are busy being angry at him they can't be feeling sorry for him. It works, too, didn't you notice?'

Lineham was silent for a few moments. 'Yes, I suppose you're right.' A further silence, then he burst out, 'Why can't I ever see things like that for myself?'

'Practice, I suppose. I've been at it longer than you have.'

'No point in trying to make excuses for me. It's always happening, however hard I try.'

'Perhaps you're not trying in the right way.'

'What do you mean?'

'Well, back there . . . You found you were getting angry, right?'

'Right.'

115

'So, then what? You reacted by speaking out, didn't you?'

'Yes. And I shouldn't have, I know.'

'So what should you have done?'

Lineham stopped walking and turned to face Thanet. 'What do you mean? Kept my big mouth shut, of course.'

Thanet shook his head. 'No, that's not what I mean. That's a negative reaction, and I'm looking for a positive one.'

'Sorry, you've lost me. I got angry, right? So I either allow myself to show it, or I don't. How else could I have reacted?'

'There are a couple of alternatives. Look, you know the anger is unconstructive, don't you? So you have to defuse it. And you do this either by trying to understand your own reaction, just why you are getting so annoyed, or by asking yourself why it is he finds it necessary to behave so provocatively. In this particular instance the answer wasn't hard to find. Nobody likes to be pitied. Better, by far, to make people angry, irritate them so that they won't come back again . . .'

'I wonder if that's why he got up Mrs Salden's nose.'

'Could be one of the reasons. I shouldn't think she'd take kindly to being made fun of . . . Anyway, as you see, it's all a question of not allowing yourself to react blindly, of trying to analyse what's going on instead.'

Lineham was shaking his head. 'Sounds beyond me.'

Thanet moved on again, quickening his pace. There was a great deal to do today. 'Nonsense. I've told you before, it's all a question of practice. A skill to be learned, like any other. The more interviewing you do, the better at it you get.'

They had reached the car.

'Where next, sir?'

'I think it's time we found out how Josie Trimble and Councillor Lomax fit into all this, don't you?'

THIRTEEN

If this was the reward in the trap which Marcia Salden had baited for Lomax, Thanet thought, he wouldn't be surprised if the councillor had succumbed to temptation. Josie Trimble was a succulent morsel indeed, if you liked smooth young flesh, downy as a peach, curves that were neither skimpy nor over-generous, huge dark eyes and a tumble of luxuriant curls to match.

The proprietor of the unisex hair salon ('Call me Gary') hadn't been too pleased to see them and they had been whisked at high speed past clients and pot plants alike into a small room at the back of the premises which obviously doubled as laundry and staff room; towels whirled in a pair of automatic washer-dryers and a girl and a young man were seated at the formica table, drinking coffee and smoking.

Gary advanced, teeth bared in false bonhomie. 'Sorry to interrupt your break, darlings, you'll have to tack an extra few minutes on to your dinner hours.'

They cast resentful glances at Thanet and Lineham, stubbed out their cigarettes and left without a word.

'Josie hasn't been a naughty girl, I hope.' The fashionable quiff at the front of Gary's head quivered with anxiety. At sides and back his hair had been cut very close, practically shaved. Thanet wondered how the hairdresser would describe the effect. 'Sculptured', perhaps? He was in his mid-thirties, colourfully dressed in purple velvet trousers and canary yellow open-necked shirt.

Thanet had murmured appropriate platitudes and Josie had duly been produced. At a glance from Thanet Gary had retired, leaving the door slighly ajar behind him.

Without a word Lineham had got up and closed it.

'Now then, Miss Trimble,' said Lineham.

Thanet had decided that in view of their conversation after the interview with Greenleaf it would be a good idea for Lineham to conduct this interview. From time to time the Sergeant needed a boost to his self-confidence. The girl was obviously nervous and Thanet watched with approval as, handling her gently, Lineham established the basis of her relationship with Marcia Salden ('Ever so kind to me, she was'), gradually working around to the events of Tuesday evening.

'So you arrived at the Manor at what time?'

'Mrs Salden told me she wanted me to be there on time, so I got there dead on half-past seven.'

Thanet noticed the careful aspirate. Marcia's teaching had obviously begun to pay off.

'You walked up from the village?'

She nodded. 'Along the footpath. Mrs Salden said I could use it whenever I liked.'

A touch of pride, there. Josie had obviously enjoyed the privilege.

'See anyone, on the way?'

She hadn't.

When she got to the Manor, Mrs Salden had told her that Mr Salden had been called to see Mrs Carter, who had taken a turn for the worse. It had been too late to contact Mr Lomax, so they were going to go ahead with the dinner party and Mrs Salden might pop down to the village later to see her mother. At that point Mr Lomax had arrived and they'd all had drinks.

'You'd met Mr Lomax before.' Lineham made it a statement, not a question.

Josie nodded and lowered her head a little so that her hair fell forwards to screen her face.

'Often?'

She shrugged and murmured something.

'I'm sorry, I didn't catch that.'

She raised her head. 'I said, a few times.'

'Where did you meet him?'

'Mrs Salden introduced me to 'im at a cheese and wine she took me to.'

Interesting, thought Thanet. The aspirate had slipped. Josie was getting nervous.

'When was this?'

She licked her lips. 'Christmas.'

So, four months ago.

Unobtrusively, Thanet edged his chair back. He wanted to be able to see Josie's feet. Feet are often excellent registers of emotion. He was in luck, she was wearing open-toed sandals. As he expected, her toes were tightly bunched up. What was she afraid of?

Abruptly, she stood up. 'Sorry, I need to go to the toilet.' And without waiting for permission she blundered out of the room.

Lineham raised his eyebrows. 'What was all that about?'

'Interesting, wasn't it? Lomax, d'you think? Or something else?'

But whatever it was, Josie wasn't giving it away. When she returned, Lineham continued to probe, without success. She and Lomax had met a few times at functions when she had been accompanying Marcia. Three, perhaps four times in all. She didn't know nothing about any business dealings between them. Yes, Mrs Salden had left for the cottage at around twenty to ten, saying she'd only be gone ten or fifteen minutes and that she especially wanted a word with Josie when she got back. When she failed to return Josie and Mr Lomax had naturally assumed that it must be because Mrs Carter was very ill indeed.

'It must have been rather awkward for you.'

'Awkward?'

'Being left to entertain Mr Lomax on Mrs Salden's behalf.'

'Oh . . . No, not really. It wasn't as though we was complete strangers.'

'I suppose not. Did Mrs Salden ring, to apologise for being held up?'

The dark curls bounced as Josie shook her head. 'We wasn't surprised, if her mum was that ill . . . In the end Mr Lomax decided to go, but I 'ung on because I'd said I would.'

'I understood that you eventually gave up and went home.'

Her expression changed. 'I waited for an hour or more after Mr Salden rung up,' she said defensively.

Lineham smoothed ruffled feathers. 'It's all right. It's perfectly understandable that you went home. You couldn't have been expected to wait up all night.'

'Didn't know what was 'appening, did I? I mean, when Mr Salden rung about half ten, to ask me to tell 'er he was staying and not to wait up, we thought she must still be on her way 'ome. When she didn't come, well, I thought I must have got it wrong, some'ow. Or that she'd changed 'er mind, turned round and gone back to 'er mum's.' The girl was becoming agitated and now her eyes filled with tears. ''Ow was I to know she'd fallen in the river?' She began to cry in earnest, reaching blindly for a box of tissues on the table.

Thanet pushed them towards her groping hand. 'Miss Trimble . . . Josie . . . Would you mind if I called you Josie?'

She shook her head, wiping her eyes.

'Look, Josie, I hope you're not blaming yourself for what happened to Mrs Salden.'

'If I'd called someone right away, it might have been in time to save 'er!' she sobbed.

'Called who?'

'Anyone! The police?'

'And what good would that have done? What would you have said to them?'

She shrugged. He had her attention now and her sobs were abating. She wiped her eyes and blew her nose.

He pressed home the advantage. 'That Mrs Salden was walking home from the village alone in the dark? D'you think they'd have taken you seriously, done anything about it? Turned out to look for a grown woman who hadn't been missing more than ten minutes? Of course they wouldn't. There's never any point in trying to be wise after the event, is there? So come on, cheer up. Whatever happened, it wasn't your fault. You do see that, don't you?'

But she was avoiding his eye, seemingly unconvinced. Perhaps . . . He glanced at Lineham, who raised his shoulders. *Carry on if you want to.*

'Josie . . . I think there's something you'd like to tell us, isn't there?'

And yes, that was an unmistakable flash of fear.

'No! What d'you mean?'

'You may have heard rumours . . .'

'What rumours?' Her lips barely moved and she was staring at Thanet as if suddenly mesmerised.

'About Mrs Salden's death.'

'Ah.' A slow exhalation. She shook her head, once, a slow, almost dreamy movement. She was still gazing at him but her stare had lost its fierce intensity. Then puzzlement gradually crept into her eyes. 'What rumours?' she repeated.

'That it may not have been an accident,' put in Lineham.

Thanet hoped they were doing the right thing in perpetuating those rumours. But the girl was frightened of something, was hiding something, he was sure of it. The affair with Lomax, perhaps?

'Not an . . . accident?' she whispered, staring at him.

'So you see, we have to ask you. Do you know if Mrs Salden had any enemies, anyone with a grudge against her?'

You could see her working it out. Accident . . . Enemies . . . The colour ebbed away from her face, leaving the skin chalk white. 'Grudge. . . ?'

Lineham caught her as she slid off the chair.

FOURTEEN

'I always wanted to do that,' said Lineham with a grin as they stepped out into the street.

They had arranged to return in an hour, when Josie would have had time to recover, having temporarily abandoned her to Gary's ministrations amidst disapproving looks which clearly hinted at police brutality.

'Catch a maiden in distress in your arms, you mean? A very pleasant experience, I imagine. And neatly done, if I may say so.' But Thanet's teasing was half-hearted. He was thinking of something else.

'Sir . . .'

'Mmm?'

'Where are you going? The car's this way.'

Thanet woke up. 'Mike, how many times have I got to tell you?' He stopped, pointed at his feet. 'You know what those are? Yes, we are going to see Lomax, but it'll be quicker to walk than drive round the one-way system. You'll lose the use of your legs before you're forty, at this rate.' And he set off again, briskly.

Sturrenden was at its best on a clear, bright morning like this, the picturesque jumble of Tudor and Georgian, black and white timbering and mellow bricks and tile preening themselves to face yet another spring. A strong conservationist lobby had averted too many contemporary disasters. Thanet gazed about appreciatively. How fortunate he was to work in a place like this!

'I just like driving, that's all,' grumbled Lineham, hurrying to catch up.

Thanet grinned. 'Stop sounding like a five-year-old who's

had his favourite teddy taken away, Mike, and tell me what you thought of the luscious Miss Trimble.'

'Well, she obviously knows someone who had it in for our Marcia.'

'Hmm. I wonder why she passed out just then.' Thanet was satisfied that the faint had been genuine.

'A subconscious means of avoiding the issue,' said Lineham with the smug smile of a conjuror who has just pulled off a particularly difficult trick. 'She knows – or suspects – who the murderer is but she doesn't want to tell us.'

'I'm not sure . . . I'm inclined to think it was because she had just realised who the murderer might be.'

'Isn't it practically the same thing?'

'Not really, no. But whichever it is, I think it means that this person is someone close to her. She lives with her mother, doesn't she? Did Miss Phipps mention any brothers or sisters?'

'I don't think so, no. Could be Lomax, sir.'

'Possibly. In fact I was wondering if what she was really frightened of, all the time we were talking to her, was whether or not we knew about her and Lomax. Ah, here we are.'

Thanet had got one of his men to do a little digging on Lomax. The councillor was sixty-four, married, with two sons, both now with families of their own and settled some distance away. He and his wife lived in a bungalow on one of the more established small new estates on the edge of Sturrenden. He owned a radio and TV shop called Sturrenden Audio in one of the town's side streets.

Business wasn't exactly booming, by the look of it, thought Thanet. The place was going to seed. The glass of the window was grubby and smeared where fingers and noses had been pressed against it over a long period; dead flies which looked as though they had been there since last summer lay scattered on the faded blue paper which lined the window, and the few radios and television sets looked dusty and out of date. The shop appeared to be empty. A bell pinged as they went in.

Nothing happened. There was a distant sound of pop music.

Lineham rapped on the counter. 'Shop!'

Still nothing.

The door behind the counter was ajar and Lineham put his head through and shouted. 'Hello.'

A sound of movement and a moment later a spotty youth appeared with a screwdriver in his hand. 'Sorry.'

'Mr Lomax in?' asked Lineham.

'Just popped out. Won't be long.'

'We'll wait.'

The boy looked at the screwdriver, then at Thanet and Lineham. His dilemma was apparent. There was work to be done, but he couldn't leave the shop unattended with potential thieves in it. 'He might be quite a while.'

Lineham grinned, pulled out his warrant card. 'It's all right, son, we're not going to walk off with the stock, such as it is . . . Been working here long, have you?'

'Six months.'

'Like it?'

The boy pulled a face, shrugged. 'It's a job, in't it?'

'Repair work, serving in the shop, that sort of thing?'

'Yeah.'

'Get on well with Mr Lomax, do you?'

The lad hesitated.

'You can be frank with us. We won't get you into trouble with him, I promise.'

Another shrug. 'So-so.'

'No more than that?'

'Like I said, it's a job. You can't be too choosy these days.'

'No . . .' Lineham leaned forward a little across the counter, glanced over his shoulder at the street as if to check that there was still no sign of Lomax, then lowered his voice as he said, 'You'd have a pretty good idea of his comings and goings, I suppose.'

'I suppose,' said the boy, warily.

'And of his visitors, too – people who come to see him here at the shop.'

'Well . . .'

'A certain young lady, now . . . About eighteen or nineteen, very pretty, long curly hair . . .'

The boy had immediately recognised the description. But

there was a spark of something else in his eyes, too. What was it?

He nodded. 'Can't think what she sees in him. He's old enough to be her grandfather.'

Jealousy, then. And pique?

'Until the day before yesterday it was all hush-hush. They meets each other most dinnertimes, see, but she never comes in here. Ten past twelve, regular as clockwork, she walks past the shop and a few minutes later off he goes.' The boy snorted. 'Thinks I'm stupid or something!'

'Until the day before yesterday?' said Lineham.

The day Marcia Salden died.

'Yeah. She rings up, see, middle of the morning. Never done that before. Wants to speak to him, urgent. Well, I tells her, he's out, gone to pick up a TV. Half an hour later, she's on the phone again and he walks in while I'm telling her he's not back yet. When he hears who's on the line he sends me off to the workroom, but I listens. Well, I wants to know what's going on, don't I? "I thought I told you never to ring me at work," he says. Then he listens for a sec, and he says, "Oh, my Gawd, oh my Gawd," over and over. Then he says, "Look, we can't talk now. I'll see you in your lunch hour as usual. And don't worry, I'll see you right." ' The boy glanced into the street, then leaned forward and said confidentially, 'D'you know what I reckon? I reckon he's knocked her up.'

'*I'll see you right.*' The most likely explanation, certainly. Maybe this was what Josie had been afraid of revealing when they had talked to her earlier on. And it opened up a number of interesting avenues of speculation. If Josie was pregnant, had she told Marcia? And if so, was the matter brought up at the ill-fated dinner party that night? And if it had been, and Marcia had tightened the screw on Lomax by hinting at publicity should he fail to swing the planning permission for her, how would Lomax have reacted? Difficult to tell, without ever having met the man. Would he have been upset? Angry? Desperate, even? Pretty agitated anyway, surely. Mrs Pantry said Lomax had left the Manor at around a quarter or twenty past ten that night. Thanet's imagination conjured up

Lomax's car speeding down the drive, turning right towards the village . . . But not, that wouldn't work. Lomax lived in Sturrenden. He would surely have turned left, towards the main road. And if so, he and Marcia wouldn't have met at all. Unless he had deliberately gone looking for her . . .

The door bell pinged. A customer wanting a 13-amp plug. Thanet and Lineham stood aside while she was served. Almost at once, and before they could resume their conversation, the bell pinged again. Thanet could tell by the way the boy stiffened that this must be Lomax.

During the introductions he was interested to note that although Lomax tried to hide it beneath a mask of bonhomie, the man was definitely on the defensive.

'Ah yes, I've been expecting you. What you call "routine enquiries", I suppose.' His laugh had a hollow ring. 'Go and buy yourself a doughnut, Kevin, will you, while I talk to the police and do my duty as a good citizen.'

A Kentish accent, Thanet noted, somewhat rough at the edges.

Kevin duly departed and Lomax flipped the notice on the door to CLOSED. Then he turned, rubbing his hands and sporting a look of bright expectancy tempered with appropriate solemnity. Quite a feat, Thanet thought. He had disliked the man on sight, slotting him at once into the category which his own father, now dead, had classified as 'the type I wouldn't buy a second-hand car from'.

Lomax, like his shop, had the air of going to seed. His clothes — navy blue blazer, linen trousers, striped tie, white shirt, were of good quality but slightly scruffy, his hair, although well cut, a little too long. A bright yellow silk scarf patterned with large red polka dots was draped around his neck. How did people like this get into such positions of power in local government? Thanet asked himself. Because those of the right calibre were too busy or too uninterested to stand? Thanet had met one or two truly admirable councillors, men and women dedicated to the ideal of public service, but they were all too few and far between.

Lomax now affected the hollow tones of an inexperienced newsreader reporting a disaster. 'It's about Mrs Salden, I suppose. Such a sad business. She was so young . . . and such a brilliant businesswoman. Such a waste . . .'

Such a treacly voice, Thanet parodied in his mind. Such a charming, man . . . He could hear Lineham saying, 'Yuk!' But he could understand why Josie had been taken in. Lomax would be so different from the boys with whom she normally came into contact. She would look no further than the surface, be dazzled by his status as a councillor, by the apparent gloss of sophistication. A few trips in that Jaguar parked outside, a few dinners at expensive restaurants . . .

Lomax wilted under Thanet's unwavering stare. He cleared his throat, moved uneasily from one foot to another and ran a hand over his hair. His soft brown eyes, which in a romantic novel would no doubt be described as 'melting', were like muddied pools with all kinds of unpleasant things stirring at the bottom.

'You were a guest at Mrs Salden's house that evening, I believe?'

'Yes, that's right.'

'Your wife was not invited?'

'No . . . She . . . It was more of a business arrangement than a social occasion.'

'I see . . . May I ask the nature of this business?'

He hesitated, his eyes flickering around the room as if searching for non-existent eavesdroppers. 'Confidentially, Mrs Salden was negotiating to buy this business.'

Thanet allowed his surprise to show. 'She was branching out into electronics?'

Lomax shook his head and sniggered as if Thanet had made a dirty joke. 'Nooo. It was the premises she wanted. She was planning on opening a vegetarian restaurant. There isn't one in the entire area. Said it was a natural progression from the health food shops and it was a good time to do it. There is so much interest in vegetarian food these days. I thought she was on to a winner, myself.'

Thanet had to admit it sounded plausible. Could he have been wrong in suspecting Marcia of planning to blackmail Lomax? But even if she hadn't, she could still have intended to suborn him. Buying his shop and paying well over the odds for it could have been a neat way of handing over a bribe without seeming to do so. 'These negotiations . . . They were far advanced?'

'Progressing satisfactorily, shall we say? Though whether they'll go ahead now is another matter. Her husband may want to scrap the whole idea.'

'May I ask how much Mrs Salden was prepared to offer you?'

'You can ask, but you won't get an answer. I can't see it has anything to do with . . . with the matter in hand.'

'That remains to be seen. You do realise, don't you, that we are treating this as a suspicious death?'

'Suspicious death?' Lomax's ruddy complexion was turning the colour of dough.

'We have to be satisfied that it was an accident – if it was an accident, in fact.'

'If?'

'Naturally, we have to consider the alternatives. Suicide, for example . . .' It would be interesting to see if Lomax took the bait.

He didn't.

'But . . .' Lomax shook his head.

'Yes, Mr Lomax?'

'I was only going to say that Mrs Salden would be the last person to commit suicide.'

'Yes, that does seem to be the general consensus of opinion. Which leaves us with the third alternative.'

Lomax was staring at Thanet like a rabbit at a stoat. 'You can't mean . . .'

Thanet wondered why this particular snatch of conversation always sounded so clichéd. Simply because he had heard it so often? Yet there was no other way to put it. 'Yes,' he said quietly. 'That's precisely what I do mean. Murder. You must see that we have to take that possibility into account. Which is why we are looking very closely into the movements of everybody she saw on Tuesday.'

'You can't possibly be suggesting that I . . .' There was a strange, dry, clicking noise from the back of Lomax's throat.

'We're not suggesting anything at this stage, Mr Lomax.

Just enquiring. So perhaps you'd be good enough to answer just a few more questions. Now, what time did you leave Telford Green Manor on Tuesday night?'

There was definitely a flash of fear in Lomax's eyes before they slid away. 'Somewhere around twenty past ten, I should think. Soon after I'd finished my coffee. I didn't think it was on to hang about any longer.'

'Not "on"?' What, specifically, was Lomax afraid of? Thanet wondered.

Lomax's shoulders twitched impatiently. 'Not polite. With Mrs Salden's mother being ill . . .'

'I see . . . When Mrs Salden left to go down to the village to see her mother, did she tell you she was going on foot?'

Lomax's reaction looked genuine enough. 'She *walked*?'

Thanet nodded. 'Along the footpath.'

'But why? We assumed she'd drive down.'

'Her car wouldn't start.'

'Then why didn't she come and ask me if I'd run her down? It'd only have taken a few minutes.'

That was a point which, oddly enough, had not occurred to Thanet. Why, indeed? He shrugged. 'No idea. What, exactly, did she say, when she left?'

'Just that she was popping down to see her mother and she wouldn't be long – ten or fifteen minutes at most. I said in that case we'd best be getting off home but she said, no, she didn't want to break up the party and that she especially wanted a word with Josie when she got back. That's why Josie stayed on when I left, or I'd have given her a lift home.'

'Did you think it odd, that Mrs Salden neither came back nor rang to explain why?'

'A bit, yes. But then we thought, well, it would be understandable if she forgot about us, if her mother was desperately ill.'

'And when you yourself left, did you go straight home?'

'More or less.' Lomax's voice had thickened.

'More?' said Thanet pleasantly. 'Or less?'

'I'm sorry?'

Thanet sighed. 'If you didn't go straight home, where did you go first?'

'For a drink.' It was as though the words were squeezed out of him against his will.

Thanet suddenly understood Lomax's apprehension and he knew the answer to the next question before he asked it. 'Where?'

'At the Crooked Door.'

'I see . . .' Thanet allowed the silence to stretch out. Then, eventually, 'So you drove through the village.'

'Yes, of course.' Lomax was sullen now. He resented being forced to yield up information he had hoped to keep hidden.

'Pass anyone?'

'I don't know. I can't remember. I hadn't thought about it.'

'Well, think now.'

Silence. Lomax screwed up his face and gazed into the middle distance.

Thanet and Lineham hid their eagerness. If Marcia had left her mother's cottage at around twenty past ten, even if Lomax had not committed the crime himself he could have been on the bridge at around the crucial time, seen something which could give them a vital lead.

'Yes . . .' said Lomax slowly. 'There was . . . Yes, I remember now. There were two men, outside one of the cottages, before you get to the bridge. I had the impression they were drunk.'

'Why?'

'I'm not sure. One seemed to be holding the other up.'

If so, they had probably come from the pub. More potential witnesses?

'Can you tell us anything about them?'

'It was just a glimpse. And I wasn't paying much attention because I'd just spotted the first of the DANGER notices and I was wondering what was up. That bridge is difficult enough to negotiate at the best of times.'

'Did you see anyone else? On or near the bridge, for example?'

Lomax was already shaking his head.

'You're sure?' But already Thanet was adjusting to the disappointment.

'No. Though . . . Wait a minute . . .'

130

'What?' Thanet and Lineham spoke together.

'I've just remembered. That secretary of Mrs Salden's. I passed her just as she was turning into the gates of the Manor, near the lodge.'

'You're sure it was her?' said Lineham.

'Certain, yes.'

'She was on foot?'

'Yes.'

'Coming from which direction?'

'From the village.'

And Edith Phipps claimed she hadn't been out that night. Interesting.

'Did you see Mrs Salden further on, in the village?' A pointless question, really, and Thanet wondered why he had bothered to ask it. Even if Lomax had seen her, he would deny it.

'No!'

'How well do you know Miss Trimble, Mr Lomax?'

Lomax blinked at the abrupt change of topic. He was beginning to sweat, Thanet noticed. 'I . . . er . . . I've met her a few times. Chiefly when she's been with Mrs Salden.'

'Chiefly?'

Lomax folded his arms, as if to put up a barrier against this new line of attack. If Josie was pregnant, Thanet could understand the man's difficulty. If he told the truth, he would lay himself open to a lot of unpleasant questions. Also, his wife might find out. But if he lied, and the police learnt the truth later, it might lead to even worse trouble. On the other hand, they might never find out . . .

Lomax shrugged. 'Mostly, yes. She went about with Mrs Salden quite a lot.'

'But you have met her alone, too.'

'I . . .' He couldn't bring himself to utter the direct lie, for fear of future consequences. 'I may have done.'

Thanet didn't want to make things awkward for young Kevin by betraying the source of his information, so this was a little tricky. 'Oh come, Mr Lomax. Miss Trimble is a very attractive young woman. Surely you can remember whether you've been out alone with her or not.'

131

'Well, perhaps on the odd occasion, yes.'

'Mr Lomax, I don't think you're being completely frank with us . . .'

Thanet waited, but Lomax said nothing, just stared at Thanet with a fearful fascination. The moment was right, Thanet judged. 'I have to tell you it's common knowledge that you and Miss Trimble have been seeing a lot of each other.'

Lomax took refuge in anger. 'Common knowledge, my foot. I knew it! You've been listening to that madwoman, haven't you?'

Madwoman? What was Lomax talking about? Thanet knew when best to keep his mouth shut.

'I knew she wouldn't be able to resist putting her spoke in! Pretending to be so self-righteous. As if she doesn't know what her precious daughter gets up to!'

Light dawned. Lomax was talking about Josie's mother. But how did Mrs Trimble fit in to all this?

Best to allow Lomax to go on thinking they knew all about it. Thanet looked amused. 'I gather Mrs Trimble's been having a go at you.'

'Josie's nearly nineteen, you know. Nearly nineteen! And that old bat expects to be able to keep her under lock and key!'

And it looked as though Mrs Trimble's anxiety had been justified. With a stab of fierce protectiveness towards Bridget, Thanet wondered how Lomax would have felt if it had been his daughter who was being wined and dined by an ageing Casanova old enough to be her grandfather. But, of course, he and Mrs Lomax had had only sons.

And if Josie were pregnant, did her mother know about it?

Lomax was still being indignant. 'She practically demanded Josie put her coat on and come home then and there! Of course, Josie refused. She'd promised Marcia to wait until she got back.'

Thanet did a double-take. 'Just a moment. When was this, Mr Lomax?'

'When was what?'

'When did Mrs Trimble try and get Josie to go home with her?'

'On Tuesday night, of course.'

'Let me make sure I've got this straight. Mrs Trimble actually went up to the Manor on Tuesday evening during the dinner party and made a scene?'

'Yes.'

'Objecting to the fact that her daughter was going out with you?'

'That's what I've been saying, haven't I?' Lomax was, perhaps understandably, becoming exasperated.

'All right, calm down. I just wanted to make sure I hadn't misunderstood . . .'

'Here, just a minute. Didn't Mrs Trimble tell you about this herself?'

No, you told me yourself, just now. 'Does it really matter who told us, Mr Lomax? We know, that's the point . . . Can we get back to Tuesday evening, please? What time was this, when Mrs Trimble arrived?'

Lomax shrugged. 'Must have been about ten or five to ten . . . The housekeeper tried to stop her, but she just came barging in . . .'

'How long did she stay?'

'Five minutes or so. Josie refused to listen to her, sent her off with a flea in her ear.'

'How had she got there?'

Lomax gave a laugh that was also a sneer. 'Well, she didn't drive up, that's for sure.'

Thanet closed his eyes, trying to work it out. At ten o'clock Grace Trimble leaves the Manor. At twenty past Marcia Salden leaves her mother's cottage to return home via the footpath. Yes, providing Mrs Trimble hadn't walked too quickly, it was possible that they could have met on the bridge. If Mrs Trimble was still overwrought, humiliated at being shown the door by Josie and angry with Marcia for having encouraged the affair with Lomax . . .

Lomax was still looking aggrieved. 'As soon as she'd gone, I got out, I can tell you. I'd just about had enough.'

FIFTEEN

'I wouldn't trust him further than I could spit!' said Lineham.

They were discussing Lomax on their way back to Telford Green. They had returned to the hairdressing salon to see Josie only to be met by a defiant Gary. 'I sent her home, poor love. There was no point in her staying on at work, was there, she was too upset . . .'

Thanet hadn't bothered to make a fuss. He wanted to go back to Telford Green anyway, to see Betty Pantry. Now that he knew more about what had happened on Tuesday night there were a number of questions he'd like to put to the housekeeper.

'Maybe not. But that doesn't necessarily make him a murderer.'

'It makes him a potential murderer, though, doesn't it?'

'Oh come on, Mike. They say that everyone is a potential murderer, given the right circumstances.'

'You think so? You really think so?'

'I don't know. I'd like to think not. I'd like to believe that I would never go over the edge, however hard I was pushed. But how can you ever know, unless you actually find yourself in that position? It's like condemning someone for being a thief because he steals bread to feed his starving children. If my children were starving, would I steal, to keep them alive?'

'I hope you don't mind me saying so, sir, but when I hear you talk like this it makes me wonder why you're in the police at all.'

'I wonder myself, sometimes . . . But to get back to Lomax . . .'

'Well, there is just one thing in his favour.'

'That he wouldn't have wanted to kill off the goose that was going to lay the biggest golden egg he was ever likely to see, you mean?'

'That's right. Unless . . .' said Lineham slowly.

'What?' Thanet could guess what was coming.

'Well, unless he found that Mrs Salden was becoming too much for him to handle.'

'Let's pull into that lay-by for a few minutes, shall we?'

Lineham glanced in the mirror and signalled left. The lay-by was empty and he switched off the engine. The sun was warm through the glass and they wound down the windows. Sweet, fresh air rushed in and the car was filled at once with the sound of birdsong. Thanet located its source, a thrush sitting on the topmost branch of a hawthorn tree in the hedge. Reluctantly he turned back to Lineham.

'Go on.'

'Well, I was thinking. Suppose Mrs Salden and Lomax set up this deal – she'll buy his shop at a grossly inflated price if he'll wangle that planning permission . . . As extra insurance she introduces him to Josie and tells Josie to keep him happy. Then, say, he gets cold feet. Perhaps someone begins to suspect what's going on, drops a few hints . . . Lomax decides to back out. He doesn't want to end up on a corruption charge and anyway power is sweet, he likes playing God on the Borough Council . . . He tells Mrs Salden that he's changed his mind. Naturally she's furious, she can see her quarter of a million floating away out of her grasp. At this point Josie discovers she's pregnant. She tells Lomax, who is appalled and Mrs S, who is privately delighted. Here is the lever she wanted. Out come the claws and she tells Lomax that if he pulls out of the plan he'll be seeing some interesting headlines in the local paper shortly. She's got him over a barrel. She's been careful to keep all the paperwork regarding the purchase of his shop above board, so he has nothing on her. It's his word against hers. Whereas she has Josie and the soon-to-be-obvious pregnancy on her side . . . Now, in those circumstances he'd be prepared to take pretty drastic action, don't you think?'

Lineham was looking very pleased with himself for producing such a neat and cohesive theory.

Thanet refrained from saying that he'd worked all this out himself some time ago. 'Very convincing, Mike. Well done. I agree, it's a possibility we have to keep in mind.'

'A very strong possibility, surely! Motive, means, opportunity, he had them all! If he left the Manor by car between a quarter and twenty past ten . . .'

'Agreed, but there is one snag.'

'What's that?'

'We're basing all this on a possible false premise.'

Lineham raised his eyebrows.

'That Josie is pregnant. That's pure assumption, at the moment.'

'Maybe. But surely, even if she isn't, Lomax could still have decided to pull out and Mrs Salden could still have turned nasty.'

'True . . . Well, we'd better be getting on.'

Lineham started the engine and checked his mirror. 'Now we know about Mrs Trimble's visit to the Manor on Tuesday night . . . You remember you said you thought Josie passed out because she had just realised who the murderer might be, that he must be someone close to her . . . D'you think it was her mother she had in mind?'

'Possibly. A bit far-fetched, though, don't you think? Plenty of parents get steamed up about their offspring's girlfriends or boyfriends, but they don't go around murdering the person who introduced them.'

'Unless they're unbalanced. And Lomax seemed to think Mrs Trimble is.'

'That may have been a figure of speech. Anyway, we'll soon find out, won't we? With any luck she'll be at home.'

But their luck was out, it seemed. A red-eyed Josie answered the door. The house was small, Victorian and semi-detached, built of ugly yellow brick, with a skimpy front garden in which regimented tulips stood stiffly in rows. The cramped living-room into which she led them was spotlessly clean and looked as though it was rarely used. A three-piece suite covered in brown moquette, back and arms protected by antimacassars, stood on a faded Art Deco carpet square in shades of green. There were no signs of occupation, not even a television set, and very few ornaments. Net curtains shielded the room from prying eyes.

Mrs Trimble, Josie told them, worked as a cleaner four mornings a week. On Thursdays, like today, she always went shopping in Sturrenden and didn't get back until half-past five.

'I see . . . look, Josie, I'm sorry to trouble you again so soon, but there are some more questions we really must ask you.'

She gave a tight little nod, a barely perceptible movement of her head. She was sitting perched on the edge of the armchair, arms tightly folded, legs tucked sideways. It was a stiff, uncomfortable pose, with tension in every line. She had changed into jeans, track shoes and sweater, and had caught the luxuriant mass of her hair back into an elastic band at the nape of her neck. She looked young, defenceless and forlorn. Thanet experienced a pang of conscience. Should he have brought a policewoman with him, instead of Lineham? But despite her appearance Josie was an adult, he reminded himself, and this was potentially a murder case. He would press on.

'You told us that when Mr Salden rang at about half-past ten, and you told him Mrs Salden had not yet arrived home, you both assumed she was still on her way.'

'That's right, yeah.'

'Did you know she'd had to walk down because her car wouldn't start?'

A shake of the head. 'No, she didn't say.'

'So you thought she'd be turning up any minute, I suppose.'

''S right.'

'So, when she didn't, why didn't you ring Mr Salden, to tell him?'

'I told you. I thought she'd changed her mind, didn't I, gone back to the cottage.'

For a moment Thanet thought she was going to start crying again, but she took a deep breath, held it and exhaled slowly.

'Look,' she said, 'I been thinking. It's easy to look back and say, "I should've done this" or "I should've done that". But at the time you, well, you just go on from minute to minute, if you see what I mean. On Tuesday, well, it'd been an 'orrible

137

day, one way and the other, and I was dead tired, all I wanted to do was go 'ome and go to bed. But I'd said I'd stay till she got back, so I 'ung on and 'ung on . . . And when she didn't come I just got madder and madder. I really did think she must've got part of the way 'ome and then turned round and gone back, meaning to ring us when she got there. And then she found 'er mum had taken a turn for the worse and she'd decided to stay, forgot all about us. After all, 'er mum must've been pretty bad that night, mustn't she, she died later on, didn't she? Anyway, I worked all this out, but at the same time I couldn't 'elp being mad with 'er for not ringing and letting me know . . . And like I said, the longer I waited the madder I got. So in the end I decided to come 'ome.'

'Yes, I see. But if you felt like that why didn't you simply ring the cottage to say you were tired and couldn't wait any longer?'

Her eyes went blank, flickering from side to side as if seeking a means of escape. This was a question whose answer she didn't want to admit even to herself. The silence stretched out. 'Didn't like to, did I?' she said at last, in a voice blank of emotion. 'Didn't think it was right, not if 'er mum was that ill.' She shook her head, a brief, violent movement as if to clear it of confusion. 'No!' she burst out. 'That in't right. I was sick and tired of being kept dangling, that's the truth. And I thought, if she can't be bothered to ring me, then I'm damned if I'll ring her. And if she's cross when she gets back and finds I didn't wait, then too bad!'

'And now you're feeling guilty.'

She nodded, lips compressed, the tears starting to flow again.

'You think that if only you hadn't allowed yourself to be angry, if only you'd rung Mr Salden, Mrs Salden might still be alive.'

More nods as she wiped her eyes, snuffled, blew her nose.

Thanet sighed. 'Well, I can understand how you feel, but the fact of the matter is, there's just no reason why you should. To put it bluntly, Mrs Salden couldn't swim, she would have drowned very quickly, and quite soon after leaving her mother's cottage. It's even possible she might already have been dead by the time Mr Salden rang you at half-past ten. So you see . . .'

She had given an involuntary shudder of distress while he was talking, but at least she had stopped crying. 'You mean that?' She gave her nose one final blow and sat up a little straighter.

'I wouldn't have said so, if I didn't. All the same . . .'

'What?'

'I'm afraid that doesn't let you entirely off the hook. Josie . . . why weren't you frank with us about your relationship with Mr Lomax?'

A wary look crept into her eyes and the muscles along her jawline clenched. 'What d'you mean?'

'You told us you'd only met him three or four times in all, and always when you were with Mrs Salden.'

She tried to bluff it out. 'But I did meet 'im when I was with 'er . . .'

'Josie . . .' Thanet was reproachful. 'Come on, now. We're not stupid, you know, and we do have ways of finding things out. What about all those lunch hours, for example?'

She stared at him for a moment longer and then tossed her head. 'I didn't think it was any of your business.'

'Maybe not, in normal circumstances. But these are not normal circumstances.'

Her flash of defiance had gone and once again she was looking frightened, vulnerable. 'You said . . .'

'Yes?'

'The last time I saw you . . . At the salon . . . You said, it *may* not've been an accident.'

'That's right, yes.'

'But you're not sure?'

'Not yet, no.'

'Oh . . .' She looked relieved.

'But it's still a possibility we have to consider. Which is why I asked you if you knew of anyone who had a grudge against Mrs Salden.'

'I've been thinking . . .'

'Yes?' Thanet could see quite clearly what Josie was up to. She had decided to employ diversionary tactics in order to steer their attention away from her affair with Lomax and also, perhaps, away from her mother. All the same, this could be interesting.

'Well, I don't know if I ought to tell you . . .'

Thanet smiled. 'I can't let you get away with that, now can I? Not now you've begun . . .'

'It's just that . . . Well, I was up at the Manor that afternoon and I 'appened to oyer'ear something . . .'

She glanced from Thanet's face to Lineham's, as if to ensure that she had their complete attention.

'Marcia — Mrs Salden — was going on at 'er secretary, that Miss Phipps . . .'

'. . . We've lost it, d'you realise that? Lost it! An absolutely prime site in Week Street in Maidstone, and we've lost it. And why? Because someone else got a written offer in ahead of us! And what is more, Edith, my dear, efficient little secretary, you may be interested to hear that my written offer never in fact arrived. NEVER ARRIVED! Now why do you suppose that is?'

'I don't understand.'

'Of course you don't understand. You never do understand, do you, when things go wrong because of your inefficiency? Well, it occurs to me that the reason why it never arrived could just be because it was never posted. Where's that so-called handbag of yours? Go on, get it. My God, beats me how you ever find anything in it. Now empty it out on the desk. Empty it out, go on. Ah . . . Surprise, surprise. Three unposted letters. One of which is addressed to Page and Wells, Estate Agents, 52–54 King Street, Maidstone. What have you got to say about that? Not a lot, obviously.'

'Marcia, I'm sorry, I really am. I can't think what could have happened.'

'Oh, but I can. It's quite simple, isn't it, Edith? You just forgot, as usual. Well, let me tell you this. I've had it up to here with your little lapses of memory, and this time they've cost me just too much. I've wanted a Week Street site in Maidstone for years, and if it hadn't been for you I'd have got it.'

'Couldn't you. . . ?'

'It's not your business to tell me what I can or can't do!'

'I was only going to suggest . . .'

'To hell with your suggestions! I don't need a secretary to make suggestions. I need a secretary who is efficient, who does what I want her to do when I want her to do it. Such as posting important letters when they're written. No, I'm sorry, Edith, I've put this off as long as I can, but I'm afraid I shall have to ask you to look for another job.'

'But . . .'

'No! I'm not going to listen. I know you're in a difficult position, but you've become too expensive for me. I have the business to think of. I haven't put years of my life into building it up to have it undermined by your inefficiency. You can have a month to find somewhere else.'

Josie stopped talking. Her eyes still glittered with the excitement of recounting the drama she had overheard.

Thanet remembered Edith Phipps's prim, tight face, the undertone of resentment, jealousy, even, as she had talked about Marcia's success. Then there was her invalid mother, the convenience of working so close to home . . . Would she have had to move out of the gatehouse, if she had lost her job?

And she had lied about not going out that night.

Like Lomax, means, opportunity and now motive, she had had them all.

SIXTEEN

'She's not back from lunch yet.' Mrs Pantry's eyes flickered in the direction of the avenue of trees, as if she half-expected to see Edith Phipps walking up the drive. Despite the fact that it was pouring with rain, she did not ask them in. The sun had suddenly clouded over and a heavy April shower had materialised with very little warning.

Thanet hunched his shoulders against the water which was trickling down the back of his neck. He and Lineham had unwisely not bothered to put on their raincoats for the short distance between house and car, and Mrs Pantry's inhospitality had caught them unprepared. He was annoyed that she had not invited them to take shelter from the downpour and annoyed, too, that he had not thought of calling in at the gatehouse on the way. He had, after all, been well aware that Edith always spent her lunch hours at home.

Still, there were various points he wanted to raise with the housekeeper.

'In that case, I'd like another word with you, while we're waiting.'

Grudgingly she opened the massive door a little wider and moved aside to allow them to pass. They stepped inside, brushing the rain off their jackets and wiping their faces.

There was a pungent smell of polish in the hall and halfway up the staircase lay an open tin and some dusters. Without asking permission, Mrs Pantry climbed the remaining stairs, plumped down on her knees and resumed the task which they had evidently interrupted. 'You won't mind if I get on with my work?'

Thanet was about to protest that yes, he did object, when he changed his mind. This was more than Mrs Pantry's natural ungraciousness, it was a calculated snub, and it intrigued him. He would play it her way, for the moment. What had aroused her hostility? he wondered. Despite Edith Phipps's brief account of Mrs Pantry's unhappy past, Thanet found that his dislike of the housekeeper had not diminished. What was it about her that provoked this instinctive recoil? It certainly wasn't her size. He had met any number of large women in the past, and some of them he had found very attractive. Nor was it the fact that she was physically unprepossessing. Perhaps it was her lack of femininity, her gracelessness, her uncompromising harshness. Or perhaps it was no one thing, but a combination of many. Irrelevantly, he found himself wondering about the husband who had absconded. What sort of man would be attracted to a woman like this?

Anxious to avoid the sight of her massive buttocks and tree-like thighs advancing slowly towards him down the stairs, he crossed to the oak table against the wall on the other side of the hall and hitched himself up on to it. From here he had a good view of her profile through the banisters. Lineham stationed himself beside the staircase, his head just below the level of hers.

'Is Mr Salden about?' Thanet wanted to be sure that this conversation was not going to be overheard.

'No, he's gone into Sturrenden to make the arrangements for his mother-in-law's funeral.'

All clear, then.

She was pretending to concentrate on her work, her shoulders moving rhythmically as she applied the polish in small circular movements. He must begin by somehow breaking down that barrier of hostility. But how?

By making her angry, perhaps?

'You're in a rather unique position in this house, aren't you, Mrs Pantry?'

She stopped polishing and cast him a suspicious glance through the banisters. 'What d'you mean?'

'Well, you come into contact with everybody, you know what's going on . . .'

She put down her duster and knelt up, leaning her arms on

the rail and glowering at him. 'I'm in a good position to spy on people, you mean.'

'If that's how you choose to put it, yes.'

'How else am I supposed to put it? Oh yes, I've heard about all these questions you've been asking.' She snorted, an ugly porcine sound. 'All those nasty' — she sought the right word and found it, triumphantly — '*insinuations.*'

'What nasty insinuations, Mrs Pantry?' said Thanet, all innocence.

'About certain people.'

So that was it. She was angry with him because she thought he suspected Salden of killing Marcia. 'What people? Really, you are being very mysterious, aren't you? How can I answer your allegations, if I don't know what they are?'

Anger propelled her to her feet. 'You know perfectly well what I mean! And Mr Bernard is the kindest man in the world. He'd never hurt a fly!'

'But who has suggested he would — or did?'

'And anyone who says there was any trouble between him and Mrs Salden don't know what they're talking about! Like you said, I'm here all the time, and I know.'

'As a matter of — '

'I'm not saying they was all lovey-dovey, mind, but they got on all right, they understood each other, you know what I mean? And there was never any rows or anything like that, and if anyone says any different they're lying in their teeth.'

'No one has . . .'

'And you ought to have seen what he's been like since it happened! Doesn't know what to do with himself, he's so cut up about it. Can't eat, can't sleep . . .'

'MRS PANTRY!'

She blinked. 'Yes?'

Thanet crossed to look up at her, resting one hand on the newel post. 'Look, I just want to make one thing quite clear. I have not come here to question you about Mr Salden.'

She frowned. 'You haven't?'

'No.'

She descended one or two steps, warily. 'What did you want to talk about, then?'

144

'Chiefly about what happened on Tuesday.'

'Oh.' She sat down abruptly on the fourth or fifth step up from the bottom and Thanet, averting his eyes from unwelcome vistas of straining tights and large expanses of underwear, went up to sit beside her.

'We keep learning bits and pieces, you see. And we thought you might be able to fill in the gaps.'

She still looked suspicious, but the frown lines on the broad, flat forehead were beginning to ease away. 'What gaps?'

'Well, to begin with, I understand that Mrs Salden had a row with Miss Phipps on Tuesday afternoon.'

Mrs Pantry's eyes gleamed. 'Yes, I thought she must have. Who told you? Josie Trimble, I suppose.'

'You didn't hear it, then?'

'No, but I saw Edith Phipps go home in tears.'

'Do you know what it might have been about?'

'No idea.' She was enjoying being so unhelpful.

Pity. He would have liked to have another version of the quarrel, to compare with Josie's. 'If we could move on to the evening, then . . . I understand Mrs Trimble, Josie's mother, came up at some point.'

Questioned about this, Josie had been distinctly unforth-coming, playing down her mother's anger and making light of the whole incident.

'Been busy, haven't you? Yes, she did.'

'Why didn't you tell us this when we talked to you yesterday?'

'Didn't ask, did you? Anyway, I didn't think it mattered. Oh, I *see* . . . Yes, well, I didn't know, then, that Mrs Salden's death was anything but a straightforward accident.'

'We don't *know* otherwise now.'

'No, but you must think there's something fishy about it or you wouldn't still be going around asking all these questions, would you? Stands to reason, don't it?'

'We just have to be sure, that's all. So, to get back to Mrs Trimble . . . What time did she arrive?'

'About ten, I should think.' Mrs Pantry smiled, revealing an unprepossessing row of nicotine-stained teeth. 'In a fair old state, she was.'

'About?'

'Mr Lomax carrying on with that precious daughter of hers. That Josie.' She almost spat the word out. 'Little slut.'

'Oh come on, that's a bit strong, isn't it?'

'Is it? I'm not blind, Inspector, and I'm not deaf, either, though no doubt some people like to pretend I am . . .'

Thanet suspected that if he betrayed too much interest Mrs Pantry would dry up out of sheer perversity, the last thing he wanted now that she was starting to loosen up. He continued to look sceptical.

Mrs Pantry leaned a little nearer. 'Did you know there's a flat over the old stables at the back?'

Thanet shook his head.

She lowered her voice to a near whisper. 'Mrs Salden gave Josie a key. It's been going on for months, her and that Mr Lomax.' Her face twisted. 'Disgusting, I call it. He's old enough to be her father – no, her *grand*father.'

If Mrs Trimble had got wind of this arrangement it was scarcely surprising that she had been sufficiently angry with Marcia to march up to the Manor and confront her and Lomax together. He could imagine how enraged he would have been if Bridget had been exploited in this way . . . Which reminded him . . . He glanced at his watch. Yes, just about now Joan would be entering the headmaster's study. What could Mr Foreman be wanting to discuss with her?

With an effort Thanet wrenched his mind back to the present.

'Was Mr Salden aware of this . . . arrangement?'

Mrs Pantry shook her head vigorously. 'Oh no. They was careful only to come when he wasn't here – he's out a lot with his charity work, you know, he's on a lot of committees and that, and does a lot of fund-raising.'

'You don't think he would have approved?'

Another shake of the head. 'I never did understand what Mrs Salden was thinking of, to allow it.'

'So what exactly happened when Mrs Trimble came on Tuesday night?'

'She asked for Mrs Salden. I told her she was out, that she'd had to go down to the village because her mother'd taken a turn for the worse, but she wouldn't believe me, thought I was just trying to give her the brush-off. Before I could stop her, she'd ducked under my arm and rushed into the drawing-room. I went after her. Josie and Mr Lomax was both sitting on the settee, him with his arm around her. Grace Trimble started shouting at Mr Lomax, calling him a dirty old man and saying he ought to be ashamed of himself, messing about with a young girl like Josie. Then she got hold of Josie by the arm and tried to drag her away, saying she was coming home at once, and this was the end, the finish, she'd never see Mr Lomax again. Josie was struggling with her mother and screaming at her to let her go. In the end Josie managed to get free. You should have seen her! She looked a real sight. Hair all over the place, mascara running down her cheeks. And all the while Mr Lomax just sat there like a stuffed prune . . . I tell you, I wouldn't have missed it for the world!'

'So what happened, in the end?'

'Josie refused flat to go home with her mother. Said she was over age and could do what she liked. Her mother could like it or lump it.' Mrs Pantry shrugged. 'There was nothing Mrs Trimble could do about it, was there? So she just left.'

'What sort of state was she in?'

'Quiet. Defeated, sort of. I felt sorry for her really. Offered her a cup of tea, but she refused.'

'How long would you say all this took?'

'No more than a few minutes, I shouldn't think. I mean, a lot happened, but it was all over very quick.' Mrs Pantry shook her head reminiscently. 'I tell you, we've never had a night like that since I've been here. All those comings and goings . . .' She gave Thanet a sly, knowing look. 'Just like *Dallas*, it was. Real action-packed.'

Surely she wasn't implying . . . 'All those comings and goings?'

She smoothed the skirt over her knee, looking almost coy. 'Well, first Mr Salden going, then Josie and Mr Lomax coming, then Mrs Salden going, then . . .'

He had been expecting her to say, 'then Mrs Trimble coming,' but she had stopped deliberately. 'Then. . . ?' he prompted.

She folded her arms and leaned back against the banisters with a self-satisfied smile. 'Then, of course, there was Mr Hammer.'

Hammer. The name sounded vaguely familiar. Who was he? Mrs Pantry was enjoying this, dangling the information tantalisingly in front of his nose. Struggling to suppress his rising irritation, Thanet said, 'Mr Hammer?'

'Reg Hammer, I believe it is. His mother lives in the village — lived, I should say. She died last Monday.'

Thanet remembered now. The first of the three deaths the Vicar had mentioned. Mrs Hammer, Mrs Carter, Marcia Salden. Was there a connection?

'He came here on Tuesday evening too?'

'Just said so, didn't I?'

'What did he want?'

'To see Mrs Salden.'

'What about?'

A shrug. 'No idea.' She was obviously determined to make him work for the information.

'Did she speak to him?'

'No. They were in the middle of dinner.'

'This was fairly early in the evening, then?'

'Yes.'

'When, exactly?'

'About half-past eight, I should think.'

'So what happened?'

Another shrug. 'He went away.'

'Before that, I mean. What was his attitude, when he asked to see Mrs Salden?'

That sly smile again. 'He wasn't too happy, I'd say.'

'He was angry, you mean?'

'You could say that.'

'With Mrs Salden?'

'I suppose.'

'But he didn't say why?'

'No. Just said he wanted to see her, urgent.'

'And what message did she send back?'

'That he was to ring up in the morning, make an appointment.'

'How did he react to that?'

'Called her some four-letter names and drove away. Wonder he wasn't picked up. He wasn't fit to drive.'

'He'd been drinking, you mean?'

'Reeked of it.'

'And you're sure you've no idea why he wanted to see Mrs Salden?'

'Haven't a clue.'

The front door opened and Bernard Salden came in, his eyebrows going up at the sight of his housekeeper and Thanet sitting side by side on the stairs. He didn't look too pleased to see the police again so soon and his tone was distinctly frosty. 'Good afternoon, Inspector.'

Thanet returned the greeting and descended to the hall. 'I was hoping for another word with you, sir.'

Salden gave a resigned sigh as he handed his raincoat to Mrs Pantry. 'Very well. But d'you mind if we talk outside? It's stopped raining and I could do with a breath of fresh air.'

'Not at all.'

Salden led the way.

SEVENTEEN

Outside the air was still charged with moisture, but the sun was just beginning to emerge from behind the heavy bank of cloud which had brought the showers, stippling the drowned landscape with random patches of brilliant light.

It was too wet to walk on the grass and they strolled across the forecourt in the direction of the drive. Salden sighed again. 'What is it this time, Inspector?' He had changed out of the casual clothes he had been wearing earlier into a formal dark suit, white shirt and black tie.

'Fresh information keeps coming in, and I need your help, to understand how it fits in.'

Salden gave him a wary glance. 'What information?'

'About your wife's affairs — business affairs, that is,' he added hastily as Salden's eyebrows shot up. 'And as they're presumably your affairs too . . .'

'Not necessarily, Inspector. We were partners in the health food business, yes, but Marcia had various schemes on hand of which I knew very little. But if I can help you, I will.'

'Inspector Thanet!' Mrs Pantry had emerged from the front door, waving. 'Telephone.'

Could it be Joan, calling about Bridget? No. His movements at work were so uncertain that she rarely attempted to contact him during the day, except in cases of emergency. 'You take it, Mike, will you?'

Lineham loped off and Thanet and Salden continued their stroll, entering the avenue of beeches which were still dripping after the rain. From time to time they had to take out their handkerchiefs and mop their faces. 'Did you know that your wife had had a row with Miss Phipps on the afternoon of the day she died?'

Salden stopped walking. 'Really? No, I'd no idea. What about?'

'Miss Phipps had forgotten to post your wife's written offer for a shop in Week Street, Maidstone, and someone else got the lease.'

'She forgot to post it! No wonder Marcia was angry. I was wondering why we hadn't had a reply.'

'You knew about it, then?'

'About the shop? Yes, of course. We'd been hoping to get a Week Street site for years, but they'd always been too big or too small or in the wrong position . . . This one was perfect for us.'

'Apparently your wife was so angry that she fired her.'

'Fired Edith? Are you sure?'

'That surprises you?'

'It certainly does. They'd known each other for years, you know. As a matter of fact, they were at school together.'

'Yes, Miss Phipps told me.'

'Did she tell you about this herself — about being fired, I mean?'

'No. Someone overheard the quarrel.'

'Mrs Pantry, I suppose.'

'As a matter of fact, no, it wasn't.'

'Then it must have been Josie.'

'Does it matter?'

'Not really, I suppose. Except that you have only her word that it ever took place.'

'Mrs Pantry saw Miss Phipps go home in tears afterwards.'

'Edith, in tears? Then I suppose it must be true. But I must say I'm astounded, I really am.'

'The impression I had was that this was only the latest in a long series of blunders. The last straw, so to speak.'

'I must admit Marcia had been complaining about her rather a lot lately, but I didn't think she was that fed up with her. In fact, I had the impression she was rather sympathetic towards her. Edith — Miss Phipps — doesn't have much of a life, you know. She's very tied to her mother, who's an invalid, and lately, for the last year or so, she's been having rather a bad time with the menopause. It's true that she has been increasingly forgetful . . .'

'But Mrs Salden said nothing to you that evening about having fired her?'

'We hardly saw each other. I'd been out, to a committee meeting in Sturrenden, and I didn't get home until six thirty. Marcia was having a bath and I had to bathe and change as well . . . We scarcely exchanged more than a few sentences.'

'I see.'

There were hurried footsteps behind them and Lineham came puffing up. Thanet walked back a few paces to meet him. 'You're out of condition, Mike. You should take more exercise.'

Lineham rolled his eyes. 'I will if you will,' he managed to say between gasps.

'Anything urgent?'

Lineham glanced at Salden, who had strolled on, and lowered his voice. 'Doc Mallard, with a verbal on the PM.'

'And?'

Lineham shook his head. 'Not a lot. Except that she was definitely dead before she went into the water. That blow to the right temple.'

'Ah. Nothing else?'

'Just one interesting thing. You remember Mrs Pepper said the Saldens had been keen to have more children after the first one died – that Mr Salden had even suggested adopting?'

'Yes. What about it?'

'Well, according to Doc M, Mrs Salden had been sterilised, some time ago. Had her tubes tied or something.'

'Really?' Thanet glanced at Salden who had stopped walking and was waiting for them. In his dark, formal suit he looked out of place in the setting of grass, trees and parkland. Was it possible that he was unaware that his wife had had this operation? If so, and if what Mrs Pepper said were true and he really had longed for another child, how would he react to this news?

He had evidently become tired of waiting and was walking towards them. 'We might as well go back.'

Thanet agreed, glancing back down the drive at the lodge.

He had intended to call in and see Edith Phipps after finishing with Salden, but he could easily drive down. Why was she so late returning to work? he wondered. She should have been back an hour ago.

'I was thinking, while you were talking,' said Salden. 'Assuming it's true that my wife and Edith did have this quarrel . . . I hope you're not implying that this means Edith could have had anything to do with her death.'

'I'm not implying anything. I told you, at the moment we're just trying to gather together as much information as we can. Though I have to tell you that we've just had the results of the *post mortem*, and I'm afraid it has been confirmed that your wife did not die by drowning.'

Salden stopped walking. 'She didn't drown?'

Thanet shook his head. 'No. She was dead before she went into the water.'

'But . . . Then how. . . ?'

'She was killed by a blow to the right temple. I'm sorry.'

Salden swallowed hard, almost gulping in air as though his throat had suddenly closed up, making it difficult for him to breathe. His face was the colour of parchment. 'A blow. . . ?' He swayed slightly.

Thanet put out a hand to steady him. 'Yes – but perhaps not in the sense you think. You know we think she went into the river through the gap in the parapet?'

Salden nodded, a barely perceptible movement of the head, as if even the effort required for this minute movement were too much for him.

'We think she banged her head – her temple – against a sharp piece of projecting stone.' Thanet decided against giving further details. Salden's skin had taken on an unhealthy, almost luminous tinge. 'I'm sorry. But I felt you had a right to know.'

'You're saying that this . . . blow might not have been deliberate? That it might have happened when she . . . slipped?'

'Or – it has to be said – was pushed.'

Salden stared unseeingly at Thanet for some moments, apparently adjusting to this new information. At last he said,

'I see.' And turning stiffly like someone awakening from a dream he began to walk once more towards the house.

Thanet and Lineham fell in alongside him in silence.

They had covered more than half the distance towards the end of the avenue of beeches before Salden spoke again.

'All the same, the idea that Edith could have had anything to do with my wife's death is ludicrous. If you knew her as well as I do . . .'

Thanet wondered just how many times he had heard precisely this sentiment expressed of a murder suspect. 'May I just ask . . . Will you allow her to keep her job, now?'

Salden looked at him suspiciously. 'I suppose if I say yes, it won't really help her in your eyes. All the same, it's pointless to mislead you. Yes, I expect I shall – and what is more, I'm convinced that I shall be doing exactly what Marcia would have wished. I don't suppose for one moment that she really meant what she said – that is, assuming she said it. It's exactly the sort of thing one comes out with in the heat of the moment and then regrets. I've no doubt that if she'd lived she would have changed her mind by next morning and I'm sure Edith would have known that.'

'You may be right.' On the other hand, with home, livelihood and the welfare of her invalid mother at stake, Edith might not have been willing to risk it. In any case, it was clear that at least two people who had good reason to wish Marcia dead, Harry Greenleaf and Edith Phipps, had in fact gained considerably by that death. Thanet closed his mind against the unlikely, even crazy notion that they might possibly have joined forces to bring that death about. He decided to change tack.

'This shop you were buying, to turn into a health food restaurant . . .'

'What about it?' Salden sounded wary.

'. . . from Councillor Lomax.'

'Yes?'

'Would it have been part of the scheme we were discussing this morning, the one you didn't fully approve of?'

'It seemed a sound enough business proposition,' said Salden stiffly.

'That isn't exactly an answer to my question.'

'I'm sorry, Inspector, I don't know what you're talking about.'

Salden had evidently decided that ignorance was the safest course.

'A sound business proposition, you say?'

'We wouldn't have been contemplating it otherwise, obviously. There isn't a single other health food restaurant in the area. We thought it had a good chance of success.'

'You'll have gone into the financial side of it, of course.'

'Naturally.'

'What price was Mr Lomax asking for his premises?'

'I'm sorry, I can't see that that has anything to do with my wife's death. To be blunt, Inspector, it's none of your business.'

'We could examine your papers . . .'

'That wouldn't help you. Negotiations were only at the verbal stage.'

'I see.'

He obviously wasn't going to get anything more out of Salden on that topic at the moment. 'Did you know that Josie's mother came up to the house the night your wife died?'

Salden blinked at the abrupt change of subject. 'Mrs Trimble? What on earth for?'

'Apparently she is very upset at the association between her daughter and Mr Lomax.'

'Between . . .' Salden was apparently taken aback. 'You must be joking. He's older than I am.'

Thanet shrugged. 'Maybe. But it seems her suspicions are justified. I gather they've been meeting in the flat over the coach house.'

Salden came to a dead halt again. '*Our* coach house?'

Thanet nodded.

He was shaking his head. 'I don't believe it. You're making this up, aren't you? Playing games with me.'

'No games, Mr Salden. If Mrs Pantry is to be believed, Josie has a key to the flat. She and Lomax used to meet there regularly when you were out.'

'Josie has a *key*?'

Salden was silent, working it out. It was obvious that if the girl had had a key, Marcia must have given it to her.

'Understandably, Mrs Trimble must have been rather angry with your wife.'

The word *procuring* hung unspoken in the air between them. Salden gave Thanet an uncomfortable, almost shame-faced glance. 'So what did Marcia say to her?'

'She didn't see her. This was latish in the evening, at about ten o'clock. Your wife was down in the village at the time.'

'But Lomax and Josie were there . . .' The look on Salden's face indicated the degree of his distaste.

Perhaps he shouldn't have mentioned the matter, thought Thanet. Perhaps he should have allowed Salden to keep his illusions about his wife intact. If he had had any . . . 'Yes, they were. I gather Mrs Trimble tried to insist that Josie go home with her, but Josie refused.'

Salden was shaking his head. 'Poor kid. She's the loser in all this.'

Especially if she's pregnant, thought Thanet. But if she were, it looked as though Salden might be prepared to attempt to make amends for his wife's behaviour by giving the girl a helping hand. In which case, he, Thanet, would have done Josie a good turn by making Salden aware of the situation. He felt a little better about bringing the matter up. Marcia was beyond help, but Josie was not.

They were almost at the end of the avenue of trees and suddenly the last of the wispy clouds which had been drifting across the face of the sun cleared away and it burst through in full strength, streaming in great shafts of light between the interlacing branches overhead.

Thanet paused to admire the effect before saying, 'There's just one other point I wanted to ask you about . . . What does the name Hammer mean to you?'

Salden frowned. 'There's an old lady in the village, Mrs Hammer. Or there was. She died earlier this week.'

'Do you know her son? Reg, I believe he's called. Short for Reginald, I presume.'

'I didn't even know she had a son. Why?'

'Well, apparently he came here on Tuesday evening too, wanting to speak to your wife. According to Mrs Pantry he was very angry with Mrs Salden for some reason.'

'Angry with Marcia?' Salden was shaking his head. 'I can't imagine why. You'll have to ask him.'

'I will, of course.'

They were nearing the front door. The heat of the sun was causing ground water to evaporate so fast that a haze of low mist was rising from the paved path along the front of the house.

Salden paused with one hand on the bleached oak of the front door. 'Well, if that's all, Inspector . . .'

'Mmm? Oh, yes.' Thanet's mind was elsewhere, preoccupied with two questions. 'May I use your phone?'

'Of course.' Salden led them inside. 'You can use the one in my office.'

This was a small, businesslike room at the back of the house, with modern desk, computer and a couple of filing cabinets. Thanet tried the Probation office first. Joan was there.

'Luke! I was wondering if you'd ring.'

Having realised that Thanet was talking to his wife, Lineham tactfully withdrew.

'How did you get on?'

'You're not going to believe this.'

A stone suddenly appeared in the pit of Thanet's stomach. 'What?'

'Our darling daughter has been playing truant.'

'*What?*'

'True. Honestly. I just couldn't believe it. Just sat there with my mouth open. Well, we knew things hadn't been going well for her, but . . .'

'How long has this been going on?'

'For the last few weeks, apparently, on and off.'

'Why on earth didn't the school let us know before?'

'That's what I said. It seems they only found out by chance, yesterday. One of the teachers had a dental appointment and saw her in the town.'

Yesterday. Thanet remembered Bridget's reluctant back as she had walked towards the school gates. As soon as he was out of sight she must have turned around and headed for the town. The deception hurt. If she was as unhappy as that, surely she could have confided in them. And what about Ben? Did he know about this?

'She's been forging notes, apparently.'

'She's *what*?'

'Been forging notes from me, saying that she was ill. I know. Unbelievable, isn't it? I mean, *Bridget* . . .'

'What worries me is why.'

'I know. And that she couldn't trust us, to talk to us about it.'

'Yes.' To feel that you'd failed, as a parent, when your child evidently needed you most. That really hurt . . . Thanet said so.

'I know.' Joan was subdued.

'We'll have to talk to her.'

'Yes. Tonight.'

Thanet rang off and then sat looking at the receiver, thinking back over the conversation. He still felt stunned.

Lineham came back in. 'You all right, sir?'

'What? Oh, yes . . .' With an effort Thanet focussed his mind on the case again and remembered his other anxiety. 'Anyone mention Miss Phipps? Has she rung to say why she's not back yet?'

'Haven't seen anyone, to ask.'

Thanet nodded at the telephone directory. 'Look up her number, will you? She should have been back a couple of hours ago.'

Lineham grinned. 'If this were an episode in one of those detective series where bodies are scattered around like confetti we'd know what's happened to her, wouldn't we?' He spread his hands in a dramatic gesture. 'We'd dial her number and the phone would ring and ring in a silent house. The camera would pan through the empty rooms and finally come to focus on her body . . .'

'I think you'd better change your viewing habits, Mike. And look up that number before I decide to do it myself!'

It was all very well to make jokes about it, he thought, but where was she? One woman had been murdered, why not another? The palms of his hands were clammy as he dialled the number Lineham dictated to him.

EIGHTEEN

'Miss Phipps?'

'Yes?'

She sounded out of breath. The dialling tone had sounded at least a dozen times before she lifted the phone. Perhaps she had been in the garden, Thanet thought with relief.

'Detective Inspector Thanet here. I'm up at the house. Are you coming to work this afternoon? I'd appreciate another word with you.'

'No, Mr Salden gave me the afternoon off. Could you come down to the lodge?'

'Yes, of course. We'll be there shortly.'

She opened the front door before they could knock and with a finger to her lips led them into a small square kitchen overlooking the drive. A door leading into a narrow walk-in larder in the corner was open and she was obviously half-way through cleaning it; a lightweight aluminium stepladder stood near by and all the upper shelves were empty, their contents stacked on the table in the middle of the room. On top of the pile of bottles and packets lay a neatly folded print apron, removed no doubt in expectation of their visit. Today her square, dumpy body was encased in a drab, rather shabby crimpelene dress in two tones of blue.

She apologised for the muddle, smoothing her hands down her skirt as if ashamed of her appearance, too. 'I thought I'd take the opportunity to do a bit of spring-cleaning.'

Thanet grinned. 'My wife says spring-cleaning the larder is the job she hates most of all. That's why she always starts with it, to get it over and done with.'

'I feel exactly the same!' She glanced at the single chair. 'Is this going to take long, Inspector? If so, I'll fetch a couple

160

more chairs. We don't spend much time in here. I think I told you, my mother's an invalid and we eat together in the other room.'

She glanced nervously at the door as she spoke. Presumably she was hoping her mother would remain unaware of their presence. He wondered why, if she had nothing to hide. In his experience, housebound people welcomed any interruption of their monotonous existence. And why suggest holding the interview here at the lodge, if she didn't want her mother to know about it? Perhaps she was now regretting having done so. 'No, don't worry, we can stand. But do sit down yourself.'

But she, too, chose to stand and they disposed themselves about the room, leaning against various work surfaces.

'Your mother's not confined to bed all the time, then?'

'Oh, no, but movement is very difficult for her, very painful. She's badly crippled with arthritis and her heart is failing. She has a walking frame and she does try to get about a little – they say you have to, or you'll seize up altogether – but naturally she reserves the effort for essentials.'

'She goes to bed quite early, I imagine.'

Edith Phipps was no fool. Her eyes narrowed and she adjusted the tip-tilted spectacles as if hoping to see more clearly into Thanet's mind. 'I usually settle her down about nine o'clock, yes.' She paused. 'Is that an . . . oblique way of asking for an alibi, Inspector?'

It was always a relief to come across a witness prepared to say exactly what she thought.

'I'll be frank with you, Miss Phipps. When we last met I asked you if you had been in all evening, the night Mrs Salden died. You said yes. I thought at the time that you were holding something back. Now I have to tell you that you were seen, that night, walking from the village towards this house, at about twenty-five past ten.'

'By whom?'

She hadn't denied it, he noted. He shook his head. 'That's irrelevant. What is not irrelevant is why you found it necessary to lie at a time when there was only the merest suspicion that Mrs Salden's death was anything but an accident.'

'Do I gather that you are now sure that it was not?'

161

'Shall we say that at the moment it seems necessary to continue the investigation.'

She stared at him in silence, thinking.

Eventually, 'I'm still waiting for an answer, Miss Phipps.'

She sighed and lifted her shoulders slightly. 'Stupid of me not to be frank with you, wasn't it? I'd only been to post some letters. I'd . . . forgotten to do it, earlier.'

And presumably hadn't wanted to risk incurring Marcia's wrath again, just in case overnight she changed her mind about firing her, thought Thanet. But although the errand may have been innocent it could have culminated in tragedy. The two women could have met on the bridge.

'Marcia! Look, you didn't mean what you said this afternoon, did you? I mean, it was just because you were angry, wasn't it?'

'You're damned right I was angry. Still am. When I think what your carelessness has cost us . . .'

'I'm sorry, Marcia, truly I am. It'll never happen again, I promise.'

'It certainly won't. Because I'm not giving you the chance. I meant what I said, Edith. This sort of thing has happened once too often. Now, please let me pass.'

'But what'll I do? Where shall we go? You know how difficult it is, with Mother . . . Marcia, please. I've always done my very best for you, haven't I?'

'Well, your best turned out not to be quite good enough, didn't it?'

'It's only because I haven't been well. If you knew how ill I'd been feeling . . .'

'I'm sorry, Edith, but you've used that excuse just once too often. And I've tried to make allowances, but this time . . . No, the sooner you get used to the idea that you're leaving, the better. Now, if you don't mind, let me pass. I have guests waiting . . .'

Thanet became aware that Edith Phipps was gazing at him expectantly, awaiting his reaction. 'It was rather foolish of you not to admit to so innocent an errand. Why didn't you?'

'Edith?' A querulous voice calling from another room.

Edith grimaced. 'My mother. Sorry, I'll have to go and see what she wants.' She hurried out.

'Seems to be our day for interruptions,' grumbled Lineham. 'And always at just the wrong moment.'

'Don't suppose it matters much. She's not going to run away, is she?'

'She didn't try and wriggle out of it,' Lineham conceded. 'Pretend she'd forgotten she'd been out that night.'

'Quite.'

'What d'you think, sir? You think she might be the one?'

Thanet lifted his shoulders. 'She had a lot at stake, if Marcia Salden stuck to her guns.'

'Just because she'd lost her job it doesn't mean they'd have had to leave this house, surely?'

'I've no idea. But I should think it might be on the cards. Marcia doesn't exactly sound the tender-hearted type. Look at what happened with Greenleaf.'

'Sorry.' Edith came back in, looking flustered. 'What were you saying?'

'I was asking why you lied to us about going out that evening. Posting letters is an innocent enough occupation.'

'I know.' She caught her underlip beneath her teeth, shook her head. 'It's just . . . I was frightened, I suppose.'

'Of what?'

'You'd just told me that Marcia's death might not have been an accident. And, well, to be honest . . .' She gave him an assessing look. 'I was glad she was dead,' she said quietly. She shifted uncomfortably, brushed back a stray strand of hair. 'Now you know,' she added. Then without warning her face suddenly contorted into a mask of distress and, covering her eyes with one hand, she sank down on to the chair, fumbling in her pocket for a handkerchief to wipe away the tears. It was some minutes before she recovered sufficiently to go on. Eventually she blew her nose, shook her head and said, 'Sorry.'

'No need to apologise. I presume that what you're trying to say is that because you were glad she was dead you felt guilty and because you felt guilty you thought we might suspect you of having something to do with her death.'

She nodded gratefully.

'Something of an overreaction, I would have thought.'

She shrugged. 'People don't always act logically. That was how I felt.'

'Why were you glad she was dead?' Thanet awaited her reply with interest. Would she now confess that she had had a motive, that Marcia had sacked her? To her knowledge no one else knew. She must realise by now that Marcia hadn't told Bernard and she might well believe that with any luck the police would never find out. So if she did tell them it would weigh heavily in favour of her innocence.

She compressed her lips and shook her head.

'You really can't make a statement like that and refuse to amplify it,' said Thanet gently. 'Especially in these circumstances.'

'Well, perhaps I was putting it a little too strongly. Perhaps what I really meant was that I wasn't sorry she was dead. It was a shock at first, of course, but once the news had sunk in I found I was really rather . . . relieved.'

'Any particular reason?' He couldn't give her a more specific lead than that. But she was shaking her head. She wasn't going to take it.

'Not really. I just didn't like her. She was hard. Very hard. Look at the way she treated Harry Greenleaf, who never did any harm to anyone . . . And she was very difficult to work for. Very demanding, hyper-critical.'

Thanet waited but she said nothing more. She had definitely decided against telling them, then. Interesting. The question now was, should he bring the matter up himself? Lineham was watching him, clearly wondering if he was going to.

'Perhaps I ought to tell you,' Thanet said slowly, 'that your conversation with Mrs Salden on Tuesday afternoon was overheard.'

The breath caught in her throat. 'Which conversation?'

'The one you're afraid I'm referring to. The one in which she fired you.'

She seemed to stop breathing, to move into a state of suspended animation. For a minute or more she gazed at Thanet unblinking. Then at last she stirred, sighed, glanced down at the sodden handkerchief in her lap. 'I see . . .'

There was a further, brief silence, then she said, 'How long have you known?'

'Since this morning.'

'Mrs Pantry, I suppose.' But there was no bitterness or animosity in her tone, merely a weary resignation.

'Actually, no . . .'

She shook her head. 'It doesn't really matter . . .' She gave a wry smile, the first glimmer of humour she had shown since the interview began. 'Now all I have to do is convince you that whoever it was who pushed Marcia off that bridge, it wasn't me.'

'Was it?'

She shook her head. 'Even if it was, would you really expect me to admit it? But no, Inspector, it wasn't.'

'It obviously wouldn't surprise you if somebody did.'

'Not really, no. Marcia was the sort of person to arouse strong passions. She was very stubborn and she liked to get her own way. And she didn't really care what people thought of her.'

'I gather she'd made herself pretty unpopular in the village.'

Edith pulled a face. 'I'll say. But you couldn't blame her, really.'

'What d'you mean?'

'For not caring what local people thought. I mean, they weren't exactly welcoming when she and Bernard bought the Manor, you know. They couldn't really stomach someone from the cottages buying "The Big House". Honestly! In this day and age . . . Well I knew just how much that house meant to Marcia, as I told you, so I was firmly on her side, prepared to back her to the hilt. All that drawing aside of skirts made me so angry . . . And I do think that if only she'd been prepared to be patient, give them time to come round, they would have accepted her in the end. But she wasn't the patient type and I suppose her reaction was predictable. "I'll teach them," she said to me, after one particular snub. "Just you wait and see." That was when she decided to close the footpath. And then it was just one thing after another.'

'So you think she did care what local people thought about her, underneath?'

'Oh yes, she did, beyond doubt. It was a shame, really. For her, buying the Manor was the proof that she'd really made it, the fulfilment of a life-long dream.'

'And the dream went sour.'

'I'm afraid so. And it soured her, too. She became much harder, more ruthless. And much more impatient, liable to lose her temper.'

Which could be important in their understanding of this particular crime, thought Thanet. If, as he suspected, Marcia's death had happened as the result of a quarrel, her attitude could have played a crucial part in precipitating the tragedy. That barely suppressed anger and resentment simmering away just below the surface would have been all too likely to erupt if someone challenged her or took her to task.

'Can you think of anyone in particular who had a grudge against her?'

Edith frowned, shaking her head. 'Strangely enough, no. Apart from Harry Greenleaf, of course, and I'm sure he couldn't have been involved. He wouldn't hurt a fly. Naturally I've been thinking about it, I've thought about it a lot, and I've come to the conclusion that Marcia tended to take on people collectively rather than individually. Which doesn't really help you, of course.'

'What about her husband?' The last time Thanet had spoken to Edith she had said that she wasn't prepared to discuss the Saldens' private life, but that she might reconsider if Marcia's death did turn out to be murder.

'Oh no. Not Bernard. He's just not the type to resort to violence under any circumstances. And although I wouldn't say they were really close, I can honestly say I never heard them quarrelling.'

'I have the impression he wasn't too happy about some of his wife's business interests.'

'Maybe, but you're not trying to tell me he'd resort to murder to stop her!'

'Not in cold blood, perhaps. But I'll be frank and tell you that in my opinion this was no premeditated crime. Someone quarrelled with Mrs Salden, grabbed her by the arm, perhaps, and she tried to get away, slipped . . .'

Edith folded her arms across her plump body and shivered. 'And then he just walked off, without raising the alarm, leaving her to drown.'

Thanet had no intention of telling Edith that Marcia had been dead before she reached the water. 'I'm afraid so, yes.'

She was shaking her head. 'I just can't see Bernard doing a thing like that. He's . . . well, not only is he the type of man to do everything he can to avoid a quarrel, but I just can't see him leaving anyone to drown, let alone his wife, not under any circumstances.'

'What can you tell me about a man called Hammer?'

The question surprised her. 'Reg Hammer?'

'Yes. His mother lived in the village. She died earlier this week.'

'What do you want to know about him?'

'Anything, really.'

'Well, he was born and brought up in Telford Green. He's married and lives in Sturrenden. Used to work at Chatham Dockyard, but was made redundant when it closed a few years ago and hasn't been able to get work since . . . Funny you should ask, really.'

'Why?'

'I saw him in the village yesterday, for the first time in years. He and his wife were clearing out his mother's cottage.'

For some reason she suddenly understood why he was enquiring about Hammer. Thanet saw the comprehension in her eyes.

'He wasn't a regular visitor to his mother, then?'

'No. Which I expect is one of the reasons why . . .' She stopped short.

'What were you going to say just then?'

'When?'

'You said, "Which I expect is one of the reasons why . . ." Then you stopped.'

She shrugged. 'It was automatic, I suppose. A sort of built-in reaction. I don't normally gossip about my employers' business.'

'This isn't gossip, I assure you. It could be highly relevant.'

'I suppose there's no reason why you shouldn't know. It's all in the files up at the house. I was merely going to say, I supposed the fact that Reg never bothered to visit his mother was one of the reasons why Mrs Hammer applied to join Marcia's Golden Oldie scheme.'

Thanet raised his eyebrows.

'It was one of Marcia's new business ventures. Lately she'd been getting a little bored with the health food business. It was very successful, yes, but the thrill of building it up had gone.'

'I thought she was contemplating moving into health food restaurants.'

'That's the latest idea, yes.'

'Do you know anything about the negotiations with Mr Lomax, by the way? What price he was asking, for example?'

'I don't think they'd got as far as that, not on paper anyway. Bernard is doing a feasibility study.'

'Sorry I interrupted. You were talking about Reg Hammer's mother . . .'

'Well, as I say, Marcia had been looking for ways to . . . diversify, I suppose is the best way of putting it. She spent some time considering various ideas and eventually she decided that the best investment these days is property. So she thought up this scheme.'

'The Golden Oldie scheme.'

'Well, that was her private name for it, yes. Officially it was Salden Investments Ltd. The idea was that she would approach elderly people living in small period village properties, terraced houses chiefly, which as you know have rocketed in price lately, and would propose to them a scheme whereby they would sell her their house but would retain the right to continue to live in it until they died. In return, instead of an outright payment of the full market value of the house, Marcia would offer them a lump sum down and a guaranteed annual income for life. It was a gamble, of course. The pensioner could continue to live way beyond the age at which Marcia would have made a profit out of the deal, or he could die soon after the agreement was made and she could make a killing.'

Not the happiest expression in the circumstances, thought Thanet. 'Perhaps you could give us an example?'

'Well, she was careful always to choose someone well into their seventies and without any close family likely to make a fuss if they felt they'd been deprived of their inheritance.'

Thanet was beginning to see where Hammer came into the picture.

'Take Mrs Hammer, for example, though she was a little different in that, as I say, she approached Marcia, not the other way around. She'd heard about the scheme from some friend of hers and she was seventy-seven when Marcia first heard from her earlier this year. She was in very good health for her age and I know Marcia calculated on her living another ten years. The old lady was very hurt at her son's neglect and had no compunction about applying to join the scheme. She positively jumped at the offer Marcia made. Marcia offered her £5,000 down and £3,500 a year for life. For pensioners these are substantial sums of money, perhaps more than they have ever seen in their lives. With that sort of guaranteed income on top of their pension, even allowing for income tax they can afford luxuries they may never have been able to enjoy before. The scheme hasn't been going long, and of course it's all properly drawn up by solicitors, but out of the fifteen people Marcia approached only one turned the offer down.'

Lineham had been working it out. 'So if a cottage was worth £50,000, she would calculate on paying out £5,000 down and a further £35,000 over ten years, making an expenditure of £40,000 in all.'

'That's right.'

'So she'd make a tidy profit as well as cashing in on the fact that house prices are rising by between ten and fifteen per cent a year here in the South-east.'

'True. But you must remember that her capital would be tied up for a period of ten years — and don't forget that the scheme only worked because the elderly people welcomed it. And Marcia was very fair about it. She never tried to mislead

169

them. I always went with her, when she approached people and explained how the scheme worked, and she always presented the snags of the scheme as well as the advantages. But it really seemed to appeal to them. It gave them more money in their pocket than most of them had ever had before, together with the guarantee of being able to stay on in their own homes for the rest of their lives — which is, above all, what most old people want. Given that, they just didn't care whether or not they would receive less than the market price for their properties. It really was a scheme which benefited everybody.'

'Everybody except the heirs,' said Lineham.

'True. But, as I say, Marcia was careful to approach only those who appeared to have no family or were estranged from them . . . Do I gather that Reg has been kicking up a fuss?'

'Not surprising, is it?' Lineham sounded indignant on behalf of the unknown Reg. 'Presumably Mrs Salden in effect bought his mother's cottage for £5,000.'

'And half the first annual payment of £3,500.'

Lineham waved a dismissive hand. 'Even so.'

'What I can't understand,' said Thanet, 'is why, if Mr Salden is the accountant for all their business affairs, he didn't know about this.'

'Marcia never bothered to consult him on her pet projects. He does the annual accounts for them, of course, and keeps an eye on the books from time to time, but the payments to Mrs Hammer only went through earlier this month, so they wouldn't have filtered through to him yet.'

'Edith?' The quavering voice again.

They had finished here for the moment. Besides, time was getting on and Thanet was anxious to get home early tonight because of Bridget. He had to ring Draco too, give him a brief progress report for the media statement. And he wanted to see Reg Hammer, first.

They thanked her, asked for directions to Mrs Hammer's cottage, and left.

NINETEEN

'You really wouldn't believe a house like that could be worth £50,000, would you?' said Lineham.

He had parked across the road from Mrs Hammer's cottage, which was in the middle of a terrace of eight, on the Manor side of the bridge.

It certainly had very little to recommend it in Thanet's eyes, being only about fourteen feet wide and built of ugly yellow Victorian brick with a slate roof. Prices indicated, however, that people were queueing up to buy such houses, village properties being especially in demand. 'The property world's gone mad,' he agreed.

'There's the Vicar,' said Lineham as they got out of the car. He grinned. 'Looks as though his car's gone wrong again. Can't say I'm surprised.'

Fothergill had just come into sight around the bend which lay between them and the bridge, and was heading in their direction on a bicycle. Thanet and Lineham waited for him to pass, but he raised his hand in greeting and pulled up beside them.

'We really must stop meeting like this,' he said with a cheery grin.

'What happened to the car?' said Lineham, grinning back.

Fothergill gave him a reproachful look. 'You are insulting the vehicle I love. She is sitting in the garage at the Vicarage, resting after her exertions. We had to go to Canterbury this morning. Anyway, I never use her for visiting within the village. Much too extravagant. I told you, vicars have to be seen to be poor. Makes people respect them more. How's it going?'

'Slowly,' said Thanet. 'We were just talking about the

171

ridiculous price of terraced cottages these days. Especially in the villages.'

Fothergill held up a hand. 'Don't start me off. That's one of my favourite hobbyhorses. People have these fantasies about living in a village, about enjoying the peace and quiet and the rural life. The young people especially are soon bored stiff and depart to the town again, looking for more excitement. They're not usually interested in village life at all. They don't join the village organisations or come to church. They don't realise that living in a village is like marriage – the more you put into it, the more you'll get out. The other thing, of course, is that it means all the old village families are disappearing. When the local young people get married they simply can't afford to buy anything and unless they're lucky enough to get a council house – and there are far too few of them – they have to move away.' He grinned. 'I told you, once I get launched . . . Anyway, I mustn't stand here gossiping. See you around.'

He wheeled his bicycle to the last cottage in the row, propped it against the fence and disappeared around the side.

There was no reply to their knock at Mrs Hammer's front door.

'Must've finished clearing up and gone home,' said Lineham. 'There's no car parked in front.'

'He may not have a car. He's supposed to be unemployed, remember. Try again.'

But there was still no answer and they turned away. As they were walking down the path, Thanet glanced over his shoulder and caught a glimpse of movement behind the net curtain at the downstairs window. He caught Lineham's sleeve. 'There's someone in there.'

They marched back to the door and knocked again, loudly. Still no reply.

'Try once more, then call "Police" through the letterbox,' said Thanet.

Lineham complied and this time they heard movement within.

The door opened a crack. A middle-aged woman peeped out. 'What do you want?'

'Mrs Hammer?'

'You want the old lady? She's . . .'

'No. We're looking for her son. Sturrenden CID.' Thanet produced his identity card.

'He's out.'

The door began to close, but Lineham stuck his foot in the gap, quickly.

'A brief talk with you, then,' said Thanet.

Slowly, the door opened, revealing the reason for her reluctance. One side of her face was badly bruised, from forehead to chin. Avoiding Thanet's eye she stood back. 'My husband said not to let anyone in.' Unconsciously, her hand went up to her face, touched her cheek. She was in her late forties, wearing a tight, shoddy black skirt and a short-sleeved scarlet sweater which had seen better days. Her hair was an improbable shade of orange, a frizzy uncontrolled bush, and she was heavily made up. Despite the gaudy, defiant colours, her shoulders sagged and she exuded an aura of defeat.

Inside, the house was in good repair, freshly decorated and comfortably, even luxuriously furnished, with a thick new fitted carpet and new dralon-covered three-piece suite. Presumably Marcia would have taken over the maintenance of the fabric of the house and Mrs Hammer would have been able to afford to indulge herself in the choice of furnishings. The curtain poles were bare and the room stripped of ornaments. Several overflowing cardboard boxes stood by the door, waiting to be taken away.

Mrs Hammer stood in the middle of the room, arms hanging loosely at her sides, clearly uncertain as to what should happen next.

Thanet gestured at the chairs. 'May we sit down?'

She shrugged. 'Help yourself.'

She dug a hand into her pocket, brought out a pack of cigarettes and lit one, inhaling the smoke greedily.

'I believe your mother-in-law died earlier this week.'

'So?' She perched on an arm of the other chair.

Expressions of sympathy would evidently be pointless. 'You've been busy.' Thanet nodded at the boxes.

'Nothing wrong with that, is there?' She was very much on the defensive.

'Of course not, no. Not a very pleasant job, though.'

She shrugged, drawing on her cigarette. 'Got to be done, hasn't it?'

'Have you nearly finished?'

'Just about.'

'Surprising how much people accumulate, isn't it, even in a small house like this? How long has it taken you?'

She gave him a puzzled glance. 'We started yesterday.'

'You arrived here yesterday morning, then?'

'No, Tuesday. Tuesday morning.'

If Mrs Hammer had died on Monday they certainly hadn't wasted much time moving in on what they must have thought of as Reg's inheritance. 'And on Tuesday afternoon you went to see the solicitor.'

She frowned. 'Yeah. So what?'

'And discovered that your mother-in-law had sold the cottage to Mrs Salden, without telling your husband.'

She was scowling heavily. 'Senile old bitch. Going behind Reg's back like that . . .'

So this woman's resentment was directed at her mother-in-law, not at Marcia. Predictable, perhaps. And her husband's? 'I understand your husband went up to the Manor to speak to Mrs Salden about it on Tuesday evening?'

That look of surprise was genuine, he would swear to it. 'You didn't know?'

She shook her head. 'He didn't tell me.' There was a long grey worm of ash on her cigarette and she looked around vaguely for an ashtray. Failing to see one, she tapped it into her cupped palm.

'You knew he was out that evening.'

'He said he was going to the Door.'

The local name for the pub, Thanet assumed. 'What time did he get home?'

Her cigarette had burned down. 'Excuse me. Must go and put this out.'

She went into the next room, leaving the door open, and they heard the brief hiss of a tap being turned on and off.

'About half-past ten,' she said as she came back in. Her eyes turned to the window as an old grey van pulled up outside. A man got out.

'There's Reg now.' Her hand went up to her cheek again in that unconscious gesture.

'Don't worry, I'll explain,' said Thanet hurriedly as the key sounded in the lock. He and Lineham rose as the door opened.

Hammer checked on the threshold, glancing from the two men to his wife and back again. 'Who the hell. . . ?'

He was a big man, well over six feet and a good eight or nine inches taller than his wife, with a drooping grandad moustache and a belly which hung over the waistband of his trousers. Thanet disliked him on sight.

Quickly, Thanet introduced himself.

Hammer looked accusingly at his wife.

'Don't blame your wife for letting us in. She had no choice. We would have found you sooner or later anyway.'

Hammer's expression changed to wariness. 'What d'you want to see me about?'

'Mrs Salden.'

'What about her?'

'Shall we sit down, Mr Hammer?'

He, too, was smoking and needed an ashtray. He flicked a glanced at his wife and without a word she got up, went to one of the cardboard boxes by the door and rummaged about until she found a saucer. She put it into his outstretched hand and he took it without word or look of acknowledgement. He sat down in the second armchair, balanced the saucer on the arm and folded his arms belligerently. 'Let's get on with it, then.'

Thanet glanced at Lineham and the Sergeant took up his cue, opening his notebook and glancing down at some imaginary notes. 'We understand you went up to the Manor on Tuesday night, to see Mrs Salden.'

'What if I did?' He stubbed his cigarette out, lit another.

'Would you mind telling us why?'

'Why should I? It was private business.'

'Reg,' said his wife.

'Keep your nose out,' he flung at her.

'But Reg . . .'

'I told you. Shurrup.'

'Mr Hammer,' began Lineham.

'Reg, they *know*,' said his wife, desperately.

There was a brief silence.

'Know what?' he said to her.

'About your mum signing the house over.'

He gave Lineham a venomous glare. 'Trying to catch me out, were you?'

'Merely trying to give you a chance to tell the story in your own words.'

Hammer gave a mirthless shout of laughter. 'Want a story, do you?' He ground out his half-smoked cigarette in the saucer and leaned forward, fixing Lineham with a basilisk stare. 'OK, I'll tell you one. Once upon a time there was an evil bitch who got her kicks out of making money. She got her biggest kicks of all when her victims was poor and downtrodden. She really rubbed her hands with glee the day she hit on a scheme for taking away the very roof over their heads. Now, there was one poor bloke who'd lost his job, through no fault of his own. His firm closed down, see, and he was made redundant. And he just couldn't find work 'cos unemployment was sky-high because of the bloody Conservative government what was in at the time. In the end the DHSS wouldn't go on paying his mortgage, so the building society took his house back and him and his wife and kids had to go and live with her mother in a poky little two-bedroomed flat. The council waiting list was as long as your arm, so it looked as if this situation would go on for ever. Then, unexpected-like, his mum dies. He was sorry, of course, he thought she'd go on for years, but looking on the bright side he thinks, at least I'll now have a home for my family. And what does he find? He finds that that bitch, that bloody bitch has snatched the house away from under his very nose with some crooked scheme what no one in his right mind would have taken on . . . Do you realise,' he went on, stabbing the air with his forefinger to emphasise the point, 'exactly how much Mrs Salden paid for this cottage? £5,000 down and half the first annual instalment of £3,500 – £1,750, that is. In other words,

£6,750 in all! 6,750 quid! And do you know how much the cottage is worth? £50,000!' He clutched his hand across his stomach and groaned, as if the thought gave him physical pain.

As well it might, thought Thanet. 'We're not here to discuss the rights and wrongs of the scheme, merely to . . .'

'Oh, I see,' said Hammer. 'The police force is no longer interested in justice.'

'In this instance, what you need is a solicitor, not a policeman.'

'Bloody solicitors! Fat lot of good that stuffed shirt Bassett is.'

Oliver Bassett, precise, prissy, conventional and well-tailored, had been a suspect in one of Thanet's cases. He and Hammer would be chalk and cheese.

Hammer was still fulminating. 'They're all the same. Make you pay through the nose just to say good morning to them. Carrion crows, that's what they are.' The phrase seemed to please Hammer and he repeated it, nodding emphatically. 'Carrion crows, picking over the leavings of the dead.'

Thanet glanced around the stripped room.

Hammer had the grace to flush.

'You haven't quite finished your story,' said Thanet.

'Oh?'

'On the night the poor honest labourer discovered the way in which he'd been cheated of what was rightfully his, the wicked witch died.'

'And good riddance, too.'

'But unfortunately for him, there was some doubt about her death.'

A brief silence, then 'Doubt?' said Hammer. He glanced at his wife. but she was staring at Thanet as if mesmerised.

It was interesting, Thanet thought, that the Hammers hadn't heard the rumours flying around the village. Perhaps it was a measure of Reg's unpopularity with neighbours who might have resented his neglect of his mother. 'That it may not have been an accident.'

Hammer gaped at him for a moment, then leapt to his feet. 'Now look here!' he shouted. 'What you getting at?'

In such a tiny room the effect was overpowering and it was difficult not to shrink back from the towering figure looming over them. 'Nasty temper you've got there, Mr Hammer,' said Thanet quietly.

Hammer glowered down at him then, without a word, returned to flop down into his chair. He lit another cigarette.

'Now, if you've calmed down, perhaps we can get this over with. All I want is a brief, factual account of your movements on Tuesday evening.'

Hammer's story was that he had left the house just after eight and had gone to the pub for a drink before going up to the Manor to see Marcia.

Dutch courage, no doubt, thought Thanet. 'One drink? Or two? Or more?'

'May have been two.' Hammer was sulky.

'Beer? Whisky?'

'Whisky.'

'Singles or doubles?'

Aware no doubt that all this could be checked, Hammer muttered reluctantly, 'Doubles.'

He had then driven up to the Manor and had asked for Marcia. He used her Christian name this time, Thanet noticed. Of course! He was the right age. They might well have been at school together. He wanted to think about this and signalled for Lineham to take over the questioning again. They knew that Marcia and Edith Phipps had both attended the village school. Now there was Reg. How many other people still living in the village had shared their childhood and adolescence with her? Marcia had lived at home until she got married, at eighteen. Was it possible that the roots of this present tragedy went deeper into the past than Thanet had so far considered?

Listening with one ear to what Hammer was now saying, Thanet gathered that, denied entry by Mrs Pantry ('rotten bitch'), he had resorted once more to drink, going directly back to the Crooked Door and staying there until closing time.

They would check at the pub, of course, but meanwhile . . .

'I suppose you knew Mrs Salden well at one time, Mr Hammer?'

He looked taken aback. 'Pretty well, yes. We was at school together.'

'Yes, I thought you might have been. What was she like, then?'

He gave a cynical sort of laughter. 'A prig and a swot, if you must know. Always did have her sights set upwards, did our Marcia.'

Mrs Hammer stirred.

'Yes, Mrs Hammer?' said Thanet.

'I was only going to say,' she said with a nervous glance at her husband, 'that she wasn't snooty, though, was she? I mean, you told me she . . .'

'Never mind what I told you,' snarled Hammer.

She subsided with a little shake of the head.

'What was the name of the headmaster at the village school in your time?' said Thanet.

The unexpectedness of the question brought an immediate response. 'Mr Pringle.' A brief pause, then, 'Why?'

'Just wondered. He'd be retired now, I suppose.'

'I suppose,' echoed Hammer.

'D'you happen to know where he's living?'

'Haven't a clue.'

Thanet's beeper went and Mrs Hammer jumped. 'It's all right,' he said, 'I'll have to get to a phone, that's all.' They'd finished here, anyway. He glanced at Lineham, raising his eyebrows. *Any more questions?* Lineham shook his head.

He used the phone box outside the Crooked Door. There was a message for him to ring home. What could be wrong? He felt slightly sick as he dialled the number.

Joan answered on the first ring.

'What's the matter, darling. What's wrong?'

'It's Bridget. She's not home yet.'

He glanced at his watch. 'It's only half-past five. She could have gone to Amanda's house. Or Sheila's.'

'I've rung around, and she's not with any of her friends. And she hasn't been at school today, remember. She could be anywhere. Oh Luke, I'm sorry to fuss, but I can't help

179

worrying, in the circumstances. I mean, she knew I was seeing the headmaster this afternoon . . . What if she's afraid to come home?'

'I'll be there as soon as I can.'

TWENTY

All the way home Thanet's unruly imagination ran riot. He was fully aware of the growing problem of runaways who, unable to cope at home, make their way to the nearest big city and end up by being sucked into prostitution or worse. And there was no point in telling himself that it couldn't happen to a girl like Bridget, from a stable, loving home. It was true that most of these youngsters ran away because of irreconcilable differences with either father or mother, but Thanet himself had dealt with at least two cases where the parents were just like himself and Joan, and completely bewildered as to what had gone wrong.

And in one of them, the child, a boy of thirteen, had never been seen again.

The very thought brought an uprush of panic and he took a deep breath and told himself to calm down. Like Joan, he was overreacting, of course. It simply would not, could not happen to them. Bridget wouldn't have expected her mother to be home before a quarter or ten to six, so there was no reason why she herself should turn up before then. After all, she wasn't a baby any more. At fifteen she shouldn't have to account to them for every minute of her time. He and Joan had always striven to strike a sensible balance between being over-protective and allowing too much freedom. No, by the time he got home she would have arrived, safe and sound.

But she hadn't. Joan came out to meet him and it was immediately obvious from her face.

'Tell me I'm blowing things up out of all proportion,' she said with an attempt at a smile when they had kissed.

He put his arm around her. 'Come on. Let's go inside.'

Joan had rung everywhere she could think of and it was

181

pointless to consider requesting official help from the police at this stage. Thanet knew that in similar circumstances he would expect a girl of Bridget's age to be a minimum of three or four hours overdue before mobilising his men, and probably much longer. And in any case, if Bridget were making an innocent visit somewhere, she would justifiably be furious if she discovered that an official search had been organised just because she was a couple of hours late getting home from school. Thanet said so.

'I know that. But if ever she's going anywhere, she always lets us know.'

'There has been the odd occasion in the past when she hasn't.'

'But not in these circumstances. I'm just worried in case, guessing why Mr Foreman wanted to see me this afternoon, she feels she can't face us. After all, she must have felt she couldn't confide in us up to now, if things have got so bad that she's been driven to playing truant.'

'Did Ben know about that?'

'I don't think so, no. He says not, and I believe him. He says he knew something was wrong, but thought it was just exams.'

They were in the kitchen. Thanet sat down heavily on one of the chairs. 'He's right, in a way, of course. There's no doubt that it's the prospect of GCSEs looming that's done the damage.'

'But we've done everything we can to stop her getting too worked up about it.'

'I know, and let's face it we've failed dismally, haven't we? Just look at the way she's been going on! Sitting up till all hours sweating over her books, and if you dare suggest she ought to give up and go to bed you either have your head bitten off or she dissolves into floods of tears . . . D'you know, the night before last she was still working at midnight and when I went along I just didn't have the nerve to tell her it was time she stopped, in case it upset her!' He shook his head in disbelief. 'I suppose if we had any sense we'd have seen this coming.'

'But what could we have done about it, even if we had?'

Thanet shook his head. 'I don't know.'

'She's too conscientious, that's the trouble. Takes things too much to heart.'

'But she didn't do impossibly badly in her mocks at Christmas.'

'She felt she had. She only had reasonable grades in two subjects out of seven.'

'But all her teachers said she had a fair chance of achieving considerably higher grades in the summer, if she worked hard.'

'Which is precisely what she's been doing, of course. Honestly, Luke, I sometimes think it would have been better if the results had been so appalling that she'd given up hope of doing any better.'

'You don't really mean that.'

'I suppose not.'

'After all, under this new system, her continuous assessment is supposed to be equally important, and that's been quite good.'

'Let's face it, average, at best.'

'Well, all right, average. There's nothing wrong with that.'

'No, of course not.'

'One thing's certain, we're going to have to try and work something out. If she goes on like this for another couple of months, we'll all have nervous breakdowns!'

'Just let's get her back, that's all I can think of at the moment. Oh Luke, what d'you think we ought to do?'

He stood up. 'I'm going to go out and have a scout around for her. Would you mind staying here? I think one of us ought to.'

'I agree. No, I'll stay.'

At least he knew where to look, he thought as he set off. He'd done this often enough before. But never when it was his own child who was missing, never with quite this sense of urgency.

It was now half-past six and his task was made easier by the fact that the streets of Sturrenden were virtually deserted. It was the dead time of day between the rush home from work and the start of the evening's entertainments. He began with the cafés. In one or two there were little groups of teenagers lingering over cups of coffee, reluctant to go home, but he didn't recognise any of them as Bridget's friends and he didn't approach them. At this stage he wanted to keep things as low-key as possible, in case it was a false alarm.

After his round of the cafés he decided to quarter the town systematically. There was no point in trying the pubs. The fact that she was still in her school uniform precluded them, she wouldn't even be allowed in. It was that uniform his eyes were seeking, he realised, and once or twice his stomach lurched as one was sighted; each time he was disappointed.

Where could she have gone? He'd now been right around the town twice and there was no sign of her. It was pointless to continue.

At home Joan came to the front door as soon as she heard the car, her look of disappointment when she saw he was alone reinforcing his anxiety as he realised that she had no news either.

'No luck?'

It was almost a whisper and automatically he lowered his voice as he said, 'No. Why are we talking in undertones?'

She glanced back over her shoulder along the hall. 'Vicky's here.'

Thanet groaned. 'Oh, no.' Vicky Younghusband's post-natal depression was the last thing he felt able to deal with at the moment.

'I couldn't just turn her away, could I?'

'I suppose not. It's just that . . . Have you told her Bridget's missing?'

'No. There's no point. It's not the sort of news she can cope with, the state she's in. And it would look as though I was trying to get rid of her, say, "Sorry, I've no emotional energy to spare for you just now." '

'Which would be true! How on earth can we deal with this situation in whispers? It's bad enough as it is without having to lurk in corners to discuss it.' They were still standing in the hall. 'Where is she?'

'In the kitchen. I decided to start supper. I had to have something to do.'

Thanet nodded understanding. A thought struck him. Cooking . . . 'Have you tried Helen Mallard?'

'No, I haven't!' She hurried to the phone and Thanet followed, hovered as she spoke into it. In a few moments she shook her head at him.

He waited while she finished the call.

She glanced at the closed kitchen door. 'I thought, if I served supper . . .'

'I'm not hungry.'

'No, neither am I, that's not the point. I thought, if I served supper Vicky might take the hint and go . . . Oh dear, that does sound callous, but . . .'

'Good idea,' said Thanet. 'Yes, do that. I suppose I'd better say hello to her.'

They went into the kitchen. Vicky Younghusband was sitting at the table, hands in lap. She was almost unrecognisable as the lively, attractive, cheerful young woman of a few months ago. Her loose blouse was stained with milk and baby's vomit, her hair uncombed and unwashed. She wore no make-up and the flesh beneath her eyes was dark with the bruises of sleeplessness and despair. She even smelt, Thanet realised with a shock, sour and unwashed. Since the baby was born he had seen her only when she was with Peter, when presumably an effort had been made to make her presentable. He could now understand Joan's anxiety and resolved to talk to Peter the minute he got home.

She attempted a smile in response to his greeting, but it was no more than a mechanical lifting of the corners of her mouth.

'How's the baby?' said Thanet.

'The baby?' Her forehead creased and she looked around vaguely, as if expecting to see him somewhere in the room. 'Oh, he's fine. He's asleep,' she added, after a pause. 'Yes.' She nodded. 'Yes, asleep.'

'Good.' Thanet heard the tone of his own voice, over-hearty, and hated himself for it. 'When's Pete due back?'

Another pause. 'Not until the weekend.'

Briefly, something frantic peeped out of her eyes, then was gone.

Had he imagined it? 'Where's he gone?'

'Uhh . . .' She put her hands up to her head and pressed her fingers against her temples, as if trying to squeeze the answer out. 'Scotland,' she said at last.

'Scotland!' Thanet was startled. Uneasy, too. He wasn't happy about Peter being so far away, with Vicky in this state. 'A bit off his usual beat, isn't it?'

'It's the annual sales conference.'

'I see.' Thanet glanced at Joan, who was clattering saucepans. 'Where's Ben?'

'Upstairs, doing his homework.'

'I'll go and have a word.'

Ben was lying on his bed, reading a book. He laid it face down on the bedspread. 'She not back yet?'

Thanet shook his head. 'We'll be having supper soon.'

Ben rolled off the bed and stood up. 'I'm not hungry.'

And that, thought Thanet, was a telling admission. Ben's appetite was constant and voracious. He must be very worried indeed.

'Ben, d'you have any idea at all of where she might have gone?'

'No. Unless . . .'

'What?' Thanet couldn't hide the hope in his voice.

'I was wondering . . . She did say she wanted to see *Crocodile Dundee*. She missed it first time around.'

The cinema! Of course. Why hadn't he thought of that? It was dark, warm, anonymous . . . A comfortable place in which to hide, to lick one's wounds. 'Like to come with me, to see?'

Ben was eager. 'Sure.'

They set off, Thanet careful to take the route she would follow if she were walking home from the town.

'Dad?'

'What?'

'I'm not sure this is such a good idea after all.'

'Why not?'

'They have separate performances. The last one would have finished by now and the next won't start till eight. The usherettes would have checked that nobody . . . Dad, look! There she is!'

Ben was right! There she was, walking towards them some two hundred yards ahead on the other side of the road, shoulders hunched, feet dragging. He and Ben exchanged a jubilant glance. The uprush of relief, however, was immediately followed by a swell of anger. How could she have done this to them? Furious words and phrases began to run through Thanet's mind. Then, as he checked for traffic, and did a U-turn, he had a brief, vivid image of the photograph he had seen in the paper after the disappearance of a French girl in London. She had been the same age as Bridget and had been missing for over twenty-four hours before being found safe and sound, sleeping rough. The photograph had shown her struggling in the street with her father, determined, apparently, not to return home. Like other parents right across the land, Thanet had sympathised with the man's dilemma. Understandably, the Frenchman couldn't bear to let his child walk off into the London jungle unprotected, and had in fact manhandled her back into the flat. But Thanet had wondered at the time what would happen. How long would it be before the girl disappeared again?

No, anger was not the answer. This situation must be handled with kid gloves. He said to Ben, 'OK, Ben, now look, we'll play it cool, right? She's in a pretty fragile state of mind at the moment . . .' He pulled up alongside her and said, 'Hello, love.'

She stopped, glancing from him to Ben. She looked wary, apprehensive.

As well she might, he thought. 'Come on, hop in.'

She hesitated a moment longer, then climbed into the back.

No reproaches, Thanet reminded himself as they headed for home. But he couldn't think of anything to say which might not be construed as such. Safer, then, to say nothing. He could see Bridget's face in the driving mirror. She looked thoroughly miserable.

The silence became oppressive.

'I went to see *Crocodile Dundee*,' she said at last. She was defiant, aggressive, almost. Obviously anticipating trouble and prepared to meet it.

Ben gave his father a triumphant glance and Thanet accorded him a congratulatory nod. *Well guessed.*

'Next time, give us a ring, let us know where you are.' His tone was mild, almost casual.

He caught her startled look in the mirror. *Surely they're not going to let me off as lightly as that?*

Their swift return brought Joan to the front door again. Her look of joy when she saw that Bridget was with them was one that Thanet would never forget. He sent her an admonitory glance and recognised the effort it cost her simply to say, with admirable restraint, 'Ah, there you are, then, Bridget. Well timed. Supper's ready.'

On the way in Joan caught Thanet's hand and squeezed it as they exchanged a look of relief.

'Vicky gone?'

She nodded.

'Good.'

Despite their attempts at conversation, supper was a silent meal. Guiltily, Thanet found himself ravenous. Ben, too, was eating heartily, he noticed, whereas Joan and Bridget merely toyed with their food. Halfway through, Bridget laid down her knife and fork. 'Why don't you say it?' she burst out.

Thanet and Joan glanced at each other.

Joan spoke for both of them. 'Say what?'

'How can you sit there, pretending nothing's the matter?' She glowered at them. 'I thought this was supposed to be a great family for talking things out, for "communicating". So go on, communicate!'

Joan abandoned any pretence at eating. 'If that's what you want.'

'Oh!' Bridget jumped up out of her seat and took a few agitated paces around the room. 'Why are you always so *reasonable*?'

'You make it sound like a crime,' said Thanet.

'Why don't you ever shout at me, or swear, like other people's parents?' She was practically in tears.

'That's what you'd like?'

'At least I wouldn't feel so guilty.' She glanced from Thanet to Joan and back. 'Can't you *see*?' And she rushed out of the room.

Ben had gone on eating steadily.

'Is that how you feel too, Ben?' said Joan.

He considered, chewing away, cheeks bulging. 'Sometimes, I suppose. Occasionally it's nice to have someone to kick against and have rows with, get it out of your system. But most of the time, no. Is there any pud?'

Joan shook her head. 'Sorry, not tonight, no. You can be thankful you got anything to eat at all! Have an apple or an orange.'

He slid out of his chair. 'Right.'

Left alone, Thanet and Joan looked at each other.

'Now we know!' said Joan.

'Honestly, you can't win, can you? If you shout at them you're being tyrannical, if you try to be reasonable you're not exerting enough authority!'

'I know. So what are we supposed to do now, about Bridget?'

Thanet considered. 'I think she wants to talk.'

'I agree. Probably wants to get it over with.'

He grinned. 'So do I!'

Joan stood up. 'Come on, then.'

Bridget was lying on her bed, staring at the ceiling.

'We've come to communicate,' said Thanet with a smile. 'If that's what you want.'

No response for a moment, then she rolled over to sit on the edge of the bed. She looked sullen, unresponsive, rebellious. Thanet's heart sank. If she continued in this mood they weren't going to get very far.

Joan evidently felt the same. '*Is* that what you want?'

Bridget shrugged. 'It's up to you.'

Her mother frowned. 'No, it's up to you. We'll have to talk about it sooner or later, and we thought you'd prefer it to be sooner rather than later. But we don't mind, if you'd rather put it off.' She glanced at Thanet and after waiting for a moment and receiving no response they began to move towards the door.

Bridget glanced up. 'No. Wait. I . . .' She shrugged. 'Better get it over with, I suppose.'

'Look,' said Thanet. 'I'm not sure it's a good idea to chew it over just now, when we're all feeling a bit het up. On the other hand, we don't want you lying awake all night worrying about it. So I'll just say this. Your mother and I were naturally very upset to hear you'd been playing truant. And the reason we were upset was because you hadn't felt able to come and talk to us about it, despite the fact that you were obviously feeling pretty desperate. Now, I want to make one thing clear. As far as we are concerned, we don't care if you don't get a single decent grade in your GCSEs, if worrying about it is going to have this effect on you. Academic grades are not everything — you've got plenty of other talents and lots of qualities that employers would value. So just stop worrying about it. No exams in the world are worth this sort of stress and strain.'

'As far as we're concerned,' Joan added, 'this incident is over and done with. Unless you want to bring it up again some time, it's finished. So long as you understand that we both mean what your father said. Is that clear?'

Bridget nodded slowly. 'Thanks.'

She said nothing more and reluctantly they left her.

'What else could we have done?' whispered Thanet as they went downstairs.

Joan shrugged. 'Nothing, as far as I can see.'

Thanet felt for his pipe. 'Let's have some coffee and watch something mindless on television. I've had more than enough emotional traumas for one evening.'

They went into the sitting-room.

'Which reminds me,' said Joan. 'I saw your new Superintendent on *Coast to Coast* this evening, giving a statement about your case. He was . . . What's the matter?'

Thanet had just remembered: he hadn't written up a single report today.

Draco would be furious, in the morning.

TWENTY-ONE

'What sort of example d'you think you're setting?'

Draco *was* furious.

The Superintendent raked his hand through the cropped, wiry black curls and glowered at Thanet. 'You heard what I said, the other day in this very room.' His finger stabbed at the desk as if to impale the memory. 'Reports, I said, are the key. Detailed, literate and accurate reports. Now, I can understand if, on the odd occasion, you're pushed and have to put in something a bit sketchy, but you're telling me you haven't done *any* for yesterday. And on a murder enquiry!'

Ejected from his chair by the strength of his emotion, Draco leapt up and began to pace agitatedly about. The size of the office restricted his movements and Thanet began to count: two paces from desk to window, four from window to door, three from door to desk. Draco sat down with a thump.

'What sort of excuse have you got?'

'None that you would find acceptable, I'm afraid, sir.'

Draco expelled air through his nostrils in an affronted hiss. If he'd been a dragon the flames would have reached across the desk to burn Thanet to a crisp. His eyes bulged slightly. 'Think I'm that unreasonable, do you, Thanet?'

Thanet saw his mistake. 'No, sir, I didn't mean that. I simply meant that . . . well, I was judging by my own standards. I always tell the men that they should try not to let personal problems interfere with their work.'

'Personal problems! I hope you're not sitting there telling me that the reason why these reports are late – no, the reason why they don't even *exist* – is because you're having personal problems!'

'Well, not exac– '

'My God, what's the world coming to?' Draco was up out of his chair again. 'When an experienced officer like you . . .' He stopped and resting both hands on the desk he leaned forward, looming over Thanet like an avenging angel. 'You've got problems? Everybody's got problems. I've got problems. But do I let it interfere with my work? No, I do not. And do you know why, Thanet? Or should I say, how?'

Thanet had given up for the moment. He shook his head dumbly.

Draco straightened up, standing almost to attention. 'Self-discipline, that's how. When I walk in through that door I say to myself, "Goronwy," I say, "that's it. Put it all behind you now, boyo." And I do, Thanet, I do. And so should you. Compartmentalise, that's the answer, compartmentalise.'

So that was how you pronounced Draco's apparently unpronounceable Christian name, thought Thanet.

On the 'p' of 'compartmentalise' flecks of saliva flew across to spatter themselves over Thanet's face and he had to restrain both an urge to wipe them ostentatiously away and a desire to burst out laughing. Draco was rapidly becoming a sit-com character. Thanet almost expected him to say, like Reggie Perrin's boss, 'I didn't get where I am today by . . .'

And yet, in another way, it just wasn't funny. This man had power over Thanet's career, Thanet's life. A good working relationship with him was essential to Thanet's peace of mind. And at the moment Thanet was feeling anything but peaceful. He was aware of the signs of mounting stress in himself: clenched hands, a thrumming of blood in his ears, a tension and rigidity throughout his body. Careful, he told himself. Don't let him get to you. Don't say anything you'll regret later. And, above all, calm *down* . . . Deliberately he uncurled his hands, relaxed, expelled held breath in a long, unobtrusive exhalation. 'Yes, but it's not . . .'

Draco waved a hand and sat down again. 'Oh, I know what you're going to say. "It's not easy", that's what you're going to say. Of course it's not, but it shouldn't stop us trying. A bit of practice and self-discipline, that's all . . .' His eyes narrowed. 'Not marriage problems, I hope?'

'No, sir,' said Thanet stiffly. 'In fact, I was about to explain that it was strictly a one-off situation.' *I hope.*

'I'm very glad to hear it. Crisis over now, then, is it?' Draco was visibly deflating, leaning back in his chair and steepling his hands beneath his chin.

'Oh yes.'

'I see. Good. Good. Well, I've made it clear, I hope, that I don't expect this to happen again.'

'Yes, sir.' *Abundantly.*

It had already been decided during the briefing, earlier, that the Salden investigation was to continue. The fact that Marcia had been dead before she entered the water had ensured that. With relief, Thanet escaped. Outside in the corridor he rolled his eyes in despair. It looked as though Draco was becoming his daily cross.

Upstairs he cast a longing glance at the sanctuary of his room. The decorators had finished the woodwork and were now painting the walls. Tomorrow, they assured him, by tomorrow afternoon at the latest, he should be able to move back in.

Spirits rising, Thanet returned to the CID room. He and Lineham had already discussed the timetable for the day and there was one interview, later on in the morning, that he was especially looking forward to. Meanwhile, another visit to the Hammers was indicated. Enquiries had established that Hammer had indeed been in the Crooked Door most of Tuesday evening, for the last hour or so muttering incomprehensible drunken complaints about some bitch who had stolen what was his by right. The landlord had assumed he was referring either to wife or girlfriend. There was one interesting discrepancy, however: soon after ten the landlord, judging that Hammer had had more than enough to drink, had refused to serve him any more and had 'chucked him out'. Which could have placed Hammer in the vicinity of the bridge around the time when Marcia was crossing it.

'And his wife says he didn't get home till around half-past,' said Lineham.

'Yes, interesting, isn't it? Twenty-five minutes to half an hour to walk a couple of hundred yards.'

'Wonder what he was up to?'

'If only we could get some more precise timings,' Thanet sighed as he and Lineham set off for Telford Green.

'I know. They all say "around such and such a time", don't they? Not surprising, of course, not many people go around checking the exact time for no particular reason. But it does mean you have to allow five or ten minutes either way . . . The one thing that does seem certain is that they were all in the right place at approximately the right time. Salden claims to have been sitting on a bench only a couple of hundred yards away, Edith Phipps was posting her letters, Josie's mother was on her way home from the Manor, Councillor Lomax was on his way to the pub and now we find Reg Hammer was around too.'

'What did you think of him, Mike?'

There hadn't been time, yesterday, to discuss their visit to the Hammers.

'I bet she didn't get those bruises by walking into a door.'

'A wife-beater, if ever I saw one,' agreed Thanet.

'I can never understand why women put up with it.'

'It's a very complex matter, as you well know. Straightforward fear, in a lot of cases, I imagine, that they'll have to suffer even worse violence if they leave or take legal action. And we both know how justifiable a fear that is. The number of cases you hear of, where a woman is harassed or beaten up or even killed by a violent ex-husband who won't leave her alone. And it's well known that some women just seem to go for violent men, repeating the same pattern over and over again.'

'Is this Mrs Hammer his first wife?'

'That was the impression I had, from Edith Phipps.'

'Anyway, it did occur to me, a man like that, who's used to hitting women around . . . We did say we thought that was probably how Mrs Salden died, when someone just lashed out at her during a quarrel . . .'

'It's a distinct possibility, I agree.' Thanet wound down his window. It was a sparkling April day with a frisky wind chasing puffy white clouds across a sky the colour of the forget-me-nots in the cottage gardens.

194

'In fact, the only suspect who doesn't seem to have been around at the right time is Harry Greenleaf.'

'The way things are going, I shouldn't count on it.'

They drove in silence for a while, then Lineham said, 'Sir . . .'

'Yes?' An uncharacteristic diffidence in the Sergeant's tone alerted Thanet to the fact that this was nothing to do with work.

'I just wanted to say . . . Well, Louise and I had that talk, and you were right . . . I didn't realise just how bored and frustrated she is. As I said, it's not that she doesn't love the kids, it's just that . . . Well, we said it all the other night, didn't we? Anyway, I think we've got something sorted out. She's going to look around for a part-time job in September, when Mandy starts playgroup.'

'And no more talk of you leaving the police?'

'No.'

'Good. Excellent.' Thanet couldn't help feeling a self-congratulatory glow.

The old grey van was drawn up in front of Mrs Hammer's cottage. Hammer and his wife were struggling with the base of a divan bed.

'Having problems?' said Thanet pleasantly.

'Nothing we can't deal with. Hold that leg up higher, Dor, and twist it a bit to your left. To your left, you stupid cow, not to your right! Now pull!'

Pull?

The bed slid out like a cork out of a bottle and Mrs Hammer went down on one knee. She had exchanged the black skirt for some faded jeans, the red sweater for a collarless man's shirt rolled up to just below the elbows. Hammer glowered impatiently at her and she scrambled up, putting up a hand to lift the bush of hair out of her eyes. The wide sleeve of the shirt fell back, revealing fresh bruises in the tender flesh of the upper arm. She saw Thanet noticing and flushed, quickly lowered her hand.

The van, Thanet realised, was crammed with household goods.

Hammer picked up one end of the bed. 'Come *on*,' he said to his wife. She stooped to lift the other end and they started off up the short path to the open front door.

'Moving in?' said Thanet.

He and Lineham followed the Hammers up the path.

Hammer dropped his end of the bed with a crash and straightened up, turning to face Thanet with a belligerent expression. 'What if we are?'

'Rather pointless, in the circumstances, isn't it? I imagine Mrs Salden was very careful to make sure the legal agreement over the purchase of the cottage was watertight. You'll only have to move out again shortly.'

'Don't you believe it! Yesterday I got to thinking. What is the point in clearing the house out and leaving it empty? I'd just be handing it to them on a plate. I ought to be on the spot, defending my right to my property.' Hammer cast a proprietorial glance over his shoulder. 'No, if they want a fight, they can have it. I'm going to make that pouf Basset's life hell until we find a way around that agreement.' He took a dog-end from behind his ear and lit it, blowing smoke into Thanet's face. He grinned. 'Anyway, you know what they say, about possession being nine points of the law.' He turned to pick up the bed again. 'So now, if you don't mind . . .'

'Just one or two questions, Mr Hammer,' said Lineham quickly.

Hammer turned. 'What now?'

'It's about Tuesday night,' said Lineham. 'Mrs Hammer, you said your husband arrived home at . . .' He pretended to consult his notebook. 'At about half-past ten.'

She darted an uneasy glance at Hammer. 'Yes, he did.'

'But according to the landlord of the Crooked Door, Mr Hammer, you were asked to leave soon after ten.'

'Was I?' Hammer shrugged. 'If he says so. I can't remember a blind thing about it. I was blotto.' He folded his arms across his chest and a smug, self-congratulatory smile lifted the corners of his mouth.

Presumably he thought it was macho to get drunk, thought Thanet.

196

'We were wondering how it could take you nearly half an hour to walk a couple of hundred yards.'

Hammer lifted his shoulders again. 'Search me. Can't remember the first thing about it.'

'Uh . . .' said his wife.

All three men looked at her and she shifted uncomfortably. 'I was only going to say . . . I think someone brought Reg home, on Tuesday.'

Of course! Thanet remembered the two men Lomax had seen in front of these cottages on his way to the pub that night. Why hadn't he realised before that Hammer must have been one of them? But in that case, who was the other?

Hammer and Lineham spoke together.

'You never said . . .'

'You didn't mention this before . . .'

She ignored Lineham, answered her husband. 'You never asked me.'

'Who was it?'

Thanet wondered if Hammer ever addressed her in anything but that rough, almost brutal tone.

'Dunno, do I?'

'Stupid bitch,' muttered Hammer as Lineham said, 'When you say you *think* someone brought your husband home, what do you mean?'

'Someone knocked at the door. When I opened it, Reg was sitting on the doorstep, leaning against the doorpost. And a man was walking away. He was disappearing around the bend by then, on his way to the bridge.'

'And you've no idea who it was?'

But she didn't reply. She was staring at her husband.

Hammer was gazing fixedly into the middle distance, mouth slightly agape, eyes narrowed, as if a thought had just struck him.

'Mr Hammer?' he said.

Mrs Hammer clutched at her husband's arm. 'What's the matter, Reg?'

He shook her off. 'Nothing.'

'But you . . .'

'I said, it was nothing!'

'Remembered something, have you?' said Lineham.

Hammer's gaze focussed on the Sergeant. 'If you think I've remembered shoving Marcia off the bridge, you've got another think coming. Look, we've still got a lot to do here. If you've quite finished . . .'

'You must realise that things don't look too good for you, Mr Hammer,' said Thanet. 'If you remember anything, anything at all, that you might have seen or heard on your way home from the pub that night, please let us know, immediately. It could be in your own interest.'

'Don't worry. I'm a lot more interested in saving my neck than you are.'

'I hope you're not thinking of leaving the area at the moment.'

'If you want me, you'll know where to find me.'

'I should think Mrs Hammer's mother is down on her knees praying he gets that cottage,' said Lineham as they drove away. 'Imagine having a son-in-law like that! Especially living in the same house!'

'Don't! It doesn't bear thinking about.'

But Thanet sounded abstracted. His mind had already moved ahead to the next interview.

This was the one he was looking forward to.

TWENTY-TWO

'He's in the garage.'

Mrs Pringle, wife of the former headmaster of Telford Green primary school, was a little dumpling of a woman with sausage-like curls and cheeks as rosy as a Spartan apple. She was leaning on an aluminium walking stick with a fat rubber tip.

Thanet was intrigued by her expression as she told them where her husband was: a mixture of resignation, indulgence, and yes, he was certain of it, amused anticipation.

What could Pringle be up to in the garage?

'I'll take you across.'

'There's no need, I'm sure we'll find him.'

But she insisted and Thanet and Lineham followed her slow but determined progress along the concrete path in front of the bungalow. Whatever Pringle did in his retirement, it wasn't gardening. The small patch of grass in front of the house was raggedly mown and any flowers in the weed beds which surrounded it had long ago given up.

They saw the long, low pre-cast concrete structure as soon as they rounded the corner of the house. It was at least twice as long as any normal garage. On the side facing the back garden was an unusually large window and Thanet was interested to see that steel shutters similar to the type used to protect lock-up shops had been fitted to roll down over both this window and the sliding entrance doors.

What could Pringle keep in there?

Possible answers flicked through Thanet's mind: a vintage car of exceptional value? Only the other day he had seen a photograph of a 1925 silver-plated Phantom Rolls in the paper. Bought for £2,000 in 1970, it was now worth £100,000. But here, in the garage of an old-age pensioner in Telford Green? Or perhaps Mr Pringle was one of those zany inventors who spends all his days engaged in working on some hopelessly impractical Icarus-style prototype, valuable only in his fevered imagination.

'Gerald?'

Mrs Pringle was struggling with the heavy door and Lineham went to help.

She stood back, steadying herself on her stick as the door slid back, watching their astounded expressions with a mixture of triumph and amusement.

Lineham gasped.

The entire garage was taken up by a waist-high, landscaped model railway layout of incredible size and complexity: hills and valleys encircled a small town of houses, shops, hotels, pubs and car parks; there were tunnels, bridges and viaducts; stations and sidings; row after parallel row of rails; and, above all, dozens of exquisitely fashioned goods and passenger trains, many of which were racing around the tracks in dizzyingly impressive patterns of movement. In the centre space, supervising all this frantic activity with an expression of blissful absorption, stood a tall, crane-like elderly man with sparse grey hair and benign blue eyes which swivelled now in the direction of his wife as she spoke.

'Someone to see you, Gerald.'

Lineham had forgotten about work. Like a man in a dream he stepped forward, eyes devouring the wonders laid out before him. He shook his head in amazement. 'I've never seen anything like it,' he breathed.

Pringle recognised genuine enthusiasm when he saw it and within seconds he and the Sergeant were involved in a conversation larded with technical terms Thanet never knew existed. Amused, he waited patiently. It would be easy this time to get the witness to open up to them; Lineham was preparing the ground beautifully.

'D'you hear that, sir? Seven hundred and fifty feet of track!' Lineham turned a dazed face towards Thanet, his expression changing as he registered the look on Thanet's face. He glanced back at Pringle, then at the layout. 'Sorry, sir,' he muttered. 'Got a bit carried away.'

'And why not?' Thanet smiled at Pringle. 'It's not every day one sees something like this. To someone keen on model railways it must seem like one of the Seven Wonders of the World.'

Pringle was beaming with pride. 'It's taken me thirty years to build.'

'And the Inspector'll be standing here for another thirty listening to you talk about it if you have your way!' said his wife, her tone that of an indulgent mother addressing a wayward child. 'It's half-past ten, time for elevenses. Come into the house, Inspector, you'll be more comfortable there.'

Pringle ducked out of sight and a moment or two later crawled from under the layout.

'Getting a bit old for this,' he grumbled as he slowly stood up, unfolding his angular frame as if it were hinged rather than jointed. He took his wife's arm, adjusting himself to her pace as they set off along the concrete path, looking for all the world like Jack Sprat and his wife after an especially amicable meal.

'Didn't know you were keen on model railways,' said Thanet to Lineham in an undertone.

Lineham looked a bit sheepish. 'I don't actually collect any more. Can't afford to. But I will again one day, when the children are off our hands. I've got all my stuff packed away in boxes.'

'You start the questioning,' Thanet said hurriedly as they approached the front door. 'After that, we'll play it by ear.'

'OK.'

'You go in there and sit down,' said Mrs Pringle, 'and I'll make some coffee.'

'There' was a cosy book-lined sitting-room overlooking the wilderness of a back garden. The three men sat down in comfortable chintz-covered armchairs, leaving a conspicuously orthopaedic chair for Mrs Pringle if she chose to join them. Despite the warmth of the day the gas fire was full on and the room was uncomfortably hot.

'It's about Marcia, I suppose.' Pringle leaned sideways to take a pipe out of his pocket and began to scrape it out, tapping the dottle into a thick glass ashtray on the table beside his chair.

Thanet immediately began to wish he could smoke as well, but it was too early in the interview, the atmosphere was not yet sufficiently relaxed for him to suggest it. Besides, two pipes in one room . . . Lineham would hate it.

'I gather you're not satisfied it was an accident.' Pringle was looking at Thanet.

'Not yet, anyway.'

'We've heard the rumours, of course. You can't have secrets in a place the size of Telford Green.'

'What rumours exactly?' said Lineham.

Pringle blew through the stem of his pipe to make sure it was clear and flicked a mischievous glance at Thanet. 'That Marcia was variously shot, strangled, stabbed or − most mundane and therefore probably true − pushed off the bridge.'

Lineham raised his eyebrows. 'By. . . ?'

'The most popular choice is her husband.'

'Any particular reason?'

Pringle shrugged. 'Not really. Because he was closest to her, I suppose, and therefore the obvious person. But there have been one or two outsiders coming up on the rails over the last twenty-four hours. Reg Hammer, for instance. Old Mrs Hammer was as good as a public-address system and she made no secret of the fact that she'd applied to join Mrs Salden's house-purchase scheme. Everyone was wondering what Reg would do when he found out, and the fact that you've been to see him has not passed unnoticed. Then there's Edith Phipps, because Marcia apparently gave her the sack that afternoon. Don't ask me how that whisper started. And there's Grace Trimble, too. Rumour has it that she went up to the Manor that night breathing fire. Perhaps she doesn't approve of the amount of time Josie seems to be spending up at the Manor . . .'

'Have you any particular favourite yourself?'

'Not really. Marcia always did have a talent for putting

people's backs up. Well no, that isn't strictly true. Perhaps it would be more accurate to say that she always did have a complete disregard for other people's feelings. Anyway, I never could understand why she was so popular.'

The door had opened and Mrs Pringle came in, pushing a trolley. 'She certainly wasn't popular when she first started school, remember. For two or three years she was practically an outcast. I used to feel so sorry for her . . .' She handed out coffee, freshly filtered by the smell of it, and homemade biscuits with cherries in the middle.

'Why?' said Lineham.

Mrs Pringle lowered herself carefully into the orthopaedic chair and picked up her coffee. 'Various reasons, really. I suppose chiefly because of her father. He used to beat her mother up, you know. And if Marcia got in the way . . . Many's the time I've seen that child come to school covered in bruises.'

'Wasn't he reported to the NSPCC?'

'Oh yes. They were always hovering around in the background. But Marcia was never taken into care or anything like that. It wasn't the kind of deliberate and persistent cruelty you hear so much of these days, but all the same . . . I often used to think how much she must dread Friday nights, when he got his pay packet and headed straight for the Door.'

'And of course, she was badly undernourished, wasn't she, Gwen?' said Pringle. 'There was never enough money left over for food. Marcia didn't qualify for free school dinners because theoretically at least her father earned enough to pay for them. So I think she lived chiefly on bread and margarine – if she was lucky. She used to bring a bread and marge sandwich to school for her dinner and quite often she'd hide behind her desk lid to eat it before school, she was so hungry. And then, of course, she'd have nothing to eat all day and precious little to look forward to when she got home from school at night . . . She used to look so pasty and unhealthy. We resorted to all sorts of stratagems for slipping her food on the quiet, so that she wouldn't be too shamed in front of the other kids, didn't we Gwen?'

Mrs Pringle wrinkled her nose. 'And she used to smell! I

don't think her mother ever bothered to bathe her or change her knickers. And you know how cruel kids can be . . . In the end I resorted to buying half a dozen pairs of knickers for her myself and putting a clean pair on her each morning when she got to school. We never had any children ourselves, and it really used to upset me seeing that poor little scrap treated as a pariah through no fault of her own.'

No wonder Marcia had been so determined to succeed, thought Thanet. That sort of childhood puts grit into the soul.

'Didn't her mother care?' said Lineham.

'I think Mrs Carter was so browbeaten she'd given up caring about anything. You should have seen the state their house was in, in those days! Honestly, it seems a terrible thing to say, but it was a blessing for her when her husband was killed in that accident. After that, she was a changed woman. But that wasn't till much later, after Marcia was married. She married very young, of course. Couldn't wait to get away from home.'

'What you're saying doesn't exactly square with her being popular,' said Thanet.

'Oh, that was later,' said Pringle.

'After we'd done something about it,' said his wife. 'It was obvious things weren't going to improve at home, and in the end Gerald had this brilliant idea. When Marcia was about eight, old enough to bathe herself, he had a hygiene campaign at school. He got the health visitor to come and talk to the children, sent out leaflets to all the parents, that sort of thing. Well Marcia was no fool and the message got through. Before long the improvement in her was noticeable. She was clean, she didn't smell, she even managed to wash her hair and come to school in clean clothes. We were thrilled to bits, weren't we? She looked a different child. And it was interesting to see how the other children reacted. It was such a transformation they didn't quite know what to make of it. At first they just sort of circled around, keeping their distance, then they began to make little approaches . . .'

'How did Marcia react?'

'Very wary at first, wasn't she, Gerald? Suspicious. And off-hand, always off-hand. I think that was what intrigued them, the fact that she didn't seem eager to welcome their advances. In the end she had them vying for her favours. Extraordinary, wasn't it, Gerald?'

'Fascinating.'

Not so surprising, really, thought Thanet. He'd seen it so often before, the self-centred person who has everyone running around in circles trying to please him, and gets away with it every time. But in Marcia's case understandable, surely. When life is as difficult as hers had been, the one thing that matters is self-preservation. Ironic that in the end it could perhaps have been this very trait which destroyed her.

'Forgive my asking, Mrs Pringle, but you talk as if you were very much involved with the life of the school. Did you teach there too?'

She laughed, the rosy cheeks bunching up to look more apple-like than ever, and glanced at her husband.

Pringle shook his head. 'No, she didn't. But in those days we lived in the school house, which was part of the school building. Now, of course, like so many other village schools, it's been converted into a private home. A crying shame, I think. The old village schools were so much the heart of the community. Like the church, they linked village people in a way that no one at the time quite understood. Practically every household in the village used to have a child or a grandchild or a niece or a nephew at the school and even if they didn't everyone certainly knew at least one child who attended it, probably more. When they closed down, something crucial to village life was lost. Anyway, in those days, as I say, the headmaster's house was part of the school building and the headmaster's wife couldn't have got away from the children even if she'd wanted to. She was surrounded by them all day long and knew them as well as the staff did.'

Lineham said, 'When the other children had got used to this transformation you were talking about, did Marcia end up with her own special little group of friends?'

'Her own "gang", you mean? Yes, there were four of them.' Pringle ticked them off on his fingers. 'Edith Phipps, Reg Hammer, Grace Gates — Grace Trimble, she is now — and Henry Gates, Grace's brother.'

'What happened to Henry?' said Lineham. 'Is he still around?'

'Ah, well, that was rather sad,' said Pringle. 'No, he's not. No thanks, love, not for me.' He shook his head at his wife, who was offering more coffee, waited while she refilled Lineham's cup, handed another biscuit to Thanet. Pringle's pipe was drawing well, Thanet noticed enviously.

'What happened to him?' said Lineham.

'Predictably, he fell in love with Marcia. This was much later, of course, when they were in their teens. At first they were all just friends, kids playing together. Edith's father was head gardener up at the Manor, and the five of them used to spend a lot of time in the Manor grounds. They used to keep well out of the way of the owners, of course, but as you can imagine they were the envy of all the other kids in the village for enjoying this privilege. And you'd often see the three girls around together, or the two boys. But of course, as they became adolescents, sex raised its ugly head and altered things between them. First Edith fell for Henry. They went out together for, oh, around six months, wouldn't you say, Gwen?'

'Something like that. The trouble was it was one-sided, really. Henry just went along with it, but it was Edith who was really smitten.' Mrs Pringle sighed and brushed some biscuit crumbs off her ample lap. 'Poor Edith, I don't think she ever got over it.'

'Unfortunately, Henry then fell for Marcia, in a big way.'

'Marcia shouldn't have encouraged him,' Mrs Pringle said tartly.

'Wouldn't have made any difference. He'd have left Edith anyway.'

'Still, Marcia was supposed to be Edith's friend. It was all such a *pity*. As you can imagine, Inspector, Edith hasn't had much of a life, looking after her mother all these years. Henry Gates was the one bright spot in it. And,' she added indignantly, 'it wasn't even as if Marcia really wanted him. The minute a better prospect came along, she dropped him like a hot potato.'

'Which is rather a circuitous route to answering your

question, Sergeant,' said Pringle. 'Henry Gates left the village when Marcia threw him over, and never came back.'

'And it wasn't just Edith who was upset,' said Mrs Pringle. 'Grace, his sister, was in a terrible state too. Their father had died not long before and their mother had died when they were thirteen or fourteen. So when Henry went off she was left entirely on her own.'

'And Reg Hammer wasn't too pleased, either. He and Henry had been bosom pals for years. He never did find another friend, and until he moved away he used to hang around the village looking like a lost sheep.'

'Henry was such a good-looking boy,' said Mrs Pringle reminiscently. 'Not like Reg. A great lump of a boy Reg was, wasn't he?'

Pringle laid his pipe down in the ashtray. 'And he hasn't changed much, so far as I can see. Always had a foul temper, too . . . Inspector, while we've been sitting here I've been wondering . . . Why did you come to see us? I can't imagine that all this stuff that happened thirty-odd years ago is relevant to Marcia's death last Tuesday.'

'Background,' said Thanet. 'I'm trying to understand what sort of a person Marcia was, and you've helped me immensely.' He stood up. 'Thank you, both of you.' He smiled at Mrs Pringle. 'The homemade biscuits were delicious.' He glanced at Lineham, who was still sitting down. 'Sergeant? There's something else you want to ask?'

Lineham was going pink. 'Er . . . yes, sir. But it's nothing to do with work.'

Thanet grinned and Pringle beamed. 'You'd like to come back and take a closer look at my railway! Any time, Sergeant, any time.'

Thanet was anxious to be off. His hand was in his pocket, closed around the comforting familiarity of the bowl of his pipe. He was itching to take it out and smoke it. And it was lunchtime, possibly a good time to catch Grace Trimble at home, the only person in that little group that he had not yet met — apart from her absent brother, of course. Lineham was still talking and Thanet gave him an unobtrusive nudge. *Come on.*

He was eager to see if Grace lived up to her name. As mother of the luscious Josie she might well be something rather special.

TWENTY-THREE

But the genes which had given her brother and daughter their good looks had unfortunately passed Grace Trimble by. She was a tall, big-boned woman with dowdy clothes, a dour expression and prematurely greying hair scraped back into a bun. And she looked strong, easily strong enough to have miscalculated a push in anger and sent Marcia slipping backwards on the icy road through that fatal gap in the parapet.

As soon as he saw her, Thanet's pre-conceived notion of Josie as a spoiled only child and of her mother as a weak, somewhat hysterical single parent had disappeared. Far more likely, he thought, that Josie had been over-protected and suppressed and was now busy kicking over the traces.

After waving them into armchairs in the bleak sitting-room where they had interviewed Josie the previous day, Grace Trimble picked up a small upright chair which stood against the wall and placed it in front of the fireplace in the exact centre of the fawn hearth rug. Then she sat down facing them, back ramrod straight, ankles crossed, hands folded in lap.

And waited.

Thanet was tempted to wait too, see which of them broke the silence first. But he wasn't here to play games. It was irritating that she should have taken the psychological advantage by choosing an upright chair, but he had no intention of allowing himself to be disconcerted. Nor of being manipulated into going away without the information he came for.

This woman intrigued him. He had the impression that she would lose her temper rarely, but that when she did the explosion would be all the more violent because of her habitually rigid self-control.

And it was obvious that there was no point in beating about the bush.

'I understand you paid a visit to the Manor on Tuesday evening, the night Mrs Salden died.'

'What if I did?' She was cold, hostile, her voice grating on his ear like over-smooth chalk on a blackboard.

'Would you mind telling us of the purpose of that visit?'

'Yes, I would mind. It was private business.'

'Would it help if I told you that we already know why you went and what happened when you got there?'

'If you know it all, why are you asking me about it?'

'We would like to hear your side of the story, Mrs Trimble.'

No response.

'We're only trying to understand it from your point of view.'

'Understand? What is there for you to understand? It's no business of yours.'

'Ah,' said Thanet softly, 'but I'm afraid that's where you could be wrong.'

'What do you mean?' Her expression changed. 'Nothing's happened to Josie?'

'No. Josie's fine, so far as I know.'

'Then what did you mean?'

'Mrs Trimble, you may or may not realise that we are treating Mrs Salden's death as suspicious. That means that we are not satisfied yet that it was an accident. Which in turn means that, until we are, we have to talk to all those people who could conceivably have had a reason for being glad she is dead.'

'There's no need to wrap it up. You're saying it could be murder, and I'm a suspect.'

'Possibly, yes.'

Further silence. Thanet gave her a few moments to think about it, then said, 'So if there's anything you'd like to tell me . . .'

'There's not. You can think what you like.'

Thanet tried another tack. 'I understand you used to be quite friendly with Mrs Salden at one time, when you were children.'

He saw at once that it had been the wrong thing to say. No doubt he had resurrected memories of the other injury Marcia had done her, in driving her brother away.

'I don't see what that's got to do with it.'

He might as well accept that she wasn't going to unbend. Extract as many facts as he could, then, and get out.

'You left the Manor at around ten past ten on Tuesday evening, I believe.'

'So?'

'What time did you arrive home?'

She shrugged. 'Twenty to half-past ten, I suppose. I don't know. I didn't look at the clock. No reason to.'

'Which way did you go up to the Manor? Alone the main drive, or along the footpath?'

'Along the footpath.'

'And you came back. . . ?'

'The same way.'

'Did you see anyone, either on your way up or on your way back?'

Thanet had given up hoping for anything interesting to emerge during this interview. Grace Trimble's next words were therefore all the more a shock.

'Only Harry Greenleaf.'

Greenleaf, the suspect with perhaps the most powerful motive of all! Thanet resisted the temptation to look at Lineham. He knew that the Sergeant would be remembering what they'd been saying only a couple of hours ago.

'In fact, the only suspect who doesn't seem to have been around at the right time is Harry Greenleaf.'

'The way things are going, I shouldn't count on it.'

It was an effort to keep his voice casual. 'I see. And was this on the way up, or. . . ?'

'On the way back.'

'And where, exactly, did you see him?'

'He was standing on the bridge, looking at the river.'

'Leaning on the parapet?'

'Yes.'

'On which side?'

'The far side.'

'By "far side", you mean the opposite side from the broken parapet?'

'Yes.'

'Are you sure it was Greenleaf?'

'Certain. He was wearing that balaclava thing he always wears when he comes into the village.'

An excellent disguise, thought Thanet, if someone else had wanted to give the impression that Greenleaf was abroad that night. But that would imply premeditation, and he had been certain all along that this had been a crime of impulse, if crime it was. Marcia had simply been unlucky. Time, circumstance and contiguity had conspired to produce a fatal result.

'When he heard me step on to the road he glanced over his shoulder and then slipped away, quick as a flash. He doesn't like meeting people, does Harry.' And I don't blame him, her expression said.

'In that case, it's surprising he hadn't gone before you got to the top of the steps,' said Lineham. 'He must have heard you coming.'

She was shaking her head. 'He wouldn't have heard me earlier because I was walking on grass. And while I was climbing the steps a couple of cars went over the bridge.'

'Rich pickings,' said Lineham, when they were outside. 'Though it's a pity those car drivers haven't come forward.'

Appeals had been put out on TVS and Radio Kent.

'Yes. Not that this information about Greenleaf really makes much difference in practical terms. We're no nearer to proving anything.'

'We do now know that Greenleaf was lying, when he said he didn't go out that night.'

'True.'

'So are we going to see him next?'

'Who else? But we'll get something to eat at the Crooked Door first.'

They got into the car and headed for the pub, but halfway through the village Thanet said, 'Just a minute. Pull in, will you?'

212

They had stopped in front of what was recognisably once the school, though there were curtains at the windows and the playground had became a lawn, surrounded by flower borders. Thanet guessed that the projecting arm of the 'L' had once been the school house, where the Pringles lived.

'Pringle's right, it's a shame so many village schools have closed down.'

Thanet gazed at the building, imagining it as it once was, with the sound of children's voices floating through those open windows, the noise of shouts and laughter enlivening the midday hush which lay now over the village like a pall.

And it was here, within those thick stone walls, that Marcia, Edith, Grace, Reg and the long-lost Henry had spent the years of their youth, seeing each other daily, linked by the tight ties which used to bind the small rural communities. This school, this village, would have been Marcia's whole world and it was scarcely surprising that she had wanted to return to flaunt her success before the people who would once have regarded her as the lowest of the low. And her former school friends, how would they have felt when they learned that it was Marcia who had bought the Manor? None of them had made very much of their lives. Wouldn't they have found it galling, to know that the child who had once come to school bruised and hungry and smelling of stale urine had out-stripped them all? And they surely wouldn't have forgotten their ancient grudges against her? She had, after all, stolen Edith Phipps's one and only chance of happiness, robbed Grace of her brother and Reg of his best friend.

And she had then proceeded to threaten to injure them further. Edith was to lose her job, Grace her daughter and Reg his inheritance.

Had the memory of those old wounds served to underline and reinforce the inevitable feelings of anger at these new and latest injuries?

Thanet suggested as much to Lineham.

'Could be, sir. In each case they were going to lose what they valued most. But unless we can come up with some evidence, whoever did it is going to get away with it.'

213

'*Nil desperandum*, Mike. Drive on. After a certain point my brain can't function properly without food and drink.'

The pub had featured so much in this case that Thanet looked around with more than customary interest when they went in, but there was nothing special about it: heavy oak beams, gaudily patterned carpet, veneered oak tables and the usual pub smell of beer, smoke and furniture polish. The food was good, though – generous portions of quiche and a salad which was rather more adventurous than the universal offering of a lettuce leaf topped with a few slices of tomato and cucumber. Apart from three young men at the bar it was deserted. The landlord recognised Lineham and they were swiftly served.

Half an hour later they were walking up the sloping meadow towards Greenleaf's hut. The place seemed deserted.

'There's no sign of him,' said Lineham. 'Perhaps he's out.'

Thanet hoped not, but if so, there was nothing they could do about it. It would be pointless to wait, for all they knew Greenleaf could be gone all day. 'Let's hope he hasn't skipped!'

'No, look, the door's open!' said Lineham. 'He can't be far away.'

'Try calling him.'

It was evident that Greenleaf had been sawing logs. There was a wide scattering of fresh sawdust around a chunk of tree trunk which had evidently been used as a sawing horse; saw and axe lay near by, ready to be taken up again at a moment's notice. The freshly cut logs had been stacked beneath an open-sided shelter at the back of the hut.

Lineham cupped his hands around his mouth and shouted Greenleaf's name a few times, swivelling to project the sound in different directions. In the distance a dog began to bark.

'Greenleaf's dog?' said Lineham.

Thanet shrugged. He was standing at the door, looking into the hut. Greenleaf lived a spartan life. There was a canvas camp bed, a pile of neatly folded blankets at one end, a pillow at the other, no sheets; an old leather armchair with the stuffing coming out; a formica-topped table with a small Calor gas cooker on top, and an upright chair; a tall storage

214

cupboard which probably served as a larder; a wooden box about two feet long by eighteen inches deep; and a transistor radio. A knitted balaclava helmet hung on a nail by the door.

Thanet and Lineham looked at each other.

'Are you thinking what I'm thinking, Mike?'

Lineham grinned. 'Seems a pity to miss such a good opportunity.'

'Call him again.'

Lineham obliged, but there was still no response.

'I'm just going to take a look around out here,' said Thanet.

Another grin. 'Right, sir.'

Thanet wandered off to look at the chickens, keeping an eye open in case Greenleaf suddenly emerged from the woods. He thought that he would probably hear the man coming, though; up here it was very still. And the view was remarkable. For someone who didn't need the company of others, or who shunned it for some reason as Greenleaf did, this was as pleasant a place as he could hope to find. How badly had Harry wanted to stay here? Badly enough to kill, when the opportunity offered itself?

Thanet glanced at the hut. Lineham was kneeling in front of the wooden box.

The goat's stake, Thanet noticed, had been moved since the last time they were here, a good ten feet further away from the hut, and the animal was busy cropping the new grass near the perimeter.

'Sir!'

Thanet swung around. Lineham sounded excited. The Sergeant was hurrying towards him, waving a book.

A book?

'Look!' Lineham opened it to the flyleaf and thrust it towards him. A square label pasted inside informed him that on 18 July 1951 this book had been awarded to Henry Gates, for the best work in his class.

Henry Gates?

Henry . . . Harry . . .

Was it possible that Harry Greenleaf, the recluse, was really Henry Gates, Grace Trimble's brother? Henry, who had been Reg Hammer's best friend, Edith and Marcia's first love?

TWENTY-FOUR

Thanet stared at the label, mind racing. If Greenleaf was really Henry Gates, it would explain why he had chosen Telford Green as his sanctuary. After the trauma of the fire and no doubt many months of surgery he would have needed the comfort of familiar surroundings. Thanet closed the book, read the title. *Palgrave's Golden Treasury*. Typical of school prizes given at that time.

'What d'you think, sir? Think he could be Gates?'

'Greenleaf could have picked this up at a jumble sale in the village.'

Lineham's excitement visibly waned as he considered this proposition. 'Possible, I suppose.'

'Likely, even. On the other hand . . .'

'If he is Gates, why d'you think he didn't go back to his family?'

'There was only his sister to go back to, remember. And frankly, from what we've seen of her, if I were Greenleaf I'd prefer to live up here by myself.'

'The Pringles said she was very fond of him.'

'True. Though that's not the same as saying he was fond of her.' Thanet shrugged. 'Perhaps he just didn't want to make himself known, wanted to hide himself away from everybody. It would be understandable, considering the degree of his disfigurement.'

'You don't think. . . ? No.'

'What?'

'I was wondering if his sister did know who he really was, if he might have told her. But if so, I shouldn't think she'd have dropped him in it by telling us he was on the bridge that night.'

'No.' Ironic, that, if Harry was Gates: brother and sister

meeting on the bridge where they must have lingered so often as children, Harry knowing that the following day he would have to leave Telford Green for the second and perhaps last time. Had he been tempted to approach Grace, tell her who he really was? He would then have been able to move in with her, stay on in the village legitimately. He would have been a nineday wonder, true, but once the sensation became everyday reality people would no doubt have accepted him back as Henry Gates, one of them. Sympathy for him would have run high. He wasn't stupid, must have realised all this. Why, then, if he was Gates, had he not declared himself?

Perhaps he wasn't Gates after all, really had picked the book up at a jumble sale. Thanet glanced down at it. The cover was bent, worn and stained. If Greenleaf was Gates it must have accompanied him through all the intervening years, perhaps the only memento of his childhood.

Thanet suddenly became aware that the distant barking had become louder and a few moments later Harry's black and white mongrel shot out of the wood and tore up to them, barking furiously. A couple of feet away it skidded to a halt but continued barking.

It didn't look as though the animal was going to attack them, but it seemed politic to stand still. Harry couldn't be far away.

A couple of minutes later he emerged from the wood, bent almost double, both hands clutching the rope over his right shoulder. In a moment Thanet could see that he was dragging a sizeable log. He lowered it to the ground and straightened up.

'Jack! Enough!'

The dog stopped barking immediately, like a radio that had been switched off. Then it looked at its master and, nose to the ground, ran up to the hut, sniffed around inside, then returned to sniff at Lineham's trousers. The message was clear.

Greenleaf hadn't needed it, however. His eyes were on the book in Thanet's hand. 'Got a search warrant, have you?'

Thanet was in the wrong and he knew it. But if he admitted it, Greenleaf could prove difficult. He was just the type to make an almighty fuss. Better to counter-attack. If they were wrong about his identity, of course, their ammunition would be useless. But it was worth a try.

'Ah, there you are, Mr Gates. We've been waiting for you for some time.'

'Gates? What are you talking about?'

Thanet held up the book. 'This is yours?'

Harry glanced towards the door of the hut. 'You should know.'

'Your name is inside.' Thanet opened the book and held it out, displaying the label.

Harry barely glanced at it. 'Ha, ha. Very funny.'

'You don't deny that you are Gates, then?'

'You can think what you like, mate.'

Thanet sensed Lineham tense beside him and cast him an admonitory glance. It was one of the Sergeant's weaknesses that he took it as a personal insult when witnesses were rude to Thanet. Why on earth, he wondered, had various people he had spoken to about Greenleaf said that he was a mild, gentle man, the type who "wouldn't hurt a fly"? Perhaps, in normal circumstances, he was. Perhaps it was only when he felt threatened that he threw up this barrier of implacable hostility like a hedgehog extending its bristles. Once again Thanet regretted the impossibility of reading the man's reaction from his expression. That stretched, shiny skin was about as responsive as a balloon. He heard Mrs Pringle's voice, *Henry was such a good-looking boy . . .*, and firmly suppressed the pity which once again threatened to get in the way of handling the situation correctly. If Harry, or Henry, were a murderer, he would have to take his chance with the rest. And if not, well, he seemed quite capable of looking after himself.

'If you prefer, we can go back to Headquarters to talk about it.'

Harry's sudden stillness told him that this was a highly unwelcome suggestion.

'Or we can discuss it here. Providing that you are willing to cooperate.'

Harry stared at him for a moment longer, then shrugged. 'Let's get it over with, then, I've got work to do.' He strolled across to the hut, picked up an old guernsey sweater from the chair near the door and pulled it on. Then he turned, leaned against the outside wall of the hut and folded his arms. 'Well?'

Lineham took out his notebook.

Harry still hadn't either admitted or denied that he was Gates, Thanet reminded himself.

'Look, it would be a simple matter for us to check whether you really are Greenleaf or not. One phone call to the Records Office would do it.' If they were lucky. 'But I would like to emphasise that even if you do choose to live up here under an assumed name there is no reason whatsoever for us to make this public unless you are involved in our investigation.'

'That's all right then, in't it? I'm not.'

'In that case you have nothing to worry about. And nothing to hide, either. You are Henry Gates?'

Gates looked away from Thanet, down towards the village. Then, with a resigned sigh he shrugged. 'Yes . . . You did mean what you said, about not telling anyone?'

It was the first sign of vulnerability he had shown.

'Of course. So long as you are not involved . . .'

'How many more times do I have to tell you? I'm not!'

'Oh come on, Mr . . . I'll call you Harry, shall I? It'll be simpler. Come on, Harry, we both know that's not true. You were seen.'

'When? What are you talking about?'

But the note in Harry's voice told Thanet that he knew quite well.

'When we were last here, you told us that you had been at home on Tuesday night, packing up, that you hadn't gone out. That was a stupid thing to do. You knew you'd been seen in the village by at least one person. Why lie about it?'

'Why d'you think? Because any fool could see that with the motive I had for wanting to get rid of her, if I told you I'd been down to the village that night, I'd be inside quicker than I could say "Marcia"! I thought it was worth taking a chance you wouldn't find out.'

'So what time did you go down?'

He had set off, it seemed, at about a quarter to ten. He wanted to take a last look around Telford Green before moving on next day. He had left Jack behind because people tended to stop and chat when he had Jack with him and he didn't feel like talking to anyone that night.

'So how long would it have taken you to get down to the village?'

'Five minutes or so.'

Harry had then walked first up to the far end of the village, getting back to the bridge probably soon after ten. Pressed for a firm time he became irritable. 'I wasn't looking at a bloody watch all the time, was I? Haven't even got one.'

Lineham was tense, Thanet could tell. At around a quarter past ten Marcia had left her mother's cottage, only a few minutes away from the bridge, and shortly afterwards had fallen or been pushed through that gap. If Harry had been hanging about the village it was possible that, even if he hadn't had a fatal quarrel with Marcia himself, he might have seen what happened to her.

'Go on. And take your time. Tell us in detail what you saw and heard as you were approaching the bridge.'

'Well, just as I was passing the pub the door opens and a coupla men come out. One of them was drunk and the other just propped him up against the wall outside and said, "Go on then, Reg. Home." And back he goes inside. Reg just stands there for a minute and then his knees sort of fold up and he slides down till he's sitting on the floor. Then he doesn't move.'

'So what did you do?'

'Nothing. Not then, anyways. I sort of hesitated a bit, then I thought, someone else'll be out in a minute, they'll see him home. So I walked on to the bridge and stood looking down at the water.'

He hadn't heard Grace coming up the steps from the footpath on the other side of the bridge because a couple of cars went by, and it was not until she stepped on to the metalled road that he was aware of her presence. He recognised her at once, and slipped away, went to hide behind some bushes near by.

'It didn't occur to you to tell your sister who you are – I'm assuming she didn't know? – and move in with her?'

Harry moved his shoulders uneasily against the wooden

wall of the hut. 'I did think about it, yes. But I'm used to living by myself. I like it. I like the freedom. You don't have to account to nobody, up here.'

Thanet understood. Harry had escaped from his sister once and didn't want to risk being enmeshed again.

'So then what did you do?'

He could see it all as clearly as if he were there, hiding behind the bushes himself: the bridge, with the warning lights around the broken parapet; the receding figure of Grace. Any second now Marcia would come into sight . . .

'Well, Grace went off home, in the other direction, and there was Reg still sitting on the floor outside the pub across the road . . . Well, I wasn't doing nothing, and once upon a time me and Reg was best mates. So I goes across, says, "Come on, me old mate." I manage to get him on his feet and off we stagger.'

The whole scenario sounded all too likely. Thanet remembered that curious look on Hammer's face, as if he thought that his memory must be playing tricks on him. If, in his drunken state, he had recognised the voice of the childhood friend he hadn't seen for years, he might well have wondered later if he had been dreaming. 'You took him all the way home?'

'It's only a coupla hundred yards. Yeah. Rung the bell and dumped him on the doorstep.'

'Mrs Hammer says he didn't get home until half-past ten. Nearly half an hour, to cover that distance. . . ?'

'It must've taken me getting on for five minutes to get him to his feet and get him on his way. And then . . . Ever tried moving a drunk? He's a dead weight, believe me. Reg is a big man, and he kept on falling down.'

'While you were helping him along, did you look back at the bridge at all?'

Harry shook his head. 'Had my hands full, didn't I?'

'Or hear anything?'

'Reg was singing, on and off. And I really wasn't paying attention to what was going on behind me. If I'd known there was going to be a murder, and I was going to be a suspect . . . !'

No point in saying that strictly speaking they still weren't sure that there had been one. Harry probably wouldn't have believed them anyway.

'While you were in the village, did you see anyone else about?'

Harry frowned, thinking. 'There was a woman . . .'

Thanet and Lineham spoke together.

'When?'

'Where?'

'As Reg and me staggered across the bridge. She was posting a letter.'

Edith? Thanet had checked. The post box was on the Manor side of the bridge. Unless Edith had seen Marcia coming and had walked on to the bridge to accost her, there would be no reason for them to have met.

'Did you recognise her?'

'No. There's no lamp on that side of the bridge and the light is bad. And she was turning away from the box at the time. I only saw her back. Anyway, I wasn't paying much attention.'

'Could it have been Edith Phipps?'

'Might have been. But I couldn't swear to it.'

'Where did she go?'

'Walked away down the road.'

'Towards the Manor gates?'

Harry shrugged. 'I dunno. She went off ahead of us around the bend. Could've been going to the cottages for all I know.'

'Did you see anyone else?'

'No.'

'You're sure?'

'I told you, no!'

They left him to his sawing and walked down to the river bank.

'We need to talk,' said Thanet. 'Might as well sit down here for a while.'

The grass was dry, the sun warm. They took off their coats and Thanet lit his pipe. They sat for a while in silence, gazing at the water. Eventually Lineham stirred, picked a piece of grass and began to chew it.

'What d'you reckon, sir?'

Thanet shrugged. 'About what Harry said? It's all credible enough. Mrs Hammer told us someone had brought Reg home, and it would be typical of Harry to ring the bell and walk away before the door opened.'

'It was probably them that Lomax saw, in front of the cottages . . . If it was murder it's essential to know whether Harry's speaking the truth, isn't it? Perhaps more than any other witness so far.'

'For elimination purposes, you mean. Yes.'

'Both he and Hammer would be out, for a start . . .'

'Unless they were in it together.'

Lineham raised his eyebrows. 'Hadn't thought of that. Bit unlikely, don't you think?'

'Yes, I do, actually. Go on.'

'And it would cut out Grace Trimble, too. Because she would have left the bridge before Marcia Salden arrived.'

'And if the woman Harry saw posting the letter was Edith Phipps . . .'

'It certainly narrows the field down, doesn't it, sir? It only leaves us with Councillor Lomax and Salden.'

'*If* Harry is telling the truth, Mike. I think we have to accept that if Marcia was murdered and he or any of his old pals were involved, he'd have very good reason for lying. He's not crying over Marcia's death, in fact it came at just the right moment for him. So if someone obliged him by getting rid of her he's not going to give that person away, especially if he or she is a childhood friend. And all those old pals had very good reasons for wanting to get rid of Marcia, remember.'

'True. But let's look just for a moment at the possibility that everything he's told us is true, and only Lomax and Salden remain. As we've already said, in every case but Salden the suspect had a reason, what you always call the trigger factor. With Lomax we think it was probably the threat of blackmail or scandal if he didn't toe the line over the planning permission; with Harry it was the threat of eviction and with Grace the damage being done to her daughter and that nasty scene with Josie up at the Manor; with Reg it was having his inheritance snatched from under his nose and with Edith it was losing the job and possibly the home which suited her and her invalid mother so well. In addition, all these people but Lomax are old mates of Marcia's and have long-standing grudges against her . . . But with Salden. . . ? Nothing, so far as I can see.'

'As we've said before, in a detective novel that would automatically make him suspect number one,' said Thanet with a grin.

Lineham gave a slight frown, as if to indicate that this wasn't the moment for jokes. 'He stands to inherit the business, yes, but I can't see that as a reason. In fact, as his wife seemed to be the driving force behind it, he stands to lose in the long run.'

'Perhaps he'd just reached the point where he was fed up with her. She does sound pretty overpowering.'

'Plenty of men have overpowering wives, but they don't go round bumping them off.'

Thanet restrained himself from giving Lineham a sharp glance. Had that remark been uncomfortably heartfelt?

'No,' Lineham went on. 'In a case like this you've got to have something which finally pushes the murderer over the edge.'

Thanet remembered the scene he had envisaged between Bernard Salden and his wife, in which Bernard gets angry with her for going back to her guests at the Manor instead of staying with her mother. It all seemed rather tame, now, in comparison with the powerful motives of the other suspects. 'I wonder . . .'

Lineham turned an eager face. 'What?'

'Mrs Carter, Marcia's mother . . .'

'What about her.'

'Everyone's taken it for granted that she wanted to see Bernard Salden that night because she was so fond of him. Which could well be so. But what if there was another reason? What if she wanted to see him because she wanted to tell him something before she died?'

'What, for instance?'

'It would have to be something about Marcia which she knew and he didn't, something she felt was important to him . . .'

They stared at each other, then suddenly Lineham's face lit up. 'The sterilisation! What if she wanted to tell him Marcia had been sterilised?'

'It's a possibility. But why would she want to do that? It would cause him nothing but pain, and problems in his marriage too.'

'Because she thought it was cruel for him to go on hoping for a child of his own, when there was no possibility of it happening? Everyone says how fond of children he is, how much he longs for one . . .'

Thanet frowned, considering. 'She'd be betraying her own daughter. Would she do that, for her son-in-law?' Impossible to speculate on such a matter without knowing the people involved personally.

'Marcia and her mother weren't exactly fond of each other, were they? I mean, everyone agrees she did her duty by her, but I've never had the impression there was much feeling between them. It is a possibility, sir, don't you think?'

'Anything's possible, Mike. It would certainly explain Salden's behaviour that night – why he seemed so upset when he left Mrs Carter's cottage, why he went for a walk and sat around brooding on the river bank instead of putting in an appearance at home.' Thanet heaved himself to his feet, rubbing his backside. The grass had been wetter than he thought. 'We'd better go and have another little chat with him, hadn't we?'

TWENTY-FIVE

They walked into the village to pick up the car, then drove to the Manor.

Mrs Pantry looked harassed. She was wearing a surprisingly smart navy blue dress with white collar and cuffs and was balancing two plates of sandwiches covered in cling film in one hand. 'Yes, he's in.' Her usual grudging manner.

In the hall Thanet could see through an open door that a table had been set out with plates of sandwiches and cakes, cups and saucers.

Mrs Pantry followed his glance. 'Mrs Carter's funeral is later on this afternoon, and people are coming back here.'

'How is Mr Salden today?'

Her expression lightened and she was uncharacteristically forthcoming. 'He must be feeling a bit better, I think. He's been on the phone all morning.'

Thanet wasn't surprised to hear it. He knew that at times like this people often found work a salvation. 'Good. Where is he?'

'In his office.' She put the sandwiches down on the long oak table in the hall. 'I'll tell him you're here.'

In a few minutes she returned. 'You can go in.'

She was right. Salden did look better. He was again neatly dressed, presumably for the funeral, in a well-cut grey suit and black tie. And, although there were dark smudges beneath his eyes, the dazed look was less evident. He was seated at his desk as though he had been working but there were no papers about except for a closed notebook exactly in the centre of the desk blotter.

'I hope this won't take long. I have a funeral to attend.'

Thanet shook his head. 'I shouldn't think so.'

He and Lineham sat down.

'Mr Salden, it has occurred to us that you haven't told us why your mother-in-law wanted to see you on Tuesday night.'

'I don't see what possible relevance that could have to your investigation.'

'You must allow me to be the judge of that.'

Salden compressed his lips. 'She merely wanted to say goodbye.' He looked away, out of the window. 'She knew she was dying, and we were very fond of each other.'

'There was nothing special she wanted to tell you?'

'No.' Salden's head swung back and he looked at Thanet with eyes narrowed. 'Why do you ask? Was there something?'

Was the enquiry genuine? Thanet didn't particularly like the idea of breaking the news of Marcia's sterilisation to Salden, but the man would have to know some time; the information would emerge at the inquest anyway.

'I only wondered because . . . Mr Salden, were you aware that your wife had been sterilised?'

Salden's reaction gave him the answer. Unless the man was a superb actor there was no doubt that this was news indeed. His jaw dropped and his eyes dilated, then he became perfectly still, staring at Thanet. Only the expression in his eyes changed, from shock and disbelief to pain, anger and finally to acceptance. And to something else less definable. At last he ran his tongue over his lips and said, 'The *post mortem*?'

Thanet nodded. 'Yes.'

There was no point in prolonging the interview. And Salden had a funeral to face yet, this afternoon. They left.

Thanet glanced at Lineham's face as they got into the car. 'Cheer up, Mike, it was a good idea.'

'No point in having good ideas if they don't work out. You believed him then, did you, sir?'

'Didn't you? Yes, I'd swear it was a complete surprise to him. A terrible shock, in fact.' He wondered how Salden would feel about Marcia now, knowing that she had deceived and betrayed him over something which meant so much to him.

'I agree,' said Lineham gloomily. 'So where does that leave us?'

'Up a gum tree as far as Salden's concerned, I should say.'

They had reached the end of the drive and pulled in to allow the funeral cortège to pass by. Mrs Carter was going to set off for her last resting place from the Manor. Bernard was doing her proud.

Thanet could see Edith Phipps watching from the kitchen window. She was wearing a black hat with a feather in it. No doubt Bernard had offered to pick her up on the way past. 'I suppose we could console ourselves by the fact that, even if he had known about the sterilisation and even if we had got him to admit that it was in order to tell him about it that Mrs Carter sent for him that night, there is still no way that we could prove that it was he who committed the murder. And at the moment the same thing applies to all the others. We've got to come up with something concrete, Mike.'

'What, for instance?'

'Your guess is as good as mine. We'll really have to put our minds to it.'

They drove in silence for a few minutes, then Thanet said, 'Perhaps we've been barking up the wrong tree all along. It's happened before. Perhaps Marcia wasn't murdered at all and it was a simple accident.'

'Difficult to see how it could have been, under the circumstances. Anyone passing that gap in the parapet would have been hyper-careful.'

'Oh, I don't know. She could have been crossing the bridge towards the footpath entrance, which is right alongside the broken section. A car could have come along too fast and she could have jumped back to avoid it, slipped on the icy road . . .'

'Are you suggesting we give up, then, sir?'

'Not yet, no. But I'm beginning to wonder if we might have to. If we don't come up with any better ideas . . .'

'Meanwhile, what?'

'Bring Draco up to date and then it's time for a session on reports, I think. And there's no point in groaning. Have you got a better suggestion?'

In the past they had often found that if they were stuck a thorough sifting of everything that had come in so far was a useful way of breaking the impasse. Up until now reports on the Salden case had been read as they came in, in dribs and drabs. Now, with any luck, discrepancies might be spotted that had earlier been missed and a fresh overall view would suggest new insights, new avenues to explore.

'It'll be impossible to concentrate in the main CID room,' said Lineham hopefully.

'Then we'll commandeer one of the interview rooms,' said Thanet.

So they did. But to no avail. At seven o'clock, Lineham put his head in his hands and groaned. 'I don't know about you, sir, but I can't think straight any more. I'm just not taking this in.'

Thanet closed the file he was reading and tossed it on to the desk. 'Neither can I. We'll call it a day.' He pressed his fingers into the deep, dull ache across the small of his back. He longed to lie down, preferably flat on the floor, and allow his muscles to relax. He decided that when he got home he'd go up to the bedroom and do just that.

Joan was in the kitchen, busy with supper. 'Twenty minutes,' she said, after one look at his face. 'Plenty of time, if you want to crash out for a while.'

At the door he turned. 'Bridget in?'

Joan nodded. 'In her room.'

'How is she?'

Joan pulled a face. 'Subdued.'

'Only to be expected, I suppose.'

In the bedroom he lowered himself to the floor and began his relaxation routine. Right leg, stretch . . . and relax. Left leg, stretch . . . and relax . . . Breathe in, breathe out . . . He was beginning to float when the back door slammed, interrupting his concentration. He tried to ignore it. The telephone pinged in the hall, then there was a rush of feet on the stairs and Joan's voice, jagged with emotion.

'Luke! Luke!' She burst into the room.

His eyes snapped open. 'What?'

'It's Vicky. I think she's taken an overdose.'

'Oh God.' Thanet rolled over, got up. 'Is she still alive?'

'Just, I think. I've rung for an ambulance.'

Bridget appeared at the door, looking frightened. 'What is it? What's the matter, Mum?'

There was no way she could wrap this up, protect Bridget from the harsh reality. 'It's Vicky, darling. I'm afraid she's . . . well, it looks as though she's taken an overdose.' She glanced back at Thanet. 'I heard the baby. He was screaming his head off, that's why I went across . . . I must go and get him.'

And she was gone.

Bridget said: 'Dad, how awful! What can we do?

They started downstairs.

'Not much, at the moment. We'll have to look after the baby, obviously. I expect he's hungry. Go and put the kettle on. Just as well she isn't breast-feeding.'

Everything seemed to happen quickly. Joan arrived with the screaming baby and within minutes had changed his nappy and made his bottle. Meanwhile the ambulance arrived. Thanet let them in next door and watched them take away an unconscious Vicky. He then took a quick look around to see if there was any clue to Peter's whereabouts. To his relief, by the telephone he found a clear list of dates, times and places; Peter had wanted to be certain that Vicky would at least be able to contact him each evening. But it hadn't been enough, Thanet thought sadly as he dialled. At this particular time in her life Vicky had needed a much stronger lifeline than a voice on the telephone once a day. It was unfortunate that both sets of parents lived some distance away. They were all good, decent people and would be desperately upset about this. Thanet didn't envy Peter, having to break the news to them.

At home peace had descended. Bridget was nursing the baby and Joan was putting on her coat.

'I managed to get hold of Peter,' said Thanet. 'He's coming straight home.'

'Good. What time will he be here?'

'In the early hours, he thinks. You're going to the hospital?'

'Yes, I must. You do realise, don't you, that it's my fault she's there? The least I can do is be with her.'

'What do you mean, your fault?'

230

'I just didn't make enough time for her. She was sending out all the signals and I just ignored them. If only I'd — '

'Joan!' Luke took her hands. 'When will you learn that you are not responsible for the well-being of the whole world? You've spent a lot of time with Vicky, taken endless trouble over her. It's her illness that has put her in hospital, not you.'

Joan bit her lip. 'That's not how it feels to me at the moment. I should have gone over to see her as soon as I got home from work. I'd have found her that much earlier and she'd have had a much better chance.' She snatched up her bag. 'I'll see you later.'

'Ring me,' Thanet called as she hurried to her car.

Ben arrived home soon afterwards and they had supper. Thanet fetched further supplies for the baby from next door and at ten o'clock he and Bridget between them fed and changed him, Thanet remembering ruefully how adept he had once been at handling his own children.

At eleven Joan rang. 'She's come round.'

'Thank God.' Thanet was relieved not only for the sake of the young family, but for Joan. If Vicky had died . . . 'Are you coming home now?'

'No, someone must be here with her, for moral support. I'll wait until Peter arrives. Is he coming straight to the hospital?'

'I don't know, he didn't say. I imagine so . . . How is she?'

'Drowsy. She doesn't really know what's hit her yet. Poor Vicky. When I think how happy they were, when she first knew she was pregnant . . .'

'I know. Well, I suppose the only good thing to come out of this is that now she will at last get some psychiatric treatment. The hospital will make sure of that before they release her.'

'True. That doctor of hers ought to be struck off!'

'I'm sure Peter'll see that she's transferred to that woman doctor I was telling you about.'

'I do hope things improve for her.' Joan suddenly sounded very low.

'Cheer up. They will. Post-natal depression doesn't go on for ever.'

They chatted for a few minutes longer, then Joan said she must get back to Vicky.

In bed, Thanet could not get to sleep. Without Joan beside him he felt bereft, incomplete, and found himself listening out all the time for her return.

Eventually, after an hour of tossing and turning, he decided to get up. He went downstairs, made himself some tea and sat down at the kitchen table to drink it. A moment later he decided he might as well wait in comfort in the sitting-room. He didn't feel like reading, and although he had never watched television at this hour before he switched the set on. They were showing a film of a nineteen fifties musical. Sinking into an armchair he drank his tea then slipped into a half-awake, half-asleep state in which he drifted in and out of consciousness. Images from the dramatic events of the evening mingled with sentences read during the report session this afternoon and snatches of conversation from the last few days. Some time in the small hours he fell asleep and dreamed that Marcia was floating down the river towards him, that he was reaching to pull her out. But when he finally got her out of the water he discovered that she was Vicky. 'What shall I tell Peter?' he moaned. 'What shall I tell Peter?'

Someone was shaking him by the arm and he blinked awake. Joan's concerned face hovered over him.

'You were dreaming.'

He shook his head to clear it. 'Yes, I . . .' He stopped, groping to recapture the dream before it faded.

'What?' She looked exhausted. 'Luke, what is it?'

He didn't reply, scarcely heard her. An astounding thought had just struck him. Was it possible?

'Luke?' Joan was tugging at his sleeve.

He glanced at his watch. Half-past three. Louise would not appreciate it if he rang Lineham now. And this certainly wasn't the moment to start propounding theories to Joan. Somehow he would have to wait until morning.

Suppressing his excitement, he shook his head. 'Just an idea,' he said. 'Come on, let's get you to bed.'

TWENTY-SIX

At half-past nine next morning Thanet and Lineham were knocking at Mrs Pepper's door. The pink and scarlet tulips in the tiny front garden were looking somewhat the worse for wear after the torrential rain the other day. The weather today didn't look too promising either; the early morning sunshine had long since faded and ominous-looking clouds were building to the west.

Mrs Pepper looked surprised to see them. She was even smaller than Thanet had remembered. She had exchanged the green tracksuit with orange trimmings for a purple one with yellow trimmings. Thanet was glad to see that beside her was Spot, old Mrs Carter's dog. Nurse Lint must have persuaded Mrs Pepper to take him on.

'No, we won't come in, thank you. There's just one question we wanted to ask you.'

He told her what it was and her eyebrows went up. 'What on earth d'you want to know that for?'

'I'm sorry, I can't say. But if you could just tell us . . .'

Her answer was just what he wanted to hear. He and Lineham exchanged jubilant looks.

They left her gazing after them, puzzled.

Next stop was the Vicarage.

'Let's hope he's in,' said Thanet as they walked across the green. 'If I hadn't had to attend the daily meeting . . .'

'We couldn't have left any earlier anyway, we had to make that phone call.'

'True.' Thanet was edgy. What if Fothergill were out? They already had sufficient confirmation of his theory — Fothergill's evidence would really just be the icing on the cake. But he had a feeling amounting almost to superstition that he must have the answers to every single query he had listed before tackling the murderer; he wanted to be as sure of his ground as possible.

Telford Green Vicarage was a compact modern house which had been built in the grounds of the large, draughty, Victorian vicarage next door.

There was no response to their ring.

Thanet shifted impatiently from one foot to the other. 'Come *on*, Mr Fothergill.'

'I'd settle for Mrs Fothergill. At least she could tell us where he's likely to be.'

'Vicars!' said Thanet, scowling. 'He could be anywhere. He could be away at a conference.'

'Or at the Diocesan Synod.'

Thanet raised an eyebrow. 'Didn't know you even knew such a thing existed, Mike.'

Lineham grinned. 'Just a little information I picked up.' He rang the bell again. 'I haven't the faintest idea what it is, though. What is it?'

Thanet was saved from having to reply by the young woman who now walked through the gate. She was wearing jeans and a sweatshirt and was pushing a pushchair with a baby in it. 'Can I help you?'

'Mrs Fothergill?' said Thanet with relief. He introduced himself. 'We'd like a word with your husband.'

'I'm sorry, he's out.' Then, looking at their faces, 'But he should be back shortly. He'd better be! I need the car to go to Sturrenden and do the weekly shop. Would you like to wait inside?'

She showed them into the sitting-room, made them cups of coffee, then excused herself. 'I'm sorry, but there's rather a lot to do before I go.'

'Just forget we're here,' said Thanet, smiling.

Ten minutes later a series of explosions heralded Fothergill's return. Lineham jumped up and went to the window. Thanet joined him. Fothergill spotted them and raised a hand, ostentatiously patting the car before coming into the house.

'Is she really going shopping in that?' said Lineham.

'Don't suppose she has much choice.'

'Sorry!' Fothergill breezed in. 'Hope I haven't kept you waiting too long.'

'Not at all. We've only been here ten minutes and your wife very kindly gave us some coffee.'

'Good. Excellent. So?' Fothergill looked from one to the other. 'How can I help you?'

'There was something we wanted to ask you . . .'

Five minutes later they were back in the car.

Lineham's eyes were sparkling. 'Pretty conclusive, don't you think, sir?'

'I hope so, Mike. I hope so.' Over the years Thanet had learned to trust his intuition. 'Never underestimate those gut feelings,' he had once been told by a policeman he very much respected. And he was certain about this now, in his own mind. But to satisfy the law was another matter. He said so.

'So what do we do? Wait until we have some evidence that'll clinch it?'

'The trouble is, I don't see much prospect of getting any. No, I think our only hope is to try and manoeuvre a confession.'

'And if one isn't forthcoming?'

Thanet shrugged. 'We'll just have to play it by ear.'

Back, then, through the village which had become so familiar to them, past the cottage where Marcia had spent the miserable childhood which had spurred her on to success beyond her dreams; past the pub where Salden, Hammer and Lomax had in turn drowned their sorrows on the night of what Thanet was now convinced was a murder; over the bridge – now being repaired, Thanet noticed – where Marcia had met her death; past the Hammers' cottage and the lodge where Edith lived, to the house with which Marcia had fallen in love all those years ago.

As they emerged from the avenue of trees, huge spots of rain began to spatter the windscreen. Remembering their previous experience when Mrs Pantry had kept them standing on the doorstep in a downpour, this time they pulled raincoats on. By the time they reached the front door it was pouring.

Mrs Pantry was as unwelcoming as ever. 'He's out.'

It was an anticlimax. Hunching his shoulders against the

water trickling down his neck, Thanet tried to suppress his disappointment.

'Where's he gone?'

She planted herself a little more firmly on her solid legs, as though preparing herself against an onslaught, and folding her arms across her chest said belligerently, 'Can't you leave the poor man alone? After all he's been through.'

'I assure you we wouldn't be wanting to talk to him if it weren't absolutely necessary. Where is he?'

'You're the detective. Well then, detect.'

Thanet suppressed his rising anger. 'Mrs Pantry . . .'

'What is it, Mrs Pantry? What's going on?' It was Edith Phipps. 'What on earth are you thinking of, keeping the Inspector and the Sergeant standing out there in the pouring rain? Look at them, they're half drowned. I can't think what Mr Salden would say. Come in, Inspector!'

Thanet shook his head. 'Thank you, no. We wanted to speak to Mr Salden, and I believe he's out. Do you know where he is?'

Edith gave Mrs Pantry an admonitory look. 'He's gone fishing.' She wrinkled her nose. 'Not exactly ideal weather, but it never seems to bother him. He's got one of those big umbrellas.'

'Where does he go, do you know?'

'Not really. Down to the Teale, that's all.'

'So he'll be somewhere in the grounds.'

'Oh yes, I'm sure of it.'

'Great!' said Lineham when they were back in the car. 'So all we have to do now is walk along about a mile of river bank in the pouring rain.'

'I don't know about you, but I couldn't get much wetter than I already am.'

'True.'

'So we might as well do it.'

'Why not?'

They decided to drive back to the bridge and start from there. He'd been wrong in thinking he couldn't get any wetter, thought Thanet as they trudged along, their wellingtons swishing through the sodden grass. He must be mad. Why couldn't he have waited? The rain would stop soon enough and then they could have made this trek in comfort. But having come this far he certainly wasn't going to turn back now.

Ten minutes later they spotted the blue and yellow segments of a big umbrella tucked under the lip of the river bank fifty yards ahead.

'It might not be him,' said Lineham.

But it was. Salden looked cosy enough, well wrapped up in waterproof jacket and trousers, a steaming cup of coffee in his hand. Thanet looked at it enviously. He could hardly expect to be offered a cup, and even if he were he wouldn't be able to accept, in the circumstances.

'You look a little damp, Inspector.' There was a glint of amusement in Salden's eyes. 'This is surely devotion well beyond the call of duty. Would you like to share my umbrella? I'm sure we could all squeeze underneath.'

'There are some trees over there,' said Thanet.

He and Lineham waited while Salden reeled in his line and propped his rod against the overhanging bank, then they headed for the trees. It was only marginally drier here; the leaves were not yet fully unfurled, the summer canopy not yet established.

Thanet decided that there was no point in wasting time. Shock tactics might in any case prove more effective. He nodded at Lineham.

'Bernard Salden, you are not obliged to say anything unless you wish to do so, but what you say may be put into writing and given in evidence.'

Salden looked — what? astounded? appalled? It was difficult to tell, with the rain streaming down his face.

He looked from one to the other. 'What?'

'Mr Salden. Before you tell us exactly what happened on Tuesday night, let me say off the record that I'm sure you will find any jury sympathetic to your case. Any man who suddenly discovers that his daughter has been murdered . . .'

Salden was galvanised into life. 'Murdered? What are you saying? Who told you that?' He grabbed Thanet by the shoulders and shook him. He looked frantic.

Thanet was nonplussed. He didn't know what to say. In a matter of seconds his neatly constructed edifice had been demolished. His whole case rested on the premise that, in an abnormal state of mind as a result of severe post-natal depression, Marcia had killed her baby daughter and disposed of the body. With no one else to turn to she had then run to her mother for sanctuary, confessed her crime and sworn Mrs Carter to secrecy. This, he had been convinced, was what Mrs Carter had wanted to tell Bernard before she died and this, he had been certain, was what had prompted that fatal quarrel between Salden and his wife. But if Salden hadn't known. . . ? He stared at Salden. Should he back down, apologise? No. Facts were facts. Doggedly he recounted them.

'That charade your wife played, when she came back to Telford Green, claiming the baby had died. We checked with the Records Office, and no death certificate exists. We spoke with Mrs Pepper, who attended the "funeral". The "ashes" were not buried in the churchyard. In that case the vicar would have needed a copy of the death certificate, and of course Marcia didn't have one. A convincing little ceremony was held on the village green instead. No doubt your wife intended to deceive her mother, too, but somehow she must have let the truth slip out. Mrs Carter might have carried the secret with her to the grave, but her conscience wouldn't allow her to. She . . .'

'Just a minute, let me get this straight. Are you suggesting my wife *murdered* Clare?'

'I told you, the death certificate doesn't exist . . .'

Something was happening to Salden's face. The flat planes were cracking, breaking up. He collapsed into a sitting position on the ground, hunched forward with hands over face, shoulders heaving.

Thanet and Lineham looked at each other. Now what? They stood staring down at Salden. And then Thanet realised. Those snorts and sniffles were not the sounds of grief.

Salden was *laughing*.

Oblivious of the rain, Thanet realised that at last it really had happened; his famous intuition had let him down and one

238

of his theories truly was just as preposterous as it sounded. He remembered the struggle he had had to convince Draco of its credibility, and his soul shrivelled with embarrassment. He cursed himself now for not keeping his mouth shut until he was certain. Yes, he had to face it. He had made a fool of himself in a big way. He risked a glance at Lineham, but the Sergeant was avoiding his eye.

Salden was wiping his eyes, shaking his head. He held out a hand and Thanet helped him to his feet. 'Sorry about that. But you really had me worried there, for a minute, Inspector.'

'I'm sorry,' said Thanet stiffly.

'Oh, it's OK. Don't worry. As soon as I realised you were talking about the past, not the present . . .'

'What do you mean?'

'I thought,' said Salden, with the patient air of someone spelling something simple out, 'that you meant you'd just heard that my daughter had been murdered.'

Just heard? Thanet tried to remember exactly what he'd said. *Let me say off the record that I'm sure you will find any jury sympathetic to your case. Any man who suddenly discovers that his daughter has been murdered* . . . But if Salden had thought that . . . And Salden hadn't queried what Thanet had said about the death certificate . . . A tiny bud of hope began to unfurl in his chest as he adjusted to new possibilities.

'You did know that your daughter is still alive, then?'

There was a brief silence. In Salden's eyes was the look of a man who suddenly realises that he has said too much.

'So that was what Mrs Carter wanted to tell you on Tuesday night. I see.' Thanet did see. He saw that here was another motive as strong as the last. Whatever Marcia had done with the child, Salden would have been furious with her for deceiving him so, for depriving him of almost thirty years of fatherhood.

'I don't know what you're talking about.'

'Oh come, Mr Salden. I'm not stupid. You gave yourself away there, didn't you? What did your wife say she'd done with the baby? Given her to a childless couple, perhaps, who were so desperate for a child that they would take her with no

239

questions asked? No? Surely she didn't just abandon her?'

Despite his attempt at self-control, Salden's expression gave him away.

'No,' said Thanet firmly, knowing that if this bluff failed all was lost. 'That can't be true.'

'Why not?' The words seemed forced out against Salden's will.

'Because in that case your wife would have been traced. A woman can't just disappear, leaving a child behind her ... No, I'm afraid you've been badly deceived.'

'What do you mean?'

'That your wife was desperate enough at that time to have been driven to take far more drastic action than that. Naturally she wouldn't have told her mother the truth.'

'You're trying to tell me you have proof that Clare is ... dead?'

Thanet said nothing.

'No!' said Salden. 'That's not true! There's some mistake! She left her, I know she did. In the foyer of a hospital, where she would be found and looked after.'

The fear that Thanet could be right had made Salden throw discretion to the winds. Even now he did not realise that he had betrayed himself.

It was essential to press on without allowing Salden time to think. Hating himself, Thanet said, 'Where was this? In the town where you were living?'

'No. She wanted to get right away. She couldn't risk leaving her anywhere in Bradford, she afraid she might be traced.'

'Where, then?'

'York. She caught a train to York. She'd heard it was a nice city, she said.'

She said?

They had him! There was only one possible occasion when Salden and Marcia might have discussed this subject: after he had seen his mother-in-law on Tuesday night.

'Who said? Your mother-in-law?'

'No! Marcia! My wife. She told me herself and I believed her.'

'When?' said Thanet softly. 'When did she tell you?'

Salden opened his mouth to reply, then closed it again. His face betrayed the fact that he knew he had given himself away.

TWENTY-SEVEN

'So what happened then?' said Joan. 'Here, mash these potatoes, will you, while I do the sauce?'

Thanet took the saucepan, added margarine, black pepper, milk. With two cooks in the house you couldn't help learning something.

'He just caved in, confessed.'

'He needn't have, of course.'

'Why not? He'd given himself away, hadn't he?'

'He hadn't actually admitted that he'd heard about all this from his mother-in-law that night.'

'True.'

'So all he had to do was say that his wife had told him ages ago.'

Thanet froze. 'That's true. You're right! I didn't even think of that! How stupid can you get!' If Salden's wits had not been blunted by pain, grief and confusion he could have got away with it, at the very point when Thanet thought he had him. Thanet's scalp prickled with sweat as he realised how close a shave he had had.

'You're lucky he didn't think of it either! Have you finished with that?'

Thanet held out the saucepan. 'Will this do?'

'Fine, yes.' Joan was stirring vigorously. 'Put the lid on, I'm not quite ready.'

Thanet was recovering. 'We caught him off balance and he wasn't thinking straight. And also I think it was a relief to him to confess, get it off his chest. He's not the sort of man to live comfortably with a secret like that on his conscience.'

Joan took the plates out of the oven and began dishing up.

'So what did happen that night, exactly?'

'Well, if you remember, Salden had been sitting brooding on a bench on the river bank a few hundred yards away from the bridge on the other side from the Manor. Around twenty past ten he decided he really ought to get back to his mother-in-law's house. He was worried about her and, besides, there was an unseasonable frost that night and he was feeling thoroughly chilled.

'He was climbing the steps from the footpath when he heard footsteps approaching from the direction of the village. As he came up on to the bridge he saw that it was his wife. Because of the broken parapet she had been walking on the side nearer to him, but now she was crossing the bridge diagonally, making for the opposite flight of steps which lead down to the footpath to the Manor. He called her name and hurried to intercept her. When they met she was standing right next to the warning lights with her back to the gap in the stonework.'

'Marcia! What are you doing here?'

'What d'you think? I've been to see my mother.'

'Did she tell you why she wanted to see me?'

'No, she was asleep. Anyway why should she?'

'Because it concerned me.'

'Concerned you? What d'you mean? What are you talking about? Look, couldn't we discuss this later? We've got guests, in case you've forgotten. I can't think what they'll think of us. You don't turn up at all and then I walk out on them.'

'To hell with them! Who cares what they think? I don't. But I can tell you this, Marcia. I cared about what your mother told me. I really did care about that . . . What did you do with her, Marcia? What did you do with our daughter? With Clare?'

'Clare's dead. She died thirty years ago . . .'

'Don't give me that! I won't let you get away with any more lies. To think I believed you, unquestioningly . . . What a fool I was . . . So tell me. What did you do with her?'

'Let go of my arm. You're hurting me.'

'What did you do with her? Tell me!'

'I . . . took her to York.'

'York? Why York?'

'I don't know.'

'There must have been a reason why you chose York.'

'I think . . . Someone once told me it was a nice place . . .'

'Where did you go, in York?'

'My arm . . . Please . . .'

'Where?'

'A hospital. I left her . . . in the foyer . . .'

'Which hospital? Which hospital?'

'I can't remember. I don't know. I didn't notice. Please. You're really hurting me. Let go . . .'

'He claims he can't remember very clearly what happened then. She was struggling to get away, pulling and tugging, and he thinks she gave an especially violent wrench just as he finally let go. The road was slippery and she lost her balance, doubling up as she fell backwards through the rope barrier. She'd disappeared through the gap in the parapet almost before he realised what was happening.'

'You believe him?' Joan had finished serving and had put the plates of food in the oven to keep warm while Thanet finished his story.

'I don't know. I'm not sure, how can I be? He may have shoved her away, in disgust or anger . . . Whatever happened, I do believe it was an accident, a result of the quarrel.'

'In that case, why didn't he try to do something to save her, call for help?'

'He says that for a moment or two he couldn't believe his eyes. One moment she was there and the next she was gone. He'd been so wrapped up in what they'd been saying that he hadn't been aware of the gap in the bridge wall behind her and he couldn't understand what had happened. For a moment he just stood there. Then he rushed to the parapet and looked over. There was no sign of her. Neither of them could swim, the river was running high because of the rain and he realised at once that it would be pointless to go for help, it was already too late.'

'He should have, all the same.'

'Of course he should. I think the truth is that, even though he may not deliberately have pushed her, at that point he still felt so angry and cheated that he just didn't care if she was alive or dead. A child of his own would have meant so much to him. If his wife had lived I don't think he could ever have forgiven her for what she did.'

'I expect he'll get a verdict of manslaughter. I wonder if he'll go inside.'

Thanet shrugged. 'Depends on the judge. He might get a suspended.'

'Highly probable, I should think. From what you say, he isn't likely to be a danger to the public.' Joan grinned. 'Though I wouldn't say that was exactly the impression conveyed by Superintendent Draco on *Coast to Coast*.'

'You saw him?'

'Wouldn't have missed it for the world! Anyone would think he'd conducted the entire investigation single-handed!' Joan came and put her arms around Thanet's neck. 'It's not fair. You should have got the credit.'

'Some credit! When I think how I was within a whisker of it going the other way, and I didn't even realise. . . !'

Joan kissed him. 'Well, it didn't. Tell me, what put you on to him in the first place?'

They moved apart and sat down.

'Oddly enough, it was Vicky, poor girl. I was thinking about her a lot last night, of course, while you were at the hospital. While I was waiting for you to come home I dozed off and I had a rather nasty dream in which she turned into Marcia. I suppose that, subconsciously, I had spotted the similarity between them: they'd both had severe post-natal depression. Vicky had been driven to try to kill herself. What if Marcia actually had killed her baby?

'You see, I knew she hadn't wanted that baby. I also knew that she'd been very ambitious, that she'd hated living up North and that when her husband was posted abroad and she was left alone there with the baby it must have been the last straw. Looked at like that, the baby's death had been very convenient for her. It had meant that she was free again to pursue whatever career she wanted, and that she had an excuse to run away from the area she hated and return to Kent. In the circumstances no one would blame her.

'Well, we checked, and discovered that the death had never been registered. The fact that there'd been a funeral, presided over by the vicar and witnessed by at least one neighbour who couldn't possibly be suspected of complicity, was a bit of a stumbling block. Until we discovered that it hadn't been a proper burial service in the churchyard at all – the vicar would have needed a death certificate for that – but a simple sort of blessing ceremony, a scattering of the ashes on the village green . . . Stupid of me, really. I just assumed the baby was dead, it never occurred to me that she could have just abandoned it. I can imagine how Salden felt when he found out. He adored that child, by all accounts.'

'So how is he taking this now?'

'All he can think of is how to trace his daughter. He'd already started making enquiries.'

'That won't be an easy road. And if he does succeed, who knows if she'd want to be found?'

'Quite. Still, that's his affair. As I say, I can understand how he feels . . . Which reminds me . . . I think I've had a brilliant idea, about Bridget's problem.'

'Oh?'

'What if we said to her, "Look, what if you planned, afterwards, to do something for which you don't need to do particularly well in these exams, would that help you to stop worrying?" '

'Such as?'

'Well, we've always thought in terms of catering college, haven't we? But there's no reason why we shouldn't consider sending her to one of the private cookery schools. Some of them have excellent reputations. And I read somewhere that their academic entrance requirements aren't too exacting. In any case, with all Bridget has already achieved in the cookery field, I'm sure they'd be only too delighted to take her.'

'Could we afford it? They're terrible expensive.'

'But wouldn't it be worth it?' Thanet took Joan's hands. 'I know it wouldn't be easy, we'd have to make economies, but later on, if Ben manages to get to university, we'll have to help him through, and over the three years that would mount up. Most of these Cordon Bleu courses are only a year, or less. Surely we ought to be prepared to spend the same on Bridget.'

'True. It's just that it's a new idea . . .' Her tone became more positive. 'It would certainly take the pressure off her as far as these exams are concerned.'

'Exactly! Then, if she did pass . . . Well, I suppose then we'd have to leave it to her to choose which she wanted. We could hardly offer her the chance then take it away if she passes!'

'Quite. Oh darling, the more I think about it . . . Let's go and talk to her now, before we have supper, shall we? She badly needs cheering up.'

'If you like.'

Faced by the sight of both parents entering her room, Bridget's look was less than welcoming.

'It's all right,' said Thanet. 'This isn't what you think.'

'No *post mortem*,' said Joan. 'Daddy's come up with a brilliant idea.'

'Oh?' Bridget was wary. She looked ill, Thanet thought, pale and listless. He couldn't bear the thought that his bright, lively daughter had been reduced to this. He began to explain his idea. 'Your mother and I wondered . . .' He watched her face as he talked. Almost at once her cheeks became tinged with colour, her eyes began to sparkle and before he had finished she jumped up out of her chair and flung her arms around his neck. 'Oh Dad, what a wonderful idea. That would be terrific!' She turned to her mother, hugged her too. Then she stood back to study their faces. 'You mean it, don't you? You really mean it!'

Thanet and Joan, relieved and delighted at her reaction, beamed at her and at each other. They both nodded. 'We certainly do,' said Joan. 'We thought it would take the pressure off you. As Daddy says, even if you didn't do too well in your exams, you'd be sure to get in, after winning that cookery competition and writing the column for the *Kent Messenger*.'

'Terrific!' Bridget's look of excitement faded. 'But wouldn't it be terribly expensive?'

Joan explained what Thanet had said about Ben's

247

education. 'It won't be easy, there's no point in pretending it will. But we see no reason why you shouldn't have the same chance as Ben, in a different way.'

Bridget burst into tears.

Joan got up and took a handkerchief from a drawer, handed it to her.

She wiped her eyes, smiling and biting her lip. 'It's such a relief . . .'

Joan reached for Thanet's hand and squeezed it.

He smiled and returned the pressure. It looked as though another of life's minor crises was over.

DEAD BY MORNING

To Jenny and Ian

ONE

Thanet lifted the edge of the curtain aside and peered out into the dark street. 'It's nearly half-past twelve. Where can she be? She's never been as late as this before. And – yes – it's beginning to snow, look!'

Joan joined him at the window. 'So it is. The temperature must have risen.'

Earlier on it had been freezing hard.

She returned to her seat by the fire. 'Darling, do come and sit down, you're driving me mad prowling about like that.'

'How you can sit there so calmly I just do not know. She's always home by half-past eleven. Anything can have happened.' Thanet, who had seen far more than his share of broken bodies during his years in the police force, blanked off hideous images of Bridget mutilated, injured, suffering appalling pain or even now dying, perhaps. He plumped down beside Joan on the settee and, leaning forward, put his elbows on his knees and his head in his hands.

Joan put her hand on his shoulder. ' "Anything" includes perfectly ordinary things like being delayed at work, Tim's car not starting, being held up because they witnessed an accident . . .'

Their daughter Bridget was now nearly seventeen. She had managed to scrape one or two respectable grades in her GCSEs last summer and, always keen to have a career in

1

cookery, was taking a year off to gain some practical work experience in the kitchens of a local restaurant before starting a year's Cordon Bleu course in September. Tim was one of the waiters, and gave her a lift home each night that their stint of duty coincided.

Thanet's shoulder twitched impatiently. 'Yes, I know . . . But in that case, why hasn't she given us a ring?' Perhaps Tim wasn't as trustworthy as he had appeared. A married man with two children, he had seemed a decent enough young man, but what if his offer of lifts for Bridget had had an ulterior motive, what if . . . ?

Thanet jumped up and crossed to peer out of the window once more. 'It's coming down more heavily now.'

The snow was already beginning to lie, mantling the ground with a thin gauzy veil of white. Huge soft wet flakes swirled around the fuzzy orange globe of the street lamp on the pavement outside their house and hurled themselves silently against the windowpane like moths attracted to the light, melting from the contact with the warm glass as they slid down. Thanet peered hopefully down the street. Nothing.

'We should have refused Tim's offer, insisted on fetching her ourselves.'

'That would have looked really churlish, as he actually has to pass our house on his way. Anyway, it's ridiculous turning out late every night if we don't have to.'

'Better than having to sit here and wonder where she is and what's happened to her.'

Joan laughed. 'It looks as though you're in for a really bad time.'

'What do you mean?'

'Don't look so alarmed! I simply mean that this is only the beginning. We've been unusually lucky up to now but no doubt this is only the first of many, many nights over many, many years when we're going to lie awake waiting for the sound of her return, wondering where she is, if she's all right . . .'

'How can you make so light of it?'

'I'm not making light of it. It's just that I . . . well, I'm a little more resigned to it, I suppose. I can remember how my own parents used to fuss when I was late home after going out with you.'

'Do you? Did they? I never knew that.' Thanet took her hand, momentarily distracted.

'They certainly did. But I wasn't going to tell you, naturally. It would have made me sound like a little girl, to be fussed over.'

He grinned. 'The ultimate insult.'

'Exactly. And that's precisely how Bridget will take it if she gets home and finds us sitting here like a reception committee.' Joan stood up, decisively. 'So come on, let's go to bed.'

'But . . .'

'Luke! Come *on*.'

Grudgingly, he allowed himself to be persuaded upstairs. 'But I'm not going to let it go, mind. If she's going to be late like this she really must let us know.'

'All *right*. I'll speak to her about it. Tactfully.'

Thanet caught her eye and grinned. 'Not too tactfully.'

She smiled back. 'Agreed.'

They had just got into bed when outside in the street a car door slammed. A few moments later they heard the front door close. Quickly, Joan switched off the bedside light. When Bridget had crept past their door on the way to her room, Joan said, 'That wasn't all that was worrying you tonight, though, was it?'

Thanet turned to face her in the darkness. There was no point in denying it. 'No,' he admitted.

'Draco again.'

' 'Fraid so.'

'Why didn't you say?'

'I should think you're sick and tired of hearing about him.'

'Nonsense. It enlivens my days no end.'

3

He could hear the laughter in her voice.

'Seriously, though,' she said. 'What's he been up to this time?'

'That's the trouble, we're not sure. There're all sorts of rumours flying around. Some new campaign he's planning . . . But one thing's certain, it's sure to make life even more uncomfortable for the rest of us.'

Just over a year ago Superintendent Parker had retired and Goronwy Draco had taken over at divisional headquarters in Sturrenden, the small country town in Kent where Thanet lived and worked. The new Superintendent was a fiery, dynamic little Welshman who was firmly of the opinion that a new broom should sweep clean as quickly as possible. Suffering under the new regime of regular morning meetings and tighter control, Thanet had grudgingly to admit that under Draco's ever-watchful eye divisional headquarters at Sturrenden had become a much more stimulating place to work. Enlivened by newly-decorated offices and higher standards of cleanliness and efficiency, the place now crackled with a new energy and there had been a gratifying increase in crimes solved and villains safely ensconced behind bars. Draco may not be popular, but he certainly got results.

Thanet sighed. 'I expect we'll survive.'

As soon as he opened his eyes next morning he was aware of the difference in the quality of the light. There must have been more snow overnight. He hoped that the fall had not been heavy. Snow was very picturesque but it brought problems. However hard the local authority tried, it never seemed to make adequate preparation for bad weather. A mere skim of snow brought its crop of traffic jams and minor accidents; anything over six inches, severe disruption. And of course, there was the cold. Thanet hated the cold and the tip of his nose told him that the temperature in the bedroom was at a far from acceptable level. February was definitely bottom of his personal popularity chart of favourite months. He

4

allowed himself the indulgence of a few more moments in the warm cave that was the bed, then braced himself and slid out, careful not to allow a gush of cold air to disturb Joan who was still sleeping peacefully. He padded across to the window. Might as well know the worst.

Despite his dislike of the inconvenience snow brought in its wake he could not escape the inevitable sense of wonder at its transforming beauty. Beneath its mantle of pristine white, his familiar world preened itself in the first rosy light of a clear winter dawn. He peered at the roof of the garage, trying to gauge the depth of the fall: not more than a few inches, by the look of it. Good. It shouldn't take too long to clear the drive, with Ben's help. And the gritting lorries had been out last night, so the roads shouldn't be too bad.

Three-quarters of an hour later, fortified by the porridge that Joan had insisted on making, he and Ben had almost reached the front gate. Up and down the road warmly-clad figures shovelled and swept drives and pavements. In the road cars seemed to be making slow but steady progress.

Joan appeared at the front door. 'Luke? Telephone.'

'Finish it off, will you, Ben?'

Ben, thirteen, gave a reluctant nod.

'Sergeant Pater,' said Joan, handing over the receiver.

The Station Officer. Something out of the ordinary, then, to necessitate an early morning call, in view of the fact that Thanet was due at headquarters in half an hour or so.

'Thanet here.'

'Morning, sir. Just had the report of a body in a ditch at the side of the road, out at Sutton-in-the-Weald. Found by a man walking his dog.'

As in his last case, Thanet thought. If you were a dog owner you certainly seemed to run a greater risk of stumbling over a corpse than most.

'You've reported it to the Super?'

'Yes, sir. He says he's going out there himself.' Pater's tone was carefully non-committal.

'Ah.' Thanet's heart sank. This was new. What was Draco up to now? He remembered wondering, when Draco first arrived, just how long the new Superintendent would be content to sit behind a desk. All that restless energy needed numerous outlets. Thanet hoped that active participation at ground level wasn't going to be one of them. It would be impossibly inhibiting to have Draco breathing down his neck.

'Apparently there's been quite a bit of snow out there, fifteen inches or so, with some pretty deep drifts in places, so it's going to make transport a bit tricky. The Super's put through a request to the Council to clear the road as soon as possible and he's asked for a couple of Land Rovers to be laid on for you. He wants you to meet him here and he'll go out with you.'

'I see. What time?'

'Eight-thirty.'

'Right, I'll be there. Have you contacted Sergeant Lineham?'

'I'll do that next, sir. I'll arrange for the SOCOs and the CCTV sergeant to come in the other Land Rover, and pick up Doc Mallard on the way. I thought I'd let you know first.'

So that Thanet wouldn't be late for Draco, no doubt.

'Thanks.'

Grateful that he had already had breakfast and that the driveway was clear, Thanet put on thick socks, wellington boots, sheepskin jacket, gloves and woolly hat in anticipation of hours of standing around in the snow. 'I feel like the Abominable Snowman,' he said as he kissed Joan goodbye.

She grinned. 'You look like him. Here.' She handed him a Thermos.

'Thanks, love. Oh, hang on. Better take some shoes, in case. I can't go tramping in and out of houses in these.'

'Sure you wouldn't like me to pack a suitcase for you?'

'All very well for you, in your nice, centrally heated office.'

Joan worked as a Probation Officer in Sturrenden.

'Courtroom actually.'

'Courtroom, office, what's the difference, it'll be *warm*.'

'Stop grumbling,' she said, pushing him out of the front door. 'Go on, you don't want to keep Draco waiting, do you?'

Thanet rolled his eyes. 'Heaven forbid.'

As he got into the car he realised that he had been so put out by the prospect of Draco's presence that he had forgotten to ask whether the body was that of a man or a woman.

It was another couple of hours before he found out.

The journey out to Sutton-in-the-Weald had been irritatingly protracted. The first few miles hadn't been too bad but then the snow had begun to deepen and a little further on they had caught up with the snow plough sent out at Draco's request. After that they had resigned themselves to travelling behind it the rest of the way, at a snail's pace. Fortunately a local farmer with a snow-clearing attachment on the front of his tractor had eventually turned up coming the other way and after a certain amount of manoeuvring they had been able to proceed more quickly.

There then followed a long wait for the second Land Rover bringing Doc Mallard and the Scenes-of-Crime officers. Meanwhile, there had been little to do. The body lay in a roadside ditch backed by a high stone wall, only a few yards from the lion-topped pillars at the entrance of the driveway to Longford Hall Country House Hotel. From the road nothing could be seen but the upper surface of a sleeve in distinctively bold black-and-white checked tweed, lying along the edge of the ditch as it had been uncovered by the dog. Although the arm was patently stiff with rigor mortis, PC Yeoman, the local policeman who had been first on the scene, had understandably cleared the snow from the man's face, to make quite sure that he was dead. The rigid features, pallor of the skin and open, staring eyes had told their own tale and thereafter he had left well alone, winning Thanet's approval by erecting a temporary barrier of sticks stuck into the snow and linked by string.

7

Despite his years in the force Thanet had rarely been able to overcome a dread of his first sight of a corpse, but today, uncomfortably preoccupied by Draco's presence, he had approached the body with no more than a twinge of trepidation and, gazing down at the dead face set deep in its ruff of snow, he felt no more than his usual pang of sorrow at a life cut short. Blurred as the man's features were by snow, it was difficult to estimate his age with any accuracy, but Thanet guessed that he had been somewhere between forty and sixty. Time, no doubt, would tell.

No further attempt had yet been made to clear the snow from the rest of the body. Thanet wanted photographs taken first. Not that he thought this very important. Covered with snow as it was, the body had obviously been placed or had fallen into the ditch before or around the time the snow started. Still, one never knew. It paid to be scrupulously careful and, with Draco taking in every move, Thanet had every intention of playing it by the book.

In any case, the marks in the snow told their own story: a scuffled, disturbed area betrayed the dog's excited investigation of this interesting and unusual find and there were two sets of approaching and departing footprints, belonging to Mr Clayton, the dog's owner, and PC Yeoman. Thanet, Draco and Lineham had been careful to enquire which were Yeoman's tracks, and to step into his footmarks when they approached for their brief inspection of the body.

As yet the snow had kept most people indoors and there had been little traffic up and down the road. Half an hour ago a tractor had begun clearing the hotel drive and any minute now Thanet expected someone to arrive and demand an explanation of the activity just outside the gates.

'Where the devil are they?'

Draco, who along with Lineham and Thanet had been stamping up and down the road in an attempt to keep warm, was finding it difficult to contain his impatience. 'They should have been here half an hour ago.'

'Perhaps Doc Mallard was out on a call.'

Draco snorted, two dragon-like puffs of condensation emerging from his nostrils. Short, square and dark and sporting an astrakhan hat and a heavy, fur-lined overcoat, he looked like a Russian statesman awaiting the arrival of foreign dignitaries. The backdrop of snow served to heighten the illusion.

'Like some coffee, sir? I've got some in the Land Rover.'

'Thank you. Excellent idea. Should have thought of it myself.'

'My wife's, actually.'

Thanet fetched his Thermos from the Land Rover and he, Draco and Lineham took it in turns to sip the steaming liquid. Lineham had been very quiet so far, subdued no doubt by Draco's presence. Thanet had to suppress a grin at the memory of Lineham's face when he had seen Draco climb into the Land Rover. The sergeant evidently hadn't been warned.

A vehicle could be heard coming down the hotel drive and a moment later a Range Rover pulled up between the stone pillars. A man and a woman jumped out.

'What's going on here?'

It was, unmistakably, the voice of authority, cultured and self-assured. Its owner, clad in country uniform of cords, thick sweater, Barbour and green wellies, was in his late forties, tall and well built with slightly receding dark hair and slate-grey eyes which quickly summed up the situation and unerringly selected Draco as the person to approach. 'What's happened?'

Draco handed the Thermos cup to Thanet and, drawing himself up to his full height, announced, 'Superintendent Draco, from divisional police headquarters at Sturrenden . . .'

But the man wasn't listening. He had caught sight of the arm in its boldly checked sleeve and his expression changed. 'My God, that's . . .'

He spun around, putting out his hand to prevent the woman behind him from coming any closer.

9

'What is it, Giles? What's the matter?'

Clear, ringing tones, another Barbour and more green wellies. A beautiful woman, this, a little younger than her husband, in her early forties, Thanet guessed. She, too, was dark, her long hair swept back into a thick French plait, accentuating the classic bone structure of her face. She would look much the same, he thought, twenty years from now.

'I think you ought to get back into the car, darling,' said her husband.

She shook off his restraining arm impatiently. 'What do you mean, what are you talking about?'

The movement gave her a clear view of the arm for the first time and she gasped. 'My God, that's Leo's coat.'

Draco stepped forward. 'Leo?'

'My brother.' Her gaze was riveted to the arm, her eyes appalled. She clutched at her husband, who put an arm around her. 'Is he . . . ?'

'Dead?' said Draco. 'I'm afraid so. If it is your brother, I'm sorry that you had to learn of it like this.'

'But why are you just standing around drinking coffee, for God's sake! Why aren't you trying to get him out? You can't just leave him there!' She grabbed the stick marker nearest to her, tugged it out of the snow and, tossing it impatiently aside, started towards the ditch.

The three policemen darted forward to stop her, but it was her husband who grabbed at her coat and tugged her back. 'No, Delia. Can't you see? If it is Leo, there's nothing anybody can do now.'

'But it's awful! It's . . . inhuman, just leaving him buried in the snow like that!' She turned on Draco, her eyes blazing. 'How dare you!' Her contemptuous gaze swept around the little group of policemen and returned to Draco. 'The Chief Constable is a personal friend of ours. I shall report you to him. Immediately!'

Thanet studiously refrained from looking at Lineham.

She turned to her husband. 'Come on, Giles. We'll go back

10

to the house and get something done about this absurd situation.'

And with another furious glance at Draco she swung herself up into the car and sat gazing stonily through the windscreen as her husband manoeuvred the Range Rover around and drove off.

'A lady who's used to getting her own way, I presume,' said Draco, apparently unruffled. 'You're going to have your hands full with her, Thanet.'

Just what Thanet had been thinking. Though the prospect intrigued rather than dismayed him. He raised an eyebrow at PC Yeoman. 'Who are they?'

'Mr and Mrs Hamilton, sir. Owners of Longford Hall. She runs the hotel, he runs the estate.'

'There are the others now, sir,' said Lineham.

'About time, too,' growled Draco.

Doc Mallard's half-moon spectacles glinted through the windscreen as the Land Rover drew up.

'Where the devil have you been?' snapped Draco as Trace, the SOCO sergeant, got out, followed by his team.

Mallard accepted Thanet's steadying hand. 'My fault, I'm afraid, Superintendent. Blame it on a doctor's irregular lifestyle. I was out at a confinement. Woman was on her way to hospital, but the ambulance got stuck in the snow. Luckily I just got there in time.' He beamed. 'Bouncing baby boy, mother and child both right as rain, I'm glad to say. Nothing like bringing life into the world to cheer you up, you know.'

'I'm sure.' Draco turned to Trace. 'Well, let's get on with it now you are here. If we have to stand around out here much longer we'll all turn into blocks of ice.'

TWO

By the end of another hour Thanet felt as though Draco's prophecy were coming true; his feet were numb, he felt chilled to the bone and he had long since regretted using up his precious flask of coffee so early. Perhaps, soon, they would be able to go up to the hotel and have a hot drink.

There had been much to do. Screens had been erected, photographs of the relatively untouched area of snow had been taken, Doc Mallard had officially pronounced the man dead and then there had been a long wait while the Scenes-of-Crime officers had patiently scooped the snow away from the body, pausing to take samples or more photographs when necessary. Eventually the corpse was completely exposed, proving to be that of a man of around fifty with thinning brown curly hair, dressed in well-cut cavalry twill trousers, Aquascutum sports jacket and the black-and-white checked tweed overcoat. A wallet in his breast pocket contained twenty pounds in notes, various receipts and other scraps of paper and, more importantly, a driving licence and several credit cards in the name of Leo Martindale. It was always a help to establish identification at the outset of a case.

There were no visible marks on the body until it was lifted carefully out of its snowy grave for transfer to the waiting ambulance. Then Doc Mallard had spotted an area of matted blood on the back, left-hand side of the scalp, and there had been some excitement when the SOCOs had found some flakes of rusted paint-coated metal, two caught up in a tear in the back of the overcoat and another on the ground beneath.

'Presumably snagged in the cloth on impact,' said Draco as they gathered around to peer at the samples in their plastic envelope. 'If so, forensic will find out. Hit and run?'

'Looks like it. Though if so . . .' Thanet was thoughtful.

'What?'

'I was only thinking . . .'

Draco shifted impatiently. 'Come on, man, spit it out.'

'Well, the injury is to the back of the head, and the tear is on the back of the overcoat . . .'

'So?'

'The implication is that he was struck from behind. I'm just trying to visualise what happened. If he was knocked into the ditch by the impact, you'd expect him to be on his face or his side, or crumpled into a heap, not neatly laid out on his back.'

'What are you suggesting? That whoever knocked him down then stopped his car, got out and dragged the body into the ditch?'

Thanet shrugged. 'It's a possibility, isn't it, sir?'

'One among many, I suppose. But it is surely equally possible that he could have been thrown into that position by the collision?'

Thanet disagreed. But it would not have been politic to say so. Draco did not appreciate opposition. 'I expect we could do some experiments, sir.'

'Quite. And then, it's also possible that he wasn't killed outright by the impact. He could have remained conscious – or regained consciousness – and crawled or staggered to the ditch in order to get off the road, and lain down in it in the most comfortable position, which just happened to be on his back.'

This was much more likely. 'True.'

'Or,' said Lineham, contributing to the discussion for the first time, 'he could have been deliberately run down.'

13

This earned him a scowl from Draco. Murder investigations were both time-consuming and expensive. 'Anyway, if these metal flakes are from a car we shouldn't have any problems in tracing it.'

Thanet nodded. They all knew that it was a relatively straightforward matter these days to trace a vehicle from paint samples. Forensic science has reduced it to a fine art.

They all peered again at the largest sample. 'Looks like a mid-grey. And definitely going rusty,' said Lineham.

'I'll get forensic to hurry it up,' said Draco.

'Thank you, sir.' There were, apparently, advantages in having the boss along.

'You'd better do a house-to-house, get the men to check all local vehicles. Radio in for reinforcements. I'm going back to headquarters now.'

Another bonus. Thanet suddenly felt a lot more cheerful. Even his toes didn't seem quite so cold.

One of the ambulancemen approached. 'We're ready to leave now, sir.'

Draco glanced at Thanet. 'Might save time if you got Hamilton down from the hotel first, see if he can make a formal identification.'

Thanet had every intention of doing so. 'Right, sir.' And to the ambulanceman, 'If you could just wait a little longer . . .'

'Good. Good.' Draco gave a little bounce on the balls of his feet, preparatory to departure. The thought of his snug office must be enticing. 'I'll take one of the Land Rovers and get it sent back, in case you need it to get off the beaten track. Can I gave you a lift, Mallard?'

'Thank you. Be glad to get back to civilisation.' Mallard picked up his bag, brushed snow off the bottom.

'Just one thing, Doc,' said Thanet.

Mallard twinkled at Thanet over his half-moons. 'Thought you wouldn't let me get away without asking. Time of death, right?'

Thanet nodded.

'Well I'm afraid you're going to be disappointed. In these particular circumstances it's virtually impossible to hazard a guess.'

'All the same . . .' pressed Thanet.

'Really, Luke . . . Well, I suppose the best I can do is to say that it must have been some time last night. Say, any time between six o'clock and . . .' Mallard shrugged. 'What time did the snow start, do you know?'

'Around half-past twelve, in Sturrenden. Could have been earlier here, of course.'

'Well, you'll have to check. But it's obvious that most of the snow fell after the body went into the ditch. Say between six o'clock and four a.m., then, to be on the safe side. Not much help I'm afraid. Sorry, but I have to allow for the fact that it might not have been the accident that killed him. He could have died of hypothermia.'

Draco was shifting from one foot to another in his eagerness to be off. 'Right, then, Thanet. Keep me informed – in fact, you'd better report in at about five. Interesting to get back to grass roots for a while.'

'Let's hope he's had enough of grass roots,' said Lineham, gazing after the departing Land Rover. 'What now?'

'Better call in for those reinforcements. Tell them to come up to the hotel.' Thanet beckoned to PC Yeoman who had kept well away from Draco and was now patiently waiting near the entrance to the hotel drive. 'I hope you're not frozen stiff.'

'No sir, I'm fine.' Yeoman didn't look it. His narrow face was pinched with cold, his nose red-tipped, eyes watering.

'You did well here, before we arrived.'

'Thank you, sir.' A faint flush warmed the pallor of his cheeks.

'I gather Mrs Hamilton's brother, if that's who the dead man is, was a stranger to you.'

'I knew she had a brother but I've never set eyes on him before. I've only been here two years and he left the village ages ago; everyone assumed he was dead.'

15

'Black sheep of the family, was he?' Thanet scented an interesting story.

'I believe so, yes. Pretty unpopular generally, from what I can gather.'

'Why was that, do you know?'

Yeoman shook his head. 'Not specifically, no. It's just the impression I've got.'

'Part of your job will be to find out, listen to the gossip. There's bound to be a lot of talk in the village after this. Meanwhile, nip up and fetch Mr Hamilton, would you? We'd like him to identify the body. Afterwards, if the SOCOs have finished you can come up to the hotel with us and have a hot drink.'

'Thank you, sir.' Yeoman set off up the hotel drive at a brisk pace, slipping and sliding on the snow.

Thanet glanced around. 'You finished here, Trace?'

'Almost, sir.'

'Right. Get those paint samples to forensic as soon as you can, won't you?'

'Yes, sir.'

Twenty minutes later the Range Rover returned. Hamilton jumped out and the ambulancemen slid the stretcher out and uncovered the dead man's face. Tight-lipped, Hamilton nodded. 'That is my brother-in-law.'

'Leo Martindale,' said Thanet.

Hamilton looked startled. 'How did you ... ? Oh, I suppose he had identification on him.' He sighed and shook his head. 'The last of the line.' He grimaced. 'Sad, isn't it? There have been Martindales at Longford Hall for over two hundred years.'

'He was unmarried, then?'

'So he told us.'

'You had any reason to doubt him?'

Hamilton looked uncomfortable. 'Oh no. No. It's just that ... Well, I suppose you're bound to hear. He wasn't exactly the most reliable of men.'

'I see. We'll need to talk to you and your wife, of course, so perhaps we could now go up to the house.'

'Of course.' Hamilton glanced at the Land Rover into which the SOCOs were loading their equipment. 'You seem to be without transport at the moment, Inspector. I assume that will shortly be remedied but meanwhile may I offer you a lift?'

Thanet would have liked to take his first look at the Hall in his own time, but it would have seemed churlish to refuse and he didn't want to antagonise the man. Besides, the thought of getting out of the cold more quickly was enticing. 'Thank you.'

They climbed into the Range Rover and set off up the drive, which was fenced on both sides and wound across open parkland. Before the great storm in October 1987 this would no doubt have been graced by stands of mature oak and beech, but now it was virtually bare, only the odd solitary survivor lifting its branches into the winter sky. Here and there broken and splintered trees still lay about in disarray, testament to the devastation suffered by the whole of this south-east corner of England on that one night. It was said that it would take three generations for the landscape to recover. Hamilton was evidently doing his bit to ensure that it would. An extensive programme of replanting was obviously under way, in the shape of groups of young saplings protected from the depredations of rabbits and livestock by square enclosures of wood and close-meshed wire netting.

'I suppose you lost a lot of trees in the storm?' said Thanet.

Hamilton sighed. 'Like everyone else, yes. Around eighty per cent, actually, and, as you see, we still haven't got around to clearing away all the casualties. It's a mammoth task and is costing a fortune so we're doing it bit by bit. We've tended to concentrate on replanting.'

The house had just come into view and Thanet was aware of Lineham behind him leaning forward to take a better look.

17

If they'd been alone he knew exactly what the sergeant would have said. 'They can't be short of a penny!'

And it would have been true, of course. Longford Hall was not exactly a stately home, but it was certainly the house of an English Country Gentleman; built, he would guess, at the end of the seventeenth or early in the eighteenth century, the rich rose-red of its brickwork enhanced by the mantle of snow which now surrounded it. Its proportions were perfect: the rows of white-painted sash windows, the flat-topped, steeply pitched roof with dormer windows, the stone balustrade running around the roof ridge all combining with the graceful flight of steps leading up to the front door to create a perfect harmony of shape and form often striven for but rarely achieved.

'What a beautiful house,' Thanet murmured.

Hamilton lifted an eyebrow, as if surprised that a policeman should appreciate architectural genius. 'It is, isn't it. Built by Hugh May in 1675.'

And now a Country House Hotel. Thanet wondered how it must feel to have to turn the house that has been your family home for generations into a haven for rich tourists and tired businessmen. He knew that a number of these Country House Hotels now existed but he had never been inside one before. Should be interesting.

They had arrived. Hamilton pulled up in front of the steps, which were being brushed clear of snow by a tall, thin man wearing a padded anorak and a navy blue woollen cap below which his ears stuck out like those of a garden gnome. He gave them a curious glance as they passed, breaking the rhythm of his movements and straightening up to pull out a handkerchief and blow his nose.

'Who was that?' said Thanet in an undertone when they had gone by.

'Byfleet, our handyman-cum-chauffeur.' Hamilton pushed open the front door with a proprietorial air and, after stamping the snow off their boots, they followed him into a broad inner lobby that bore no resemblance to the entrance to any hotel Thanet had ever been in before. If he hadn't known it was one he would have thought that he had stepped into a private house. Ranged along the right-hand wall was an orderly litter of gumboots, croquet hoops, umbrellas, walking sticks; exactly as if at any moment members of the family might come out and equip themselves for whichever outdoor activity they had in mind. To the left, a long wooden rail screwed to the wall sported a row of hooks from which hung an assortment of well-worn Barbours, Burberries and tweed caps and hats.

There was no time for more than a quick glance around. Hamilton kicked off his boots and the three policemen followed suit. Hamilton slipped on a pair of shoes he had left beside the door and Thanet, shooting an apologetic glance at Lineham, unwrapped the parcel containing his shoes, which he had removed from the Land Rover before Draco left, and put them on, glad of his foresight. He wouldn't have fancied conducting an investigation in a place like this in the indignity of stockinged feet. Lineham was no doubt wishing he'd done the same.

Hamilton flung open the inner door and led the way into a spacious hall from which a graceful staircase curled up to the first floor. Thanet blinked, overwhelmed by the assault on his senses. The scent of potpourri and burning applewood hung on the warm air, Persian rugs glowed on the stone-flagged floor, antique furniture adorned with elaborate flower arrangements gleamed with centuries of polishing and everywhere was a profusion of fine paintings, decorative objects and porcelain ornaments. In the distance someone was playing the piano. It was like stepping back in time to a more leisured and gracious way of life.

'Just a moment,' murmured Hamilton, and he left them to speak to a young woman seated at a leather-topped desk in the left-hand corner of the room. The hotel receptionist, presumably, the first discreet indication that Longford Hall

19

was a commercial undertaking. As if drawn by a magnet the three policemen moved in the direction of the log fire burning in the huge stone fireplace in the right-hand wall. Two women, one young, one middle-aged, were sitting on the long chintz-covered settee in front of it.

'Say,' drawled the older woman, 'you poor men look frozen to the eyeballs. Come right on over in front of the fire, and warm yourselves up.'

American, by the sound of it. A guest, presumably.

Thanet smiled. 'You're certainly in the best place, on a day like this.' The warmth of the fire on the backs of his legs was sheer bliss.

The girl pouted. She was in her late teens, small and dark, with the beautifully white even teeth Thanet for some reason always associated with Americans. 'Just our bad luck, you mean. We'd planned a trip to Canterbury today. How long d'you think it'll be before the roads are clear?'

Thanet shrugged. 'Sorry, I don't know. Could be this afternoon, could be – '

Hamilton approached. 'If you'd like to come this way, Inspector, I've arranged for some coffee to be brought. You could do with a hot drink, I expect.'

The two women exchanged glances. 'Inspector!' said the younger one, scenting diversion. 'Does that mean . . . ?'

Hamilton turned on all his charm, gave her a melting smile. 'I'm sorry. There's been an accident . . .' And, like a sheepdog herding a small flock of wayward sheep, he urged the policemen towards a door to the right of the stairs. 'If you'd like to sit down . . .'

It was a small sitting-room, elegant in blue and gold.

'When you've had coffee I'll fetch my wife.'

'Is she very upset?'

'Depends what you mean by "upset". Shocked, yes, grief-stricken – well I don't think she would pretend to that. After all, until this week she's thought her brother dead for many years now, so you could say she's had time to get used to the idea.'

There was a knock at the door and a girl in housemaid's uniform of long black dress, frilly white apron and cap entered with a tray of coffee. Gratefully they all accepted the proffered porcelain cups of steaming liquid. Thanet waited until she had gone, then said, 'When, exactly, did she learn he wasn't dead after all?' His fingers and toes were aching now as they thawed and it took considerable self-control not to betray the fact. He didn't want to do anything to distract Hamilton's attention from the conversation.

'Day before yesterday.' The muscles of Hamilton's face tightened, betraying the tension their unexpected visitor had caused. He and his wife had obviously not been exactly overjoyed at her brother's resurrection.

An interesting thought crossed Thanet's mind. What if Leo had been the rightful heir to the Longford Hall estate . . . ? Here was a motive for murder if ever there were one. Questions crowded into his mind. He flicked a glance at Lineham. *Take over.* He wanted to think.

'He just turned up out of the blue, without warning?' said Lineham.

Hamilton seemed surprised by the change of questioner. 'Yes.'

'After – how long?'

'Twenty, twenty-five years. I lost count long ago.'

Why come back now, after all these years? Thanet wondered.

'Why come back now, after all this time?' said Lineham.

Hamilton shrugged. 'He'd been living abroad for some time, apparently, only returned to England a week ago. Went to the barber's and saw an article on Country House Hotels in one of the Sunday supplement magazines. Longford Hall was featured in it.'

Hamilton's tone had subtly changed. Suddenly he had become guarded.

'I saw that article,' said Lineham. 'Chilston Park was in it too.'

21

This was another well-known Country House Hotel in Kent, notable in that it was owned by the Millers, publishers of the famous *Antiques Price Guide*.

'That's right.' Hamilton was obviously relieved to be distracted from the direction the conversation was taking.

But Thanet wasn't going to let him get away with it so lightly. By now he was sure he was right. Leo *had* been the heir. Another glance at Lineham. *I'll take over again.* They had been working together for so long that this unspoken communication had become second nature to them.

'How long has the Hall been a hotel, Mr Hamilton?'

'Two years.'

'What made Mrs Hamilton decide to make the change?'

He was rewarded by the answer he expected.

'Her father died four years ago and there was no way she could have kept it on without making it pay its way.'

'Was Mr Martindale aware that his father was dead?'

This was delicate ground. Hamilton's tone was carefully casual as he shook his head. 'Apparently not. As I say, he'd been living abroad for a number of years, in the South of France, although we didn't know that at the time. Everything possible was done to try and trace him, without success. Apparently the villa in which he was . . . staying, was very secluded, up in the hills. His hostess was French and they had very little contact with the local community.'

For 'hostess' read 'mistress', Thanet guessed.

'So it must have been a considerable shock to Mr Martindale, to learn that his old home was no longer a private house.'

'I suppose so. Though he didn't seem at all put out by the fact.'

'Really?' Now if true, that *was* interesting. Had Leo hoped to cash in on all the hard work his sister must have put in to make this place into the going concern it presumably was?

'And of course to learn of his father's death,' said Thanet.

'Yes.'

An uncomfortable monosyllable. Hamilton must know what was coming next.

'The estate was left to your wife, not her brother?'

'No.'

Even more terse.

'So,' said Thanet delicately, 'there must have been a certain problem of inheritance.' He awaited Hamilton's reaction with interest.

But he was disappointed. Hamilton must have prepared himself for this moment for he simply smiled, a bland, meaningless stretching of the lips, and said, 'Not at all, Inspector. Sorry to disappoint you, but I'm sure we could all have come to some amicable arrangement. To put it baldly, it's a good-sized cake, there was plenty for everybody.'

It depended, Thanet thought, on how large a slice Leo Martindale would have wanted to cut for himself. 'How large, exactly?'

'Two thousand acres.' Hamilton smiled, the lazy, replete smile of the predator who has caught and eaten his prey. 'And the house, of course.'

Not to mention its contents, thought Thanet. They alone, from what he had seen of them, would be worth a pretty penny. He wondered how Hamilton's wife had reacted to all this.

As if on cue the door opened and a sleek dark head appeared. 'Ah,' said Delia Hamilton, 'there you are, darling. Sorry to interrupt, but there's a minor crisis. The butcher's just rung to say his van is stuck in the snow. D'you mind if Byfleet borrows the Range Rover for half an hour to go and collect the meat?'

THREE

At Thanet's request Delia Hamilton returned after giving permission for Byfleet to borrow the Range Rover. She sat down beside her husband with an embarrassed laugh. 'I suppose you think I'm very unfeeling, Inspector, to be worrying about such trivial matters after what's happened. But the fact remains that I'm still responsible for the running of this place and we do have guests. Not many at the moment, fortunately, but still . . .'

She had changed from her outdoor clothes into an elegant tweed skirt, pearls and a smoky-green cashmere jumper the colour of her eyes. Her dark hair was now folded back into a smooth pleat. Immaculately groomed, she looked every inch the country lady, an image no doubt carefully calculated to impress her guests. Of grief there was no sign.

'How many, exactly?' said Thanet, ignoring the spurious apology.

'Only eight. It's usually pretty quiet at this time of the year.'

'And they are . . . ?'

'Four Americans – a married couple and a mother and daughter – then there's a family of three and a single man, all British.'

Should make the task of interviewing easier, thought Thanet. If it had been a bank holiday weekend, now . . . 'We

24

understand from your husband that your brother arrived unexpectedly the day before yesterday, that until then you had thought he was dead.'

'Which is why I can't pretend to be devastated now. Leo was dead to me for so many years that it was his being alive I found difficult to take in.' The embarrassed laugh again. 'I suppose you think I'm pretty hardhearted, but there's no point in being hypocritical about it, is there?'

Thanet made no comment. There had been, he noted, no further word of a complaint to the Chief Constable. Perhaps it had been made and dismissed?

'Could you give us some idea of his movements since he arrived?'

She put up a hand to brush back an invisible strand of hair. 'I'll do my best, though we didn't spend that much time together. I still had the hotel to run and Leo seemed quite content to wander around by himself, renewing old acquaintances, no doubt, and revisiting his old haunts.'

'If you could just give us some idea . . .'

She glanced at her husband. 'Well, let me see . . . He arrived unexpectedly, early on Monday evening, shortly before dinner.' She grimaced. 'Shortly before we had dinner, I mean. We always dine at a ridiculously early hour so that I am free to be around while our guests have drinks and their dinner later on.'

'By "we" you mean . . . ?'

A glance at Hamilton. 'My husband and I.'

'There are no other members of the family living here at present?'

'There's Tessa, our daughter, and our son Adam is here at the moment, too. But he didn't arrive until last night. He's away at boarding school but it's his half-term and he spent the first few days of it with a friend. And Tessa was out as usual, she'd been up to town for the day and didn't get back till late.'

'By "town" you mean London?'

'Of course. Look, is all this relevant? I can't see why it matters what we did the night before last, it's last night that matters, surely.'

'I'm just trying to get the picture, so bear with me, please. Mr Martindale gave you no warning of his arrival, you say?'

She shook her head. 'No. Just turned up out of the blue.'

'It must have been a shock for you, if you had been so certain he was dead.'

'It certainly was . . . A nice one, of course.'

'Of course,' echoed Thanet, hoping the sarcasm was not noticeable in his tone. 'Anyway, I imagine Mr Martindale would have been shown up to his room, when he arrived.'

'Briefly, yes. All the rooms are always kept in a state of readiness, so there was no problem there.'

'And then you had dinner. That would have been at . . . ?'

'Six-thirty, as usual. It was something of a celebration, of course, we opened a bottle of champagne. Return of the prodigal and all that.'

Thanet couldn't imagine that Leo had really been welcomed with open arms, but they had presumably gone through the motions. 'And afterwards?'

'We always have drinks with any of the guests who choose to join us in the drawing-room at seven-thirty. They like that, it fosters the private house image we try to cultivate.'

'Did your brother join you that evening?'

'Yes, he did. The idea seemed to amuse him.'

'And afterwards?'

She shrugged. 'It was business as usual.' She glanced at Hamilton. 'I believe you did some paperwork in your office, didn't you, darling, and I stayed around, generally keeping an eye on things. Leo went off to the pub in the village. He got back about nine, then disappeared to his room.'

'And yesterday?'

Delia Hamilton put a hand up to her head and said irritably, 'I saw him around from time to time, but I didn't exactly keep a diary of his movements, why should I? And I did have work to do, you know, this place doesn't exactly run itself.' Mention of her domestic duties made her glance at her watch. 'Look, can't we hurry things up a bit, we'll be here all day at this rate.'

Hamilton stirred. 'And I have things to attend to, as well. Do you really need me here any longer? I can't see that there's much I can contribute. I'm out on the estate most of the day.'

'I appreciate that, sir, but I'd be grateful if you could stay just a little longer. You might be able to clarify or corroborate what happened last night.'

Hamilton settled back in his chair, frowning. 'Very well, but let's get a move on, shall we?'

Thanet had no intention of being hurried. 'If we could go back to yesterday morning, then . . .'

Delia Hamilton frowned and sighed. 'If we must. I'm sure our housekeeper could help you more than I.'

'That would be . . . ?'

'Mona Byfleet. She's married to our handyman-cum-chauffeur.'

'You saw him outside, if you remember, Inspector,' said Hamilton.

'Ah, yes. Perhaps I could talk to Mrs Byfleet later. But meanwhile . . .'

Delia Hamilton sat up straighter, as if to flex the muscles of her memory, then said rapidly, 'Leo had a lie-in, I believe, and breakfast in bed. I saw him mid-morning and he said he was going to wander about, revisit his old haunts, as I said. At lunch he told me he'd been for a long walk on the estate. He said he was going down to the village in the afternoon and I assume he did. Then in the evening we had dinner together . . .'

Some memory was making her uncomfortable, Thanet could tell, by the whitening of her knuckles as her clasped hands tightened, the way she adjusted her position in her chair.

'You, your husband and your brother?'

27

'That's right,' she said impatiently. 'Really, Inspector, you do like to dot your i's, don't you?'

'You said your daughter was here?'

'She'd gone off to visit friends again.'

'In London?'

'No, locally.'

'What did you talk about at dinner, Mrs Hamilton?'

She met his gaze squarely but Thanet saw the toe of her shoe tilt as her toes bunched up in tension. Feet, he found, were always an excellent indicator of state of mind. 'This and that.' Her chin lifted and her tone was cool. The message was plain. *I don't see that it's any of your business.*

Thanet ignored it. 'Such as?'

She shrugged. 'Just general chat about what we'd been doing while he was away, what he'd been doing. We had a lot of catching up to do.'

Thanet decided not to probe any further for the moment. Later, if necessary, he promised himself. At the moment he just wanted to get the general picture. 'I see. And later, after dinner?'

'I didn't see him again after dinner.'

'And you, Mr Hamilton. Did you?'

'See him again?' Hamilton shook his head. 'No, I didn't.'

'Didn't you think that strange?'

This time they both shook their heads, spoke together.

'Not at all, no . . .'

'Not in the least. Why should we?' This was Delia Hamilton. 'This isn't a council house, Inspector, we're not exactly tripping over each other all the time. And there are a number of ways in and out, you could go all day without seeing someone else who is living in the house if your activities didn't happen to coincide.'

'Did he say what he intended to do, after dinner?'

More headshakes.

'And you, what did you do?'

The Hamiltons looked at each other. 'You drove to the

28

station, to fetch Adam, didn't you, darling?' said Hamilton.

'Yes.'

'What time would that have been, Mrs Hamilton?' Thanet sensed the heightening of Lineham's attention, quite rightly. Any mention of either of the Hamiltons driving anywhere the previous evening could be highly relevant.

'I must have left about twenty-five past seven. Adam's train was getting in at seven-thirty and it takes about five minutes to get to the station.'

Thanet remembered what Doc Mallard had said. *Say between six o'clock and four a.m., then, to be on the safe side.*

'So you would have arrived back about twenty to eight?'

'Something like that, yes.'

'And you didn't pass your brother on the way, either going or coming back?'

Delia Hamilton's eyes snapped. 'Don't you think I would have said so, if I had? I told you, I didn't see him at all after dinner.'

'What about you, Mr Hamilton?'

'I was working in the office. I usually do, in the evenings.' Hamilton's eyes narrowed. 'Look, why all the questions about what we were doing?' His voice grew a little more strident. 'For that matter, now I think about it, why all the questions about what Leo was doing during the day yesterday? What possible relevance can it have? I appreciate that you need to find out about his movements last night in order to discover how the accident happened, but surely it should be enough for us to say that the last time we saw him was at dinner?'

'I'm afraid it's not quite as simple as that.'

'Why not?'

'Yes, why not?' said Delia Hamilton.

They both stared at him, waiting for a reply.

Thanet hesitated. How much should he say, at this stage?

'Well?' said Delia Hamilton impatiently.

29

Thanet shrugged. 'A man has died, Mrs Hamilton, and it's our job to find out how and why. I can't tell at this stage what information might be relevant.'

'But it was a simple hit and run, surely,' said Hamilton. 'Unless you're suggesting . . . ?'

'It's a little difficult,' said Thanet carefully, 'to see how Mr Martindale could have landed in that ditch in the position in which he was lying without, shall we say, a little help.'

' "A little help" . . .' said Hamilton. 'My God, Inspector, you're surely not suggesting that someone *put* him there?'

Thanet shrugged. 'I'm afraid I can't say any more at present.'

'But – '

'Look here – '

Again, they spoke together. Delia Hamilton deferred to her husband with a glance.

'Are you saying,' he said incredulously, 'that Leo was *murdered*?'

Thanet was saved from a reply. The door, which must have been unlatched, was pushed open and a head appeared.

'Sorry, couldn't help hearing. Why the surprise, Dad? You always did say Uncle Leo would have come to a bad end.'

It was a boy of fourteen or fifteen, though you would never have guessed it from the way he was dressed. Hair slicked down with brilliantine, he was wearing a navy-blue pin-striped suit, white shirt and narrow knitted tie. A white silk scarf hung loosely around his neck and he was carrying a trilby hat tucked under one arm and a silver-topped walking stick. Coming further into the room he posed with one hand on the stick, the other shoved into his trouser pocket.

There were further shocks to come. 'Sounds interesting,' said a female voice, and a girl of seventeen followed him into the room. She, too, was apparently making a statement of some kind by her appearance, though Thanet couldn't quite make out what it was. Rebellion against her upper-crust background, perhaps? She sported hair in stiff porcupine

30

spikes, skull-like make-up with hollowed cheekbones and shadowed eye-sockets and an all-black outfit of high heels, tights, sweater and mini-skirt so short that it was more of a frill than a garment.

Thanet sent up a silent prayer of thankfulness that so far Bridget's adolescent revolt had gone no further than a mild flirtation with heavy eye make-up.

With a glance at Thanet Hamilton stood up. 'Were you two listening at the door?' he said angrily.

'Oh come on, Dad,' said Adam. 'Eavesdropping will get you everywhere, you know that.' He gave Thanet an amused look. 'As in this case. You're the fuzz, I suppose?'

'As you say,' said Thanet drily, casting a warning glance at Lineham. The sergeant, ever-sensitive to insults to his superior, had stiffened. PC Yeoman's expression, he noticed with amusement, was suitably wooden.

'Out!' said Hamilton, advancing menacingly on his off-spring. But they stood their ground.

'Stop coming over the heavy father, Dad,' said Tessa languidly. 'We've merely come to offer our assistance, like good citizens. I should've thought you would approve. You're always trying to get us to conform.'

'That's enough,' said their mother sharply. 'You heard what your father said. Off you go. Now!'

Reluctantly they began to turn away. 'Just when the conversation was getting interesting,' muttered Adam.

Thanet looked at the Hamiltons. 'I'm sorry, but would you mind very much if I did have a word with them? They might be able to help.'

'Great!' said Adam, dropping his pose and displaying a child-like eagerness to be in on the action.

The Hamiltons exchanged glances.

'How can they possibly help?' said Delia.

'Oh Mum!' Tessa was scornful. 'How can he tell unless he tries to find out?'

And without waiting for further permission they crossed to

a settee at right angles to the one on which their parents were sitting and sat down, looking at Thanet expectantly.

Hamilton stood up. 'I'm going!' he said in disgust. 'If you don't mind,' he added sarcastically.

Thanet waved a hand. 'Fine.'

'But I've got to go too!' said his wife. 'There are masses of things to be done.'

But her objection was too late. Hamilton had already left.

'I don't think there's anything else I want to ask you at the moment, Mrs Hamilton,' said Thanet. 'So if you'd prefer to leave . . .'

She shot her children a furious glance, clearly torn between her need to attend to her duties and a reluctance to leave the young people alone with the policemen, for fear of what they would say. 'No, I'll stay a little longer.'

'He won't eat us, Mum, you go,' urged Tessa.

Delia pressed her lips together, shook her head and settled back into her chair. Her children exchanged glances, rolled their eyes and sighed.

'Oh, *Mum*,' said Adam.

'Well now,' said Thanet, and introduced himself and Lineham. 'PC Yeoman you already know, no doubt.'

They glanced at Yeoman and nodded.

'Actually,' said Thanet, 'I'm not sure whether you can help us much, Adam.'

The boy's face fell. 'Why not?'

'Well, I gather you didn't get home until twenty to eight last night, so unless you saw your uncle after that . . . Did you?'

Adam shook his head reluctantly. 'No. I did go and knock on his door some time during the evening, but there was no reply.'

'What time was that?'

He frowned. 'Let me think. I had something to eat, then I went up to my room and unpacked . . . It must have been between half-past eight and nine.'

'Was the door locked?'

'Yes.' A defensive glance at his mother. 'I tried the handle because I thought he might have been in the bathroom, and not heard me.'

And he might have been, thought Thanet, and locked his door against just this type of eventuality. So they were no further forward.

'And now, of course, I'll never know what he was like.'

It sounded like genuine regret. To a boy of Adam's age the mysterious wicked uncle who disappeared into the blue never to be seen or heard of again was no doubt an intriguing figure.

He turned on his sister. 'And you can stop looking so smug! Just because you happened to be here — '

'Adam!' said his mother sharply.

'What about you, Tessa?' said Thanet.

But before she could reply there was a knock on the door.

'Come in,' said Delia, with evident relief.

A maid entered. 'Sorry to interrupt, ma'am, but a lot more policemen have arrived.' A glance at Thanet. 'They're asking for the Inspector.'

'Thank you,' said Thanet. 'Tell them I'll be out in just a few minutes.' He turned back to Tessa and raised an expectant eyebrow. 'Did you see your uncle last night?'

'Not last night, no. But I did have a natter with him earlier.'

'Oh, when was that?' said her mother sharply.

'I ran into him on my way downstairs yesterday morning, so naturally I introduced myself and he suggested coffee in the conservatory.' She rolled her eyes. 'He was real dishy.'

'Tessa!'

'Well, he was! So smooth and . . . well, he was *int*eresting. I mean, he'd travelled all over the place, seen everything, done everything . . .'

'And everyone!' murmured Adam, *sotto voce*.

'What was that?' snapped his mother. 'What did you say?'

33

Adam and his sister flicked amused glances at each other. 'Nothing, Ma, no need for convolutions of the under-garments.'

'Adam!'

Lady Bracknell couldn't have put more disapprobation into those two syllables, thought Thanet.

'I would remind you,' she said furiously, 'that this is an official interview.' She cast a disgusted look at Lineham's notebook. 'So just watch what you are saying, if you don't mind.'

'Don't worry, Mrs Hamilton, I have teenaged children of my own,' said Thanet. He could imagine Ben's comments if he saw these two. 'Couple of *posers*!' Ben would say.

He turned back to Tessa. 'Did he give you any details of his activities over the last few years?'

She shook her head and the black spikes quivered. 'Not really, no. Just that he'd been living in the South of France.'

'Did he say what he'd been doing for a living?'

Tessa gave a shout of laughter. 'Work, you mean? You must be joking. Dear Uncle Leo was what Grandmother's generation would have called a lounge lizard.'

'Tessa!' Her mother again.

'Oh, come off it, Ma. What's the point of pretending? I'd guess he lived off women, rich widows mostly, I should think.'

Delia Hamilton stood up, propelled by the force of her indignation. 'That's enough, Tessa! I won't hear your uncle slandered in this way. The interview is over, Inspector. Come on you two, out. And this time I really mean it.'

'But Ma,' Tessa protested, 'that wasn't slander. Slander is false report and that was – '

'ENOUGH!' said Delia. 'Just go, will you?'

And this time, they went.

FOUR

'So what d'you think, Mike?'

They were eating sandwiches provided for them by Mrs Hamilton while awaiting the arrival of the housekeeper, Mona Byfleet. PC Yeoman had been despatched to the village to help Thanet's men in the house-to-house enquiries, while others had been detailed to locate and examine all the vehicles at Longford Hall in an attempt to find the grey one suspected of running Martindale down. DC Bentley had been allocated the task of interviewing the guests, DC Swift the rest of the staff.

'No one's exactly broken-hearted, that's for sure. Mmm, these sandwiches are good.' Lineham lifted the upper layer of bread and peered inside. 'Tuna, sweetcorn and mayonnaise, I'd say. Good combination. I'll have to tell Louise.'

'If you could drag your attention away from the ingredients of your sandwich, Mike, I'd be interested to hear if you think there might be a case to answer.'

'Sorry, sir.' Lineham shrugged. 'As you would say, it's early days yet. But it seems to me that Martindale wasn't exactly the type to endear himself to people, was he? And there is the question of a nice juicy inheritance at stake.'

'Quite.'

'It'd be interesting to know whether the matter was actually discussed.'

'Exactly.'

'I mean, I can't see the Hamiltons being overjoyed at the prospect of going halves in the hotel and presumably the estate, can you, sir, whatever Mr Hamilton says about there being plenty to go around.'

'For that matter, from what we've heard of Martindale I can't really see him being happy to relinquish half of what was rightfully his, however much work his sister and brother-in-law had put in over the last few years.'

'No. And leaving the financial aspect aside, I shouldn't think Mr Hamilton would be too pleased to lose his position as squire, so to speak. He looks the type who rather enjoys the role.'

'I agree. It'll be interesting to see what Swift learns from the staff. In a place like this they'll be pretty thick on the ground, I should think. They might well have picked up some interesting snippets.'

'True.' Lineham yawned. He was looking tired, Thanet noticed.

There was silence while they finished the sandwiches and mulled over what they had learned.

'About time that housekeeper turned up,' said Thanet, draining his coffee cup. He would have liked to smoke his pipe but there wasn't time. He stood up. 'Let's go and see where she's got to.'

They went out into the entrance hall, which was empty of guests. It was now 1.15 and they were presumably at lunch. A man in formal butler's uniform of black jacket, striped trousers, white shirt and black tie was just disappearing through a door at the far side.

They crossed to the receptionist's desk.

'D'you know if anyone's managed to locate Mrs Byfleet yet?' said Thanet.

'Yes, we have. She does know you want to see her, she'll be here as soon as she can.' An apologetic smile. 'A minor crisis with one of the guests. Perhaps you'd like to wait by the fire. . .?'

'You may be able to help us.' Thanet smiled back at the girl, who was in her early twenties, small and well-spoken with a cloud of dark hair and bright dark eyes. She looked intelligent and observant. 'Were you on duty when Mr Martindale arrived, the day before yesterday?'

'Yes, I was.'

'It was about 6.15, I believe?'

'That's right. He turned up out of the blue, with no warning. I thought he was just another guest, though they usually book ahead, of course. He asked if we had a room for the night, and I booked him in. Then he asked for Mrs Hamilton.'

'What did he say, exactly?'

'Just said, "Is Mrs Hamilton around?" And when I said yes, I could find her if he wanted to speak to her, he said yes, he'd like to. And then he said, "Tell her her brother is here." I was surprised. I didn't even know she had a brother.'

'Did you see them meet?'

'Yes. When I gave Mrs Hamilton the message on the phone she sounded very taken aback, then she said, "I'll be down right away." '

'Did she seem pleased to see him?'

'Yes, she did. Though . . .' The girl hesitated, then bit her lip.

'What?'

She shook her head. 'Nothing.'

Thanet guessed that she had noticed a certain falseness in Delia's professed pleasure at her brother's arrival.

'What was Martindale wearing?'

She shrugged. 'Sports jacket, I think. And a black-and-white checked tweed overcoat. I remember that because he took it off and laid it across the corner of my desk.'

'Did he say anything else?'

She shook her head. 'I don't think so. Oh, there was just one thing . . .'

'Yes?'

'While he was waiting for Mrs Hamilton – just before she

arrived, in fact — Mrs Byfleet came out into the hall from the drawing-room with a young man, and he nodded at them and said, "Who's that?" So I told him, it was Miss Hamilton's boyfriend. He was just going to say something else when Mrs Hamilton arrived.'

'This young man, who is he?'

'Toby Fever. He's local. His father has a business in the village, he's a haulage contractor.'

Not quite Tessa Hamilton's class, thought Thanet. He wondered why Martindale should have been interested.

'Did you see Mr Martindale talk to him at all?'

'No.'

'Or anyone else, for that matter? You must see all the comings and goings, here.'

'He passed the time of day with one or two of the guests, that's all. Ah, there's Mrs Byfleet now.'

Thanet and Lineham turned to look at the woman coming down the staircase. Delia Hamilton hadn't been too pleased at the prospect of their interviewing her. 'She's not been too well lately, and I don't want her upset. She's . . . well, she's pregnant, with their first child, and she's in her thirties, she's finding it hard going. And I don't want to lose her. She's very efficient and hardworking, she'd be very difficult to replace. It's not easy finding suitable staff for a place like this.'

It was true that Mrs Byfleet didn't look well, thought Thanet. She was, he guessed, about six months pregnant, though her long, dark green dress in some stiff silky material was well cut to conceal the fact. But her narrow face was pale, her short brown hair, despite its good styling, dull and lifeless.

'Mrs Byfleet?' He stepped forward to introduce himself. 'Perhaps we could go into the small sitting-room we've been using . . . ?'

After a brief word with the receptionist she accompanied them back into the little blue-and-gold room, choosing an upright armchair into which she sank with a little sigh.

38

'Hard morning?' said Thanet with a smile.

'One of the guests had a fall. She's all right, though, thank heaven, just twisted her ankle. She's lying down now. But I shall have to go up and see her again shortly.'

'We won't keep you long. We just wanted to ask you if you could give us any idea of Mr Martindale's movements yesterday.'

'Let me see . . .' She passed a hand over her forehead as if to collect her thoughts. 'Well, he had breakfast in his room at nine, then I next saw him in the conservatory. He was having coffee with Tessa, Miss Hamilton. Then I saw him go out – for a walk, I assumed. He came back for a light lunch with Mr and Mrs Hamilton, then he went out again, to the village, that time.'

'He told you he was going to the village?'

'Yes. I was in the hall and he stopped for a chat, said he was going to see how much it had changed. I told him I thought probably very little. That was all. Then . . .' she faltered.

'Then?'

She shook her head. 'I was just trying to think. I'm not sure when he got back, but he had dinner with the Hamiltons again.'

'And afterwards?'

'I don't know what he did afterwards.'

Alerted by some evasiveness in her tone, Thanet persisted. 'Did you see him again at all, after he'd had dinner?'

'No.'

She met Thanet's eye almost defiantly. She was lying, Thanet was sure of it. But what about? Had there been an incident she didn't want to tell him about, out of loyalty to the Hamiltons?

'Were Mr and Mrs Hamilton pleased to see him?'

'Of course.'

But there was a note of falsity in the affirmation.

'It was a shock to them, of course, they thought he was dead, it would have been a shock to anyone . . .'

'You didn't see any sign of . . . shall we say, disharmony, between them?'

She shook her head. 'No.' Her tone lacked conviction, but she obviously wasn't going to go back on what she had said.

'You like working here, Mrs Byfleet?'

For the first time a genuine smile gave warmth to her response. 'Yes, I do. It suits us very well – my husband and I have a flat over the old stables, he looks after maintenance, and acts as chauffeur when necessary. It's a lovely house to work in, so many beautiful things, and Mrs Hamilton is a good employer, very fair. She expects you to work hard, but she works just as hard herself, so you don't mind.'

'How long have you been here?'

'Just over three years.'

And according to Giles Hamilton Delia's father had died four years ago. She hadn't wasted much time in getting things moving. With an estate like this there must have been considerable legal battles to be fought, in view of the fact that the heir was missing, before she got permission to proceed with her plans.

'And you opened two years ago, I believe?'

'That's right.'

'So you helped get it off the ground, so to speak?'

'Yes. Mrs Hamilton worked like a slave; we all did.'

'It must be very satisfying to see it become such a thriving business.'

'Oh yes, it has been. We're quiet at the moment, of course, mid-February isn't exactly the most popular time for a break in the country, but we've built up a very good reputation, I think, and for most of the year we're pretty busy.'

Which explained why the housekeeper clearly felt such a fierce loyalty to her employer. Having been in on the project since the beginning, she must feel an almost proprietorial interest in its success.

Thanet rose. 'What I should like to do now is take a look at Mr Martindale's room. It's all right,' he added, seeing the

40

hesitation in her face, 'Mrs Hamilton has given permission.'

'Of course.' She rose, a little clumsily, pushing herself up on the arms of her chair. 'I'll take you up.'

'You've worked in the hotel trade long?' said Thanet conversationally, accommodating his pace to hers as she led them up the graceful staircase.

'All my life, you could say. My parents ran a hotel. Not like this one, of course.' And she glanced around at the profusion of expensive hot-house flowers, the oil paintings on the walls, the gleaming antiques and rich variety of decorative objects.

'Forgive my asking, but aren't the guests ever tempted to walk off with any of these?'

'Not the guests,' she said wryly.

Meaning that the staff were, thought Thanet. Scarcely surprising, really. With so much on display there must be a temptation to think that the odd piece of porcelain or silver might not be missed.

'The guests are usually overwhelmed by it all,' she went on. 'Especially the Americans. They've never actually stayed anywhere quite like this before and they often walk around in a sort of daze for a day or two, just looking and looking.' She gave a little laugh. 'It's interesting, in a very old house like this there are bound to be inconveniences you wouldn't find in a modern hotel, but in all the time I've been here I've never had anyone complain. They just accept it as part of the general, well . . .'

'Ambience?' supplied Thanet.

'That's right. They're almost, well, in awe of it, I think, and either complaining or stealing anything would be a sort of sacrilege.'

At the top of the staircase they had turned left along a broad landing and at the third door along she stopped. 'Here we are. I put Mr Martindale in the Chinese suite.' She pushed open the door and stood back. 'And now, if you don't mind . . .?'

41

'Ah yes, your invalid. Just one other point before you go. Staff. How many are there?'

'Theoretically there should be thirty in all. I say "theoretically" because in practice it's very difficult to recruit staff for a place like this, so we're always a few short – we're rather isolated here, you see, there's nothing for them to do when they're off duty, and many of the younger ones can't afford cars, so they get bored and leave.'

'So at the moment you're how many, in all?'

'Eight in the kitchen, we're two short there, and seventeen in the house, we're two housemaids and one parlourmaid short.'

'So apart from the kitchen staff you have a butler, a footman – '

'A head footman,' she corrected him, 'then a footman, six housemaids, four parlourmaids, two receptionists, my husband and myself. Then outside there's the gardener – groundsman rather, I suppose you'd call him – and his assistant.'

'And how many of those live in?'

'Ten, excluding my husband and myself.'

'I see. Thank you, you've been very helpful.' Thanet dismissed her with a nod and a smile.

Inside the Chinese suite Lineham looked around and said, 'Wow! Some hotel room!'

There was only one word to describe it, thought Thanet: sumptuous. His living-room would have fitted into it three times over and there was so much for the eye to feast upon that it was difficult to take it all in. He pivoted slowly, looking.

Predictably the wallpaper was Chinese, in a pale celadon-green with a delicate design of bamboo and herons etched in cream. On the wide, highly polished oak floorboards lay a silky cream carpet with a green and rose design, and the elaborate hangings of the four-poster bed and the long draperies at the windows were in deeper shades of green and rose. On either side of the bed stood low round tables covered with circular floor-length rose-coloured cloths topped with smaller cloths in creamy lace. Half the room was furnished as a sitting-room, with deep, soft sofas and armchairs grouped around a leaping log fire protected by a brass fireguard. There were a number of paintings, including two Chinese scroll paintings of misty mountain landscapes and a series of framed prints of ancient Chinese costumes. Various pieces of antique furniture, including a slender writing desk supplied with headed notepaper and envelopes, were scattered around the room. Everywhere were small personal touches: apart from the ubiquitous television set and a fine enamelled clock, there were pot plants; two arrangements of fresh flowers, in various tones of cream and pink to match the decor; a small wicker basket of wrapped sweets; a bowl of fruit with plates, damask napkins and fruit knives beside it; a tray of drinks; a pile of books both non-fiction and fiction, the latter all recently published novels; and an array of new magazines.

'Wow!' said Lineham again. 'Wonder how much it costs to spend a night in a place like this?'

'We'll pick up a brochure on the way out,' said Thanet.

'I'm serious!' said Lineham. 'If I started saving now, for our wedding anniversary . . . Louise would love it!'

Thanet rather wished he'd had that idea himself and irritation that he hadn't made him terse. 'Come on, Mike, just remember why we're here, will you? Let's see what we can find out about Martindale.'

It looked as though Martindale had intended to stay some time. The old-fashioned leather suitcase plastered with airline stickers which had been stowed on top of the wardrobe was large, and the wardrobe and chest of drawers were full of clothes, all expensive if somewhat the worse for wear. As well as a dinner jacket, there were several tailor-made suits and Thanet looked into an inside pocket for the tailor's label: *Filligrew and Browne, Sporting Tailors. Conduit Street*

21.9.72. Quickly, he examined the others. None was more recent than 1981. The shoes, six pairs, all Church's, were well-worn, some of the shirts were beginning to fray at collar and cuffs and the underclothes definitely needed replacing.

'Looks as though he was a bit short of the ready,' said Lineham. 'He must have nearly fallen out of that barber's chair with delight when he read that article.'

'Quite. Short of the ready but definitely not at his wits' end. If he had been he would have pawned those long ago.' Thanet nodded at the objects scattered on the chest of drawers: a pair of silver-backed hairbrushes, silver hip-flask, and gold cufflinks.

'True.'

Thanet wandered into the bathroom which displayed the same attention to detail: bowl of potpourri; cut-glass dish of cotton puffs; posy of cotton buds; little basket of toiletries – shower caps, shampoos, foaming bath oil, and a selection of Floris soaps. The towels were thick, soft and in plentiful supply and two luxurious towelling robes with *Longford Hall* embroidered across the pockets hung behind the door. Martindale's possessions were scattered about: razor, shaving cream, badger shaving brush, aftershave, toothbrush, toothpaste. His sponge bag held supplies of paracetamol, Rennies, Alka-Seltzer, and antiseptic cream.

'Nothing much here, Mike.'

There was no reply and it occurred to Thanet that all sounds from next door had ceased. Raising his eyebrows he returned to the bedroom to find that Lineham was asleep on the sofa in front of the fire.

'Mike!'

Lineham awoke with a start. 'Oh, sorry, sir. I must have dropped off. The fire . . .'

'You did drop off. And I'm the one who's sorry. Sorry that you are so tired you actually fall asleep in the middle of a murder enquiry!'

'We don't know that it's a murder enquiry yet, sir.'

44

Thanet waved a hand irritably. 'A potential murder enquiry, then. You know perfectly well what I mean. And stop avoiding the issue.'

'I really am sorry . . .'

'It's an explanation I want, Mike, not an apology.'

Lineham rubbed his eyes. 'It's my brother-in-law.'

Thanet gave an exasperated sigh and sat down in an armchair facing the sergeant. 'What's that supposed to mean?'

Lineham yawned. 'I was up half the night talking to him. He's having problems with his marriage and he just turned up on our doorstep last night with a suitcase.'

'Left his wife, has he?'

Lineham shrugged. 'Temporarily, anyway.'

'Look, Mike, I'm sorry your brother-in-law is having marital problems and I don't want to appear unsympathetic, but this really will not do, you know. I simply cannot have you dozing off in the middle of an investigation, murder or otherwise.'

'Yes, I realise that, sir. It won't happen again.'

'Won't it? Leaving the question of your brother-in-law aside, I've noticed that you seem to have been looking very tired lately. So what's wrong?'

'Nothing, sir. Not *wrong*, exactly. It's just that Richard still hasn't settled at school yet. I don't think he gets on with his teacher, she seems to have taken against him. So he isn't sleeping very well, wakes up every night crying, that sort of thing. We take it in turns to get up, but it's pretty tiring, never getting a decent night's sleep. Last night put the lid on it, I think.'

'OK, I understand. I've got something similar going on at home myself, as a matter of fact. Ben's just changed schools, as you know, and he's finding it pretty difficult having much stiffer competition. At his last school he could just coast along, but now . . . Anyway, I appreciate your difficulty. But Mike, you're going to have to do something about it. Discuss

45

it with Louise, go and see the Headmaster, but do *something*. And as far as your brother-in-law is concerned, well, I'm sure you'll find a tactful way of ensuring that any discussions you have are before bedtime. Right?'

'Yes, sir, of course. Really, it won't happen again, I promise.'

'I hope not. Now, what have you got there? Is that the key to Martindale's suitcase?'

Dangling from Lineham's hand was a tiny key on a leather thong. 'I should think so. It was in the toe of one of his socks.'

'Let's take a look.'

'Ah,' said Lineham with satisfaction as it turned sweetly in the lock.

'Now this looks a bit more interesting,' said Thanet.

Inside was Martindale's passport and a large brown envelope which looked much handled and which crackled when he picked it up. They sat down side by side on the sofa to examine their finds. The passport didn't tell them anything useful. It had been issued only a year ago and bore no stamps; if Martindale had done any travelling since then it had presumably been in the European community, most of whose member countries no longer bothered to stamp the passports of internal travellers.

There remained only the envelope. Thanet tipped out its contents. These looked more promising: an address book, a bundle of letters and postcards, and another, smaller envelope of photographs.

Lineham picked up the address book and flicked through it. 'We're going to have our work cut out if we have to check all these.'

Thanet split the bundle of letters in two. 'Take a quick look at these, will you? We'll go through them thoroughly later. Put them in chronological order, if you can read the date stamps.'

They were all, they discovered, from women and almost all of them were addressed to hotels or readdressed from one hotel to another. The theme was almost always the same, regret that the sender had not heard from Martindale as she had hoped to, coupled with anxious requests for news of him. Several of them delicately referred to 'loans' made to him, and one or two were more strongly worded requests for information about 'investments' made by him on the sender's behalf.

'Love 'em and leave 'em was certainly his motto,' said Lineham.

'Preferably with a pocket full of cash, by the look of it.' Thanet tapped one of the postcards, most of which were of the 'wish you were here' variety. 'Looks as though this one was the last.'

The card was date-stamped 10.11.84 and was a photograph of the Byron Hotel in Worthing. The message on the back read, *Room ready for your return. Roll on the 23rd.* It was signed 'B' and addressed to the Hôtel Paradis in Nice.

'Looks as though at some point he spent some time in Worthing,' said Lineham. 'It'd be a good hunting ground for Martindale's type, I should think.'

'You're assuming the room she's talking about is in the Byron Hotel. But it could simply mean that the sender was staying in the Byron when she wrote the card, and that the room she's referring to is in her own home.'

Lineham pursed his lips. 'It could, I suppose. But isn't the other interpretation much more likely?'

'No way of telling. In any case, after this there are no more letters or cards.'

'Perhaps it was at the Hôtel Paradis that Mr Martindale met this Frenchwoman he's supposed to have been living with.'

Thanet shrugged. 'Who knows? But I agree, it's a possibility. Pity there's no indication of who she is or where she lived.' He bundled the letters up and emptied out the envelope of photographs. Predictably, these were almost all of women, either alone or with Martindale, posing against

47

varying backgrounds. A few, though, were obviously older, smaller, of poorer quality and with curling corners. Thanet picked these up and studied them more closely. 'I think this must be Martindale and his sister, look.'

They were recognisably the same pair, both wearing riding breeches and sitting on the steps leading up to the front door of Longford Hall; Delia with a cloud of dark hair framing those classically beautiful features, Leo handsome and carefree, one arm resting lightly across her shoulders.

'And these must be their parents,' said Lineham.

Tea on the lawn this time, the man lounging in a deck chair, the woman elegantly erect, caught in the act of pouring tea. They were a handsome pair, and Thanet, always interested in the quirkiness of genes, noted that it was her father Delia resembled, and Leo his mother. He wondered how the Martindales would have reacted to this present situation: with dignity and the famous British stiff upper lip, he imagined.

'Pretty pathetic, really, isn't it?' said Lineham, gesturing at the letters, the photographs.

'What do you mean?'

'Well, presumably this stuff, the stuff that's here, in this room, is all the gear he had.'

'I imagine so, yes.'

'I mean, someone like him, with his sort of background . . . What went wrong, I wonder?'

'What made him leave it all behind, you mean?'

'Yes.'

'With any luck, we'll find out.'

But Lineham was right, it was pathetic. And something more, too. Thanet couldn't believe that this small pile of letters represented the sum total of Martindale's correspondence over twenty years or so, or that there hadn't been many more photographs than this. No, in his view, they were the end result of a fairly ruthless weeding-out process. What had been Martindale's criterion? One letter or card, one photograph per woman? What Thanet was holding, he realised, were the trophies of one man's amorous past. He had a sudden, vivid picture of Martindale sitting in a chair, glass of whisky in hand, poring over them with a small, self-satisfied smile on his face. With a shiver of distaste he began to bundle them all back into the envelope. Later he would sort out which leads were worth following up, if any.

There was a knock at the door.

'Come in.'

It was one of the DCs, accompanied by a housemaid.

'What is it, Markham?'

The girl turned away and the constable shut the door behind him before saying, with understandable triumph, 'We think we've found the car, sir.'

Thanet stood up. 'Oh?'

'Well, a van, actually, sir. It was parked at the back of the hotel. A 1981 Bedford HA. It's grey, going rusty and we found a couple of threads which look as though they might match the victim's overcoat snagged on a piece of flaking metal just beside the front offside headlight.'

'Excellent. Who does it belong to?'

'The hotel, sir.'

'Right. Let's go and take a look, shall we?'

FIVE

Thanet and Lineham returned to the lobby near the front door to put on their boots. While they were doing so Tessa Hamilton passed through with a young man in tow, presumably the one in whom Leo Martindale had shown an interest. What had Mrs Byfleet said his name was? Fever, that was it. Toby Fever. Thanet caught no more than a glimpse of him, but there was something vaguely familiar about his features. Could he have a record, perhaps?

As the three policemen stepped outside the young people drove off in a newish Ford Escort, its wheels skidding on the packed snow of the drive.

After the warmth of the house the icy air was a shock to the system and Thanet turned up the collar of his sheepskin jacket, casting an apprehensive look at the sky which had that ominously leaden look which heralds snow.

'Looks as though we might get some more,' said Lineham.

'Hope not.' Thanet raised his voice to speak to Markham who was leading the way along the front of the house like an eager dog guiding its master to a particularly exciting find. 'This van. Who normally drives it?'

Markham slowed down. 'Chap by the name of Tiller, apparently, sir. He's the groundsman. This way.'

They turned right, along the side of the house.

'Ah, yes.' Thanet remembered Mona Byfleet mentioning him. 'He's got an assistant, I believe.'

'I don't know about that, sir. Someone's gone to fetch Mr Tiller, he should be there by now. Your Land Rover's back, by the way, sir.'

'Good.'

They rounded the back corner of the house and a large cobbled yard opened out before them, surrounded on three sides by a range of low, picturesque buildings in brick and tile. At the far side, standing around a small grey van, was a group of policemen stamping their feet against the cold. Amongst them was a man in boots, parka and cloth cap.

'Yes, that'll be him,' said Markham with satisfaction.

As they drew closer Thanet saw that Tiller was in his sixties, a burly figure with weatherbeaten face and angry blue eyes.

'Mr Tiller?' said Thanet.

The man thrust his chin forward aggressively. 'You in charge of this lot? What the hell's going on?'

'I'm sure you've heard about Mr Martindale's . . . accident, by now, Mr Tiller. We need to ask you some questions. Perhaps we could go somewhere a little warmer? A garage, perhaps, or a stable?'

Tiller stood his ground. 'Why?'

Thanet walked around the van and inspected the spot indicated by one of his men. It looked as though they were right and this was the vehicle they were after. A couple of threads of cloth were caught up in a snag of rusty metal. Thanet looked closer. Yes, black-and-white tweed by the look of them. He nodded at Lineham and the sergeant took out a pair of tweezers and a plastic sample bag.

Thanet straightened up.

'Mr Martindale appears to have been run down by a vehicle and it seems possible that it was this one. As you are apparently in charge of it – '

'Now just a minute. Are you suggesting . . . ?' Head down like an angry bull, Tiller appeared ready to charge.

Thanet sensed the tension in his men. The situation must

51

be defused. He smiled. 'I'm not suggesting anything, Mr Tiller. I merely want to ask you some questions. I'm sure you're as anxious as we are to get at the truth of the matter.' He turned to one of the policemen. 'Arrange for the van to be towed in, for inspection.'

Tiller hesitated, his eyes searching Thanet's face for any sign that he was being misled. Abruptly he turned away. 'This way,' he said gruffly.

He led the way to one of the outbuildings and pushed open the door. It was a storage shed for gardening equipment, with tools, work bench stacked with flower pots and other clutter, sacks of peat, fertiliser and compost leaning against the walls and several motor mowers of assorted shapes and sizes. It was only marginally less cold than outside.

Tiller leaned against the bench and folded his arms. 'Well?'

No point in beating about the bush or attempting to soften the man's mood. Thanet glanced at Lineham to check that he was ready to take notes. 'Tell us about the van.'

'What d'you want to know?'

'I understand you're in charge of it?'

'Sort of.'

'Meaning?'

'Everybody uses it. So why pick on me?' Tiller was becoming belligerent again.

'Please, Mr Tiller, do understand that I'm not accusing you of anything.' *At this stage, anyway.* 'I'm merely trying to find out who drives it, when and for what reason, that's all. And the sooner I find out the sooner this interview will be over. So if you could just give me the information . . .'

'Mr and Mrs Hamilton, Mr Talion, Mr and Mrs Byfleet, Andy – the lad who helps me. That's it.'

Thanet's heart sank. 'I see. All of them have keys to it?'

'Yes – except for Andy. He borrows mine, when he needs it. The van stands out there in the yard, and whoever wants to use it uses it.'

'Mr Talion. He's . . . ?'

'The farm manager.'

'I thought Mr Hamilton managed the estate.'

'Mr Hamilton *administers* the estate. It's Jack Talion who actually runs it.'

'I see. And where does Mr Talion live?'

'In Home Farm.'

'And where is that?'

Tiller waved a hand. 'Over the other side of the Hall.'

'And you?'

'Where do I live, d'you mean?'

Patience, Thanet told himself. 'That's right, yes.'

'Here, in the stable yard. They converted one of the outbuildings,' he added grudgingly.

'I see.' Thanet did see. This meant that everyone who had keys to the van lived sufficiently close to have had access to it last night.

'So, did any of them use the van last night?'

'How should I know?'

Thanet sighed. It looked as though every drop of information was going to have to be squeezed out of Tiller. He signalled to Lineham to take over.

'What about you, Mr Tiller? Did you use it?'

'What if I did? I had every right, didn't I?'

'No one is saying you didn't. But in the circumstances . . .'

'Why don't you come right out with it? You think I ran him down, don't you? Go on, admit it.'

'Mr Tiller, as Inspector Thanet has explained, we have no preconceived ideas about what happened last night – '

'Don't give me that guff. In that case why aren't you talking to the rest of them, eh? Go on, tell me why.'

'Because,' said Lineham with admirable restraint, 'we have only just discovered that it is likely to be this particular vehicle that was involved in the . . . accident.'

'You did it too, didn't you?' said Tiller triumphantly.

'Did what?'

'Paused before you said "accident".' His eyes flicked at

53

Thanet. 'Just like he did, just now. Go on, admit it, you don't think it was an accident at all, do you? You think it was deliberate.'

'Mr Tiller, can't you understand that at this stage we really don't know what happened? We are, I repeat, merely trying to find out. We shall of course,' said Lineham, raising his voice as Tiller again opened his mouth to interrupt, 'be talking to all the other people who have access to the van, but as you are nominally in charge of it we came to you first. So if you could just tell us if you did use it last night, where you went and what time . . .'

Tiller was shaking his head in disbelief and shifting impatiently from one foot to the other.

'Very well, Mr Tiller,' said Thanet. 'If you don't choose to tell us at present, that is your prerogative. But we must have this information, so if you'd be so kind as to accompany us back to headquarters we can all wait in greater comfort until you are ready to give it to us.'

Tiller was nodding his head with satisfaction. 'Just as I thought. Arresting me, aren't you?'

'Not at all.' Thanet was holding back his exasperation with difficulty. 'In fact, if you'd just give us the information we need we'd all be able to get on with our work that much quicker.' Then, as the man still remained silent, regarding him suspiciously through narrowed eyes, 'Come on, man, let's get it over with. As I said before, the sooner you tell us, the sooner we'll be finished, can't you see that? If you have nothing to hide there's nothing to worry about.'

Tiller gave a contemptuous snort and turned his back on them to gaze out at the yard through the cobwebbed window.

Silence.

Then, just as Thanet was about to give up and hand the man over to be taken back to Sturrenden to cool his heels for a while, Tiller swung around. 'I suppose you're right,' he said reluctantly. 'If I've nothing to hide . . .'

Thanet nodded. 'That's right,' he encouraged.

Tiller hesitated a moment longer. 'As a matter of fact I did use it last night. I went to the pub.'

The atmosphere eased. 'Good,' said Thanet.

'What time was that, Mr Tiller?' said Lineham.

'Half-past eight or thereabouts.'

Tiller, it seemed, usually spent Tuesday evenings in the village pub with a woman friend called Sonia Rankle, who also lived in Sutton-in-the-Weald, half a mile out on the Sturrenden road. He would pick her up soon after 8.30 and take her home at around 10.30 before returning to his own quarters at Longford Hall.

'And this was what happened last night?' said Thanet.

'Yes.'

'Now think very carefully, Mr Tiller. Did you, either on your way to the pub or on the way back, see Mr Martindale at all?'

The answer, of course, was predictable.

'No, I did not!'

A thought struck Thanet. 'You do know who I'm talking about, don't you?' To the groundsman Martindale might just have been one amongst a number of guests.

'I know him.' Tiller's response was wooden, arousing Thanet's interest.

'You mean, you know him because you've seen him around over the last couple of days, or because you knew him when he used to live here?'

'I'm local. I knew him before.'

Thanet strained to catch the overtones in Tiller's voice which, in contrast to all his previous responses, continued to be strictly neutral.

'And you're absolutely certain you didn't see him when you were out last night?'

Suddenly the man's belligerence returned in full force. 'I've bloody told you, haven't I? I knew you wouldn't believe me.'

'Is there any reason why we shouldn't believe you, Mr Tiller?'

'No! There is not!'

'In that case, we'll get on with our work. Come on, Sergeant.'

Tiller unfolded his arms as it dawned on him that the need to be on his guard was over. 'You mean, I can go?'

'Certainly. Thank you for your cooperation.'

They left him gazing after them in apparent disbelief.

SIX

'Interesting,' said Lineham, as soon as they were outside.

'What, specifically, Mike? The fact that he was so on the defensive or the fact that he clammed up when I asked if he knew Martindale before?'

'Both. I'd say he definitely has something to hide, wouldn't you?'

'No doubt about it. But it won't do any harm to let him stew for a bit while we find out if anyone else drove the van last night.' Thanet frowned. 'Pity so many people had access to it, though.'

'Who're we going to see first?'

'Out of courtesy it'd better be the Hamiltons. We'll start with him, I think. Presumably he is officially its owner.'

They went back into the house to find out where Hamilton was and were told that in the afternoons he usually worked in the Estate Office, which was in the stable block at the back of the house.

Retracing their steps Lineham said suddenly, 'So did Mrs Byfleet, for that matter.'

Like the partners in a long-established marriage, able to take up and lay down a thread of conversation without ever having to spell it out, Thanet knew at once what Lineham meant. 'Yes. I suspect she's either seen or heard something which she thinks would present the Hamiltons in a bad light.'

'She obviously feels a very strong loyalty towards Mrs Hamilton, at least.'

'Quite. That's an interesting point, actually. She hardly mentioned him.'

'Don't suppose she sees much of him, it'd be Mrs Hamilton she works with.'

'True.'

'There's the office, over there.'

Preoccupied earlier with Tiller and the van Thanet had not noticed the tastefully discreet OFFICE sign screwed to the wall beside one of the doors in the stable block. Guests at the hotel presumably shouldn't be made to feel that this was too much of a commercial enterprise.

Hamilton was seated at his desk dealing with paperwork. 'Ah, Inspector.'

'Sorry to trouble you again, Mr Hamilton.'

'Not at all, I was hoping for a word with you.' He waved a hand. 'Please, sit down.'

It was an attractive place in which to work, thought Thanet as he and Lineham sat down on a couple of upright chairs facing the desk. The original brick stable walls had been painted white, the overhead beams sandblasted to a smooth honey, the old granite floor sets cleaned and polished. Sturdy pine furniture and a huge map of the estate added to the atmosphere of prosperous country living. Even on a day like today the room was comfortably warm.

'I saw your men towing away our van. Do I gather that you think it was involved in the accident?'

'It seems possible,' said Thanet carefully. 'That's why I wanted to see you.'

'Oh?'

'We're trying to find out who drove it last night, and I gather that a number of people have keys to it, yourself included.'

'That's true.' Understandably, Hamilton's tone was now guarded.

'Did you, in fact, drive it last night?'

Hamilton hesitated only for a moment, presumably realising that sooner or later the truth was bound to emerge. 'Yes, I did, as a matter of fact. I went to pick up my daughter from Ashford, at about, oh, it must have been a quarter past eleven.'

Well within the time limit set by Doc Mallard.

'She doesn't drive?' Thanet was surprised. He would have expected a girl like Tessa to have taken her driving test soon after her seventeenth birthday, and he wouldn't have thought that there would be a shortage of vehicles for her to borrow, if she hadn't already been given a car of her own. Perhaps she was younger than she looked.

'Yes, of course she does. And last night she borrowed the Range Rover. Unfortunately, when she was ready to come home, she found it wouldn't start. So naturally she rang to ask if someone could come and collect her.'

'It seemed to be working all right this morning.'

Hamilton shrugged. 'It's a bit temperamental sometimes. Last night it was a very simple matter. When I got there I checked the sparking plugs' – he gave a self-deprecating smile – 'that's about my limit as far as mechanical failure is concerned. Anyway, I was in luck, one of them was loose and she was able to drive it home.'

'You'll understand that I must now ask if you saw your brother-in-law either on your way out or on the way back.'

'No I didn't. Anyway, what on earth do you think he would have been doing, wandering around outside at that hour on a freezing night like that?'

Thanet shrugged. 'What time did you get back?'

'Around ten past twelve.'

'Was it snowing then?'

'It was just starting as I turned into the drive.'

'Do you know of anyone else who drove the van last night? Presumably, when your wife went to pick up your son from the station, she would have used her own car.'

Hamilton's lips tightened. It was obvious that he had been expecting this. 'As a matter of fact no, she didn't.'

'She used the van?'

'Yes. The car she usually drives, the BMW, is in for repair. Some idiot backed into it when it was parked in the Stoneborough Centre in Maidstone last week. And of course, Tessa had the Range Rover.'

'And the BMW is the only car you have, apart from the Range Rover?'

'Well, there's the Rolls, but that's used strictly for business, to meet hotel guests or ferry them about. It's one of the luxury services we offer. She certainly wouldn't use it to pick Adam up from the station. Anyway, it wasn't here. Byfleet had driven it to Gatwick, to pick up the Americans and he didn't get back till eight.'

The door opened and Delia Hamilton came in with a flurry of cold air. 'Giles, what's all this I hear – ' She broke off when she saw Thanet and Lineham. 'Ah, Inspector. Why have they taken the van away? Is it anything to do with my brother's accident?'

Patiently, Thanet went over it all again, the strong possibility that the van had been involved, the necessity of finding out exactly who had driven it last night.

Delia had crossed to stand behind her husband, one hand on his shoulder as if to draw strength from the physical contact. 'Giles, have you told them that I . . . ?' She faltered.

'That you drove it last night?' He reached up to lay his hand reassuringly on hers. 'Yes, I have. So did I, if you remember.'

She paled, the beautiful bone structure of her face suddenly accentuated, briefly almost skull-like. 'Oh my God, so you did. To fetch Tessa.' She put up the other hand and pressed her fingers into her temple as if to ease a sudden onset of pain. 'I'd forgotten.'

'It's unfortunate that so many people have keys to the van,' said Thanet. 'I understand that apart from yourselves and Mr

Tiller, who presumably uses it most, both the Byfleets drive it and so does the farm manager, Mr Talion.'

'Jack! Oh God, he used it last night too! I didn't bother to tell you,' she said to her husband, 'because it didn't seem of any importance at the time.'

She and Hamilton exchanged a look full of unspoken messages which Thanet tried to read and failed. One thing was certain, however. For some reason the farm manager's name had some special significance for them, in this context. 'Jack? Would that be Mr Talion?'

'Yes.' Delia was still looking at her husband. 'Just after I got back from the station with Adam someone rang to say that some of our sheep had got out on to the road near the Linklaters' house — that's close to the junction with the Ashford Road,' she explained to Thanet. 'Jack — Mr Talion — had walked across from Home Farm to join us for a drink before dinner, he often does, and he said he'd attend to it. Of course, he didn't have his car with him so he went in the van.'

'That would have been at what time?'

She shrugged. 'Five minutes or so after I got back.'

'And that was about twenty to eight, you say? So, say a quarter to eight.'

'Something like that, I suppose.'

'And how long was he away?'

'I haven't the faintest idea. You'll have to ask him.'

'He's been with you long?'

'For years. He was farm manager in my father's time, and stayed on when my husband took over.'

'How many years?'

Delia frowned. 'I'm not sure, exactly. He came when I was a child. Twenty-five, thirty years, something like that. Again, you'll have to ask him. Or I suppose we could look it up in the records.'

'No, it doesn't matter. As you say, I can ask him.'

But it was interesting to learn that Talion, too, would have known Leo Martindale before he left the area.

'I didn't ask before, but why, exactly, did your brother go away?'

Delia gave an embarrassed laugh. 'I'm afraid my father's patience ran out. Leo was always a bit wild and Daddy was forever having to bail him out of one scrape or another. In the end, after he'd paid off his debts for the umpteenth time, he gave him a final warning: if he didn't mend his ways he would be out on his ear, no allowance, nothing.' She shrugged. 'Leo didn't pay any attention to the warning and out he went.'

'I assume your father therefore also cut your brother out of his will.'

Delia looked uncomfortable. 'Well no, he didn't. He couldn't. The Hall is entailed.'

'I thought most of those old entails were broken long ago.'

'Yes, most of them were, in 1925 I think Daddy said. But unfortunately ours was a little more complicated than that.'

'In what way?'

'I can't see how all this can possibly be relevant,' said Hamilton.

'It may well not be, Mr Hamilton. But I'd be grateful if your wife would explain, all the same.'

Delia Hamilton looked at her husband and he gave a reluctant nod.

'Well, it's a question of something called an entailed trust, actually, and as a matter of tradition the arrangement has been continued from one generation to the next, right from the time Longford Hall was first built. What happens is this. On the twenty-first birthday of the heir, the trust would in each generation be renegotiated so that before anyone actually inherited it, it was tied up for the generation beyond.'

'So that if, in fact, the heir ever wished to sell it, he couldn't?'

She nodded. 'That's right. Because it would be impossible to know exactly how many children he's going to have until he's dead. It's a very unusual arrangement, but it's what we've always done.'

'So you're saying that the trust had been renegotiated with Mr Martindale on his twenty-first birthday?'

'Yes.'

'And once set up it couldn't be broken?'

'That's right.' She sighed. 'Of course, no one envisaged a situation in which the heir couldn't be found. As it was, obviously someone had to administer the estate so the trustees allowed us to do so in my brother's absence.'

'And if he hadn't turned up by the time seven years had passed he would presumably have been assumed dead and the estate would have come to you?'

A tight nod.

No doubt they were all thinking the same thing, thought Thanet. *As it now does.*

'I see. Well, there's just one more question I must put to you.' And in the circumstances it was very difficult to think of a way of putting it tactfully. 'If it does turn out, as seems likely, that it was your van that ran your brother down, is there any reason why any of the people who have access to it wouldn't be sorry to see him dead?' *Apart from you, of course, with the king-sized motive which you've just handed to us.*

His delicacy was wasted. They were intelligent people and saw at once what he was asking, and its implications. They stared at him, in apparent disbelief.

'Let me get this straight,' said Hamilton at last. 'I asked you earlier if you were suggesting that Leo might have been murdered. I couldn't believe then that you were serious and I can't believe it now. But you are, aren't you? What you're really asking is whether or not any of these people – including us, I presume, as we also drive the van – had a motive for killing him?'

'This is crazy!' said his wife, clutching her head. 'I can't believe what I'm hearing. My brother has a perfectly straightforward accident and before we know where we are we're accused of murdering him!'

'No!' said Thanet. 'You're jumping to conclusions. I'm accusing no one of anything at the moment, I'm merely looking at all the possibilities. That is what I'm paid to do. And you must see that – '

There was a knock at the door.

'Come in,' called Hamilton, a little too heartily; relieved, no doubt, at the interruption.

It was Bentley. 'Sorry to disturb you, sir, but . . .' It was obvious that he had come across something interesting.

Thanet stood up. Clearly he wasn't going to get anything more out of the Hamiltons at present. 'All right, Bentley, we've finished here for the moment.'

Outside the light was fading and it was beginning to snow. Thanet turned up his collar again and pulled on his woolly hat. No point in freezing in order to look dignified. 'What is it?'

'One of the guests told me that he was out for a walk yesterday morning and he saw Mr Martindale having a blazing row with somebody.'

'Who?'

'He couldn't remember his name, though he had heard it – he saw him again last night when they were having drinks before dinner, and they were introduced. Anyway, he says he's the farm manager.'

'Talion,' said Lineham. 'Well well. I noticed the look Mrs Hamilton gave her husband when his name came up, didn't you?'

'Yes. Was this guest close enough to hear what the row was about?'

Bentley shook his head regretfully. 'No, unfortunately. But he did say that there was another man nearby, a tractor driver. Apparently the farm manager and this man were talking when Mr Martindale joined them. The farm labourer moved a little way away, tactful-like, and soon afterwards the row started.'

'But your witness thinks this tractor driver would still have been close enough to hear what was said?'

'Yes, sir.'

'In that case,' said Thanet, 'perhaps it would be a good idea to have a word with him first, before seeing Talion.'

He glanced at his watch. Ten to four. With any luck they might catch the tractor driver before he finished work for the day. Presumably the place to look for him would be at Home Farm.

Sam Tiller was crossing the yard carrying a shovel, heading for the storage shed in which they had interviewed him earlier, and Thanet called him over. To get to the Home Farm, they learned, they could either walk through the grounds of the Hall, a distance of about half a mile, or drive down to the road and take the first turning on the left.

With a glance at the leaden sky and the thickening snow Thanet decided to take the easy way out. After a word of thanks to Bentley he and Lineham headed for the Land Rover.

SEVEN

'Marvellous, isn't it?' said Lineham gloomily as they set off down the drive. 'Not only do we discover that six people had keys to the van, but that four of them actually used it last night. And we haven't asked the Byfleets yet.' He slowed down as they reached the main road. The red Ford Escort with Tessa Hamilton and her boyfriend inside turned into the drive as he pulled away.

Thanet lifted a hand in response to her wave.

'Those two young Hamiltons could put you off parenthood for ever,' said Lineham.

Thanet laughed. 'Bit late for that, isn't it, Mike?'

'All I can say is, I hope Mandy doesn't look like that when she's seventeen. . . . Anyway, the whole thing seems pretty hopeless to me. Even if we do suspect who was actually driving the van when Mr Martindale was hit, we haven't got a hope of proving it. No witnesses, nothing.'

'Come on, Mike. It's early days yet. You never know what the house-to-house enquiries will turn up and there's always forensic. If Martindale was actually put into that ditch as we suspect . . .'

'Hmm. Ah, here we are.'

He swung the Land Rover into a lane with HOME FARM stamped in black on a wooden sign. There were well-maintained wire fences on either side of the road, with snow piled against them where tractors had no doubt cleared the way. Ahead was a cluster of farm buildings and in a few hundred yards the track divided, one arm entering a drive leading to a red brick-and-tile farmhouse, the other widening out as it entered a broad yard surrounded by barns and sheds.

Over to the left a tractor with a forage box attached was moving very slowly along the wide central aisle of a long cattle shed. Thanet and Lineham walked across, hunching their shoulders and keeping their heads down against the swirling snow. At the entrance to the shed they stopped. On either side were stout iron barriers behind which black-and-white cattle on thick beds of straw were lined up munching the silage feed being spewed out of the forage box into the pens along a narrow conveyor belt.

Lineham wrinkled his nose. 'Phew! What a stink! How do these farmworkers stand it?'

'I suppose they're used to it.'

The tractor had now reached the far end of the aisle and with a roar it accelerated, described a wide arc in the open space beyond the shed and headed back towards them at a fair speed, its task presumably now completed. They stepped back as it approached and Thanet held up a hand. The driver stopped and switched off the engine.

'Yes?'

The sudden silence was a relief. Thanet stepped forward. 'We're from Sturrenden CID.' He introduced himself and Lineham. 'We're looking into the death of Mr Martindale, from the Hall.'

'Oh yeah.' The driver remained firmly planted in his seat, one hand on the steering wheel and the other on the ignition, as if ready to take off again at any moment.

'Was it you who was with Mr Talion yesterday, when he had that row with Mr Martindale?'

'Cor, was that him? I didn't realise.'

'Would you get down, please? We'd like a word.'

With a practised movement the man swung around and jumped down beside them. 'Why?'

He was in his forties, Thanet guessed, with the weathered skin of a man used to working out of doors, wearing a bulky ancient parka the colour of mud and an incongruously cheerful bobble cap in red and white stripes. A large dewdrop hung from the tip of his fleshy nose and he wiped it away with the back of his gloved hand. Almost immediately another began to form.

The smell of silage, whether from the forage box, the cattle pens or the man's clothing, was overpowering.

Thanet stamped his feet. 'Is there anywhere a bit less exposed where we could talk, Mr . . . ?'

'Mardy. Jim Mardy. I can't hang about. I got work to do.'

'It won't take long.'

Mardy hesitated a moment longer and then, without speaking, led the way across the yard to a small shed constructed of tarred weatherboarding and pushed open the door. There were no windows and inside it was very dark. Mardy twisted a switch and a single, feeble electric light bulb strung up on one of the rafters revealed a row of nails on which hung several pairs of overalls and an assortment of scruffy coats. Spaced out around the walls on a floor of beaten earth were a number of bales of straw on three of which lay plastic lunch boxes and Thermos flasks. Mardy crossed to one of the bales, picked up a Thermos, sat down and poured himself a cup of steaming liquid. Thanet and Lineham watched enviously, Thanet making a mental note to make sure that tomorrow, if the case continued, he would come well supplied with hot drinks. Lineham, he was sure, would be making a similar resolution.

Mardy was watching him expectantly over the rim of his mug. Thanet sat down on one of the bales and signalled to Lineham to begin.

Lineham remained standing, shoving his hands deep into

his pockets. 'We understand that you were talking to Mr Talion when Mr Martindale arrived.'

' 'Sright. Some of the fencing needs renewing, we'd gone to take a look at it.'

'What time was this?'

'Just before me dinner break. Getting on for twelve o'clock, it must've been.' Mardy wiped away another dewdrop.

'Could you tell us what happened?'

The glint in the man's eye told Thanet that Mardy had now realised the purpose of this conversation. The question was, would he be cooperative or obstructive? It all depended, Thanet guessed, on Mardy's character and on his relationship with his employer, whether loyalty would win over the desire to give an account of the drama.

'What d'you mean?'

The man was playing for time, still hadn't quite made up his mind. Thanet opened his mouth to intervene then closed it again. It wasn't fair to Lineham to jump in whenever the going became sticky.

Lineham had noticed and gave Thanet an uncertain glance. Thanet looked at the ground. *Go on.*

'We thought you might be able to tell us what the row was about.'

Mardy shrugged. 'No idea.'

'You heard what was said, though.'

'Some of it.'

'Perhaps you wouldn't mind telling us what you did hear.'

Silence. Mardy took another slow, deliberate swig from his cup, then screwed it back on to the Thermos. 'Why don't you ask Mr Talion?'

'We shall.'

'In that case,' Mardy stood up, 'there's no point in me telling you, is there?'

For a few minutes longer Lineham persisted but it was

useless. Now that Mardy had made up his mind nothing would shake him.

'Very well,' said Lineham eventually. 'Just tell me one thing. How long did this conversation last?'

Mardy hesitated, weighing up the pros and cons of answering this question and apparently deciding that it was harmless. 'Not more 'n a few minutes.'

'And would you say they'd met before, recently?'

Again a hesitation. Then Mardy shook his head. 'The other bloke, Mr Martindale, started off by saying, "Hullo Talion. Long time no see." '

'And what did Mr Talion say?'

Realising that he was imperceptibly being drawn into giving away information he had decided to withhold, Mardy headed for the door. 'I gotta get on.'

Thanet and Lineham returned to the Land Rover and watched him roar off on his tractor into the gathering dusk.

'I blew it, didn't I?' said Lineham. 'Sorry, sir.' He thumped the steering wheel in frustration before turning on the windscreen wipers to clear the thin film of snow which had built up while they had been talking to Mardy. 'I jumped in too quickly. If I'd begun as I ended, I might have got somewhere.'

'No point in worrying about it now. The main thing is, you can see where you went wrong. And those last two questions were very useful.'

'I just thought it would be interesting to know how long they'd been talking before the row broke out,' said Lineham eagerly. 'And whether or not it was the continuation of a recent row.'

'Quite. And apparently it wasn't. The implication being . . .'

'That whatever the issue between them, it was a pretty powerful one. I mean, you don't meet someone after an interval of twenty odd years and plunge straight into a row unless you've got a very good reason.'

'Also, it sounds as though it might have been Talion who had the grudge. Martindale's greeting sounded friendly enough.'

'Mr Talion now, then?'

Thanet nodded and they drove out of the farmyard and into the driveway of Home Farm. Inside the house a dog started barking as they approached the front door. The barks grew louder and the man who answered their knock made no attempt to stop the noise until Thanet had introduced himself.

'All right, Rhett. Enough!'

The dog, an Alsatian, at once fell silent but remained wary, watching the two policemen for any threatening move.

'You'd better come in.'

Talion opened a door to the right of the small hall, switching on the light, and they followed him into a cold gloomy dining-room furnished with heavy oak table and chairs, carpet square and skimpy unlined curtains patterned with orange and yellow flowers. The room looked as though it was rarely, if ever, used and as if no one had cared what it looked like for a very long time.

'What is it?' He was in his sixties, short and stocky, dressed in well-worn corduroy trousers, pullover and tweed sports jacket. He looked like a man who had long ago forgotten how to smile; all the lines in his face drooped and there were deep creases between his eyebrows. He did not invite them to sit down and agreed only reluctantly when Thanet asked if they may. The dog flopped down at Talion's feet and buried its nose in its paws.

The door was pushed open and a woman came into the room. 'Who is it, Jack?' She was small, pale and thin, her clothes nondescript, her grey hair pinned back in a meagre bun.

At once his whole demeanour changed and in a flash he was up out of his chair and putting an arm protectively around her shoulders. 'It's all right, Meg, it's only business, it

71

won't take long. You go back in the warm.' Gently, he urged her into the hall and through the door at the far side.

'I don't want my wife upset,' he said as he came back in, shutting the door firmly behind him. 'Her health isn't too good. Heart trouble.'

'I'm sorry to hear that.'

Thanet was sincere, but Talion gave him a sceptical glance as he sat down again. 'Well, what did you want?'

'You'll have heard of Mr Martindale's death?'

A flicker of – what? Satisfaction? Some even stronger emotion? – in Talion's eyes. He nodded. 'Hit and run, wasn't it.'

Statement, not question, Thanet noticed. And still no hint of regret, false or otherwise.

'That's what we're trying to find out.'

Talion was looking disconcerted. 'What do you mean?'

'What I say.' Thanet paused. 'It looks as though he was knocked down by the Ford van they use at the hotel as a general runabout.'

He watched Talion apparently assimilate this information and remember that he had used the van himself last night.

'So?'

'So naturally we are talking to everyone who drove it last night. As I understand you did.'

'Yes, that's true. I did. What of it?'

'Mrs Hamilton tells us that you had to go to check on some sheep that had got out on to the road.'

'That's right.'

'You left at about a quarter to eight, I believe. What time did you get back?'

Talion shrugged. 'I wasn't away long. Twenty, twenty-five minutes, perhaps.'

'So you were back by, say, ten past eight?'

'I suppose. What does it matter?'

'I'm just trying to get a clear picture of the van's movements last night. And naturally I have to ask you if you saw Mr Martindale, while you were out.'

'No, I didn't.'

'You'd seen him earlier in the day, though, I understand?'

'Who told you that?'

'One of the hotel guests saw you together.'

Talion said nothing.

'He said that you were arguing.'

Still no response.

'Having a row, in fact?'

'What of it? Aren't I entitled to have an argument with someone without the police taking an interest?'

'Not,' said Thanet, 'if that someone happens to be killed later on that same day.'

Talion stood up and, as if pulled by an invisible string, the dog rose too. 'Now just a minute ... What are you suggesting?'

The dog's hackles were rising, Thanet noticed. 'Nothing, Mr Talion. Merely enquiring. What, exactly, was the row about?'

'It's none of your bloody business!' he snarled.

Lips curling back from teeth, dog and master looked remarkably alike. A low growl issued from deep in the animal's throat.

'That's not true, I'm afraid,' said Thanet mildly. 'Everything to do with Mr Martindale is police business now. A suspicious death means a complete loss of privacy for everyone concerned.'

Talion laid a hand on the dog's head. 'All right, boy, it's all right. Lie down.' He sat down himself as the dog subsided and for several moments remained silent, staring at the table. Eventually he stirred. 'I suppose,' he said, 'if I don't tell you now, you'll be back, until you get what you want.'

Thanet said nothing. He guessed that Talion was remembering that there had been a witness to the argument and, unaware that they had already interviewed Jim Mardy without success, was thinking that it would be best to get in first with his own version.

'So I might as well tell you. Mr Martindale told me that he

was thinking of staying on for good, now he'd come back. I told him that he'd do better to take off again, the sooner the better as far as everyone around here is concerned.'

'He was that unpopular?'

Talion shrugged. 'Let's just say he had a knack of getting up everyone's nose.'

'And that's it?'

'Well, he wasn't very pleased, naturally. Said after all this time we ought to be able to let bygones be bygones. I couldn't agree and said so.'

'You make it all sound very calm, very rational. But it wasn't, was it?'

Talion said nothing, just shrugged again.

'Our witness was some distance away, but it was obvious to him that you were having a heated argument.'

Talion's mouth set in a stubborn line. 'That's all that was said.'

Now for the really important part. Thanet didn't think that he was going to get anywhere, but he had to try. 'I can't believe that you were concerned only in a general way, for the good of the community. I assume that if Mr Martindale said you ought to let bygones be bygones you had a personal reason for being so against his settling here again?'

The silence stretched out, became protracted. Thanet waited. And waited.

Eventually Talion stood up. 'Sorry, but I've said all I'm going to say.' He thrust his chin forward and his voice rose. 'And as I said before, it's really none of your bloody business. So get out, will you?'

The dog was on his feet again, barking this time, the fur along his back standing up in ridges.

It was pointless to persist. Slowly, almost casually, giving the dog no cause for alarm, Thanet rose. Lineham followed suit and they left. Outside, Lineham released pent-up breath. 'Phew. I thought he was going to set the dog on us in the end, didn't you?'

'Doesn't look as though either of us is doing too well at the moment, Mike.'

Back in the Land Rover Thanet looked at his watch. Four-thirty. If he was to report back to Draco as ordered at five they would have to get a move on. And he was chilled to the bone. The thought of home, warmth and hot food was irresistible.

He decided to call it a day.

EIGHT

As usual, however, the lure of home had to be resisted. By the time Thanet had reported to Draco, chewed over the day's findings with Lineham and written up the 'detailed, literate and accurate' reports upon which Draco invariably insisted, it was nearly nine o'clock. Fortunately the threatened heavy snowfall had not materialised and all the main roads were relatively clear. Thanet hoped that they would stay that way.

His own street looked unfamiliar, its pavements lined with humps of piled-up snow where householders had tossed it aside to clear their driveways.

Inside the house the warmth and savoury smell of food were like a benediction. He shrugged off his sheepskin jacket and hung it in the cupboard under the stairs, his stomach rumbling in anticipation.

Joan had heard him and came out into the hall. She was wearing a new jumpsuit which they had chosen together the previous Saturday, in a soft, misty blue which enhanced her delicate skin tones and hair the colour of clear honey.

'Mm,' said Thanet as they kissed. 'You look gorgeous. Smell gorgeous, too.'

'I just had a bath.'

'What are you doing?'

'Nothing much. I'm giving myself an evening off.'

'Were you watching something you wanted to see, on television?'

'Nothing special.'

She led the way into the kitchen, took his supper out of the oven and put it on the table where his place was laid. 'I had it on a very low heat but it's a bit dried up, I'm afraid.'

'Looks delicious,' said Thanet. It was steak and kidney pie, his favourite. 'Just what I need.'

'I thought of you today, tramping about in the snow. Was it grim?' She knew how he hated the cold.

Thanet grimaced. 'This morning was.'

'How did you get on with Superintendent Draco breathing down your neck?'

She poured the tea then sat down opposite him and they chatted about the day's events while he ate. When he had finished telling her about the case she sat thinking for a while. Eventually she stirred. 'He sounds a pretty sad sort of person. The victim.'

'That wasn't the impression I got from the people I talked to.'

She shook her head. 'No, I don't mean the impression he gave other people, I mean what he was really like, underneath.'

'You mean, because I said that no one has yet shown any sign of sorrow over his death?'

'Partly, I suppose. It must be awful to think that there isn't a single person who cares if you're alive or dead.'

'We don't know that that's how it was with him. There might be other people, in other places . . . No, well, I admit it does seem unlikely. He was very much a rolling stone, by the sound of it. But if you'd seen the pile of letters — carefully hoarded — from all his conquests, perhaps you wouldn't feel quite so sorry for him.'

'Oh, I'm not trying to defend all that. I'm just saying it must be sad to feel so alone.'

Thanet laid down his knife and fork. 'He certainly seems to

77

have succeeded in making himself thoroughly unpopular in the area. And now . . .'

'What?'

'I'm just trying to work it out. Yes, I feel as though they're all drawing closer to each other in a tight circle to prevent me from finding out the truth.'

'And what d'you think the truth is?'

Thanet shrugged. 'No idea.'

'You're not suggesting that it was a communal plot to get rid of him!'

'No. Oh no, nothing as bizarre as that. It's just that I'm beginning to suspect that everyone is really rather relieved that he is dead and therefore feels a degree of gratitude to whoever was at the wheel of that van when it happened. So there's a . . . well, a conspiracy of silence, if you like, to protect that person. No one wants to be suspected himself, but he's going to make sure he doesn't point the finger at anyone else. So far the only useful leads we've had are from outsiders.' He sighed. 'If it continues like that, it'll be hard going. Any more tea in the pot, love?'

She took his cup and he watched her pour it, grateful for a relationship in which each performed such small services for the other when they needed it without a second thought. It had taken them a long time to reach that plateau. For many years he had, while paying lip service to Joan's need for a satisfying career of her own, inwardly been the original male chauvinist pig he outwardly professed to despise. But now . . . He caught her hand, kissed it. He was a lucky man.

'The house is very quiet tonight. Bridget out?' He knew that it was her evening off.

'Yes. And Ben's doing his homework.'

'Still?'

They grimaced at each other. The days of Ben's skimping his homework had long gone. The higher academic standards and level of attainment in his new school had seen to that. At first Thanet and Joan had been delighted at his new

78

seriousness over his work but by now they were becoming concerned about it. They'd had enough trouble over Bridget, when she sat her GCSEs, to be concerned lest Ben should go the same way.

'I'll pop up and say hullo.'

Ben was sitting at his desk, hunched over his books.

Thanet sat down on the bed. 'Still at it?'

'Yes. I've nearly finished.'

Ben looked tired, Thanet thought, remembering anew with a lurch of anxiety how obsessive Bridget had become over her work last year, how it had nearly ended in disaster. Questions he longed to ask, things he longed to say, tumbled through his mind but he held them back. He and Joan would stick to their original resolution, to give Ben six months to settle down in his new school before reviewing the situation. He stood up. 'Good.'

Ben looked up. 'There's a chap in my class, Fellows ... He's asked if I'd like to go ice-skating at Gillingham on Saturday. His brother's got a car.'

With difficulty Thanet refrained from asking how old the brother was, how long he'd been driving, how many of them would be going. This was the first time Ben had mentioned a specific friend at the new school. He smiled. 'Sounds fun.'

Downstairs he flopped down on to the settee beside Joan and told her about the proposed expedition.

'Oh good! I am pleased. I think that's what he's found hardest of all, having none of his old friends at the same school.' She frowned. 'Though I'd like to have known how long it is since the brother passed his test. Still, as you say, it really will do him good.'

'Did you have the chance of a word with Bridget about last night?'

She shook her head. 'No. She was in the bathroom, as usual, when I got home and then she came down in a tearing hurry, said she was meeting Diana at seven.'

'Where were they going?'

79

'I didn't have a chance to ask. She was gone practically before I could open my mouth.'

Thanet frowned. 'I don't like not knowing where she is.'

'I know.'

'And it's not the first time it's happened. She's got to realise she must always let us know who she's with and where they're going.'

Joan sighed. 'I have tried. But she just says, how can she tell me if she doesn't know herself? She says they never decide in advance, just see how they feel when they meet.'

'I can understand the difficulty but all the same, it's not good enough. We really must try and work out some system.' She could be anywhere, Thanet thought. How would we begin to know where to look for her, if she just didn't come home?

'Perhaps it would be better if you spoke to her, Luke. She's so touchy with me these days. If ever I say anything like that to her she just says, "Oh Mum, don't fuss", or "Other people's mothers don't go on like that".'

'I don't care what other people's parents do,' said Thanet grimly. 'While she's living under our roof we do have a right to know where she is. I'll see what I can do.'

'Don't be too heavy-handed, will you? We don't want her saying, "If that's how you feel I'm moving out." '

'D'you think she would?'

Joan considered, head on one side. 'No, I don't think so. No, I'm sure she wouldn't. After all, on the whole, we get on pretty well. If you think of some of the problems other parents seem to have with their children . . .'

Thanet sighed. 'I suppose that's true. It's just that there always seems to be something . . .'

Joan grinned. 'At the risk of sounding hackneyed – *C'est la vie.*'

Thanet smiled back. 'That's one of the things I love about you. Your truly original mind.'

She raised a provocative eyebrow. 'What are the others?'

'Which would you prefer?' said Thanet, putting an arm around her. 'Demonstration or exposition?'

She snuggled closer. 'Oh, demonstration, definitely.'

Next morning Thanet set off for work early. There would be a stack of reports to read from Bentley, Swift, and the men who had been working on the house-to-house enquiries, and he wanted to skim through them before the morning meeting with Draco at 8.45. He hated facing the Super's early morning ebullience ill-prepared. He was thankful to note that the temperature had risen and the snow was beginning to thaw. He'd remembered to make two large flasks of coffee but it looked as though it wouldn't be quite as miserably cold today.

Lineham had not yet arrived. Thanet hoped that the sergeant had managed to sort out his problems with his brother-in-law and get a good night's sleep. He lit his pipe, considerately leaving the door open so that Lineham would not be greeted by a smoke-filled room, and settled down to read.

A number of interesting points had emerged.

One of the guests had seen the housekeeper, Mona Byfleet, coming out of Martindale's room at 7.15 on the night he died. This meant that she was, so far, the last person to have seen him alive. Thanet sat back and gazed up at the coils of smoke lazily intertwining above his head, remembering.

'*I don't know what he did afterwards.*'

'*Did you see him again at all, after he'd had dinner?*'

'*No.*'

And he distinctly remembered knowing that she was lying and wondering why. At the time he had thought that perhaps she had overheard some snatch of conversation, some argument, even, between Martindale and the Hamiltons, but now he wondered. Had she simply not wanted him to know that she had seen Hamilton again after dinner? But why not?

81

Thanet shook his head. No, it was much more likely either that she had been making a routine check on the room or that Martindale had called her in to solve some small domestic problem, and the incident had been so trivial that it had slipped her mind.

He picked up the next report.

The Byfleets claimed that neither of them had driven the van last night, Byfleet stating that he had left the Hall at 5.30 in the Rolls to pick up some guests from Gatwick Airport and had arrived back just before eight. The guests had confirmed this. All very well, thought Thanet. That still meant that apart from the time when Tiller had been using the van to go to the pub, they had both been free to drive it later on in the evening, if they had so wished.

He moved on to the house-to-house reports.

The landlord of the village pub had mentioned Tiller and Mrs Rankle, his woman friend, as being among the regulars who had been in that night. They always came on Tuesday evenings, he said, and had arrived at their usual time, around twenty to nine. Also . . . Thanet's eyes widened.

'Morning, sir.' It was Lineham, looking, Thanet was pleased to see, somewhat fresher this morning.

'Listen to this, Mike. The landlord of the pub says that Mrs Rankle – Sam Tiller's girlfriend – always borrows his van some time during the evening to nip home. Apparently she's got a handicapped son and she likes to check that he's OK.'

'And did she borrow it on Tuesday?'

'Apparently she went out for a short while as usual, and he assumed that was where she'd gone. She's usually away for twenty minutes or so.'

'Wonder what sort of a driver she is. The roads were pretty icy that night.'

'Quite. We'll have to go and see her, obviously.'

Lineham picked up a batch of reports and sat down. A few minutes later he looked up. 'Sir! This is interesting . . .'

It was the report of an interview with a Mrs Doreen Victor,

who lived in the village. She claimed to have seen Martindale (identified by his distinctive black-and-white checked overcoat) twice that afternoon. On the first occasion he had been talking to Mrs Fever, wife of a local businessman (and mother of Toby Fever, Tessa Hamilton's boyfriend, Thanet wondered?) who had been filling her car up with petrol at the garage. On the second occasion Mrs Victor had seen him having what appeared to be a heated exchange with Mrs Rankle, Sam Tiller's friend. Unfortunately they had been on the other side of the street and she had been unable to hear what the argument was about.

'An argument,' said Thanet thoughtfully. 'You don't walk up to a perfect stranger in a village street and have an argument with her, do you?'

'He must have known her before,' said Lineham eagerly. 'When he lived here. And she drove the van that night . . .'

'Quite . . . . What about this Mrs Fever? Did the witness have the impression Martindale knew her too?'

'She doesn't say,' said Lineham regretfully.

'Did you happen to notice if the petrol pumps at the garage are self-service, Mike?'

'No, I didn't. You mean, there might have been an attendant, who could have overheard the conversation?'

'It's possible. A lot of the smaller garages in the villages haven't switched to self-service yet. We'll check.'

Lineham made a note.

Thanet was now glancing through Swift's reports of interviews with the staff at Longford Hall. 'Ah, listen, Mike. One of the housemaids saw Martindale having a row with a Mr Fever – this woman's husband, I presume – at about a quarter past six that evening. She was in the library, checking that everything was in order, and Martindale was there. Fever apparently came barging in and laid into him, telling him to keep away from his wife.'

'What did Martindale say?'

'He was very cool apparently, tried to play it down, laugh

83

it off. Said there was no harm in saying hullo to an old acquaintance, was there? Fever nearly went through the roof.'

'What happened?'

'Mrs Hamilton came in and shooed the girl away, so she didn't hear any more.'

'So Mrs Hamilton knew about this and didn't say a word.'

Thanet sighed. 'It's just as I thought. I was saying to Joan last night, I suspect we're going to have our work cut out trying to get people to talk. Our main hope is through outsiders like this Mrs Victor, or the pub landlord, and this housemaid.'

'They're not exactly outsiders.'

'By outsiders I mean people who didn't know Martindale before.'

Lineham pulled a face. 'You may be right. If so, as you say, it'll be hard going.'

Thanet checked the time. Eight-thirty-five. 'Let's just glance through the rest of these. I'd like to be up to date before the meeting, and know roughly what our plans are for today.'

They hurried through the remainder of the reports. The only other item of any interest was Swift's account of an interview with another member of staff, who had overheard Sam Tiller delivering an ultimatum to Delia Hamilton: if Martindale stayed, he, Tiller, would go.

'Mr Martindale certainly wouldn't have won a popularity poll around there!' said Lineham.

'No.' Thanet shuffled the papers together. 'Right, Mike. Go over these again while I'm in the meeting, check we haven't missed anything. We'll have to interview a lot of these people again, see if we can get any more out of them – that's Mrs Byfleet, Mrs Hamilton, Mr Tiller. And we must also try and fit in Mr Tiller's girlfriend, Mrs Rankle, both the Fevers and of course this Mrs Victor, in case she can tell us anything more. It sounds as though she could be an interesting source of gossip, perhaps we ought to try and see her first. So ring and get the interviews set up.'

Thanet glanced at the clock again. 'Sorry, must dash.' One minute to go. If he was late Draco would be furious and they'd waste half the meeting listening to a lecture on the importance of punctuality.

NINE

Thanet made it to the meeting with ten seconds to spare. He slipped into his seat and noted Draco's customary glance at the clock. After murmured greetings all round Draco picked up the sheaf of papers lying exactly in the centre of the blotter on his desk and cleared his throat.

Apart from Draco and himself there were two other men in the room: Chief Inspector Tody, who acted as Draco's deputy should the Superintendent be unavailable; and Inspector Boon, Thanet's long-time friend and colleague. Each was watching Draco in characteristic manner, Tody with an ingratiating half-smile, Boon with an ironic twinkle in his eye.

There was a sense of expectation in the air, Thanet realised. Something was up. He looked at Draco again and yes, the signs were there: the familiar glint of self-satisfaction overlaid by missionary fervour, the almost audible crackle of energy which emanated from him. It looked as though the long-rumoured new campaign was about to begin. Mentally, Thanet braced himself. What now?

'Good morning, gentlemen. Incidentally, I think that we should soon try to amend that state of affairs. There should, if we are to keep abreast of the times, be at least one woman present. That is, however, not what I want to talk to you about this morning. This morning I want to talk to you about a scheme for further improving the efficiency of our police force here in Sturrenden. Oh, I know what you're saying to yourselves.'

Draco's Welsh accent was becoming more pronounced, Thanet noticed, a sure sign that he was getting into his stride. He often felt that the Superintendent's style was more suited to the pulpit than the police force.

'You're saying, "Haven't we had enough changes for the moment? Don't we need – indeed deserve, a bit of a break?" '

Draco brought the flat of his hand down upon his desk, making everyone jump. 'No! That is the very moment, I tell you, when standards begin to slip. Complacency is our enemy. It leads to lazy minds, lazy work practices and, above all, lazy policing.'

Draco sat back, tucking his thumbs into the armholes of his waistcoat and deliberately looked at each man in turn. 'Now I'm not denying that you've all worked very hard to make this a more efficient force over the last year, and the results show, as I'm sure you'll agree. But I think you'll also agree, when you've heard my new proposals, that there are a number of areas in which there is room for further improvements.'

You had to admire the man's enthusiasm if nothing else, thought Thanet. Must remember to give those cards and letters to Swift, he reminded himself, concentration flagging as Draco carried on in the same vein, see if he can track down any of Martindale's old girlfriends. Not that at this stage there would appear to be any urgent reason for doing so, but it was a lead, however unpromising, that ought to be followed up.

Draco was still on his preliminary speech. *Oh, do get on with it, you Welsh windbag*, Thanet urged silently.

He was thinking about Martindale, about how extraordinary it was that anyone could arouse in so many people such a degree of animosity that it could survive apparently undiminished an interval of more than twenty years, when, with a loving glance at the papers in his hand, Draco finally came to the point.

'After considerable thought I have identified the three main areas in which improvements need to be made. Organisation, Delegation and Documentation.' He spelt it out letter by letter. 'O-D-D. Which, as you'll no doubt realise, spells "Odd".' He waited for the small ripple of amusement before smiling himself. 'Yes, I thought you'd appreciate that. And if the acronym affords the men some light relief, then that's all right by me. I don't in the least mind appearing a figure of fun so long as they buckle down and get on with implementing my proposals. It will, of course, be up to you to see that they do.'

He stood up and handed a sheet of paper to each of them. 'Here they are. I'd like you to take them away and study them and come back to me tomorrow with comments – constructive, of course. No, don't read them now, there's no time, you'll all be wanting to get back and get on with your work. So, briefly, could we have your reports, please.' He sat back, folding his hands over his waistcoat.

Although he made it as succinct as possible Thanet's report was of necessity the longest, the finding of Martindale's body in the ditch being by far the most important of yesterday's events. He wondered if Draco was going to raise any objections to an intensive investigation, but apparently the discovery of the fibres on the van had convinced the Superintendent that for the moment at least Thanet and his team were justified in devoting their energies to finding out exactly what had happened.

'I might even pop out to Sutton myself later on,' said Draco, causing Thanet's heart to sink. 'You'll be needing to see several of these people again, as well as interviewing new witnesses. I suggest you begin with the chap who barged into the hotel and had a row with Martindale – what's his name? Fever, was it? And with this woman Rankle.'

Thanet forbore to say that by now Lineham should already

have a series of appointments set up. If Draco came looking for them, with any luck he wouldn't find them. If this made the Superintendent mad, too bad. Hoping that he wouldn't have to waste too much time in elaborate games of hide and seek with Draco, he made his way back upstairs to his office, where he found Doc Mallard talking to Lineham. As usual the little police surgeon was looking spruce and cheerful and was scarcely recognisable as the sardonic scarecrow of a man he had become after the lingering death of his first wife. Thanet never ceased to marvel at the miracle which remarriage had wrought in his old friend.

'Ah, Luke. Just telling Lineham here that the PM is set for this afternoon. I'll let you know the findings as soon as I can.'

'Thanks Doc.'

'How's it going?'

Thanet shrugged. 'All right, so far. Did Lineham tell you we found the van?'

'Yes. Belongs to the people at Longford Hall, I gather. Does the plot thicken?'

'I'm not sure, yet. It could have been a simple hit and run.'

'As non-committal as ever,' said Mallard, twinkling at Thanet over his half-moons. 'How you ever have the nerve to complain when I can't be too precise about time of death I don't know.' He picked up his bag. 'Well, I'll be in touch later, then. Happy hunting.'

When Mallard had gone Lineham gestured at the paper in Thanet's hand. 'Anything interesting, sir?'

'The Super's latest campaign.' Thanet handed it over. 'Haven't looked at it myself yet.'

Lineham took it eagerly. 'Thought something was brewing.' He grinned. 'Does he realise . . . ?'

'Oh yes. ODD. It's his crafty way of taking the sting out of it all.'

Lineham, reading, groaned.

'Don't tell me,' said Thanet. 'I'm not going to read it until I'm feeling stronger.'

'At this rate we're going to end up doing so much paperwork there won't be any time for policing. Do you realise . . .'

'Mike, I said, don't tell me. At the moment I don't want to know. Now, did you get those interviews set up?'

'All except the ones with Sam Tiller and Mr Fever. I'm still trying to get hold of them.'

'Right. You carry on while I have a word with Swift. I want to put him on to tracing some of Martindale's former girlfriends. Are we seeing Mrs Victor first?'

'Yes. At eleven.'

'Fine.'

By 10.30 they were on their way. The sky had cleared, the sun had come out and in the town the few remaining areas of blackened slushy snow were thawing fast. Out in the country it was a different matter. Along the sides of the lanes, where the sun had not yet penetrated, the snow still lay in drifts, piled up against tangled brown hedges on which there was as yet no hint of green. In the open fields it had melted in patches, stippling the brown of ploughed earth and tender green of winter wheat with random frostings of white. Tall trees stood winter-stark against a sky the milky blue of opals.

'What I can't get over,' said Lineham, pulling into the side of the road to allow a lorry to pass, 'is the degree of bad feeling against Martindale. Sam Tiller obviously felt so strongly about him that he threatens to leave if Martindale stays on, Jack Talion tells him bluntly he isn't wanted, this Mr Fever barges up to the Hall and has a row with him because Martindale passes the time of day with his wife, and even Sam Tiller's girlfriend launches straight into some kind of argument when she bumps into him in the village. It's incredible! Really makes you wonder what he'd done.'

'I was thinking the same thing myself, earlier. I'd really like to know just what all these people had against him. And was it the same thing, or did they all have different, individual grudges? The trouble is, I suspect it's not going to be easy to find out.'

'Perhaps it doesn't matter, sir. Perhaps it'll turn out to be a simple accident. Someone ran into him by chance – the roads were very icy that night, remember – and couldn't face owning up. So when they discovered he was dead they just dragged him into the ditch and left him there.'

'Could be. Though in that case we haven't a chance of finding out what happened unless a witness turns up or someone actually walks into the police station and confesses. Still, we'll just have to see. What did you say the Victors' house is called?'

'Casa Mía. And it's a bungalow, at the far end of the village. There's a For Sale sign outside, apparently.'

They were just entering Sutton and Lineham slowed down. Like so many of the smaller villages in Kent it had no obvious centre and consisted of a straggle of houses, a pub, a garage, a church and a village school, now converted into a private dwelling.

The severe shortage of building land in the South-East meant that Casa Mía, like most new houses in rural areas, had been squeezed into what had evidently been the garden of the older house next door. It had been built, Thanet guessed, by someone who had cherished the dream of a villa in Spain and had had to settle for the next best thing. Its Moorish arches and wrought-iron embellishments looked as out of place in this very English setting as a tart at a vicar's tea party.

Lineham parked the car in the road and they got out. The inappropriately tall iron gates were flanked by brick pillars topped with stone pineapples.

'Delusions of grandeur,' murmured Thanet.

A curtain twitched as they walked up the drive and Thanet just had time to realise that the doorbell chimes were playing 'Home Sweet Home' before the door opened.

'Mrs Victor?'

The woman patted her towering beehive of dyed blonde

hair and gave a coy smile, revealing suspiciously white and even teeth. She was, he guessed, in her late fifties, and many sessions on either sunbed or beach had tanned her skin to a deep, rich brown, unfortunately drying it to the texture of a prune in the process. She was carefully if heavily made up and was wearing unsuitably youthful clothes – tight trousers and flower-strewn sweater. Thanet gave her a warm smile as he introduced himself. She looked exactly as he had hoped she would, a woman with too much time on her hands and little to do but take an interest in her neighbours' affairs.

She peered anxiously over his shoulder down the drive before inviting them in. 'I'm expecting my hubby home any moment.'

It was clear that she didn't want the interview to begin until he arrived. In the living-room the Spanish theme continued, with heavily carved furniture in dark oak, incongruously juxtaposed with the ubiquitous dralon three-piece suite, and a garish painting of a Spanish flamenco dancer over the synthetic dressed stone fireplace. Mrs Victor fussed about, settling them comfortably and insisting on providing them with unwanted cups of coffee. 'It's all ready, it won't take a tick.'

'Wonder if her husband was due home anyway?' said Lineham, when she had left.

'Or if she rang him after you set up the appointment, you mean?'

'And if so, why?'

Thanet shrugged. 'Perhaps she's the little woman type, doesn't feel comfortable unless her husband is at hand to give her moral support.'

Lineham's lip curled. 'I thought that sort of attitude had gone out with the ark.'

'I can't see why you're so surprised at the idea. There must be thousands of women – Isn't that a car in the drive?'

Lineham half rose to glance out of the window. 'Jaguar, E reg. Must be doing well.'

Outside in the hall footsteps went past towards the front door and there was a murmur of voices.

Of all the many different aspects of his work interviewing was the one Thanet enjoyed most and it was with a keen sense of anticipation that he stood up as the Victors entered the room

TEN

'Inspector Thanet?' Hand outstretched, Victor advanced, picture of an honest citizen eager to do his duty.

Thanet, experienced in encounters of this kind, sensed a secret bubble of excitement in the man. Was it merely that Victor was relishing the drama of being involved, however peripherally, with the death which must be the talk of the village, or was there something more?

Short and burly with sparse curly hair and copious side-whiskers, he was formally dressed in dark suit and discreetly striped shirt. Only his tie, vividly patterned in orange and mustard-yellow whorls, betrayed the taste which had bought and furnished Casa Mía.

'The coffee's all ready,' murmured his wife, and by the time the three men were seated she had brought it in.

Victor began conventionally enough. 'Naturally the wife was wondering what you wanted to see her about.' He took a cautious sip of the scalding liquid. 'I mean, she told the policeman who called yesterday everything she knew about this Mr . . . What was his name?'

'Martindale.'

'That's right, yes. Which wasn't much. I mean, she'd never set eyes on him before Tuesday afternoon and at the time, of course, she didn't realise who he was. It was only when his coat was mentioned . . .'

'Black-and-white checked tweed,' said Mrs Victor, entering the conversation for the first time. 'Very nice, too.'

'Yes, Dor, we know that.' A hint of impatience, there. He turned back to Thanet. 'So . . . ?'

'We just wanted to clear up one or two points, sir. Clarify your wife's impressions.'

'I see.'

Obviously he didn't, but he pressed gamely on. 'Well, any way we can help, of course . . .'

And there was that glint of excitement again, as if Victor was hugging some secret knowledge to himself. Thanet began to wonder if the man's presence had nothing to do with his wife and he was really here because he had a titbit of information to impart. If so, no doubt he would come out with it in his own time.

'Thank you. Now I understand, Mrs Victor, that on Tuesday afternoon you saw Mr Martindale twice?'

'Yes.' She put her coffee cup down on the low carved oak table beside her and looked at her husband, waited for his encouraging nod. 'I had to go to the post office, see, to get some stamps. It's at the far end of the village so of course I had to pass the garage. That was where I first saw this man, this Mr Martindale. At least, I suppose it was him?' She glanced doubtfully at her husband.

'Tell the Inspector what he looked like, Dor,' said Victor, as if encouraging a child who lacked confidence.

'He was in his late forties, early fifties, I should say. Medium height, brown curly hair, going a bit thin on top.' An involuntary glance at her husband's own sparse locks before she hastily averted her eyes. 'I didn't see him all that clearly then; it was later, after he'd been talking to Mrs Rankle, he passed quite close to me.'

Victor glanced at Thanet for confirmation and he nodded. 'Sounds like him.'

'I noticed him,' said Mrs Victor, getting into her stride, 'because of course he was a stranger and we don't get many around here, we're a bit off the beaten track. So naturally I wondered who he was. Especially . . .' She pulled herself up. 'Well, no, not especially, I suppose . . . But anyway, he was talking to Mrs Fever.'

Thanet, intrigued, tried an oblique approach. 'Mrs Fever is a friend of yours?'

'Oh no! It's just that . . .' She stopped, looked to her husband for help.

He sniggered and said, 'Fever has a reputation for being jealous as hell. His wife can't so much as look at another man without him going off the deep end, so she tends to avoid little tête-à-têtes with anything in trousers.'

Interesting. 'You've actually seen him lose his temper over this?' Thanet wondered if Victor had made a pass at Mrs Fever himself, and had learnt about Fever's possessiveness the hard way.

'Not exactly. We don't mix much, in the village.' He glanced at his wife and gave a bitter little laugh. 'To be honest, they're not exactly a welcoming lot around here. Keep themselves to themselves and if you're a newcomer . . . Doreen and me've got fed up with it. We've decided to move back to Maidstone.'

'So how did you find out that Mr Fever was inclined to be jealous of his wife?'

'That was me,' said Mrs Victor. 'One day when my car was in for repair I had to go into Sturrenden on the bus and I heard two of the women from the village talking . . .'

'But you can tell by the way he watches her,' said Victor. 'We've been to one or two dos in the village, the church fête and that, and he never takes his eyes off of her.'

'So when you saw Mr Martindale talking to her on Tuesday afternoon, Mrs Victor, you were naturally intrigued?'

She nodded. 'Yes. That was another reason why I specially noticed him.'

'I see. Were you close enough to hear what they were saying?'

She shook her head with a tinge of regret. 'No.'

'She was filling her car with petrol, I believe you said?'

'That's right. Well, she wasn't actually doing it herself, Bert was. The garage attendant.'

'I see.' Good. With any luck Bert would be able to tell them more. 'And they were just passing the time of day, so far as you could tell.'

'Well, I'm not sure. I wouldn't put it quite like that. He seemed to be doing the talking and she was shaking her head.'

'As if he was trying to persuade her to do something?'

'Could have been. Something like that, anyway.'

'Were they talking long?'

'Just while her car was being filled up. I looked back when I got to the post office and she was just driving off.'

'Did you have the impression they knew each other?'

'Oh yes. Definitely.'

Thanet glanced at Lineham and raised his eyebrows. *Anything else?*

Lineham shook his head.

'Right, thank you. Now, I assume that it was when you came out of the post office that you saw him again, this time talking to Mrs Rankle?'

'That's right. When I went in Mrs Rankle was there, being served. She went out, I bought my stamps and when I went out again there they were, having this argument.'

'Where was this? Were they on the same side of the road as you?'

'Yes. He must've crossed over while I was inside.'

'How far away from you were they?'

She screwed up her face in concentration and glanced at her husband as she said doubtfully, 'Fifty yards?'

'Dor's not very good at distances,' said Victor with an apologetic little laugh.

'It doesn't matter. Were they near enough for you to hear what they were saying?'

'Not really, not most of it, anyway. But you could tell they were arguing. And I did hear Mrs Rankle say, "How you've got the cheek to show your face here again I just don't know." '

'She raised her voice, presumably? Yes. Did you hear any more?'

Mrs Victor shook her head regretfully. 'I was sticking the stamps on my envelopes before posting them and if I'd gone back along the pavement the way I'd come, well, I'd have had to pass quite close, you see, and it was so obvious they were rowing ... It would have been embarrassing, trying to pretend I couldn't hear. And it would have looked a bit obvious if I'd crossed the road just to avoid them. I didn't know quite what to do, so in the end I just stayed where I was and made out it was taking a long time to stick the stamps on.'

'Yes, I see.' Pity, but still ... 'So then what happened?'

'She went off, well, flounced, really, I suppose you'd say, in a temper. And he came on towards me and went into the post office. That was when I got a better look at him.'

'Did he seem upset?'

'Yes, he did a bit. Well, I mean, it'd be understandable, wouldn't it, after being told to your face you're not wanted.'

She and her husband exchanged glances. *We know all about being not wanted.*

'Is there anything else you can recall?'

A shake of the head. 'No, I don't think so.' Then another glance at her husband, a slight lift of the eyebrows. *Are you going to tell them?*

Might as well make it easy for him, Thanet decided. 'I believe you were out yesterday, when our man called, Mr Victor?'

'That's right, yes.'

'So is there anything you can add to your wife's statement?'

'Well there was something, as a matter of fact. Though I don't know if it's of any importance.'

'If you could tell us anyway . . .'

Victor passed the tip of his tongue over his upper lip and leaned forward, relishing his moment centre stage. 'I was in the pub on Monday night – '

'Sorry to interrupt, but I just want to make sure I've got this straight . . . You're talking now about the night before Mr Martindale had his accident?'

'Yes.'

Thanet remembered Delia Hamilton saying that Martindale had gone down to the pub that first evening, and had got back about nine. 'Go on.'

'Dor'd gone to her Keep Fit class in Ashford, so I went along for a drink, about eight it must've been. Place was pretty crowded, there was a darts match on. Anyway, this chap was at the bar, by himself.'

'Mr Martindale, you mean?'

'Yep. Though I didn't know it was him, if you get my meaning. At first I thought he was a stranger, just dropped in for a drink as he was passing through the village, then I began to realise there was more to it than that.'

'What do you mean?'

'Well, after a while it dawned on me that all the locals, the older ones, anyway, were avoiding him. It was unnatural, like. They didn't look at him and when they wanted a refill they'd deliberately go to the end of the bar away from him.'

'How did he react?'

'Just sat there drinking as if he didn't notice what was happening. I wondered if I was imagining it at first, but after a while I was sure I wasn't and I began to feel sorry for him. I'd just made up my mind to go and stand next to him, have a chat, perhaps offer to buy him a pint, when Sam Tiller came in – he's groundsman up at the Hall.'

'Yes, I know. Go on.'

'Well, he comes in and goes straight to the bar, to the space next to this man. Martindale looks round and says, "It's Sam,

99

isn't it? Sam Tiller! How are you?" Tiller looks at him and sort of freezes . . . I swear, if looks could kill . . . Tiller doesn't say a word, just moves away, to the other end of the bar. No one says anything, but all the locals were watching, to see what Martindale would do.'

'And what did he do?'

'Just finished up his drink and left.'

So, a public snub, thought Thanet. And more than that, a warning?

'What happened after that?'

'Sam paid for his drink and went across to join some of his pals.'

'Nothing was said, that you could hear?'

'No. But one of them clapped him on the back and said something, and they all laughed.'

'I see. Well thank you very much, both of you. You've been very helpful.'

'There's just one point . . .' said Lineham, as they all stood up. 'When you came home on Monday night, Mr Victor, did you happen to mention this incident to your wife?'

'Yes, I did. Well, like I said, I felt sorry for him.'

'I was just wondering why you didn't mention it to the PC who interviewed you yesterday, Mrs Victor?'

She looked confused. 'I don't know. I didn't think . . . He said they were trying to trace Mr Martindale's movements during the day he died, so I just told him what I'd seen.'

'But when I got home from work and heard what had happened,' said Victor, 'that this chap was dead and the police had been round asking questions, I thought perhaps I ought to tell you. If you hadn't made this appointment I was going to give you a ring.'

'Quite right, too,' said Thanet. 'We need all the help we can get.'

In the car Lineham said, 'What d'you think, sir? Think Mrs Fever was an old flame of Martindale's?'

'Possibly. Anyway, it certainly confirms that both Fever

and Tiller have some explaining to do, doesn't it? What time is the appointment with the Fevers?'

'Twelve-fifteen.'

Thanet glanced at his watch. Twenty to twelve. 'Just time for a word with that mechanic first.'

ELEVEN

The local garage did nothing to enhance the meagre charms of Sutton, being no more than a large weatherboarded hut tacked on to the end of a row of cottages in the centre of the village. At some point the peg tiles had been stripped off the roof and replaced with green-painted corrugated iron. Outside were two antiquated petrol pumps with a notice saying PLEASE HOOT FOR SERVICE, inside was the usual acrid smell of oil and metal.

Business did not appear to be thriving. There was only one car in the workshop and one pair of legs sticking out from beneath it. Bert, presumably.

Lineham advanced. 'Bert?' He stooped, peered underneath the car. 'Sorry, I don't know your surname.'

The legs slid forward, a torso emerged clad in mechanic's overalls, then a head.

'Seller.' The man squinted up. 'What d'you want?'

He was in his thirties, Thanet guessed, with longish, greasy black hair and pinched ferrety features.

'Police, Mr Seller.' Lineham held out his warrant card.

The man glanced warily from Lineham to Thanet and back again. 'If it's anything to do with the business you'll have to wait for Mr Stake. He's gone into Ashford to pick up a spare part.'

'No, it's nothing to do with the business. It's you we wanted to see.'

'Oh ... ?' Seller scrambled to his feet as Lineham introduced himself.

Thanet was intrigued by the overtones of wariness in Seller's voice. Had Lineham noticed?

Seller crossed to a bench, put down the spanner he was holding and wiped his hands on an oily rag.

'We're looking into the death of a Mr Martindale, the night before last.'

'The hit and run.'

'Yes. During the afternoon he was seen talking to Mrs Fever here at the garage.'

He was nodding. 'That's right. She'd stopped for petrol, and he came over.'

'Could you tell us about the conversation, please?'

'Well ...' He squinted into the middle distance, considering. 'I was just starting to fill Mrs Fever's car when he came across.'

'Across the road, you mean?'

'Yeah. He was walking towards the post office, on the other side of the road. I'd noticed him because he was a stranger and we don't get many around here. Anyway, he must've spotted Mrs Fever because suddenly he stops, looks, and then crosses the road. He nods at me then he bends down and says through the car window, "It is Yvonne, isn't it?" Well, she looks up and goes white as a sheet. She doesn't say a word, but it's obvious she'd recognised him and he says, "Yes, it's me. Leo."

'She still doesn't say nothing, but she opens the door and gets out, and moves away a bit with a look at me as if to say, "I don't want him to hear this." ' Seller grinned. 'Out of luck, wasn't she? Hear a pin drop at fifty yards, I can.'

'So what happened then?' said Lineham.

Seller glanced from one to the other, obviously gratified by their rapt attention.

'The chap runs after her, doesn't he? "Aren't you pleased to see me?" he says.'

'Where on earth have you sprung from, Leo?'
'Oh come on, 'Vonne. What sort of a welcome is that?'
'Why have you come? What do you want?'
'Which question would you like me to answer first?'
'Leo, please!'
'It's quite simple, my sweet . . .'
'Don't call me that!'
'Very well. It's quite simple. I've come home for good.'
'Oh God, no . . . But why? Why now, after all these years?'
'Shall we say I recently learned something to my advantage?'
'You mean, you didn't know your father was dead?'
'Not until last week.'

'I'd finished filling up with petrol by then and Mrs Fever asked me how much it was. She paid me and I had to go into the office to fetch her change,' said Seller regretfully. 'Then the phone rang and I had to answer it. When I went out again he was trying to persuade her to go to tea with him. For old times' sake, he said.'

'Did she agree?'

'No. He was still trying to get her to change her mind when she got into the car and drove off. Pretty upset she looked, too.'

'Then what?'

'He looks at me, grins, shrugs and says, "Ah well, you can't win 'em all." Then he crosses the road and goes on his way towards the post office.'

Thanet was surprised that Seller had been so forthcoming. Initially he had thought that Lineham might have problems in getting the man to talk. He remembered Seller's uneasiness when Martindale was first mentioned. Was all this loquacity a smokescreen for something else? He watched carefully as Lineham continued the questioning, and became convinced that the man was hiding something. Seller had apparently worked in the village for only two years and at first had had no idea who Martindale was.

'When did you find out?' said Lineham.

'I mentioned it to Mr Stake when he came back.'

'Mentioned what, exactly?'

'That this Leo character had been chatting Mrs Fever up.'

'And he knew who he was, straight away?'

'Oh yes. Said, "Leo Martindale back? I hadn't heard. That's a turn-up for the book." '

'Mr Stake has lived here a long time, presumably.'

'All his life. His dad had the garage before him.'

'How old is he?'

Seller looked surprised, shrugged. 'Fiftyish?'

Contemporary with Martindale, then, thought Thanet.

'What else did he say, when you told him?'

'Not much. Just said he hoped he wasn't going to start causing trouble again.'

'What sort of trouble?'

'He wouldn't say.'

Lineham glanced at Thanet, raised his eyebrows.

'Mr Seller,' said Thanet, 'did you by any chance mention this incident to anyone else?'

On target! Seller's expression changed and he shuffled his feet, looked uncomfortable.

'Yes, Mr Seller?'

Seller was still hesitating.

'Let me guess, then,' said Thanet. 'You thought you might stir things up a bit by telling Mr Fever, didn't you?'

'He's such a prick!' Seller burst out. 'Always throwing his weight about, thinks he's so great! I thought it would do him good, take him down a peg or two. How did I know he'd react like that?'

'Like what? When was this?'

'Outside the Drovers. I went along for a pint, after work. I ran into him in the car park.'

'So what, exactly, did you say to him?'

'Nothing much! Just said I'd seen an old friend of his wife's, that afternoon. The man's a nutcase!'

'What did he do?'

'Grabbed me by the collar and said, "What the hell do you mean by that?" '

'And?'

'I tried to back-pedal, play it down, but he wouldn't have it. He made me tell him what I'd heard.'

'And then?'

'He got straight back into his car and drove off.'

'In the direction of the Hall?'

Seller nodded sullenly. 'Like I said, he's a nutcase.'

Thanet considered that after such deliberate malice Seller had been lucky to get away so lightly. He said so to Lineham, outside.

'I should think Fever was much more interested in tackling Martindale, sir. He must have rushed straight up to the Hall to have it out with him.'

'Sounds like it. But in any case Martindale was alive and well for some time after Fever tackled him at – what time was it? Six-fifteen?'

'Yes. He had dinner with his sister and Hamilton after that.'

'Of course, it's always possible that Fever went back later. Though that still wouldn't put him behind the wheel of the van.'

'We're still not a hundred per cent sure that it was the van, are we, sir? When d'you think forensic will come up with the confirmation?'

'The Super said this afternoon, if we're lucky. If not, tomorrow morning. I'd be very surprised indeed if it doesn't turn out to be the vehicle we're after. Anyway, we'll see what Fever has to say for himself. It's nearly a quarter past, we'd better get a move on.'

The Fevers lived in a large modern house set in generous

gardens next to the dilapidated range of farm buildings from which he ran his haulage business.

'Wonder how on earth he got planning permission for that,' said Lineham as they parked on the wide gravelled sweep of drive. 'Bet a bit of palm-greasing went on there.'

'Not necessarily, Mike. If you look at the centre section you'll see the brick is older than the rest. I think it's an ambitious conversion.'

'Pretty well done, then,' said Lineham grudgingly.

Thanet awaited the sergeant's next remark with an inward smile. It came.

'Can't be short of a penny,' said Lineham. 'There must be money in haulage.'

'Thinking of buying a lorry and setting yourself up?' Thanet rang the door bell and this time was rewarded with a rendering of the opening bars of 'My Old Man Said Follow The Van'.

'Very appropriate,' said Lineham with a grin.

The door was opened by Toby Fever, Tessa Hamilton's boyfriend. 'Come in.'

A good-looking young man, thought Thanet, nagged once again by the feeling that he might have seen him somewhere before. He wondered what the two families thought of Toby and Tessa's friendship. For various reasons, not much, he imagined.

'I'll tell Dad you're here.' Toby opened a door to the right of the hall, ushered them into the room then went off towards the back of the house.

It was a large sitting-room, at least twenty feet square, with windows overlooking the garden on three sides. It had considerable potential, Thanet thought, but whoever chose the furnishings had played too safe with neutrals and pastels; although the thick carpet, heavy curtains and three-piece suite were of good quality the effect was dull and lifeless. Mrs Fever, he guessed, lacked sufficient confidence in her own taste to indulge it.

'Inspector Thanet?'

For the second time today Thanet was greeted by an outstretched hand. In the case of a man at whom the finger had been pointed, like Fever, such bonhomie invariably made him suspicious.

And Fever himself was a surprise.

It was interesting, Thanet thought, how one could build up an image of someone through other people's accounts of him, and how completely wrong one could be. He'd had a very clear picture of Fever as a great lumberjack of a man, overpowering as much by his physical size as by the force of his personality. Apart from his age, which Thanet guessed to be around fifty, the reality was completely different. Fever was at most five five in height, and wiry as a whippet. He was wearing expensive casual clothes – slightly baggy gaberdine trousers and high-necked cashmere sweater over soft-collared shirt. Beneath the surface affability he was, Thanet thought, distinctly wary.

A woman had come into the room behind him.

'And this is my wife. I believe you did want to talk to her as well?'

Like the Princess in the fairy tale guarded by a dragon, Thanet had expected Mrs Fever to be beautiful and she did not disappoint him. Well, perhaps not exactly beautiful, he corrected himself, but very attractive, certainly. She was perhaps an inch or two taller than her husband, with a beautifully proportioned figure, a cloud of dark hair and soft deep-velvet-brown eyes. She seemed to exude not sex-appeal but something much more subtle, a fragrant femininity enhanced by the flared suede skirt which flowed about her as she walked, the high-heeled shoes and silk blouse. She might not give her husband cause for jealousy but Thanet could understand his fear of losing her to another man.

They all sat down, Fever and his wife side by side on a settee.

'As you've no doubt realised, we're looking into the death

108

of Mr Leo Martindale,' said Thanet. 'And at the moment we're trying to build up a picture of his movements on Tuesday.'

'Excuse me interrupting, Inspector,' said Fever. 'But why? By all accounts it was a hit and run accident. Surely you ought to be concentrating on motorists passing through the village that night?'

'Among other things, yes, we are. Unfortunately it looks as though it might not be as simple as that. It's difficult to see how Mr Martindale could have got into the position in which he was lying without, shall we say, a little help.'

Mrs Fever's eyes widened as she understood the implications of what he was saying and her hands, clasped together in her lap, tightened their grip on each other. Thanet saw the knuckles whiten.

Fever's eyes narrowed and he sat forward. 'Now wait a minute. What are you saying? Are you implying that it wasn't an accident, that . . . ?'

'We're just trying to find out exactly what did happen. It's possible that it was an accident, that the driver panicked when he got out to investigate and discovered that Mr Martindale was dead, moved the body into the ditch to prevent anyone else running over him.'

'But it's also possible that he was deliberately run down. That is what you're getting at, isn't it?'

Fever was becoming agitated.

Here we go again, thought Thanet. The interview was already beginning to follow a pattern that had become all too familiar over the last couple of days. 'Anything is possible, Mr Fever. You must see that at this stage we have to keep an open mind . . .'

'Don't give me that guff!' Fever sprang up and began to pace about. 'That's really why you're here, isn't it? You heard I had a bit of a barney with Martindale on Tuesday and you want to pin his death on me!'

Mrs Fever made an inarticulate little sound of distress then put out her hand towards her husband and said, 'Lewis, please.'

Fever ignored her. 'Well you won't get away with it! If every time two men had an argument one of them is accused of murder, the place would be littered with corpses!'

'We're only interested in one corpse, Mr Fever, Mr Martindale's. As I say, we're not yet satisfied that his death was an accident and we are only doing our duty in trying to find out precisely what did happen.'

'Duty! Is this what you call duty, coming into a man's home and accusing him of murder!'

'Mr Fever!' Thanet was capable of showing steel when he wanted to and had no intention of being browbeaten into going away without what he had come for. 'I am accusing no one of anything. Would you please sit down and allow us to have a rational conversation, or – '

Fever ran his hands wildly through his hair. 'Rational! What's rational about – '

For the second time in two days Thanet was driven to a course of action he normally regarded as the last resort. He stood up. 'Very well. If that's the way you want it. I shall have to ask you to accompany us back to headquarters, for questioning.'

Mrs Fever jumped up and grasped her husband by the sleeve. 'Lewis, please, they're only doing what they have to . . .'

He shook her off and stood glaring at Thanet.

There was a tense silence and then he plumped down on the settee, folding his arms belligerently across his chest. 'I don't seem to have much choice in the matter, do I?'

'On the contrary,' said Thanet, sitting down again. 'The choice is yours. Here . . . or there.'

'Here, there, what's the difference? In any case I have nothing to hide, so for God's sake let's get on with it, shall we?'

In the event, there was little more that they could add to

what Thanet already knew. Mrs Fever confirmed the substance of the conversation with Martindale at the garage, studiously avoiding looking at her husband while doing so, and Fever, keeping his volatile temper barely under control, gave a brief account of his visit to the Hall. His intention, he swore, had merely been to warn Martindale to keep away from his wife, to frighten him off.

'You've all known each other for years, I gather, since before Mr Martindale went away?'

Fever's face went curiously wooden. 'That's right, yes.'

Mrs Fever cast an anxious little sideways glance at him.

'You were friends, at that time?'

'Friends! Leo didn't have any friends, believe me.'

'Why not? What did people have against him?' Thanet didn't have much hope of an honest answer and he didn't get one.

'Let's just say he had the knack of putting people's backs up.'

And Fever gave a smile that was more a baring of the teeth, reminding Thanet of Jack Talion's reaction.

Thanet stood up. 'That sounds like an understatement to me.'

They all rose. 'Think what you like,' said Fever. 'That's the way it was. But if you're looking for a scapegoat, Inspector, you won't find him in this house.'

'Charming,' said Lineham, when the front door had slammed behind them. 'D'you think he's our man, sir?'

Thanet shrugged. 'As I said before, not unless we can put him behind the wheel of that van. And even then . . . I don't know, Mike. I suppose I can see him running Martindale down while he was still all steamed up, but not calmly sitting about considering it and going back to do it in cold blood. We'll just have to see. What's next on the agenda?'

'Mrs Hamilton at 1.30.'

It was now 12.45.

'Time we visited the local, I think, Mike.'

TWELVE

Like so many country pubs the Drovers had suffered from modernisation in the sixties and seventies. The ancient floorboards had been covered with heavily patterned carpets, sections of wall faced with synthetic boarding and the bar tarted up with a collection of dangling keyrings. At this hour on a weekday there were only three other customers. The food, however, was good and the beer acceptable.

Thanet took an appreciative mouthful of roast beef sandwich seasoned with French mustard. 'What did he say?'

Lineham had been deputed to ask the landlord why he had not mentioned Martindale's ostracism by the locals on Monday night.

'Same old story. "Nobody asked me . . ." ' Lineham loaded his crusty French bread with butter, cheese and pickle. 'Think the Super will turn up?'

Thanet grimaced. 'Hope not.'

Lineham grinned. 'Perhaps there'll be a mini crime wave in Sturrenden and he'll be too busy.'

'I'll pretend I didn't hear that remark, Mike.'

Lineham chewed thoughtfully for a while and then said, 'What about this van, sir? Think there's any hope of proving which of them was driving it?'

'Ridiculous, isn't it? Six people have keys and we already know four of them drove it on Tuesday night – as well as Mrs Rankle, who borrowed it to check on her son.'

112

Lineham ticked them off on his fingers. 'Mrs Hamilton went to fetch Adam from the station at 7.25. When she got back at about 7.40, Mr Talion used it to check on the sheep that had got out. He took about — how long did he say?'

'Twenty-five minutes or so.'

'So he would have got back at around ten past eight. Then it stood idle for twenty minutes or so until Sam Tiller went to pick up Mrs Rankle. Then at 9.15 or thereabouts she borrowed it . . .'

'Passing the entrance gates of the Hall on her way. And she wasn't exactly on friendly terms with Martindale, by the sound of it. I wonder what she had against him?'

'Think there's any hope of finding out?'

'Not much, the way things are going. It's like trying to get blood out of a stone, trying to find out why they were all so anti Martindale, isn't it?'

'Never mind. As you would say, it's early days yet.'

Thanet grinned. Lineham's unfailing optimism was one of the reasons why he enjoyed working with him. 'True. Anyway, you were saying . . .'

'Sam Tiller drove it next, to take Mrs Rankle home and then go home himself. Leaving the pub at . . . ?'

'Ten-thirty, I think.'

'And finally Mr Hamilton used it at 11.15, to go and pick up Tessa, when the Range Rover wouldn't start. Think that's true, sir?'

'We must check with her. But I shouldn't think he'd risk involving her in lying for him.'

'So really its movements are pretty well accounted for, except for twenty minutes or so between ten and half-past eight and the three quarters of an hour between 10.30 and 11.15. Time enough in both cases for any one of them to have driven it down to the gates and back.'

'Yes, but who? Let's see, what did they all claim to be doing between those times, Mike?'

'Mr Hamilton said he was working in his office during the

earlier period. He must have been alone or he would presumably have mentioned that someone was with him. He could easily have slipped out. He and Mrs Hamilton stood to lose a packet, if Martindale had claimed what was rightfully his. Say Hamilton looked out of the window and happened to see Martindale leaving the house, to go to the pub, perhaps . . .'

'I doubt that he would have gone to the pub, Mike, after getting the cold shoulder the night before.'

'Oh, I don't know. He sounds pretty thick-skinned to me. Anyway, he needn't have been going to the pub. He could have been meeting someone . . .'

'Who, for example?'

'I don't know. I'm only making suggestions, sir.' Lineham was beginning to sound plaintive. 'He could just have been going for a walk.'

Thanet shrugged. 'True. All right, Mike, go on.'

'So,' said Lineham, leaning forward eagerly as he warmed to his theory, 'Hamilton sees the perfect opportunity to get rid of him. Everything's quiet, the guests are at dinner . . . He gets to the van without being seen and drives off. He catches up with Martindale at the bottom of the drive and runs him down. He gets out to check that Martindale is dead, then drags him into the ditch so he won't be found by anyone else coming in or out of the Hall gates that night. Into the van, up the drive, back into his study and he's home and dry. It need only have taken ten or fifteen minutes in all. What d'you think, sir?'

Thanet took out his pipe, tapped it, inspected it, blew through it and began to fill it. 'Unless it was a straightforward accident, I should think it must have happened like that. But the trouble is, you could apply the same scenario to any one of them. We don't know what Mrs Hamilton was doing just then, or Sam Tiller, or Jack Talion . . .'

'Or the Byfleets, for that matter,' Lineham conceded gloomily. 'He's supposed to have got back from Gatwick

114

about eight, so they were both around between ten and half-past eight as well. And the van stands near where they live in the stable yard.'

'Unfortunately the van was conveniently accessible to the lot of them,' said Thanet with a sigh. 'We've got a tremendous amount of checking to do, Mike. It would help if we had some idea what time Martindale was knocked down, but as yet we haven't a clue. After that early dinner, which was over by about seven, no one seems to have seen him.'

'Except for Mrs Byfleet. She was seen coming out of his room at 7.15, remember.'

'I know, but it could just have been a routine check. The room might well have been empty.'

'We both thought she was lying about something.'

'I know. Ah well, come on Mike, drink up. I don't think Mrs Hamilton is the type to appreciate being kept waiting.'

'Don't suppose we'll get much out of her,' grumbled Lineham.

'You never know. We have got one or two cards up our sleeve, remember,' though Thanet wasn't feeling too optimistic about the coming interview. Mrs Hamilton wouldn't easily be manoeuvred into telling them anything she didn't wish to divulge.

In the car park Thanet came to a sudden halt. 'It's just occurred to me . . .'

'What?'

'The van. Apart from the twenty minutes or so when Mrs Rankle used it, it was standing out here in the pub car park all evening, between say 8.45 and 10.30. During that time anyone could have borrowed it and unless they were actually spotted no one would have been any the wiser.'

Lineham groaned.

Delia Hamilton was waiting for them in her office, a pleasant, sunny little room tastefully furnished with antiques and country house chintzes.

She rose to greet them. 'I hope this won't take too long, Inspector. How are you getting on? Have you found out what happened?'

She was as immaculately groomed as ever, her hair in a smooth chignon today, wearing a simple, elegant dress of raspberry-coloured wool with long sleeves and a cowl neck. Pearls and a beautiful enamelled antique fob watch completed the English country lady image.

'Not yet, ma'am. But don't worry, we shall.'

She waved them to two upright chairs already in position in front of her desk and sat down behind it. She raised her eyebrows expectantly. 'Well?'

'One or two things have emerged . . .'

'Such as?'

'I understand that there was an argument that night, between a Mr Fever, who lives locally, and your brother.'

'So I believe.'

'Can you tell us anything about it?'

'I wasn't present, so no, I'm afraid I can't.'

'Can you think of any reason why Mr Fever should have been so angry with your brother?'

'I haven't the faintest idea.' She waved a hand, dismissing the matter as of no importance. 'Fever has the reputation of having what is commonly called a short fuse. I suppose Leo had done something to annoy him. I shouldn't place too much importance on it, if I were you.'

'Mr Fever's wife, Yvonne . . .'

Delia Hamilton's delicately arched brows rose again. 'What about her?'

'Your brother seemed to know her. We understand they met in the village on Tuesday, and he greeted her like an old friend.'

'Sutton is a very small community, Inspector. Yvonne Fever has lived here all her life. As children we all knew each other.'

'Was there anything special between them?'

116

'Special?'

'Was she his girlfriend, before he went away?'

Delia laughed. 'I wouldn't put it quite like that. Let's just say that Leo was a very attractive young man and I've no doubt that at one time or another he took most of the local girls out. But a special girlfriend . . .' She shook her head. 'It wouldn't have been suitable.'

Because of the difference in class, presumably. A rather naïve view, Thanet felt. He was pretty certain that if Leo had fancied a girl he wouldn't have hesitated to break the rules. Besides, he suspected that the question had made Delia Hamilton uneasy. Because of Yvonne Fever, or had there been another scandal to do with Leo and a local girl? Sam Tiller's daughter, perhaps, if he had one? Or Jack Talion's?

'So to your knowledge there is no particular reason why Mr Fever had a grudge against your brother?'

She shook her head. 'No.'

'What about Sam Tiller?'

'Sam Tiller?' Briefly, she looked disconcerted.

'Someone overheard Sam Tiller telling you that if your brother stayed, he would leave.'

A flash of anger, quickly suppressed. At being put in the difficult position of having to explain, presumably. 'You shouldn't listen to gossip, Inspector. You can't believe half of what you hear.'

'You deny that this conversation took place, then?'

'I didn't say that.'

'Or that Sam Tiller did in fact present you with this ultimatum?'

'I'm the one who presents ultimatums around here, Inspector.'

'You haven't answered my question.'

She hated being pinned down like this, obviously wasn't used to having anyone press her for an answer which she didn't want to give.

'What question was that?' But there was the beginning of

117

resignation in her eyes. She could see he wasn't going to let her wriggle out of it.

Thanet was rather enjoying this duel of wits. 'Did Sam Tiller tell you that if your brother stayed, he would have to hand in his resignation?'

'What if he did? What possible relevance could it have?'

'Did he, Mrs Hamilton?'

Anger sparked in her eyes as she capitulated. 'If it's so important for you to know . . . Yes, he did.'

But the battle was only half won. Thanet still had to find out what he really wanted to know. 'Why was that?'

She shrugged, lifting elegant shoulders. 'How should I know?'

'*Do* you know?' he pressed.

'I've no doubt he had his reasons.'

'What were they?'

Her self-control was admirable but her fury and tension showed in the unnatural rigidity of her posture, the clenching of the muscles along her jawline.

Thanet waited. Was she going to tell him, would he have to press her further or would she lie? It was, he felt, absolutely crucial that he win this battle. It would be the first crack in the barrier of silence which everyone who knew Martindale seemed to put up when being questioned about the general hostility towards him.

He allowed the silence to prolong itself for a little while longer then sighed. 'Mrs Hamilton,' he said gently. 'You're not really asking me to believe that if you didn't already know, you wouldn't have asked why Sam found the idea of working for your brother so unacceptable?'

'I'm not asking you to believe or disbelieve anything.'

Thanet tried a different tack. 'I'm beginning to wonder if you really do want us to find out about your brother's death.'

That had stung. Her lips tightened. 'You can't fool me, Inspector. You don't believe anything of the sort. You're just trying to goad me into telling you what you want to know. If it's so important, why don't you ask Sam himself?'

'If you don't tell me, I shall. But I assume that as you're so keen to protect him you really don't believe he can be involved. In which case you would be doing him a good turn by telling me, instead of my having to ask him straight out. I assume that it is a matter which has caused him some distress, in the past?'

Still no answer.

'I shan't give up until I find out, you know.'

Silence. She rose with an exasperated sigh and went to stand looking out of the window with her back to them.

Thanet waited, glancing at Lineham, who grinned and raised a triumphant thumb. Thanet pulled down the corners of his mouth and shrugged. *We mustn't count our chickens* . . .

Finally she turned to face them, leaning back against the windowsill. Sunlight haloed her hair. 'Just why is it so important?'

'We don't know that it is. It's just that it could be.'

'Because you suspect Sam of running Leo down.'

'It's one possibility among many.'

She gave a wry smile and returned to her seat. 'Well, Inspector, I can see that as you say you're not the type to give up. As you will have gathered, I don't like talking about my employees behind their backs. In my view loyalty is a two-way process. But I suppose you might as well hear the truth from someone who will give you an unbiased account of it.'

And a vested interest in diverting attention away from herself, Thanet reminded himself as she began to speak. But he had won!

'Sam wasn't always in such a . . . well, menial position. He once ran his own farm. It was only a small farm, but it had been in his family for several generations. . . . He also had a passionate and life-long ambition, to breed a prize bull. Oh, you may well smile, Inspector, but believe me there was no more serious subject in the world to Sam.

'Well, to skip all the years of trial and error, of complete failure and near misses, and to cut a long story short, in the end he did it. His bull won the prize of Supreme Champion at the Royal Show at Stoneleigh. It's the most prestigious prize of all and Sam was walking on air. Stud fees, he knew, would make him a rich man, but best of all was the knowledge that he had done it, he alone by his own efforts had made it. You understand what I mean?'

Thanet nodded.

'The week after the show my dear brother left open the gate of the field in which the bull was kept. I don't know if you've ever seen one of these creatures, Inspector, but believe me they are massive. It was unfortunate that an articulated lorry happened to be coming along at the time. The bull ran straight out into its path. The animal wasn't killed outright but it was so badly injured that it had to be put down. You can imagine how Sam felt.'

'It was carelessness on your brother's part?'

'Oh I don't think it was deliberate, if that's what you mean. But it was carelessness, yes, sheer, criminal, absolutely inexcusable carelessness. My father paid heavily in compensation, tried to smooth things over, but of course it couldn't make up to Sam for all those years of single-minded endeavour. It just about broke his heart, finished him. He couldn't face starting all over again. He let things slide, the money dwindled and dwindled and in the end he went bankrupt. Just about then his wife died and he went to live with his daughter. For years he got occasional jobs as tractor driver or farm labourer, and then when my father died and I decided to turn this place into a hotel I needed someone to look after the grounds. There was accommodation available in the stable block and I felt an obligation to Sam . . . He took some persuading but by then there was friction with his son-in-law and he was tempted, as I hoped he might be, by the prospect of independence. He's been here ever since.'

'I see.' Thanet did see. Long years of bitterness could

shrivel a man's soul. To Tiller the prospect of working for the man who had ruined him would have been unendurable. Faced with having to abandon for the second time the life he had built for himself and presented with the opportunity for revenge he could well have succumbed to temptation.

'Oh, I know what you're thinking, Inspector. It's why I didn't want to tell you. You're thinking that if the opportunity presented itself Sam might well have been tempted to run Leo down. But he's not like that. He's a good man, kind . . .'

Remembering Tiller's defensiveness, his aggression and hostility, Thanet wasn't so sure. He said as much to Lineham, outside.

'I agree. Though how we'd ever be able to prove it, if it was him – ' Lineham broke off. 'Oh, no . . .'

Thanet turned to look. A police Land Rover was coming up the drive. It was just close enough for him to recognise the passenger.

Superintendent Draco had arrived.

THIRTEEN

Draco sprang out of the Land Rover and came bouncing towards them across the gravel. Energy emanated from him in almost visible waves. 'Ah, there you are, Thanet. How's it going?'

'We're just going to have a word with the groundsman, Sam Tiller, sir.'

They waited while two of the guests, a middle-aged couple dressed for a country walk in wellington boots and anoraks, came out of the hotel and passed them, casting curious glances. Then Thanet gave a brief account of the conversation with Mrs Hamilton.

A delighted smile spread across Draco's face. 'That's a new one. Revenge for the death of a prize bull, eh? Thought I'd heard them all, but this really takes the biscuit.'

They headed for the stable yard.

'Even if Tiller did run Mr Martindale down we're going to have a hard time proving it. Have you heard anything from forensic yet, sir?'

'No. I was on to them again just before I left. Usual story, snowed under with work etc. But they promise the results by tomorrow.'

Draco was glancing about curiously as they walked. He looked as though he was thoroughly enjoying himself.

Thanet again remembered wondering, when Draco first

came, how long the Superintendent was going to tie himself to his desk. He hoped this visit wasn't heralding a new era of involvement on the Superintendent's part in the day-to-day progress of cases in his division.

'There was one point, though.' Draco fished in his pocket, produced a piece of paper. 'Bentley thought you might be interested to know that Mr . . .' He consulted the paper. '. . . Mr Talion had sacked a farmhand a couple of weeks back. Here's his name and address.' He handed the paper to Thanet. 'He thought it might be useful to interview him, in view of the fact that Talion and Martindale had had a row and you hadn't been able to find out why. He thought the man might possibly know the reason for any animosity between them and if he's still feeling sore he might be tempted to talk. I told him to go ahead. I hope that's OK by you.'

It wasn't. Thanet did not appreciate Draco giving his men orders. Who knew where it would end? He swallowed his resentment and said non-committally, 'It could be useful.' But again, it might not. It depended, Thanet thought, on how long the man had lived in the area and how much he knew about the grudge which Talion evidently harboured against Martindale. Still, he admitted reluctantly, Draco was right, it was worth following up.

The stable yard appeared deserted.

'He may be in the outbuilding where we interviewed him yesterday,' suggested Lineham.

They walked across and knocked. A moment later the door opened. Tiller scowled. 'Oh, it's you again. What d'you want this time?'

'Another word, if you don't mind. This is Superintendent Draco.'

Was that a flash of fear as Tiller glanced at Draco? If so, it was immediately replaced by the old sneering belligerence. 'Come to arrest me, have you?'

'Just a word, as I said.' Thanet was at his most benign.

Grudgingly, Tiller stood back.

He had been cleaning his tools, sharpening a spade with a whetstone. Not much could be done outside in this weather, Thanet supposed. It was a good time for ensuring that equipment was in good order for the rush of work when spring arrived.

Draco's arrival had given Thanet little time to consider how he was going to tackle Tiller. He felt inhibited by the Superintendent's presence, despite the fact that Draco had tactfully withdrawn into the background and was pretending to examine the tools arrayed on hooks on the walls. With an effort he tried to put the Superintendent out of his mind, pretend that he wasn't there.

He decided to take the bull by the horns. Suppressing a wry smile at the appropriateness of the metaphor he said, 'You told Mrs Hamilton that if Mr Martindale stayed on here, you would leave.'

Tiller leaned back against his work bench and folded his arms. 'So?'

'We know why, Mr Tiller.'

A spasm of — what? Anger? Fear? — briefly contorted the man's features. 'If you're so clever I don't know why you bother with pretending you want to talk to me. Go on, admit it, you've made up your minds I ran him down, haven't you?' His gaze encompassed all three policemen then focused again on Thanet.

Thanet sighed. 'If my mind were as closed as yours, Mr Tiller, I'd have a string of false arrests to my credit. And that's not the way I work. I repeat, we're merely trying to find out the truth. And I would like to point out that if you were not involved in Mr Martindale's death it is in your own interest for you to cooperate with us as fully as possible.'

Silence while Tiller considered the logic of what Thanet had said. Finally he unfolded his arms and took a pipe from his pocket.

Thanet immediately wanted to follow suit. If Draco hadn't

124

been present he might in fact have done so. Such a small act of sharing a mutual enjoyment could create a common bond and lower the emotional temperature of a difficult interview by several degrees. Once again he cursed Draco's presence.

Tiller was stuffing tobacco into the bowl with practised fingers, taking matches from his pockets. He waited until he had lit up and then, gazing up at the coils of smoke swirling lazily above his head, said, 'You could have a point there.'

Thanet knew when to keep silent and he continued to wait patiently, acutely conscious of Draco behind him. He could rely on Lineham, but the Superintendent was a different matter. Patience was not his strong point and if he said or did anything at this crucial moment ... He wouldn't, surely? Thanet reminded himself that Draco hadn't reached his present rank without good reason.

Tiller's gaze slowly descended to linger on Thanet's face. 'All right, then. What d'you want to know?'

There was a distinct easing of the atmosphere. But they were not there yet. Slowly now, Thanet warned himself. 'We're still trying to check the movements of the van that night. You said you left here at 8.30 to pick up Mrs Rankle?'

Tiller nodded, puffing rhythmically at his pipe.

'And left the pub at around 10.30, to take her home before returning here?'

Another nod.

'When did you last use it, earlier in the evening?'

Tiller considered, then took his pipe out of his mouth. ' 'Bout five o'clock. To run Andy home – the young lad who helps me. He usually cycles, but his bike's out of commission at the moment.'

'And after that the van stood out in the yard, as usual?'

' 'S right.'

'Do you know of anyone else who used it, that night?'

Tiller hesitated.

No point in reversing the man's mood and making him dig his heels in again out of mistaken loyalty to Delia Hamilton.

'Mrs Hamilton told us she used it to fetch her son from the station just before half-past seven. Also, Mr Talion used it to check on some sheep that had got out on to the road, some twenty minutes later. After that it stood idle until you left at 8.30, so far as we know . . .'

No response.

Thanet tried again. 'Do you know if anyone used it either before Mrs Hamilton or during those twenty minutes between ten and half-past eight?'

Tiller was shaking his head. 'Not so far as I know. Someone could have, of course.'

'Does your cottage overlook the yard?'

Tiller nodded, eyes narrowing.

'Even if you didn't actually see anyone getting into or out of it, or driving it, did you happen to glance out at any point and notice that it was gone?'

Tiller considered. Finally he shook his head. 'Earlier on I was having my tea in the kitchen at the back of the house. Then I watched telly until about eight, when I went upstairs to have a shave and get ready to go out. And it was dark, of course, the curtains was drawn.'

Pity. 'Did you hear anything, then, while you were in your bedroom? An engine start up?'

'Nah. Had the radio on.'

'What about later on, after you got home? Did you hear anything then?'

Tiller started to shake his head again, then stopped. 'There was something,' he said slowly.

'When was that?'

'Soon after I got into bed. I was just dozing off. Must have been about a quarter past eleven. I heard a car start up.'

'Ah, yes, that was probably Mr Hamilton. Miss Hamilton had borrowed the Range Rover and she couldn't get it to start. Mr Hamilton went to help her. You might have heard them come back.'

'Not me. Went out like a light, I always do.'

'What about earlier, before you went to bed?'

Another shake of the head. 'Sorry.'

Dead end, there. Move on, then, to the more delicate topic of Mrs Rankle borrowing the van. Would it be best to try to get Tiller to volunteer the information, and risk arousing his anger again if it was necessary to press him, perhaps catch him out in a lie, or to ask him outright? Either way he was likely to erupt. Marginally better, perhaps, to avoid putting him in the wrong.

'I understand that when you and Mrs Rankle go to the pub she usually borrows the van some time during the evening to go and check that her son is all right. He's handicapped, I believe?'

Tiller's reaction was instantaneous. Ignoring the last question he took his pipe from his mouth and straightened up, glaring at Thanet. 'So what? I've got every right to lend it to whoever I like.'

'I'm not questioning your right to lend it . . .'

'I should hope not. Because you ask Mrs Hamilton. Go on, ask her. I wondered about Sonia driving it because of the insurance, see, I wasn't sure who was covered, so I asked Mrs Hamilton's permission and she told me the cover was comprehensive and I could use it as I liked. "Off duty you must treat the van as yours, Sam," she says. "Just use your own discretion." '

Thanet held up his hand. 'All right, all right. I accept that. I told you, I'm not questioning your right to lend it to whoever you want to lend it to. All I'm trying to find out is whether Mrs Rankle drove it on Tuesday night.'

If Tiller had been playing a game of Statues he couldn't have frozen into immobility more quickly. Only his eyes seemed alive, small black burning coals in an expanse of paralysed flesh. Then a hiss escaped through his slightly parted lips, his left eyelid twitched and he took a deep breath. 'Just what,' he said through his teeth, 'are you implying?'

The waves of antagonism emanating from him were so

powerful that it was with difficulty that Thanet stood his ground. 'Asking, Mr Tiller. Not —'

Tiller took a step forward and Thanet sensed Lineham tense beside him. 'Just leave Mrs Rankle out of this, d'you hear me? LEAVE HER OUT OF THIS!'

'That may not be possible, Mr Tiller.'

Tiller made an inarticulate sound that was almost a growl and, bunching his hands into fists, took another step forward.

Lineham also moved forward and Thanet was suddenly conscious of Draco flanking him on the other side. Three against one, he thought. Not very fair. He suppressed a desire to laugh. How impressed the Super must be with his handling of this one!

He was opening his mouth to speak when Draco intervened. 'Come now, Mr Tiller. That wouldn't be very sensible, would it? Assaulting a police officer and all that?'

'Look,' said Thanet, humiliated and seething, trying to ignore the fact that Draco had spoken at all, 'I can imagine how you feel . . .'

'Can you?' snarled Tiller. 'How would you like it if someone you knew died in an accident and before you could turn round you're suspected of murdering him? Or if not you, your girlfriend or wife, perhaps. Just think about it! How *would* you feel?'

'If I were innocent — furiously angry, outraged, helpless, frustrated, hurt, confused, misjudged . . .'

'Well then!'

'But if I were guilty . . .' Thanet allowed the pause to lengthen then said softly, 'If I were guilty, then I would put on a good show of feeling all those things, in order to proclaim my innocence.'

Tiller stared at him. Then his shoulders drooped and he turned away. 'I can't win, can I? I can't bloody win!'

'You don't help yourself by getting all worked up like this, that's for sure,' said Thanet gently. 'And I do assure you that

128

we are putting precisely this kind of question to everyone who had access to the van that night. Everyone. Sooner or later the truth will come out. And I meant what I said. If you are not involved you have nothing to fear and everything to gain by cooperating with us in full.'

Tiller made a dispirited gesture. 'I've told you all I know. But if you want to ask questions about other people you'll just have to go and talk to them yourself, because I can't and won't answer.'

There really was no point in continuing. 'Very well, Mr Tiller, I can understand that.' Thanet glanced at the others. *Ready to go?* 'We'll leave you to get on with your work.'

Outside they crossed the yard in a tense, embarrassed silence. After a few moments Draco cleared his throat.

'I owe you an apology, Thanet.'

Thanet said nothing.

'I shouldn't have interfered. I was most impressed by the way you handled him.'

Apologies didn't come easily to Draco and Thanet felt appeased. 'I admit he had me worried for a moment there, sir. I was glad you and Lineham were present.'

'Tricky customer. And no fool. With a chip as big as a mountain on his shoulder. If that's the degree of antagonism Martindale was capable of arousing, it wouldn't surprise me in the least if someone grabbed the opportunity to get rid of him. Think it was Tiller?'

'I just don't know, sir. What do you think, Lineham?'

Lineham was pleased to be included in the discussion, Thanet could see, but the sergeant was as undecided as he was himself.

'If Mr Martindale happened to be walking down the drive when Tiller drove down to collect Mrs Rankle, well, I could certainly see him being tempted. But I don't know that he would deliberately have planned to do it.'

'I agree.' Thanet sighed. 'If only we had a better idea of Martindale's movements . . .'

'What's your next move, Thanet?' Draco was still being conciliatory.

'I thought we might go and see Mrs Rankle.'

Thanet held his breath, praying that Draco wouldn't say he would accompany them.

They had reached the front drive and Draco stopped. 'Right, I'll leave you to it, then, I've got to be getting back.'

Relief. 'Right, sir.'

One foot in the Land Rover, Draco turned. 'And as I said, Thanet, well done.'

Thanet raised a hand in acknowledgement and watched the Land Rover drive off.

'Think he'll give you a medal, sir?' said Lineham.

He ducked as Thanet threw a mock punch at him and tension dissolved into laughter.

FOURTEEN

'Pretty uphill work, isn't it?' said Lineham as they set off down the drive.

'I feel as though I'm swimming against the tide most of the time,' Thanet admitted. 'I can't ever remember a case in which we've had so many hostile witnesses. I just wonder . . .'

Lineham glanced at him. 'What?'

Thanet shrugged. 'I was wondering if this means we're barking up the wrong tree. That it was after all just a simple hit and run accident.'

'I'm not quite with you, sir.'

'Perhaps I'm being fanciful, and I don't quite know how to put this, but . . . Well, if someone had killed Martindale, his anger against him would be defused. It wouldn't still be around. But most of these people, they're still so angry it's like handling a lot of unexploded bombs. D'you see what I mean? It's almost as if . . .'

Lineham raised his eyebrows.

Thanet gave an embarrassed little laugh. 'It's almost as though their hostility towards Martindale has been redirected, at me.'

'Are you suggesting we should abandon the investigation?'

'Absolutely not. In fact, the harder it gets the more determined I become to find out the truth.'

'I wonder if there'll be any response to the TVS appeal.'

They had arranged for a request for all motorists passing through Sutton-in-the-Weald between the hours of seven p.m. and two a.m. on Tuesday night to come forward.

'We'll just have to wait and see.'

'That'll be Mrs Rankle's cottage, I think.'

Lineham pulled up in front of a pair of semi-detached cottages. In the garden of one of them, a youth, warmly wrapped up in rug, anorak and bobble hat, was sitting in a wheelchair parked in front of a rapidly thawing snowman. He was leaning forward and patting it.

'Hullo,' said Thanet, smiling.

The youth's head swung around and Thanet saw that he was much older than Thanet had thought, in his late twenties, perhaps, with the vacant stare of the mentally handicapped. He looked upset, on the verge of tears.

'What's the matter?' Thanet squatted down in front of him.

'No gone.' The words were barely intelligible.

Thanet frowned, trying to understand.

'Who are you? What do you want?'

The voice was shrill with alarm. A woman was standing at the open door of the cottage. She started towards him as Thanet stood up.

'Mrs Rankle? Sorry, we didn't mean to startle you.' He introduced himself. 'Your son seems upset.'

She was in her late fifties or early sixties, thin and slight, with untidy brown hair and a worn, lined face. There were deep creases between her brows and she looked as though she carried the sorrows of the world on her bowed shoulders. She wore no make-up and was dressed in a shapeless brown skirt and fawn jumper matted by many washings. She fished a handkerchief out of her pocket and briskly wiped the young man's cheeks. 'He's upset because the snow is melting, aren't you, Vince? You thought it was lovely, didn't you? Come on, we'd better go inside, you're getting cold.'

132

She turned the chair and began to push it across the soggy lawn. It was hard going and Thanet said, 'Let us do that for you.'

Between them he and Lineham manoeuvred the chair on to the path and in through the front door. Mrs Rankle went ahead of them, along a short passage. She flung open the door. 'In here.'

It was a squarish kitchen-cum-living-room, old-fashioned but adequately furnished with central table, china-clay sink, gas cooker and antiquated refrigerator. A small coal fire burned in the black cast-iron grate and there was a wooden armchair beside it, complete with cushion and curled-up cat. It should have been comfortable enough, cosy even, and yet ... Thanet, ever-sensitive to atmosphere, looked about, searching for clues to his unease. The place felt curiously empty, bleak. Perhaps it was because the room was not only spotlessly clean but immaculately tidy. There was none of the clutter that Thanet associated with living – books, newspapers, magazines, plants, and no signs of any kind of activity on the part of either Mrs Rankle or her son. What did they do all day in this small bare cell?

Stupid question, he realised. Mrs Rankle had been removing Vincent's hat and coat and now she went to the huge television set, which Thanet had noticed but not really registered, and switched it on. A gardening expert was explaining how to care for pot plants. Then she manoeuvred Vincent's wheelchair so that it was positioned squarely in front of it. 'All right, love?' She ran her hand over his hair in a gesture of affection before turning to Thanet. 'What did you want?'

'May we sit down?'

She looked around. 'We need another chair.' She started towards the door. 'I'll get one from the front room.'

'No, don't bother,' said Lineham. 'I can stand.' He went to lean against the sink.

'You're sure?' She sat down in the armchair, Thanet in the

single upright chair beside the table. Didn't they ever have visitors? he wondered.

'As you've probably guessed, we're looking into the death of Mr Martindale, on Tuesday night.'

He paused. What was the expression that had flitted across her face? Satisfaction?

'And one of the things we're trying to do is piece together his movements during the day.' He gave her no chance to ask him why. 'You were seen talking to him in the village that afternoon . . . Having an argument with him, in fact.'

No response.

'We wondered why . . . Why you were arguing with him, that is.' He waited for denial, prevarication, outright refusal to discuss the matter. It would only be par for the course.

She glanced at Vincent who was apparently absorbed in how to take geranium cuttings, her mouth settling more firmly into bitter lines. 'No reason why I shouldn't tell you. If I don't, you'll hear soon enough from someone else, I've no doubt . . .'

She gestured at her son. 'Leo Martindale did that to Vince.'

Thanet was shaken. What did she mean?

'You'd never believe it to look at him, would you, but until he was nine he was a perfectly normal, healthy little boy.' Briefly the sour lines around her mouth slackened, then tightened again. 'One day, nearly twenty-five years ago, we were visiting my mother, in this cottage. We didn't live here then. We had a council house in Cranbrook . . . While we were here Vince went out to play. We'd told him not to go out on the road but you know what boys are. The first we knew, there was a squeal of brakes and a crash . . . We went rushing out. Vince was lying in the road and Leo Martindale's sports car was slewed across, nose in the hedge.'

In a brief, vivid flash of memory Thanet remembered the heart-stopping moment when Ben, aged about nine himself, had been knocked off his bicycle by a tractor. His stomach clenched as it had then and he was not surprised that as she recalled the incident, even now after all this time, Mrs Rankle's hands were moving in desperate wringing movements painful to watch and her eyes had filled with tears. She dashed them angrily away. 'He'd been drinking,' she said bitterly. 'There was a girl with him. They were both all right, of course, but Vince . . .' She glanced at him again, immobile in front of the flickering screen. 'We thought he was going to die. He was in a coma for weeks, and when he recovered . . .' She shook her head and gave a cynical little laugh. 'Recovered! Not a very good choice of word, as I think you'll agree.'

What could he say? What did one say, in such circumstances? 'It must have been a terrible time for you.'

'I can't tell you . . .' She glanced at him assessingly, as if suddenly aware of whom she was talking to, and he could see her wondering whether to continue. Strictly speaking, of course, he had got at least part of what he wanted, the fact that she had a powerful motive for wanting Martindale dead: revenge. He could understand now that look of satisfaction earlier, when he had mentioned Martindale's death. Even if she hadn't been at the wheel of the van herself there must be for her a delicious irony in the fact that he had himself been killed in a road accident similar to that in which he had maimed her son. Thanet knew that he should now go on to question her about her use of the van that night, but something held him back. There was more that she wanted to tell him, he was sure of it. It occurred to him that it must be rare indeed now for her to have the opportunity to talk about the tragedy that had surely blighted her life. The local people must all know about it and would scarcely welcome hearing the same old story over and over again, and she could hardly go up to a total stranger and buttonhole him like the Ancient Mariner.

'It wasn't as though it was over, when he came out of the coma,' she said in a low voice. 'It was only just beginning. When we found he was permanently brain-damaged and would never walk again, my husband . . . He just couldn't take it, you see. He stuck it out for a couple of years and then walked out.' Her mouth twisted and she snapped her fingers. 'Just like that. One day he was there, the next he was gone. Leaving me stuck . . .' She pulled herself up. 'Not that Vince isn't a good boy, he is. Very loving and obedient, but . . . It's just that there's no relief. You know it's going to go on and on and on, day after day, month after month, year after year . . .'

Her voice was rising and the desperation in her face gave Thanet a glimpse of the endless, unremitting years of selfless commitment she had had to endure. How could she bear it? 'Don't you have any help at all in looking after him?'

'A couple of times a year they take him into residential care while I have a break, but that's all. There just isn't enough manpower to give people like me any help on a regular basis, it's as simple as that – especially in a rural area like this. And the fact of the matter is, that so long as you're coping, you'll be left to get on with it.'

'And you wouldn't want him to go into residential care.' Thanet made it a statement, not a question.

'I've thought about it, often. And I have got as far as making enquiries once or twice when I've been feeling really desperate, but you wouldn't believe the waiting lists, for people in far worse case than Vince. Besides, he's happy here and so long as I'm able to look after him . . . When you have kids you can't just opt out of your responsibilities when the going gets tough, can you?'

An understatement if ever there was one. Thanet shook his head sympathetically. 'Was there a prosecution?'

She grimaced. 'Yes. All he got was a six-month suspended sentence and his licence taken away for eighteen months . . . It still makes me mad to think about it. Oh, it wasn't so bad when Mum was alive. Vince and me moved in here with her and she used to look after him while I went out to work part-time. But since she died, ten years ago . . . No one can imagine, who hasn't been through it . . .'

136

And with no prospect of relief in sight, thought Thanet. It wouldn't have been surprising if, hearing that Martindale was back and faced with the opportunity to avenge the long purgatory of looking after a son born perfectly fit and healthy and now reduced to helpless dependency, she had succumbed to the impulse to run his destroyer down. He hoped very much that this was not what had happened. How could he live with his conscience if she were convicted and Vincent's only prop were removed?

Come on, he told himself. You're not here to judge, simply to discover the truth. And whether you like it or not, that's what you have to do.

Closing his mind with difficulty to the rumblings of his conscience he said quietly, 'Mrs Rankle, I understand you borrowed Mr Tiller's van on Tuesday night, to come back here and check that Vincent was all right?'

She blinked at the change of subject. 'Yes, I always do. It's the only night of the week I go out.' She was on the defensive now. 'I put Vince to bed a bit early on Tuesdays. He can't move about by himself, you see, so he's perfectly safe. But I do like to check he's OK, halfway through the evening.'

'I'm not questioning the care you take of him. It's obvious he's very well looked after, it's just that . . . did you see anybody, on your way here, or on your way back to the pub?'

She frowned, thinking. 'Not so far as I can remember. It was very cold, the roads were icy and I was concentrating on driving, I don't drive much, you see . . . Oh!' Her eyes widened as she realised where this could be leading. 'Just a minute . . . I was wondering why you'd come. You're not trying to tell me it was Sam's van that knocked him down?'

'We're not absolutely certain yet, but it looks that way, I'm afraid.'

'Oh, my God.' She glanced at Vincent then shrank back in her chair, looking near to panic.

Thanet saw her throat move as she swallowed convulsively

and she put her hand over her mouth as if she were about to be sick. Her eyes above it were wide and staring. If she were acting, he thought, it was a first-rate performance. He sincerely hoped she wasn't.

Then she sat up again, making a visible effort at self-control. 'You . . .' she whispered, running the tip of her tongue over dry lips, 'Surely you're not suggesting . . . ? Oh God, you are, aren't you? You think I might have run him down.'

'Mrs Rankle, I assure you that at this stage we're not suggesting anything. We're merely trying to find out what happened.'

A thought struck her. 'Sam . . .'

'Several people drove the van that night, Sam included. We're talking to all of them.'

Now that she was over the initial shock she was rallying. He could see it in the straightening of her back, the tilt of her head, the hardening of her expression. She was a fighter, he reminded himself. If she wasn't, she would have given up long ago.

'That's why you were asking about the argument.' Her voice was much stronger, almost belligerent as she said, 'Well let me tell you this. I may have no reason to love Mr rotten Martindale, but that doesn't mean I'd run him down in cold blood. And in case you're wondering, I didn't knock him down accidentally, either.'

Suddenly she leaned forward, eyes gleaming. 'You said, "All of them". That several people had driven the van that night and you were talking to all of them. Does that include Lewis Fever?'

Thanet saw Lineham, behind her, stiffen.

'What do you mean?' It was scarcely surprising that she should try to use diversionary tactics, but this could be an unexpected break for them. If Tiller had lent Fever the van on Tuesday night they had both kept very quiet about it. Presumably Mrs Rankle felt no such loyalty to Fever.

'He borrowed the van that night too. He came into the pub, about . . .' She put her hands to her temples, pressed them as if trying to force her memory to function efficiently. 'Let me think. It was . . . Yes, it was before I came to check on Vince.' The words began to tumble out as she recalled the incident more clearly. 'It must have been about, oh, around a quarter to nine. He came into the pub and asked Sam if he could borrow it. He and Sam are old mates . . . He'd just heard his mother-in-law had been taken ill and he wanted to run his wife over to see her.'

'Why didn't he use his own car, or his wife's – I presume she's got one?'

'Yes, but Toby had borrowed it. They'd set out in his car, Lewis's that is, but as they were driving through the village he realised he'd got a slow puncture. He didn't want to waste time changing the wheel and he saw Sam's van in the car park at the Drovers so he came in to ask if he could borrow it for half an hour. Of course, Sam said yes.'

'Where does his mother-in-law live?'

'Ashford.'

So Fever would have had to pass the gates of the Hall on his way. 'How long was he away?'

'Only half an hour or so, as he promised. As soon as he got back I drove home to see if Vince was OK.'

Outside in the car Lineham said resignedly, 'I just don't believe this. How many more people d'you suppose drove the wretched thing that night?'

'The Byfleets?' said Thanet.

'How much d'you bet?'

'I'm not a gambling man, as you well know, Mike. But the way things are going the odds in favour seem pretty high. We need to find out if she actually saw Martindale that night when she went to his room, anyway, so let's go and ask them, shall we?'

139

FIFTEEN

On the way back up the drive they passed the middle-aged couple they had seen earlier, returning from their walk, and in the stable yard Adam Hamilton was mooning about, kicking a stone. Thanet scarcely recognised him at first; he had discarded his bizarre outfit of yesterday in favour of jeans and a scruffy sweater – a discard of his father's? – which hung on him in folds and with sleeves so long that they completely covered his hands. He came over as they parked the car.

'Hey, Inspector, how're you doing?'

'Fine, thanks.'

'Found out who dunnit yet?'

'Done what?' Though it was clear what Adam meant.

'Oh come on! Bumped off dear Uncle Leo, of course. It's obvious that, as Eliza Doolittle would say, someone done 'im in.'

'What makes you say that?'

'Stands to reason, doesn't it? I keep my ear to the ground and the word is he really stirred things up in the short time he was here.'

'And who's the popular choice of villain?'

Adam shrugged. 'You pays yer money and you takes yer choice ... I couldn't care less as long as it wasn't the old man.'

His tone was flippant but briefly Thanet glimpsed the fear behind the façade. Adam, whether he knew it or not, was looking for reassurance that his father wasn't involved. Unfortunately Thanet couldn't give it to him, not at this stage. His own tone was correspondingly light as he said, 'You think it might have been?'

The boy shrugged, looking suddenly very young and defenceless. 'Had a bloody good motive, didn't he?' He rallied, flinging his head back and gesturing theatrically about him. 'The old ancestral acres and all that.'

Thanet took pity on him. 'I shouldn't lose too much sleep over it just yet. As you say, your uncle seems to have stirred up a good many sleeping dogs in the short time he was here and anyway there's no indication yet that it wasn't an accident, pure and simple . . . Look, I wanted a word with the Byfleets. Do you happen to know where they might be at this time of day?'

'Since Mrs Byfleet's been in pod Ma's insisted on her having the afternoon off, so she might be in the flat. I don't know about him, he could be anywhere around.'

'Where do they live, exactly?'

Adam pointed to some windows above a row of stable doors. 'Over there. You go in through the right-hand stable, there're some steps leading up.'

Thanet thanked him and he and Lineham began to walk in that direction. Adam fell in beside them.

'It's pretty boring hanging around here at half-term. Trust me to be away when something really exciting happened for once. So if I can help at all . . .'

'Go on keeping your ear to the ground. And if you come across anything interesting, let me know.'

'Anyone special you'd like me to keep an eye on?'

'Not at the moment, thanks.'

Adam looked disappointed and walked moodily away, hands in pockets, in the direction of the house.

'Poor kid. Must be worried sick,' said Lineham.

'You noticed, then. Yes. But there's not much we can do about it at the moment.'

The door Adam had indicated was propped open with a stone and led into a long building divided off on their left into a series of stalls where horses had once been kept. This end section had been gutted and a sturdy wooden staircase with wide, open treads and a handrail had been fixed to the right-hand wall.

'Pretty dark in here,' said Lineham. 'Wonder if there's a light.'

He looked about and found one, just inside the door. He clicked it on and a bulkhead light fitment at the top of the staircase came on, illuminating the door beside it. Byfleet answered their knock and when he saw who it was stood back without a word. He led them through a tiny vestibule into a large sitting-room which ran the whole depth of the building with windows to front and rear. It was, Thanet thought, a delightful room, the sort of room he would be very happy to live in himself, with beams overhead infilled with rough plaster painted a rich, creamy white. Overflowing bookshelves stood between the windows, and the colours in the flowery chintz curtains were echoed in the comfortable, slip-covered armchairs and the patterned rugs on the wide, highly polished floorboards. There were brightly coloured cushions, plants and flowers and, in addition to a small portable television set, there was a modest stereo system and an extensive collection of records and tapes on specially constructed shelves. A bundle of lacy white knitting lay on one of the chairs and a low table with an unfinished game of chess laid out on it stood nearby. On another table stood a beautiful blue-and-white ceramic bowl heaped with odds and ends – some coloured pebbles, a silver nutcracker, a corkscrew, a pocket diary, a brass doorknob, a screwdriver and a pair of pink baby's bootees. Table lamps cast welcoming pools of light. It was a living-room in the best sense of the word, a room for enjoying life. The contrast with Mrs Rankle's bleak kitchen was almost painful.

'Did you want to speak to my wife?'

'We'd like a word with both of you, actually, Mr Byfleet.'

Up until now Thanet had had little more than an occasional glimpse of the housekeeper's husband and he studied him with interest. Without the bobble hat his ears did not stick out quite as much as Thanet remembered, and the man was younger than he had thought, in his late thirties, perhaps. Divested of his anorak he was even thinner than Thanet expected, a tall, bony, gangling individual whose joints seemed articulated rather than smoothly linked by muscle and tendon. He looked tense, but there was no special significance in that. Most people were tense when interviewed by the police, innocent and guilty alike. And perhaps Byfleet was feeling especially protective towards his wife at the moment, as she'd been having a difficult time with her pregnancy. His next words confirmed this.

'She's having a rest.' He glanced at his watch. 'But she should be up soon. She asked me to call her at a quarter to four.'

The implication was clear. He didn't want to wake her before time. Thanet glanced at his watch. Three-thirty. 'That's fine. We can talk to you first, while we're waiting.'

They all sat down.

Byfleet looked expectantly at Thanet but as prearranged it was Lineham who spoke. 'We understand you picked up some guests from Gatwick last night, Mr Byfleet.'

'That's right.'

'You took the Rolls-Royce, I believe.'

'I usually do when I'm collecting guests.'

'I bet they love it.'

'They do seem to appreciate it, yes.'

'You're a lucky man. It's one of my life-long ambitions, to drive a Rolls – oh, don't worry, Mr Byfleet, I'm not hinting. But even a humble copper can have his dreams.'

This brought a faint smile to Byfleet's face.

Well done, Mike, approved Thanet. Lineham had done well to get Byfleet to relax even to this degree.

'Anyway,' Lineham went on, 'you got back at around . . .' He pretended to consult his notes.

'Five to eight,' said Byfleet. 'Or thereabouts.'

'Did you meet Mr Talion going down the drive in the van? He had to go and check on some sheep that had got out on to the road about then.'

Thanet was sure that Lineham was well aware that Talion had left a good ten minutes earlier.

Byfleet was shaking his head. 'I didn't meet anything coming down the drive. But even if I had I wouldn't have known Mr Talion was driving. It was dark.'

Lineham shrugged. 'But your headlights would have been on. You might just have recognised someone. Anyway, if you say you didn't meet anything . . .'

'I didn't.'

Thanet missed the next exchange. He was wondering if Martindale had realised that the approaching van was going to run him down. Thanet imagined the scene: Martindale walking through the darkness, the sound of his footsteps crisp in the frosty night. Then, from behind him, the sound of an approaching car, its headlights casting long fingers of light towards the entrance gates. Martindale would have stopped walking, perhaps moved in close to the fence at the side of the road for the car to pass. At what point would he have realised that it wasn't going to, that he himself was its target? Perhaps he never had realised. The tear in his overcoat was in the back. Perhaps he had been hurled all unawares into Eternity. Of course, it was possible that it had been an accident after all. The driver could have seen the pedestrian ahead, braked too fiercely in order to pass him, and found himself skidding on the icy road. And of course the entire incident could have taken place on the main road and not in the drive at all. In any case it was highly unlikely that Martindale would have glimpsed the face of his killer.

144

Thanet switched his attention back to the interview.

'If you had happened to look out of any of the front windows, would you have been able to recognise anyone crossing the stable yard? How well lit is it at night?'

Lineham had evidently been asking if either of the Byfleets had seen anyone drive the van away.

'Very well lit really. Mrs Hamilton had extra lights installed when a guest twisted her ankle on the cobbles last year.'

'Who is responsible for switching them on?'

Byfleet shrugged. 'Theoretically I am. But if I'm not here when it gets dark one of the others will do it.'

'Were they on when you got back that night?'

'I think they must have been, or I'd have noticed.' He thought for a moment. 'Yes, they were.'

'Your wife was already here when you got back?'

'Yes. She knew I'd be back about eight, so she came over to finish getting supper ready.'

Had Thanet imagined it, or was there a touch of unease there? Any mention of Mrs Byfleet seemed to disturb her husband. It would be interesting to see them together.

'And you say you sat down to supper straight away?'

In the kitchen, presumably, thought Thanet. There was no dining table in here. Unless they had eaten off trays. He opened his mouth to ask then thought better of it. Perhaps this point had already been covered in the brief snatch of conversation he had missed while thinking about the accident. He mustn't let his attention wander again.

Lineham had noticed and raised his eyebrows. *You wanted to ask something?*

Thanet shook his head.

'How long did you take over supper?'

Byfleet shrugged. 'Not that long. Twenty minutes, half an hour perhaps.'

So, over the crucial period when the van had stood idle Byfleet was claiming that he and his wife were enjoying a cosy domestic interlude.

Lineham hadn't missed this point. 'You usually eat at that time?'

'Generally between eight and half past, yes. By then the guests are usually at dinner, and my wife is free.'

'And she goes back over to the Hall afterwards?'

'For an hour or so, yes. From around nine to ten.'

'She works long hours.'

'She does have the afternoons off. And at least one full day every week.'

Delia Hamilton commanded an astonishing degree of loyalty from her employees, thought Thanet. So far he hadn't heard a single grumble about her.

Lineham glanced at his watch. 'Well, thank you, Mr Byfleet. It is ten to four now, so perhaps you wouldn't mind waking your wife?'

Byfleet frowned then stood up, reluctantly. He hesitated then said, 'Look . . .'

Thanet and Lineham said nothing, waited.

'My wife . . . She's not been well.'

'Yes, Mrs Hamilton told us,' said Thanet.

'I don't want her upset unnecessarily.'

A touch of belligerence there.

'We're not inhuman, Mr Byfleet. We just want to ask her one or two simple questions.'

Byfleet looked embarrassed. 'I'm sorry. It's just that . . . Well, this baby . . . it's . . . We've been married five years and we'd given up hope, you see, and then . . .'

'I understand.'

Byfleet hesitated a moment longer, as if in need of further reassurance, then turned away and disappeared through a door at the far side of the room, closing it behind him.

'Bit jumpy, isn't he?' said Lineham.

'Mm. I can't make up my mind if he's got something on his mind or if it's just that he's concerned that all this shouldn't upset his wife. He obviously feels very protective towards her.'

'Understandable, I suppose. They're both getting on, for a first baby, and the pregnancy hasn't been straightforward, apparently.'

'Quite. Er . . . I'm afraid my attention wandered for a few minutes back there, Mike. Where did he say they were while they were having supper?'

'In the kitchen at the back of the building.'

Thanet got up and wandered over to the bookshelves. He was always interested to know what people were reading. The Byfleets seemed to have pretty catholic taste. There was biography, mostly fairly light, a modest collection of poetry, a whole shelf of non-fiction covering topics ranging from travel to do-it-yourself, and row upon row of fiction, both classical and contemporary. On the bottom shelf, below a row of romantic historical novels, were a few children's books. Thanet squatted to inspect them: Alison Uttley, Beatrix Potter and the once despised but now reinstated Enid Blyton. Smiling reminiscently he picked out *The Famous Five Go Adventuring Again*, one of his own favourites. Inside the front cover was written in neat, carefully rounded script:

> Mona Taylor
> The Limes Preparatory School
> Burgess Road
> Brighton
> Sussex
> England
> The British Isles
> Europe
> The World
> The Universe.

He smiled and held it out to show Lineham. 'Things don't change much, do they? I remember writing this myself, and I bet you do, too. And so did Ben and Bridget.'

'Yes. No doubt my two'll get around to it in due course. Pretty nice place they've got here, haven't they? Bit unexpected, really. For that matter, he's not exactly your typical handyman, is he?'

'Presumably he likes the life. Perhaps they just enjoy working together.' Thanet was now glancing at the records and tapes. Popular classics, Gilbert and Sullivan, old pop songs, none of the more recent stuff. He could almost hear Ben and Bridget chanting '*bor*ing'.

'Taking their time, aren't they?' Lineham was getting restless.

'If she's been asleep she'd have to have a few minutes to collect herself.'

'Is the Super expecting you to report in again today?'

' 'Fraid so.' Thanet returned to his seat.

Lineham groaned. 'It's getting beyond a joke. Think he's going to turn up every day, like he did today?'

'I sincerely hope not! I'm trying to tell myself the novelty'll soon wear off.'

'It'd better, or he'll be having a mutiny on his hands.'

'Now now, Mike. You didn't say that. Or if you did, I didn't hear it. And do stop prowling around like that, you're getting on my nerves.'

'You were prowling yourself until a minute ago!' Lineham plumped down on his chair looking disgruntled. 'I hate hanging about like this.'

'I wonder if they've finished the post-mortem yet.'

'Should have, by now.'

'Doc Mallard said he'd let us know if there was anything interesting and there hasn't been a word, so it doesn't look as though we're going to get much help there. I'm beginning to think this case might be a non-starter, Mike.'

'It's not like you to say that. But I see what you mean. And I agree, there doesn't seem to be much prospect of proving who did it even if we do find out. Still, we've had cases before when we've said exactly the same thing and we've made it in the end – or you have, at least.'

'Mm.' Thanet was beginning to feel drowsy. If he had to sit

in this very comfortable chair much longer he would fall asleep. The first couple of days of this type of investigation were always very tiring. There were so many people to see, so many leads to follow up, so many judgements to make, impressions to absorb. It was fine so long as you kept going, but once you stopped and lost your impetus . . . Abruptly he got up and crossed to the window in an attempt to rouse himself. 'They are taking a long time . . .'

'Perhaps they've knotted sheets and climbed out of the window,' said Lineham with a grin.

'Ha ha. Very funny.' Thanet peered out into the stable yard. The sky had clouded over and once again it was getting dark early. Tiller emerged from his work shed and crossed the cobbles, trundling a wheelbarrow. From here there was an excellent view of almost the entire yard, across to the back of the house. Tiller's house was at the end of this same side and Hamilton's office in the block at right angles. All of them would have had a clear view of Martindale if he had come out of the back door, especially if the yard had been well lit. Thanet said so.

Lineham came across to look. 'Yes. And in that loud checked overcoat of his he would have been easily recognisable. But why come out of the back door, not the front?'

Thanet shrugged. 'He didn't feel like running into guests in the foyer? It can't be easy, finding your home overrun by all and sundry who feel they have as much right there as you have. Or —'

They both turned as the door opened and the Byfleets came in. Byfleet's arm was around his wife's shoulders. She was wearing the same long dark green dress, her housekeeper's uniform, presumably. Her eyes were still puffy with sleep and she looked alarmingly pale and fragile.

'Sorry to keep you waiting, Inspector,' she said with a smile. 'I'm afraid it takes me a little while to get going after a rest, these days.'

'It really doesn't matter, Mrs Byfleet. I'm sorry to trouble you again, but I'm afraid there are one or two small points . . .'

'I understand.'

She and Byfleet sat down. He took her hand. Side by side Thanet noticed that they were already beginning to acquire that uncanny resemblance sometimes found in married couples who are very close to each other. He had noticed it before and wondered once again exactly wherein it lay. In facial expression, attitude, in tiny gestures or habits unconsciously picked up from each other? Did he and Joan have it?

'It's just that we are still trying to piece together Mr Martindale's movements on Tuesday, and when we saw you yesterday you forgot to mention that you had seen him after dinner that evening.'

He watched the slow tide of colour suffuse the pale, almost translucent skin and wondered if she could remember their conversation yesterday as clearly as he did.

'*Did you see him again at all, after he'd had dinner?*'

'*No.*'

She shook her head in embarrassment. 'I expect you're wondering why I didn't mention it before, but . . .' She glanced at her husband and Thanet saw the grip on her hand tighten as Byfleet nodded.

'It's just that it was so awkward, so embarrassing . . .'

Surely Martindale hadn't made a pass at her, in her advanced state of pregnancy?

'I was just doing a routine check around the house as I always do at that time, to make sure that everything is in order – lamps lit, curtains drawn, that sort of thing – and as I was walking along the corridor past the Chinese room the door opened and Mr Martindale looked out. He said he wanted a word with me, so I went in. He . . .' She glanced at her husband again and took courage. 'It was horrible! He began to – well – quiz me, about the hotel. He began by asking how long I'd been here, whether I liked it and so on

150

and then he started asking very specific questions about the number of staff, about how many guests we had, about staff wages and holidays and things like that . . . I just didn't know what to say . . .'

She was becoming agitated and Byfleet put an arm around her shoulders again. She shook her head. 'I mean, I know he was Mrs Hamilton's brother, but I just didn't feel he had the right . . . I tried to be polite, or pretend I didn't know the answers but he just persisted . . . In the end I said I was sorry, but I just didn't feel I could give him that sort of information without Mrs Hamilton's permission, and he said I'd better get used to the idea that from now on I would ultimately be responsible to him, not to her . . . I asked him if that meant Mrs Hamilton wouldn't be running the place any longer and he said yes, she would, but that he was the owner and everyone was going to have to adjust to the fact. I said that I still felt I would have to get Mrs Hamilton's permission to give him the sort of information he was asking for. I was a bit nervous when I said it — after all, if he really did own the place, he was my employer and I thought he might be angry, ask if I was calling him a liar or something, but he just laughed and said to go ahead and ask her, that he admired loyalty in members of staff and would see me again when I had spoken to her.'

'And did you speak to her?'

'Not immediately. I met a guest on the way, who delayed me for a few minutes, then I found Mrs Hamilton had gone to the station to meet Adam. Then when she got back she went straight into the drawing-room to have drinks with the guests — she always does, before dinner — and then I had to come back here to get your supper, didn't I, Des, so it wasn't till just after nine that I eventually saw her.'

'And she confirmed what he had said?'

'Yes.'

'Why didn't you tell me this yesterday?'

She shrugged. 'It didn't seem relevant.'

Thanet sighed. 'I wish people would let me decide what is relevant and what isn't.'

She bit her lip. 'I'm sorry.'

'Never mind, you've told me now ... We asked your husband, earlier, if he happened to notice the van drive out of the yard during the evening. He said no, but did you?'

She shook her head.

'What about later on? Sam Tiller drove it back from the pub at 10.30.'

'I didn't notice,' said Byfleet. 'Did you, love?'

Another shake of the head.

'And after that?

She hesitated. 'I did hear something ...'

'When?'

'Shortly after we went to bed. Somewhere around a quarter past eleven. I heard a car start up and drive off, and come back some time later.' She gave a rueful smile. 'I don't sleep too well these days.'

Thanet remembered Joan's restless nights during the latter months of her pregnancies. 'No ... Did you hear one car return, or two?'

'Two, I think.'

'And that was when?'

'I'm sorry, I didn't notice. I didn't think it was important.'

Thanet rose. 'There is just one question I must put to you both. Did either of you, for any reason, drive the van that night?'

They obviously realised the significance of the question. Neither looked at the other as they shook their heads in unison.

'We had no reason to,' said Byfleet stiffly.

Picking their way carefully down the staircase outside Lineham said, 'Did you believe them, sir?'

Outside Thanet took deep breaths of the clear, cold air. He shrugged. 'Difficult to tell. She's so obviously unwell and he's so on edge about her ...'

'Of course, what she told us does give them some sort of a motive, doesn't it, sir?'

'You mean, they might have been afraid that they would lose their cosy billet if Martindale took over? Bit thin, isn't it? A good housekeeper and chauffeur/handyman can always find a job, surely.'

'When she's pregnant and her health isn't too good? Not as easy as all that, I shouldn't think.'

'Perhaps not.'

As they got into the Land Rover the lights in the courtyard came on. Byfleet was right, the whole area was well illuminated. Had Martindale strolled across this very spot on the way to his death?

As he had said to Lineham, earlier, Thanet was beginning to wonder if he would ever find out.

SIXTEEN

Arriving home at around 8.30 Thanet was surprised to find Bridget in the kitchen with Joan. He kissed them both, then said, 'I thought you were on duty tonight, Bridget.'

'Mandy wanted me to swap with her, so I worked the lunchtime shift today.'

Thanet nevertheless wouldn't have expected to find her in – but managed not to say so. Bridget led such an active social life. At seventeen she was blossoming into womanhood – face and figure were fast losing the plumpness which had bedevilled her mid-teens and she always managed to look stylish when going out even though her wardrobe could hardly be called extensive. Tonight she was wearing jeans, trainers, a collarless man's shirt and a baggy sweater which practically reached her knees, sleeves pushed casually up to just below the elbows.

He plucked at it. 'This looks familiar.'

She flung her arms around his neck in mock humility. 'I knew you wouldn't mind. You don't, do you?'

'Can't call a thing your own in this house, these days.'

'Don't tell me!' said Joan. 'We haven't eaten, by the way. We thought we'd wait till nine to have supper, in the hope that you might be back in time. It's ages since we all had supper together.'

Thanet beamed. 'Lovely.' His irregular hours had always meant that family meals were a hit-and-miss affair but when

154

the children were younger he had at least known that if he did manage to get home at a reasonable hour they'd all be able to eat together. But lately, especially since Bridget had left school and begun working in the restaurant, this had become an increasingly rare event. 'What about Ben? Has he managed to last out?'

'I stuffed him with baked beans and toast when he got home from school,' said Bridget with a grin.

'I'll go and wash my hands, then.'

Upstairs he remembered that he and Joan had promised themselves a serious talk with Bridget about late nights and jaunts to destinations unknown, and his heart sank. It would be a pity to spoil the pleasure of an evening together. Perhaps they could put it off to another time? He scowled at himself in the bathroom mirror as he shook his head. No. For his own peace of mind it had to be done. The problem was, how to choose the right moment.

By the time he came down supper was ready.

'This looks good,' said Thanet. 'What is it?'

Bridget looked pleased. 'Chicken with paprika and onions.'

'Bridget cooked it,' said Joan. 'Don't gobble, Ben,' she added.

Ben scowled and went on shovelling food in as fast as he could. 'I've still got homework to do.'

'Don't know how you can taste it when you eat at that speed,' said Bridget.

'It's all right for you. You're finished with all that, aren't you? Nothing to do but enjoy yourself these days.'

'I wouldn't put it quite like that. I do work, you know.'

'Call that work? A few hours a day? I should be so lucky.'

'That's enough,' said Thanet. 'Bridget had to go through what you're doing now, remember.'

Ben laid down his knife and fork. 'Any pud?'

'All in good time,' said Joan. 'We're still eating.'

Ben pushed his chair back and stood up. 'Well I can't hang around. I'll have it in my room, while I'm working.'

'You will not!' said his mother. Then, more gently, 'Look, Ben, it's ages since we all had supper together. Let's just relax and enjoy it, shall we?'

He gave her a black look. 'I'll go without, then!' And he stumped off.

'Ben!' Thanet half rose, then sat down again with a rueful look at Joan. 'May as well let him get on with it. I can quite see he finds it difficult to enjoy a leisurely meal with work hanging over his head.'

'He's absolutely impossible these days,' said Bridget.

'He's finding it difficult settling in to the new school, as you well know,' said Thanet. 'We have to make allowances.'

'But he's always having a go at me! It's my clothes, or my make-up, or I'm taking too long in the bathroom, or – '

'I think,' said Joan, beginning to clear the plates, 'that his nose is put out of joint.'

'Oh, why?'

'Well you used to get on so well together. Now you don't have time for him any more – or so he feels.'

Now Bridget was getting cross. She stood up and picked up the other plates, clashing them together in a way which made Joan wince. 'What am I supposed to do? Take him with me? Who wants a kid brother hanging around their neck all the time?'

She flounced out and Joan gave Thanet an exaggerated shrug of mock despair. 'I always put my foot in it these days. No,' she said as he stood up, 'don't bother to come out. We can manage.'

She and Bridget returned with the pudding, a lemon meringue pie, and the dessert plates. Joan began serving in an uncomfortable silence.

'Look,' she said, 'I'm not suggesting you should let Ben tag along with you, of course I'm not. But he is going through a bad patch and if you could find a little more time for him . . .'

'But he's always working! And if he's not, I'm out.'

Thanet caught Joan's eye and an unspoken message passed between them.

Don't forget we've got to talk to her . . .

I know.

Bridget wasn't stupid. 'What was that supposed to mean?'

'What?' said Joan.

'That look. You and Dad looked at each other.'

Thanet sighed. There wasn't going to be a right moment to discuss this. Should they leave it? But the subject had come up and if he were realistic, he realised, there never would be a right time for what he had to say. Why did adolescents have to be so difficult? But he refused to give in to moral blackmail and fail to broach delicate subjects for fear of provoking an outburst of bad temper.

'Well, now that you mention it . . .'

Bridget rolled her eyes. 'What now?'

'Bridget, I do think that's unreasonable!' Uncharacteristically, Joan was now becoming angry. 'How many restrictions do we place on what you do, where you go, or who you go with?'

'Hah. So that's it!' Bridget laid down the spoon she had just picked up, sat back and folded her arms. 'Well, let's have it. What have I done now?'

Pleasant family meals were evidently a thing of the past, thought Thanet with regret as he said sharply, 'That's enough, Bridget. Your mother and I wanted to have a sensible, adult discussion with you. Please, try to calm down.'

'By "sensible discussion" I suppose you mean you're going to lay down rules that I'm supposed to follow?'

'Well you suppose wrong. I meant exactly what I said, a sensible discussion. That is, a discussion in which both sides put their point of view and a compromise is reached. Now, are you going to listen or are you going to behave like a spoilt adolescent?'

She glared at him. 'Oh, so that's what I am now, is it? A

spoilt adolescent?' She pushed back her chair preparatory to getting up.

Thanet put his hand on her arm, detaining her. 'No, Bridget, wait. Just answer me one question.'

'What?' She was still glowering at him.

'Can you honestly say we've been the sort of heavy-handed parents who lay down the law and expect you to accept what they say whether you like it or not?'

Pause. She chewed the inside of her lip, poised for flight yet unable honestly to answer in the affirmative. Eventually, 'I suppose not,' she said grudgingly.

'Well in that case, can't you at least listen to what we have to say, see if you think we're being unreasonable this time?'

Another hesitation, then he felt the rigid muscles in her arm relax. But she was still sulky as she said, 'Go on, then. Let's get it over with.'

Thanet paused for a moment, marshalling his thoughts. He had to get this right first time.

'Can you accept that as your parents we're bound to worry about you?'

'Oh, *Dad*!'

'Yes, I realise you must find that irritating. When you're young you don't want to have limitations put on your freedom – and I want to make it clear that that's not what we're after. We know you, and trust you to be sensible, but at the same time we'd like a little more peace of mind ourselves. So what we're asking is this: if you know you're going to be late, could you give us a ring to let us know, and if you're going out, we would like to know who you're going with and where you're going. That's it.'

'But that's impossible!' Bridget burst out. 'I've told Mum over and over again! How can I tell you where I'm going if I don't know myself! You don't understand! Say I'm meeting Sue. She may have arranged to meet some other people as well and when we're all together we say, Right, where shall we go tonight? It could be bowling, or to a pub – oh, don't

158

look like that, Dad. It's different nowadays. Everyone goes to pubs and yes, I know I'm under eighteen and I promise you I don't drink alcohol, I really don't, but that's where people get together these days . . . Or we might go to McDonalds or if one of us has a car we might drive over to the Chimneys in Biddenden or over to that Hungarian restaurant in Tunbridge Wells . . . And you needn't worry about that, either. Whoever's driving never drinks. We make sure of that. We don't want to end up in the mortuary, either.'

'Look love, you're wrong in thinking we don't understand. We do. And we do see the problem. We know that that's how things work, and one of the reasons why we've never brought the matter up before is because we really couldn't see any solution to it. But now, well, I think I've thought of a possible answer. But before I see what you think of the idea, I would just like to know if you can understand why we're making a fuss about it. Can't you see that not to know where you are, to think that we wouldn't even know where to begin looking for you if by any chance something went wrong and you just didn't come home – and don't roll your eyes like that! I'm better placed than most people to know just how often these things do happen. If you'd met some of the frantic parents I have . . . But anyway, do you understand what I'm trying to say?'

'I suppose so.'

'Well then, this is what I suggest. That you carry on as usual. You meet your friends, you go wherever it is you want to go, with one small difference. That when you get there you make a phone call, just a brief one, telling us where you are. That's all. It need take only a few seconds and it would help us to stop worrying.'

'Everyone would fall about laughing!' She mimicked a child's voice: ' "Excuse me, everyone. I've got to go and ring my Mummy and my Daddy, to let them know where I am." '

'Would it really be so impossible? You needn't tell them who you're ringing. Or you can make us out to be ogres if you like, lay all the blame on us. We wouldn't mind . . .'

She bit her lip, thinking about it.

What, exactly, would he do if she refused? Thanet wondered. He had no intention of playing the heavy father and laying down ultimatums which it would be impossible to keep. They never worked and would have a disastrous effect on what he liked to think, despite the present problem, was basically a good and sound relationship.

'Look,' he said, as the silence stretched out. 'Would you at least agree to give it a trial run? For a week, say? If it didn't work, and you really did find it too embarrassing, we could think again, see if we can work something else out. Or if you've got an alternative suggestion . . . ?'

She shook her head. 'I can't think of anything at the moment . . .' Suddenly she capitulated. 'OK, then. I'll give it a whirl. Why not?'

The sense of relief was overwhelming. Thanet felt as though he'd just run an exhausting race. 'Good! Terrific!' He looked at his untouched piece of pie. Now he would be able to enjoy it. And afterwards, he'd take a slice up to Ben.

He and Joan usually did the washing up together after supper but tonight Bridget insisted on doing it all.

'Go on, relax while you can! I'll bring you in some coffee later.'

Thanet and Joan plumped down side by side on the settee. 'She's OK really, isn't she?' said Joan. 'If you look about you and see the sort of mess so many young people get into, we're very lucky.'

'So far.'

'So far. It's just that at the moment I seem to get on her nerves all the time.'

'Perhaps she's too like you to be able to forgive you your faults at present. She'll grow out of it, later on.'

Joan sighed. 'I suppose so. Yes. I remember someone telling me once about his daughter. Apparently, in her late teens, she was absolutely impossible, made life hell for them.

And a few years later, when she was in her mid-twenties, she was a completely different girl: kind, thoughtful, considerate, a joy, in fact. And she actually said to him, "You know Dad, when I look back and think what I was like as a teenager, I don't know how you and Mum put up with me." So when Bridget and I have an argument or I feel I can't do anything right as far as she's concerned, I just remind myself of what he said and tell myself that if I grit my teeth and hang on it'll all work out in the end.'

'You're right. I really do believe that.' Thanet yawned hugely. 'Sorry.'

'You're tired. You look tired, actually. Bad day?'

Bridget came in with two cups of coffee. 'I'm going to have a bath and wash my hair.'

'All right, love. Thanks.' He waited until she had gone, then said, 'Not bad, no. But you know how it is at the beginning of a case. And the Super hasn't helped.'

'Oh, why?'

'ODD.' Which reminded him, he really must take a look at the information sheet Draco had handed out.

'What is?'

'His new campaign. I told you one was brewing. Well, that's it. ODD. O-D-D. Standing for Organisation, Delegation and Documentation. Stop grinning like that. The acronym, I might add, was deliberate. He thought it might afford the men some light relief! Oh, he's cunning all right. Knows how to sweeten the pill. Though in fact – and you may not believe this – he actually apologised to me this afternoon!'

'He did *what*?'

'It's true.'

Joan wriggled into a more comfortable position, tucking her stockinged feet up beneath her. 'Tell me!'

She was always a gratifying audience. As he talked Thanet thought how much it meant to him to have her there, to be able to share these rare, quiet evenings at home together. He felt sorry for Martindale, who had apparently never known the pleasures of domesticity. No one seemed to mourn his passing – quite the reverse, in fact. A number of people must secretly be relieved or even pleased that he was dead. Thanet wondered what influences had worked upon Martindale to make him the man he was, a man apparently incapable of making lasting relationships or even, indeed, of needing them. Though he did seem to have remained attached to his last, French mistress. Or perhaps it was simply that he had found a comfortable billet and made sure he didn't lose it. Knowing Martindale, that was much more likely. Thanet said so, to Joan.

'Mm.' She was thoughtful. 'He certainly doesn't sound the most sensitive of souls. Practically everyone he met seems to have had a row with him.'

'Quite. At first I thought it strange that people would dive straight into resurrecting old grudges as though they had happened only yesterday, but when Mrs Byfleet told me how he had tried to pump her, quite unashamedly, it does seem that although he could presumably turn on the charm when he wanted to, if it didn't suit him to do so he really couldn't have cared less if he upset people or not.'

'Yes, but we're not exactly talking about trivial matters, are we? Crippling that poor boy for life and destroying his mother's marriage, causing the death of Mr Tiller's prize bull after all those years of effort, making a pass at a married woman whose husband has a reputation for jealousy . . .'

'He might not have known Fever was the jealous type.'

'Even so . . .'

'Then there's Jack Talion, the farm manager. We still don't know what he had against Martindale.' Thanet sighed. 'Anyway, as I was saying to Mike, I'm beginning to wonder if we're going to get anywhere on this one.'

'Oh come on, darling! You've only been working on it for forty-eight hours. And if you gave me a pound for every time I'd heard you say that . . . Nearly every time, at some point in

162

a case, you start having doubts about whether you'll be able to solve it.'

'I suppose that's true.' Joan was right, he had to admit it. 'But the problem is that this time, even if I do find out who killed him – assuming it wasn't a straightforward accident, that is – I don't see any prospect of proving it.'

'And I've heard that before, too! You'll get there in the end, I know you will. You're just tired, that's all. We'll have an early night and you'll feel quite different in the morning, you'll see.'

Thanet hoped she was right.

SEVENTEEN

As usual, Joan was right. Although Thanet had lain awake for some time while the crowded impressions of the day jostled through his mind, in the end he did manage a good seven hours' sleep and by next morning his pessimistic mood had vanished. After all, he reminded himself as he squinted into the shaving mirror, he was far from at a dead end. Reports should now be in on a number of enquiries that had been set in motion, including the interview with the farm-hand Jack Talion had sacked. Thanet was hoping that this was a local man who would be able to shed some light on the reason for Talion's animosity towards Martindale. Also, the forensic evidence on the van and the results of the post-mortem should be in today.

Outside, Thanet's spirits rose further. The sun was shining, the sky was clear and it was several degrees warmer. The last of the snow had gone and they would be able to discard the Land Rover in favour of a car. Lineham would be pleased.

Whistling, Thanet set off for work. But his buoyant mood was soon to be severely tested. In good time when he left home, he was only halfway when there was a squeal of brakes ahead of him and the cars in front braked sharply. Thanet sucked in his breath as there was a dull ominous crunch and his car lurched. The driver behind had reacted too slowly and failed to pull up in time. There followed a time-consuming exchange of names, telephone numbers and details of insurance companies, as a result of which Thanet finally arrived at work only a matter of minutes before he was due at the morning meeting. It was unfortunate that as he hurried in Draco happened to be talking to the Station Officer in the Reception area. The Superintendent's hairy eyebrows elevated themselves in pained surprise, and he glanced pointedly at the clock.

To compound his problem the sight of Draco reminded him that he'd completely forgotten after all, last night, to read through Draco's information sheet on ODD. He wasn't exactly going to be top of the Superintendent's popularity poll this morning.

Muttering under his breath Thanet raced upstairs to his office, removing his coat as he went. Lineham glanced up, startled, as he burst in.

Thanet tossed the coat on to a chair. 'No time to stop,' he panted. 'Minor accident on the way. No, it's all right, I'm fine. Anything it's absolutely essential for me to know before the meeting?'

Lineham glanced at the papers littering his desk. 'Interesting but not essential.'

'Fine. See you shortly.'

Down the stairs again with seconds to spare. Outside Draco's door Thanet pulled up and paused long enough to take a couple of deep breaths before going in. Once again he was last.

Draco shot him a sideways glance but made no comment. He waited until Thanet was seated then said, 'Right, well now that you've had twenty-four hours to think over my suggestions, perhaps we could begin by having your thoughts on ODD.'

Thanet slid down an inch or two in his chair, unconsciously betraying his desire to become invisible. Draco noticed and gave him a sharp glance. Thanet sat up again, straightening his shoulders. *Face it like a man*, he told himself with an inward grin, in a Midwestern drawl. And then, with a spurt of resentment, *I have had more important things on my mind.*

Tody and Boon had obviously done their homework. In turn they came up with constructive comments while Thanet continued inwardly to justify himself.

'Thanet?'

'Er . . .' Might as well come straight out with it. 'I'm afraid I've been so busy with the Martindale case that I clean forgot you were expecting our comments today, sir.'

Draco's nostrils flared. 'I see.'

There was a brief, pregnant silence before the Superintendent went on, 'Well in that case perhaps you could tell us what you have been doing.'

Ignoring the emphasis on 'have' Thanet launched into an account of yesterday's activities. The others listened, asked pertinent questions and then Draco said, 'Anything interesting come in overnight?'

'I'm afraid there hasn't been time to check yet, sir.' Thanet was furious. Having seen him arrive only moments before Draco must have known he wouldn't have had time to read any reports. It had been a deliberate ploy to put him further in the wrong. Perhaps the Superintendent was paying him back for having wrong-footed him yesterday. 'I was involved in a minor accident on the way to work and there was some delay.'

'Not your fault I hope, Thanet.'

'No, sir.'

'Good. Don't like my officers to be seen to be infringing the law.'

The meeting broke up, but Draco called Thanet back. He clasped his hands behind his back and gave a little preparatory bounce, as if to lend more weight to his words. 'Look, Thanet, I do understand that you are very busy with this Martindale investigation, but it won't do to let other things slide, you know.'

'No, sir.'

Bounce. 'I don't think you quite appreciate the importance of this new initiative of mine. It doesn't do to let the grass grow under one's feet.'

'No, sir.'

Bounce. 'One has to keep a sense of balance, of proportion. It's so easy to become so obsessed with one aspect of one's work that one lets others slide. Not that I'm suggesting you do that, of course. It's just that one has to be on one's guard against it. . . . Perhaps by tomorrow you'll have had time to come up with some thoughts on ODD.'

'I'll try, sir. But . . .'

Bounce. 'I'll look forward to hearing them, then. Good. That's all.'

Thanet fumed silently all the way back upstairs and into his office.

Lineham took one look at his face and said, 'Been having fun?'

'Don't joke about it, Mike!' Thanet reached for his pipe and began filling it, stuffing the tobacco in with angry stabs.

'Bad as that, was it?'

'Let's just say it was an experience I shouldn't care to repeat too often.'

With an upsurge of the resentment common among smokers against a world which was making them feel more and more like social outcasts, Thanet lit up. Lineham could put up with it for once.

The door opened and Doc Mallard came in.

'Faugh!' he said, waving his hand to disperse the coils of smoke drifting towards him. 'At it again, Luke? How often do I have to tell you – ?' He broke off. 'Do I detect a chill in the atmosphere?'

'He had a minor accident on the way to work,' said Lineham.

'Really?' Mallard advanced, concerned. 'You all right, Luke?'

'It's not that,' said Thanet irritably. 'That was nothing, I'm perfectly all right.'

'Sure? You don't want me to look you over?'

'No, no. If you must know, I've just been hauled over the carpet, that's all.'

'Oh dear. Our zealous Superintendent on the warpath again. What have you been up to this time?'

Thanet shook his head. 'It's not important. Any news for us, Doc?'

'Here's the PM report. I meant to give you a ring yesterday afternoon, but one or two things cropped up . . .'

'That's all right.' Thanet knew that if there had been something important to tell, Mallard wouldn't have forgotten. 'So there was nothing unexpected?'

'Not really. It's all there, but shall I give you a quick summary in layman's terms?'

'Please.'

'Well, as seemed likely from the tear in the overcoat and the head injury, the victim was struck in the back. My guess is that when the car hit him he was tossed upwards and backwards and struck the back of his head on the front offside corner of the roof.'

'That's right,' said Lineham. He glanced at Thanet. 'The forensic report on the van came in this morning.'

'Well, as I say,' said Mallard, 'the main impact was to the back left side. There was considerable muscle bruising, kidney damage and – this was the worst injury – partial dislocation of the spine. The scalp wound was relatively superficial, a glancing blow.'

'So he might have recovered consciousness?'

'He did.' Mallard hesitated. 'That's the unpleasant part.'

'What do you mean?'

'Work it out for yourself. Assuming that he was put into that ditch immediately after the accident . . .'

'Just a minute,' said Thanet. 'You said "put". The spinal injury meant that he wouldn't have been able to put himself in?'

168

'He certainly wouldn't have been able to walk. He could have dragged himself a short distance, but there were no cuts or abrasions on the palms of his hands. On the other hand, there were particles of dirt under some of his fingernails . . .'

Thanet stared at Mallard, appalled, his imagination at once conjuring up the scene: the injured man in the ditch, a thin mantle of snow covering his face, the gradual awakening, the increasingly despairing attempts to sit up, the dawning consciousness of his situation before the frantic scrabbling of fingernails against the frozen sides of the ditch and the final slide into numbing unconsciousness and death.

'If he'd been taken to hospital right away he'd be in pretty bad shape but at least he'd still be alive. Or if it had been summertime and the weather had been warmer . . . As it was, of course, he didn't have a chance and it's not surprising that he was dead by morning.'

Thanet shook his head to try and dispel the grim images lingering on the screen of his mind. 'I suppose you still can't be very precise about time of death, in the circumstances?'

'No. But from the rectal temperature and the tests on the eye fluid the findings are consistent with death occurring sometime in the early hours of the morning.'

Thanet was still feeling shaken. He took the report Mallard held out. 'Well, thanks for coming in, Doc.'

'You're sure you're all right, Luke, that you don't want me to take a look at you?'

'No, really. Some idiot behind me didn't brake quickly enough, that's all. The only damage was to the rear of my car.'

'It's the inconvenience of sorting it out that's the nuisance,' said Mallard sympathetically. 'Well, if there's nothing else . . . ?'

Thanet watched him go and then in contrition laid down his pipe. There was no reason why Lineham should suffer because of Draco's unreasonableness.

'Nasty,' said Lineham.

'Very. Hardly bears thinking about, does it?' Then, with an attempt at briskness, 'Right then, Mike. What have we got?'

'Various bits and pieces. As I said, forensic have confirmed that it was the van that knocked him down.'

'Good. Anything else there?'

'Hundreds of fingerprints, of course, all useless. So many people used it legitimately . . .'

'Quite. Never mind, at least we're now certain we're on the right track, and it wasn't just a passing motorist. And talking of passing motorists, anything come in as a result of the TVS appeal?'

'Nothing useful, sir. Of course, it was a bitterly cold night and I suppose most people were at home by the fire, watching television. And it's not exactly a major road, it's mostly local traffic along there.'

'Pity. We could just do with an independent witness.'

'Doesn't look as though we're going to get one. It's been two days now . . .'

'Don't rub it in, Mike. Anything else?'

'Several things, actually.'

'So? Come on, man, we haven't got all day.'

'There's an interesting report on an interview with the parlourmaid who served dinner to the Hamiltons and Martindale the night he died. She says she definitely heard him tell them that he was going to be staying on at the Hall and – get this – that he would be establishing his right to sole ownership.'

'Really? How did she hear all this? They wouldn't have talked about it openly in front of her, surely?'

'I don't know, sir. I have the impression that people like that think servants are pretty well invisible. But no, they didn't discuss it openly. It's just that she could tell there was a bit of an atmosphere and sensing that there might be some interesting gossip, she eavesdropped.'

'I see. Who interviewed her?'

'Swift, sir. I had a word with him and I gather it took a little while to winkle all this out of her.'

'Turned on the boyish charm, I suppose. She was young, I imagine?'

Lineham grinned. 'Yes. And pretty.'

'Why didn't she come up with all this before?'

'She was off duty the day the body was discovered, so he didn't see her till yesterday.'

'So what else did she hear?'

Lineham sat back and grinned. 'Only that Martindale informed them that they were welcome to stay on and work for him, if they liked.'

'His sister to run the hotel and Hamilton the estate?'

Lineham nodded.

'So much for all that "I'm sure we could all have come to some amicable arrangement." And, "It's a good-sized cake, there was plenty for everybody." '

Lineham was still nodding. 'Quite. It's a classic motive, isn't it? Two thousand acres and Longford Hall.'

'It certainly is. I must admit I was a bit suspicious when Mrs Hamilton told us about Sam Tiller and his bull. Oh, I know she put up a good show of reluctance, but I'm pretty sure that she still wouldn't have given in if she hadn't had a good reason.'

'To deflect attention away from herself, you mean?'

'Yes. Did the girl say how they reacted to the good news?'

'Unfortunately she doesn't know. She had to go and fetch the next course. But she didn't think there'd been an open row about it, judging by their behaviour when she went back.'

'I imagine they'd have been too subtle for that, tried persuasion first, or sought legal advice.'

'Quite.'

'We'll have to talk to the Hamiltons again, obviously. If only we could find out what Martindale was up to after Mrs

Byfleet left him at 7.15 . . . Well anyway, was there anything else?'

'Swift is still trying to trace Martindale's former lady loves. The address book was pretty useless, most of the stuff was way out of date. He thinks it might well take several more days yet. Some of the names were non-starters, of course. Just a postcard, with no address. Some of them were guests at the hotels Martindale stayed in, often some time ago, so it's a long job. Records have been lost or destroyed or the hotel's changed hands, or the women have moved . . .'

'Yes yes, I get the picture. Has he managed to get any positive results yet?'

'Well, some of them were manageresses or even the owners of the hotels, so they're still around. Not surprising, really. Martindale was only fifty and he would have gone for middle-aged widows mostly, I should think. And if they owned hotels they wouldn't be likely to have retired yet. But some of them are now married, so it's proving a bit tricky. Swift's made a list.' Lineham shuffled through the papers on his desk and picked out a sheet of paper. 'Here we are.' He handed it over.

'Mm.' Thanet read out the names. 'Mrs Mary Wix in Norwich, Mrs Elizabeth Johnson in Broadway, Mrs Jeannette Martin in Eastbourne, Mrs Brenda Taylor in Worthing, Mrs Caroline Dempster in Folkestone, Mrs Kathleen Jackson in Bournemouth.' None of them rang a bell. But then, why should they, and what possible relevance could they have? Perhaps Swift was wasting his time. Thanet said so. 'What d'you think, Mike?'

'Well I agree, it does seem an awful lot of time spent to little purpose. I'm not quite sure why you thought it important.'

'Not important, just a loose end to be followed up. But if it's going to be as time-consuming as that I'm not sure it's justified.' Thanet tapped the report. 'Did he actually learn anything useful from any of them?'

'Not really. Reactions varied, apparently. One or two refused to talk. As soon as they heard Martindale's name they slammed the phone down. One — Mrs Dempster, in Folkestone — was rather pathetic apparently, eager for news and pretty upset to hear he was dead. A couple more said they didn't want to talk about it, they were now happily married ... No, I agree. I don't think there's much point in wasting any more time on it.'

'Pull him off it, then. That the lot?'

'Not quite.'

There was a glint in Lineham's eye which Thanet had seen before. It looked as though the sergeant had saved the most interesting item till last. 'What have you got up your sleeve, Mike? Ah, don't tell me. That sacked farmhand ...'

'Right!' Lineham selected another report, opened it. But he didn't hand it over. Obviously he wanted to tell Thanet himself, watch his reaction.

Thanet decided to indulge him. 'Well?'

Lineham leaned forward. 'Talion's daugher Rose committed suicide when Martindale ditched her.'

EIGHTEEN

Thanet remembered the satisfaction in Talion's eyes when Martindale's death was mentioned, the man's bitter hostility when questioned, the bleakness of the atmosphere in Home Farm, the frailty of Talion's wife, his protectiveness towards her. Had Rose been their only child, he wondered? And had her suicide cast over her home and family a blight from which they had never recovered?

'When was this?'

'Nineteen sixty-four. She was seventeen.'

Bridget's age. How would he feel about a man who drove her to suicide? Thanet shivered.

'Explains why Talion was so hostile, doesn't it, sir? Especially when we told him it was the hotel van that ran Martindale down and he knew he'd used it himself that night. No wonder he didn't want to tell us what he had against him. He must have known we'd consider it a strong motive.'

'True. All the same, it doesn't necessarily mean he did it. He might quite simply not have wanted to have what must have been a very painful business resurrected.' Thanet sighed. 'I must say, Martindale didn't do things by halves, did he? He seems to have left a trail of shattered lives behind him. Sam Tiller, Mrs Rankle, now Talion . . .'

'We'll have to go and see Talion again.'

'Obviously.' Thanet grimaced. 'He'll probably set the dog on us. But I want to see the Hamiltons first.'

'Shall I fix up appointments?'

'No. We'll take pot luck. It doesn't really matter which order we see them in. If we can't find one we'll try another.'

It was a real pleasure to drive out to Sutton-in-the-Weald this morning. The countryside basked in the sunshine and it was possible to believe that spring really was just around the corner. Soon now the sheep grazing in the fields would be surrounded by lambs, the woods and hedges misted over with the tender green of young foliage. Thanet loved to watch the progress of the seasons and pitied city dwellers who depended on parks and gardens for visible evidence of nature's annual rhythms.

Longford Hall was at its best today, its rosy brick mellow in its serene setting of park and woodland. Far away over to the right tiny figures toiled on the Sisyphean task of clearing up the storm damage. Thanet wondered aloud if Hamilton were among them.

'Doesn't matter if he is. We can see Mrs Hamilton first.'

'If she's there.'

She wasn't, but was due back shortly, apparently. Thanet had noticed Toby Fever's car outside and thought that while they were waiting they might take the opportunity to clear up one or two minor points with him and Tessa.

The receptionist frowned. 'I'm not sure where they are. I think they said they were going up to see Nanny.'

Nanny! Thanet's ears pricked up. He wondered if, by any stroke of luck, she had also been Delia and Leo's nanny. Sometimes, in families like this one, the nanny became so much part of the household that she stayed on when her charges were grown up and then looked after their children. Such elderly retainers were a dying breed, of course. Today's nannies rarely stayed more than a few years at most, then moved on to fresher and perhaps more lucrative pastures. But in a house like this . . . 'Where would we find her?'

'I'm not sure that . . . Oh, I don't suppose she'd mind.' The girl laughed. 'In fact, come to think of it, she'd probably enjoy it! She's pretty lively still, it's only her arthritis that keeps her confined to her rooms. She's in the day nursery. I'll get someone to show you.'

A trim housemaid led the way up seemingly endless flights of stairs and along interminable corridors to a bright, sunny room on the south-east side of the house. At this hour in February the sun was streaming in and Thanet blinked, momentarily dazzled. The room seemed full of people but when his vision cleared he saw that there were only four: Adam, Tessa, Toby and an elderly woman in an orthopaedic wing chair near the fire. The room was comfortably but plainly furnished with sturdy central table and chairs and a number of sagging armchairs with worn loose covers. Adam and Tessa were seated in two of them and Toby was sprawled on the hearthrug in front of the fire, which burned brightly in a black Victorian cast-iron grate surrounded by glazed green tiles with animal motifs. A tall brass fireguard stood in front of it, relic of the days when the room really was a nursery and now presumably retained as a safeguard against the nanny's disability.

They were all clearly enjoying this cosy relaxed domestic interlude. They had been sharing a joke and the faces they turned towards the two policemen were still smiling.

'Inspector!' Adam jumped up. 'Allow me to introduce you to the love of my life, Nanny Foster. Nanny, this is Inspector Thanet, that I was telling you about, and his faithful sidekick, Sergeant Lineham!'

Gone were the dandy and the waif. Today Adam was very much the son of the house in cavalry twill trousers, tattersall shirt, old school tie and tweed sports jacket. Which persona would eventually emerge? Thanet wondered. Tessa, too, looked different today. The stiff spikes of hair were now horizontal instead of vertical, sticking out above her ears on either side, as if a mysterious force had visited her in the night, altering their disposition. If anything her mini was even more minimal; the expanse of inner thigh seemed to go on for ever, leaving little to the imagination.

'That's enough, Adam,' said the woman, smiling. 'The Inspector will think I never taught you any manners.'

She was alarmingly frail, her thin body bent and twisted by the disabling disease, her hands as gnarled and misshapen as old tree roots. But there was plenty of evidence that she was well looked after. She was neat and clean, her sparse white hair neatly combed back into a bun. Beside her chair was an adjustable spotlight on a stand and a three-tiered trolley laden with books, magazines, radio, photograph albums, and all the cluttered pill and potion paraphernalia of an invalid's day. Nearby stood a hospital-type table which would swivel across her knees. On it was a half-completed jigsaw.

They all settled down, Thanet and Lineham on upright chairs at the table.

'I hope you don't mind us intruding, Miss Foster, but there are one or two minor details we wanted to check,' said Thanet. But his mind was only partly on what he was saying. When he'd come in just then and glimpsed Toby from that unfamiliar angle he had once again experienced that curious shock of recognition. He *had* seen the young man before, he was certain of it. But where? Toby was still on the floor but was now sitting up, elbows hooked over knees, leaning back against Tessa's armchair. Thanet glanced at him again and suddenly it came to him. Of course!

'Not at all. The children have told me about you and it's nice to meet you in the flesh, though I could wish it was for a happier reason.' Her face was sombre.

'You've been here a long time?' The question was mechanical. Thanet was still preoccupied with his revelation. He realised that Lineham, always sensitive to the nuances of his behaviour, had noticed and given him a questioning glance.

'Forty-six years. I came when Leo was four.' Briefly her face contorted and her lower lip trembled.

With an effort Thanet focused his mind on the conversation. He would think about the implications of his discovery later. Registering her distress he guessed that she was remembering those early, presumably happy days and wondered if this was, after all, a good idea. It was in any case difficult to talk to her as he would wish, with the young people present.

'He had wings and a halo then, didn't he, Nanny?' This was Tessa.

Adam laughed. 'Used to bore the pants off us with stories of Ma and Uncle Leo, didn't you, Nanny?'

'All very well for you to laugh, you two, but they were happy days. Right up until your grandmother died.'

'Ta-ra-ra, ra-ra ra ra.' Adam scraped away at an imaginary violin.

'Adam!' she said sharply and for once he actually looked a little shamefaced.

'You ought to be ashamed of yourself,' she snapped. 'It's all very well for you, brought up with the security of your mother and father behind you. Your Uncle Leo wasn't so lucky.'

Tessa sighed. This was obviously an old theme, retold so often that for them it had lost its impact. 'Nanny's trying to say that after Grandmother died Uncle Leo became a Deprived Child.'

'He did!' said the old lady. She put her hands on the arms of the chair and shifted herself into an almost imperceptibly different position.

Thanet recognised the signs. She was settling herself into a narrative mood. He hoped none of the young people would sabotage it.

Tessa and Adam exchanged glances. *Shall we go?*

Thanet willed them to leave but to his disappointment they stayed, through sheer inertia he imagined. It was comfortable in here and any entertainment was better than none. Tessa presumably didn't have a job, but what about Toby?

As if he had tuned in to Thanet's question Toby uncurled himself and stood up. 'I'd better be off. I'm supposed to be halfway to Maidstone by now and I'll have Dad on my tail. No,' to Tessa, 'don't bother to come down. I'll see you tonight. About half seven?'

She nodded. 'Fine.'

Thanet glanced at Lineham and gave an almost imperceptible nod at the door. *Go and ask him.*

Unobtrusively Lineham followed Toby out. Thanet saw that Tessa was frowning. The little exchange had not escaped her.

'Sorry, Miss Foster,' he said. 'You were saying, about Mr Martindale . . . ?'

'He was unlucky, that's all. As so often happens, the father favoured the daughter and the mother the son. Leo was the apple of Mrs Martindale's eye and I'm afraid she spoiled him rather. Over-indulged him. I don't blame her, mind, it was always very hard to say no to Leo. He was such a handsome lad, he could have charmed the birds out of the trees if he'd set his mind to it. But I'm afraid it set his father against him. It was the old story, really, I've seen it so often, the father jealous of the son . . . So when Mrs Martindale died, when Leo was twelve, he had a rough time.'

'In what way?'

'He was shoved off to boarding school for a start,' said Adam. 'Like poor little me.'

'You hadn't just lost your mother,' said Miss Foster reprovingly. 'And you'd boarded at your prep school, too. Leo had been a day boy until then.' She shook her head. 'Of course, he hated it, just went haywire. Personally, I think his behaviour was so impossible because he was hoping they'd throw him out and he could live at home again. He loved it here. But his father wasn't having that. Every time Leo was expelled he was just sent off to another school.'

Lineham came back in and sat down again.

'Every time?' said Thanet.

179

'Well, it sounds worse than it actually was. He was expelled from three. After that I think it dawned on him that there really wasn't much point, he might as well settle down. But he was never happy. Did as little work as possible and then went to Cirencester, where he started the Estate Management course. Threw it in at the end of the first year and came home, lazed around doing nothing very much. His mother had left him enough for him not to have to work.'

'Sounds great!' said Adam. 'Wish somebody'd leave me enough to doss around and do nothing.'

'You'd be bored out of your tiny mind by the end of the first week,' said Tessa. 'I know. I've tried it. I'm off to Art College in September,' she said to Thanet, her eyes alight with the first sign of enthusiasm she had shown.

'Good!' he said. 'Where?'

'St Martin's School of Art.' There was pride in her voice now.

Obviously he had done her an injustice and he was careful not to sound condescending as he said, 'You must be good. It's very difficult to get in, I believe. Fashion?'

'Textile design.'

'It's all very well for you,' said Adam sulkily. 'You've always known what you wanted to do. There's nothing that really grabs me like that.'

'Give it time,' said Miss Foster, smiling. 'Just keep on doing as well as you are at school and who knows, you could end up Prime Minister!'

'Heaven forbid!' said Tessa. 'The imagination boggles!'

'I don't suppose,' said Thanet, anxious to lead the conversation back to Martindale, 'that Mr Martindale senior was too pleased, when his son dropped out of college.'

'He was furious. Barely spoke to him for weeks. There was always a clash of personalities between them but after that things were worse than ever. Mr Martindale was a good employer and I don't really like saying this, but he seemed to have this blind spot as far as Leo was concerned; couldn't see

180

anything good in him at all. And that just made Leo behave more badly.' She shook her head sadly. 'It was a vicious circle, really.'

'And once he'd set his foot on the slippery slope . . .' said Adam. He made a sliding motion with his hand. 'Oops, it was downhill all the way.'

'I've never discovered why he finally went away for good,' said Thanet. He'd be interested to hear Miss Foster's version of the rift between father and son.

Miss Foster pursed her lips and shook her head.

'Simple,' drawled Tessa. 'Oh do stop looking so disapproving, Nanny. If we don't tell the Inspector someone else will. Can't you see, he's not the type to give up? It happened really because he ran out of money. Grandmother Martindale had apparently been rather unwise and instead of setting up a trust fund from which he had the income until he reached the age of wisdom – though from what we know of Uncle Leo I don't suppose he ever would have – she left him a capital sum outright. He had a whale of a time: wine, women, song, fast cars, expensive clothes, the lot. Grandfather kept on baling him out of debt but when he started betting on the gee-gees it was the last straw. I believe he gave him one more chance and when he finally blew it, to the tune of several thousand pounds – and that was an awful lot of money in those days – that was it. Grandfather did the "Never darken my doors again" act, and Uncle Leo never did.' She shrugged. 'We always felt deprived about that, didn't we, Adam, thought our lives had lacked a certain spice.'

Adam nodded. 'That was why I was so disappointed not to have seen him when he came back. Ah well, that's life, I suppose. Incidentally, Tess, you forgot to put the finishing touch to the scenario. When he went, he took half the family silver with him.'

'All right, that's enough!' said Miss Foster. 'I let you run on, Tessa, because I could see you were right and Inspector Thanet would have gone on asking until someone had given him the information. But I won't sit here and listen to you running poor Leo down any longer. I know he was bad in many ways but it wasn't his fault. Children aren't born spoiled, you know, it's adults that make them so. And in your uncle's case . . . to be so over-indulged and then suddenly to find himself out in the cold for good . . . I'm not a bit surprised he went off the rails, even if I couldn't approve of some of the things he did. No, I felt sorry for him, still do. He missed so much in life, through no fault of his own. And if you're not careful, Adam, you'll go the same way, with all this smart-Alec nonsense.'

Adam jumped up and went to lay his cheek against her hair. 'Not true, Nanny! You know that at heart I'm pure gold, right through.'

'That's a matter of opinion.' But the smile she gave him showed that she agreed, really.

Thanet decided to change the subject. 'Tell me, Tessa, when you drove home that night, did you happen to notice anything out of the ordinary on the way?'

'Such as a body lying at the side of the road, you mean! Honestly, Inspector, you can't really believe I wouldn't have got Dad to stop if I had!' Tessa was scornful and Thanet felt that her opinion of him had just taken a nose-dive. He didn't care, it had just been a way of leading into his next question.

'Of course, your father was with you . . . The Range Rover had broken down, I believe.'

'Yes. Infuriating. It was nothing serious, only a loose sparking plug apparently, but I'm not mechanically-minded, I'm afraid. So I rang Dad and asked him to come and fetch me. I knew he'd still be up, he never goes to bed very early. Anyway, he managed to fix it.'

Thanet was certain that she was telling the truth. He had never really believed that Hamilton would stoop so low as to get his daugher to lie for him in case someone had seen him driving the van that night. And Mrs Byfleet had heard both cars return.

182

'What time did you get back?'

She shrugged. 'Soon after twelve, I think. I rather lost track of time, hanging around waiting for Dad.'

'Was it snowing when you got home?'

'Yes. It had just started.'

On the way back downstairs Lineham said, 'We still can't rule Mr Hamilton out, though, can we? He'd have had plenty of opportunity earlier on.'

Thanet sighed. 'What did Toby say?'

Lineham waited while a chambermaid went by. 'He confirms what Mrs Rankle told us. He did borrow his mother's car that night, to go to Canterbury on business for his father to discuss a haulage job with a chap who was unavailable during the day. His father was supposed to go, apparently, but then they had that phone call to say Mrs Fever's mother had been taken ill and he asked Toby to go instead. Toby couldn't use his own car because he was working on it and it was jacked up.'

'Cars, cars . . . They seem to crop up everywhere in this case. Should be just up your street, Mike.'

They had reached the head of the staircase and Thanet paused, glancing around to make sure no one was in earshot. Downstairs in the hall the receptionist was at her desk and a group of guests was seated around the fire, a tray of coffee on the table between them.

Thanet lowered his voice. 'By the way, I wanted to ask you . . . Did I mention to you that I thought Toby looked familiar, that I had a feeling I might have come across him before somewhere?'

'No, why? Have you?'

'No. But just think, Mike. Doesn't he remind you of someone else in this case? Not all the time, but just in fleeting moments?'

Lineham frowned. 'I don't think so. Who?'

'It didn't dawn on me till just now. And then . . . Well, first of all, when we went in, he was lying down, and then he sat up. Both positions were the same, you see, that was what made me realise . . .'

Lineham was still puzzled. 'Sorry, I just don't see what you're getting at.'

'The first time we saw Martindale, lying in the snow . . . And then that photograph we saw in his room, the one of him and his sister, sitting on the steps . . .'

Lineham's eyes widened. 'You mean . . . ?'

Thanet nodded. 'I think Toby might be his son.'

NINETEEN

Lineham was still looking stunned. 'But . . .'

Thanet knew how he felt. The implications were so complicated and far-reaching that it was difficult to take them all in at once. 'I'd like to discuss this with you before seeing Mrs Hamilton. Also, there's a check I'd like to run . . . Let's go outside.'

Delia Hamilton was back, apparently. Thanet asked the receptionist to tell her that he had an urgent call to make before seeing her, then he and Lineham went out to the car. There he put in a request for two pieces of information – Toby's date of birth, and the date of his parents' marriage. 'As fast as you can, please.'

'Will do.'

Lineham waited until he had finished before saying, 'If you're right, sir, do you think any of them realises?'

'Ah, now that's the million-dollar question. I haven't had time to think about it properly yet, but I doubt that the Hamiltons know. Otherwise they wouldn't be too keen on Tessa going out with him.'

'You mean, because they're first cousins . . . Sir!' Lineham's eyes widened in shock.

'What?'

'Do you realise what this could mean? No, perhaps it wouldn't. I don't know . . .'

'You're being incoherent, Mike. Start again.'

'Can illegitimate children inherit?' said Lineham.

Thanet could see why the sergeant had looked so thunder-struck. This had not yet occurred to him. If Martindale had been the owner of Longford Hall, and Toby was his son . . .

'I believe they can. Wasn't there an Act, to make it legal?'

'I remember something about it . . . In that case, perhaps the Hamiltons do know,' said Lineham. 'I should think they're pretty snobbish and I always did wonder if they approved of Tessa going out with Toby. But now . . . Perhaps they actually encouraged it, knowing that it was just possible that one day Toby could be heir to the whole estate.'

'Let's not speculate on that one until we're sure of our ground. We might well find that the fact that his mother and Martindale never married would rule him out.'

'All the same, I find it difficult to believe that Mrs Hamilton wouldn't have spotted the resemblance between Toby and her brother before now, if you cottoned on to it as quickly as you did.'

'I don't know. For one thing you and I are trained to look for connections, to be actively on the alert for them. And the fact that we are strangers means that we look at everyone with a fresh eye. The Hamiltons will have watched Toby grow up as just another village boy, remember, and probably always accepted him on face value as the Fevers' son. It isn't as if the resemblance is striking – and let's face it, I could be wrong.'

But he wasn't – or at least, it didn't look as though he was. A few minutes later the information came through: Toby's date of birth was 9.1.66, that of his parents' marriage 4.8.65.

After their initial elation that it seemed Thanet's hunch was correct, Lineham sobered. 'Doesn't necessarily mean he's Martindale's son, of course. He could still be Fever's – or anybody else's, for that matter . . .'

Thanet shook his head. Logically Lineham could be right, but Thanet knew in his bones that he wasn't.

Lineham grinned. 'OK, I give in. I've never known you

wrong about something like this. So let's see . . . Martindale left in 1965. Right? And if Toby was born in January 1966 he would have been conceived in April 1965. I wonder in which month Martindale left.'

'We'll ask his sister.'

'In the summer, probably, if the Fevers were married in August. The sequence of events probably went: in April Yvonne becomes pregnant and in June she tells Martindale. That same month Martindale is thrown out of the ancestral home because of his debts – perhaps he was only too glad to get away, in the circumstances! – but Yvonne thinks he's gone away because of the baby, so she marries Fever who is waiting in the wings.'

'She might not have discovered she was pregnant until after Martindale had gone,' said Thanet. 'In which case he might never have known about the baby.'

'The question is, did he?'

'And if so, when did he find out? Before he left, while he was away, or after he came back?'

'It's all so complicated,' said Lineham with relish.

'I know. It's just occurred to me . . . perhaps you're right, and he did know about the baby before he left. Let's just accept, for the moment, that he did. You remember what the receptionist told us, about Martindale asking who Toby was, when Toby was talking to Mrs Byfleet? Perhaps there was something about the boy that reminded him of himself as a young man, and made him wonder . . .'

'I don't know.' Lineham was doubtful. 'Isn't it usually considered rather difficult to recognise a resemblance to yourself?'

'Possibly. But if Martindale knew he had a child, and was on the lookout for him . . .'

'Or her . . .'

'All right Mike, or her, but anyway, on the lookout; then when he saw this young man of the right age, he could have thought, I wonder . . .'

187

'It's possible. And then, of course, when the receptionist told him who Toby was, he'd have known this was his son — no, hang on, sir, he wouldn't, would he? Not unless he knew Yvonne had married Fever. And even then he couldn't have been sure — for all he knew, the Fevers could have had several children.'

'I think, for the purpose of this argument, we will assume that he did know she'd married Fever and that they'd had no other children. After all, Mike, if he knew she was expecting his baby, he might well have made it his business to keep an eye on her from afar, so to speak, find out what happened to her and the child. If he didn't know, this whole scenario collapses anyway. Still, we might as well follow it through for the moment. So, you were saying . . .'

'Well if he did find out who Toby was, by asking the receptionist, I was just thinking it might have whetted his appetite to get to know him. So I was wondering if, when he ran into Mrs Fever in the village next day, he could have told her he'd seen Toby and wanted to meet him, make himself known to him, as his real father. Mrs Victor said it looked as though he was trying to persuade Mrs Fever to do something she didn't want to do.'

'The mechanic said that was because she was refusing to go and have tea with Martindale, Mike.'

'But the mechanic wasn't present during the whole conversation, was he? He had to go into the office to get change. After all, it's not the sort of thing Martindale would have been likely to discuss with anyone within earshot, is it? He might just have pretended to have been asking her to go and have tea with him, to fool the mechanic when he came back.'

'Mm. Could be, I suppose. All right, let's accept that Martindale was saying that he intended to tell Toby he was his father. . . . Let's think. According to the mechanic, it was after he teased Fever about Martindale's encounter with Mrs Fever that Fever went rushing off — as we know, up to the

Hall, to tell Martindale to keep away from her in future. Say Fever then went home and had a row with his wife about it . . .'

'Fever must have known Toby wasn't his son, if his wife was four months pregnant when he married her, mustn't he, sir? If he's as jealous as people say, I expect he would have gone on and on at her until she told him who the real father was, and she may well have thought it was safe to tell him as Martindale had gone away, apparently for good. And if Fever did know Martindale was Toby's father, it would explain why he reacted so strongly when he heard Martindale was back and had been chatting Mrs Fever up. And then, when Fever went home afterwards and started going on at his wife about her talking to Martindale, in order to distract him she could have told him that Martindale had suggested making himself known to Toby . . .'

'Yes. I always think it must be pretty devastating when someone turns up on the doorstep claiming to be a long-lost son or daughter, father or mother. It must put all the family relationships in a turmoil, especially if the one who is being claimed had been kept in ignorance.'

'Of course, in all this we're assuming Toby has no idea who his real father was.'

Thanet frowned, thinking. 'I don't think he does. After all, if he had known Martindale was his father you'd have expected him to try to make contact with him when he came home, or at least to be affected to some extent by his death, but he seems completely unconcerned by it all. Anyway, assuming Martindale did suggest telling him the truth and Mrs Fever then told her husband, Fever could have been fuming about it all evening. And then, on his way back from Ashford in the van, if he saw Martindale ahead of him on the road . . .'

They looked at each other in silence.

'It's convincing,' said Thanet at last. 'But let's remember that at the moment it is still pure speculation and far from the only possibility. But it will be interesting to see what Mrs Hamilton has to say about it.'

They were shown into her office again. Her desk was littered with papers and she wasn't too pleased at the prospect of having to spend more time answering questions. 'I hope this isn't going to take long, Inspector. I really have a great deal to do today.'

It looked as though she had just been to the hairdresser's. Her hair was loose for once, framing her face and falling to her shoulders in carefully casual waves. It made her look younger and more vulnerable. She was wearing a finely pleated skirt in red wool and a long matching cashmere cardigan over a silky cream blouse with a finely scribbled abstract pattern in red and black.

'No longer than I can help,' said Thanet politely. 'May we sit down?'

She gestured impatiently. *If you must.*

No point in beating about the bush. 'It must have been a shock to you, to learn that your brother intended staying on and taking over his inheritance.'

A flash of anger, quickly suppressed. 'You've been listening to gossip again, Inspector. Do you enjoy scrabbling around in the refuse of people's lives?'

This accusation had been levelled at Thanet too often for him to be moved by it. 'Not at all, Mrs Hamilton. I'm only too well aware of the fact that after a sudden death, and especially a violent death, people close to the victim are often in a state of shock. To be honest, there are times when I find my work very distasteful.'

Recognising his sincerity Delia Hamilton had the grace to look discomforted, but she quickly recovered. 'It wasn't that much of a shock, to learn he intended staying on. My husband and I always knew that it could happen. We would have worked something out.'

'My information is that Mr Martindale suggested that you should continue to run the hotel and your husband the

190

estate as his employees, and that you quarrelled about it.'

Again that flash of anger before she said coolly, 'Then your information is wrong, Inspector, or at least misleading.'

'You deny that there was an argument?'

'No. There was an argument, yes, I admit it. But arguments need not end in disharmony. On this occasion I think we managed to get my brother to see that in view of all the hard work Giles and I have put in, it would be a little unfair for us not to benefit by it, at least to some extent.'

'You're saying that you reached an agreement?'

'Let's say we were well on the way to it.'

'Despite the limitations imposed by the Trust?'

'Despite the limitations imposed by the Trust,' she echoed firmly.

No doubt Hamilton would back her up, but Thanet was certain that she was lying.

'Would you mind telling us the terms of that agreement?' He didn't think for a moment that she would, but there was no harm in asking.

'That's out of the question! It was an entirely private matter, and I . . .'

The phone rang and, with a muttered 'Excuse me', she picked it up and held a brief conversation about proposed repairs to the roof. After a moment she began shifting papers about on her desk and peering underneath. Then suddenly she tutted as if she had just remembered something, and stopped looking. A minute or two later she put down the receiver and said, 'While I think about it, Inspector, I've been meaning to ring up and ask . . . Did your men find a pocket calculator in the van? It's about so big,' and she made a window about three inches by two and a half with her fingers. 'My name and address are tucked into the inside flap.'

'I don't think so, no.' Thanet raised his eyebrows at Lineham, who shook his head. 'We'll ask, if you like, when we get back.'

'I'd be grateful. I really must buy another, it's just a question of remembering, when I'm in town . . .'

'You think you dropped it in the van when you went to fetch Adam?'

She shrugged. 'Well, it's several days now and it hasn't turned up anywhere else. I'm lost without it, it's just the right size to carry in my pocket. I've thought and thought and I know I had it just before dinner on Tuesday and that it was missing later on that evening.'

'Before your early dinner, you mean?'

'Yes. Anyway, if you'd just check . . .'

'Of course.' Thanet caught Lineham's eye. They had already arranged that the sergeant should question her about the two periods when the van had stood idle in the yard.

'You may be interested to know, Mrs Hamilton, that it has now been confirmed that it was your van that ran your brother down. We don't yet know whether this was deliberate or an accident, but in any case, as we explained before, it does seem from the position of the body in the ditch that whoever was driving must have moved it afterwards and can't claim ignorance of the accident. So we are questioning again everyone who had access to the van.'

He paused.

Delia Hamilton's lips had tightened, but she said nothing.

'We have therefore been trying to draw up a timetable of the van's movements on Tuesday evening. And there are two gaps unaccounted for, when the van was standing outside in the stable yard, unattended. So naturally we are now concentrating on those gaps.' He made a pretence of consulting his notebook. 'The first is between 8.10 and 8.30 that evening, the second between 10.30 and 11.15. Now, when we first talked to you, you told us that you got back from meeting Adam's train at twenty to eight, but unfortunately Adam and Tessa interrupted us before you could tell us what you did after that. We know, from what you told us subsequently, that you joined your guests for drinks, so if you

192

could give us a summary of your movements from, say, eight o'clock onwards . . .'

'I see. So this is the inquisition, is it?'

'I wouldn't put it quite like that, ma'am.'

She stood up abruptly, folding her arms as if to protect herself. 'This is preposterous. I refuse to answer any more questions without my solicitor present.'

'It's up to you, Mrs Hamilton. You have every right to do that, if you wish, but . . .' Lineham glanced at Thanet.

Thanet intervened. He knew that the sergeant was asking his senior officer to use his authority to back him up on this.

'Mrs Hamilton, Sergeant Lineham is simply trying to say that although the choice is yours, there really is no need for you to take this attitude. These are routine questions, which we are asking of everyone who had keys to the van.'

'I'm not stupid, Inspector! I appreciate that, but at the same time it does seem to me sensible to protect my own interests.'

'Not if you have nothing to hide,' said Thanet.

There was a brief silence.

'Very clever, Inspector. By implication, if I still refuse, then I do have something to hide.' She sat down in her chair again, an angry, petulant movement, and tapped the polished wood of the desk with one crescent-shaped fingernail. The tiny, repetitive clicking was like the ticking of an alarm clock – or perhaps a bomb, thought Thanet. He watched her with interest. Would she explode?

Suddenly she folded her arms with that same defensive, self-protective movement he had noticed before. 'Oh very well. It irritates me to play your game, but when all's said and done, you're right. If I have nothing to hide there's nothing to be afraid of. And as I don't have anything to hide . . . From eight o'clock onwards, you say? Let me see. I know it's only a few days ago, but in a place like this our routine is such that one evening tends to merge into another . . .'

193

But it didn't take her long to work it out. After the guests went into dinner she had gone along to the kitchen to check that everything was running smoothly. At around five past eight she had gone up to have a brief word with Adam and make sure he had everything he needed before she retired to her room for half an hour. This was her usual practice, apparently, one of the rare periods of the day when she had time to herself, to relax.

'That would have been from, say, ten past eight until around twenty to nine?'

She pulled a face, aware that this covered the first period in question. 'Yes.'

After that she had gone down to the dining-room to check that all was running smoothly, then watched television with Adam and her husband until ten o'clock. After another trip downstairs she had retired to her room to take a leisurely bath before an early night. She had, she claimed, been in bed by around ten to eleven. She gave a wry little laugh and said, 'Hence my irritation just now, Inspector. I suspected that I might be unlucky and have no one to confirm my movements during the two periods in question.'

Thanet made no comment. Delia Hamilton qualified as a suspect in any case, having driven the van during the crucial period. Finding out what she had been doing during those two blank periods was at this stage not as important as it could have been. On the other hand it could prove vital later, if for example a witness was found who claimed to have seen Martindale leaving the house during one of them. 'What about your husband?'

She shrugged. 'I've no idea. This is a big house, we don't exactly live in each other's pockets. He has a bed in his dressing room and if he's late coming to bed for any reason he sleeps there, so as not to disturb me. He did that night, after going to fetch Tessa.'

'So you don't know what he was doing, during either the earlier or the later period in question?'

194

She shook her head. 'You'll have to ask him.' She reached for a sheaf of papers, pulled them towards her. 'And now, if you don't mind . . .'

'I'm sorry,' said Thanet, 'we're not quite finished yet.'

She gave an exasperated sigh. 'For heaven's sake . . . I'm never going to catch up on my work at this rate.'

'One or two more questions about Mr Martindale. He left the area in 1965, didn't he? Could you tell me exactly when? Which month, I mean.'

She frowned. 'What on earth d'you want to know that for?'

'Please . . .'

'It was the end of June.'

'Can you remember who his girlfriend was, at the time?'

The frown was deeper now.

'The last time we talked to you we asked if Yvonne Fever had been your brother's girlfriend, before he went away . . . We have reason to believe that you were less than frank with us.'

'Really, Inspector, what can it possibly matter? We are talking about twenty-four years ago . . .'

'Let me put it this way. Mr Martindale left in June 1965. The Fevers were married in August. Toby Fever was born in January 1966.'

He let her work it out for herself. Delia Hamilton was no fool and he was rewarded by seeing the colour seep out of her face, leaving it chalk white. He saw her throat move as she swallowed.

'You're not suggesting . . .' It was scarcely more than a whisper.

Thanet said nothing. He had his answer. He stood up.

She put out a hand. 'No, wait . . . You've . . . Have you . . . Does anyone else know about this?'

'That,' said Thanet, 'is what we would like to know.'

He and Lineham turned to leave but she rose, pulled by invisible strings. 'Will you tell them?'

'That depends, I'm afraid.'

'On what?'

'On whether it becomes necessary.'

She sank back into her seat and he left her sitting at her desk, motionless as a statue.

TWENTY

By comparison with the last time they'd been in, the Drovers seemed positively crowded. There were eight other customers, five of them a group of young men in near-uniform of formal suit, white shirt and sober tie. Salesmen attending a conference nearby?

Sam Tiller was also there, enjoying a lunchtime pint with a couple of cronies. He gave the two policemen a hostile glance before firmly turning his back on them.

Thanet and Lineham waited until they had collected their beer and sandwiches before continuing their discussion. Delia Hamilton's reaction had convinced Thanet that the idea of Toby being Leo's son was entirely new to her, but Lineham was sticking to his guns.

'I think she'll tell whatever lies are necessary to get her off the hook.'

'Telling lies is one thing. Changing colour like that is another. I'd say it was virtually impossible to do it at will.'

'I don't know. Actors and actresses cry real tears.'

'Maybe. But they have years of practice, of thinking themselves into other people's skins, other people's moods. I imagine even the most experienced actor would need at least a few seconds to produce real tears, longer, probably. And she reacted just like that.' Thanet snapped his fingers in the air. 'One second she was her normal colour, the next she was white as a sheet.'

'I suppose so.' Lineham was still grudging, reluctant to relinquish his conception of Delia as a devious, scheming woman.

Thanet was shaking his head. 'Come on, Mike, you can't tell me she could have faked that.'

Lineham took a huge mouthful of sandwich and began to chew thoughtfully. A moment later he made an inarticulate sound.

'What?' said Thanet.

The sergeant's eyes were bulging with frustration as he tried to reduce the quantity of food in his mouth to manageable proportions.

'Serves you right,' said Thanet with a grin. 'I bet you tell the children never to bite off more than they can comfortably chew.'

Lineham swallowed, chewed, swallowed again. 'It's just that it occurred to me . . . The fact that Mrs Hamilton doesn't know Toby is her nephew doesn't mean that Mr Hamilton doesn't.'

Presumably the three negatives made a positive. 'You mean, perhaps he does know?'

'Yes. Leo Martindale could have told him.'

'And Hamilton didn't tell his wife? I doubt it, Mike. They seem pretty much in cahoots, those two.' Thanet took a thoughtful swig of beer. 'Besides, come to think of it, I'm not sure why it's especially important anyway for us to decide whether they knew or not. It's interesting, I grant you, but is it relevant to the case? If we're right about this and Toby really is Martindale's son, it could certainly matter whether Martindale himself knew, and also whether Fever knew. But the Hamiltons? I'm not so sure.' He paused. 'In fact, it could even be a point in their favour. Surely, if there was even the slightest chance of Toby inheriting the Hall the last thing they'd want to do is to get rid of Leo. At least with him in charge they'd be able to stay on, carry on their lives much as before, but with Toby installed there they would presumably

198

have had to get out . . . We really must check whether or not he could inherit.'

'So are we going to see Mr Hamilton now?'

Thanet chewed the last mouthful of his sandwich – ham and pickle, this time – while he considered. 'No. I don't think we're going to get anything new out of him at the moment, I think he'll stick to whatever story he and his wife have prepared. If you're feeling brave enough to face the dog, I think we'll go and see Jack Talion next.'

'Are you, sir? Feeling brave enough, I mean?'

Thanet laughed. 'I'm counting on you to protect me, Mike. What else are sergeants for?'

Privately, Thanet wasn't looking forward to this interview. If Talion's daughter really had committed suicide because of Leo Martindale, it wasn't surprising that Talion had been dead against the idea of Martindale settling down in Sutton again. But that didn't necessarily mean he had killed him and, if not, Thanet hated the idea of reopening old wounds best left undisturbed. On the other hand, if Talion were guilty . . . Thanet sighed. He had meant it when he told Delia Hamilton that he sometimes found his job distasteful.

It took them some time to track Talion down. The farmyard at Home Farm was deserted and when they went up to the house there was no answer to their knock. Thanet shivered while they waited. During the morning the sky had clouded over again, the sunshine become fitful and now, suddenly, a chill wind began to blow.

Thanet turned up his collar. 'We'll have to come back later, Mike. Let's see if we can find Fever instead.'

They were heading back to the village when Lineham spotted a tractor coming towards them. 'Wonder if this chap works for Talion. If so, he might know where he is.' He flashed his lights, sounded his horn and pulled up. The tractor stopped and Lineham got out of the car.

'Have you any idea where we can find Mr Talion?'

Talion, it seemed, was repairing fences and after following

the tractor driver's directions they donned their boots and had to plod across two huge fields of winter wheat. It was hard going. The soil, sodden and sticky in the aftermath of the snow, adhered to their boots in heavy lumps and after a few hundred yards it began to feel as though their feet were weighted down with blocks of concrete.

'Should be at the far side of the next field,' panted Lineham.

'Mm.'

The interlude had given Thanet time to think and he was beginning to wonder if this was a good idea. It was all very well to joke about the dog, but it was distinctly inhibiting to have to watch every word he said in case he provoked a hostile reaction from its master.

'There they are.'

They had reached another five-barred gate set into a thick hedge backed by post and wire-mesh fencing. On the far side of the next field were a tractor and trailer and a group of three men working on the boundary fence nearby.

The words were no sooner out of Lineham's mouth when a furious barking confirmed his guess and Talion's Alsatian jumped out of the trailer and began to streak towards them. The two policeman faltered. Would Talion call the dog back?

Talion allowed the dog to get halfway across the field before shouting a command. 'Rhett! Stay!'

To Thanet's relief the dog skidded to a halt.

'Rhett! Here!'

Reluctantly, it seemed, the animal turned back and trotted towards its master. Thanet and Lineham exchanged relieved glances before continuing on their way. After a word to the other two men Talion advanced to meet them with the measured stride of a countryman, the dog beside him.

'Sorry to interrupt your work, Mr Talion,' said Thanet when they were within speaking distance.

'Sit!' said Talion as they came up to him, and the Alsatian obeyed, ears pricked.

Thanet gave the animal a wary glance. This was definitely a bad idea. It was virtually impossible to concentrate out here in the open with the rising wind whistling about his ears and the dog alert to every move. It would have been more sensible to ask Talion to come into headquarters to make a statement. Here, on his own ground, legs planted firmly apart, Talion looked as sturdy and unlikely to bend as one of his own oak trees.

'Well?' said Talion, shoving his hands deep into the pockets of his windproof jacket. His eyes were wary, hostile.

'There are one or two more questions . . .'

Talion said nothing, merely raised his eyebrows a fraction.

'We're still checking on the movements of everyone who has a key to the van.'

Still no reaction.

'Could you give us an account of your movements after you returned to the Hall that night.'

'Why?'

'A man is dead, Mr Talion. It has been confirmed that he was knocked down by the van. We now also know, from the post-mortem, that it was not the impact which actually killed Mr Martindale. After the incident his body was moved into the ditch where he was found, and where he later died from exposure. This is therefore now definitely a murder investigation, and the movements of every person with access to the van naturally have to come under close scrutiny. So if you would just give us the information we need . . .'

Talion shrugged. 'I don't see that it'll help you much, but for what it's worth I went straight home, and spent the rest of the evening there.'

'You walked?'

'Yes.'

'Which way?'

'Along the footpath which links Home Farm with the Hall.'

'Is there anyone who can confirm that you were at home all evening — apart from your wife, that is?'

Talion's expression hardened. 'No. And I don't want you bothering my wife, either. I told you, she's not well. You'll just have to take my word for it.'

'It would only be to . . .'

'No!'

The dog's hackles were up and it again gave that alarming deep-throated growl. Thanet could see the muscles in its front legs bunch as it tensed, ready to spring on command. Time for a strategic withdrawal, he decided. The death of Talion's daughter would, understandably, be a very touchy subject indeed, and even to mention that they now knew Talion had good reason for hating Martindale and therefore a possible motive for leaving him to die would provoke the man even further. Thanet had no intention of putting either Lineham or himself at risk. From now on, if they wanted to talk to Talion it would be on Thanet's terms.

He shrugged. 'We'll have to leave it there for the moment, then.'

Moving with unprovocative care he and Lineham turned away. They had gone only a few paces when Talion shouted after them. 'Remember what I said. Just keep away from her!'

Thanet raised a hand in acknowledgement but did not look back until he and Lineham were safely in the next field. Talion and the dog had almost reached the tractor and as they watched the animal leaped up to its former position. Thanet could see the silhouette of its head and shoulders above the boarded side of the trailer. It seemed to be watching them.

Lineham grinned with relief. 'I was beginning to work out when I'd had my last tetanus jab.'

'Yes. Not very clever of me, was it, to interview him on his own ground again. Talk about inhibiting! If there has to be a next time, it'll be safely back at headquarters, minus that dog.'

They began to plod back across the fields, collecting more mud on their boots on the way.

'D'you think there will have to be a next time, sir?'

Thanet shrugged. 'Difficult to tell. We haven't exactly made much progress with him, have we? But he's got as good a motive as anyone.'

'Will we talk to his wife?'

'Not at this stage. No point in provoking him unnecessarily.'

'Beats me why people keep animals like that,' said Lineham as they struggled on. 'I wouldn't trust that dog within a mile of my kids.'

'Ditto.'

'Let's hope Mr Fever is feeling a bit more cooperative.'

'It would make a change!'

Back at the car they changed into their shoes, banging their boots on a fence post to remove the worst of the mud then wiping them roughly on the grass.

'Give me a nice warm office every time,' said Lineham as he slammed the car boot.

It was a relief to get into the car, out of the wind.

Thanet glanced at his watch. Half-past one. Unless Fever's lunch hour was from one to two, he should be back at work by now. Anyway, if not, the house was only a stone's throw away. 'We'll try the yard first.'

Most of the farm buildings from which Fever ran his haulage business looked on the verge of collapse. The old Kent peg tiles had been stripped off and replaced with corrugated iron – a common sight since the hurricane, when the value of the old tiles had tripled overnight – and there were ragged gaps in the traditional weatherboarding. Lineham swung in between the open double metal gates which fronted the yard and parked alongside a small brick twin-kilned oast house marked OFFICE, the only building in reasonably good repair. As they got out of the car they became aware of raised voices within. The door was slightly ajar and as they drew closer Thanet put a warning finger to his lips.

'Honest, Mr Fever, I swear I never – '

203

'Don't give me that guff! Think I was born yesterday? I been over and over those records and there's no way I can come up with any other answer. If you think I'm going to sweat my guts out supplying easy money for toe-rags like you, you've got another think coming!'

'But – '

'But nothing! I've said all I'm going to say. That's it. Finish. There's your card, there's your money up to date. Now get out!'

Silence, then the sound of a door closing and footsteps approaching. A typewriter started clattering. Fever's secretary starting work after listening to the row?

Thanet and Lineham stepped back as a man emerged. He was grossly overweight, his belly hanging over the waistband of his low-slung trousers, his round moon-face wearing a hangdog expression. After a flicker of surprise at the sight of the two policemen he slunk past them and walked away through the gates, hands in pockets, shoulders slumped.

Thanet knocked at the door and they went in.

They were in a short, uncarpeted corridor floored with scuffed, grubby vinyl tiles. To their left was a closed door, to their right a notice saying ENQUIRIES stuck on to a glass partition through which they could see a girl typing on an antiquated machine. It was increasingly obvious that however freely Fever lavished money upon his private life, he didn't believe in spending it on his working environment. Presumably most of his business was conducted by telephone and as there was no one to impress he didn't think it worth the expenditure.

Lineham tapped on the glass and the girl looked up, then came to slide a section of the partition open.

'Yes?'

She was young and plain, shoddily dressed in a short, tight black skirt and striped acrylic jumper.

'We'd like a word with Mr Fever.'

Her eyes darted anxiously to the door across the corridor. 'I'll see if he's free. Who shall I say?'

'Detective Inspector Thanet and Detective Sergeant Lineham, Sturrenden CID.'

She looked alarmed. 'Yes,' she said. 'Right. I'll . . . er . . . I'll just go and see.'

She came out into the corridor and crossed to knock at the door on their left.

'Come in.'

With a nervous glance over her shoulder at the two policemen she opened the door just wide enough to sidle in, closing it behind her. After a brief murmur of voices she came out again, holding it wide open this time. 'Mr Fever can see you now.'

Fever was seated at a paper-strewn desk. He cast up his eyes. 'This is all I need.'

'Trouble?' said Thanet benignly. 'I'm afraid we couldn't help overhearing. The door was open.'

'Nothing I can't handle.' He waved a hand at a spindly metal stacking chair with a plastic seat. 'I'm afraid there's only one chair.'

Personal appearance mattered to him. His clothes, by contrast with the tattiness of his surroundings, were again sleek and expensive: creamy silk polo shirt and soft beige suede jacket. His rather sparse brown hair was well-cut, if rather long for Thanet's taste, and a faint aroma of aftershave hung in the air.

'Not to worry.'

Thanet sat down and Lineham moved across to lean against the windowsill, taking out his notebook.

'Right, Mr Fever, now perhaps we can start again.'

Fever's eyes narrowed with suspicion. 'What d'you mean?'

'Some rather interesting information has come to light since we saw you last.'

'Oh?' said Fever, warily.

'Yes. First, it has been confirmed that Mr Martindale was knocked down by the Ford van from Longford Hall Hotel.'

'So?'

'The one used principally by Sam Tiller.'

Something flickered in Fever's eyes. Dismay? Guilt? Fear? Impossible to tell. His facial expression did not alter. He had himself well under control. He raised his eyebrows in polite enquiry. *What has this got to do with me?*

'Secondly, we have also learned, from the post-mortem, that Mr Martindale did not die as a result of the collision. After the "accident" ' – Thanet's voice implied inverted commas around the word – 'his body was placed in the ditch where it was found next morning. He died from exposure, Mr Fever.'

'Too bad. But . . .'

The man's indifference infuriated Thanet and, longing to puncture it, he cut in. 'We understand that at some point he must have recovered consciousness and tried to get out. Unfortunately his spine was broken and he couldn't.' Fever, he was glad to see, was looking shaken. 'A very unpleasant death, as I'm sure you'll agree.'

'Poor bastard . . . But I still don't see what all this has to do with me.'

'Well, as I was explaining, you must see that this is therefore now a murder investigation.' Thanet paused, sat back and folded his arms. 'We were interested to learn that you drove the van that night, Mr Fever.'

The implication was too obvious to ignore. Fever sat up with a jerk, looking suitably outraged. 'Now look here . . .'

'No, you look here, Mr Fever. You admit, do you, that you drove the van that evening?'

'Well yes. But I had a perfectly good reason . . .'

'So I believe. But that is beside the point. The point is that you did drive it. I think you'll have to admit, it doesn't look good for you. First of all you have a blazing row with Mr Martindale, telling him to keep away from your wife . . .'

'Why shouldn't I – ?'

'Then,' Thanet raised his voice, cutting Fever off, 'only a

few hours later, Martindale is knocked down by a van which you admit to driving that same evening.'

Fever's face had become suffused with colour and his eyes bulged slightly as he said through his teeth, 'I refuse to put up with this.' His hand went out to the telephone. 'I'm going to call my solicitor.'

Thanet sat back, folding his arms. 'Do, by all means. But it might be a good idea to hear the rest of what I have to say, first.'

Fever's hand hovered above the instrument then fell back. 'Spit it out, then, why don't you?'

'It's obvious, surely. Means, motive, opportunity.' Thanet ticked them off on his fingers. 'I think you'll agree, you had them all.'

'Agree! Like hell I will.' He gave a cynical bark of laughter. 'Motive, indeed. What motive? Just because I told him to keep away from my wife?'

'Partly, perhaps. But I think we both know it goes a lot deeper than that.'

Fever was suddenly motionless, his eyes gleaming. 'What the hell,' he said softly, 'do you mean by that?'

'You had good reason to be jealous of Martindale, didn't you, Mr Fever?'

'What's that supposed to mean?'

'Oh come on, let's not play games. We both know what I'm talking about.'

'Do we?'

About to deliver a mortal blow to Fever's pride, Thanet steeled himself. Aggression did not come easily to him and it was only the knowledge that with this particular man he couldn't afford to let up for a moment that enabled him to sustain the attack. And if Fever were guilty, if he had indeed dragged an injured man into a ditch and left him to die, then he deserved all he was getting. But if not, if he were innocent . . . Thanet was well aware that Fever's hostility might well be a defence mechanism to cover up his vulnerability, that the man could have been more sinned against than sinning.

'I must admit that I was a little surprised that a few minutes' conversation in public between your wife and Martindale was enough to send you to rushing off to have a row with him . . .'

Fever was very still, waiting.

'And then this morning, of course, I realised why you had reacted so strongly.'

The tension in the air was almost tangible.

'What did Martindale say to your wife that afternoon, Mr Fever, to make you so angry?' Thanet paused before playing his trump card. 'Did he threaten to tell Toby that he was his father?'

'No!' With the explosive monosyllable Fever was on his feet, hands gripping the edge of his desk. 'Who the hell . . .' he shouted and then, remembering his secretary's proximity, 'who the hell,' he hissed, 'do you think you are, coming here like this, poking your nose into my private life, making irresponsible accusations right left and centre . . . ?' His eyes were wild and flecks of spittle flew in Thanet's direction.

Thanet didn't flinch. 'Irresponsible, Mr Fever?' he said softly. But, although he didn't show it, for a moment he wavered. What if he were wrong?

'Yes!'

'You deny, then, that Toby was Martindale's son?' Thanet held up a hand. 'And, before you say "yes", I must warn you that this is not just idle speculation. We have been in touch with the General Register Office to check dates and so on.'

Fever stared at him, the anger gradually dying out of his eyes, to be replaced with despair. Then he slowly subsided into his chair and putting his elbows on the desk buried his head in his hands.

The silence was sufficient answer. Thanet was relieved. At least he hadn't been wrong in this. He glanced at Lineham who gave a satisfied nod.

Thanet waited a moment or two longer and then said,

'Look, Mr Fever, whether you believe it or not, I'm not enjoying this. I don't get a kick out of other people's misery and I'm not here either to make judgements or to broadcast people's secrets unless it is absolutely necessary. I am merely trying to discover the facts but you must see that until I do I can't even begin to decide whether this matter is relevant or not.'

Fever was listening, he could tell. Encouraged, he went on. 'I've had to be rather hard on you because, as I'm sure you'll admit, you weren't exactly in a cooperative mood. But if we could now have a sensible and rational discussion . . .'

Fever raised his head and looked at Thanet, a long, assessing look. *Can I believe what you're saying?*

Thanet waited, meeting Fever's gaze squarely and hoping that his expression was suitably frank and open.

After a moment or two Fever sat back, lifting his hands a little way off the desk and dropping them again in a gesture of surrender. He shrugged. 'OK. What do you want to know?'

TWENTY-ONE

As the tension in the room began to ebb away Lineham shifted his stance and cleared his throat, unconsciously signalling the fact that one phase of the interview had just ended and another was about to begin. Briefly Thanet wondered if highly-charged emotion actually generated its own − what? − static electricity? Magnetic field? He didn't know. He felt depleted, suddenly aware of an ache in the small of his back, always his weak spot. He longed to get up and ease it, to walk about, light his pipe, relax, but he couldn't afford to do any of these things. It was important not to lose the impetus he had won.

Fever, by contrast, had now given up. Slumped in his chair, he was waiting for Thanet to begin, eyes dull, hands clasped loosely across his stomach.

'I'll be as brief as I can. Toby is Martindale's son?'

A tightening of the lips, a nod.

'And you've known this right from the beginning.'

Another nod.

'Does Toby know?'

This brought a reaction. Fever straightened up. 'No! And I − we, don't want him to know.'

'You've brought him up as your own son?'

'Yeah.' A wry attempt at a smile. 'We always thought if he took it into his head to count up on his fingers, he'd simply work out we'd enjoyed a bit of hanky-panky before we walked up the aisle.'

'You had no other children?'

Fever shook his head. 'No such luck. So it was all the more important that Toby never suspected . . .'

'Yes, I can see that. All the same, a bit risky, wasn't it?'

Fever shrugged. 'Even if he'd been adopted we wouldn't have told him till he was at least four. By then Leo'd been gone nearly five years and as time went on it seemed less and less likely he'd ever come back.'

An uncomfortable thought struck Thanet. 'Does anybody else know, or suspect?'

Fever was shaking his head again. 'Not that I know of. It's never even been hinted at. There was a bit of ribbing, of course, when Toby was born only six months after the wedding, but we just let everybody think we'd been at it before we should've.'

Oh God, thought Thanet. And I've told Delia Hamilton. What would she do, if anything? He shook his head, to clear it. He'd have to think about that later. Ought he to mention it to Fever? No, not now, when the man was being cooperative at last.

'I'm not sure of the legal position of an illegitimate child, but did you ever think that you could be depriving Toby of a fine inheritance?'

'Well yeah, that did worry us, I must admit, but we took legal advice, confidential-like, when old Martindale died, just for our own peace of mind. Anyway, we discovered Toby didn't have no claim at all, in law. According to the solicitor, illegitimate kids can now inherit, but only if the parents are together. To be honest, we was relieved. Having kept it from him all that time . . . And the last thing we wanted was a legal battle on our hands, that sort of thing can drag on for years. Besides, Toby's happy as he is. He's got everything he wants or needs. He's a good lad, we get on well together, he enjoys working in the business with me ... Nah, we decided ignorance was bliss and to leave well alone.'

'You implied just now that one of the reasons why you'd never told Toby was because you thought Martindale would never come back.' Now for the important question. 'Does this mean that Martindale knew your wife was pregnant by him, before he went away?'

It was clear that the thought of Martindale impregnating his wife was even now, after all these years, painful to Fever. He compressed his lips and shook his head.

'You're sure?'

'Of course I'm sure! We just thought that if Leo did come back he might work it out for himself.'

'And did he?'

'No!'

Thanet didn't think he was lying. But what if, knowing her husband's jealous nature, Yvonne had told Martindale before he went away, but had never had the nerve to admit it to Fever? Remembering Martindale's questioning of the hotel receptionist in regard to Toby's identity, Thanet considered this possible.

Thanet tried to work it out. If Fever truly believed that Martindale had never known and had therefore never been in the position to threaten to tell Toby, the case against him was strongly undermined. Though there still remained his jealousy. Would that have been enough to drive him, on impulse, to murder? Remembering Fever's reaction just now Thanet thought that it might. For Fever to have stepped in and married Yvonne the moment it became obvious that Martindale had abandoned her, it was more than likely that Fever had been in love with her for some time, that he had had to stand back and watch helplessly while she was swept off her feet by the son of the big house. Jealousy was a cruel emotion, a classic cause of murder. In the case of a man like Fever, whose reputation was such that his wife scarcely dared even speak to another man in his presence for fear of

212

provoking an outburst, the reappearance of Martindale, who had once actually possessed Fever's wife, perhaps stolen her from under his very nose while he looked impotently on, could well have reactivated all his original resentment and hatred of the man. Jealousy had certainly driven him to an immediate confrontation with Martindale. Thanet wondered exactly what had been said during that row, how Martindale had reacted to Fever's warning. Could he have laughed at him, thus provoking him even further and sending him away in an even greater rage? If so, and if, later, on his way back from taking his wife to her mother's house in the van, Fever had been presented with the spectacle of Martindale walking along the road ahead of him, alone ... Yes, it was still possible that Fever was their man.

Thanet became aware that both Lineham and Fever were watching him, intrigued by his long silence. He stood up. 'Right, thank you.'

Fever came to his feet. 'That's it?'

'For the moment, yes.'

They left him staring after them with a puzzled frown.

'No point in asking him if he'd seen Martindale later, when he borrowed the van. He'd only have denied it,' said Thanet as they got into the car. He wound down the window and took out his pipe, began to fill it.

Lineham was nodding agreement. 'He could be our man, though.' He smacked his clenched fist into the palm of the other hand. 'If only we had some hard evidence against one of them. Just one tiny scrap!'

'I know.' Briefly, at the very back of Thanet's mind something flickered. What was it? He struggled to grasp it, drag it out in order to examine it but already it was gone. Had he imagined it?

Lineham was watching him. 'What?'

Thanet shook his head. 'It's gone.' He struck a match, lit his pipe.

'Where now, sir? Hamilton?'

Thanet shook his head. 'Not much point. You realise I've put my foot in it there, Mike?'

'By telling Mrs Hamilton about Toby? I can't see that you've done much harm.'

'In any case, it's done now. There's no point in worrying about it, I suppose.'

'It'll give them a few uncomfortable moments, I dare say. But I can't say I feel much sympathy for them. They haven't done too badly, have they?'

'I wasn't thinking of them, I was thinking of Toby.'

'I shouldn't lose any sleep over it. The Hamiltons aren't exactly about to shout it from the roof-tops, are they?'

'No. All the same, for Toby's sake I think I'll have to have a word with Mrs Hamilton.'

Lineham's expression indicated that he thought Thanet overscrupulous on this point, but he merely said, 'So what now?'

Thanet glanced at his watch. Two-thirty. 'Might as well go back to headquarters, have a session going over the papers. There could be something we've missed. And I really ought to glance at the Super's directive on ODD. He'll go through the roof tomorrow morning if I still haven't got around to it.'

It was a silent journey back, each of them preoccupied with his own thoughts. Back at the office they wrote their reports on the morning's interviews, then settled down to work systematically through the considerable stack of papers which had accumulated since the case began. They were methodical, both going through each report in turn, in case one of them spotted something the other had missed. In this particular case, when suspects were many and hard evidence against any one of them sadly lacking, it might well happen that some tiny detail which at the time had seemed of no importance could prove to be of crucial significance. The atmosphere in the room was heavy with concentration, the silence broken only occasionally by a murmured comment or enquiry. From time to time Thanet stood up and walked about, conscious that the dull ache in the small of his back was intensifying. He longed to stretch out on the floor, relieve tense muscles of the downward tug of gravity. Instead, he would sit down, pick up the next sheaf of paper and carry on the task.

By twenty to five he had to admit defeat. Nothing of any importance had emerged. Both he and Lineham were bleary-eyed, their thought processes clogged with the mass of information through which they had sifted. He put down his pen, rubbed his eyes, sat back and stretched. Time to glance at Draco's notes on ODD before going down to report to the Superintendent at five. 'See if you can rustle up some tea, Mike, while I look at this.'

When Lineham got back Thanet was looking much more animated. 'Something occurred to you, sir?'

'Not to do with the case.' Thanet tapped the ODD directive. 'Did you have any thoughts on this, Mike?' He took the cup Lineham was offering him. 'Thanks.'

Lineham sat down. 'Not really. Why, have you?'

'Possibly. Organisation, Delegation and Documentation. Now, the whole point of this campaign is to improve efficiency. Which one of those three would you say is the most time-consuming?'

'Documentation, I suppose.'

'Exactly!' Thanet leaned forward across his desk. 'Now tell me this. How much time is wasted in the front office looking through the files for, say, a key-holder's card for shop or office alarms that has been put back in the wrong place by some officer in a hurry?'

'Quite a bit, I'd say.' Everyone in the situation had ground his teeth over this particular bit of inefficiency, at one time or another.

'Well, why don't I suggest that all that information is put on the computer, instead? It's being done more and more – Maidstone introduced it a couple of years ago, for example.

And not only key-holders' lists, but names and updated addresses of station staff, charge cards, details of emergency action plans . . .'

'But if all that information was stored on the computer what happens if you need it in a hurry when the computer operator is away at lunch or, even worse, off sick?'

'Obviously it would mean that everyone in the station would have to be trained to use the computer.'

Lineham groaned. He wasn't into computers. 'Oh, no!'

'Come on, Mike, don't be faint-hearted. It would all be in a good cause and besides, it wouldn't be too difficult. Not if we got hold of a simple, user-friendly system. Just think how much time it would save in the long run!'

'Well . . .'

'I think I'll suggest it. If Draco doesn't like the idea, then too bad, but at least I'll have come up with a positive suggestion.' Thanet glanced at his watch. Two minutes to five. 'I'd better go down to give my report.'

At the door he turned. 'Oh, by the way, while I'm away, give Mrs Hamilton a ring, tell her her calculator wasn't in the van.' This was clear from the report on the van's contents. Thanet had checked. 'She must have dropped it somewhere else.'

On the way downstairs he was again conscious of that strange, almost physical sensation at the back of his mind. He had felt it before, many times, and it meant that his subconscious had registered something which his conscious mind had not, and the information was trying to get through. Experience had taught him that it was pointless to try and work out what it was. Sooner or later it would surface in its own good time and the best way to speed up the process was to think of something else.

Outside Draco's office Thanet paused, braced himself. What sort of a mood would the Super be in this afternoon? A better one than this morning, he hoped. He knocked.

'Come in.'

216

Draco was sitting in front of an immaculately tidy desk, pens and pencils neatly aligned, in-tray empty, out-tray full, empty blotter before him. He looked relaxed, composed, positively benign. 'Ah, Thanet. How's it going?'

Thanet gave a succinct summary of the day's findings, Draco nodding from time to time, putting in a question here and there. It looked as though the session was going to go off without incident and, encouraged, Thanet decided to float his new idea.

'By the way – '

'Just a minute . . .' Draco held up a hand. He was peering out of the window, which overlooked the main entrance to the building and enabled the Superintendent to keep a watchful eye on comings and goings. If anyone sneezed in this building, Draco liked to know about it. 'Sorry to interrupt, Thanet, but who's that?'

Thanet rose and crossed to the window. Walking towards them were two men deep in conversation, one in uniform, the other in civilian clothes. He assumed Draco wasn't referring to Inspector Storey, an old friend of Thanet's now working in Maidstone, and he'd never seen the civilian before. 'Sorry, I don't know. Some member of the public coming to – '

'No, no,' said Draco testily. 'That's Councillor Watford, I know him. The other man, in uniform.'

'Inspector Storey. He's one of the instructors at the Police Training School in Maidstone.' The words came out mechanically. Thanet was barely aware that he had spoken. He was staring at the two men, dumbfounded.

Of course! Why hadn't he seen it before?

'Wonder what they're doing here,' muttered Draco, heading for the door. 'Was that the lot, Thanet?'

'What? Oh, sorry, sir. Yes.' His suggestion could wait until the morning meeting tomorrow. Besides, he couldn't wait to tell Lineham . . .

He followed Draco out of the office and took the stairs two at a time.

Lineham glanced up, startled, as Thanet burst into the office.

'Mike! Listen to this!'

Thanet watched the light dawn in Lineham's face as he talked.

'I see! Brilliant, sir! So what do we do now?'

Thanet told him.

TWENTY-TWO

'Let's hope they haven't gone to bed.'

'Shouldn't think so, Mike, it's only ten o'clock.'

It was five exhausting hours later. After making the necessary appointment, clearing it with the Sussex police and ringing Joan and Louise to tell them they'd be late home, Thanet and Lineham had set off on the longish drive to Worthing. The interview there had verified Thanet's hunch and presented them with a clear motive where none had apparently existed before. Now they were about to put his theory to the test.

Thanet shifted in his seat in an attempt to ease his back and rubbed his eyes, which were beginning to feel gritty with fatigue. He was glad he wasn't driving. He glanced across at Lineham who still looked relatively fresh.

'I gather you got the problem with your brother-in-law sorted out?'

'Yes. Or at least, he did. Went back to his wife this morning.'

'Good.'

Lineham leaned forward to wipe the windscreen, which kept on misting up. Since darkness fell the temperature had plummeted rapidly and along the sides of the lane the grass and clumps of tangled undergrowth were encrusted with frost.

The sergeant was driving carefully, leaning forward slightly to peer at the road ahead. 'Lucky we haven't had any rain today, or it'd be like a skating rink.'

'Mm.' Thanet was preoccupied with the interview to come.

'Of course, it still doesn't necessarily mean one of them did it,' said Lineham, for the third time.

Thanet realised that the sergeant was merely armouring himself against disappointment. 'I'm aware of that, Mike,' he said patiently. 'But it's a powerful motive, you must admit. And I've just got this feeling . . .'

The gateposts at the entrance to Longford Hall loomed up ahead and Lineham put his indicator on. 'Even if you're right, I still don't see how we're going to prove it.'

Ay, there was the rub indeed. 'I know.'

'I mean, we've no more evidence against them than against any of the others.'

Yet again Thanet experienced that flicker at the back of his mind. What was it that he was trying to remember? Was it possible that there was something he had missed, some minute scrap of evidence that could turn the tide in his favour? Not that, if his theory proved correct, an arrest would give him much satisfaction. After the initial excitement over that flash of inspiration he had felt progressively more and more depressed and now he felt only a dragging weariness at the prospect of the interview ahead. He braced himself as Lineham drove into the stable yard and parked. Whether he liked it or not, he had to go through with it. Murder had been done and if one of these two were guilty it was his clear duty to bring the perpetrator to justice, whatever his personal feelings in the matter.

They walked across the cobbles to the stable block, climbed the indoor staircase and knocked at the door at the top.

It was a few minutes before it was opened by Desmond Byfleet, peering out into the semi-darkness. 'Oh, it's you, Inspector.'

220

'May we come in?'

Byfleet stood back to let them pass, closing the door behind them. 'We were just about to go to bed.' He was in his shirt-sleeves, tieless, carpet slippers on bare feet. Without a jacket he looked thinner than ever and more vulnerable, as if with the outer layer of cloth he had peeled off his defences.

'I'm sorry to trouble you so late, but we'd like a word with you both.'

'Do you have to see my wife? She's very tired.'

Thanet shook his head. 'I'm sorry,' he repeated. He meant it. 'I'll have to talk to her sooner or later. Better to get it over with.'

Byfleet hesitated a moment or two longer, apparently trying to make up his mind whether to refuse point-blank, the muscles in his cheeks moving as he clenched his teeth. Then he turned away and flung open the sitting-room door, switching on a light inside. 'I'll go and see.'

The sight of the cosy, welcoming room reinforced Thanet's distaste for the coming interview. He strolled restlessly about, his gaze wandering abstractedly over the attractive soft furnishings, the books, plants, records, chess-game, bowl of odds and ends on the coffee table. He sat down heavily, his back protesting at the softness of the cushions. 'I'm not looking forward to this, Mike.' What if he were wrong? He could see the headlines. WOMAN MISCARRIES AFTER POLICE HARASSMENT. He rubbed his eyes, shook his head in an attempt to clear it. It had been a long day.

Lineham had chosen an upright chair which stood in front of a small writing desk. He picked up one of the ornaments on it, a glass paperweight, and peered into it as if it were a crystal ball. 'Fascinating things, these.' He put it down hastily and stood up as Byfleet entered the room, followed by his wife.

Thanet rose too. 'I apologise for disturbing you at this hour, ma'am.'

She attempted a smile but said nothing, walking past him

to sit on the settee. She was wearing a man's woollen dressing gown, her husband's presumably, loosely tied across her protruding belly. The shade, a drab fawn, did not become her, leaching any colour from her sallow skin and from the lank, lifeless brown hair.

She looked as tired as he felt, thought Thanet. Scarcely surprising, really. If he was right, she couldn't have had much sleep over the last few days.

Byfleet sat down beside his wife and covered her hand with his.

Thanet glanced at Lineham to check that he was ready and the sergeant nodded. *Go ahead.*

'There's no point in beating about the bush, so perhaps it would be best to begin by telling you that we have just come back from Worthing, where we have seen your mother, Mrs Byfleet.'

Mona Byfleet blinked and blindly put out her other hand to her husband who took and clasped it. Neither of them said a word, just stared at him, awaiting the next blow.

'She was naturally very distressed when she heard what had happened. She realises that you and your husband had no idea, when you married . . . It must have been an awful shock for you.'

Thanet paused expectantly. He didn't want to spell it out if he didn't have to.

Desmond Byfleet cleared his throat. 'We don't know what you're talking about, Inspector.'

Thanet shook his head wearily. 'It's no good taking that line, Mr Byfleet. We know, you see.'

'Know . . . what?' Mona Byfleet spoke for the first time, in a near-whisper.

'That your mother told Mr Martindale and that he must have told you, Mrs Byfleet, when he called you into his room, the night he died.'

'We still haven't the faintest idea what you're on about, Inspector.' Byfleet's voice was stronger now. He had obviously decided on the line he was going to take and was sticking to it.

His wife was less certain. She shot him an agonised glance and said, 'Des . . .'

Byfleet gave no overt sign of having realised that she was on the point of capitulation. There was no frown, no shake of the head, just a brief exchange of glances. But the message still came over loud and clear. *Stand firm.*

She glanced back at Thanet. *Don't say it*, her eyes pleaded. *Please, don't say it.*

But he had to, somehow, Thanet realised, or they would get nowhere. He sighed. 'Perhaps it will help if I tell you a story.'

Byfleet clicked his tongue impatiently but his wife, re-cognising perhaps that Thanet was proposing an oblique approach to the subject in order to cushion the blow, laid a restraining hand on his arm.

'Once upon a time,' said Thanet, 'there was born in London's East End a girl called Brenda. She had eight brothers and sisters and her father was a drunkard who couldn't keep any job down for more than a few weeks at a time. Needless to say she couldn't wait to get away from home and in 1949, at the ripe old age of seventeen, she married the first man who asked her and moved to the Midlands.

'Unfortunately it wasn't long before she discovered that she had jumped out of the frying pan into the fire. Her new husband was a bully and a brute and not long afterwards, when she was seven months pregnant, he beat her up so badly that the baby was born prematurely.'

He had their attention now. They were gazing at him as if mesmerised.

'This was the last straw as far as she was concerned. In hospital she refused to see her husband again and on the day she was due to be discharged she left earlier than the time arranged and, having borrowed the train fare from one of the other women in the ward, came straight to London, leaving her baby boy behind. Being premature, of course, he would in any case have had to remain in hospital for some time but this was, she felt, the only way she could get away from her husband and be certain that the baby would be well looked after. She had had this plan in mind right from the moment of that last, brutal beating and although the baby seemed healthy enough she insisted on his being christened immediately after the birth. In fact, the husband refused to have anything to do with the child, who was brought up first in a children's home then in various foster homes.

'Meanwhile, Brenda changed her surname and, despite the nationwide appeal for her to come forward, disappeared into the lowest stratum of London's catering trade where employers didn't bother about National Insurance cards and were only too glad to get cheap labour. For some time she washed dishes, waited at tables in the smallest and meanest cafés and then, when she felt it was safe, reverted to her married name, legitimately got hold of a National Insurance card, and began to work in earnest towards furthering the career she had meanwhile decided to pursue. Shrewdly, considering her lack of qualifications, she chose the hotel business. I won't go into the details. It's enough to say that beginning on the bottom rung and by working twice as hard as anyone else, in five years she managed to work her way up to Housekeeper in a smallish hotel. During this period she also divorced her husband. Then, late in 1954, she managed at last to get the kind of job she'd always been aiming for, a post as Housekeeper in a hotel out of London, on the South Coast. At this time she was still barely twenty-three and perhaps it's not surprising that now, for the first time, romance entered her life. It was a small, family-run hotel, and the Assistant Manager was the son of the owners. In due course Brenda and he were married and the following year they had a daughter.' Thanet paused. 'In a minor way a fairy-tale ending, as I think you'll agree. Unfortunately, the story doesn't end there.

'In due course first the owner and his wife were killed in a holiday air crash and then Brenda's second husband died, so the ownership of the hotel passed to her. Her daughter grew up and when she left school worked in the hotel with her mother. Although she wasn't exactly antisocial she was never the type of girl to have lots of boyfriends and it wasn't until she was in her late twenties that at last she met a man she liked. He had recently moved down to the South from Birmingham. For some reason – shyness, perhaps? – she kept their association a secret. Finally, when they began to talk of marriage, she broke the news to her mother and asked her to meet him. She was taken aback by her reaction. From the outset, before she had even met him, Brenda seemed prejudiced against him. The girl put it down to over-protectiveness of an only chick and told herself that when her mother met the young man and saw how respectable and hardworking he was she would become reconciled to the idea. Instead, the meeting merely served to harden her mother's attitude. The young man, she insisted, was unsuitable, completely wrong for the girl.

'Naturally, the daughter thought that her mother was being totally unreasonable. But in fact, she was misjudging her. Brenda was against the marriage for quite another reason.

'As soon as she heard the man's name – a fairly unusual one – she had realised to her horror that he could be the son she had abandoned long ago and there was a real possibility that brother and sister were planning to marry.'

TWENTY-THREE

With an abrupt, desperate movement Mona turned her head and buried her face in Desmond's sleeve as if ashamed to look Thanet in the eye any longer. Desmond shot Thanet a furious, resentful glance and put his arm around her.

Thanet took a deep breath and attempting to ignore the pity that was churning his stomach said softly, 'It would perhaps be more accurate to say, "half-brother", and it is clear that the young people were entirely the innocent victims of tragic circumstance. Although Brenda had confided the details of that early, disastrous marriage to her husband, she had never told her daughter about it. All that, she had thought, was behind her, best forgotten. Now . . . Well at first, of course, she couldn't be sure that her suspicions were justified. So she agreed to meet the young man and when she did knew at once that he was her son. He was the spitting image of his father. That, together with his name . . . She may have abandoned him, you see, but she'd never forgotten him, and ironically her daughter's name had even been chosen in a rather subtle way to complement his.'

Desmond and Mona glanced at each other as they worked out what he meant and the name shivered unspoken in the air between them. *Desdemona.*

'A few questions about his background convinced Brenda that she was right. Now she was in a real dilemma. If she told

226

her daughter the truth, the girl would never forgive her for not having been frank with her from the beginning. If she didn't, her daughter would think that she was against the marriage for far more trivial reasons. Either way she ran the risk of losing the only person she really loved. It wasn't surprising that that night she tried to drown her sorrows in drink, but it was unfortunate that she did so in the company of one of the guests in the hotel, a man by the name of Leo Martindale. He was a confidence trickster who made a habit of preying on lonely middle-aged women and she was his favourite type, the hotel owner who was reasonably well off and might be sweet-talked into parting with some money if he played his cards right.

'In Brenda's case he had got as far as hinting at marriage and had managed to worm his way into her bed. On this particular evening, more than a little drunk and desperate to share her problem with someone, she confided in him and asked his advice. He did in fact tell her that he thought it would be best to tell the girl the truth but when it came down to it Brenda couldn't bring herself to do it. Finally, just when she had screwed up sufficient courage to do so, she found it was too late. Furious at her mother's opposition to the marriage, the daughter had decided to elope. The young people were both over age and there appeared to be nothing to prevent them marrying. For marriage in a registry office couples do not have to produce birth certificates unless they are under 23 years of age, so in all innocence they went through the ceremony and as far as the mother was concerned, just disappeared. Eventually they found work as a husband-and-wife team here, at Longford Hall.'

For the first time Thanet addressed the Byfleets directly. 'Ironic, wasn't it, that you chose this particular hotel, Martindale's family home. The owner's name, of course, was different, Hamilton, so you had no reason to connect your new employer with the man your mother hoped to marry, and it must have been a shock when he turned up as Mrs

227

Hamilton's brother . . . And even more of a shock when he told you what he had learned from your mother, Mrs Byfleet.'

Mona was staring miserably down at her lap now, twisting the cord of the dressing gown round and round one finger, releasing it, twisting it again. Still she did not speak and, meeting Byfleet's stony stare, Thanet realised with something like despair that if they chose to remain silent there was absolutely nothing he could do about it. So where did he go from here? He had no stomach for browbeating these people into a confession, they were suffering enough as it was. And, too, there was the possibility that he was wrong and they had had nothing to do with Martindale's death.

Lineham was watching him, aware no doubt of Thanet's predicament. The silence in the room stretched out uncomfortably.

He had miscalculated, Thanet realised. He had thought that informing the Byfleets that he knew their unhappy secret would be such a shock to them that they would break down and confess, especially if he could do so in such a way as to convince them that he was sympathetic to their predicament. To this end he had put all his ingenuity into devising a way of breaking the news gently – too gently, perhaps. Compassion may have made his efforts self-defeating. In any case, he had not thought beyond that point.

Well, they had reached it and it had got him nowhere.

If only, he thought desperately, he could remember whatever it was that had been eluding him. It was, he was sure, highly relevant. He could feel the knowledge struggling to surface, lacking that final impetus which would bring him enlightenment. He glanced around the room seeking inspiration but seeing only an Eden that was for the Byfleets perhaps forever lost.

It was pointless to prolong the interview. He was about to rise, had actually put his hand on the arm of his chair preparatory to levering himself up when his gaze fell upon the blue-and-white ceramic bowl of odds and ends and, at last, he spotted it.

Of course! That was what his subconscious had registered, the last time he was here!

Despite the pity he felt for the couple still clinging on to the shreds of their dignity, for the second time that day he experienced the unique explosion of triumph which invariably accompanies such rare flashes of understanding – followed at once by doubt.

What if he were wrong?

He longed to put out his hand and pick the object up, his fingers actually ached with the need to do so, to open it, examine it, verify that it really was what he thought it was.

Lineham was now watching Thanet intently. After years of working together he was attuned to even the slightest shift in Thanet's mood and he knew that something of significance had just occurred to him.

Thanet glanced at the Byfleets. They too were watching him, still warily but with the beginning of hope that the worst was over. What should he do? Should he risk making a monumental fool of himself?

His heartbeat accelerated as alternative ways of approaching the subject flashed through his mind.

He took a deep calming breath and exhaled slowly. Then he said, 'The last time I was here I asked if either of you had driven the van the night Mr Martindale died. Now I'd like to ask you again. Did you?'

They did not look at each other but he sensed the unspoken communication which flashed between them before they shook their heads. Thanet waited a moment and then, with a complete change of tone, leaned forward and pointed. 'Is that yours, Mr Byfleet?'

'No. It's my wife's.'

Mona twisted to look up at him. She frowned. 'No it's not, Des. Mine's back at the hotel, in my office. I was using it this evening and that one's been there for a couple of days. I thought it was yours.'

Now it was Byfleet's turn to look puzzled. He leaned forward and reached out to pick the object up, but Thanet put out a hand to prevent him from touching it. Their eyes locked and for a moment there was an unspoken battle of wills between them, Byfleet's hand hovering uncertainly over the coffee table. Then he capitulated, leaning over and pulling towards him the jacket which was lying across the arm of the settee. He patted one of the pockets, put his hand in and took out a virtually identical small black object. Then he looked back at the one in the bowl. *So whose is that?* His wife was looking at it too, but Thanet guessed that she at least now knew the answer and that the question in her eyes was, *How did it get there?*

Now for the moment of truth. Taking a polythene bag from his pocket Thanet slipped it over his hand and then, with care, picked up what he had first thought was a diary, flipped it open. Relief that he had been proved right mingled with regret as he saw the slip of paper tucked into the flap. Even before he carefully extracted it with a pair of tweezers he knew what would be written on it.

Delia Hamilton's pocket calculator had turned up.

Briefly he held out the paper for the Byfleets to read the name and address on it. Their bewilderment was now mixed with apprehension. They couldn't understand why the calculator was important but Thanet's behaviour showed them that it was.

'Where did you get this?' Thanet tossed the question at them both.

They looked at each other. 'I really have no idea,' said Mona Byfleet. But Thanet could tell that in her husband's mind a memory was beginning to stir.

So Byfleet was their man.

Thanet breathed a silent prayer of thankfulness that at least he would not have to charge a pregnant woman with murder. If she were completely innocent and knew nothing of what her husband had done that night this was going to be a terrible shock to her, potentially disastrous as far as the baby was concerned, and it would be better if she were to leave them now. Perhaps he should insist that she do so. But it was still possible that she was an accessory after the fact. Byfleet was not the sort of man to commit a murder and return home with no sign of distress, and given the closeness of their relationship Thanet thought it highly unlikely that Byfleet would have been able to hold back from telling her what had happened. No, she would have to stay for at least a little while longer.

'Perhaps it would be best if I spell this out. I can see, Mr Byfleet, that you now remember just how Mrs Hamilton's calculator got here. On the night Mr Martindale died she distinctly remembers using it just before she drove to the station to pick up her son. Later, after hunting for it everywhere – as I'm sure you know, Mrs Byfleet, she realised that she must have dropped it in the van. Mr Talion didn't notice it when he used the van a little later but you, Mr Byfleet, I'd guess that after you put Mr Martindale in the ditch you quickly checked to see if you'd dropped anything and seeing this familiar object on the floor picked it up and put it in your pocket. I also think that you were so shaken by what had happened and in such a hurry to get back to the stable yard before anyone realised that you'd used the van that you scarcely realised what you were doing and later, when you found two calculators in your pockets, simply thought that you must have picked your wife's up by mistake. So you put it in the bowl there and she, of course, thought it was yours, and left it there.'

During this brief speech the expression on Mona's face had gradually changed from puzzlement to horrified realisation. Now she looked up at her husband who was staring down at his lap, chewing the inside of his lip. He shook his head in defeat and after a moment Thanet nodded at Lineham, who came forward and delivered the caution.

Mona Byfleet burst into tears.

Her husband put both arms around her and drew her close to him, smoothing her hair. 'It's all right, love. Hush. It's going to be all right.'

Thanet and Lineham exchanged uncomfortable glances. Thanet longed to get up and walk out, leave the whole miserable situation behind, but duty kept him pinned to his seat. Whatever he did now, sooner or later Mona was going to have to face the consequences of what had happened that night. It wasn't surprising that she had been looking so ill. Ever since she had learned the appalling truth from Martindale she must have been in a state of turmoil, worried sick about the health of a child born of an incestuous union and terrified of the effect of this new knowledge upon their future. And then, on top of that, to know that her husband had committed a murder ... The last few days must have been a torment for her. What would become of her, he wondered – and of the child?

The ragged sobbing was beginning to abate. Byfleet was still trying to soothe her and now he took a handkerchief from his pocket, moved slightly away from her and began to mop the tears gently from her face. Finally she took the handkerchief herself, blew her nose and looked at Thanet. 'You ... You don't understand. It wasn't the way you think. It ... It was an accident, wasn't it, Des?' And she gave her husband such a look of love and faith that Thanet could hardly bear to see it.

'It was because I was so upset, you see.' She blew her nose again, wiped her eyes and sat up straighter. 'He ... Mr Martindale ... was so foul to me.'

'When he called you into his room, you mean?' Thanet attempted to make his tone both matter-of-fact and sympathetic. It was important to try to lower the emotional temperature.

She nodded. 'It was an awful shock when he turned up at the hotel. I never liked him and he didn't like me – I think he

232

knew I saw through his smarmy ways.' She shuddered and made a little moue of distaste. 'I knew he'd recognised me, of course, in the foyer.' Her voice was getting stronger now as she regained control. It was clear that she wanted to set the record straight, to state the facts in such a way as to present her husband's behaviour in as good a light as possible.

'At first I thought Mum had found out where we were, and had sent him to check up on me. When I left home he seemed to be pretty well dug in there and I'd often wondered if they'd got married. Then when he turned up here and someone told me he was Mrs Hamilton's brother, I didn't know what to think . . . In any case, I wasn't too surprised when he called me into his room. I was glad of a private word, really. I wanted to find out what the situation was, and if he and Mum weren't together I wanted to make sure he didn't tell her where we were . . .

'At first it was all right. We just chatted, and I was relieved to find he had been living in France and had lost touch with my mother soon after I left. Then it was just like I told you before, he started asking questions about the hotel and when he got on to things that I didn't feel I ought to tell him, I said I couldn't answer any more questions, if he wanted to know he'd have to ask Mrs Hamilton, she was the boss, after all. He just laughed.

'That's what you think, Mona. Things are going to change around here from now on. My dear little sister isn't going to play at God any more.'
'What do you mean?'
'Simply that I've come home to stay. And to claim, somewhat belatedly, my inheritance. So you see, I'm going to be in charge here from now on and I have every right to ask you whatever questions I choose.'
'I'm sorry, I'm afraid I shall still have to talk to Mrs Hamilton first.'

'Think I'm lying, do you? Well I'm not, as you'll soon find out, perhaps to your cost.'

'What do you mean?'

'Simply that I could find your excessive devotion to my sister rather tiresome. And if you should find it impossible to transfer your loyalty to me, it might be necessary for me to look around for another housekeeper. You're not exactly the ideal candidate anyway, are you?'

'Because of the baby, you mean? I've never let my work suffer because I'm pregnant. Ask Mrs Hamilton.'

'I wasn't talking about the baby, not exactly, anyway.'

'What do you mean, not exactly? What were you talking about, then?'

'I was thinking more on the lines of bad moral influence.'

'Bad moral influence?'

'Yes. My God, you still don't know, do you?'

'Don't know what?'

'Why your mother was dead against you marrying Byfleet.'

'And then he . . . he told me . . .' Even now, when it was out in the open, Mona couldn't bring herself to say it. She was shaking as she relived what must have been the worst moment of her life. 'It . . . Oh, it was horrible.'

'I don't believe you.'

'Ah, but it's true, my dear.. Ask your mother. She'll give you chapter and verse all right. So unless you want the whole world to know the truth about you and your so-called husband, I suggest you remember to toe the line, as far as I'm concerned. Both of you.'

Mona was twisting and tugging at Desmond's handkerchief and now there was a small tearing sound as the material ripped. Engrossed in her story, she didn't even notice.

'I ran away, then. I couldn't bear to stay there a moment longer, to see that . . . triumphant look on his face. I came back here and waited for my husband.' She looked up at Desmond. 'It seemed such a long time before you got here, but I suppose it wasn't, really.' She turned back to Thanet. 'He could see at once I was in a state and then . . . when I told him . . . He was so upset . . . and angry because Mr Martindale had been so foul to me . . . And then, when I told him what Mr Martindale had said, about the whole world knowing the truth . . . Suddenly he just took off . . .'

'It was all such a shock,' Byfleet broke in. 'I hardly knew what I was doing. I couldn't keep still, I was walking about, and while my . . . wife was talking I'd happened to glance out of the window and see Mr Martindale crossing the stable yard, heading towards the drive: I stood there, watching him and listening to what she was saying and, a few minutes later, when she told me what he'd said about telling everyone . . .'

Byfleet's voice broke and he dropped his head in his hands. Now it was Mona's turn to give comfort and she stroked his back, gently, as if soothing a frightened animal.

How was he going to make this arrest with equanimity? Thanet wondered.

Byfleet straightened up again. 'In all my life this is the first place I've really felt I could call home. We've been so happy here. Haven't we, love?'

Mona nodded, biting her lip.

'The thought that it was all going to end, that he had ruined it all . . . And my wife was in such a state . . . I'm not trying to excuse myself, but it's true, it really was an accident.'

'What actually happened?'

Byfleet was shaking his head. 'I don't know what came over me . . . I suppose I just felt I had to do something, anything . . . So when Mona said that, about him threatening to tell the whole world . . . I just rushed out. I wanted to have it out with him at once, then and there. When I got down in the yard he was out of sight and the van was just standing there so I jumped in. I always carry the keys in my pocket.

Then the damn thing wouldn't start. It was so cold, that night . . . Anyway, it fired in the end and I went after him. When I was nearing the end of the drive I could see him ahead and I slammed on the brakes. I suppose I left it too late and had to brake too hard . . . Anyway, the van skidded and went out of control. He'd glanced around when he first heard me coming, and moved right in to walk at the side of the road, but there was nothing I could do to prevent myself hitting him.' Byfleet closed his eyes as if to block out the memory.

Mona Byfleet pressed her husband's arm.

Thanet waited.

'It was like a bad dream. It all happened so fast . . . It was over in a flash, in a matter of seconds . . .' Byfleet put up his hands and massaged his temples as if to erase the shock and bewilderment he still felt. 'I got out of the car. He was lying at the side of the road. I tried to find a pulse and couldn't . . . I realised he was dead, that I'd killed him . . .' Byfleet shook his head in despair. 'I'm afraid I just panicked. I knew that at any second someone could come along and . . . We were near the gates and I thought, the roads are so icy, if I put him in the ditch just outside the gates, it would look as though anyone could have done it . . . So . . . So that's what I did.'

'You see, Inspector. It *was* an accident.' Mona Byfleet was still holding on to her husband's arm, as if clinging to the wreckage of their life. 'The roads were icy and Desmond wasn't drunk . . .'

'It's all true, Inspector. It happened exactly as I've told you, I swear it.'

'Maybe so, but I'm afraid it's not quite as simple as that,' said Thanet, bracing himself to deliver the blow.

'What . . . What do you mean?' said Mona.

They stared at him with identical expressions on their faces. The likeness between them had never been more apparent.

'If it happened just as your husband told us . . .'

'It did!' broke in Byfleet.

236

'I believe you,' said Thanet. 'And if you had immediately gone for help . . .'

'But he was dead!' Byfleet was leaning forward now in his eagerness to convince Thanet of the innocence of his intentions. Then he sat back. 'Oh hell, why not admit it, you're right, I know you are. Even though there was nothing to be done for him . . .'

'Unfortunately, that's where you're wrong.'

Again that identical expression, an unspoken question in both their eyes. Perhaps they dared not ask it. Suddenly the tension was back in the room, the air was thick with their fear.

Thanet steeled himself. There was no way to soften the impact of what he was about to say and in any case it was true that it was Byfleet's action that had cost Martindale his life. 'I'm afraid Mr Martindale wasn't killed by the collision with the van,' he said. 'When you put him in the ditch he was still alive, but then it snowed, of course . . .'

He hesitated. Should he tell them that Martindale's spine had been injured, that he had recovered consciousness and been unable to get out of the ditch? No, at this point he couldn't bring himself to do it. They would learn, soon enough.

'So after lying outside all night in those conditions it's not surprising that he was dead by morning,' he concluded.

Mona fainted.

TWENTY-FOUR

Noon next day, Saturday.

Thanet laid down his pen, sat back, stretched, then reached for the telephone.

'Joan? It's me.'

'Hullo. How's it going?'

'Just finished. I was thinking . . . Fancy an afternoon out?'

'Lovely! Where?'

'What about Rye?'

'Bit chilly, d'you think?'

'Nice and quiet, though. No tourists.'

'True.'

'If there's anywhere you'd prefer . . . ?'

'No. I like Rye, as you know.'

'Yes. That's why I thought . . .'

'Good. That's settled, then.'

'What about the children?'

'Ben's going ice-skating in Gillingham, remember?'

'Ah yes, of course. And Bridget? Think she'd like to come?'

Much as he loved his daughter, Thanet hoped she wouldn't. There was so rarely time these days for him and Joan to talk, just to enjoy being alone together.

'She's going shopping with Mandy this afternoon.'

'Fine.'

'What time will you be home, then?'

'Soon as I can. Twenty minutes?'

Outside on the steps Thanet stopped to inhale appreciatively. It was a perfect winter day: crisp cold air, blue sky decorated with puffs of cotton-wool cloud, and a sun which was doing its best to make you forget that it was February.

By 1.30 they were on their way, with a delicious feeling of escape. Across the Weald the landscapes immortalised by Rowland Hilder basked in the unaccustomed warmth, the bare trees casting long shadows across furrowed fields and empty roads.

For a while they drove in a contented silence, relishing the sense of freedom, and then Joan stirred.

'Feel like telling me how you worked it out?'

Thanet would have preferred to forget about work this afternoon but it was part of the pattern of their lives to have a 'post-mortem' at the end of every case and Joan, he knew, would be disappointed if he demurred. 'If you like.'

He paused, ordering his thoughts. 'Actually, believe it or not, it was the Super who finally put me on the right track.'

'Really? How?'

'Oh, I don't mean he did it consciously. No, it was just that while I was talking to him, yesterday afternoon, we saw two visitors coming in – his window overlooks the forecourt, as you know. And as you also know, he likes to know every last thing about what is going on in the division. So I wasn't in the least surprised when he said, "Who's that?" and because I didn't know one of the men I assumed he was referring to him. Then I discovered he was referring to the other chap.'

'I don't get it. How did that help?'

'Well, when Leo Martindale arrived at Longford Hall on Monday evening he saw Mona Byfleet, the housekeeper, talking to Toby Fever in the entrance hall, and he asked the receptionist the same question: "Who's that?" Mona was wearing her housekeeper's dress and the receptionist therefore took it for granted that Martindale would realise who she was and that he must be referring to Toby. So she told him it

239

was Miss Hamilton's boyfriend. Then she said, "He was just going to say something else when Mrs Hamilton arrived." '

'And you think the "something else" would have been, "No, I don't mean him, I mean the woman with him." '

'Exactly. In other words, it was Mona Byfleet who interested him, not Toby, and when I realised that I naturally asked myself why? If she'd been an attractive woman, the sort that Martindale was always on the lookout for, it would have been a different matter, but she's fairly plain and heavily pregnant. So it seemed to me that the most likely answer was that she interested him because he had recognised her and wondered what she was doing there. Until then, you see, I had assumed that the Byfleets couldn't possibly have had any motive for wanting him dead because they didn't appear to have any connection with him, past or present.'

'So then you asked yourself what that connection could possibly be?'

'Yes. We knew that Martindale had been abroad for several years but before that, when he was in this country, he tended to move from hotel to hotel, living on any pickings he could glean from women he met, mostly wealthy widows or middle-aged spinsters. They're always the most vulnerable, the most susceptible. Well, Mona didn't really fit that pattern but it did occur to me that her mother might. I knew that Mona had been to school in Brighton and that her maiden name was Taylor – I saw it in the fly-leaf of one of her old books – and then I remembered that one of Martindale's former women friends had been called Taylor and ran a hotel in Worthing, which is near Brighton.'

'So you thought, Aha, I wonder if she was Mona's mother and that was where Mona and Martindale met?'

'Precisely.'

'But even so, what possible relevance did you think it could have?'

'I didn't know. But if the connection had been entirely innocent I didn't see why Mona shouldn't have owned up to it.'

'Not necessarily, surely. If I became innocently entangled in a murder investigation I'm not sure that I'd be particularly anxious to volunteer information that could connect me with the victim, would you?'

That was a tricky one. 'I don't know. It would depend on the circumstances, I suppose. But in this case I just felt that this particular connection could be important.'

'Your intuition again.'

'Probably.'

'I once read that a policeman should never underestimate the value of intuition.'

'I think I'd agree with that. Though I know a lot who wouldn't, who are distinctly suspicious of it.'

'Why is that, d'you think?'

'Probably because nobody quite understands how it works.'

'I suspect,' said Joan slowly, thinking aloud, 'that although it sounds very vague it's really a perfectly logical process. Without our even being conscious that it's happening, the brain takes note of facts, impressions, expressions, reactions and then assesses them all and comes up with a conclusion.'

'I think that just about sums it up. An article I was reading the other day claimed that the brain is infinitely more powerful than the computer and that we only ever use a minute fraction of its potential.'

'I'm sure that's true. So anyway, your intuition told you you were on to something . . .'

'Yes. I'd put DC Swift on to checking back on Martindale's women friends and Mrs Taylor was one of the ones he'd managed to track down, so we rang her up, made an appointment, and went to see her.'

They had reached Appledore and Thanet stopped talking while they drove through the picturesque village, pausing to admire a pretty Georgian house built of rose-red brick with a For Sale notice outside.

'My ideal house!' sighed Joan.

241

'Mm.' It was Thanet's too, but a policeman's pay was unlikely ever to stretch to their buying anything like it.

As they turned into the Military Road to Iden Lock and drove along parallel to the Royal Military Canal, Thanet told Joan the sad tale of Brenda Taylor's two marriages and the disastrous meeting of the son she had been forced to abandon and the daughter ignorant of her mother's past.

'Bit of a coincidence, wasn't it? That they should meet at all?'

Thanet shrugged. 'Coincidences do happen. And I've often thought that the danger of this sort of thing, the innocent coupling of close relations, is going to become more and more frequent as time goes on. With divorce and remarriage becoming more common, artificial insemination by donor and surrogate motherhood . . . It would be a miracle if half-brothers and -sisters didn't occasionally meet.'

'And become attracted to each other for that matter. With all those genes in common . . .'

'Yes. I noticed the resemblance between the Byfleets the first time I met them, you know, but I didn't realise its significance. Just thought how interesting it was that some husbands and wives do grow to resemble each other.'

Joan grinned. 'D'you think we have?'

He smiled back. 'Don't know. I suppose we'd be the last to see it even if we had.'

'So, all right, you'd discovered that the Byfleets had a possible motive for the murder. You assumed that Leo Martindale had recognised Mona Byfleet, and had told her the truth about Desmond being her half-brother. Presumably you also thought he must have threatened to blackmail them in some way with this knowledge?'

'I didn't know. I just felt that it was a potentially explosive situation.'

'But how did you guess which of them had run him down? Or did you think they'd acted together?'

Thanet shrugged. 'Again, I didn't know. At that stage

neither of them was even admitting to having driven the van that night and at one point in the interview, I really thought I wasn't going to get anywhere. All along, you see, Mike and I had been saying that even if we did find out who'd actually killed Martindale, there'd be no means of proving it. All the other suspects had admitted driving the van but even so there was no specific evidence, or so it seemed, to link any of them with the crime.'

' "Or so it seemed . . .". There was something, then?'

'Yes. And I knew it. But I simply couldn't put my finger on it. It was just nagging away at the back of my mind . . . Infuriating.'

'So put me out of my suspense. What was it?'

Thanet told her about Delia's pocket calculator, picked up in the van by Desmond and mistaken by Thanet for a diary when he first saw it in the Byfleets' sitting-room. 'A diary and a calculator can look extraordinarily alike.'

'True.'

'Though when I looked more closely at it, of course, even without picking it up I could see that it wasn't a diary.'

'Bit of a gamble, though, wasn't it? You were only guessing that it was Mrs Hamilton's.'

'I know. I had a few nasty moments there, I must admit. But as soon as I started questioning them about it, it became obvious at once that each thought it belonged to the other and that it therefore belonged to neither. I knew then that I was probably home and dry.'

'Because you could then definitely prove that they were lying and that one of them must have driven the van that night – no, wait a minute. Not necessarily, surely. Desmond could still have claimed that he'd picked the calculator up somewhere else, and you'd never have been able to prove it.'

'Not really. Because then he'd have *known* it wasn't Mona's. And as I said, they'd both already revealed that each thought it belonged to the other and the only way that could have happened was if one of them had acquired it unconsciously, when they were too agitated to know what they were doing.'

'It could still have been Mona, though.'

'Less likely, I thought, because Delia had told her the calculator was missing and she was on the lookout for it. But the last place she'd have expected to find it would be in her own sitting-room, obviously.'

'So when you'd proved that they'd lied about having been in the van that night, Desmond confessed?'

'Well it was his wife, really. She just broke down. The past few days had been a terrible strain. I honestly don't think she could have gone on indefinitely, living with the knowledge that Desmond had killed someone. It was only her genuine belief that it had been an accident that had enabled her to keep quiet as long as she did.'

'I should have thought that would be the very reason for getting him to own up! After all, no one knew about the connection between her and Martindale.'

'I don't think she was thinking straight at the time. Not surprising, really, after what she'd just learned. Her whole future had just collapsed around her ears and I suppose she must have thought, illogically, that if Desmond did own up the truth would come out. But I agree, if he'd only called an ambulance and said it was a straightforward accident, a skid on icy roads, then that would probably have been the end of it.'

'I notice you're saying "she" all the time. Are you implying what I think you're implying? That Desmond either ran Martindale down deliberately or at least knew that he was still alive when he put him in the ditch?'

'Well, I must admit I can't help wondering if he did genuinely believe Martindale to be dead. After all, Martindale alive was an unexploded bomb as far as he and Mona were concerned, whereas Martindale conveniently dead would enable them to decide in their own time and on their own terms what would be their best course of action in the light of what they had just learned. If Martindale were unconscious but still breathing there must have been considerable temptation simply to leave him out in the cold and let nature take its course. And Desmond did move him, remember, put him in the ditch, where he was less likely to be found before morning. And that's what is going to put him in the dock. If only he hadn't moved him, if Martindale had simply died in hospital as a result of the accident, Desmond would probably have got away with it. As it is, because Martindale wasn't dead when he was moved to the ditch we've been able to charge Desmond with manslaughter, on the basis of recklessness in regard to his post-accident conduct.'

'You're still on tricky ground there, though, surely. Doesn't it depend whether or not Martindale would have died anyway from his injuries?'

'Doc Mallard says he wouldn't.'

'Maybe, but will he be prepared to stand up and say so in the witness box? You know how reluctant expert witnesses are to commit themselves on matters of opinion in Court. And the Defence might well be able to dig up someone to disagree with him. I can imagine a good Counsel having a field day over this.'

'The Prosecution too, for that matter. I can imagine them pulling out all the stops, playing on the jury's emotions by painting a horrendous picture of Martindale struggling to get out of that ditch with an injured spine ... It's something that's going to haunt me for a long time yet.'

Joan shivered. 'I know. But if Desmond continues to swear that he thought Martindale was already dead when he put him in the ditch ... Surely, if he can convince the jury of that it would make a considerable difference to his sentence?'

'Yes. If he could pull that off and if there was some doubt as to whether or not the injuries would have been fatal anyway ... I suppose he could get as little as two years suspended ... Otherwise he'd get between three and seven, don't you think?'

'Between three and four, I'd say.' Joan sighed. 'Poor things. What will become of them, d'you think? How is Mona?'

'Still in hospital, under observation.'

'They're still afraid of a miscarriage?'

'Yes.'

'What will she do? What will they do, even if he does get off?'

'I know.'

'What is the legal position of a couple in a prohibited relationship innocently marrying?'

'The marriage is null and void from the beginning, I gather. And in this case there's obviously no question of prosecution because both parties were ignorant of the connection between them.'

But in any case, the future for the Byfleets looked pretty bleak. Thanet thought of their pretty, comfortable sitting-room with its evidence of a rich, satisfying life and mourned the bitter blow which fate had inflicted on them. He would never know for sure whether or not Desmond had dumped Martindale in that ditch knowing that he was still alive, but in any case they were to a large extent the innocent victims of a past tragedy not their own and he couldn't help feeling sorry for them.

They were coming into the outskirts of Rye now and with an effort he shut his mind to repercussions of the case. This was a rare treat and he was going to make sure they enjoyed every moment of it.

In summer Rye is always a magnet for tourists but at this time of year it was blissfully empty and they spent the remainder of the short winter afternoon wandering through the steep cobbled streets, gazing in shop windows, browsing in the second-hand bookshops. Before setting off for home they indulged in a cream tea.

In the car Joan settled back into her seat with a smile. 'I did enjoy that.'

He leaned across and kissed her. 'We ought to do it more often.'

As they drove through the darkening countryside, ahead of them like a welcoming beacon shone the thought of home, of the pleasure of a leisurely evening together, of drawn curtains, lamplight, a blazing log fire.

Thanet could think of no better way of spending the evening. He glanced across at Joan's serene profile and gave a sigh of pure contentment. With the case behind him he would be able to relax at last.

He felt at peace with the world.